STEPHEN DONALDSON

Stephen Donaldson was born in 1947 in Cleveland, Ohio. From the age of three until he was sixteen he lived in India, where his father worked as an orthopaedic surgeon. He now lives in New Mexico.

His work includes the two award-winning *Thomas Covenant* fantasy trilogies; a collection of short stories, *Daughter of Regals*; the two books in the bestselling *Mordant's Need* series, *The Mirror of Her Dreams* and *A Man Rides Through*; and *Strange Dreams*, a selection of favourite fantasy short stories.

This Day All Gods Die – which spent more than two months on the *Sunday Times* hardback bestseller list – is the fifth and final volume in the *Gap* series, the acclaimed epic science-fiction adventure that begins in *The Real Story* and continues in *Forbidden Knowledge*, *A Dark and Hungry God Arises* and *Chaos and Order*.

THIS DAY ALL GODS DIE

'Donaldson's stunning epic of futuristic anarchy and intrigue finally comes to an end, and doesn't let the series down one bit. Action-packed, complex and filled with betrayals and shadowy agendas . . . Donaldson's *Gap* sequence will still be selling by the bucketload a decade from now, and deservedly so.'   *Northern Echo*

'The *Gap* series is easily the most interesting thing he's done since the Thomas Covenant stories that made his name. In a year or two they'll be calling these classics.'
The Dark Side

Further reviews overleaf

THE GAP SERIES

'The *Gap* series is the best work of his career. Donaldson displays a real and rare gift for depicting intrigue, deception, betrayal and the dynamics of the multiple double-cross, and the dizzyingly complex back-stabbing arabesques of his cast of resourcefully vicious interstellar slimeballs make this series as funky, grungy and down-and-dirty as space-op ever gets. This sequence has me hanging by my thumbs waiting for the next instalment.'

Time Out

'The essence of Donaldson's artistry – and the key to his success – is his ability to construct narrative crescendos that build and build and keep on building, unremittingly, until they have reached a pitch which no composer of texts has ever attained before.' *Interzone*

'Stephen Donaldson, a master of cybernetic horror, writes in overdrive . . . corruption is rife, gangsters and fraudsters abound, layer upon layer of environmental and moral pollution . . . life in the uncontrollably fast lane.'

Daily Telegraph

'Vicious corporations, aliens, pirates, power politics, police and a wealth of characters you wouldn't want your children to bring home to dinner . . . good stuff, precisely what Donaldson fans keep coming back for.'

Kirkus Reviews

'Fascinating . . . the best thing Donaldson has ever done.' *Oxford Times*

THE GAP SERIES

'The world Donaldson creates is entirely credible . . . fast, furious and very frightening . . . extraordinary for both its detail and its sense of realism.'   *Bookcase*

'Expands even further the author's complex mind-game universe . . . looks set to be the biggest space epic of all time.'   *Manchester Evening News*

'Ambitious and imaginative . . . Donaldson's impressive adventure should more than satisfy his legion of fans.'

Northern Echo

'Gripping, utterly relentless . . . bravura crescendo. In the grips of a complex story none of them understand, and a crescendo they all feel building in their savaged and weary bones, every single character in the sequence operates under some terrible duress. Everyone is imprisoned, or zone-implanted, or bribed, or trapped, or betraying, or without money, or fuel, or a gap drive, or sleep, or a gun. Everyone has been driven to the edge of endurance. Everyone sweats fear, loathing, self-betrayal, anguish, heat. And no one knows what anyone else knows, or is bondage to, or committed to accomplish, or on whose behalf any of the betrayals and reversals have been prepared – a nightmare of stress . . . a small miracle.'   JOHN CLUTE, *Interzone*

'Complex, carefully plotted and richly detailed . . . excellent . . . a rewarding experience.'

British Fantasy Society Bookshelf

Works by Stephen Donaldson

The Chronicles of Thomas Covenant, the Unbeliever
1. Lord Foul's Bane
2. The Illearth War
3. The Power That Preserves

The Second Chronicles of Thomas Covenant
1. The Wounded Land
2. The One Tree
3. White Gold Wielder

Short Stories
Daughter of Regals and Other Tales
Strange Dreams (Editor)

Mordant's Need
1. The Mirror of Her Dreams
2. A Man Rides Through

The Gap Series
1. The Gap into Conflict: The Real Story
2. The Gap into Vision: Forbidden Knowledge
3. The Gap into Power: A Dark and Hungry God Arises
4. The Gap into Madness: Chaos and Order
5. The Gap into Ruin: This Day All Gods Die

STEPHEN DONALDSON

THE GAP INTO RUIN

THIS DAY ALL GODS DIE

HarperCollins*Publishers*

Voyager
An Imprint of HarperCollins*Publishers*
77–85 Fulham Palace Road,
Hammersmith, London W6 8JB

The *Voyager* World Wide Web site address is
http://www.harpercollins.co.uk/voyager

Special overseas edition 1997
This paperback edition 1997
1 3 5 7 9 8 6 4 2

First published in Great Britain by
Voyager 1996

ISBN 0 00 647023 8

Set inPostscript Galliard by
Rowland Phototypesetting Ltd, Bury St Edmunds, Suffolk

Printed and bound in Great Britain by
Caledonian International Book Manufacturing Ltd, Glasgow

To
Sensei Mike Heister
and
Sempai Karen Heister:
two of the best

ACKNOWLEDGMENTS

I wish to thank Douglas A. Van Belle and Mark Woolrich – as well as the entire HIT-list – for their efforts to relieve some of my ignorance. The Dancing Wu Li Masters would be proud of them. Any evidence of incomprehension which remains is entirely my own responsibility.

THE GAP INTO RUIN

THIS DAY ALL GODS DIE

HASHI

It was typical of Hashi Lebwohl that he did not report to Warden Dios as soon as he returned to UMCPHQ.

He wasn't trying to avoid another confrontation with the man who had outplayed and, in a strange, piquant sense, shamed him. On the contrary he felt remarkably sanguine about the prospect of talking to the UMCP director. He simply made no effort to bring about a conversation himself. He assumed that Warden Dios was perfectly capable of recognizing an emergency when he saw it – and that he wouldn't hesitate to summon Hashi when he wished to speak to his DA director.

A kaze had attacked the Governing Council for Earth and Space in extraordinary session, apparently intending to exterminate Cleatus Fane, the First Executive Assistant of the United Mining Companies. Only Hashi's personal intervention had prevented serious – not to say embarrassing – bloodshed. And as a direct result of the attack the GCES had voted to reject Captain Sixten Vertigus' Bill of Severance. Indeed, the Members had been stampeded into clinging to the status quo for their lives; to Holt Fasner and the UMCP. None of them had wanted to take on the responsibility for their own safety – and certainly not for the safety of human space.

If Warden didn't call this an emergency, he must have lost all contact with the world of factual reality. Or else his game was deeper than anything Hashi had dared to imagine. Perhaps it was deeper than he could imagine.

Neither prospect offered reassurance. On the whole, however, Hashi preferred the latter. That which he found impenetrable today might well appear transparent tomorrow. And he could always push himself to expand his own capacities. The challenge might conceivably be good for him. In the meantime he could endure the shame of being outplayed.

But if Warden Dios had lost his grasp on events –

From that fount endless disasters might spring.

This was all speculation, of course. Still Hashi wondered – and worried. The quantum mechanics of his conundrum remained as Heisenberg had defined them. By his own efforts he had taken hold of events in flux in order to name them accurately; establish them in their positions. Therefore he was prevented from knowing where those events tended. Certainty precluded certainty.

He chose not to report to Warden on his own initiative because he wanted to know how long Warden would wait before summoning him. That interval would reveal more surely than words the extent to which Warden had been taken by surprise.

In any case the DA director still had plenty of work to do in order to ready himself for Warden's summons; to confirm and solidify what he'd learned on Suka Bator. No one would criticize him for spending every available moment on an effort to be sure of his facts.

Using a tight-beam transmission coded exclusively for Data Acquisition, he'd begun speaking to Lane Harbinger as soon as the UMCP shuttle had left the GCES island and broken free of Earth's gravity well; supplying her with preliminary data; preparing her for the research he required. He felt some discomfort as he did so because he wasn't alone on the shuttle. Protocol Director Koina Hannish rode with him, accompanied by her retinue of aides and techs. And UMCPED Chief of Security Mandich was also aboard: he was on his way to explain his failures to Warden Dios, since his immediate superior, Min Donner, was absent from UMCPHQ. He'd left Deputy Chief Forrest Ing in charge of Security's version of 'martial law' on Suka Bator.

At the best of times Hashi disliked being overheard – unless he had some use for his eavesdropper. But his present circumstances didn't supply privacy, or justify delay. He owed Warden restitution for his earlier mistakes. Instead of waiting for the shuttle to reach UMCPHQ, he kept his exchanges with Lane as brief as possible; and when he spoke, he employed the impermeable jargon of DA to disguise what he was saying.

To all appearances Koina ignored him completely. No doubt she had more than enough to occupy her contemplations. Although she was new to her duties, she'd acquitted herself admirably during the extraordinary session. And she had reason to be grateful to Captain Vertigus, despite the failure of his proposed legislation. On the other hand, Hashi deemed that most of her thoughts were more troubled. He knew her well enough to suspect that she feared her performance before the Council may have triggered or catalysed the kaze's attack. For her it must have been easy to believe that the men who'd sent a kaze against the GCES would not have felt compelled to go so far if they hadn't been surprised or frightened by her declaration of the UMCP's neutrality in the debate over a Bill of Severance; her declaration of Warden Dios' independence from Holt Fasner.

Hashi knew better. Earlier he'd been uncertain: now he was sure. Her performance may in fact have been a catalyst. Nevertheless it was essentially incidental. The men responsible for Clay Imposs né Nathan Alt could not have known that Sixten Vertigus, Senior Member for the United Western Bloc, would introduce a Bill of Severance. In addition, Imposs/Alt had been moving past Captain Vertigus toward Cleatus Fane when Hashi had accosted him. Therefore Captain Vertigus wasn't the intended target. The motivations behind the kaze's attack operated independently of the UWB Senior Member and his bill, as well as of Warden Dios' neutrality.

Hashi said nothing to reassure Koina. She hadn't asked for anything of the kind. And she would hear what he'd learned soon enough.

In contrast Chief Mandich studied Hashi narrowly while

he spoke to Lane. Clearly Mandich was waiting for a chance to talk to the DA director.

A pox on the man, Hashi thought with unwonted vexation. The Chief of Security's rectitude was as ironclad as Min Donner's, but he lacked her flexibility of intelligence, her capacity to acknowledge concepts which violated her personal reality. For example, Hashi didn't doubt that if Mandich were suddenly exalted to the position of UMCP director, the man wouldn't hesitate to fire Hashi for having done things which disturbed the Chief's scruples. Min Donner, on the other hand, might well retain Hashi in DA, even though she knew far more about his actions and policies, and therefore had experienced far more outrage to her peculiar sense of honor.

Still Hashi did nothing to fend off Chief Mandich. Instead he made himself accessible as soon as he'd finished his interchange with Lane.

The Chief took the opportunity to move to a g-seat beside Hashi, belt himself down. 'Director Lebwohl,' he began without preamble, 'I need to know how you knew that man was a kaze.'

Hashi's blue eyes glittered dangerously behind his smeared lenses. 'Do you?' he countered in a tone of false amiability. No doubt Mandich meant, How were you able to spot him when we couldn't?

'I do.' Chief Mandich was a blunt man with a blunt face; stolid as bone. His nearly colorless gaze had the dull tenacity of a pit bull's. 'And then I need to know why you didn't do anything to stop him sooner.

'Something about him made you suspicious. You left your seat and moved around the hall specifically so that you could get close to him. But you didn't *say* anything.' Mandich spoke with undisguised bitterness. He hated his own failures. 'We're just lucky nobody in the hall was killed. If you'd bothered to warn us, a GCES Security guard would still be alive. Ensign Crender would still have his left hand.

'With respect, Director Lebwohl,' he sneered, 'what the hell did you think you were doing?'

12

A tremor ran along Hashi's frame. His own reaction to the danger and indignity of the past few hours seemed to shrill inside him. 'Very well.' He folded his thin hands in his lap to conceal their indignation. 'You answer my questions, and I will answer yours.

'To use your phrase, Chief Mandich, what the hell did you think you were doing when you assigned a whelp like Ensign Crender to take my orders?'

Mandich's eyes widened.

Wheezing sharply, Hashi sent his words like wasps into the Chief's blunt face. 'I made my needs known explicitly to Deputy Chief Ing. I informed him that I desired him and his men to stand ready to carry out my requests and instructions.

'He replied that he could not comply without consulting you.

'I did not consider that adequate. "If I ask you to 'do something', I will need it done without the delay of applying to your Chief for permission." Those were my exact words. I told him plainly that I did not know what to expect, but that I wished to be prepared for whatever might transpire.

'Still he hesitated. I answered, "Then kindly inform Chief Mandich that I require him to assign personnel to me who have been given his authorization to do what I tell them." Again those are my exact words.

'Director Hannish supported my wishes.'

Obliquely Hashi observed that Koina was staring at him, her lips slightly parted in surprise. It was probable that in the years she'd worked with him she'd never heard him sound so angry.

An undignified flush stained Chief Mandich's neck, mottled his cheeks with his own anger. He opened his mouth to deliver a retort. But Hashi wasn't done. He didn't give the Chief a chance to speak.

'How did you respond?' he went on harshly. 'By assigning to me a boy so untried that he was unable to react without hesitation – hesitation which could well have resulted in murder in the meeting hall of the Governing Council for Earth and Space.

13

'True, he mastered his hesitation. He took the action necessary to save lives. For that I honor him.

'But I do not honor *you*, Chief Mandich.' If Hashi hadn't controlled his hands, they would have flown like stings at the Chief's eyes. 'I am the United Mining Companies Police Director of Data Acquisition, and you did not take my stated requirements seriously enough to assign personnel capable of prompt obedience.

'Shall we discuss our separate motivations now, or do you prefer to wait until we can explain them in front of Director Dios?' Hashi shrugged dismissively. 'For myself, I am content to wait.'

Chief Mandich closed his mouth. Congested emotion made his features appear swollen. Poor man, he was cursed with a sense of probity so strict that it left him defenseless. Min Donner would have faced down Hashi's challenge in order to pursue the answers to her own questions; but her Chief of Security couldn't do the same.

After a moment he murmured through his teeth, 'You have a valid grievance, Director Lebwohl. If you want to censure me, I won't fight it.'

Stiffly he unclipped his belts and drifted back to his former g-seat.

Oh, censure you, forsooth, Hashi thought in the direction of the Chief's retreat. I would not trouble myself. Our present circumstances are accusation enough. We confront a dilemma which censures us all.

Honesty with himself forced him to admit that he'd enjoyed scathing Chief Mandich.

Koina met Hashi's look when he glanced at her. Gravity and speculation darkened her gaze. 'Aren't you being just a little disingenuous, Director Lebwohl?' she asked crisply. 'Even a "whelp" like Ensign Crender wouldn't have hesitated if you'd told him what you were looking for.'

Hashi spread his hands as if to show her that his equanimity had been completely restored. 'My dear Koina, have you studied Heisenberg?'

She shook her head.

'A pity.' He settled himself in his g-seat to await the shuttle's arrival at UMCPHQ. 'If you had, you would understand that I could not possibly have known what I was looking for until I found it.'

That may have been as close as he'd ever come to telling her the truth.

Lane Harbinger met him at the dock as soon as the shuttle powered down its systems and the space doors of the bay sealed to restore atmosphere.

On Suka Bator he'd supervised the essential chore of placing Imposs/Alt's earthly remains in a shielded, sterile bodybag and loading them into the shuttle's cargo space. Now he watched over the delivery of the bodybag into Lane's care.

A glance at the corridor in which the kaze had been detonated had assured him that too many people had trampled too much evidence – and indeed that the corridor itself was too large – to permit the kind of meticulous scrutiny Lane had given Godsen Frik's office. Of necessity he'd surrendered his desire for some form of microscopic data from the region around the body, and had instead concentrated on Imposs/Alt's corpse – on the smears of his blood and the mangled mess of his tissues. The body itself had been simply scooped into the bodybag with a sterile shovel. But every streak or droplet of blood Hashi could locate had been cut out of the concrete with a utility laser and added to the bodybag's contents.

He hoped devoutly that these remains would enable Lane to find the answers he needed.

No, not the answers: the proofs. He already knew the answers.

A fuming nic dangled from her mouth as she joined him beside the cargo space. Her eyes glittered like shards of mica – a sign that she rode levels of stim and hype which would have poleaxed anyone whose metabolism hadn't been inured to them. In the pockets of her labcoat her fingers twitched as if they were entering data on a purely metaphysical keypad.

While the bodybag was being loaded onto a sled for transport to her lab in Data Acquisition, she asked tensely, 'You sure of his id?'

'My dear Lane,' Hashi chided gently. She knew as well as anyone who worked with him that he was unlikely to mistake an id.

She shrugged like a twitch. 'Just checking. If you're right, my job's that much easier.'

Certainly she would be required to spend less time waiting for Data Storage to run its vast SAC routines.

'Any chance I'll find a detonator?' she continued.

Hashi made a conscious effort to remain calm; amiably unruffled. He didn't want to be infected by her congenital tension. 'Who can say?' There were too many factors: the type of explosive, its brisance, the shape of the charge, blast reflection from the nearby walls. 'But if you do,' he went on more sharply, 'the information will be vital. Do you understand me, Lane?'

She sucked on her nic. 'What's to understand? Isn't that what it all hinges on?'

'Not all,' he countered with a shake of his head. 'But enough.' He knew the truth: whatever Lane learned wouldn't change it. Nevertheless the proof he wished to give Warden Dios depended heavily on what Lane could discover.

'In any case,' he added, 'these will be of interest.'

Casually, almost covertly, as if he didn't wish to be seen, he slipped Imposs/Alt's clearance badge and id tag into Lane's pocket.

She identified them with her fingers, nodded decisively. 'I'm sure they will.'

The sled was ready to go. Lane moved to accompany it. Despite the nature of the emergency, however, and his own desires, he called her back. Camouflaging his seriousness with his peculiar sense of humor, he told her that he wished to see her results 'relatively instantaneously. Engage your gap drive, Lane. Defy time if you must.'

He wanted her findings before Warden summoned him.

She replied with a snort of smoke. 'Don't I always?'

He wheezed a laugh. 'You do. Indeed you do.'

He waited until she and her sled had left the dock before shifting himself into motion.

By then he'd already begun to wonder how much longer Warden would delay.

More than an hour passed before a call from the director of the UMCP reached Hashi, instructing him to present himself immediately to one of Warden's private offices.

Hashi hadn't wasted the time. First he'd issued a number of Red Priority – 'screaming red,' as it was sometimes called – security locks: one for every communications channel and computer that belonged or connected to Anodyne Systems, the UMC subsidiary which manufactured SOD-CMOS chips; one for the UMCP's own personnel files; and one for each of Holt Fasner's Home Office personnel, payroll, and Security Liaison computers. A screaming red security lock didn't prevent anyone else from looking at electronic files or using communications linkups; but it blocked changes of any kind to those files, or to any transmission logs and records. At the same time it warned DA that changes had been attempted, and traced the codes and routing of the attempt backward.

He was morally certain that the Dragon's HO techs could disable or deactivate a Red Priority security lock, no matter how loudly it screamed. At the same time he was quite sure that this would not be done, first, because Holt Fasner would hardly imagine that crucial records were in any danger of exposure, second, because Holt would believe that any embarrassment which might arise from his files could be quashed through Warden Dios, and, third, because as a matter of policy the Dragon liked to preserve an illusion of openness and honesty. Rather than resistance Hashi expected passive acceptance: another illusion.

An illusion which would reveal itself as murderous fury against Hashi himself when the UMC CEO determined that Hashi no longer represented a threat.

This prospect didn't trouble Hashi. He could say with considerable accuracy that he did not fear the Dragon in any ordinary sense. The possibility of intellectual inadequacy gave him far more distress than a merely physical threat.

When his security locks were in place, he used his authority under the provisions of Red Priority to compile the most complete dossiers which Data Storage, joined by microwave downlinks to GCES Security and Anodyne Systems, could provide on both Nathan Alt and Clay Imposs.

Warden's summons found him just as he was finishing.

More than an hour since the shuttle had docked: several hours since the kaze's blast. Apparently Warden hadn't been taken by surprise to any meaningful extent.

That was good and bad; better and worse. The delay had allowed Hashi to complete his immediate research. On the other hand, a longer delay might have given Lane time to produce the results Hashi craved.

Despite the plain urgency of the summons – and the necessity of obedience – Hashi took the time to call her.

Her voice over the intercom was brusque and focused; deep in concentration. 'Make it quick. I'm busy.'

Hashi couldn't restrain himself: his personal imp of perversity made him say, 'Too busy to talk to *me*? Lane, I'm crushed.'

She let out a sigh that sounded like smoke. 'If you want me to work fast, I have to be careful. If you want me to work faster than the speed of light, I have to be more careful than God.'

He relented. 'I understand perfectly.' Above all he valued Lane for her meticulousness. 'Nevertheless I must appear before Warden Dios in a matter of moments. The time is apt for results. *He* will certainly desire results from *me*.'

'Then let's not waste each other's time. Here's what I have so far.

'The id tag and clearance badge were easy.' She didn't need to organize her thoughts. Hashi suspected that she permitted herself no disorganized thoughts. 'They're legit. I mean Clay Imposs is – or maybe was – a real GCES Security guard with a good record. He's been with them for years. The tag and badge say they're his. But the body isn't.'

'You were right, it's Nathan Alt. Gene scan matches exactly.

'So how did he get through his own Security?' She asked Hashi's next question for him. 'Right after that first kaze attacked Captain Vertigus, GCES Security started using retinal scans to confirm id. That should have stopped Alt cold.

'The answer is, this is a new id tag. Made for the job. It says it identifies Clay Imposs, but the retinal signature and the rest of the physical id belong to Alt.'

'Is that possible?' Hashi inquired. He knew it was.

'Sure. It worked because the physical id was generated by the same code engine that drove Imposs's clearances. Everything looked legit on the surface. GCES Security didn't know they had to run a full playback from the SOD-CMOS chips and compare it to Imposs's original data to catch the switch. Hell, Hashi, we aren't doing that *here*. It would take hours to clear anybody.'

Sadly, that was true. Indeed, the only reason GCES – or UMCPHQ – Security functioned at all was that the expertise needed to circumvent it was so specialized; and so closely guarded.

'Are you performing this playback? I require evidence.'

'One of my techs is.'

'And –' Hashi prompted her.

'We haven't found anything yet.'

'Have you encountered any patches, or other signs of tampering?'

As Hashi had told Koina before the extraordinary session, the code-strings Lane had extracted from the credentials of Godsen's killer were current as well as correct. If that code engine had been patched or altered – lawfully or otherwise, by GCES Security, Anodyne Systems, or anyone else – the change would have been apparent. Such adjustments transformed source-code as much as mutagens transformed human RNA.

But only older code required patching.

Lane restrained impatience poorly. 'Not yet.'

'Very well.' He let that question go. 'And the code engine itself –?' he probed.

19

'It's valid,' she returned at once. 'Current and correct. Which means exactly what you think it means.

'But if you want confirmation,' she continued without pausing, 'the source-code strings we've picked up from the id of the kaze who killed Godsen are a perfect match.'

Hashi nodded to himself. 'Confirmation is always welcome. However, this is hardly a surprise.'

'No,' Lane acknowledged.

He cast a worried glance at his chronometer, then asked, 'Have you gleaned any other data?'

'That's what I'm working on,' she retorted. 'The body.'

As she spoke, he heard a subtle shift in her tone; a change of intensity. So far the results she'd given him had been relatively routine, despite their importance: any of the techs in her department could have supplied them. But now she sounded more personally engaged; perhaps excited. At once he became convinced that she was on the track of something vital.

'But I can tell you right now,' she went on, 'we aren't going to find a detonator.

'The bomb has to be shielded in the body. Otherwise Security would catch it. And you know what that kind of shielding is like.' Hashi did know. Angus Thermopyle's body was full of it. 'It has to appear organic in order to pass scan. On top of that, it has to reflect back what scan expects to see. Unfortunately – for us – any shield contains the blast when the bomb goes off. Maybe only for a millisecond or two, but that's enough to throw some of the force back onto the bomb itself. And the detonator. On a molecular level, I'll be able to find all the pieces you want. But I won't be able to reconstruct the device those pieces came from.

'So I'm concentrating on biochemistry.'

Her voice conveyed an almost subliminal frisson, like a distant electrostatic discharge. Despite the numbers ticking away on his chronometer, he listened harder.

'His blood is a real witches' brew. Which is exactly what you would expect if he was in a state of drug-induced hypnosis. I haven't had time to identify even half the chemicals his body shouldn't have had in it.' She paused to emphasize what

20

followed. 'But there's one detail that looks a little strange. Or a little stranger than the rest of it.'

'Tell me,' Hashi put in as if he thought he could hurry her; as if he didn't know that she was already moving as fast as she could without stumbling into disorganization.

Instead of hurrying, she began to speak a bit more slowly, articulating each word with deliberate precision.

'There's a coenzyme spike in his blood spectrum. I mean a major spike. Of course, it's a *co*enzyme. It's inert. And it isn't even remotely natural. But it combines with some natural human apoenzymes to produce an artificial holoenzyme, and that one *is* active. It bears some interesting resemblances to pseudoamylase, which is one of the enzymes we use to produce shielding in cyborgs, but there are significant differences, too.'

Involuntarily Hashi drummed his fingers on his desk. He needed to answer Warden's summons. 'Lane, please make your point. I am not in good odor with our esteemed director. This delay while we talk will doubtless vex him.'

'I'm trying, damn it,' she snapped. 'Nobody but you ever gets to think around here.'

He swallowed a burst of ire. He had called her before she was ready to report. Her findings were partial or unclear. Naturally she wished to express them cautiously. He would gain nothing by reproaching her.

'If there were more resemblances,' she explained stiffly, 'I would probably assume this particular coenzyme is there because of the shields. But it wouldn't work well for that. The differences are too significant.'

Again she paused. In another moment or two, Hashi thought, he would have no choice but to shout at her.

More slowly than ever, she went on, 'If I were asked to come up with a use for the holoenzyme this coenzyme creates, I might say it would make a good chemical trigger. Release it into the bloodstream, and one or two heartbeats later you get a big bang. Like an orgasm so intense it kills you.'

Without transition his irritation vanished. Lane Harbinger,

he hummed to himself, you are a marvel. Is it any wonder that I endure your eccentricities?

Almost singing his excitement and pleasure, he said, 'Check his teeth, Lane.'

Where could a coenzyme be concealed so that a man in a state of drug-induced hypnosis would be able to ingest it on some preconditioned signal? Where else but in his mouth? And absorption into the bloodstream would be slower. Ten or fifteen seconds at least. Safer for the man who gave the signal.

'What's left of them,' she returned. 'I'm already working on it.'

In a glow of perverse gallantry, he answered, 'Then please do not allow me to interrupt you. Perhaps when your efforts are complete you will let me persuade you to marry me.'

So that he wouldn't hear her laughing in scorn, he silenced his intercom.

No doubt she could never prove the conclusions he drew. When her research was complete she would probably be able to demonstrate that this particular holoenzyme would serve well as a chemical trigger. Sadly, logic would preclude her from concluding that this holoenzyme *did* serve in that fashion.

Nevertheless what she had learned was enough for his immediate purposes.

Gathering his rumpled labcoat around him, Hashi Lebwohl left his office and walked as quickly as his untied shoes allowed to his meeting with Warden Dios.

CIRO

Vector had told him he was cured. Mikka told him over and over again, holding him in her arms and rocking him as if he were a baby.

Ciro knew better. The walls of his doom had closed around him like the claustrophobia of Mikka's embrace. His bunk was a coffin. Of course he knew better.

Sorus Chatelaine had injected a mutagen into his veins: he understood that in the genetic programming of his DNA; understood it more profoundly than anything anyone could have said to him. No mere words could outweigh his cellular comprehension of the way he'd been betrayed.

Somehow Morn had lured or tricked him into revealing what had happened. Now everyone knew. By the hour his doom became more certain, not less.

Of course she'd asked Vector for help. Why not? Why should she grant Ciro the simple decency of facing his shame and horror alone? No one had ever taken him that seriously.

And when the dilemma had been explained to him, Vector had proposed giving Ciro some of Nick's antimutagen. Vector had said, *The drug is essentially a genetically engineered microbe that acts as a binder. It attaches itself to the nucleotides of the mutagen, renders them inert. Then they're both flushed out of the body as waste.* As he spoke, the man who'd once been Ciro's mentor and friend had sounded confident and calm, inhumanly sure of himself.

But his reassurances meant nothing. Ciro couldn't hear them through Sorus Chatelaine's threats.

Her words were infinitely stronger.

The mutagen stays in you, it stays alive, it works its way into every cell and wraps itself around your DNA strings, but it doesn't change you as long as you have this other drug in your system. The drug she'd offered him in exchange for his compliance. *How long the delay lasts depends on how much of this other drug you have in you – or how often you get it. You can stay human until you're cut off from your supply. After that you're an Amnioni.*

That's why I serve them, Ciro. If I don't, they'll cut me off from the antidote.

And that's why you're *going to serve me.*

When she'd injected him – while Milos Taverner had held him – he'd grasped that she was telling him the simple truth. He would stay human as long as his supply of the other drug lasted.

He knew what he had to do.

She wanted him to sabotage *Trumpet*'s drives. Both of them. That was her price for keeping him human.

He would do it if he ever got the chance.

Kill everyone aboard; murder them –

Even Mikka.

Especially Mikka. The more she knew about her danger, the more stubborn her loyalty to *Trumpet*'s people became. She stood by them despite the fact that her interference was going to kill him.

She didn't understand. How could she? She was stronger than he was. They were all stronger. Instead of leaving him alone – hadn't he begged her to leave him alone? – she'd daunted him with her strength; smothered him with her devotion. She'd prevented and prevented him. Gripped him in her arms to comfort herself. And all the time his doom had continued counting down; approaching ruin.

Here, Vector had commanded when he'd returned from examining Ciro's blood in sickbay. *This is a dose of Nick's antimutagen.* He'd thrust a capsule at Ciro. *Take it. Then come with*

*me. I want to run a series of blood tests in sickbay. We'll be able
to see it working. That way you'll know you're safe.*

Ciro knew better. He'd always known better. But Mikka
and Vector were too strong for him.

While *Trumpet* ran a relatively quiet part of the swarm,
Mikka had compelled him to sickbay. At her urging, he'd
looked at the results of Vector's blood tests; seen the nucleo-
tide profiles shifting until they reached the range designated
'human normal.' He'd listlessly watched a video display which
purported to give a real-time picture of the mutagen immunity drug binding itself to Amnion RNA strings and carrying
them away.

Vector clearly believed the results. Mikka believed them.

Beyond question Ciro knew better.

*Sabotage the drives. Both of them. You've been trained in
engineering. You know how to do it. You make sure* Trumpet
can't outrun me. She's finished if she can't run.

Back in his cabin, imprisoned by his sister, he continued
waiting.

Twelve hours. Sorus Chatelaine had said, *If I don't have
what I want in twelve hours, you're on your own.* That was all.
And only a portion of it remained. Whenever he was due for
another capsule, he made Mikka release him so that he could
go to the san: he swallowed his next dose of the temporary
antidote privately. He was strong enough for that. But the
dwindling store in his vial reminded him harshly that he didn't
have much time left.

Was it already too late? He couldn't tell. Without warning
Trumpet went into battle, and he couldn't have left his
g-sheath no matter how much he wanted or needed to obey.
The whole ship was filled with the frying sound of matter
cannon, the metallic clangor of impacts and stress. Acceleration g slammed the gap scout in one direction after another.
Any fight in an asteroid swarm was a navigational nightmare.
Judging by the sounds and pressures, this one was even worse
than that. The intense, inexplicable alternation of quiet and
violence gave the impression that *Trumpet* was fighting more
than one opponent; in more than one part of the swarm.

Voices over the intercom offered partial explanations, but Ciro paid no attention to them. They were wasted on him unless they forced Mikka to go away.

Then the ship hit g so extreme that he blanked out. He no longer knew what he needed, or why it mattered. His mind was filled with death and effacement; the last, absolute relief.

He thought he'd been spared.

But of course g eased again. Thrust went on roaring in the tubes, but the pressure receded to more human levels. Beside him in the bunk, Mikka recovered consciousness. Despite her cracked skull and her exhaustion, she was stronger than her brother.

'Shit,' she breathed to him softly, as if she feared to raise her voice. 'What the hell was that?'

He didn't know. He didn't even know why she troubled to ask him.

Minutes passed. Or maybe they didn't: maybe they simply fell to the floor and lay there, swollen as tumors; thick with mutation. Was it time for another capsule? Had he been unconscious that long? No. Like the gap, the darkness of too much g felt vast – and yet it took almost no time at all. Otherwise it would have done him the kindness of killing him.

Would Mikka force him to suffer helplessly until the end? Could she be that cruel? Yes, she could. Even though she was his sister: even though he was the last of her family left alive.

If their positions had been reversed, he would have treated her more gently.

'Mikka?' Davies' voice barked unexpectedly from the intercom speaker; desperately. '*Mikka?* Do you hear me? I need you.'

Acid hope stung Ciro's heart as soon as he heard the stress in Davies' tone. Suddenly he knew he was going to get the chance Sorus Chatelaine demanded.

'And don't tell me you can't leave Ciro!' Davies went on as if in confirmation. 'Let him do his own suffering for a while! I *need* you. I'm alone here!'

Mikka tensed. Her grip on Ciro became iron. What else? She clung to him because she understood the danger he was in. The peril he represented. But there were other threats. Davies' voice made that plain. She was trapped by her own loyalty. She kept watch on her brother to protect Morn and the rest of them. But now they needed something else from her.

Ciro knew what she would do.

Davies wasn't finished. 'Vector? Vector, *move!* I can't do this many jobs at once. *I'm alone here!* If I don't get some help, it's all going to be *wasted.*'

Mikka shifted positions; faced Ciro with her bandaged glower. Conflicts twisted her familiar scowl.

He tried to make it easier for her. 'You'd better go.' Tension clutched at his throat: his voice sounded like a croak. 'There isn't anybody else. I'll be all right.'

That was a lie. He knew he was never going to be all right again. But it didn't matter. He couldn't afford honesty.

'I hear you.' The shipwide intercom channel brought Vector's voice to the cabin. He might have been shouting to make himself heard over the hull-roar. Or else all this g had brutalized his sore joints, and he shouted against his pain. 'Tell me what you want. I'll do it.'

'I can't,' Mikka breathed through her teeth. 'You're in no condition –'

'Angus is outside!' Davies retorted. 'He shouldn't be alive. But he left his pickup open. I can hear him breathing.

'Put on a suit. Go get him – bring him in.'

'See?' Ciro told her. 'There isn't anybody else.' He spoke as if her predicament were as simple as his. 'Vector has to rescue Angus. Morn can't handle hard g. Sib is gone.' Even Nick was gone. Dimly Ciro remembered hearing someone – Davies? Morn? – tell Mikka that Nick and Sib had left the ship to attack *Soar* in EVA suits. 'I'll just rest until you come back.'

'I'm on my way,' Vector replied. Even when he shouted, he didn't sound like a man who understood ruin.

With an inward convulsion, Mikka made her decision. 'Do that,' she ordered bitterly. 'Lock the door after me. Seal your g-sheath, don't get out of bed.' In spite of her wounds and

27

exhaustion, she was too strong to ignore Davies' need – or *Trumpet*'s. 'I won't be gone long. Just until we get past whatever Davies is upset about.'

Just until Ciro did what he had to do in order to save his soul.

When Sorus Chatelaine captured the gap scout, she would give him back his humanity. His sanity –

The g of *Trumpet*'s acceleration canted the cabin steeply. Brandishing her glare like a fist, Mikka rolled out of the bunk, planted her feet, and climbed to the door. When she'd reached it and keyed it open, however, she turned toward him again.

'I mean it,' she insisted. 'Don't get out of bed. You're *safe* here. As safe as it's possible for any of us to be. That mutagen is gone. This isn't something Vector could be wrong about. And you *know* him. You *know* he wouldn't lie to you.'

She might have gone on. Pronouncing reassurances he couldn't hear. He could tell she wanted to. But she must have seen that he was out of reach. Abruptly she clamped her mouth shut. The muscles at the corners of her jaw knotted dangerously as she left the cabin.

Left the cabin.

Left him alone.

She wouldn't come back: he was sure of that. Not when Davies needed her so badly. *I'm alone here. I can't do this many jobs at once.* Ciro trusted her implicitly, even though she'd nearly driven him crazy.

His heart pounded like terror in his chest. A dozen different vitriols seemed to burn through his veins.

The mutagen stays in you.

Somehow he forced himself to wait until he heard the wheeze of the lift as it strained against the fierce g. That sound meant Vector was on his way to the airlock. The central passage of the gap scout was probably clear.

At once Ciro ripped his g-sheath aside, flipped off the bunk, and flung himself toward the door like an unleashed animal; frantic for freedom.

It stays alive.

A dread coded into the most primitive structures of his DNA compelled him. Out in the passage, he moved directly to the nearest emergency toolkit. He knew where it was: in his demeaning role as *Trumpet*'s cabin boy, he'd been given the job of putting the C-spanner with which Nick had attacked Angus several days ago back where it belonged; and so he'd learned where all the toolkits were stowed.

It works its way into every cell and wraps itself around your DNA strings.

If anyone else came into the passage now, they would see what he was doing. Mikka, Davies, even Morn: any of them would try to stop him. But he ignored the danger. There was nothing he could do about it except hurry – and he was already hurrying as much as the gap scout's thrust allowed.

From its g-case he retrieved the spanner. Flakes of dried blood and a crust or two of tissue still clung to its shaft: he hadn't cleaned it very well. But that didn't matter. Angus' blood was still human. So was his scalp. Ciro tucked the spanner under his belt. Into his pockets he put a circuit probe, a small utility laser, an assortment of wires, clamps and solder.

Then he went looking for an access hatch which would let him into *Trumpet*'s drive space.

That's why I serve them, Ciro. If I don't, they'll cut me off from the antidote.

And that's why you're *going to serve* me.

The job would probably take a long time. He'd never seen the inside of the drive space; had no idea how the circuits and equipment might be arranged. And he didn't want to risk wrecking the wrong systems. The idea that he might cripple, say, life-support and leave the drives active terrified him. He would have to probe and test and search until he found the right control panels. But he knew how to do that. Vector had taught him. And he carried the vial Sorus Chatelaine had given him. He could afford to spend a few hours carrying out his mission.

In his own way, he was as loyal as Mikka.

HASHI

As he expected, he was the last to reach Warden's designated office – one of the private, utilitarian, and above all secure rooms in which the director of the UMCP officially ceased to exist for the outside world. Koina Hannish and Chief Mandich were there ahead of him.

Koina sat against the wall to the left of the door where Hashi entered: a deliberately self-effacing position which may have expressed her awareness that Protocol had only a small role to play at the moment. Opposite her stood Chief Mandich. The two of them approximately bracketed Warden's desk.

Obviously the UMCPED Security Chief was here to account for his own inadequacies in person; but he also represented Min Donner by proxy. His discomfort was plain in his refusal to accept a seat. Although his back was to the wall, he did nothing so casual as lean on it. He stood with his hands clasped behind him and his shoulders stiff. The heat which had mottled his face and neck earlier had subsided, but it remained apparent.

Warden sat behind his desk with his forearms braced on the desktop and his palms flat. His single eye glittered with penetration, complementing the resources of the IR prosthesis hidden by his patch. He was not an especially large man, but the strength of his frame and the immobility of his posture made him appear carved in stone; as unreachable as an icon.

Hashi shuffled quickly into the room, strewing apologies

in all directions, although he hardly listened to them himself. The door closed behind him: he heard the seals slot home, metallic and final. That sound gave him the unsettling impression that he'd entered the presence of ultimate questions. When he neared the front of Warden's desk, he stopped; glanced around him for a chair. But he didn't presume to sit until Warden made a gesture of permission with one blunt hand.

'Don't apologize, Hashi,' Warden said harshly. 'Explain. Tell me why we've been twiddling our thumbs here for the past ten minutes as if we didn't have anything better to do.'

Warden Dios, Hashi noted, was not in a good mood.

With an effort he stifled his impulse for obfuscation. 'Lane Harbinger has been studying the kaze's remains.' His glasses had slid too far down his nose to muffle him from Warden's gaze, but he didn't push them up. 'I waited as long as I could – until I received your summons. Then I took the time to obtain a preliminary report.'

For the sake of his own dignity, he declined to comment on whether or not Lane's report had been worth hearing – or worth waiting for.

Warden studied Hashi as he spoke, then nodded once, brusquely. 'All right. We're in a crisis – the worst crisis any of us has ever seen. But the fact that the rest of us have just wasted ten minutes probably doesn't increase the danger.'

Hashi blinked owlishly. Did Warden consider Imposs/Alt's attack 'the worst crisis any of us has ever seen'? Impossible. Surely he could not be so entirely divorced from the world of the real. To call that attack anything less than an emergency was foolish: to call it anything more was madness.

'You think we're here to discuss Suka Bator,' Warden rasped. 'And some of you' – he seemed to concentrate briefly on Hashi – 'are wondering why I took so long to summon you. Well, we are going to discuss Suka Bator. I want to know what happened. More than that, I want to know what it means.

'But an attack on the Council is only one side of our predicament. Before we go on, I'll tell you what else has

31

happened. Then you'll understand why I didn't call for you right away.'

What else has happened. Hashi smiled his relief, despite the grimness of Warden's tone. After some anxious moments, he felt suddenly sure that the UMCP director was about to justify the confidence Hashi had placed in him.

'Crudely put,' Warden announced as if he were full of a bitterness he could neither contain nor release, 'the situation is this. For all practical purposes, we are at war.'

Chief Mandich stiffened. He took a step toward the director's desk, perhaps without being aware of it. His blunt features became as hard as Warden's.

Koina leaned forward, her lips parted slightly. Her eyes were dark with shock and dread; with a human being's essential genetic horror of the Amnion.

War? Hashi's heart skipped a beat, then started rattling in his chest like an electron barrage. At war? With some difficulty he refrained from asking, Is this why you accepted Milos Taverner as a control for our Joshua? Did you foresee it? Is it what you hoped to gain?

'Two hours ago,' Warden continued, 'I received a message from Min Donner by gap courier drone from Valdor Industrial. More precisely, the message is from VI Security, but she ordered them to send it. She reports that an Amnion "defensive" has entered the Massif-5 system. A Behemoth-class Amnion warship.

'At that distance from forbidden space, I think we can dismiss the idea that she's there by mistake. According to VI Security, *Punisher* has engaged the defensive, but the fight isn't going well. *Punisher* is damaged, not at full capacity. The defensive's shields and sinks are holding. On top of that' – he paused darkly – 'she's armed with super-light proton cannon.'

Mandich swore under his breath. Hashi would have done the same if he hadn't been armored against betraying his emotions. Warden's tone conveyed images of bloodshed and destruction. They constricted the air in his small office, making it hard to breathe. A super-light proton cannon was especially fearsome because it could wreak havoc through a planetary atmosphere. Matter cannon were useless for that: air protected the surface better than any particle sink. And lasers were too precise to unleash wholesale ruin. In addition, they tended to lose coherence across large distances. A super-light proton cannon, however –

Warden didn't stop.

'VI is scrambling support for *Punisher*,' he went on. 'Unfortunately those ships aren't in range yet. For some reason the defensive isn't anywhere near the main shipping lanes – or the Station itself, for that matter. And our cruiser *Vehemence* is too far away to be involved in the action.'

How entirely typical, Hashi thought. His attention was fixed on Warden; nailed there. Nevertheless his mind ran off on several oblique angles simultaneously. *Vehemence*'s record was far from illustrious. No matter who commanded her, or how her crew was composed and trained, she seemed inherently luckless or incompetent. To all appearances Nathan Alt's months as her captain had put a curse on her.

'What are your orders, Director?' Chief Mandich put in abruptly. Tension strained his voice to a croak. 'Director Donner isn't here. I have to –'

He may have been as honest as an iron bar, but Hashi considered him inadequate to take Min Donner's place.

Koina had better sense than the Security Chief: she waited her turn.

Warden stopped the Chief with a rough gesture. The move-ment of his single eye was sharp as a slap.

'Since then,' he pronounced trenchantly, 'I've been making preliminary preparations for our defense. Our shipyards have gone to emergency work shifts. We need to get every ship we can into space. UMCPHQ is on alert. I've ordered *Sledge-hammer* back. And I've sent out drones to recall *Valor* and *Adventurous*.'

Sledgehammer was a full battlewagon, the biggest and most powerful warship the UMCP had ever built. Currently she was executing shakedown maneuvers out between the orbits of Jupiter and Saturn; training her crew to handle a vessel

33

that massive. Too near to return to Earth by crossing the gap: too far to arrive at space-normal speeds in less than days. As for the other vessels Warden named, the destroyer *Valor* was on patrol around Terminus, the station in human space farthest from the Amnion. The obsolete cruiser *Adventurous* had been assigned to supervise exercises for the cadets of Aleph Green.

Other ships were available, of course. Hashi could think of half a dozen gunboats and pocket cruisers within Earth's control space. They were paltry, however, for a task the size of defending a planet.

UMCPHQ itself couldn't do that job. The Station had scarcely been designed to defend itself. It possessed shields and sinks; cannon of various kinds; but nothing that would be effective on such a scale. Any war which came close enough to Earth to threaten UMCPHQ was presumed to be already lost.

'But,' Warden pursued, 'I don't want to leave us spread too thin elsewhere – as if we weren't already – because I don't know what the Amnion are going to do next. From a strategic point of view, VI isn't exactly a logical target for an act of war.'

Indeed. Hashi followed his director's reasoning at the same time that he chased his own thoughts. Humankind's ability to give battle would hardly be diminished – at least in the short term – by VI's complete destruction. In addition that station was too well defended, as well as too difficult to approach, for a single assailant to be sure of success. Any attack on Valdor would probably be a waste of effort.

'I have to assume,' Warden stated, 'that subsequent threats might not be logical either. I mean strategically. Since the Amnion aren't prone to either waste or foolhardiness, I also assume that this incursion doesn't imply a full-scale assault on human space. It has some other objective.

'I can guess what that is, but I can't guess where it might go. So I can't predict where to concentrate our defenses.'

Koina had been silent too long. Now her dread seemed to compel her to speak.

34

'Please tell us, Director,' she murmured softly. 'I think we need to know.'

'I'm sure you do,' Warden snorted. However, his sarcasm or disgust did not appear to be directed at her.

'You're all aware Min Donner is aboard *Punisher*,' he answered between his teeth. 'And you've probably guessed that I ordered her there to help protect *Trumpet*.'

'No, wait,' Koina protested. 'I'm sorry, you've lost me. All I know about *Trumpet* is what you and Director Lebwohl told the Council. Angus Thermopyle and Milos Taverner stole her –'

'No, *I'm* sorry,' Warden interrupted. For a moment he gave the impression that he'd been overtaken by weariness. His personal defenses had flaws he couldn't afford. 'It's all these damn secrets. I've been carrying them around too long.' With the fingers of one hand, he rubbed his forehead briefly. 'Sometimes I forget I haven't told you something critical.

'Angus Thermopyle didn't steal *Trumpet*. He's a cyborg. We welded him after we reqqed him from Com-Mine Station. He works for us. We sent him into forbidden space to carry out a covert attack on Thanatos Minor. And we sent Milos Taverner along to keep an eye on him. The story that they stole *Trumpet* was just cover. We didn't want to make the wrong people suspicious.

'If Igensard asks in front of the Council,' Warden added, 'you can tell him that.'

'But I still don't –' Koina bit her lip. 'Never mind. I'll need the details later. For now the present is more important.'

The director nodded like an act of brutality. 'I sent *Punisher* to the Com-Mine belt,' he resumed, 'to wait for *Trumpet* to escape back into human space. Then she followed the gap scout to Massif-5.

'Why *Trumpet* went I don't know.

'But if the Amnion chose to commit an act of war by entering that system – and chose to do it *now* – for reasons that don't have anything to do with *Trumpet*, it's the biggest coincidence in history. I think we can be sure the defensive is after *Trumpet*.'

Hashi felt the tension in the room. Chief Mandich radiated dismay; the anxiety of vast responsibilities. Koina struggled to manage the scale of her incomprehension. Warden had the air of a man who was determined to hold the center of a whirlwind. At the same time, however, the DA director rode an entirely private swirl of oblique inferences and intriguing possibilities. An act of war? Fascinating! Whose game was this? Warden's? Nick Succorso's? The Amnion's? – with or without Captain Succorso's participation?

Uncertainties proliferated like ecstasy, weaving unknowns out of the quantum mechanics of the known. In his excitement Hashi dared to say, 'It might be argued that we would do well to let this defensive succeed against *Trumpet*.'

Holt Fasner would surely approve.

Koina drew a sharp breath. Chief Mandich swore softly.

At once Warden's gaze focused on Hashi. He could almost feel his electromagnetic aura frying under the intensity of the director's IR sight.

'Explain,' Warden demanded.

Hashi shrugged; smiled. The risk he took pleased him: it might prod Warden to reveal more of his intentions. The director could stop him if he went too far.

He directed his words and his gamble at Warden, although they were superficially meant for Koina and Mandich.

'Director Hannish and Chief Mandich have perhaps not been informed that our Angus Thermopyle, Isaac né Joshua, has escaped forbidden space with a remarkable combination of companions. In particular I refer to Morn Hyland, first Captain Thermopyle's victim, then Captain Succorso's.

'This is an unexpected development for several reasons. On your direct orders, Isaac's datacore was explicitly written to preclude the possibility that he might save Ensign Hyland's life.' Then Warden had switched that datacore for another; a new set of instructions. But this secret was Warden's to reveal or hide: Hashi had no intention of exposing it. He used it only to put pressure on the director. 'She is – or has been – thought dangerous to our purposes. Only a strange, unforeseeable sequence of events could have led to her presence aboard *Trumpet*.'

'What "purposes"?' Koina asked quickly; intently.

Hashi ignored her to concentrate on Warden.

'In addition,' he continued, 'we have reason to suspect that she has been a prisoner of the Amnion, delivered to them by Captain Succorso to gain some end we can hardly imagine. Thus it is doubly strange that she now accompanies our Captain Thermopyle. Did she escape? If so, how? Was she released? If so, why?'

The DA director was not entirely prepared to surrender his hypothesis that Morn might be a type of genetic kaze: ruin aimed at the UMCP. Angus had rescued Morn – privately Warden had admitted as much – but that didn't erase other possibilities.

Warden frowned as Hashi finished. For a long moment he kept his grip on Hashi's eyes: he may have been searching to find out how much Hashi knew – or guessed. Then he nodded. 'I'll keep that in mind.'

'Forgive me, Director,' Koina put in insistently. She remained almost motionless in her seat, yet she gave the impression that she'd risen to her feet. A low tremor flawed her tone without softening her manner. 'Director Lebwohl said "purposes". "*Our* purposes." In what sense is it conceivable that Ensign Hyland could be a threat to any purpose of ours?

'I heard Director Lebwohl tell the Council why we let Captain Succorso have her. I didn't like that, but this sounds a lot worse. She's one of *our people*. Why in God's name would a UMCP cyborg's datacore be "explicitly written to preclude" rescuing her? I would have said that violates our *purposes* more than anything she might say or do.'

No doubt Min Donner would have approved Koina's objection. To the extent that he was capable of thinking clearly, Chief Mandich surely felt the same. Nevertheless Hashi was not swayed by it. Deliberately he pushed his glasses up on his nose. The smear of the unnecessary lenses aided his concentration.

Now more than ever he needed to understand Warden Dios.

Although Warden sat still, his frame seemed to intensify, almost to swell, as if he were taking on mass from the air and ambience of his office. He faced the PR director with an ungiving glare while she spoke. When he responded, his voice was gravid with bile and self-coercion. Each word was as exact as the flash of a laser.

'Director Hannish, how did we get the Preempt Act passed?'

She answered without relaxing her insistence. 'A traitor in Com-Mine Security conspired with Angus Thermopyle to steal supplies.' Beneath her professional polish and her womanish softness, Hashi realized, she was tougher than departed Godsen Frik had ever been. 'That scared the Council. The Members decided that if they couldn't trust local Station Security they had no choice but to expand our jurisdiction.'

Warden nodded. 'Would the Act have passed if the Council hadn't been scared?'

A twist of her mouth suggested a shrug. 'They voted it down on two previous occasions.'

'Exactly.' Warden's voice sounded sharp enough to draw blood; perhaps his own. 'But the Members were mistaken. We misled them. The "traitor" in Com-Mine Security didn't conspire with Angus Thermopyle. He conspired with *us*. We framed Captain Thermopyle to scare the Council. So the Act would pass.'

The director's compressed strength dominated the room. 'Ensign Hyland knows he's innocent,' he finished. 'She was there. And I'm sure she'll say so, if anyone asks her the right questions.

'You can tell Igensard *that*, too, if it ever comes up.'

Koina recoiled as if Warden had flicked his fingers in her face. A pallor of betrayal seemed to leach the color from her cheeks; even from her eyes. Indignation and confusion appeared to flush through Chief Mandich in waves, staining his skin with splotches like the marks of an infection. Knowledge which was commonplace to Hashi had never reached the Security Chief, or the new PR director. Min Donner and even Godsen Frik had known how to keep their hearts closed.

In one sense Hashi noticed the reactions of his companions. But in another he paid no attention to them at all. He wanted to applaud and throw up his hands simultaneously. Warden had astonished him again.

The director was willing to reveal the truth behind the passage of the Preempt Act. That was immensely exciting. It shed an amazing amount of light on the nature of Warden's game: too much light for Hashi to absorb in an instant. He found himself almost blinking in its brilliance. Yet that same revelation was also appallingly dangerous. When the truth was laid bare the UMCP director – and all his senior staff – would be summarily fired. At best. At worst they might even find themselves facing capital charges.

Just when the Amnion had committed an act of war, humankind's only defense would be plunged into total disarray.

'My God,' Chief Mandich breathed as if he were unable to stop himself. 'Did Director Donner know? Was she part of it?'

For him that may have been the essential question. Could he still trust the ED director? His rectitude was founded on hers. Could he continue to believe that she was honest?

Hashi would have dismissed the issue as trivial; but Warden faced it squarely.

'Yes.' His tone was final, fatal: it permitted no argument. 'But understand this. We did what we did on the direct orders of my lawful superior, Holt Fasner.' He stressed the word *lawful* with a bitterness like concentrated sulfuric acid. 'And those orders included secrecy. There would have been no point to it if we hadn't kept it secret.'

Did he mean to make *that* public as well? Did he intend that Koina should name the Dragon's role in the conduct of the UMCP before the Council itself?

Of course he did.

The prospect took Hashi's breath away. He flapped a hand in Chief Mandich's direction as if he were trying to shoo Security's petty honesty from the room. The nature of Warden's game transcended such considerations.

Hashi couldn't inhale enough to raise his voice. Softly he murmured, 'Yet you choose to reveal it now.'

'Yes,' Warden rasped without hesitation. 'Listen to me, all of you.' He aimed his single gaze in turn at Koina, at Hashi, at Chief Mandich. 'Get this straight. I choose to reveal it now.'

Now, when the GCES had just been stampeded into rejecting a Bill of Severance which would have broken the Dragon's hold on the UMCP.

Hashi's lungs strained for air.

Would it work? Would Warden succeed at toppling Holt Fasner with his own fall?

Perhaps. With Hashi's help: perhaps. These revelations, these unguessed gravitons of information, might well lack the force to pull Fasner from his throne unaided. The great worm was profoundly entrenched. They could be augmented, however –

An almost childlike sense of affection for his director swelled in Hashi's chest. At the same time he felt that he had been personally exalted by several orders of magnitude. Suddenly he was aware that he could comprehend and participate in the quantum energies of this crisis on a scale which would have been impossible for him only moments earlier. A blaze of illumination had effaced the shame of his incapacity to grasp Warden's game.

He found himself beaming unselfconsciously, like a senile old man. A joy as acute as terror throbbed in his veins.

He knew at once that he would give the UMCP director all the help he could.

Baffled by a rush of information he was unable to manage, Chief Mandich retreated into a pose of clenched stolidity. He belonged to ED; and as Min Donner had sometimes said, ED was the fist of the UMCP, not the brain. The Security Chief was accustomed to using his mind for his own duties,

40

not for analyzing the underlying purpose of Warden's policies. Hashi felt sure that Mandich was full of outrage. He was also sure, however, that the Chief would continue to take orders – and carry them out faithfully – at least until Min Donner returned to account for herself.

Koina may have understood Warden's intent as little as Mandich did, but she responded differently.

'Director Dios,' she said coldly, 'I'll certainly tell Special Counsel Igensard – as soon as an appropriate occasion presents itself.' The chill in her voice was extreme. Her inflections might have been rimed with ice. 'But that's a secondary issue. Under the circumstances, whether or not the UMCP has any integrity' – she froze the word to such brittleness that it threatened to shatter – 'can't be our first concern. The Amnion have committed an act of war. That's primary.

'Are you going to tell the Council?'

'Of course.' A tightening around Warden's eyes made Hashi think he found the question painful. 'That's the law. It's also my duty.

'But first I want to know where events are going, what the stakes are. If I can't tell the Members what the threat actually is, they're liable to do something stupid.'

Indeed they were. Hashi agreed completely. From an historical perspective, it was plain that elected officials acting in legislative bodies seldom did anything which could not be called stupid. And in this case the difficulties were greatly increased by the fact that many of the Members derived their positions, directly or indirectly, from Holt Fasner – who in turn derived much of his wealth and power from trade with the Amnion.

Koina appeared to grant Warden's reply a provisional assent. However, he had already moved on as if he neither wanted nor needed any acknowledgment from her.

'Which brings us,' he said mordantly, 'back to Suka Bator.

'You three were there. Chief Mandich, you've been made responsible for security on the Council island. In particular you were responsible for security during this extraordinary session of the GCES.'

The Chief tightened his lips to a pale line; but his only reply was, 'Yes, sir.'

'Director Hannish,' Warden continued, 'you were responsible for representing formal UMCP policy before the Council. Director Lebwohl' – the UMCP director paused to study Hashi momentarily – 'I will presume you were there because you're responsible for our investigation of the kazes who attacked Captain Vertigus and killed Godsen Frik.'

Hashi nodded, but he held his tongue.

'I want to know the exact nature of the threats we face. That means I want to know what the Amnion are doing. And I want to know what's behind these kazes. Who's sending them? Why are they being sent? And why are they being sent now, when the Amnion have just committed an act of war? How we respond to one is likely to depend on what we do about the other.'

Why are they being sent now? Hashi considered this interrogative a trifle specious. He was convinced that Warden understood the timing of recent events very well. He kept his belief to himself, however.

'So you tell me,' Warden concluded, 'the three of you. What happened? What the hell is going on?'

He did not single out Chief Mandich for answers. Perhaps he realized that no question he could ask would search the Chief more intimately than Mandich searched himself.

Nevertheless Chief Mandich considered it his duty to report first.

'I'm still waiting to hear from DA, sir,' he began. 'I can't account for what happened myself.' That admission came awkwardly for him. His sense of culpability was plain on his blunt face. 'We took every precaution I know of. Retinal scans. Every kind of EM probe we have available.' The kind of scanning which Angus Thermopyle had been constructed and equipped to circumvent. 'Full id tag and credential background verifications. For everybody on the island. And everybody who arrived or left. The kaze still got through. He must have been legit – even though that's supposed to be impossible.

'Since then it's been up to DA. I've sealed the island. Nobody in or out – except our own people. Some of the Members are squalling about it.' The Chief shrugged. He had no qualms about discomfiting the Members. 'They want to go hide. But if whoever is behind this is on Suka Bator, I'm going to make sure he stays there. So we can find him.'

Hashi nodded his approval. He knew that no direct evidence would be found on the island. A chemical trigger released on a preconditioned signal by a man in a state of drug-induced hypnosis would leave no traceable data. Nevertheless he wished to be certain that the responsible individual would not escape.

Casually he asked, 'Has the Dragon's estimable First Executive Assistant posed any objection?'

'No,' Chief Mandich retorted.

Of course not. In such matters Holt Fasner's aides and cohorts preserved an illusion of complete cooperation.

'I haven't had time to study the reports,' Warden put in. 'Cleatus Fane attended the session?'

He did not appear to be taken aback.

'Oh, yes,' Koina answered before the Chief could speak. Hashi suspected that she held Mandich blameless and wished to spare him unnecessary chagrin. She was capable of such consideration, even when her own chagrin ran high. 'I was surprised to see him. So were quite a few of the Members.

'Several of them had the impression he was there because he knew why Captain Vertigus had claimed Member's privilege. That doesn't make sense to me. I don't see how anyone could have known what Captain Vertigus had in mind' – she held Warden's gaze without faltering – 'unless he told them. But Fane was there anyway, emitting bonhomie like toxic radiation.'

Hashi chuckled pleasantly at her transparent dislike for the UMC First Executive Assistant.

Still facing Warden, she said, 'You know what happened.' She made no pretense that this was a question. 'Captain Vertigus used his privilege to introduce a Bill of Severance. He wants to dissolve us as a branch of the UMC and reconstitute us as an arm of the GCES.'

For his part Warden made no pretense that he had been caught unaware.

'Fane raised a number of objections,' she stated. 'Then he called on me to support him. I announced formally that our position on such matters was one of complete neutrality. I gave our reasons. Fane didn't seem to like them much.'

'I'm sure he didn't,' the UMCP director remarked acerbically. 'Maybe that explains why he's been trying to call me' – Warden indicated his intercom – 'every twenty minutes for the past two hours. Fortunately I've been too busy to talk to him.'

Maybe: maybe not. Hashi could think of at least one alternative rationale for Cleatus Fane's calls.

Apparently Koina could not. Or she saw no reason to redirect her account of the session. 'After that,' she resumed, 'Director Lebwohl spotted the kaze. He still hasn't told any of us how he managed that. But if he hadn't been there, a lot more people would have died. Some of the Members might have been killed.

'As it was, the cost was high enough.' Complex fears darkened her tone. 'GCES Security lost a man. An ED Security ensign lost a hand. And we lost the Bill. I suppose the Members believed Fane's argument that we would be weaker if we were separated from the UMC – and right now their lives depend on making us as strong as possible.'

She fell silent. After a moment her gaze shifted from Warden to Hashi.

Warden and Chief Mandich were also looking at the DA director. The time had come for him to speak.

He didn't hesitate. He was at home among the uncertainties which crowded Warden's office, the swirl of secret intentions; in his element. 'Director Dios,' he offered with a sly smile, 'you might find it entertaining to accept the First Executive Assistant's call.'

'Why?' Warden asked.

Hashi shrugged delicately. 'I suspect that his reasons for

44

wishing to address you have little or nothing to do with Captain Vertigus' Bill. The issues he hopes to obfuscate may prove to be of another kind altogether.'

Warden shook his head. He seemed to be beyond surprise. 'I want to hear your report first.'

Hashi bowed slightly. 'As you wish.'

Ignoring the pressure of scrutiny from Koina and Chief Mandich, he presented his information directly to Warden Dios.

'The means by which I identified a kaze in the extraordinary session of the GCES is easily explained. Quite simply, I recognized him. That is to say, despite his GCES Security uniform, I recognized him as the infamous Captain Nathan Alt. You would have done so yourself, had you been there.'

Koina caught her breath at the name. The Chief growled a soft curse.

Warden raised an eyebrow, but didn't comment.

Hashi warmed to the pleasure of his own explanations. 'Captain Alt's presence in the Council hall struck me as unexpected,' he expounded. 'And I admit that I was alert to all things unexpected. Director Hannish had relayed to me Captain Vertigus' fear of another attack. I considered his fears credible. That in large part motivated my presence at the extraordinary session.

'Because Captain Alt's presence was unexpected, I moved to intercept him, hoping to obtain an explanation. When I drew near enough to see him more clearly, I had no difficulty identifying the danger he represented. First, his eyes and his manner indicated that he had been heavily drugged. Second, his credentials were not those of Nathan Alt, former UMCPED captain. They were those of one Clay Imposs, a GCES Security sergeant.'

With false ingratiation, Hashi added smoothly, 'I'm sure Chief Mandich would have drawn the same conclusions I did – and taken the same actions – if chance had given him the same opportunity to recognize Captain Alt.'

Nathan Alt's name was well known in UMCPHQ. However, his court-martial had taken place several years ago;

before Koina's time. On the other hand, as a member of ED – with a personal investment in ED's reputation – Chief Mandich almost certainly remembered the former captain well enough to identify him.

Hashi spread his hands disingenuously. 'So much is simple.

'All that remains to be said of the events themselves is that before Chief Mandich's stalwarts impelled the putative Clay Imposs from the hall, thereby saving almost any number of lives, I contrived to snatch the clearance badge from his uniform, as well as the id tag from his neck.'

Now at last Warden permitted himself a reaction which may have been surprise. His eye widened: he shook his head slightly.

'So what?' Chief Mandich put in harshly. 'That tag and badge aren't going to help us. I'm sure you're right about Nathan Alt. I'm sure his credentials are legit for Clay Imposs. Otherwise he wouldn't have been cleared. And I'm sure they were doctored somehow. Otherwise he wouldn't have gotten past a retinal scan. But even if you figure out how they were doctored, you won't be able to prove who did it. His id tag and badge will just confirm what we already know. Which is that whoever's behind this has access to all the right codes.'

'You took a terrible risk, Hashi,' Koina breathed. 'You could have been killed. What did you hope to gain?'

Hashi ignored both her and Mandich. 'Since my departure from Suka Bator,' he told Warden, 'Data Acquisition has been diligent in its assigned functions. The technical aspects of this investigation I have entrusted to Lane Harbinger, whose qualifications for the task are superb. For my part, I have taken the occasion to impose Red Priority security locks on various data venues, hoping to ensure the accuracy of the information which may be obtained from them.' Briskly he named the sites he'd sealed. 'In addition I have obtained preliminary readouts from Data Storage on both Nathan Alt and Clay Imposs.'

'Go on,' Warden murmured like a man who couldn't be moved.

Hashi did. He had no intention of stopping.

'The vanished Imposs we may dismiss,' he stated. 'His records are both correct and clean. No marks tell against him. We must assume, I believe, that he is dead – a victim of intentions in which he had no other role except to die. It is likely that his body will never be found.'

Corpses which had been burned down to their essential energies, or dissolved into their component chemicals, no longer existed in any form which might be susceptible to discovery.

'Nathan Alt, as you might imagine, is another matter entirely.

'I will spare you the less relevant details of his history.' Hashi enjoyed lecturing. The more he explained, the more he understood. 'The primary facts are these. Less than a year after his court-martial, Captain Alt found employment with Nanogen, Inc., a research and development concern studying the production of microchips and electronic devices by nano-technological means. Specifically he found employment in Nanogen Security, despite – or perhaps because of – his record.

'Not surprisingly,' Hashi remarked dryly, 'Nanogen, Inc., is a wholly owned subsidiary of the United Mining Companies.

'Since then, our subject's career has been one of steady advancement through the vast hierarchy of the UMC's Security departments. Again I will spare you the details. For our purposes, the crucial point is that approximately a year ago he attained the position of Security Liaison for Anodyne Systems, the sole licensed manufacturer of SOD-CMOS chips.'

'We know what Anodyne Systems does,' Chief Mandich muttered.

Hashi didn't respond. He went on speaking to Warden as if the two of them were alone.

'I suspect that First Executive Assistant Fane will confirm this when you accept his call. One of the redoubtable FEA's duties as the Dragon's right hand concerns the oversight of Anodyne Systems.'

'We know that, too,' Warden said brusquely. 'Get to the point, Hashi.'

He didn't add, *I have an act of war to worry about.* There was no need.

Nevertheless Hashi declined to be hurried. The quantum mechanics of truth yielded its secrets only when its uncertainties were handled with care.

'Quite naturally,' he continued as if he were impervious to any exigencies except his own, 'as Security Liaison for Anodyne Systems, Nathan Alt had no dealings with us.' In his own way he considered himself as unreachable as the UMCP director. 'He had no direct contact with the UMCP at all. We supply all working personnel for Anodyne Systems. In particular we supply all security. Rather his duties involved coordinating the flow of knowledge and skill between UMC as well as UMCP cryptographers and Anodyne Systems Security.

'Specifically his responsibilities centered on the design of the embedded code engines which generate clearances for both the Governing Council for Earth and Space and the United Mining Companies Police. His assigned task – I quote from the personnel mandate of his employment – was "to ensure the highest possible level of precision and invulnerability" in those codes.

'The coincidence is intriguing, is it not? How did a man with Nathan Alt's record – and his reasons for disaffection – attain such a lofty and vital position? Perhaps Cleatus Fane will shed light on that question for us. Certainly our former captain's record suggests brilliance in code design and programming. And UMCP training is apt for security. In that sense he was well qualified for his work.

'Lest you think that we have committed some monumental blunder in regard to his involvement, let me stress that he had no power to select or alter the specific code engines employed by Anodyne Systems. Those decisions were made by Anodyne Systems Security under our explicit supervision. From our perspective Captain Alt was merely a resource which the UMC had made available to Anodyne Systems Security.

Therefore we had no reason to protest – or even to remark – his participation.

'Yet the fact remains that he supplied a substantial portion of the source-code and design for the engines currently in use. His proposals were tested and validated, and ultimately accepted, by our own Security techs. They were, in Chief Mandich's terms, "legit". Thus he has proved his value as a resource.

'Of course,' Hashi remarked casually, 'in order to make such a sensitive contribution to our own security, as well as to the Council's, Captain Alt required a complete knowledge of every facet of those code engines, including those portions which he did not supply.'

Obliquely Hashi wondered whether Koina and Mandich caught the implications. Warden assuredly did.

'What is the result?' the DA director asked rhetorically. 'Through the intervention – direct or indirect – of the Dragon, a man whom we have court-martialed for "dereliction of duty" has attained an intimate grasp on the most secret, as well as the most specialized, aspect of our procedures for self-protection.'

Now that man was dead.

His death in a state of drug-induced hypnosis suggested that he had not chosen his own end. Holt Fasner rarely inspired the loyalty for self-sacrifice.

Before Warden could insist again that he 'get to the point,' Hashi pronounced, 'Under the circumstances, we can be certain that Nathan Alt possessed both the skill and the knowledge to substitute his own physical id for Clay Imposs's credentials.'

The UMCP director appeared to study this assertion as if he had no essential interest in it; as if it changed nothing. But Chief Mandich reacted like a man who had been provoked beyond endurance.

'How?' he demanded fiercely. 'Tell me how. God damn it, Lebwohl, if you knew about this, why didn't you say something? We could have stopped him.'

Without glancing away from Hashi, Warden lifted a hand to warn the Security Chief that he went too far.

Mandich bit down his protest.

Into the space left by the Chief's silence, Koina placed a challenge of another kind.

'This doesn't make any sense, Hashi. If he could do all that, why did he choose himself to be the kaze? Don't you think that's a rather bizarre way to commit suicide?'

Warden continued watching the DA director stonily; remorselessly.

Now Hashi deigned to answer the Chief. 'There is no mystery here. If you were adept at the programming of SOD-CMOS chips, and if you held possession of both your id and mine, you would have no difficulty preparing a composite which blended my records with your physical data. In effect, the new id tag would identify you as me.'

He wished to show Warden that he could transcend Mandich's personal animosity. More than that, he wished to show that he was equal to Warden's game.

Koina's questions would answer themselves.

Warden planted his palms on the desktop in front of him – a gesture which usually indicated that he was out of patience.

'Director Lebwohl, I'm sure everything you're telling us is true.' His voice sounded guttural; angry and tense. 'And it's all important. But I don't have time for a seminar. None of us do. I need a *connection* – a real one, not some tenuous, circumstantial theory based on the fact that Fane hired a man who doesn't like us to help design SOD-CMOS code engines.'

Hashi nodded to show that he understood. 'May I again suggest,' he countered, 'that you allow the First Executive Assistant to contact you?'

Warden dismissed the idea. 'Not yet. You aren't done.'

Did it show? Hashi liked to believe that his personal IR emissions were difficult for Warden to interpret. The DA director had done studies on himself, seeking to determine how much his own aura revealed. The results had gratified him: he could tell the baldest lies without producing definable ripples along the bandwidths of Warden's sight. It was possible, however, that Warden understood the nature of Hashi's excitement in some unquantifiable and intuitive fashion.

'Very well,' Hashi acceded. 'Sadly, I cannot offer you a connection which will not appear both "circumstantial" and "tenuous" in law. Nevertheless the connection I propose has substance. It will hold.

'If we are fortunate' – he permitted himself a small grin – 'Cleatus Fane will confirm it for us.'

If the First Executive Assistant did so, that would also confirm the importance of Imposs/Alt's id tag and clearance badge.

'In no sense,' Hashi continued promptly, 'has Lane Harbinger had time to complete her study of Nathan Alt's earthly remains. However, certain of her preliminary findings may be relied upon.

'It is unmistakable, for example, that at the time of his demise our Captain Alt was deeply under the influence of hypnogogic substances. His actions in the hall were innocent of volition. He may well have both designed and carried out the procedures by which his id replaced Clay Imposs's, but his death was not a suicide. He did not elect his own end.'

If Min Donner's accusations during Alt's court-martial were accurate, the man was too much of a coward to die for any cause.

Koina sighed softly, nodding to herself as if she were relieved in some way. Idealistic images of the UMCP died hard, especially in Warden's presence. Apparently she had been quite disturbed by the idea that any UMCP officer could be so disenchanted that he would be willing to kill himself in order to harm his former service.

Because he spoke for Warden's benefit – as well as his own – Hashi didn't pause to acknowledge her reaction.

'The chemicals by which hypnosis may be induced are familiar to us. Lane will identify them precisely. However, Captain Alt's blood also holds heavy concentrations of a substance which is' – the DA director cleared his throat conspicuously – 'less commonly understood.

'That substance is a coenzyme. Inherently inert, it has no utility in itself. However, it combines with some of the human

51

body's natural apoenzymes to form an artificial holoenzyme, one which could not occur naturally. This holoenzyme is active.

'Lane's hypothesis – which I share – is that Captain Alt was dosed with this coenzyme in order to produce a holoenzyme which would serve as a chemical trigger for his explosive device.'

Now Hashi paused, maliciously allowing Chief Mandich time for some inapt remark. But the man kept silent. Perhaps he had realized that he was out of his depth.

In some indefinable way, Warden seemed to intensify. His outlines sharpened as if the light had changed: the strict shape of his face hinted at dangers and possibilities. He did nothing to interrupt or hurry Hashi.

'If our hypothesis is accurate,' Hashi resumed, 'several conclusions derive from it. First, no volition was required. It was not necessary that Captain Alt "set himself off".' Hashi articulated the colloquialism like a sneer. 'Second, the absence of some more mechanical timing device suggests that those accountable for this kaze wished to adjust the explosion to suit events. They were unwilling to guess in advance when their kaze might best be set off. Third, the use of a chemical trigger rather than a radio-controlled detonator suggests that the perpetrators felt some fear that they might be caught with the transmitter in their possession.

'Surely it is obvious that the timing of the blast could only have been adjusted to suit events by someone present in the hall.' Hashi permitted himself to elaborate this point unnecessarily while he explored some of the more obscure strands of inference spun by Lane's investigation. 'And it was surely predictable that UMCPED Security would seal the island in order to prevent any conceivable suspects from effecting an escape. Therefore the peril was real that an incriminating transmitter might be discovered.'

He glanced at Koina and Mandich as if he were asking them to fault his logic. Then he returned his attention to Warden.

'Thus the method becomes plain. Captain Alt is hypnotized

52

involuntarily. He is conditioned to respond to a specified signal – a particular word, a particular gesture. He is given – let us suppose until Lane's exploration is complete – a false tooth filled with a massive dose of the triggering coenzyme, a tooth which will break open when it is bitten. He is supplied, still involuntarily, with Clay Imposs's credentials. Then he is sent into the hall to await his signal – and his own death.

'The most obvious benefit of this method is that it leaves no evidence. The knowledge of the preconditioned signal – and of the man or woman culpable for it – dies with the kaze. No transmitter – or indeed timer – can be found.

'Coincidentally it perhaps rids the perpetrators of a man who might well have become an embarrassment to them.' A man who knew – and who therefore might reveal – how the code engines in question could be misused.

'The obvious conclusion,' Hashi stated with satisfaction, 'is that whoever gave the signal must have been within Captain Alt's clear field of view.'

Not simply present in the hall: present in plain sight from Nathan Alt's position.

Wondrous energy shells, layers of uncertainty, mapped the center of the atom; the core of truth.

Neither Director Hannish nor Chief Mandich spoke. Perhaps they sensed the presence of implications they were unable to define. Or perhaps they failed to grasp why Hashi considered these details to be so significant.

Warden's reaction was of another kind altogether.

Studying his DA director, he said quietly, 'All right. Let's see where this goes.' With a precise stab of his forefinger, he keyed his intercom.

'Director Dios?' a communications tech answered.

'I'll talk to Cleatus Fane now,' Warden announced. His tone carried the force of a commandment.

Koina settled herself back in her chair with a visible effort. Chief Mandich took another step forward as if he were ready for combat. Perhaps intuitively they both comprehended Hashi's explanations better than he realized.

'Right away, Director.' The intercom emitted thin hissings

53

and clicks as microwave relays shuttled, establishing a down-link. A moment later the tech said, 'Director Dios, I have First Executive Assistant Cleatus Fane by secure channel from Suka Bator.'

An alert on Warden's desk flashed until the tech left the line. Then the light turned green to indicate that the channel had been sealed against eavesdropping.

'Mr Fane,' Warden began bluntly. 'Sorry to keep you waiting. I've been busy.'

'I understand completely, Director Dios.' A faint spatter of static marred Fane's avuncular tones – solar flare activity, perhaps. 'Your duties have become especially complex recently. I wouldn't bother you at a time like this, but I think I have something to contribute to your investigation.' He chuckled fulsomely. 'That sonofabitch came close to killing me. I shudder to think what could have happened if Director Lebwohl hadn't spotted him. I'm very eager to make a contribution.'

Especially complex recently, Hashi thought. Doubtless Fane intended a reference to *Trumpet*, a reminder that Holt Fasner had given Warden orders. False bonhomie concealed pressure. The FEA meant Warden to understand that he could not afford to ignore anyone who spoke for the Dragon.

Warden was unmoved, however. 'I don't want to seem rude, Mr Fane,' he answered, 'but time is tight. What contribution did you have in mind?'

'Then I'll be brief. The sooner you finish your investigation, the sooner I can leave this hopeless rock.'

Not for the first time, Cleatus Fane's manner made Hashi think of a Santa Claus with fangs.

'By now, Director,' Fane began, 'I'm sure you've identified that kaze. I recognized him myself. If I'd noticed him earlier, we wouldn't have had to rely on Director Lebwohl to save us. *I* knew he might be dangerous. At the very least,' he explained, 'I knew he shouldn't be there. That would have made him look dangerous, even if I had nothing else to go on. But I didn't think to look at him closely until Director Lebwohl accosted him.

'His name is Nathan Alt. *The* Nathan Alt – the one who used to work for you. He was court-martialed for "dereliction" when he was in command of *Vehemence*. You know that. And you've had time to access his records, so you also know he's been working for us since then. I mean for the UMC. Specifically he was our Security Liaison for Anodyne Systems.'

Behind his smeared lenses and his impenetrable smile, Hashi resisted an impulse to hold his breath. Despite his confidence in the web of inferences he'd woven for Warden's benefit, he was acutely aware that he needed Cleatus Fane's confirmation. Without it he might be left looking uncomfortably like a man who grasped at straws in order to redeem his tarnished credibility.

Fane's disembodied voice continued smoothly. 'But that's not the reason I've been calling you. Aside from the fact,' he added piously, 'that we all have standing orders to give you our fullest cooperation whenever it's needed.' *We* no doubt referred to Holt Fasner's primary subordinates. 'There's something you may not know about him.'

'What's that, Mr Fane?' Warden put in noncommittally.

Fane paused for emphasis, then announced, 'We fired him six weeks ago. Threw him out.'

Koina shook her head at this information. Chief Mandich clenched his fists.

Only a conscious act of will prevented Hashi from laughing aloud.

Warden's shoulders tightened. He scowled at the intercom as if he were trying to read Cleatus Fane's aura through the blank mask of the microwave downlink.

'Why?' he demanded.

Fane answered promptly. 'I'm sure I don't need to tell you that we wouldn't have anybody working for us – certainly not in a position as sensitive as Security Liaison for Anodyne Systems – if he wasn't cleared by the most rigorous scrutiny.' An irritating fuzz of static distorted his sincerity. 'And we scrutinize everyone incessantly. Over and over again.

'Our latest – shall I call them observations? – of Nathan

55

Alt showed that over the past several months he's been in frequent contact with the native Earthers.'

The First Executive Assistant raised his voice to convey indignation. 'I don't need to remind you, Director Dios, that they're terrorists. The worst kind of scum. In the name of preserving humankind's "genetic purity", they oppose any dealings with the Amnion, even responsible trade. They oppose diplomatic relations. They oppose *us* because we do lawful, authorized business with forbidden space. And they don't hesitate to use violence of all kinds to support their policies.

'Of *course* we fired Nathan Alt. Once we knew he was in contact with the native Earthers, we couldn't trust him.'

Warden ignored Fane's outrage. 'And that's how you knew Alt was dangerous as soon as you recognized him?' he asked.

'Director Dios,' Cleatus Fane retorted strongly, 'I think the native Earthers are behind all these recent attacks. I think Nathan Alt gave them the means to supply kazes with legitimate id, and they've been using it to try to undermine both the UMC and the UMCP.

'Fortunately they can't succeed,' he added at once. 'The fact that the GCES soundly rejected Captain Vertigus' misguided Bill of Severance demonstrates that. But the danger is still real. And it must be stopped.'

Through the static he projected the righteous indignation of a man who had come close to a death he didn't deserve.

Warden grimaced at the intercom. After a moment he drawled mordantly, 'An interesting theory, Mr Fane. I want to be sure I understand it. The first attack – the one on Captain Vertigus – what was that supposed to accomplish? The native Earthers have always called him a hero.'

The FEA laughed humorlessly. 'But he hasn't done anything heroic for *decades*. He's too old and ineffectual to do them any good. They wanted to make him a martyr. His opposition to Holt Fasner and the UMC is common knowledge. They want people to think he was attacked to silence his opposition.'

Warden snorted softly; too softly to register on the intercom pickup. 'You can't apply the same argument to Godsen Frik.'

'Of course not.' Static or stress made Fane's bonhomie sound brittle. 'As a spokesman for the special relationship between the UMC and the UMCP, he's a natural enemy of the native Earthers. They wanted to use the confusion caused by Captain Vertigus' martyrdom to strike at one of their most public targets.'

For a moment Warden appeared to give this statement consideration. Then he asked, 'And the attack today?'

'An attempt to scare the Council,' Fane pronounced firmly. 'Fear breeds stupidity – and stupidity breeds native Earthers.'

Hashi considered this an interesting piece of conceptual legerdemain. From his perspective, stupidity bred rejection of Captain Vertigus' Bill of Severance.

Warden may have felt the same – Koina plainly did – but he didn't comment.

'I'll look into it,' he told the Dragon's henchman. 'But I have to say, Mr Fane, it makes me wonder why you hired Alt in the first place. You had reason to think he might not be particularly reliable.'

Cleatus Fane snorted. 'Because he couldn't meet Director Donner's standards for "conduct becoming an officer"? There aren't many men or women on the planet who can be that pure all the time. His court-martial didn't render him unfit for productive work. Or honorable work, for that matter,' Fane added.

'But the truth is' – microwave noise complicated his candor – 'his court-martial was one of the reasons we hired him. He never hid the fact that he resented the UMCP. From our point of view, that made him uniquely valuable. We wanted a man who was highly motivated to find fault with anything you people touched – especially with the security procedures designed for organizations like Anodyne Systems and the GCES. If he couldn't find chinks in your armor – so to speak – no one could. And if he could find them, we could fix them.'

The First Executive Assistant might as well have said, Don't try to challenge me, Director Dios. You're wasting your time.

Chief Mandich's features held a resentful scowl, but he didn't speak.

Warden shrugged noncommittally. 'As I say,' he replied, 'time is tight, Mr Fane. Director Lebwohl is already investigating some of the possibilities you've mentioned.' Cleatus Fane would know soon – if he didn't already – that Hashi had invoked Red Priority security locks for some of Holt Fasner's Home Office computers, as well as for all of Anodyne Systems'. 'Just one more question, if you don't mind.

'Did Alt take any of his work with him?'

'Director,' Fane answered heavily, 'nobody carries that kind of work around in his head. It's too minute and complex. His last project ran to something like eight million lines of source-code. Most of us would burn out our brains just trying to remember the design protocols.

'And we made damn sure he didn't carry it any other way. I can tell you that for a fact.'

On this point Hashi felt certain that the FEA's facts were accurate. Captain Alt's secrets – whatever they might have been – had never left the Dragon's orbital headquarters.

'Very well, Mr Fane,' Warden returned. 'I'll contact Holt Fasner directly when I have anything to report.'

He raised his hand and aimed one strong finger to silence the intercom.

On impulse Hashi left his seat so abruptly that Warden's hand stopped. In a rush Hashi reached the front of the desk and leaned over the intercom.

'Mr Fane?' he said quickly, almost breathlessly. 'Forgive the intrusion. This is Director Lebwohl. I am with Director Dios. Overhearing your discussion, I have a question of my own, if you will permit me to put it to you.'

Fane hesitated momentarily, then said, 'Go ahead, Director Lebwohl. Anything you want to know.'

Grinning past his glasses at Warden, Hashi responded promptly, 'You say that you fired Nathan Alt six weeks ago because he was in contact with the native Earthers. And you made sure – I believe you made "damn" sure – that none of his work left with him. Did you institute any other precautions to ensure the security of Anodyne Systems?'

If the First Executive Assistant was willing to go this far, surely he would go farther.

'Of course.' Fane's tone hinted at relief. He was prepared for this question. 'We made a mistake hiring Alt. We weren't going to compound it by being naive. In essence, we threw out everything he did while he was Security Liaison. I mean, we kept his ideas. Some of them were brilliant. But we erased every application he designed. We erased every application he might have touched. Then we wrote our own to replace his. And we wrote patches to alter the code engines in every SOD-CMOS chip Anodyne Systems manufactured during his tenure.

'Even if he was smuggling data and code to the native Earthers for months before we caught him,' Fane concluded, 'it's all useless to them now.'

Nodding to no one in particular, Hashi resumed his seat. He didn't trouble himself to thank Cleatus Fane.

Frowning at his DA director, Warden pursued, 'In other words, Mr Fane, you're sure the security breach which put legitimate id in the hands of three recent kazes didn't come from Nathan Alt? Directly or indirectly?'

'That's right,' Fane replied as if his credibility were intact. 'You have a traitor on your hands. That's obvious. But he isn't *here*.'

No doubt Fane meant in Holt Fasner's employ, either in his Home Office or in the UMC.

'Thank you, Mr Fane,' Warden said sharply. 'That's all.'

With a decisive stab of his finger, he toggled his intercom to end the First Executive Assistant's call.

Then he faced Hashi. His hands clenched each other on the desktop as if – literally as well as metaphorically – he needed to keep a grip on himself. His single eye caught the light like the wink of a cutting laser. Hope or fury beat visibly in the veins at his temples.

'All right, Director Lebwohl,' he said harshly. 'We've heard what Cleatus Fane has to say. What does it prove?'

Koina and Chief Mandich studied Hashi with their separate forms of incomprehension. Confusion appeared to aggravate the Chief's resentment. Perhaps he was irritated because he thought that Hashi's insistence on speaking to Fane wasted time. But Koina's bafflement was of a different kind. Hashi saw her as a woman whose primary assumptions prevented her from understanding what she heard.

'Ah, "prove",' he answered Warden. 'Nothing, I fear. We remain in the realm of the tenuous and circumstantial' – Werner Heisenberg's rich domain – 'despite the First Executive Assistant's generous confirmation. Nevertheless I believe that my conclusions are substantial. They will hold.'

Warden didn't hesitate. 'What *are* your conclusions?'

Hashi spread his hands as if to show that they were empty of subterfuge or misdirection. Enunciating each word distinctly, he announced, 'That these recent kazes have been sent against us by none other than the UMC CEO himself, Holt Fasner.'

With one forefinger the DA director pushed his glasses up on his nose to disguise the fact that he was keenly proud of himself.

HASHI

For an instant shock seemed to stun the room like a silent concussion. Then Chief Mandich demanded, '*What?*' Tensely Koina asked, 'Hashi, are you sure?'

The DA director gave them no reply. He reserved his clarity for Warden Dios.

'No doubt,' he elaborated, 'the conspiracy was carried out by Cleatus Fane – and to some extent by Nathan Alt. Nevertheless it derives both its authority and its intent from the great worm in his lair.'

Now both Koina and Mandich kept silent, awaiting Warden's reaction.

Warden allowed himself a long, slow breath. Some of the tension appeared to recede from his frame. Relief, perhaps? Or defeat? Hashi couldn't tell which. He could only trust that he had at last begun to grasp the UMCP director's game.

Quietly Warden asked, 'How do you figure that?'

He had authorized Koina Hannish to reveal how passage of the Preempt Act had been obtained. He had instructed her to admit Angus Thermopyle's innocence – and Morn Hyland's knowledge of that innocence. Hashi could think of no explanation except that Warden had decided to attempt the Dragon's downfall.

The DA director intended to give him every possible aid.

'Of the kaze who attacked Captain Vertigus,' he began, seeking precision so that everyone would see that his logic was seamless, 'nothing is known. Prior to the agreement recently negotiated by Director Hannish – the agreement which has assigned temporary responsibility for GCES Security to Chief Mandich – we lacked investigative jurisdiction. Therefore I admit frankly that any connection between that assault and those on Godsen Frik and the GCES must remain purely speculative. We will not be able to "prove" it.

'The other two are another matter. There our jurisdiction was plain. Within the limits imposed by events, our opportunity to investigate has been unimpeded.'

He paused to sort oblique strands of inference, then continued.

'Lane Harbinger has already justified my faith in her many times over.' Confidence sharpened the habitual wheeze of his voice. 'One notable example is germane. As my recent reports indicate, she has been able to recognize and preserve a minute fragment of a SOD-CMOS chip from the credentials of the kaze who slew poor Godsen Frik.' Hashi made no effort to pretend that his grief for the former PR director was sincere. 'From this fragment she has contrived to extract data.

'Need I explain why this achievement is remarkable?' He glanced at Chief Mandich's blunt resentment; returned his gaze to Warden. 'Perhaps not.

'The data is as fragmentary as the chip,' he resumed. 'Nevertheless it, too, is recognizable. Specifically Lane has identified strings of source-code which demonstrate, first, that the chip is one of ours, legitimately manufactured for us by Anodyne Systems, and second, that the chip is of recent production. The source-code is current as well as correct. It shows no indications of patching or other alteration.

'This coincides with what Lane has determined from her physical analysis of the chip.'

Gradually Hashi's manner expanded to match his subject.

'As you know, for credentials to pass scrutiny they need only be correct. Patched chips are correct. Nevertheless their source-code is not current. If it were, they would not require patching.'

QED.

'Sadly, this demonstrates little where our Godsen's killer is concerned. If his credentials were recently issued – too recently to have required the patch of which FEA Fane spoke – they would be both current and correct.

'However, Clay Imposs's credentials in Nathan Alt's possession are altogether more revealing.'

Hashi smiled to remind Warden – as well as Koina and Mandich – that he himself had preserved those credentials at the hazard of his own life.

Chief Mandich couldn't contain himself. He must have loathed hearing Hashi lecture. 'How so?' he demanded. 'I don't get it. If they were correct enough to pass, who cares how current they are?'

Hashi allowed his tone to sharpen. 'The benign Cleatus Fane helpfully assures us that Nathan Alt was fired six weeks ago. Further, he assures us that substantial precautions were taken to guarantee that Nathan Alt could not betray Anodyne Systems. I am certain that his statements will be confirmed by Anodyne Systems' records, as well as by those of the Dragon's Home Office.

'Yet I am also certain that the First Executive Assistant is lying to us.

'Clay Imposs was a sergeant for GCES Security. To attain his rank, he had served that organization for several years.' Hashi wished to appear calm; as stolid as his director. Nevertheless he couldn't stifle the throb of his excitement. 'Therefore his id tag and clearance badge would naturally have been patched six weeks ago. And yet the source-code in his credentials is both correct and current.'

Lane and her assistants could not be mistaken on such a point.

Koina caught her breath sharply. Mandich murmured an obscenity between his teeth like a man who was beginning to understand.

Warden waited without expression for Hashi to go on.

'As I have explained,' Hashi stated, 'those credentials are a composite of his id and Nathan Alt's. But such a conflation could only have been performed by someone with perfect access to the code engines themselves. It is a complete fabrication, which only an intimate knowledge of the code engines could have made possible.

'And yet the designers of those engines are ours,' he concluded in triumph. 'No one whom we did not assign has had access to the source-code – except Nathan Alt.'

The UMCP director nodded to himself. Despite the best Hashi could do, Warden still showed no surprise. Yet the easing of tension in the muscles around his eye suggested emotions which pleased Hashi more than any amount of surprise: relief; gratification.

'Well done, Hashi,' he murmured as if no one was listening. 'I wouldn't have thought of that.'

An elation like pride strained Hashi's chest until he wondered whether his old heart could bear it.

'Wait a minute,' Koina put in quickly. 'You think Alt went on working for Cleatus Fane after Fane says he was fired. How can he lie about something like that? Even if the records were changed, wouldn't our people – the designers who worked with Alt – wouldn't they be able to testify that the records are wrong, that Alt wasn't fired six weeks ago?'

Hashi offered no reply. Instead he waited for Chief Mandich to speak.

The Chief chewed bitterness for a moment. Then he said gruffly, 'No. I'm afraid not.'

Warden knew this as well as Hashi did. Like Hashi, however, he left the explanation to Mandich.

'We take every precaution we can think of to protect that work,' the Chief growled. 'It's all done from remote terminals by secure link to dedicated computers at Anodyne. First the link has to be established. Those are Administration codes. Then the remote terminal has to match the system protocols. DA supplies the codes for that. Then the terminal operator has to gain access. We' – ED Security – 'control those codes.

'It's not just that the code designers never even see each other. They don't have any way of knowing who else has access – who they're working with. Alt could have been fired years ago. He could have been working there yesterday. The design teams wouldn't know the difference.'

In disgust he added, 'It's supposed to be safer that way.'

Koina wasn't satisfied, however. 'But for Fane to tell a lie like that –' she protested. 'It's still too dangerous. He must have known he would be caught.'

'On the contrary' – at last Hashi turned away from Warden to face the PR director – 'from his perspective it must be inconceivable that he *would* be caught.

'Where could he have imagined that the evidence against him might be obtained? By their very nature, kazes destroy evidence. He could hardly have predicted that even a tiny fragment of Godsen's killer's id would survive for Lane's detection. Surely he must have assumed – anyone would have assumed – that Nathan Alt's remains, so thoroughly smashed in such a public place, would leave nothing to be discovered.

'With Captain Alt himself dead, what remains to expose Cleatus Fane's falsehood?

'He did not see me acquire Captain Alt's credentials.' Hashi suppressed an inclination to congratulate himself. 'He could not. I stood between him and his kaze. And I took considerable pains to conceal what I had done.'

When Hashi had cast himself headlong down the tiers of frightened aides and Members, he had accumulated a number of bruises. His lean frame was unaccustomed to such insults.

'Finally,' he told Koina, 'you must understand that Cleatus Fane had not meant his kaze to be exposed. He intended to apply the signal which would inspire Captain Alt to release the triggering coenzyme while Alt was near enough to be a threat – but not near enough to harm Fane's own person.

'If indeed records have been prepared to show that Nathan Alt was fired six weeks ago, they only confirm that the First Executive Assistant is lying.'

'Damn it.' Chief Mandich was convinced. In two strides he reached the edge of Warden's desk. Pointing at the intercom, he said, 'Director, with your permission, I'll call GCES Security. Tell them to arrest that oily sonofabitch. Maybe we can't prove he set Alt off, but we can make damn sure' – Fane's words again – 'he doesn't cause any more trouble.'

Warden shook his head decisively. 'No.

'As you say, we can't prove anything. And if we could, Holt would just disavow it – let us have Fane, and concentrate on looking innocent himself.

'What we *can* do,' the UMCP director added, 'is avoid telling him we know what he's done. That might give us an advantage.'

Hashi noted that Warden didn't specify what the advantage might be.

'Yes, sir.' Scowling his frustration, the Chief retreated.

'I'm sorry.' Koina leaned forward urgently in her seat. Hashi suspected that only her professional poise kept her from rising to her feet. 'It still doesn't make sense. There's something you seem to have forgotten.

'You're telling me Fane did all this to stop the Bill of Severance. You assume he knew Captain Vertigus was going to introduce that Bill. You might as well assume he knew what I was going to say when he asked us to support him.

'*How* did he know? How could he possibly have found out what Captain Vertigus had in mind?'

A frown concentrated her luminous gaze. 'Captain Vertigus didn't ask for an extraordinary session and Member's privilege until *after* he was attacked. Why did Fane send a kaze to try to stop something that for all we know Captain Vertigus didn't think of until later?'

Chief Mandich's eyes widened. He appeared to shudder like a man who was being sickened by uncertainty.

Hashi pursed his lips as if to say, Good question. In fact, however, the swirl of inferences in his head had left such issues behind a while ago. He strove to appear noncommittal because he wanted to hear how Warden would reply.

Still the UMCP director exposed nothing; kept his game hidden. He acknowledged the importance of Koina's question only by leaning back in his chair and folding his arms over his chest.

'You're the one with the answers here, Hashi,' he said impersonally. 'Go ahead. Tell Koina what you think is going on.'

Hashi was glad that Warden no longer insisted on calling

him 'Director Lebwohl'. On the other hand, he would have valued more highly some confirmation that he had indeed plumbed his director's intentions.

Obviously no confirmation was forthcoming. That in turn spun new implications which pushed Hashi's comprehension further.

Warden Dios needed help. Of course he did. Yet he preserved an essential distance from the very people who would be most inclined to assist him: Koina Hannish; Min Donner; Hashi himself.

He wished to protect his subordinates from sharing his fate if he failed. Or – Hashi went still further – from suffering the consequences if he succeeded.

'Hashi?' Koina urged tensely.

'Ah, your pardon,' the DA director wheezed. He fluttered his hands in front of his face to ward off emotions for which he had no use. 'I fear my attention wandered.'

His elation had gone sour, curdled by an unfamiliar pang of loss. He found that he did not want to lose Warden Dios.

Nor could he save him.

'You may have misunderstood me.' He let his voice buzz waspishly. Koina – or Warden – might hear it as anger; but he was ill equipped to express grief in any other way. 'I have not told you that "Fane did all this to stop the Bill of Severance." I have not remarked on his motives at all.

'Naturally you are concerned that your refusal to support the FEA's opposition to the Bill prompted that luminary to detonate his kaze.' Koina responded with a troubled nod. 'It may be so,' he continued. 'But if it is so, you provided only an occasion, not a cause.

'I do not assume that Cleatus Fane – or his master – possessed some prescient awareness of Captain Vertigus' intentions. Rather I assume that the purpose of these attacks from the first has been to solidify the special – the *dependent* – relationship between the UMCP and the UMC. To demonstrate that a relationship which has kept the GCES, if not all human space, secure until now should not be altered. True, a Bill of Severance threatens this relationship. But other threats preceded it, threats which suffice to account for the attacks. And those threats were public.'

Studying Hashi intently, Koina asked, 'What do you mean?'

'The threats were two,' Hashi rasped. 'First in time, if perhaps not in importance, is Special Counsel Maxim Igensard's investigation of "the Thermopyle case" in all its ramifications.

'Surely his inquiry threatens the Dragon's effective hegemony. Among other efforts, he seeks to req DA's financial records. If he were to obtain them, he would eventually unearth payments made to former Deputy Chief of Com-Mine Security Milos Taverner.' Hashi saw no reason why he should not verify Warden's earlier revelations. 'Conceivably the Preempt Act itself would unravel under such probing.

'The occasion is apt for some display to support the *necessity* of our special relationship with the UMC. Thus Maxim Igensard is countered without being directly opposed.'

Koina may have wished to interpose a question, but Hashi allowed her no opportunity. Wheezing sharply, he continued, 'The more recent, but perhaps more critical, threat derives from the often-discussed video conference between Director Dios and the Council.'

Hashi did not refer to Warden with so much as a glance. He had lost his taste for Warden's lack of response.

'You yourself said that you felt you were "witnessing the collapse of everything we're supposed to stand for". What, then, do you imagine Holt Fasner's reaction must have been? If you were indignant and dismayed, would he not have been outraged and appalled? The revelations of that conference undermined our appearance of honor, of probity – and our appearance of honor provides an essential validation for our dependence on the UMC.

'If we are not honorable, who may be held accountable? Why, no one – except our master, the great worm.'

Warden had played the conference beautifully. He had played *Hashi* beautifully. And kazes had ensued. Death had ensued. Yet that would be only the first of many extreme consequences.

'We have been afflicted with bombs and bloodshed in response to the same concerns which may well have inspired Captain Vertigus' Bill. In themselves, his actions are secondary. Indeed, they may be purely coincidental.' Deliberately Hashi did not look at Warden. 'Yet his concerns are shared elsewhere – for differing reasons. Hence these kazes. They are intended to reinforce our subservience to the Dragon.

'In that they have succeeded.

'If you doubt me,' he added, although he suspected that no one did, 'ask yourself who benefits from our special relationship with the UMC? Who *profits*? Who is diminished by anything which undermines us? Hardly the native Earthers.

'Consider the pattern of targets. First Captain Vertigus. Then Godsen Frik. Then – apparently – Cleatus Fane himself. GCES. UMCP. UMC. Thus all are placed beyond suspicion. No one remains to be accused except the native Earthers.

'But no one profits except Holt Fasner.'

For a moment Hashi's explanation held his listeners. Koina frowned like a woman who was so lost in what she'd heard that she could no longer frame questions. Chief Mandich said nothing.

But then Warden murmured distantly, 'Don't stop now, Hashi. Finish it.

'Why Captain Vertigus? Why not Igensard? Or someone with more influence than poor old Sixten?'

Koina turned a grateful look toward the UMCP director, as if he'd restored her capacity for thought. At once, however, she faced Hashi again, awaiting his reply.

Hashi found that he no longer enjoyed the sound of his own voice. The mechanics of his new comprehension showed that he was doing Warden's dirty work for him, naming facts and perhaps truths which Warden already knew, and which must be communicated to both PR and UMCPED Security, but which the UMCP director could not articulate himself without compromising his deeper intentions; exposing the nature of his game.

The bitterness of Hashi's grief grew more acrid.

'Who better?' he countered. Koina may have thought he

sneered at the old Senior Member. If so, she was mistaken. 'Precisely because he has become peripheral to the workings of the Council, he might be presumed to be an easy target. In addition, an attack on him is less bald, less easily interpreted, than an attempt on our fearsome Special Counsel. And, finally, Captain Vertigus is overdue for retribution. The Dragon never forgives. If he withholds his hand from those who trouble him, it is only because he bides his time.

'Upon occasion Captain Vertigus has both disobeyed and opposed the UMC CEO.'

Koina nodded. She no longer doubted Hashi: she had already been persuaded; won over. Now she was simply trying to fit the pieces of her new understanding together.

'But why Godsen, of all people?' she asked. 'That's never made sense to me. If anything, I would have said he was' – she searched for the right word – 'irrelevant. A pawn. Killing him is like shooting at the decor. It makes a mess, but it doesn't change anything.'

Hashi responded with a shrug of irritation. 'His own special relationship with the Dragon was well known. An attack on him would also appear to be an attack on his master. That is reason enough for his selection as a target.'

The DA director paused to gather his determination, then continued acidly, 'Surely it is obvious that our lamented Godsen was not meant to die? Before he was attacked, he received a summons to attend CEO Fasner. Had he obeyed, he would not have been present for assassination.

'He did *not* obey, however. The director had restricted him to UMCPHQ. He died because, and only because, he elected to honor Warden Dios' instructions rather than the Dragon's.'

Against all expectation, Godsen Frik had at last discovered his own honor. And he had acted on it by informing his director of Holt Fasner's summons.

Again Koina nodded.

Is it enough? Hashi asked Warden silently. Must I continue this charade?

Inadvertently Chief Mandich spared Hashi. Speaking in a

rush, he said, 'And Fane made himself look like a target to complete the pattern. Put himself above suspicion. I get it.

'He could be sure he wasn't in any real danger because he controlled the trigger.'

'Exactly so,' Hashi assented. He lacked the energy – or perhaps the will – to give Mandich any other acknowledgment.

Now that the Chief had finally grasped the thrust of Hashi's explanations, he seemed unable to contain himself. His blunt nature demanded action. He turned at once to Warden.

'Director, what do you want me to do? It's probably a mistake to arrest Fane. If you say so, I accept that. But we can't just sit on our hands with all this. It's too much –

'My God, it's going to make the Council reconsider that Bill.' He swallowed convulsively as the truth struck him. 'I mean, what we have is too much to ignore. But it isn't enough.' Like all of Min Donner's ilk, he instantly and passionately favored a Bill of Severance. 'We need more.'

Abruptly Warden surged to his feet. Perhaps Mandich's assertion had released a spring of decision in him. It was more likely, however, that he had heard all he needed. He had been waiting, not for Hashi's explanation, but for the Chief's comprehension of it – and for Koina's. Now he could move his subordinates to their places in his deep game.

His manner was all crisp authority as he replied, 'Getting ready for a possible war is my job.' Despite Min Donner's absence, warfare lay outside the Security Chief's province. 'Yours is to find evidence. Anything that counts as proof.

'You know what you're looking for now. Was Alt really fired six weeks ago? Who had access to his work? Did he ever leave HO? If he did, where did he go? Who did he see? What happened to Clay Imposs? You can think of other questions Security might be able to answer better than DA could.'

'Yes, sir.' The Chief snapped a salute, although Warden hadn't dismissed him.

Warden ignored the gesture. As a rule, he didn't respond to salutes. He acknowledged his people in other ways.

71

'Anything you find,' he continued, 'you'll report immediately to Director Lebwohl and Director Hannish as well as to me.'

'Yes, sir,' Chief Mandich repeated.

Warden turned to the DA director.

'Hashi, I want Lane's findings as soon as you get them. Let Koina have them, too. If Lane isn't already doing it, tell her to backtrack that coenzyme. Somebody must have done some research on it. There must be a record of it somewhere. She might be able to find it. Set up all the Red Priorities you need. That might lead us to whoever used Alt.'

Hashi assented with a nod. He was confident that Lane recognized the importance of her discovery, and knew how to pursue it.

'Other than that' – Warden indicated both Hashi and Koina – 'I want the two of you to get ready.

'Len is going to call an emergency session soon.' So much was predictable. An Amnion incursion into human space would demand action from the GCES. 'When he does, I want both of you there. I want the Council to hear you respond in person to' – he spread his hands – 'whatever comes up.

'It's still tenuous,' he added without transition. 'Circumstantial as hell. But it will help. By God, it will help.

'Koina, when the time comes, add Hashi's accusation against Holt to the list of things you tell Maxim Igensard.

'All right?' he asked rhetorically. 'Then get out of here.' His brusque dismissal made it clear that he didn't wish to hear any more questions. 'I'm too busy for all this talk.'

Too busy to grant me five minutes of honesty? Hashi asked with his eyes. Will you not share the truth, even with me?

Warden shook his head as if he understood the silent inquiry. Whatever happened to him, he meant to face it alone.

Hashi allowed himself a small grimace of pain as he rose to his feet.

Mandich reached the door first; headed away charged with his mission. Hashi bowed Koina out of the small office ahead of them. When the door had closed and sealed behind them, however, he walked with her a short distance along the corridor. He had no desire for her company. However, he had known her too long – and had profited too much from her former trust – to treat her as Warden had just treated him.

As soon as they were beyond earshot of the guards who watched over the director in his office, she put her hand on his arm. 'Hashi –' For a moment she actually leaned on him as if she feared her knees might fail. She kept her voice low in an effort to conceal a tremor of distress.

'If I tell Igensard all this, it'll ruin Warden. He won't have anything left to stand on. Even his honor. Igensard will have him up on charges in a matter of hours. Dereliction. Malfeasance. Tr' – the word caught in her throat briefly – 'treason. He'll be lucky if he doesn't find himself facing execution.

'What does he think he's doing?'

Despite its softness, her tone betrayed her. She, too, was grieving.

Earlier she'd refused to tell him something he had very much wanted to know. Now he took his revenge, although it gave him no pleasure. Warden wouldn't thank him for revealing what he guessed. And her sorrow would only be increased.

'My dear Koina, if I answer you, you will believe that we have both lost our minds.'

So that she would not pursue the matter, he disengaged his arm and walked away from her. Whatever happened, he meant to keep his own emotions as private as Warden's.

The Amnion had committed an act of war.

The director of the UMCP had chosen a terrible moment to stake all their lives against the Dragon.

ANGUS

He didn't scream; could not have screamed if he'd wanted to. But for a time that might have been long or short his body screamed for him.

Asteroids and static crashed in mad ecstasy through the dark void, shattering against each other and recoiling in their rush to answer the singularity's hunger. The black hole sucked down energy in jagged bolts like lightning; swallowed matter lurid with doppler shifts. Forces which he'd unleashed with his own hand seemed to tear him apart.

Dehydration. Intolerable g. Strange concussions of all kinds. EM violence intense enough to fry every circuit in his head. He was trapped in a crib of weight and pain so extreme that they crushed out every flicker or spasm of awareness. All his nerves became one long voiceless and unanswerable shriek.

There was no escape as long as the belt of his suit remained anchored to the ship – and no escape if it failed. Mortal bone and tissue couldn't survive the weird translations of the singularity's event horizon. Like the stars and the gap, so much gravity transcended human existence.

Infinite loss. Complete extinction. Every cell in his body wailed at the nearness of ultimate things. Perhaps he tried to twist against the strain, ease it somehow. He didn't know: his body understood only screaming.

But then his hurts began to shut down like systems going off-line. Behind its shields, his datacore registered the scale of his distress and engaged its last prewritten defense: the one protection which might keep him alive – if not sane – when he suffered this much damage. It put him into stasis. Every iota of energy which his body and his power cells could supply was focused on sustaining his autonomic functions: pulse and respiration. Everything else was canceled.

His flesh stopped its screaming because it was no longer accessible to pain. He was neither conscious nor unconscious: his mind occupied a place where such concepts had no meaning; a place beyond change or interpretation. If g crushed him to a bloody smear inside his EVA suit, he didn't know it. If the pressure released him entirely, he couldn't tell the difference. Time and space passed him by.

And there was no one who could command his zone implants to release him.

Pulse.

Respiration.

Stasis.

Nothing else.

If he could have identified where he was, he might have considered it Heaven.

At some indefinable point – after instants or aeons of intervening peace – vestiges of recognition returned. On some level which seemed to have nothing to do with his mind, he understood that he was no longer outside the ship. His head wasn't confined by a helmet. Perhaps he knew that he was alive. The knowledge had no significance, however. It conveyed nothing; required nothing.

When the DA medtechs had put him into stasis during the days and weeks of his welding, he'd been able to hear what they said in his presence. When Warden Dios had switched his datacore, the UMCP director's words had reached him clearly.

Technically, we've done you a favor. That's obvious. You're stronger now, faster, more capable, effectively more intelligent. Not to mention the fact that you're still alive –

In some sense he'd been aware of what he heard.

In every other way, we've committed a crime against you. We've committed a crime against your soul.

But he could not have reacted. Comprehension and recognition were irrelevant. No reactions were permitted to him.

It's got to stop.

Asteroids and singularities and the cold dark transcended him. The compulsions of machine logic transcended him.

After all, Heaven was indistinguishable from Hell.

Gradually he came to the perception that he wasn't alone. Two or three dark shapes hovered somewhere around him. From time to time they smeared themselves across his vision as if to prove that they weren't like him; weren't imprisoned in his skull.

Yet their presence changed nothing. He still couldn't react. He would never react again. Even the small effort of focusing his eyes was beyond him: an exercise of choice which his welding rendered unattainable.

So impalpably that there was no point at which the change could have been detected, the utter gulf outside his EVA suit had become a blank white light, sterile and unforgiving. How much time had passed? Stupid question. Or stupid to ask it. His datacore never gave him answers when he was in stasis. Counters in his head had measured the interval to the last microsecond, but they kept their data to themselves. When he was in stasis, he was presumed to need nothing except breath and blood, sustenance and elimination.

There was no one who could command his zone implants to release him. He himself, Angus Thermopyle, had erected barriers against the codes which could have coerced a response from his datacore.

Were the shapes speaking? He couldn't tell. They remained around him. He heard voices. But he had no way of knowing whether the voices came from the shapes.

'I'm trying,' one of them said. For no particular reason, Angus recognized Mikka Vasaczk. 'The computer says he can't wake up.'

Apparently he was in sickbay. Someone must have gone outside to bring him in.

While *Trumpet* was held by a singularity? Impossible.

'How bad is he hurt?'

That was Vector Shaheed. Savior of humanity. The man who'd analyzed UMCPDA's antimutagen and made the formula available. If anybody survived to pick up his broadcast.

'Severe dehydration,' Mikka reported. Fatigue and bitterness rasped in her voice. 'IVs have taken care of that. Hemorrhage – shit, he's lost liters of blood. But the IVs are handling that, too. And most of the bleeding's stopped. One of his hips was dislocated – he must have tried to use his suit jets against the pull. That's been taken care of.' The surgical table was almost prehensile: it could apply traction in any direction necessary. 'He's responding to the drugs. Metabolins. Coagulants. Analgesics. Stim.

'But the systems can't wake him up.'

Of course not.

Trumpet's sickbay had been designed and programmed especially for him. The cybernetic physicians knew him intimately: special instruction-sets and diagnostic resources had come on-line the instant he was attached to the table. They could have repaired his welding. They could have compensated for any damage the electrodes might have done to his brain. Within limits they could have corrected faults in some of his equipment.

But first they required the right codes.

'What about EEG?' Vector asked.

Maybe he didn't realize he was wasting his time.

Mikka answered shortly, 'No readings.'

'*You mean he's brain-dead?*'

Davies. The voice was unmistakable. Angus knew it well. Under the right kind of stress, it sounded like his own.

Three voices. Mikka, Vector and Davies. Presumably that meant there were three shapes instead of just two.

Where was Morn?

Dead? Lost in gap-sickness?

Angus went away inside his head. He promised himself that he was never coming back. Morn's pain hurt him too much. He didn't want to know what had happened to her. He was afraid it would be more than he could bear.

But if he couldn't turn himself back on, he also couldn't retreat, use stasis to protect him. Like a black hole, the machine logic of his equipment gave nothing; permitted nothing. No time passed before he heard Mikka reply, 'That's not it. I mean the systems can't get a reading. Apparently his zone implants are blanking out neural activity. Or masking it. As far as sickbay can tell, his head's full of white noise. He could be screaming at us in there – telling us what to do – and we wouldn't know it.'

'Angus, wake up!' Davies croaked. A jolt which might have been a slap rocked Angus' head from side to side on his slack neck. 'God damn it, we need you!'

'Stop that.' Mikka sounded sick with weariness. 'He can't hear you. He probably can't feel anything, either.'

Unfortunately she was wrong.

'Can we short out the noise?' Vector asked distantly. 'Set up some kind of interference? So the systems can get a reading? Maybe apply direct stimulation to wake him up?'

Mikka snorted. 'We might kill him. We don't know what kind of synergy connects him and his equipment. He's a cyborg. Maybe he's dependent on his computer. Maybe his zone implants are what keep him alive.'

Again she was wrong. The white noise in his head was his prison. The electrodes attached to his computer held him more tightly than arm cuffs and manacles. But she was right, too: Vector's suggestions wouldn't work. The bond between his brain and his zone implants was too intimate to be disrupted by any simple means.

Mikka and Vector and Davies could try to save him by ordering sickbay to remove the electrodes from his head. Or cut the leads from his computer. Turn him back into a human being. *Fuck* the synergy. But he didn't think that would work, either. Sickbay's programming wouldn't obey a command to unweld him, *dismantle* him, without authorization.

No one aboard *Trumpet* – perhaps no one within a hundred parsecs of the gap scout – knew the codes for that.

And if by some miracle sickbay obeyed –

All his new strengths and capabilities would be lost. Enhanced reflexes, lasers, EM vision, jamming fields, databases, computational power: he would forfeit them all. His zone implants would no longer protect him from pain; no longer focus his mind; no longer give him sleep or power or numbness when he needed them. He would be free at last, truly and completely free – at the cost of everything which made freedom attractive.

What would he do then? How could he survive? He wasn't sure that he could handle the gap scout effectively without his computer's support. He would be at the mercy of anyone with more muscle or knowledge than he possessed.

That was the way he'd lived before he met Morn; before he fell into Warden Dios' hands. Preying on those who were weaker than he was so that he could avoid those who were stronger. *Hating* everybody, weak and strong alike, because of his own weakness. Tied to the slats of the crib –

Oh, perfect. A cackle like the laughter of a ghoul echoed in his skull. Abso-fucking-lutely perfect.

Don't do it, he told the blurred shapes around him, even though his silence was so vast that no sound could cross it. Don't even try. Find some other answer.

If he laughed much harder, he was going to weep.

Don't make me go back to what I was.

Please.

Morn herself had never chosen to have her zone implant removed or neutralized. She was dependent on the artificial stimulation which had tortured and exalted her. The emissions that controlled her also gave her strength.

Abruptly Davies announced like a cry, 'No! He isn't unconscious. His zone implants are doing this to him.'

Two of the shapes gave the impression that they turned to face the third.

'He's in stasis,' Davies explained hurriedly. 'He warned Morn and me about that. Before he edited his datacore. He said some of the commands were hardwired. His zone implants obey automatically. He told us, "The whole system will freeze if you pull the chip." That's why we had to wire him in to the ship's datacore before he could work.

'Something he did outside – or something that happened to him, maybe being hurt so much – It triggered those commands. Sent him into stasis.'

Very good, Angus chuckled desperately. You're smarter than you look.

What're you going to do about it? Tell me what in hell you think you can do about it.

'But if you're right – if it's hardwired –' Mikka's voice trailed away.

'If it's hardwired,' Vector finished for her, 'we don't know how to countermand it.' After a moment he added, 'I was always pretty mediocre as an engineer. I can use systems like these' – he must have meant sickbay's – 'but I don't really understand how they work. I'm out of my depth here. Sorry.'

Passing responsibility to someone else.

'Don't look at me,' Mikka muttered. 'I thought I was at least competent as a programmer, but I didn't know it was even possible to edit a datacore.'

Only the Amnion could tamper with SOD-CMOS chips. The Amnion and Angus. But he was in no position to offer suggestions.

'Shit,' Davies said through his teeth. 'Morn's going to wake up soon. When she does – I can't tell her this. I just can't. After what she's been through –

'He's the only one who can repair the drives.'

Repair the drives?

'We don't know that for sure.' Mikka didn't sound hopeful. 'Vector and I haven't tried yet.'

Repair – ?

'So what?' Davies protested bitterly. 'Even if you can, we're helpless without him. We don't know enough about the ship. We don't know enough about what's going on. Who's he working for really? Why did they give him to Nick – and then let us take him back? Why are we on the run?'

Angus breathed a nonexistent obscenity. What happened to the drives?

'The cops are coming after us,' Davies went on. 'You know that. We're sending out a Class–1 UMCP homing signal. I can't figure out how to turn it off. If they chase us long enough, they'll catch us.

'When that happens, we're finished. We may not die out here, but we won't be able to make any choices.

'Whose side is that cruiser on? The side that sent Nick Angus' codes? The side that wants to suppress our antimutagen? The side that let Nick have Morn in the first place? Or the side that gave us the chance to set Angus free?

'We need to know what's going on.'

Davies' young voice rose as if he wanted to wail. 'I can't tell Morn that the only man who stands a chance of helping us is stuck in fucking *stasis*.'

'Try his priority-codes,' Vector suggested. His habitual calm sounded frayed.

'They're *blocked*,' Davies retorted.

'*Try them!*' Mikka snapped. 'What the hell do you think we have to lose?'

Fiercely Davies complied. 'Isaac,' he rasped. '*Gabriel*. Wake up. End stasis. Wake up!'

Angus waited in suspense. But of course the commands couldn't reach him. He'd erected a wall against them.

The Amnion had taught him well.

'Nothing.' Despair roughened Mikka's tone. 'No change. He can't wake up.'

Inside his head, he laughed until tears ran down his soul like sweat.

Davies reacted as if she were taunting him.

'God *damn* it!' he raged. 'What the fuck is *wrong* with Ciro? What was he *doing*? Didn't you tell him he's been *cured*? Didn't you at least *try* to convince him he doesn't have to take orders from goddamn Sorus Chatelaine?'

Ciro did it? Sabotaged the drives? Well, damn. That sounded like something Angus might have done himself.

'Of course we told him,' Mikka replied wearily. 'Of course we tried to convince him. Vector showed him the tests, for God's sake. The hurt's just too deep, that's all. We can't reach the place where she damaged him. *I* can't.' She may have shrugged. 'There isn't anything worse than what she did to him.'

A paroxysm of fury took hold of Davies. '*I don't care!*' he yelled. 'I'm not interested in *excuses*! We've got to *do better than this*! I would be a fucking Amnioni *myself* right now if Morn hadn't found a way to do better. She was *alone* on *Captain's Fancy*, Nick had her *locked in her cabin*! She still saved me.'

'Don't tell me how bad Ciro's been hurt! Tell me –'

Angus heard a sound like a blow. Davies stopped suddenly, as if he'd been struck. As if he'd struck himself –

'What is it?' Mikka breathed tensely.

Without transition Davies' voice changed. It became at once lighter and sharper. More like Morn's? His intensity gave him focus; seemed to give him authority.

'Vector,' he commanded, 'let's turn him over.'

'What?' Vector asked uncomprehendingly.

In silence Angus echoed, What?

'Turn him over,' Davies insisted. 'Put him on his stomach.'

Hands jerked along Angus' sides. He couldn't tell how many there were. After a moment the restraints fell away, releasing him into zero g.

'Mikka,' Davies went on at once, 'set the systems to open up his back.'

'Why?' she demanded. Vector may have been swayed by Davies' passion; but she was tougher.

Don't ask stupid questions! Angus shouted uselessly. Just do it!

'So we can pull his datacore,' Davies retorted. 'He said the stasis commands are hardwired. Taking out the chip freezes the whole system. Maybe if we unplug his datacore and then put it back, the computer will reset itself.'

Aping Mikka, he growled, 'What the hell do you think we have to lose?'

Shit! Abrupt amazement shot through Angus' trapped mind. It might work. It might –

This time he hadn't been ordered into paralysis. His programming had imposed it on him because he'd gone down one of its logic trees too far to recover. Under the circumstances, anything which forced or enabled his computer to reevaluate his condition might set him loose.

He landed on his face, felt the restraints close again.

'No good,' Mikka reported. 'The computer wants a code. Sickbay won't do it without the right code.'

Davies didn't hesitate. 'Then get me a first aid kit. I'll cut him open myself.' Muttering, he added, 'It's not like I haven't done this before.'

Only a few seconds passed before Angus felt a sharp line run along the skin between his shoulder blades. It should have hurt; but he was too far removed from it for pain. It might as well have belonged to some other reality.

All this was familiar. Alone with Warden Dios, he'd sprawled under the light like a sacrifice while the UMCP director had worked on his back: cut him open; swabbed away the blood; unplugged his old datacore; set a new one into the socket. Dios hadn't stopped talking the whole time.

If Min knew why I'm doing this, she'd turn against me herself.

We call the process 'welding'. When a man or woman is made a cyborg voluntarily, that's 'wedding'. 'Welding' is involuntary.

In essence, you're no longer a human being. You're a machina infernalis – *an infernal device. We've deprived you of choice – and responsibility.*

Davies swore steadily under his breath while he did the same things for different reasons. Back then Angus had been able to recognize the change when his datacore was taken out: he'd felt a void as deep as the gap between the stars crouching just beyond the window which linked him to his computer; poised to consume him – But now he recognized only the tug which plucked at his back when Davies pulled the chip. Nothing shifted.

He already belonged to the void. Its power over him could not be made worse.

Yet he knew that wasn't true. Trapped and suffocating *in the crib* in his EVA suit, he'd launched a singularity grenade against *Free Lunch*. And then he'd fired his portable matter cannon; fired it *accurately* despite the chaos of the swarm and the instability of cold ignition. He'd *created* that singularity by his own skill and cunning, no matter who hurt him, or why. Morn had set him free to fight for himself.

And then he'd been brought back from the edge of his personal black hole. He wasn't alone here: other people had saved him. They could have left him to die, damn right, that's what he would have done himself, get rid of the butcher the rapist the illegal who looked like a toad and stank like a pig while they had the chance, no one would ever know the difference. Gone and good riddance.

The people around him hadn't done that. They'd retrieved him from the fringes of his doom. And now they were trying to do the same thing again in another way.

Beyond question the power of the void *could* be made worse. Davies, Vector, and Mikka could fail –

Angus' terror might have eaten him alive if he'd been able to feel its full strength. His body was immune to it, however. Only his mind remained vulnerable.

'How long do we have to wait?' Mikka asked tensely.

'How should I know?' Davies retorted. 'I've never done this before. And I sure as hell didn't *design* this shit.'

Sounding unnaturally calm, Vector remarked, 'Orn Vorbuld' – a name Angus didn't know – 'used to say we have to drain the bad juju out of the chip.'

Mikka snorted. 'Orn Vorbuld was an asshole.'

Was. Dead now, apparently. Another casualty.

Like Angus himself.

Try it, he groaned. Haven't you waited long enough? Haven't you tortured me enough? *Try* it, for God's sake!

Save me or let me die –

'Fuck it,' Davies muttered through his teeth. 'I don't know

what we're waiting for. Give me a swab. I can't plug anything in if I can't see the damn socket.'

We've committed a crime against your soul.

Angus felt pressure on his back, roughly gentle, mopping blood away. The raw edges of Davies' incision seemed to sting with cold as if they froze in the air of sickbay; as if the deep chill of space leaked in to claim him for the last time.

It's got to stop.

Pressure again: harder; more focused. There, in the center of his back; at the nexus of his being.

Silence.

Mikka murmured, 'Is it in all the way?'

'I'm not sure,' Davies breathed.

Angus was sure enough for both of them.

Without transition a window opened in the darkness of his head – a window of relief so intense that he would have sobbed aloud if his zone implants had allowed it.

Before he slipped away into the dark, his chronometer informed him that he'd been in stasis for more than four and a half hours.

DAVIES

Davies stared at the bloody gap in Angus' back where he'd just reinserted the datacore chip into its socket, and waited for his heart to break.

He didn't have any other ideas. If this didn't work, Angus might as well be dead. Sickbay might keep him alive indefinitely; but no one aboard *Trumpet* would ever reach him again.

It wasn't working. Davies could see that. Held by his restraints, Angus lay like a slab of meat on the surgical table. Only the autonomic rasp of his breathing indicated that he wasn't a corpse.

Another failure. The last one: the fatal one. He hadn't been good enough to help Angus save the ship. If Morn hadn't risked gap-sickness to help him, they all would have died. For a while he'd been so caught up in his own exhaustion that he'd let Morn and Angus suffer for long, unnecessary minutes. And after that he'd had to rely on Mikka to run helm, despite her injuries and Ciro's pain, because he hadn't been able to cope by himself.

He didn't know how to repair the drives. He wasn't even smart enough to turn off *Trumpet*'s homing signal.

But there was worse.

He'd failed to understand himself. Hell, he hadn't even tried. He'd refused to look at what lay behind his fury for revenge on *Gutbuster*. Instead he'd let Nick commit his bizarre suicide. He'd killed Sib Mackern as surely as if he'd pressed the firing stud himself. And he'd taken his roiling terror out on Morn as if it were anger; as if she were inadequate in some way, not good enough for him.

I'm Bryony Hyland's daughter. The one she used to have – before you sold your soul for a zone implant.

Now he'd failed to bring Angus back from stasis. *Trumpet*'s drives were dead: the gap scout couldn't navigate; couldn't cross the gap in any direction; couldn't even decelerate. All her choices were gone. She was doomed to drift like a coffin consigned to the sea of space until death or the UMCP intervened.

He *wanted* his heart to break; wanted something essential inside him to snap. Otherwise he would have to face the consequences of all the things he couldn't do.

He wasn't listening when Vector sighed, 'Well, what do you know. Would you look at that?' Nevertheless an unfamiliar congestion in the geneticist's tone made him turn his head.

Mikka caught her breath as she followed Vector's pointing hand.

Davies blinked, but couldn't grasp what he was seeing. Apparently Vector wanted him to look at one of sickbay's status displays. Which one? What difference did it make?

'Davies Hyland,' Vector drawled cheerfully, 'my intense young friend, you are a genius. Or, as Angus will no doubt say when he gets the chance, a fucking genius.'

'The EEG, Davies,' Mikka urged quietly. She might have been on the edge of tears. 'Look at his EEG.'

Now Davies saw it.

Just moments ago that screen had been effectively blank; filled by the undifferentiated emission of Angus' zone implants. The sensors hadn't been able to penetrate the noise to detect any neural activity. But now a whole series of normal-looking waves and spikes scrolled along the EEG's bandwidths.

'He's asleep,' Vector explained before Davies could try to guess what the readings meant. 'Not blank. Not in stasis. Sleeping.' He consulted a readout, then went on, 'This isn't exactly natural. These lines' – he indicated a few of the band-widths – 'are too regular. His zone implants are doing this to him. He needs time to heal. But he isn't *blank*,' Vector insisted. 'His systems are on-line again. He'll probably wake up when his diagnostics say he's ready.'

The geneticist grinned at his companions. 'Maybe now we have something to hope for.'

Without warning a visceral relief gripped Davies so hard that he doubled over as if he were cramping. Mikka croaked his name, but he wasn't able to respond. Pains he couldn't name locked down the muscles in his chest and abdomen, pulling him into a fetal knot. He'd been under too much strain for too long; living on pure adrenaline. Flesh had limits – even his enhanced metabolism had limits – and he'd passed them long ago. Shocked by the sudden change in the stimulus of his neurotransmitters, his nerves went haywire, misfiring in all directions; clenching him into a ball. Adrift in zero g, he bobbed against the wall and bounced back as if he'd lost all mass; all substance.

'Davies!' Mikka snagged him by the arm, stopped his help-less motion. 'What's the matter? What's wrong?'

If he could have opened his throat, he would have called Morn's name. But he couldn't speak; couldn't breathe –

Vector didn't hesitate. 'I'll get some cat.' At once he started keying commands for the sickbay dispensary.

No! Davies wanted to protest, no drugs, no cat, don't *give* me anything, that isn't what I need, you don't have to be afraid of me, *I'm not like that!* Morn was the one who needed cat. To control her gap-sickness. So that she wouldn't try to kill them all.

Closed in pain as if it were a womb, his image of himself shifted.

I'm not *her.*

Here was the proof. When the universe spoke to Morn – when hard g pushed her flesh past its limits – she attempted self-destruct. Or she hurt herself in some way to deflect the impulse. But he had a completely different reaction. He became a killer of another kind altogether. Driven by his terror of the Amnion, and of their desire to use him against his entire species, he sent other people out to die. He hungered for murder, not suicide. And when his body was overwhelmed, he became a universe not of clarity but of pain: helpless as a convulsing epileptic.

He'd figured out how to bring Angus back from stasis.

And he was *not* Morn.

That knowledge seemed to reach depths in him which it had never touched before. The hurt which cramped his muscles and sealed his lungs was *his*, no one else's. It was his inability to distinguish himself from her.

He'd saved Angus.

He didn't want any goddamn cat.

Before Vector could reach him with a hypo, his chest and limbs began to unlock themselves.

'Vector, he's moving,' Mikka announced unnecessarily.

Davies drew a long, shuddering breath. Bit by bit he unfolded himself. When he could turn his head, he did his best to nod at Vector and Mikka. 'I'm all right.' He hardly heard his own voice, but at least he was able to speak. 'I don't need cat. I'm just –' Words couldn't convey what he wanted to say. I'm not Morn. That's important. 'I just need sleep.'

Vector studied him for a moment, glanced down at the hypo in his hands, then referred the question to Mikka.

'Don't look at me,' she murmured wanly. With the heel of one hand, she pressed the bandage over her eye and the corner of her forehead tighter. Maybe she thought that would make her injuries hurt less. 'We all need sleep. If he says he doesn't want cat, I say send him to bed.'

Slowly Vector nodded.

'I'm going to do that myself,' she went on. Her weariness was palpable. 'As soon as I make sure Ciro hasn't gone back off the deep end.' She sounded defensive as she added, 'We might as well rest. We don't have anything better to do until Angus wakes up.'

That was her brother's doing, but she seemed to feel responsible for it.

'You're probably right,' Vector replied as if he thought she needed the acknowledgment. 'Go ahead.' He gestured at the console behind him. 'I just want to run a few more tests, make sure he's all right.'

Mikka nodded; turned toward the door. Then she stopped to put her hand on Davies' arm.

'Thank you,' she said softly. When she looked straight at him, he could see that her good eye was full of loss. 'As long as Angus can function, we have a chance. If you hadn't brought him back, I'm not sure I could live with what Ciro did to us.'

Brusquely she opened the door and left.

When she was gone, Vector dropped his hypo into the sickbay disposal. With a nudge of his hip, he moved himself closer to the command keypad. But he didn't take his gaze off Davies.

A chance, Davies echoed to himself. Not long ago he'd been alone: alone on the bridge; alone with his failures. But now he'd recovered his father. If Morn could come back from the place where gap-sickness and her shattered arm had taken her, he might finally find it possible to be whole.

Drifting again, he swung around so that Vector wouldn't see the tears in his eyes.

Vector cleared his throat. 'You're a growing boy,' he remarked obscurely. 'Give yourself a break. I can handle things here. Do what Mikka says – go to bed.'

Sure. Go to bed.

Keeping his back to the geneticist, he pushed off from the surgical table and let himself out into the corridor running along *Trumpet*'s core.

Moisture smeared his vision. He could hardly see where he was going.

As soon as the sickbay door closed behind him, he caught a handgrip and stopped. More than anything he needed sleep. Yet he was reluctant to return to his cabin. He'd been through too much recently. His limbs and back still ached from the strain of his seizure. If he found Morn asleep, he would be afraid for her. And if she was awake, he would be afraid of her: afraid of what she'd become; afraid of her ability to pierce his heart.

Before *Trumpet*'s final escape from the black hole's g, she'd recovered consciousness briefly. *I can't do this again,* she'd said to him. *When I'm in trouble, the only thing I can think of is to hurt myself.* She'd let the singularity crush her right arm. *Self-destruct – I need a better answer.*

That made sense. Too often she'd driven herself to brutal extremes in an effort to keep him alive; keep him human. He didn't want to benefit from any more of her excruciation.

Nevertheless he didn't understand what she meant by *a better answer.* What else could she have done?

She'd gone too far beyond him. He couldn't imagine what she might have become.

Yet he'd found a way to rescue Angus from stasis. That steadied him. And by degrees the knowledge that he wasn't *her* seemed to grow stronger. Maybe it would be strong enough to help him face her.

He rubbed the back of his hand across his damp eyes, trying to clear them. Then he floated down the corridor in the direction of his cabin.

Morn blinked at him blearily as he entered, as if she'd been awakened by the sound of the door. At first she didn't appear to recognize him. After a moment, however, she murmured, 'Davies.' Her voice sounded rusty with disuse.

He shouldn't have tried to clean the blur off his vision. He didn't want to see her like this: pale as illness; her eyes like dark craters in the fragile landscape of her face. All her beauty had been whetted down to bone. In addition her entire right arm was wrapped in an acrylic cast and strapped across her chest; but she may not have been aware of it yet.

The sight wrung him. He had a strange sense of dislocation – an impression that he was seeing Angus' handiwork, and Nick's, from the outside for the first time. Somehow being caught and misdefined by her memories had partially blinded him to the cost of her ordeals. Witnessed from inside, that price was at once more extreme and less tangible.

Fresh tears spread across his cheeks. Despite his new

knowledge – or perhaps because of it – his muscles tightened again, trying to draw him back into a ball.

But he'd brought Angus out of stasis. That was one burden he no longer had to carry; one disaster he didn't have to explain. Surely he could stand the rest for a few more minutes?

He didn't try to hide what he was feeling from her. Hunched over as if he were bleeding internally, he slid to the edge of her bunk and sagged there beside her, anchoring himself with his fingers in the webbing of her g-sheath.

'Davies.' With an effort, she swallowed to moisten her throat. 'You're still alive. That's one good thing, anyway.'

'So are you.' Empathy and weariness hindered his voice; but he didn't care. 'I'm glad. You were hurt so bad – I was afraid you might die – or we all would – before I got a chance to apologize.'

Morn frowned weakly; swallowed again. 'For what?' The drugs sickbay had given her were fading, but they still affected her, clogging her reactions, slowing her comprehension.

He was tempted to say, For letting Nick go kill himself. For sending Sib out to die. But those were secondary hurts between him and her; easier to talk about. Instead he told her roughly, 'For not trusting you more. For saying all those nasty things to you.'

I'm Bryony Hyland's daughter.

'Half the time I really can't tell the difference between us. It confuses me.' Waves of pressure like little convulsions tightened his chest and belly, but this time they weren't strong enough to stop him. 'And I didn't want to think about it. I didn't want to be as scared as I would be if I thought about it.

'So I told myself we had to go after *Gutbuster* because that was the right thing for cops to do. Punish her for her crimes. And I could tell you had qualms about it. You weren't backing me up. So I treated you like you were weak – like there was something wrong with you – because you didn't back me up.

'But it didn't have to do with being a cop.' Anger and failure roughened his tone as he explained. 'It had to do with being terrified. *Gutbuster* was after *me*. She wanted to give me to the Amnion. And the Amnion want to use me to help them learn how to make themselves look just like human beings. *That's* why I wanted to kill her.

'You weren't being weak. You were thinking about larger questions. More important questions. Like whose game this is. Who's manipulating us now, and why. And what we can do about it.

'You didn't deserve the way I treated you.'

Morn listened attentively until he was done. Her wounded gaze held his face. But after he finished she didn't respond directly. Instead she murmured in a thin voice, 'You said *was*. *Gutbuster was* after you. She *wanted* to give you to the Amnion. What's changed? What's going on? Where are we?'

Maybe she was confused herself – by drugs; or by the gap in her awareness of what had happened. Or maybe she simply didn't realize that when he was separate from her he might not be sure of her forgiveness.

A wave of weariness seemed to break over his head. The muscles in his chest stopped clenching. He slumped on the edge of her bunk, shrinking into himself. Of course she wanted to know what she'd missed while she slept. He would feel the same in her place. Apologies weren't as important as survival.

For a moment he couldn't lift his head far enough above his fatigue to answer. But then he closed his eyes and found that if he concentrated just on speaking – if he didn't let himself look at her, witness her condition – he could go on a little longer.

'It's hard to describe,' he breathed distantly; putting words together one at a time in the darkness of his head. 'The good news is, we got away from Massif-5. We're coasting out in the middle of nowhere.' He'd seen the astrogation coordinates, but they meant nothing to him. 'You saved us when you activated the helm failsafes. Otherwise we would have run into an asteroid. Or gotten sucked back into the black hole.

'*Free Lunch* was gone.' Fuel for the weird energies of the singularity. 'There was no sign of *Soar*. Mikka took helm for me, ran us out to the fringes of the swarm. When we got there, we found a major battle going on. A UMCP cruiser – must have been *Punisher* – was blazing away at *Calm Horizons*. I still don't know how they found us. Or how *Soar* did. They aren't supposed to know how to follow a Class-1 UMCP homing signal. But the Amnion are so desperate to stop us, they've committed an act of war.'

'Wait a minute,' Morn interrupted. She put her hand on his arm as if she thought he might not stop for her. 'Did you say *Calm Horizons*? The same warship we got away from when we escaped Thanatos Minor?'

Davies nodded without opening his eyes. He didn't know why she thought this was important. Surely the incursion was the crucial point, not the identity of the intruder. But he didn't have the energy to ask for an explanation. His ability to tell his own story was too fragile.

Slumping deeper into the dark, he resumed, '*Calm Horizons* would have killed us.' Like Bryony Hyland. 'She had us on targ. We didn't have time to burn. We couldn't go into tach. Not even for a blink crossing. But *Soar* showed up again. She must have avoided the black hole somehow. Just when I thought we were dead, she opened fire on *Calm Horizons*.'

He didn't try to understand Captain Chatelaine's actions. They were a mystery, like the attack by *Free Lunch*, or the ability of the Amnion to locate the gap scout; impenetrable. As incomprehensible as the oblique physics of the gap.

'*Calm Horizons* had to hit her instead of us, or else the warship would have been destroyed. The Amnion couldn't take the chance they might miss us with their last shot.

'That gave us time. And *Punisher* was covering us. We burned like crazy. Then we went into tach. That brought us here.' He shrugged weakly. 'Wherever here is.'

He expected Morn to ask why *Soar* had turned against her masters; braced himself to say, 'I have no idea,' without sounding angry. But her attention remained focused on concerns he couldn't grasp.

As she climbed out of her long, drugged slumber, she recovered her urgency. Her grip on his arm tightened. In a sharper tone she demanded, 'Did *Punisher* kill *Calm Horizons*?'

He sighed. 'I hope so.' He didn't have the strength for this. He needed sleep, not more questions. 'But we didn't see it. *Calm Horizons* was hurt. *Soar* took her by surprise. *Punisher* was starting to get through. Then we went into tach. I don't know what happened after that.'

Pulling on his arm, Morn raised herself to sit beside him. He felt her draw her legs out of the g-sheath and hook them over the edge of the bunk. Her shoulder and her grasp conveyed a palpable tension.

'*Calm Horizons* is too big,' she murmured distantly, as if she were thinking aloud; trying to brace herself against a threat he couldn't see. Surely the Amnion couldn't track UMCP homing signals? 'She has too much firepower. If *Punisher* didn't kill her right away, she's probably still alive.'

Maybe not, Davies countered in silence. He was too weary to argue aloud. She was practically stationary. She doesn't accelerate fast. And *Punisher* must have called for help from VI. If more ships came – if they caught *Calm Horizons* before she could go into tach –

He wanted to finish; *needed* to finish. After that he would be able to rest. For a moment he put his free hand over his eyes in an effort to increase the darkness so that he could concentrate. Then he continued.

'Angus is still alive. God knows how he survived being outside in all that.' He hadn't suffered any more g than anyone else. But he hadn't had the support of a g-seat or bunk. And he'd been exposed to all the forces of the singularity and the swarm. If nothing else, he could easily have been crushed by rock rushing to answer the black hole's hunger. 'But Vector brought him in before we left the swarm. Sickbay says he's going to be all right.

'Other than that –'

His voice trailed away. He had more to relate; but now he needed her to ask him what it was. He didn't think he could go on unless she prompted him; pushed him.

Slowly she loosened the pressure of her grip on his forearm.

He seemed to feel some of her tightness easing. Maybe at last she'd become enough aware of him to realize that he was near the end of his resources.

'What's the bad news?' she inquired more gently. 'When people tell you what the good news is, there's always bad news.'

Again he nodded blindly. He hardly heard himself speak.

'Ciro went haywire. I guess that mutagen made him crazy. Even though he was cured, he still thought he had to do what Sorus Chatelaine told him.'

Morn shifted at Davies' side. She may have winced. Or she may have simply nodded. He didn't look to see.

'When Mikka came to help me on the bridge, Ciro left their cabin and found his way into the drive space. He must have been in there when we burned. All that g with no protection banged him up pretty good. He's lucky he didn't break any bones.

'But it slowed him down. He took too long. That saved us. Before anything failed, we were able to go into tach, get away from Massif-5.'

Davies waited while a wave of fatigue nearly washed him out of himself. Then he went on.

'He took too long, but he did it right. We've lost both drives. That's why we're coasting. There's nothing else we can do. We still have navigational thrust, that's all. We can't even decelerate. And we sure as hell can't cross the gap again.

'We haven't tried to rig any repairs yet,' he added as if he were drifting. 'Too busy taking care of our wounds.' Too tired. 'But I don't think we can do it.' Or do it in time. 'Without Angus, we can't get into the damage control databases. We don't know the codes. And his zone implants have put him to sleep so he can heal. At least that's Vector's theory. He won't wake up until they let him go.'

Davies stopped. The hollow dark inside his head seemed louder than his voice, and for a moment he feared that he might start to whimper or moan without realizing it. But he probably didn't have the energy.

After a while he heard Morn ask, 'Is that all? Is there anything else I need to know?'

He shook his head. Carried by its own momentum, his head continued rocking from side to side on his weak neck.

'Well, it's bad,' she said judiciously, as if she wanted to comfort him by not panicking, 'but we've had worse. I was afraid we were still in the swarm. Angus was dead, and we were stuck in the swarm because without him we couldn't escape.'

She paused, then mused more to herself than to him, 'I guess it's possible *Calm Horizons* is finished. That would help.'

To his surprise he found that he had enough strength left for a small pang of vexation. What was so important about *Calm Horizons*? Was that all she cared about? Didn't she understand the consequences of what Ciro had done?

He opened his eyes so that he could glare at her.

'Before he went EVA,' he rasped sourly, 'Angus activated our homing signal again. None of us can get deep enough into the command systems to turn it off. Eventually someone will come after us.' That was a safe bet. 'Maybe *Punisher*. Maybe some other UMCP ship, or one from VI.

'If that happens before Angus wakes up,' he explained with as much force as he could muster, 'or before he can fix the drives, we're out of choices. We'll be at the mercy of whoever takes us.'

The UMCP was corrupt. Vector's mutagen immunity drug proved that. Whether or not Min Donner – and therefore *Punisher* – was honest, she had to obey orders: orders which could easily come from the same source as the corruption. Holt Fasner. Possibly Hashi Lebwohl. More likely Warden Dios himself.

'They might still want to suppress what we know. No matter who they are, we'll be pawns in somebody else's game. And we can't run or fight. We don't have any realistic defense except self-destruct. But if we kill ourselves, Vector's formula dies with us.'

He sagged as another surge of exhaustion broke through

97

his thin ire. 'Out here,' he finished as if he were giving up hope, 'nobody's going to hear that broadcast anyway.'

Morn's sore gaze held his glare without flinching until he looked away. She may have been battered and abused to the core; but at least she'd had a little rest. He couldn't match her.

'I understand,' she said quietly. 'I guess I've been afraid all along that this would happen.

'So in the end it comes down to whether *Punisher* managed to kill *Calm Horizons*.'

Davies couldn't help himself: he gaped at her as if her obsession with the Amnion warship were making her alien.

Yet she must have been human enough to realize that he couldn't grasp what she meant. She smiled at him ruefully, touched his forehead as if she wanted to smooth away his incomprehension. Then she began to explain.

'Someone somewhere in the VI system is going to hear our transmission. We can't know if they'll care. Or if they'll believe us. Or if they'll try to do anything about it. At least they'll hear it. We've accomplished that much, even if we can't do more.

'But if *Calm Horizons* is still alive –'

Painful memories darkened Morn's eyes. Frowning at the hurt, she said more bitterly, 'They heard the broadcast, too. They have the formula. On top of that' – dismay at the recollection twisted her expression like a touch of nausea – 'I'm pretty sure they have samples.

'When I was their prisoner – back on Billingate – they tried to mutate me. But I didn't change. I was full of Nick's immunity drug. So they took some of my blood.'

Now Davies caught a glimpse of what she was getting at. He'd forgotten about her time in the Amnion sector of Billingate. She'd lived through horrors which for him were only nightmares; endured an experience which would have destroyed him.

'That means if they survive – if they reach Amnion space – they can figure out how to counteract Vector's formula.'

Grimly she concluded, 'Then if the wrong people get their

hands on us, stop us, everything we've done is wasted. Even if VI hears our broadcast and takes it seriously enough to follow up on it, it's still wasted. Because the Amnion will have the formula. The drug won't be safe anymore.'

Davies may have nodded. He wasn't sure: he couldn't feel his head moving. And he was no longer able to tell the difference between exhaustion and hopelessness. He'd brought Angus back from stasis: surely that counted for something?

With a thin sigh, he asked, 'What're we going to do?'

For a moment she didn't reply. Then he felt her tighten and shift against his side as if she'd made a decision.

'*You're* going to rest,' she announced in an easier tone. 'That's enough for right now. There's no point in trying to make any plans yet. We don't know how much time we have. Or who they'll send after us. Or how badly Angus is hurt. Maybe his equipment's been damaged. Maybe his *brain's* been damaged. He may have more tricks up his sleeve. Or he may not. And if he does, he may or may not be willing to do what we want.

'It's too much to worry about when you can't even keep your eyes open. You can leave it to me for a while.' She snorted softly, as if she were amused. 'If the safety of human space depended on my talent for worry, we wouldn't need cops at all.'

When he didn't respond, she left the edge of her bunk, pulling him with her.

All the resistance had drained out of him. He was weightless: only his fatigue had substance. Floating, he let her pilot him to his bunk and ease him into the g-sheath.

Her lips brushed his cheek. Close to his ear she whispered, 'Thank you. It helps to know what you were so angry about.'

Without transition he dropped into the dark as if she'd kissed him to sleep.

MORN

I need a better answer.

For some reason those words were all she remembered from the time *Trumpet* had spent in the grip of the black hole. For a while she'd regained consciousness – just long enough to speak to Davies; see that he was alive. Then the pain of her shattered arm had forced her back down into the dark. And afterward –

I can't do this again. When I'm in trouble, the only thing I can think of is to hurt myself.

Someone must have taken her to sickbay. Davies, presumably. The cast on her arm and the straps holding it across her chest were unmistakable. And the muffling of the hurt was also unmistakable. Drugs: lots of them. Otherwise she wouldn't have slept so long.

She remembered none of it, however. Only the unexpected promise she'd made to herself remained. Despite her conversation with Davies, her thoughts still moved slowly, wandering through veils of sleep and medication.

I need a better answer.

Saying that was easy. Doing it would be more difficult.

Forces she didn't know how to evaluate and couldn't control hunted the gap scout. With a Class–1 homing signal to guide them, they could hardly fail. And *Trumpet* had been damaged: sabotage. Poor Ciro – Angus surely knew how to repair her. But after his ordeal outside the ship he might not be in any condition to make the attempt. He may have been harmed in ways sickbay couldn't treat. Or his programming – or his own perversity – might interfere.

Eventually someone would have to deal with the pursuit. At the moment Morn couldn't imagine any way to do that which didn't involve sacrificing herself; buying the lives of her companions with her own.

Her arm should have hurt more than this.

If she meant to come up with a better answer, she'd better get started.

Nevertheless she spent a few minutes in her cabin with her son while he slept, reminding herself that he was alive and still relatively whole; worth fighting for.

Nearly cocooned in his g-sheath, he lay motionless, heavy with exhaustion. For a while, at least, the tension which usually drove him was gone. From time to time a brittle snore caught in his throat, then sank away.

Asleep, he looked more like a kid, less like his father – more vulnerable and unformed, less accustomed to brutality. More like he needed cherishing. Yet his parentage was clear: she saw Angus in him more than she saw herself.

Looking at him, she felt a complex pang, despite the drugs. Angus had raped and abused her; done everything in his considerable power to break her spirit. This was the result. She had a son who was precious to her. In addition she had friends now – Vector and Mikka and lost, brave Sib Mackern – who were willing to stand by her.

Yet Angus himself was still the only person aboard who might be able to save her.

The pang in her heart was complex with a vengeance. It seemed to twist simultaneously in all directions.

Driven by the necessities of his tormented soul, Angus had allowed her to guide his decisions. First he'd rescued her from the Amnion. Then he'd let her convince him to take Vector to the Lab – and to broadcast the results of Vector's analysis. During the time he'd spent taking Nick's orders, anguish had poured off him like the raw sweat of his soul.

I didn't defend myself, he'd told her, trying to persuade her to free him from his priority-codes. Com-Mine Station

Security had failed to find enough evidence to convict him of a capital crime; but still Milos Taverner had tortured him while he was in lockup, hurt and humiliated him to extract his secrets. And yet he hadn't revealed anything which might have eased his plight. *I let them do whatever they wanted to me. So you could get away.*

Why? *Because I made a deal with you. I gave you the zone implant control. You let me live.*

And I kept my end. Whether you kept yours or not.

That was true. It had to be. He'd known too much about Milos. If he'd betrayed any of it, UMCPDA's plotting with Nick and Milos would have been exposed. Then Angus wouldn't have ended up as a UMCP cyborg controlled by the man who'd tortured him.

She couldn't deny that in his own way and on his own terms he'd kept faith with her.

When I hurt you, he'd told her painfully, *I hurt myself.*

And since she and Davies had freed him, he'd done everything possible to keep her and the people she cared about safe.

She didn't know whether or not letting, helping, him edit his datacore constituted *a better answer*. That decision might yet prove to be an oblique form of self-destruct. But she didn't think so. And even if she was wrong: where else should she begin her quest to reinvent herself, if not with the man who had laid bare the shame in the core of her heart?

Unaccustomed to maneuvering in zero g with only one arm, she moved awkwardly toward the door.

At first she couldn't figure out how to anchor herself so that she wouldn't rebound from anything she touched. But then she found that she could shift her right arm a few centimeters, despite its cast and straps – just enough to hook those fingers around a handgrip. Grateful for the analgesics remaining in her body, she held herself still while she dimmed the lights so that Davies might sleep more deeply. Then she left the cabin and pulled herself one-armed in the direction of sickbay.

The unnatural silence of the ship struck her almost immediately. The low, steady hum of the thrust drive was gone. At the moment *Trumpet*'s energy cells held more than enough capacity to run the support systems – lights, warmth, air-processing, sickbay. Presumably most of the electronic equipment remained alive as well: the command boards, scan, communications, damage control. But power for the whole ship – including the gap field generator – was normally supplied by the thrust drive. The absence of that hull-noise made *Trumpet* seem irrationally desolate, almost dead, despite the obvious illumination and heat: a drifting tomb, or a derelict haunted by ghosts.

How long would the cells last? Surely no more than a day or two. If Angus couldn't repair the drives, everyone aboard might end up praying to be found, no matter who came after them.

A new urgency sharpened Morn's concentration. She began to move faster.

When she reached sickbay, she forced her right hand into another handgrip so that she could key open the door. At once she swung around the edge of the frame into the room.

Vector was there with Angus. As she stopped her momentum on the side of the surgical table, the geneticist turned away from the control panel and smiled at her.

'Morn. It's good to see you among the living. I'm sorry about your arm. On the other hand, I'm glad you're well enough to move around.'

She ignored him involuntarily: she simply had to look at Angus first.

Held by the table's restraints, he lay on his face with his EVA suit pulled down around his waist. A new bandage covered the place between his shoulder blades where Davies had once cut him to access his datacore. Spots of fresh blood marked the gauze. She could smell metabolins and antibiotics. The low rasp of his breathing lifted and lowered his chest rhythmically.

The helmet of his suit bobbed forgotten against one wall.

He didn't react to her arrival. Davies had told her that the sickbay systems said he would be all right. He must have been as profoundly exhausted as his son.

'He's sleeping,' Vector answered before she could ask a question. 'Sickbay is satisfied with his condition. But we won't really know what shape he's in until he wakes up. Right now his zone implants are in control. I assume his datacore is taking care of him, forcing him to sleep so he can heal. We couldn't rouse him unless we found some way to trigger a survival reflex in his programming. I can't begin to imagine what being outside like that, doing what he did, may have cost him.'

Vector paused for a moment, then went on with apparent detachment, 'Watching the indicators, I get the impression sickbay has run diagnostics on his equipment. That makes sense. The same people who welded him probably designed these systems to take care of him. But the panel' – Vector grimaced ruefully – 'declines to let me access the results. I guess I don't have the right codes.'

Yes, Morn thought. That made sense.

Finally she was able to turn her attention away from Angus. She lifted her head; attempted a thin smile to thank Vector for his consideration.

Now she noticed the ashen hue of his skin, the sluggishness of his movements. Despite his familiar air of calm, his blue gaze was dull, and his round cheeks seemed unnaturally sunken, drawn tight against his skull.

'Are *you* all right?' she asked. 'Davies told me you brought him in. That must have been an ordeal, with your arthritis.' Long ago Orn Vorbuld had beaten up Vector so badly that irreversible damage had been done to his joints. 'Why aren't you resting? You look like you could use it.'

Vector shrugged. Despite the absence of g, a twinge crossed his face. Distantly, as if he had no personal interest in the subject, he said, 'Bringing him in was the hardest thing I've ever done. I mean physically. We were still in the gravity well. I had to rig a winch to move us. Now I probably need half a dozen joints replaced. At the very least I should let sickbay give me a whole pseudoserotonin multicortisone series. Reduce the inflammation, if nothing else.

'But really it doesn't matter,' he added promptly. 'Zero g helps. And we all have more important things to worry about.'

Morn opened her mouth to object; but he wasn't done.

'Mikka said she was going to get some sleep' – his tone sharpened – 'after she checks on Ciro. But I don't trust her. I think she's going to make herself crazy suffering over what he did. If one of us doesn't stay awake to stop her, she'll probably go start trying to fix the drives.'

Morn frowned. Surely he didn't consider that their most important worry? But she wasn't ready to tackle larger issues yet. And she *was* concerned about Mikka – as well as about Mikka's tormented brother.

'How is Ciro now?'

Vector spread his hands. 'I have no idea. To be honest, I didn't ask. Until Mikka and Davies left here, we were all too busy.'

'Doing what?' Davies hadn't said anything about this.

For a moment Vector hesitated. He may have been wondering how much Davies hadn't explained to her – or why. Then he seemed to put the question aside with a turn of his head.

'When I brought him in' – the geneticist indicated Angus – 'he wasn't unconscious or asleep. He was in stasis. His datacore had shut him down. We couldn't figure out how to reach him. As far as we could tell, he was stuck there permanently. We spent quite a while trying to get through to him, but we weren't able to do it.

'Then Davies decided to pull the chip.' Vector's phlegmatic tone gave this detail no special emphasis. 'When he plugged it back in, Angus' computer reset itself. Came back on-line.

'After that,' Vector finished laconically, 'his zone implants put him to sleep.'

Pull the chip –? Morn thought in amazement. The muting of her mind had begun to fade: she could feel real amazement. Pulling the chip was a brilliant solution. She doubted that she would ever have conceived of it herself.

And Davies hadn't mentioned it?

'No,' she said, answering Vector's hesitation, 'he didn't tell me. He gave me a summary of what's been happening, but he kept it short.' Because – she'd assumed – he was exhausted. 'He didn't say anything about stasis. He didn't say anything about bringing Angus back.'

Vector's mild gaze offered no comment.

'Do you have any idea why he kept that to himself?' Morn pursued.

Vector pursed his mouth, studying the question. Despite the blur of fatigue, his eyes hinted at penetration.

'Your son hasn't had what I would call an easy life,' he said judiciously. 'Early on he spent most of his time helpless while you performed miracles to keep him alive. And since then he's been struggling to figure out who he is. Not always gracefully, I admit. It's not a graceful process.

'If I were in his place, I might not tell you because I didn't want to scare you. Or' – Vector faced her squarely – 'I might be trying to learn how to respect myself without outside help.'

Trying to learn how to separate himself from her.

Slowly Morn nodded. That explanation made sense to her. And it matched Davies' unexpected apology. While she slept her son had grown –

If she could keep up with him, she might yet discover a way to end her reliance on self-destruct.

'In that case,' she murmured, 'I'll wait until he brings it up before I tell him what I know about miracles.'

Rescuing Angus was as much a miracle as anything she'd ever done.

Through his weariness, Vector smiled again.

She smiled, too. However, the thought of self-destruct reminded her that she didn't have much time. While *Trumpet* coasted, helpless, other ships were moving: other forces were at work, seeking to impose their own priorities on the gap scout. She should get to work herself.

Changing the subject, she remarked with deliberate non-chalance, 'In the meantime, I probably don't have to mention that we need Angus awake.'

Vector shook his head. 'I've been giving him the occasional

cybernetic nudge' – he twitched a hand in the direction of the control panel – 'just to see what happens. So far what happens is nothing. We'll have to wait until his computer decides it's time for him to start receiving external stimuli.

'As I said,' Vector mused, 'he might wake up if his programming recognizes a survival threat. We could set off the decompression klaxon, see if that reaches him. But I don't think it's a good idea. After what he's been through, he needs the rest.'

Morn agreed. She was sure that *Trumpet* didn't have much time. But the situation wouldn't become urgent until another ship appeared on scan.

And, she admitted to herself with another pang, she wasn't in a hurry to deal with Angus again. Too much depended on what he would be like when his zone implants allowed him to awaken. Or perhaps on her ability to hold him to his obscure bargains.

Let him sleep for a while. Everyone else needed a chance to rest. And think.

'In that case,' she suggested to Vector, 'let's go to the bridge. We won't learn anything here. There we can at least sit down. Look at scan, see where we are.' See if the sensors had picked up another ship yet. 'Maybe we can start trying to figure a way out of this mess.

'And maybe,' she added, 'we can rig the command board to tell us if Mikka tries anything rash. If we can get that far into the systems.'

Vector considered for a moment, glanced at the sickbay readouts, then nodded. 'You go ahead. I'll stop by the galley first – make some coffee, bring us food. Now that I think about it, I can't remember the last time any of us had a meal.' He grimaced humorously toward Angus. 'If you don't count IVs.'

He was right. As soon as he said the words, she realized that she was acutely hungry. The prospect of coffee brought a rush of saliva into her mouth.

At the same time new pain throbbed along her arm. Sensations of several kinds began to return as the drugs withdrew their effects.

'Sounds good,' she said to cover a wince. 'Don't be long. I must be recovering, or I wouldn't be this interested in food.'

Gingerly she nudged herself toward the door.

She didn't want to use her right hand again. Without it, however, movement in zero g was tricky. The same tap which keyed open the door moved her in the opposite direction. But then a lucky thrust with her leg caught one of the surgical table supports and impelled her gracelessly out of the room.

After that progress was easier: she didn't have to deal with doors. Protecting her cast, she launched herself from handgrip to handgrip in the direction of the bridge.

On the rails of the companionway she stopped her motion in order to shift vectors toward the command station.

At once she saw Mikka.

Nick's former command second sat at the second's station with her back to Morn. Her head hung over her limp hands and the keys as if she'd fallen asleep in the middle of some task.

Another pang. As the drugs faded, Morn found more and more hurts. Vector was right: Mikka hadn't been able to let go of her grief and shame long enough to lie down on her bunk.

But she wasn't sleeping. As soon as Morn made a sound, Mikka raised her head, looked around.

Her features were drawn, haggard; sallow with exhaustion and loss. A bandage still covered one eye and part of her forehead where Angus had once hit her; nearly broken open her skull. Weariness blurred her gaze, but the distress in her good eye was too dark and deep to be hidden. Her habitual frown had lost its edge of ready belligerence: it had become a clenched effort to contain the effects of an inner crisis. She looked like a woman who'd lost her reasons for living – and hated herself for it.

'Morn' – a strained croak, barely audible. 'I'm glad –' Her voice trailed away as if she had no words for gladness.

The sight hurt Morn like her shattered bones. She pushed off from the companionway, floated to the back of Mikka's g-seat. 'Mikka –' She wanted to put her arms around the woman, try to comfort her somehow. But of course that was impossible. She needed her left to hold her at the second's station. 'You shouldn't be here. Look at you. You need rest.' A clutch of empathy nearly closed her throat. 'Good God, you need *rest*.'

Mikka made a small, aimless gesture. 'I know.' Her gaze wandered away. 'I can't.'

Morn glanced quickly at the screens, found a scan image on one of the displays. Someone – probably Mikka – had routed a steady stream of data from the sensors and sifters to that screen. As far as *Trumpet* could tell, there were no ships anywhere around her. In fact, there was nothing at all except the black void and the unreachable glitter of the stars. Only a faint spatter of dust occupied the vacuum.

No doubt astrogation could identify the gap scout's position; perhaps had already done so. But the information was useless. The numbers told Morn that the nearest hope of a star system was decades away at this velocity.

Until another ship appeared on scan, *Trumpet* had nothing to fear. And nothing to hope for.

'Mikka,' she said as gently as she could, 'you're not alone here. Vector's still up. I've had enough sleep for six people. Angus is probably going to wake up soon. You don't have to take care of everything yourself.'

'I know,' Mikka murmured. 'I'm not trying to be a martyr. But Ciro's there. In the cabin. I can't' – her head drooped as if her neck had gone limp – 'can't stand to be around him.'

'Because he sabotaged the drives?' Morn asked softly. 'Because he obeyed Sorus Chatelaine even after Vector treated her mutagen?'

Are you that angry at him?

Slowly, weakly, Mikka shook her head. 'I might have done the same thing –'

Again she trailed away. For a long moment she was silent. When she went on, her voice ached like Morn's arm.

'He did what he was told. It's over for him now. Everything's over – All he does is lie there crying.

'I don't mean sobbing. He doesn't make a sound. He just

lies there with tears streaming down his face. He won't talk to me. I'm not sure he hears me. I think he's deaf with grief.

'He's only a kid. As far as he knows, he's killed us all. That didn't mean anything to him until he did what he was told. It couldn't. Sorus Chatelaine made him crazy. But now –

'I guess he can't figure out how to live with it.'

Mikka's head hung over the console. She couldn't hold it up. 'He's all I have.' She sounded distant and worn, like the low plaint of the air-scrubbers. 'All I've ever had. And I got him into this. I talked Nick into taking him aboard. I thought I could make a life for both of us.

'Now he's gone,' she finished brokenly. 'He did this, and he can't fix it. If I can't repair the drives for him, there's nothing left.'

Pain whetted the edge of Morn's reactions. She valued Mikka too much to watch in silence while Mikka suffered. And Mikka was simply too worn out to pull herself back from the gravity well of her despair. Some kind of intervention was necessary.

'I can't argue with you.' Morn put words together carefully, hoping to string them in ways Mikka couldn't refute or deny. 'You're the only one who knows what matters to you.

'You don't want to hear about the times you've saved my life, or the times you saved this whole ship. You don't want to hear that when you talked Vector and Sib into joining you against Nick you gave us our only hope – the only way any of us has to redeem ourselves. Without you Vector and Sib would probably have been stranded on Billingate, we never would have gone to the Lab, Vector wouldn't have his formula, Nick would still be alive –

'You probably don't want to hear me say I've got about as much tolerance for seeing you like this as you have for watching Ciro,' who was by God old enough to be responsible for his own insanity.

Rough needles had begun probing the joints of her arm, the marrow of her bones. An irrational anger rose in her – a desire to yell at Mikka in order to contain her own pain. If Vector didn't get here soon with food and coffee and distraction, she feared that she might do or say something she would later regret.

'Maybe I can understand a little of what you're feeling,' she continued with as much kindness as she could muster. '*Angus* is my son's father. Whenever my gap-sickness takes over I'm in love with self-destruct. Which is about the same as killing yourself with exhaustion. But I don't believe you when you say "there's nothing left". *You're* still here. Worth caring about. Even if you can't protect Ciro from himself.'

At first she couldn't tell whether Mikka heard her. But then Mikka murmured, 'That's fine.' She spoke without bitterness; without hope. 'Until the cops get me.'

Morn groaned to herself. Mikka Vasaczk was a proven illegal: Nick Succorso's command second; a woman who'd participated in robbery, murder and treason in Nick's name.

Ciro had raised the same objection. *Why is it worse for them to die now?* – Mikka, Vector and Sib. *At least they can fight. They don't have to sit around waiting to be* executed!

At the time Mikka had responded, *I don't* care *about being executed! I don't care about anything that might happen days or weeks or* months *from now, if we're lucky enough to live that long. I care about* you!

If you want to betray us, then do it. *But don't use* me *as an excuse.*

Now she felt differently: that was obvious. The danger of being captured was at least as personal to her as it was to Morn.

Morn had no answer. She didn't trust the UMCP herself. She was in no position to promise Mikka justice – or mercy.

For a moment a clench of pain threatened to make her gasp. When she'd pushed her arm past the support of her g-seat into the grip of the black hole's gravity well, she'd shattered the bones, damaged the joints, torn ligaments, shredded cartilage. Sickbay had probably worked on her for hours to put her back together. If she had any sense, she would get more drugs right away, before the pain grew worse.

But she didn't leave the bridge. She needed the pain – not to punish her, but to teach her the consequences of her own actions. If she hadn't been so frantic to escape pain and consequences, she wouldn't have accepted her zone implant control from Angus; wouldn't have fled Com-Mine Station with Nick. Instead she would have turned herself over to Com-Mine Security; put a stop to everything which had engulfed her – and Angus – since then.

Rotating around her strapped arm as if it were her personal center of gravity, she swung away from Mikka and drifted to the command station. Carefully she belted herself into the g-seat as if she belonged there. For a moment she closed her eyes and concentrated on simply breathing; exhaling the worst of her hurt.

When she looked at Mikka again, she'd recovered her composure.

Gently again, she asked, 'What were you trying to do?'

Mikka had removed her hands from the second's console as if to disavow responsibility. Despite the absence of g, she slumped like a woman who couldn't support her own weight. But she was still Mikka Vasaczk, not some callow UMCP ensign appalled by gap-sickness and zone implants and Angus Thermopyle. Regardless of her own distress, she made the effort to reply.

'Get into the drive databases,' she muttered thinly. 'Find schematics. Diagnostic routines. Repair protocols. Anything that tells us how to work on the drives.

'Wrecking electronics is easy. Like murder. You don't need brains. All you need is a spanner. But you can't repair anything if you don't know what you're trying to fix.'

'No luck?' Morn pursued, although she already knew the answer. She wanted to keep Mikka talking until Vector arrived.

Mikka wobbled her head negatively. 'Everything that has to do with the ship is locked away. We can run helm – for whatever good that's going to do us. Targ, scan, communications. But the ship is hidden. I can't get into damage control. Hell, I can't even access maintenance. I can't find out how much food we have. I can't tell you how long our fuel would have lasted if we were able to use it.'

'Are we still broadcasting Vector's message?'

'Sure. Now that it's useless, nobody can hear it, we're screaming it in all directions.' Mikka paused, then added bleakly, 'Hell of a drain on our energy cells.'

The energy cells were all that kept *Trumpet* alive.

'Speaking of which,' Vector remarked casually, 'I've been draining them as fast as I can.'

Morn turned her head, saw him at the head of the companionway. He looked at Mikka, and his eyes narrowed. Then he shrugged himself into motion. He was carrying a tray laden with g-flasks and food-packets in retaining clips. Steam curled past his shoulders as he floated down the treads.

'Coffee,' he went on in his most avuncular manner. 'Hot soup – black bean, if you can trust the smell. Steamed sirloin bars, according to the label. Wasting power like mad. The only things I didn't cook are the nutrient capsules.'

He drifted in front of the second's station and stopped himself on the edge of the console, forcing Mikka to notice him.

'I thought you told me you were going to get some sleep,' he said sternly.

She scowled up at him: a reflex; devoid of force. She didn't say anything.

'Oh, well.' He shrugged again. 'Who am I to talk? If any of us had the intelligence God gave curdled milk, we probably wouldn't be in this mess to begin with.'

With a show of cheerfulness, he started distributing packets and g-flasks.

As soon as the steam reached Morn's nose, she nearly went blind with hunger and eagerness. Her pain seemed to vanish: for a moment her universe shrank until it contained only coffee, soup and meat. One-handed, trembling with anticipation, she set the coffee in a holder in the arm of her g-seat, pushed a couple of packets down into her lap, then raised the soup unsteadily to her mouth.

Black bean, hell. It didn't smell like that – or taste like it. It was pure Heaven. She hardly noticed that the heat stung her tongue as she drank.

Her nerves hadn't felt a thrill like this since the last time she'd turned on her zone implant.

She took several swallows before she recovered enough awareness to realize that Vector was watching her intently. Making sure she was all right –

'Vector Shaheed,' she murmured, 'you are a saint. You deserve to live forever.'

He grinned at her briefly, then coasted away to the auxiliary engineering console and anchored himself to the seat with his zero-g belt while he ate.

Morn tore open a sirloin bar with her teeth, chewed a bite of the meat. Drank more soup. Swallowed her nutrient capsules. Sipped some coffee. And found that she felt better answers might be possible after all. Food certainly seemed to be one of them. Her arm resumed its sharp pulsing almost at once: if anything her pain grew stronger as her body took in sustenance. Nevertheless it had become less threatening. She could endure it better.

At last she looked over at Mikka.

Mikka sat with her head bowed over her coffee, her face in the steam. For a while she appeared content to simply breathe the aroma. But then she took a few small sips. Slowly her head came up, and she reached for her soup.

As she ate, her skin lost some of its pallor. Her movements regained a measure of clarity. She straightened her back a bit against the support of her g-seat.

Morn gave a private sigh of relief. She didn't want to lose Mikka.

Finally she was done eating. She secured her g-flasks, crumpled her empty packets to dispose of later, and rested her hands lightly on the command board.

'Now,' she announced. 'I don't know how much time we have left, but there's nobody else on scan yet.' Numbers along the scan display confirmed the absence of blips within the sensors' reach. 'This might be the best chance we'll ever get to make some plans.'

'What plans?' Mikka snorted. Food had apparently given her the energy for bitterness. 'The drives are dead.'

Nothing was possible without power.

'And we might not be able to fix them,' Morn added for her. 'Angus might not be able to fix them. He might not even be willing. If he ever wakes up. We don't know whose side he's really on, who's responsible for his core programming,' although she suspected it was Warden Dios. 'If we start listing all the things we don't know and can't tell, we'll be here for hours.'

The pain of her arm nagged at her in waves, each crest higher than the last; reminding her of consequences.

'But I still think we should try to figure out where *we* stand,' she insisted. 'What's important to *us*. What *we* want to accomplish. If we don't, we'll never accomplish anything at all. Even if we get the chance.'

Mikka tapped a couple of keys on her board, refining the scan display. She didn't respond.

After a moment Vector cleared his throat. 'That makes sense to me,' he offered. 'But I'm afraid I don't have much to contribute. I was never a very good engineer. And I can't fight worth a damn.' He shrugged eloquently. 'For me it's all simple. My whole life is in that antimutagen. The formula. And the broadcast. I'm really not worried about anything else.' A shadow seemed to pass across his gaze. 'Except I don't want any more of us to die. I still haven't recovered from losing Sib.'

Poor frightened, valiant Sib Mackern, who had accompanied Nick Succorso in an EVA attack on *Soar* so that Nick wouldn't be able to turn on *Trumpet*; so that *Trumpet* would have a better chance to survive.

Sib's gesture, like Nick's crazy lust for revenge, had seemed hopeless, doomed; an exercise in futility. And yet it had achieved something vital. *Soar* had lost her super-light proton cannon. Nick and Sib must have damaged it somehow. They'd kept *Trumpet* alive with their deaths.

Morn had watched the Amnion inject their mutagens into her. She'd endured a terror as profound and personal as her own DNA while she waited to learn whether Nick's immunity drug would preserve her humanity. And then – for reasons which still seemed entirely incomprehensible – Angus had rescued her. Across the light-years, and despite the intervening layers of corruption, someone at UMCPHQ wanted her alive.

She knew from experience that she was too mortal – too rich with fear – to recognize doom when she saw it.

With a nod she acknowledged Vector's reply. For a moment she was silent while she settled her broken arm as comfortably as she could across her chest. Then she began.

'Sometimes I think the only things I've ever been really good at are holding grudges and being ashamed of myself.' She needed to say this so that Vector and Mikka would understand her. 'It makes perfect sense that I love self-destruct when I'm gap-sick. That's what I've been doing all my life, one way or another. Eating myself alive with misguided anger, and then punishing myself for it. Making myself a zone implant addict. Shattering my own arm –'

Vector murmured a demurral; but Morn didn't pause to hear it.

'I'm looking for better answers.'

A deeper surge of pain seemed to concentrate her mind. The distress of her damaged bones forced her to be clear.

'The UMCP has the same problem,' she pronounced. 'As far as I'm concerned, suppressing Intertech's immunity research was self-destructive. So was sending Angus against Billingate under Milos Taverner's control.' More than anything else, that single action had led to *Calm Horizons*' incursion into human space. 'If you're a cop, you can only damage yourself when you try to manipulate the definition of your responsibilities.

'In some ways, the crucial question is, where does the damage come from? Is Min Donner honest? Is Warden Dios? Has the harm been imposed by Holt Fasner, or is it more internal – more organic? Is there anyone we can trust?

'But in other ways,' she asserted, 'that question is irrelevant. We'll probably never know the answer. Or we won't know in time. We need to make our own decisions for our own reasons.'

Another crest of pain rose remorselessly through her. The tide was coming in with a vengeance. Soon she would have no choice but to retreat to sickbay for medication. But not yet. In the spaces between the waves she felt clear and sure. She seemed to see the consequences of what Holt Fasner or Warden Dios had done precisely, as if they were delineated on one of the screens in front of her.

'We may not be able to figure out what we're actually going to do until we see who comes after us.' This had to be said as well. 'I'm not sure which would be worse, *Punisher* or a ship from VI. *Punisher* fought for us against *Calm Horizons*. But she also gave Nick Angus' priority-codes.' At the same time she'd made it possible for Davies and Morn to free him from those codes. 'And Valdor is a UMC station. For all we know, they could be taking orders directly from the Dragon.'

Deliberately she dismissed the possibility of pursuit by *Calm Horizons*. To avoid distracting herself with prospects of terror, she chose to believe that the Amnion couldn't follow a UMCP homing signal. *Soar* and the Amnioni must have found *Trumpet* at Deaner Beckmann's lab by some other means.

'But we can worry about that later. For now, I'll tell you what my priorities are, what's important to me. Then you can tell me whether you agree.'

Vector nodded. Food and coffee had rubbed the smudge from his gaze. He watched Morn steadily, almost without blinking.

Mikka kept her head turned toward her console. Her fingers twitched erratically over the keys as if she felt driven to enter commands and didn't know how. Tension knotted the muscles along her jaw. The bandage covered one eye and hid the other; concealed her reaction.

Morn paused to let a harsh crest roll past her. Then she continued.

'First, I want to make sure we keep transmitting that formula. Maybe no one out here can hear it. That's not the point.' She faced Vector. 'You said you've always wanted to be the "savior of humankind". Maybe you were joking –

sometimes I can't tell – but our broadcast is probably as close as you'll ever get.'

Vector smiled ruefully. 'I know.'

But Morn didn't stop. 'If it's *Punisher* that comes after us,' she went on, 'and if Min Donner is honest, then we can probably trust *Punisher*'s datacore. Our message will be recorded. At some point it'll be played back. The formula might spread, even if we end up dying out here.'

Now she turned to Mikka.

'Second, I want to keep you two and Ciro away from some confused cop's notion of summary justice. The UMCP needs to hear what you know – about those high-g acceleration experiments the Amnion are doing, if nothing else. Probably the GCES should hear it. And they all need to hear what I have to say about you.

'I may have committed a crime or two myself, but I'm still a cop. The UMCP and the GCES ought to be told what you've done' – she quoted the official phrase exactly – '"in support of a sworn officer of the law in the performance of her duty".'

At first Mikka didn't react. Then, slowly, she lowered her hands from her board. Her head turned until Morn could see her good eye frowning like a sibyl's.

'You would do that?' she demanded in a clenched voice. 'A cop like you? If you got the chance? After what you just told us about the cops damaging themselves by manipulating the definition of their responsibilities?'

Another cutting surge caught Morn as Mikka spoke. From shoulder to wrist hot iron seethed in her arm. For a moment she lost her balance; stumbled without transition into a sea of pain and dark rage. Try me! she wanted to shout. *Try* me. Do you think I'm lying? Do you think I came through all this just so I could feed you *bullshit*?

But Vector was already answering for her.

'Stop that, Mikka!' he said with unaccustomed vehemence. 'You aren't paying attention.

'Morn can't testify for us without explaining why she was aboard *Captain's Fancy* in the first place. If you paid attention, you might understand what that means.' He faltered, then continued more quietly, 'Eventually she'll have to explain why she kept her zone implant control.'

Why she'd helped conceal evidence of a capital crime by accepting her black box from Angus. Why she'd committed the crime of using a zone implant on herself.

Now Vector turned toward Morn. 'Are you sure this is a better answer?' He sighed his concern. 'It sounds like more self-punishment to me. Aren't you offering to damage your-self so that the rest of us will look good?'

The surge receded. Morn's head cleared with a suddenness that made her gasp. Abruptly she recovered her footing.

She was in a hurry now. She needed to finish this before the next wave caught her.

And yet Mikka and Vector asked important questions; ques-tions which searched her more deeply than any of the issues she'd prepared herself to face. As deeply as Angus' appeal for freedom from his priority-codes. They required answers.

Instead of rushing to reach the point where she could with-draw to sickbay, she stood her ground.

'I don't think it's self-destructive to tell the truth,' she stated. 'And justice doesn't mean anything if it isn't based on the truth. My job is enforcement, not judgment. That means I'm supposed to arrest you because I have reason to believe you've broken the law. But it also means I'm supposed to tell the truth at your trial. The whole truth, if I can. If I look bad in the process, I probably deserve it. I've broken the law myself.

'If it'll help you feel better, I'll arrest you right now.' She was entirely serious. 'Although you might not notice any difference. As the arresting officer of record, I have certain rights. Legally they can't take my prisoners without "cause". And they can't do anything to you without my testimony. That might give you some protection.'

Unless they killed Morn herself to silence her.

To her surprise, Vector burst out laughing. He clasped his hands together, rolled his eyes upward. 'Take me now, O Lord.' His voice shook with mirth. 'First I'm declared a saint.

Then I'm placed under arrest on a ship lost in the middle of nowhere with both drives ruined. Life holds no greater riches. If I go now, I'll die happy.

'Morn Hyland,' he chuckled as he subsided, 'you are an amazing woman. Absolutely amazing.'

Mikka ignored him. Poised in her g-seat, she waited until he was done: she might have been holding her breath. Then she leaned forward to speak.

'Do you remember,' she asked Morn softly, intently, 'back when we were on *Captain's Fancy*? After Nick killed Orn? It was practically the first conversation we ever had. You asked me how often I've been raped. Then you said, "After a while you hurt so bad that you don't want to be rescued anymore. You want to *eviscerate* that sonofabitch for yourself."

'I believed you. The way you said it, I knew you meant it. You were a woman who could cut a man's guts out. That's when I first realized Nick was in trouble. He made a serious mistake bringing you aboard. I wasn't even particularly surprised when you took over the whole damn ship to rescue Davies.'

Involuntarily Morn closed her eyes. She felt another wave of pain approaching; felt the bitter waters rise around her head. She didn't want to remember that conversation with Mikka. She didn't want to think about Orn Vorbuld's attack on her – or his death. Rage already had too much power over her.

Mikka wasn't finished, however. Her tone hardened.

'But you didn't do that to Angus, did you,' she said as if she were challenging Morn. 'You could have *eviscerated* him, but instead you freed him from his priority-codes.

'Now you say you want to testify for us. Plead "extenuating circumstances", or some such shit.' She paused, then admitted more weakly, 'And I still believe you.

'Why is that? You should have ripped Angus apart while you had the chance. How can you talk about standing up for us and make me believe you?'

She might have been obliquely asking Morn for a reason not to give up on herself.

Morn didn't know how to answer.

The Amnion had injected their mutagens into her. They'd taught her that she couldn't afford to hold grudges anymore. Not against Nick or Angus: not against herself. Not if she valued her humanity. Revenge was too expensive.

As the acid surge of her hurt washed back out of her, she opened her eyes so that she could face Mikka's demand. Slowly she took a deep breath and released it, letting her anger and confusion drain away. Then she shrugged as if the issue were simple.

'I just don't want to end up like Nick.'

For all his cunning and experience, and his talent for self-preservation, Nick Succorso had been reduced to suicide by his craving for revenge on Sorus Chatelaine.

Morn knew that feeling. She had turned her back on it because she knew it so well.

'Good cops tell the truth,' she added softly. 'And they don't do vengeance.'

For a long moment Mikka held Morn's gaze, her reaction hidden by the darkness in her good eye. Then she nodded once, decisively, as if at last she understood.

'As long as we're telling the truth,' she muttered, 'I can't see how Ciro and I have earned any protection. But thanks. You can stop worrying about me. I'll do anything I can to help.'

Morn felt a pang of relief and gratitude. She ignored it, however. She knew she wouldn't last much longer. Already another crest gathered its load of agony on the horizon. Soon it would roll toward her with the force of a breaker.

'I wasn't done,' she said more abruptly than she intended. 'I want to keep broadcasting Vector's message. I want to testify for all of you. And there's one more thing. But I need to finish quickly.' She smiled like a grimace, trying to soften the edge of her brusqueness. 'The painkillers are wearing off. If I don't get more soon, I'll start to babble.'

At once Vector spread his hands as if to show that they held no more interruptions. 'Please.'

Mikka scowled in chagrin. 'I'm sorry. I didn't realize –'

She bit her lip. With a gesture that seemed to indicate the whole bridge, she added, 'This can wait. We'll still be here when you get back.'

No, it couldn't wait. Morn needed to say it now; needed to make her intentions plain before another ship appeared on scan.

Although any movement might bring on the next surge, she straightened her back and squared her shoulders like a woman who meant to fill the command station completely. As firmly as she could with so much pain looming toward her, she announced, 'I also want the GCES to hear *my* story.'

Vector and Mikka probably knew what she meant, but she explained it anyway.

'The UMCP gave me to Nick. I don't know why. But they could have stopped me before I boarded *Captain's Fancy*. Com-Mine Security must have consulted with them about me. Com-Mine wouldn't have let me go without orders from UMCPHQ.

'The GCES needs to hear that. But there's more.

'I know for a fact that Angus was framed. He may have committed every crime we can think of, but he didn't do the one he was arrested for.' Arrested and convicted. 'He says he can prove Nick was in collusion with Milos Taverner. He found a data-link between them before he was framed – a link he could have traced. I assume the evidence is in *Bright Beauty*'s datacore. But when the cops welded Angus and aimed him at Billingate' – she still didn't understand any of this – 'they sent Taverner along to control him.'

More than anything else, that single fact had precipitated an act of war.

'The more I think about it, the uglier it looks. It stinks of conspiracy. Which is just another way for the cops to destroy themselves.'

Distress began to rise around her again, shrilling along her nerves, drawing a wail from every crack and tear in her arm. She couldn't wait any longer. With her left hand, she opened her belts so that she could drift out of the command station.

Pain and consequences. Better answers.

She held onto the back of the g-seat while she finished.

'I guess what I'm saying is that I want to get back to Earth. And when I get there I want to be free to make my own decisions. I want to be able to talk to the Council without interference from corrupt cops who've been ordered to stop me by Warden Dios or Holt Fasner.

'If that means I have to patch the drives with duct tape and fight cops the whole way home, I'm willing to do it.'

That was enough. Clear enough: painful enough. She had to go now. If she stayed, she would cross the line into self-punishment; into shame and rage.

When I'm in trouble, the only thing I can think of is to hurt myself.

She pushed off toward the head of the companionway.

Vector actually saluted her while she coasted across the bridge. 'Have I ever mentioned that I like the way you think?' he called after her.

Morn reached the companionway rails and kept moving. She was sure he didn't mean to stop her.

But Mikka did. Raising her voice to make Morn pause, she asked, 'What if Angus won't go along with it?'

Morn closed her fist on one of the rails, swung around to face the bridge.

'Then I'll convince him to change his mind.'

One way or another, she was doomed to deal with Angus Thermopyle.

Moving one-handed, full of pain, as awkward as a cripple, she impelled herself in the direction of sickbay.

ANGUS

Angus Thermopyle awoke the instant Morn said his name.

Without transition his zone implants imposed new conditions on him. The regular alpha of sleep was canceled: dreams he couldn't remember stopped as if they'd never existed: his long escape from the loud ravage of the swarm and the excruciating forces of the black hole ended severely, as if it had been cut off with a knife. Emissions programmed by his computer swept safety away; snatched peace out of his synapses and ganglia. Morn said his name, and his entire neural state of being was transformed. He didn't twitch or tighten: his body remained still. Nevertheless from the depths of a fathomless, healing dark he moved instantly into light and consciousness.

Morn spoke again. 'Angus. It's time to wake up. We need you.'

He heard the anxiety in her voice, the pressure of self-coercion. He knew her too fucking well. She loathed him: she'd always loathed him. If she'd consulted only her own desires, she wouldn't have come within thirty light-years of him. She was here because she needed him. *Trumpet* needed him. The people she cared about needed him.

Yet she was here. She'd survived hard g and gap-sickness in the swarm; come through them somehow.

What had Davies said earlier? When he'd risked removing Angus' datacore? *Morn's going to wake up soon. I can't tell her this. After what she's been through* – Bitterly he'd protested, *I can't tell Morn that the only man who stands a chance of helping us is stuck in fucking* stasis.

Something had happened to her. Something brutal. Like everything Nick Succorso and Angus himself had done to her.

And still she was here.

In a flash of disgust as swift as the effects of his zone implants, he realized that he was glad.

His eyes were open. For all he knew, they'd been open the entire time. Lying on his belly on the surgical table, with his right cheek leaning into the cushions, he had a clear view of the sickbay console and readouts.

The sterile light of the room illuminated the indicators distinctly. They told him he was awake. No shit. In addition they assured him he was healing rapidly.

But Morn was on the other side of the table. Maybe she couldn't see that his eyes were open. Or maybe she hadn't looked at the readouts yet. 'Angus,' she said for the third time. 'I don't know how to do this. I don't know if you can hear me. But it's important. You've got to wake up.'

Damn right *Trumpet* needed him. *He's the only one who can repair the drives.* That brain-dead little shit Ciro had sabotaged them. Carried out Sorus Chatelaine's orders even after Vector flushed her mutagens out of him.

No one else could get past the lock Angus had set on most of the gap scout's internal systems. He, on the other hand –

He had the necessary database in his head, ready and waiting on the other side of his data-link. He could rebuild the ship from scratch without consulting damage control. Hell, he could fabricate half the goddamn parts himself, if he had to –

He swallowed to clear his throat. He was going to say, Go away, you stupid bitch. I don't care how much you need me. I don't need you. He was going to say that and fucking *mean* it.

But it was bullshit. He didn't want her to go away. He no longer had any intention of hurting her –

When he hurt her, he hurt himself.

That was the story of his whole fucking life. For years, *decades*, he'd raped and killed and beaten and destroyed with all his strength. And after every act of violence his choices had dwindled. His freedom shrank. No matter what he did, he sank deeper into his personal abyss – the void of terror and pain from which he'd always fled.

Until Morn released him from his priority-codes.

His programming still restricted him in more ways than he could count; but now no one had the power to compel his allegiance.

And he'd survived the crib. Alone outside the ship in his EVA suit, hammered by the energies of warships and the swarm and a black hole, he'd fallen into the pure, blind, helpless agony he'd always feared; and he'd survived.

He definitely didn't want Morn to go away.

But it was more than that; worse than not meaning to hurt her. He didn't want her to think she couldn't reach him. Didn't want her to feel helpless –

'I hear you.' His voice was a dry scrape in his throat. 'Don't push me. I've got a lot to think about.'

God, what was the *matter* with him? What was he going to do next – beg her to fucking *forgive* him?

No. Not now: not ever. He was *alive*, God damn it, in spite of everything. He'd survived the crib. He was *Angus Thermopyle*, not some shit-crazy philanthropist who wanted or maybe even needed to apologize for living.

'Thank God.' Morn's relief was as plain as a message from his datacore. Despite her loathing, she didn't wish him dead.

We need you. You've got to wake up.

Which didn't make any sense. Ciro sabotaged the *drives*? Then why the hell was *Trumpet* still alive? How had she *survived*? Where *was* she?

Davies had said, *The cops are coming after us.* Angus had heard that. *We're sending out a Class–1 homing signal.* Then Davies had asked as if he thought Angus had the answer hidden away somewhere, *Whose side is that cruiser on?*

What the fuck was going on?

He decided to move. But he couldn't: the table's restraints held him. He flexed against them, then remembered what they were for. To keep him still while sickbay – and Davies – operated on him. To protect him from g.

'If you'll let me out of these damn straps,' he croaked, 'I'll sit up.'

If you trust me that much.

While he waited, he asked his computer for a status report.

Internal diagnostics informed him that he'd suffered a dislocated hip (corrected), severe dehydration (treated), and massive hemorrhaging (stopped). Blood chemistry analysis reported appropriately high levels of metabolins, coagulants, analgesics, antibiotics. Prognosis: complete recovery in forty-eight hours.

All of his welded resources were functional. If he had to, he could cut his way out of the restraints.

But Morn had already begun to tug awkwardly at his fetters, releasing them one after another. The moment he was free, he rolled over and swung his legs off the table.

Pain lanced through his hip as he moved. Maybe he shouldn't have tried to use his suit jets against the singularity's pull. Or maybe that small extra support was all that had saved him.

Almost instantly his zone implants muffled the sensation. Only a residual throbbing ache remained to remind him that he needed more time to heal.

Anchored on the edge of the table, he looked at Morn for the first time since he'd left the bridge to risk EVA in the swarm.

She floated an arm's length away. 'We let you sleep as long as we could,' she said at once. Anxiety complicated her tone. She seemed to speak quickly so that she wouldn't freeze; so that her loathing wouldn't get the better of her. 'But we're out of time. There's another ship on scan. Resumed tard five minutes ago. We've got id.

'It's *Punisher*. A UMCP cruiser. The same ship we passed when we first reached human space.' She faltered, then finished, 'The same one that ordered you to give Nick your priority-codes.'

She appeared to think Angus would consider that detail significant; but he didn't. He wasn't listening.

Rest had done her some good: he saw that at a glance. The young woman's beauty of her face was gone, permanently eroded by suffering and desperation. Stark against her pale features, her eyes were as dark as caves. Nevertheless sleep or food – or both – had improved her skin-tone and restored some of the elasticity to her muscles. It had eased the deep-cut lines around her mouth, between her brows, at the corners of her eyes.

He dismissed those details as soon as he noticed them, however. His attention was caught by the cast which encased her right arm in acrylic from shoulder to wrist; by the straps which closed her arm against her chest.

At the sight black rage came to fire in him as suddenly as the explosion of an incendiary grenade. Only his zone implants kept him from launching himself at her, grabbing her, shaking her to learn the truth.

Nearly choked by dark flame, he demanded harshly, 'Who did that to you?'

In about a minute the bastard responsible was going to find himself strangling on his own balls.

A small wince plucked at the side of her face. 'I did it to myself,' she answered thinly. 'That's how I controlled my gap-sickness. While I was at the command board.'

To herself. He swore through his teeth. To *herself?* He believed her instantly. And he wanted to slap her.

'You're crazy, you know that?' he rasped. 'Out of your goddamn mind. You know what g does to you. How many times' – he started shouting, *had* to shout so that he wouldn't hit her – 'did I tell you to *leave the fucking bridge?*'

Her forehead knotted into a frown. She was afraid of him, always afraid of him. But she was also stronger than he was. Even when she was terrified, she knew how to concentrate.

'Angus,' she pronounced distinctly, 'we don't have time for this. A lot's been happening. You've been asleep for –'

'I know.' His computer supplied the information. 'Six hours.' More than enough time for every enemy he'd ever had to line up and take shots at him. 'And before that I was unconscious. In stasis.'

His fury needed a better outlet. He hungered for violence. Anything that hurt Morn hurt him, and he wanted to *repay it*. Nevertheless he made an effort to match her. *We need you.* With the support of his zone implants, he imposed calm on the avid fire crackling inside him.

'*Punisher* is after us,' he went on. 'You said that already. And Ciro sabotaged the drives. Davies said that.' Beyond question the thrusters were dead. He couldn't hear the muted hull-roar of an active drive. 'Tell me something I don't know.'

Where are we? How did we get here?

I saw *Free Lunch* die. Where's *Soar*?

What do you want from me?

Morn caught her lip between her teeth as if she were restraining a retort. With a visible effort, she swallowed her impatience. After a moment she nodded slowly.

'I'm sorry. I forgot how much I need to tell you. And we're out of time –' She grimaced. 'But I can't very well ask you to help us if I don't explain what kind of help I want.

'I was asleep myself for most of it. But Davies, Mikka and Vector told me the story.'

Angus wrapped artificial calm around his black fires and braced himself to listen hard.

'We got away from that black hole,' she reported flatly. The strain of suppressing her urgency made the darkness in the caves of her eyes seethe. 'I guess that's obvious. We knew you were still alive because we could hear you breathing over your suit pickup. By then I was' – she referred to her arm with a glance – 'finished, so Vector brought you in. Mikka and Davies took us out to the edge of the swarm.

'But we were stuck. Both *Punisher* and *Calm Horizons* were there. How *Calm Horizons* found us I don't know.' *Punisher* had followed *Trumpet*'s homing signal, of course – at least until Nick had turned it off. 'The same way *Soar* did, I guess.

'*Punisher* and *Calm Horizons* blazed at each other the whole time. According to Davies, *Punisher* was trying to cover us. But *Calm Horizons* has that super-light proton cannon. And she knew where we were. We were hidden by asteroids, but she still fixed our position somehow. There was nothing Mikka and Davies could do. But just when *Calm Horizons* was about to smash us, *Soar* showed up and opened fire on her.'

Morn raised her hands to ward off questions. 'I can't explain that either.' Angus didn't try to interrupt, however. He assumed she was telling the truth. If she lied, he could learn the truth by looking at *Trumpet*'s log. And for right now he cared only about the facts. Explanations meant nothing to him unless they helped him predict what his enemies would do.

Tensely Morn continued, 'I guess *Calm Horizons* couldn't handle both *Punisher* and *Soar*. She used her proton cannon to destroy *Soar*.

'Then she needed time to recharge. That gave us a chance. Before she could fire again, Mikka burned out of the swarm and hit the gap, got us away from Massif-5. We're 1.4 light-years out in the middle of nowhere.'

Triggered by numbers, Angus' computer began multitasking seamlessly. Involuntary astrogation databases scrolled through his head, extrapolating possible positions. Nevertheless he missed nothing Morn said; nothing she appeared to feel.

She sighed. 'So far, so good. Unfortunately no one knew what Ciro was doing. He must have thought he still had to obey Sorus Chatelaine. He found his way into the drive spaces somehow. Whatever he did to the drives knocked them out right after we resumed tard. Since then we've been coasting. Living on the energy cells.

'Now *Punisher*'s found us. And she's overtaking us fast. Give her thirty minutes, and we'll be in point-blank range. If she wants to, she can catch us in two hours – if she's willing to put off deceleration that long and brake that hard.'

130

Through his data-link, damage-control schematics overlaid potential starfields. Diagnostic parameters and repair protocols marshaled themselves for use. But he also noticed the particular tightening of Morn's muscles; the squirming shadows behind her gaze when she mentioned the cruiser.

She was a cop. She should have been fucking delighted to see a UMCP warship. But she wasn't. She dreaded that vessel more than she feared Angus himself.

This was something he needed to understand.

'What does she want?' he asked as soon as Morn paused.

Her eyes flared bitterly. 'How should I know?'

A feral grin twisted his mouth. 'What does she *say* she wants? Is she talking?'

Morn sagged a little. Apparently he was pushing close to the sources of her urgency.

'Emergency UMCP hailing,' she answered dully. 'We've been ordered to slow down, let her come alongside. Maybe her scan hasn't figured out yet that we've lost thrust.'

Again Morn bit her lip. 'This is difficult for me,' she said unnecessarily. 'I'm torn –

'Angus,' she broke out suddenly, 'Min Donner is aboard that ship. *Min Donner.*' The UMCP Enforcement Division director. 'God knows what she's doing there.' For a moment Morn sounded baffled; racked by uncertainty. Then she tapped an anger of her own. Weeks of suffering and self-expenditure had whetted her to a knife's edge. 'Somebody saw this coming a hell of a long way off. She must have joined ship before *Punisher* left UMCPHQ for the Com-Mine belt.

'She's doing all the talking. Like she thinks we wouldn't listen to anyone else.'

A long way off, shit, Angus thought. That was the goddamn truth. The same man who'd switched his datacore so that he could rescue Morn and then sent him out with Milos Taverner primed to betray him had planned for this situation as well.

Morn hadn't stopped. She was saying, 'If there's anybody honest left in the UMCP, it's her. But I'm just not sure –'

She straightened her shoulders. '*Punisher* isn't threatening us. But she has us on targ. Her matter cannon are charged and tracking. She could open fire the minute we say something she doesn't want to hear.'

Angus recognized the danger; but he refused to be deflected from what he needed to know. 'What about *Calm Horizons*?' he pursued. 'Did the cops finish her?'

That question probed Morn even more deeply. She winced in spite of her anger.

'We don't know. When we went into tach, they were still shooting at each other. Davies says *Calm Horizons* was hurt. Maybe *Punisher* got her. Or maybe not. According to Mikka, *Punisher* looked hurt herself.

'We didn't see any other ships. I guess VI hadn't had time to muster a response.'

Angus chewed his concern for Morn while his computer spun scenarios, crunched possibilities: the likelihood that he could repair the drives quickly; the risks of a second cold ignition; other, more extreme options. Despite the complexity of the programs running in the back of his head, however, his concentration on Morn held.

Was she this worried just because *Calm Horizons* had committed an act of war? No, that wasn't it. He'd missed something. She was afraid for reasons he hadn't thought of yet.

Looking for answers, he changed directions, came at her from another side.

'All right,' he said as if he'd heard enough. 'None of this makes any sense, but I can live without explanations. What do you want me to do?'

His hands gripped the edge of the surgical table, holding him there against the pressure of her alarm, his computer's demands, and his own needs.

What do you think I fucking can do under these conditions?

She took a deep breath. Her gaze sank to his hands as if she were watching his knuckles whiten. Then she lifted her eyes sharply back to his. No matter what she feared, she remained strong enough to face him.

'I want you to keep us away from *Punisher*,' she announced distinctly, as if she thought he had that kind of power. 'She fought *Calm Horizons* for us. She gave Davies your priority-codes. But she also handed you over to Nick. I don't trust her. I trust Min Donner – I think I trust her – but I do not trust whoever's giving her orders.'

Slowly Morn tightened her own fists. 'Instead of surrendering this ship,' she went on, 'or blowing her up, I want you to take us back to Earth. So I can tell our story to somebody besides the UMCP. Preferably the Council.'

His eyes widened. Behind his pose of calm, he was shocked. Tell our story –? He was an illegal to the marrow of his bones. For a man like him, talking to anybody with authority was as good as suicide. Morn might survive: she was a cop. But he would absolutely end up dead.

Roughly he demanded, 'What in hell do you want to tell them?'

'Vector's formula,' she replied. She might have been reciting a list. 'How we got it. Why the Amnion are after Davies.'

All that was bad enough; but she wasn't done. Her voice hardened as she added, 'I want to make sure somebody hears me describe what Vector and Mikka have done for all of us. I want to tell the Council that the UMCP gave me to Nick.' She faced Angus as if she were defying him. 'And I want to tell them you were framed.'

He nearly lost his grip on the edge of the table. 'Christ, Morn!' he protested. 'You can't tell them *that*.' If she did, she would have to tell them he gave her a zone implant – and she took the control. 'We'll both be executed. They'll fry our fucking brains. The cops will kill every one of us eight times before they let you say something like that out loud.'

Was this what scared her? The prospect of explaining her own crimes in front of the Governing Council for Earth and Space – condemning herself so that she could try to save her shit-crazy species from their own fucking cops as well as from the Amnion?

She nodded grimly. If she was afraid, the darkness of her gaze concealed it. 'That's why we have to stay away from them.'

Angus couldn't contain the rush of his distress. He needed an outlet. He ordered his zone implants to reduce their

133

emissions, diminish his imposed calm, so that he could shout.

'God *damn* it! Don't you know what they *got* out of framing me? No, of course you don't. You were stuck out there on *Captain's* motherfucking *Fancy* while it happened.

'They paid Captain Sheepfucker and Milos to frame me. They wanted Com-Mine Security to look bad. So the Council would pass something called the fucking *Preempt Act*.' Angus himself had been one of the first victims of that legislation. Hashi Lebwohl had reqqed him from Com-Mine under the Preempt Act. 'It gives the UMCP authority over local damn Security *everywhere in human space*! Like they *needed* more muscle – like datacores and id tags and Emergency Powers and ships like *Starmaster* and all the money in the fucking galaxy aren't enough.

'The cops,' he finished savagely, 'are *not* going to let you undermine that much power.'

Morn lowered her head. Hiding her chagrin – or simply giving herself time to absorb this information. Angus didn't know which until she looked up at him again.

Her eyes burned like the black flame of his visceral fury.

'For some sick reason,' she said through her teeth, 'I'm not surprised. But that doesn't change anything. It's got to stop. One way or another.

'We don't have the leverage to stop it. Maybe the Council does.'

It's got to stop. Despite his dismay, Angus heard echoes of Warden Dios, with his strange priorities and his secrets. Had that goddamn one-eyed terrifying sonofabitch foreseen *this* too?

He had one protest left – one last objection which might make her change her mind. Shouting only angered her, so he reimposed his artificial calm. He wanted to sound like a man she couldn't argue with.

He wanted to sound like Nick Succorso –

'I told you you're crazy,' he asserted sardonically. 'Maybe you weren't listening. Didn't you hear me explain that I *can't* go back to Earth? I thought you understood. As soon as Milos betrayed me, I became too dangerous. Whatever is chasing me, whatever I'm carrying with me, is too dangerous. That's written into my programming. I can't go back there unless somebody uses my priority-codes, orders me to do it.

'But my codes are blocked. You can yell them at me until you rupture something. I might even want to obey you. But my computer can't hear you. It still won't let me go.'

That was the plain truth. Without the authority of those codes, he couldn't override his underlying instruction-sets.

Yet Morn wasn't daunted. Even now she was more than a match for him.

'Fine,' she snapped grimly. 'I'll put Mikka on helm. I'll give her orders. All you have to do is stay out of the way.'

She did more than shock him: she shook him to the core. His grasp on reality seemed to fail under the impact of her determination. Put Mikka on helm. Stay out of the way. That would work. His programming would allow it.

Suddenly every brutal, inhuman restriction which the cops had welded into him appeared negotiable –

Without warning some of the tactical scenarios weaving themselves across the background of his mind began to look plausible. His computer and his instincts spun ruses and gambits into webs which might conceivably be strong enough to hold.

He didn't move to act on them, however; didn't let go of the table to take up Morn's challenge. He needed to understand her. If she could find his way out of his electronic prison for him, she might be capable of almost anything.

He needed to know what drove her.

'All right,' he said more quietly. 'That might work. But something about all this still sounds like bullshit to me.

'I know you,' he insisted. 'You haven't told me the whole story. There's something nagging at you. Something that scares you worse than I do. I can see it in your eyes.

'I don't want to fucking guess what it is. Just say it, so I'll know what I'm dealing with.'

He expected her to flare out at him; accuse him. You want me to trust *you*? You raped me, hurt me, damn near broke me, and you want me to *trust* you? I would rather be dead.

But she didn't. Dark as pits, her eyes held his without flinching. Muscles tightened at the corners of her jaw, forcing her chin up.

'When I was in the Amnion sector on Billingate,' she said acidly, 'they took samples of my blood. Samples with Nick's immunity drug in them. I figure they ended up on *Calm Horizons*.

'But even if they didn't, she heard Vector's broadcast.

'I want to find out if she's still alive. That's more important than anything. If *Punisher* killed her, it almost doesn't matter what happens to us. The formula will get out somehow. We may lose everything else, but we've already gained that.

'But if she survived, she might get back to Amnion space. They'll learn how to counter the drug. Vector's formula will be useless before anyone in human space ever benefits from it.'

For reasons he could hardly recognize, Angus felt a rush of relief. Was that all she feared? Then it didn't threaten him. If she was telling the truth –

He believed her. She cared about shit like that. Maybe she hadn't when they were aboard *Bright Beauty*, when she was in his power. Maybe he hadn't let her. But she did now.

He should have known she wasn't scared for herself. Her damn convictions had become too strong for that.

Those same beliefs had freed him from his priority-codes. Now they were bending the bars of his welded lockup. If he gave her enough help, they might turn him loose altogether.

'Hell, Morn,' he replied almost cheerfully, 'you can't do anything about that. There's no point in suffering over it. You don't know where she'll go from Massif-5. If she's crazy enough to commit an act of war, she's crazy enough to try anything.

'For all you know, she's still looking for *us*.

'Don't waste your time on her. Worry about something that makes a difference. Worry about what *we're* going to do.'

Her eyes narrowed suspiciously. 'Talk's cheap, Angus. What *are* we going to do?'

She meant, What're *you* going to do?

He gave her a malicious, happy grin. 'That depends,' he told her cryptically, 'on just how much damage that little shit did to the drives.'

Despite the pain in his hip, he released the edge of the table with a thrust which carried him toward the door. Reality had changed. Morn changed it. Anything might become possible.

Somehow when he'd first met her he'd put his feet on a road which had led him away from everything he knew or understood about himself. Now each step carried him farther.

MIN

Despite the precise assistance of the gap scout's homing signal, *Punisher* would never have been able to follow *Trumpet* if the encroaching Amnion warship hadn't dropped fire in order to concentrate on her own acceleration out of the Massif-5 system.

As long as the Behemoth-class defensive continued to deliver torrents of matter cannon fire, as well as super-light proton blasts like thunderstrikes, *Punisher* was forced to maintain her staggering, frantic evasive maneuvers. Even when the cruiser had accumulated adequate velocity to hunt *Trumpet* across the gap, she couldn't risk tach: not when she needed to alter her actual heading by the second in order to keep herself alive. If she'd used her gap drive to escape the defensive's guns, she would have resumed tard so far off *Trumpet*'s trail that she would have required precious hours – or even days – to reacquire the gap scout's signal. And in that time *Trumpet* might flee beyond recovery.

She might silence her homing signal, as she had once before.

Fortunately the dilemma of *Trumpet*'s departure was as urgent for the Amnioni as it was for *Punisher*. The alien warship found herself virtually stationary in a hostile star system, with her shields and sinks damaged, the target of her incursion gone, and an entire flotilla of enemy vessels burning toward her from Valdor Industrial. She had to run.

Helpless in her g-seat at the periphery of the bridge, Min

Donner focused intensely on the actions of both ships, although she couldn't do anything about them. Because *Punisher* had heard Vector Shaheed's amazing broadcast, Min feared that the defensive would commit herself to destroying the cruiser.

She also wondered how long Sergei Patrice on helm could endure the strain of this ordeal. Glessen on targ did what he could to help; but the real burden of keeping *Punisher* alive now fell exclusively to Patrice.

Min suffered from nausea and vertigo herself, despite her years of experience and her eagerness for battle. And *Punisher* was a cruiser, a quick-strike vessel: she hadn't been designed for this kind of hours-long pummeling, these brutal maneuvers.

Gradually it became clear, however, that whoever was 'invested with decisiveness' aboard the Amnioni didn't mean to prolong the battle. The defensive had other priorities. She continued to blaze at the UMCP cruiser while she shrugged her vast bulk into motion. But then, near the effective limits of *Punisher*'s ragged return fire, she broke off her side of the engagement, presumably so that she could dedicate all the power of her drives to acceleration.

Her vector away from the asteroid swarm didn't point toward forbidden space, or any other obvious destination. Instead her immediate course aimed only at escaping Massif-5 as efficiently as possible.

'Cease fire, targ,' Captain Dolph Ubikwe ordered. Immobile as stone, he sat at the command station as if he were welded to his g-seat. 'We aren't hurting her anyway. And we might enjoy being able to hear ourselves think.'

'Aye, Captain.' Glessen keyed toggles, dropped his hands from his board. At once the hot, frying hull-sound of the matter cannon ceased. Without transition the squalling of half a dozen stress and damage alarms seemed to grow louder. Nevertheless after several hours of incessant fire Min felt that the bridge had become suddenly quiet.

'Stay sharp, Sergei,' Captain Ubikwe warned. 'At the rate she's pulling away, we're probably safe from her matter cannon. But that damn proton gun can still reach us.'

Patrice mumbled a reply Min couldn't hear. He looked too tired to speak any louder. The stark lighting of the bridge gleamed in the sheen of sweat on his face.

'Maybe not, Captain,' Porson offered from scan. 'The sensors say she doesn't have a targ fix on us anymore.'

At once the data and damage control officer, Bydell, put in numbly, 'If we can trust the readings.' Remorseless pressure had worn the young woman down; but she clung to her duties. 'We've taken a hell of a beating, Captain,' she explained. 'Damage control says we have potential failure on half the receptors. Maybe she's dropped targ. Or maybe we just can't tell the difference.'

Min swore to herself. She wasn't surprised: *Punisher's* wounds could only have worsened under the strain of helm's maneuvers. Still the ED director hated anything which weakened her command; threatened her people.

As *Trumpet* fled Massif-5, the gap scout had broadcast the formula for a mutagen immunity drug. This may or may not have been what Warden wanted – *Punisher* still hadn't succeeded at deciphering the transmission which had given Nick Succorso control over Angus, so the director's real intentions remained secret – but it transformed Min's sense of her own mission.

She *hated* anything which might come between her and *Trumpet*.

'Damn her to flinders,' Dolph growled. He was studying the Amnioni's escape trajectory. 'It *galls* me to let her run. She's a goddamn loose cannon.' He may have been talking to Min. 'Who the hell knows where she'll go off next? Could be anywhere.'

Min swallowed bile and frustration. She understood his implied complaint. He might conceivably have been able to finish the big defensive – if Min hadn't ordered him to go after *Trumpet* instead of pressing his advantage when the Amnioni's sinks began to fail.

'Can't be helped,' she answered harshly. 'We're in no condition to chase her.

140

'Program a courier drone for UMCPHQ,' she went on. *Punisher* had only two left – too few – but Min didn't balk at using one. 'Bring Director Dios up to date on what's happened. Launch it. Then get after *Trumpet*.

'If the Amnion think she's worth an act of war to kill, she's probably worth anything we can do to protect her.'

Almost as an afterthought, she added, 'She probably isn't safe. We still haven't accounted for *Free Lunch*.'

Dolph swiveled his g-seat, turned his dark face toward her. A combative hunger smoldered in his eyes, promising trouble. He'd already declared his loyalty to her, however. He'd obeyed when she'd told him to turn away from the Amnioni. Despite his desire to hunt and kill the defensive, he didn't argue now. Any trouble he caused her would take some other form.

'I'm sure you're right,' he rumbled sardonically. Still holding Min's gaze, he said to communications, 'You heard the director, Cray. Code a message for Director Dios. Give him a datacore playback for the past twelve hours. We don't have to explain it for him – he'll figure it out. Tell him we're letting the Amnioni go so we can chase *Trumpet* on Director Donner's orders.' He emphasized that detail with a lift of one eyebrow, nothing more. 'Program the best window on UMCPHQ you can get from scan and data. Launch as soon as you're ready.'

'Aye, Captain,' Cray answered loudly; too loudly. She may still have been trying to shout over the absent sizzle of the matter cannon. 'Give me five minutes.'

Captain Ubikwe met Min's stare for another moment as if he were warning her. Then he swung his station to confront the main display screens.

'Take ten,' he told Cray. 'We've got time. I want to make damn sure that bastard doesn't have us on targ before we steady our course for tach.

'You hear me, Porson? Bydell doesn't trust your equipment. Oversample as much as you have to. Get me a reading we can believe in.'

'I'm not worried, Captain.' Porson was older than the rest

141

of the bridge crew; probably more experienced. 'Scan is erratic, but what I see doesn't look like sensor failure. It's probably quantum discontinuities. There's been enough matter cannon fire in this sector to charbroil a planetoid.'

Captain Ubikwe nodded. 'Just be sure.'

Porson bent over his board as Dolph turned to helm.

'Hang on, Sergei,' he said in a reassuring growl. 'You'll get relief as soon as we cross the gap. I'll take helm myself, if I have to.'

Patrice tried to smile, but his grin was sickly with fatigue. 'I'll make it, Captain,' he murmured. 'We had tougher drills in the Academy.'

That was partly true. Min had designed some of them herself. But the worst of them had been hours shorter –

As soon as she returned to UMCPHQ, she intended to give Sergei Patrice the highest commendation she could think of.

Hell, everybody aboard deserved more than mere commendation. At the very least they ought to get a goddamn parade. *Punisher* had been damaged and shorthanded before Min joined ship; but Dolph's people had risen to every demand she'd made on them. Nevertheless Patrice stood out – as did Hargin Stoval, the command fourth, who'd been injured fighting a fire which had threatened to gut the cruiser. Patrice couldn't have run helm any better if he'd been driven by zone implants.

Abruptly Porson announced, 'I'm sure, Captain. That defensive doesn't have us on targ. And there's a shift in her emission profile. The energy signature of her proton gun is gone. The cannon isn't charged.'

Dolph looked quickly at data. 'Bydell?'

'Data agrees, Captain,' the young woman reported, almost panting. Her eagerness to be out of danger left her breathless. 'We've filtered enough of the inaccuracies. And a super-light proton signature doesn't look like anything else. It's hard to mistake.'

Good enough. 'Let's do it,' Min ordered Captain Ubikwe sharply. 'As soon as that drone is away, let's get out of here.'

Her palms burned with the intensity of her desire to catch *Trumpet*.

Morn Hyland was aboard, even though – so Min had been told – Angus had been explicitly programmed not to rescue her. She had a son with her, Davies Hyland, *force-grown on Enablement Station*. According to Angus, the Amnion thought they could learn how to *mutate Amnion indistinguishable from humans* by studying the boy.

Milos Taverner had turned traitor. Directly or indirectly, that betrayal had led the Amnion to commit an act of war.

For reasons which Min still couldn't imagine, Warden Dios had given Angus' priority-codes to Nick Succorso. And yet Vector Shaheed had broadcast the formula for an antimutagen – a drug which he could only have obtained from Nick.

The entire UMCP might collapse if the GCES or Holt Fasner learned the truth behind Shaheed's transmission. Warden would certainly be disgraced; ruined.

What was Min supposed to do about that? What did the director want her to do?

And what had become of *Free Lunch*? *Punisher* hadn't seen any sign of her. The ship which had unexpectedly saved *Trumpet* by attacking the alien defensive was some other vessel. The unnamed ship had pursued the gap scout all the way from forbidden space, only to die protecting her from the Amnioni.

Too many questions, all of them urgent.

Captain Ubikwe gave his people their orders; but Min wasn't listening. Every nerve in her body was on fire to catch up with *Trumpet*.

Porson found the gap scout minutes after *Punisher* resumed tard on the track of *Trumpet*'s homing signal.

'Got her, Captain!' he said excitedly. He seemed to be the only member of the bridge crew with enough energy for excitement. 'Right where her signal said she would be.'

A burst of relief spread across the bridge. Captain Ubikwe

143

sat up straighter in his g-seat. 'Thank God,' Bydell breathed. Roughly Glessen muttered, 'It's about time.' Patrice put his head into his arms on the helm board.

Min strained against her belts, studying the screens. The end of the vertiginous stress of evasive maneuvers left her light-headed and vaguely sick; her nerves jangling. She was viscerally hungry for g.

Then Porson frowned. Almost at once he added, 'Which doesn't make sense. She's had plenty of time to hit the gap again. Even if she needed to rest for a while, she could have been long gone. But she's still on the same heading she took from Massif-5.

'We're moving faster than she is,' he finished. 'At this rate, we can overtake her in a couple of hours.'

Dolph's eyes widened as he considered the implications. 'Is she waiting for us?' he asked Min. 'Does she *want* us to catch her? After all this?'

Min didn't answer directly. Instead she turned to scan.

'What condition is she in? Is she using thrust?' Min swallowed acid and apprehension. 'Does she have us on targ?'

Porson didn't hesitate. 'We can feel her scan, Director. She knows we're here. But she isn't using targ. In fact' – he cleared his throat, looked at Captain Ubikwe – 'now that you mention it, I can't say for sure that she is *Trumpet*.

'She's in the right place,' he explained quickly. 'She's the right size. But there's no emission signature. No particle trace. As far as I can tell, her drives are cold.'

No thrust? No course alterations? The gap scout had come 1.4 light-years across blank space from the Massif-5 system – and now she was *coasting*?

Before Min could ask another question, Cray put in from communications, 'That's *Trumpet*, all right, Captain. She's still broadcasting. The same message from Vector Shaheed. We picked it up as soon as we resumed tard.

'But it isn't aimed at us,' she added. 'It's a general broadcast. So far, she isn't trying to talk to us.'

'General broadcast?' Dolph growled under his breath. 'What the hell good is that going to do out here? There's nobody –' Then he caught himself. 'Porson, are we alone? Any other ships around? Any sign of *Free Lunch*?'

Porson consulted his board. 'Negative, Captain. Nobody here but the two of us.' He shrugged. 'Of course, I'm blind on one side.' *Punisher* had lost a sensor bank to combat and fire. 'But helm still has us under rotation. That gives us a steady sweep. If we had company, we would know it by now.'

The cruiser's slight centrifugal g seemed to tug at the lining of Min's stomach, hinting at vomit. Sergei Patrice had performed one more miracle by following *Trumpet* so accurately while *Punisher* turned.

Captain Ubikwe blew a sigh past his lips. For the first time in long hours, he permitted himself to show signs of strain. He shrank slightly, as if his bones were sagging inside his bulk, and his eyelids drooped.

'All right,' he said in a slow grumble. 'Keep her on targ, Glessen. Just in case she tries to surprise us. Matter cannon charged.'

'Aye, Captain,' Glessen said. 'I'm ready.'

'Good.' Dolph seemed to be thinking aloud. 'So we're alone. Just the two of us. So far, so good. And she isn't trying to get away from us. That makes a change. In fact, she looks like she's shut down her drives. Almost like she wants us to catch her. On the other hand, she hasn't tried hailing us.'

Min needed action. 'We'll hail her ourselves,' she put in impatiently. 'I want to talk to her.'

Dolph scowled at her. 'In a minute,' he retorted. 'I have other things to take care of first.'

Brusquely he keyed open an intercom channel and announced shipwide that the cruiser was about to resume internal spin.

His response bordered on insolence – no doubt a mere foretaste of the trouble to come – but Min was forced to approve, despite her frustrated urgency. *Punisher*'s people must have been desperate for normal g – and for a chance to move around. Most of them hadn't been to the san for, hell, close to twelve hours. But Dolph hadn't risked spin before the cruiser went into tach. If he had, core displacement might have sent her off course by several hundred thousand k.

While spin alerts sounded throughout the ship, Captain Ubikwe ordered his helm second to the bridge to relieve Patrice.

'Thank you, Captain,' Patrice murmured weakly. He may have been close to losing consciousness.

'No, Sergei,' Dolph countered. Despite his own fatigue, his voice was almost loud enough to echo. 'Speaking for the whole ship, I want to thank *you*. You aren't just good. You're certifiably brilliant. If we ever get out of this mess, Director Donner and I' – he didn't so much as glance at Min – 'are going to throw you the biggest, loudest, drunkest, soppiest goddamn party you've ever seen. And I will personally court-martial anyone who doesn't end up comatose.'

Glessen grinned wearily. Cray and Porson clapped for a moment. Despite – or perhaps because of – the deep strain of her fear, Bydell laughed aloud.

'Thank you, Captain,' Patrice said again. Although his eyes were glazed, and his head wobbled on his neck, he managed a thin smile.

Shit, Dolph! Min thought bitterly. Stop this. I need to talk to *Trumpet*.

At the same time, paradoxically, she admired *Punisher*'s commander. His care for his people was invaluable. She suspected that if he'd ordered them to follow him through the gates of hell, they would have obeyed instantly.

Alerts finished warning the ship. Within her hulls, *Punisher* slowly began to revolve around her core. For a moment Min felt a sideways pressure as her inner ears and her sense of inertia – sensitized and aggrieved by so much violent motion – reacted to the change. Then the familiarity of shipboard g reasserted itself. Her viscera seemed to shift, as if they were being pulled back where they belonged.

Around her men and women groaned and sighed as they reacted to a comfort so acute that it was almost painful.

'But that'll have to wait,' Captain Ubikwe continued to Patrice. 'In the meantime get off the bridge. Emmett will be here in a minute. We can live without helm until then.'

'Aye, Captain.' Fumbling, Patrice undid his belts; lurched to his feet. At first his legs refused to hold him: he had to support himself on his console to stay upright. After a moment, however, he staggered away from his station and left the bridge.

Min didn't move. She could have stood; eased the cramps in her limbs and the fire in her nerves by walking to the communications station and giving her orders directly to Cray. But as an act of self-discipline – or self-mortification – she remained in her belts; contained her discomfort and ire by force of will.

I have other things to take care of first.

'If you're quite ready, Captain,' she said sarcastically, 'I want to hail that ship.'

'I haven't forgotten.' Dolph shifted his station to face her. 'But I'm not sure I am ready.' He made no effort to conceal his weariness. By some trick of personality, however, he appeared to draw strength from it: fatigue fed his stores of insubordinate anger. 'Earlier we were up to our ass in alligators. Well, we let that damn warship get away, but I can still feel something chewing on my hams.'

Here it comes, Min thought. Right now, while everything depended on contact with *Trumpet*, Dolph Ubikwe was about to make good on his promise of trouble.

Damn him, anyway.

'We've had to swallow a hell of a lot since you joined ship,' he began. 'Nick Succorso, who is supposed to be working for DA, just happens to be the only human being in space with a mutagen immunity drug. By some amazing coincidence, DA reacts to Succorso's presence aboard *Trumpet* by giving *Free Lunch* a contract to destroy her. But of course Succorso has his own personal geneticist with him, just in case he feels like having his antimutagen analyzed. That probably explains why Hashi Lebwohl wants to get rid of him.

'Unfortunately' – Dolph's deep, rumbling tone sharpened trenchantly – 'Director Dios is on a completely different page of the UMCP Code of Conduct. While Hashi Lebwohl tries to kill *Trumpet*, Director Dios orders us to supply Succorso with a cyborg's priority-codes. In effect, handing *Trumpet* to Succorso.

'Are we confused yet?' Captain Ubikwe drawled sourly. 'Sure we are. But there's more.

'Much to nobody's surprise – certainly not yours – Succorso heads for a bootleg lab. And when we see *Trumpet* again, Vector Shaheed is *broadcasting the goddamn formula*. Suddenly Succorso has been transformed. Now he's a philanthropist. He's an illegal and a covert operative, but he doesn't want to profit from what he knows. He wants to *share* it.

'And he's *coasting*. He's been on the run all the way from forbidden space, and suddenly he's by God *waiting* for us.'

Min clenched her fists, held herself still. Dolph obviously wasn't done.

He took a deep breath to contain – or focus – his outrage, then went on.

'Naturally *Free Lunch* has disappeared. Director Lebwohl must have canceled her contract as soon as he suspected that Succorso was going to make his precious secret drug public. That makes sense, doesn't it? Especially when you consider that as soon as this story gets out Director Lebwohl is going to spend the rest of his conniving life in lockup for malfeasance. Betraying his office, the UMCP, and most of his entire species.

'Meanwhile the Amnion have just committed an act of war, even though Thermopyle thinks they already have Shaheed's formula. In any case, if they didn't before, they do now. They heard it from *Trumpet*.'

Min tightened her grip on herself. She didn't need Dolph to remind her that her decision to abandon the attack on the alien might have serious consequences for the whole human race. However, she believed that there was more at stake than Shaheed's formula. She risked everything on that conviction.

Captain Ubikwe made a visible effort to calm himself. Slowly he sank back into his g-seat. When he spoke again, his voice was unexpectedly mild.

'Tell me what's going on here, Director,' he finished. 'I don't think I can stand any more surprises.'

Min ached to snarl at him, *Surprises? You don't like surprises?* You self-righteous, overweight sonofabitch, what makes you think I *care* what you like and don't like? But she restrained the impulse. Despite the fire in her nerves, she understood him. For him what might happen to humankind if the defensive survived with Shaheed's formula was a secondary concern. He cared more about his relationship with his people; the moral authority which empowered him to hazard their lives.

'All right, Captain,' she answered like acid. 'I'll tell you what's going on. As soon as you tell me what Director Dios' message to *Trumpet* really said.'

The words had been plain enough. **Warden Dios to Isaac, Gabriel priority. Show this message to Nick Succorso.** But they'd been embedded in some kind of machine code which Min hadn't recognized and didn't know how to interpret.

Dolph winced. Baffled indignation twisted his features. 'God damn it, Min,' he rasped softly. 'You know my people haven't had time to crack that code. They've been at *battle stations*, for Christ's sake.'

Min met his glare without remorse. 'Too bad. That's where the answers are.'

He bared his teeth. Still softly, he asked over his shoulder, 'Cray?' Deciphering code was one of communications' responsibilities.

'Aye, Captain,' Cray responded as she hunted her readouts. 'As you say, we haven't had much time. But before we went to battle stations' – she found what she was looking for; pointed at her screen while she raised her head to face Dolph – 'we set up a sequence of parameters to test the code. Turned them over to data. They should have been running all this time. Maybe –'

She glanced uncertainly at Bydell.

Flustered, Bydell croaked, 'I'm checking, Captain.' She hit keys as fast as she could; too fast. Biting her lip, she canceled mistakes, reentered commands.

'I've got the results,' she announced abruptly.

'The computer ran those tests. It doesn't recognize the code. But it thinks it's some kind of specialized programming language. Something similar to the one we use to write the instruction-sets for datacores.'

By God. Min held her breath. By God and Warden Dios. Under other circumstances – in another life – she would have flourished her fists and shouted aloud. Now she kept herself still while her heart burned like thrust and her nerves were etched with incandescence. Yes! *Programming* language. Wrapped inextricably around the words which had betrayed Angus and Morn and humanity.

Intuitively she understood what Warden had done. With one coded stroke he had outplayed Hashi Lebwohl and Nick Succorso and Holt Fasner. She thought she could feel the future he'd been striving for begin to take shape all around her; become real.

'Do you call *that* an answer?' Dolph asked in a congested voice, as if he were choking on uncertainties.

'Yes, I do,' she asserted without hesitation. 'It doesn't explain what's happened to *Free Lunch*.' Hashi's proxy had probably died in the asteroid swarm from which *Trumpet* had emerged broadcasting Shaheed's message. 'But it tells us everything we need to know about what's going on aboard *Trumpet*.'

'Which is what?' Captain Ubikwe murmured helplessly.

Min scrubbed sweat like hot oil off her palms. 'Director Dios has reprogrammed Angus Thermopyle.' She was sure. 'The same transmission that turned him over to Succorso gave him new instruction-sets. New code.

'This is Warden Dios' game.'

'Then what was the *point*?' Dolph protested. His tone hinted at anguish. 'Why did he bother giving Succorso those priority-codes at all, if what he really meant to do was to change them?'

Min shook her head. 'That's none of our business.' She didn't need inspiration to guess that the reason involved Warden's secret, unexplained struggle with the Dragon. 'The point is that this is *Warden's* game. The Director of the United Mining Companies Police,' she pronounced fiercely, 'is pulling the strings here.'

This was why Warden had sent her aboard *Punisher*: to ensure that the game would be played his way.

'He hasn't told me what his game is. Are you going to say he's wrong?' She challenged Dolph squarely. 'Are you going to claim he isn't doing exactly what his oath of office requires?'

No, Dolph wasn't going to make that claim. She could see it on his face. His resistance slumped like heated paraffin on his heavy frame. Like her, he'd been under Warden's spell for years. He would have followed Warden through the gates of hell as willingly as any of *Punisher*'s people would have followed him.

He spread his hands to concede defeat. 'Then I guess we'd better find out what's happening aboard that gap scout.' A glint of humor came back into his eyes. 'Before Director Dios decides to chew off anything the alligators haven't already eaten.'

Finally.

Min made no pretense that she wasn't in a hurry. Slapping off her belts, she flung out of her g-seat and strode swiftly toward the communications station.

By the time she reached it, Cray had already opened a channel so that she could hail *Trumpet*.

MIN

The ED director hailed *Trumpet* for fifteen minutes,
using every authorization she could think of – except
Angus' priority-codes. Then she gave up in disgust.
The gap scout wasn't answering.

All the explanations she could think of were bitter.

Trumpet's people didn't trust her.

Or everyone aboard was dead.

If Morn and her companions had been killed by *Trumpet*'s
brutal acceleration away from the asteroid swarm, the small
ship's scan would remain active. Shaheed's broadcast would
continue automatically. But failsafes would have shut down
the drives after the vessel resumed tard.

'Keep at it,' Min told communications darkly. 'Hail her
yourself. Or just play back what I've been saying for the past
fifteen minutes. If they don't answer – if they don't let us
know they're alive – that's all we can do for now.'

'Aye, Director.' Cray set to work at once.

Min turned to the command station. 'Dolph, how soon
can we catch up with her?'

'And match velocities?' he asked. 'I assume you want to
board her?'

Min nodded. Damn right she wanted to board the gap
scout.

Captain Ubikwe referred the question to the helm officer
who'd relieved Sergei Patrice. 'Emmett?'

Emmett was a stolid man with a round face and unnaturally

152

pale skin. His unreactive manner conveyed the impression that he was no match for Patrice. Nevertheless he knew his job: he already had the figures Dolph needed on one of his readouts.

'That depends on how hard you want to brake, Captain. We're overhauling her at a good clip. At this rate, we'll be alongside in an hour and a half. But if we're going to match velocities for boarding, we have to decelerate first.'

'And if we brake too hard,' Dolph muttered, 'we'll probably fall apart.'

'We can take it, Captain.' Apparently Emmett had a literal mind. 'I can put us right beside her in two hours if we start a two-g deceleration in' – he glanced down at his board – 'make it seventy-eight minutes.'

Double the effective mass of everyone aboard for forty-two minutes. They could bear it. They'd all endured much worse. Recently.

Dolph cocked an eyebrow at Min. 'Good enough?'

She acquiesced unhappily. 'But *watch* her. If she shows any sign of life, we'll have to be ready.'

'I'm on it, Captain,' Porson said unnecessarily.

'Go ahead, Emmett,' Captain Ubikwe instructed.

After a moment's consideration he toggled his intercom to inform *Punisher*'s people that they had seventy-eight minutes in which to eat something, relieve themselves, and complete their duty rotation before the ship began braking.

Because she needed to manage her tension, Min paced the bridge, working the cramps and helplessness out of her muscles, damping the fire in her hands; trying to center herself so that she wouldn't scream if she found Morn and Angus and Vector dead.

Despite the self-discipline she'd learned from years of action and experience, she felt the unexpected crackle of the bridge speakers like a jolt of stun.

'*Punisher*,' a woman's voice said distantly, 'this is *Trumpet*. We hear you. Can you hear us?'

Trumpet was too close to sound so far away. The voice in

the speakers gave the impression that the woman was reluctant to stand near her pickup. Reluctant to take this risk.

Instinctively Cray moved to reply; but Captain Ubikwe stopped her with a sharp gesture. 'Let Director Donner do it,' he told her. His deep voice had a warning tinge.

Min threw a quick look at the nearest chronometer. *Punisher* was thirty-one minutes from deceleration.

A few swift strides carried her to the communications station. Poised over the console, she answered as soon as Cray keyed the pickup.

'*Trumpet*, this is Enforcement Division Director Min Donner aboard UMCP cruiser *Punisher*, Captain Dolph Ubikwe commanding. We hear you.' Full of complex relief, she added, 'I'm glad you're alive.' Then she went on more carefully, 'Who am I talking to?'

There was a delay. Not transmission lag: hesitation. After a moment the voice in the speakers said, 'Director Donner, I'm Ensign Morn Hyland.'

Morn was alive. After all this time: against incredible odds. Despite the fact that Nick Succorso had been given the power to use Angus against her. Min closed one fist on the butt of her handgun to steady herself. Suddenly she thought that *any*thing was possible. The UMCP and humankind might survive. Warden might actually *win* –

She was in focus now, primed with flame. Her excitement and alarm seethed beneath the surface; hidden. Nothing except authority showed in her tone.

'Who else is with you, Ensign Hyland? Where's Captain Succorso? I thought he was in command.'

Again Morn paused. Afraid to answer? Wondering where Min's loyalties lay? That was likely: she had reason to be suspicious. Plenty of reason.

But when she replied, her voice had more force. She must have moved closer to the pickup.

'Meaning no disrespect, Director Donner,' she said distinctly, 'but I have some questions of my own.'

'No *disrespect*?' Dolph muttered under his breath. 'Who the hell does she think she's talking to?'

Min ignored him. Morn was saying, 'When we left Massif-5, you were engaged with an Amnion warship. *Calm Horizons.* What happened to her?'

'*Calm Horizons,*' Dolph repeated. 'We've got id. Finally.

'File that, Bydell,' he ordered. 'Add it to our records on that defensive. UMCPHQ might find a name useful.'

'Aye, Captain,' Bydell returned softly.

At the same time Min countered, 'Ensign Hyland, I'm prepared to make some allowances here.' She concentrated exclusively on her pickup and Morn's voice. 'After what you've been through, you probably deserve them. But I want answers, too. Where is Captain Succorso?'

She could almost hear Morn leave the pickup: the sense of withdrawal from the speakers was palpable. Morn didn't close the channel, but she moved out of range. Consulting with someone? Trying to decide how much to say?

Did she think she could bargain with the ED director?

What did she have to bargain with?

When it came, her response was stark and unrevealing.

'Nick Succorso is dead.' For no apparent reason, she added shortly, 'So is Sib Mackern.'

Dead? That explained a lot – and raised more questions. Succorso held the priority-codes for a UMCP cyborg. Who could possibly have gotten past Angus to kill him?

But Min didn't pause to consider the implications.

'I'll ask how he died later.' I'll ask you why you're talking for *Trumpet.* Why Angus is willing to let anyone else speak for his ship. 'First I'll answer your question.

'*Calm Horizons* survived. We had to choose between trying to kill her and coming after you. She was on her way out of the system as we left. Her course didn't reveal where she was headed.'

In the background of the transmission, a harsh male voice growled, 'Shit.'

Morn's reaction was silence.

'Well,' Dolph put in casually, 'now we know she isn't the only survivor. She may have killed Succorso and this Sib Mackern, but she didn't get everybody.

155

'You recognize the voice, Director? Was that Thermopyle?'

Maybe. Maybe not. Min couldn't tell.

She waited while her heart beat eight or ten times. Then she prompted, 'Ensign Hyland?'

Abruptly Morn's voice came back across the narrowing gap between the ships.

'Don't you care that *Calm Horizons* must have heard Vector's broadcast? Don't you care that she's probably burning for forbidden space?'

'Of course I care.' Min's tone dripped acid. 'I'm Min Donner,' God damn it. 'But *Calm Horizons* isn't my only problem.'

'You mean us.' Morn sounded like she was talking to herself. 'We're too dangerous. I knew we were in trouble. But it's worse than I thought.'

Dangerous? The ED director knew what Morn meant. But she didn't comment on that. Instead she offered, 'And it could get even worse. One of my other problems is a mercenary called *Free Lunch*. She has a contract to kill you. Have you seen her?'

Another pause: more hesitation. Min restrained an urge to shout while she waited.

Captain Ubikwe shifted forward in his g-seat as if he hoped that might urge Morn to answer. Cray frowned relentlessly past Min's shoulder. Glessen drummed his fingers on the edges of his board like a man who wanted to start shooting.

At last Morn replied, '*Free Lunch* is dead, too. We met her in the swarm. Angus killed her with a singularity grenade.'

'Captain,' Porson whispered excitedly, 'that must have been the kinetic reflection anomaly we picked up. Director Donner was right.'

'Don't remind me,' Dolph grumbled.

An edge of anger crept into Min's voice. 'Damn it, Morn, you're talking, but you aren't telling me what I need to know.' She wanted to ask, demand, With a *singularity grenade*? How in hell did he manage *that*? But she cautioned herself, No, keep it simple. Don't get distracted.

Deliberately she pushed her ire down.

'Never mind, Ensign. *Free Lunch* is something else I'll ask you about later.

'What's your condition? Have you lost anyone besides Captain Succorso and Sib Mackern?'

Why are you coasting? Who's really in command there?

Morn responded with another maddening silence.

Min allowed herself to rap the communications console with the knuckles of one fist – a small outlet for her tension.

'For a mere ensign,' Dolph observed dryly, 'that woman is certainly mistrustful of her superior officers.'

She glared at him. 'We gave Succorso those priority-codes,' she retorted. Hell, we sold her to him in the first place. So he would go along with one of Hashi's misbegotten plots. 'How much do you expect her to trust us?'

'That's a good question.' Captain Ubikwe adjusted his bulk against the arm of his g-seat. 'You called this "Warden Dios" ' game. Do you think she knows whose side she's on? Do you think she or that cyborg or any one of them has a clue what Director Dios wants them to do?'

Min didn't reply. She held herself ready for Morn's response.

The speakers emitted a whisper of static.

'Director Donner,' Morn's voice said, still muffled by her personal distance, 'what are your intentions? You have us on targ. Are you planning to open fire?'

The ED director swallowed a hot protest. 'That depends,' she snapped back, 'on whether you try to get away again.'

Who in hell do you think I *am*?

Now Morn spoke without delay. She'd already made this decision. 'We can't,' she returned flatly. 'Our drives are dead.'

Still she contrived to supply answers without telling Min what she needed to know.

Captain Ubikwe looked quickly at scan.

Porson shrugged. 'It's probably true, Captain. I can't see anything that says otherwise. Her guns aren't charged, that's for sure.'

'What if she's faking?' Dolph suggested. 'What if she shut down her drives, and now she risks cold ignition?'

This time Min made Morn wait. For a moment she wanted to hear what was being said around her.

The scan officer's face showed a perplexed frown. 'I can't imagine what good that would do her, Captain. Thrust will be unstable while her tubes are cold. She'll hardly be able to maneuver until the tubes heat. That'll give us plenty of warning. We can probably react to whatever she does.'

'We already have her at point-blank range, Captain,' Glessen put in without being asked. 'I don't think I could miss if I wanted to.'

'Don't jump to conclusions, targ,' Dolph warned sharply. 'She may be telling the truth. Stranger things have happened.

'What about her gap drive, Bydell?' he pursued. 'Can she get away from us if she just uses thrust to power her into tach?'

Bydell's eyes widened at the idea. She seemed to find it frightening. 'Not until her thrust stabilizes, Captain,' she said hurriedly. 'Otherwise it'll be like hitting the gap at random. If she can't generate reliable hysteresis, she can't be sure she'll ever resume tard.'

'And as I say, Captain,' Porson repeated, 'we'll get plenty of warning.'

Min had heard enough. She turned her attention back to the communications pickup.

'Listen to me, Ensign Hyland. We're talking to each other, but we aren't getting anywhere. We need to do better.

'You've been through quite an ordeal. And you probably think you have good reason not to trust me. I understand that. So let's not make this any harder than it has to be. Tell me what you want us to do.'

Tell me how I can keep you from fighting me.

Apparently Morn was done with hesitation – at least for the moment. Her answer returned from the speakers almost at once. 'Drop targ,' she said clearly. 'Drain your matter cannon. Stop treating us like the enemy.'

Min raised her head as if she'd been stung; faced Captain Ubikwe across the bridge.

She expected umbrage: instead he rolled his eyes humorously. 'Hell, Min,' he drawled, 'if she thinks this is how we treat the enemy, she should see us when we're in dock.'

The fire in Min's palms was as acute as a decompression klaxon, warning her of trouble. Morn's attitude didn't make sense to her. *Trumpet*'s drives were dead: the gap scout was helpless; doomed. Under the circumstances, what sane ship would insist on trying to bargain with her rescuers? What in *hell* did Morn think she had to bargain with?

Nevertheless Min put on authority as if it were confidence. 'Just do it, Captain,' she ordered.

He gave an exaggerated sigh; but he didn't argue. 'You heard the Director, Glessen. Cancel targ. Drain the guns. At least we don't have to worry about *Free Lunch* anymore.'

'Aye, Captain,' Glessen muttered disapprovingly.

'We're relying on you, Porson,' Dolph went on. 'If that damn ship lets out so much as one flicker of drive emission, I want to hear about it.'

'I'm on it, Captain,' the scan officer promised.

Min bent to the pickup again. 'We're complying now, Ensign Hyland,' she said acerbically. 'Watch scan. You'll see I'm telling the truth.'

For half a minute the bridge speakers brought in nothing from the void except random particle noise. The silence seemed hollow, devoid of life; vaguely ominous. Then Morn's voice returned.

'Thank you, Director Donner.' She sounded faint with relief or dread. 'That helps.'

Then she sighed audibly. 'There's just one more thing.'

'No, Ensign Hyland,' Min snapped. She meant to be cautious, but she'd come to the end of her patience. 'Now it's my turn.' Morn's palpable suspicion grated on her nerves – perhaps because she knew she deserved it. 'I'm trusting you. It's time for you to trust me. Then we'll consider whatever it is you want next.'

Morn sighed again. 'I'm listening.'

Gritting her teeth, Min ordered, 'Stop broadcasting Vector Shaheed's formula.'

Morn made a hissing sound – indignation or dismay. Again

Min thought she could hear a male voice swearing in the background.

Dolph cocked an eyebrow at Min, pursed his mouth. Apparently he hadn't expected this. He was caught up in the needs of his ship; hadn't thought beyond the immediate situation.

When Morn spoke again, her voice was closer: as acute as a knife. It flayed bitterly from the speakers.

'Why am I not surprised? You've been suppressing this drug ever since it was developed. You took it away from Intertech, and now you're keeping it to yourself. You would rather use it for a few covert operations once in a while than make it public and take the risk it might actually scare the Amnion into a retreat. Because' – Min tried to interrupt, but Morn overrode her – 'if the Amnion backed off, the UMCP wouldn't be so crucial. And then people might start asking questions about you.'

'Stop that, Ensign Hyland,' Min commanded harshly. 'You're talking about Data Acquisition, not Enforcement Division. *I* don't play those games.'

She probably wouldn't be playing Warden's game right now if he'd ever told her what it was.

'I swear to you on my honor as the Enforcement Division director that I am not going to suppress Shaheed's transmission. I have no intention of suppressing it.

'Even if Director Dios orders me directly to bury it,' she added for emphasis, 'I can't do it. VI has already heard it. It can't be suppressed.'

She was confident Warden wouldn't give that order. But it didn't matter whether she was right or wrong. He wasn't here.

'Then why – ?' Morn began, then faltered to silence.

'Because,' Min rasped, 'it's too goddamn loud! You can't control who's going to hear it. You say *Free Lunch* is dead. Fine – I hope you're right. But what if some illegal picks it up and decides to come after a prize like that? What if *Calm Horizons* swings around this way and uses it to locate you?

'We've got damage over here, Ensign Hyland. We can't

160

protect you. We're in no condition for another battle.

'Turn it off,' she finished with all her authority. 'Turn it off now.'

Don't force me to board you at gunpoint. Don't make me take you prisoner. You deserve better.

Dolph nodded to Min, showing her that he understood. Glancing around the bridge, he remarked generally, 'Makes sense to me,' just in case any of his people agreed with Morn.

Min whitened her knuckles on the butt of her handgun and waited for a response.

When Morn answered, her voice sounded more distant than ever: she might have been whispering. For no apparent reason, she asked, 'Do you remember my parents, Director Donner?'

Min's eyes widened. What? Your *parents?*

She recalled them vividly. Not because she had Hashi's eidetic memory: she didn't remember faces or names well. To some extent her ferocious loyalty to her own people was an attempt to compensate for a lack in herself. But years of service overcame that inadequacy. And men and women whose names or faces she sometimes forgot while they worked for her were unalterably etched in her mind by death.

Morn was testing her in some way she didn't understand.

She wasn't a woman who hesitated under pressure, however. 'Your father was Captain Davies Hyland,' she replied promptly, 'commander, UMCP destroyer *Starmaster*. He died with his ship while he was hunting Angus Thermopyle in the Com-Mine belt. You probably consider yourself responsible. And your mother was Bryony Hyland, targ second, UMCP cruiser *Intransigent*. She died saving her ship during an engagement with an illegal armed with super-light proton cannon.

'I delivered a whole satchel full of commendations and decorations for her in person when you were just a kid.' Min scowled at the memory. She hated all the duties that fell to her when her people died. For that reason she never shirked them. 'The way I remember it, you refused to look at them.

161

You were too angry to let someone like me comfort you.'

Is that it? Is that really what you want to know?

Maybe it was. Out of the void Morn breathed softly, 'What I remember is that they trusted you.'

Cray adjusted the receiver in her ear. She didn't look at Min: her eyes were busy tracking signals on her board. Abruptly she jerked up her head. 'They did it, Captain! They've stopped broadcasting.'

Min began a low sigh of relief – and realized suddenly that she wasn't relieved at all. If anything, her nerves burned hotter. An intuitive alarm she couldn't name squalled in her head. There was danger here –

What danger? *Trumpet*'s drives were dead: she couldn't charge her guns; couldn't avoid *Punisher*. And this whole sector of space was empty of other ships.

Morn's distrust ran deep. Why had she acquiesced?

Angus killed her with a singularity grenade.

If he could do that, he could do damn near anything.

No! Min told herself grimly. It didn't make sense. Any singularity which could threaten *Punisher* would swallow *Trumpet* as well. The gap scout's people had fought and suffered all this way from Billingate for no apparent purpose except to make DA's antimutagen public. They wouldn't commit suicide now – not for the small satisfaction of damaging Enforcement Division.

She looked over at Dolph. His expression was speculative, searching; but he didn't offer any comment.

No one else said anything. The bridge crew knew even less about what was going on than she did.

'We've complied, Director Donner,' the speakers announced unnecessarily. 'Now it's my turn.'

Did Morn sound scared? Or was that just more suspicion?

'What else do you want?' Min asked the pickup. How much more do you think you can get away with?

Morn had her answer prepared.

'There are six of us.' Her voice seemed to resonate softly across the gap between the ships, hinting at threats. 'Mikka and Ciro Vasaczk. Vector Shaheed. Davies Hyland. Angus

Thermopyle.' If she was scared, she didn't falter or flinch. 'I want you to take us aboard.'

Min's whole body tightened in surprise.

Bydell looked almost cross-eyed with perplexity. Glessen cracked his knuckles over his board as if he were limbering his fingers to recharge his guns. Cray gazed vaguely at Min with her mouth hanging open.

'Well, shit.' Captain Ubikwe threw up his hands, then slapped them on the sides of his console. 'Is *that* all?'

'What in hell's the *matter* with her? If we aren't going to shoot her, we for God's sake sure didn't come all this way just so we can watch her *coast*.' He paused, then wondered, 'Or is she afraid we'll only take some of them? Leave the rest to die? Does she think we've sunk that low?'

Min punched her pickup silent. 'I know what you mean,' she told Dolph sourly. 'The more she says, the less sense she makes.'

Who was Morn talking *for*? Who was really in command over there?

Did she have Angus' codes? Was that possible?

'But we still have the upper hand,' Min went on, even though her nerves flamed with warnings. 'We have guns and thrust. And Angus is alive. We know his priority-codes.' If worst came to worst, she could order him into stasis. 'We want those people.' Warden Dios wanted them. 'If we don't bring them aboard when we get the chance, they may do something really crazy.'

Like commit suicide.

Dolph spread his palms as if he were disavowing responsibility. 'You're the ED director, Min. I'm just here to follow orders. And right now,' he admitted, 'I don't want your job.

'You make the decisions.' He chuckled quietly. 'I'll be content complaining about you behind your back.'

Min had no time for his sense of humor. With a movement like a blow she toggled her pickup.

'Sorry to keep you waiting, Ensign Hyland.' Despite her apprehension, she kept her tone neutral. 'Of course you can come aboard. That's what we're here for.

'Just give us time to come alongside and match velocities. We'll use limpets to pull you to our airlock,' so we don't need to try any tricky maneuvers in our condition.

'We'll be ready,' Morn replied promptly; distantly. Apparently she'd received the answer she expected. '*Trumpet* out.'

The speakers gave a pop of static as the gap scout ended her transmission.

'I'll bet you will,' Min muttered as Cray closed the communications channel. 'I'll just bet you will.'

Morn Hyland was only an ensign, nothing more. But she'd been to the far side of hell – and come back. Now she was trying to play a game of her own: against Min and *Punisher*; against the Amnion; even against Warden Dios.

In the secret core of her heart the ED director didn't know whether to feel proud or appalled.

Punisher eased carefully toward *Trumpet* and nudged braking thrust to pace the gap scout. Emmett had brought the cruiser to within two hundred meters of her target.

He could have done better: Sergei Patrice probably could have done much better. But two hundred meters was close enough for limpets. With a damaged ship and an exhausted crew, Captain Ubikwe didn't want to push his luck by moving nearer. If *Punisher*'s core displacement worsened suddenly – if misalignment froze the bearings, halting internal spin with a screech of tortured metal and any number of injuries – she would be thrown out of control, at least temporarily. A collision was possible.

Dolph kept a safe distance; let limpets close the gap for him.

Magnets on flexsteel cables coiled out from *Punisher*'s sides toward the little ship. Guided by sensors from the cruiser's auxiliary bridge, the limpets were aimed along *Trumpet*'s flank until they reached suitable positions bracketing one of her airlocks. Then the magnets were charged, locking the limpets to *Trumpet*'s hull. After that it was a relatively simple matter to reel the gap scout in like a hooked fish.

The final adjustments took time. *Trumpet*'s airlock and *Punisher*'s had to meet and mate securely, so that they could seal against each other. But eventually the auxiliary bridge reported that *Trumpet* was in place: status indicators green; the airlock pressurized.

Captain Ubikwe blew a sigh through his lips, then turned to his intercom.

'I know you're tired, bosun,' he said into the pickup, 'but I think this might be a good occasion for a little ceremony. Muster a guard, meet our guests at the airlock. Let me know when they're aboard.' He paused for a heartbeat, then added, 'Go armed, bosun. But don't threaten anybody. I'm not expecting trouble. I just want our guests to know we're prepared to stand up for ourselves.'

'Aye, Captain.' The young man tried to stifle his weariness, but the strain in his voice was clear.

Dolph silenced the intercom.

'You don't suppose, do you,' he drawled to Min, 'that they're going to keep us waiting? After they made such an issue out of getting permission to join ship?'

Min paced the bridge to contain her impatience while other people worked. At Dolph's question she shook her head. If she'd been able to guess any of the moves Morn – or Warden – would make, she would have been better prepared for them.

'Apparently not,' Captain Ubikwe answered himself a few minutes later. His status readouts told him what was happening. 'They're in their airlock already. They're keying our side now. We're cycling our lock for them.'

Abruptly, as if he felt a sudden need for reassurance, he asked scan, 'We're still alone, aren't we?'

'We've lost our scan sweep, Captain,' Porson answered. *Punisher* had been forced to stop her rotation so that she could grapple with *Trumpet*. 'I can't be sure. But I haven't seen any hint of another ship.'

Dolph's mouth twisted. 'Charge the guns anyway, Glessen,' he ordered. 'Maybe we can believe *Free Lunch* is dead. But I don't trust *Calm Horizons* to leave us alone.'

At once Glessen's hands jumped to the task. 'Aye, Captain.'

'As soon as our lock seals, Emmett,' the captain went on, 'resume rotation. We need that scan sweep.'

'Aye, Captain,' Emmett responded stolidly.

'Cray,' Dolph finished, 'tell the auxiliary bridge to hang onto *Trumpet*. We'll piggyback her home with us.'

Cray reached for her intercom. 'Right away, Captain.'

He looked around the bridge as if to assure himself that he hadn't forgotten anything. Then he settled his back more comfortably against his g-seat while he waited.

Min feared that she was losing her self-command. At intervals she caught herself grinding her teeth as she paced. *Trumpet*'s people were playing some kind of game: she was sure of it. And she wanted to know what the hell it was.

Fortunately she didn't have to wait long. After another minute or two, the intercom snapped to life.

'Captain,' the bosun reported softly, 'they're here.'

Dolph toggled his pickup quickly. 'All six of them, bosun?' he asked in a deep growl.

'Aye, Captain. But, Captain –' The bosun faltered, then said more loudly, 'One of them – it's Captain Thermopyle – he's pretty angry. He says we're still treating them like the enemy. Because we're armed.'

The captain's eyebrows arched on his forehead. He flicked a glance at Min. 'What does he want you to do about it, bosun?'

'He wants me to disperse the guard, Captain. He says they'll find their own way to the bridge.'

For reasons she couldn't name, Min's sense of danger worsened. With his welded resources and his native hate, Angus was a kind of singularity grenade.

Dolph's rumble took on an unmistakable edge. 'Is Captain Thermopyle threatening you, bosun? Has he mentioned what he intends to do if you don't comply?'

'No, sir,' the bosun replied. 'He hasn't gone that far.'

Captain Ubikwe tapped his fingers on the arms of his g-seat. Glancing at Min again, he asked, 'Now what, Director?'

She didn't hesitate. 'I want them in front of me, Captain. I want to see their faces when they talk.'

Dolph nodded slowly. To the intercom he said, 'Remind them that an honor guard is a sign of respect, bosun. Assure Captain Thermopyle I'll dismiss the guard as soon as he and his companions are safely here. Then bring them to the bridge.

'When he gets here, he and I can discuss the protocol of joining a superior officer's ship in person.'

'Aye, sir.'

The intercom clicked silent.

Questions she didn't have permission to ask filled Bydell's face. Glessen seemed unnaturally busy at his board, giving *Punisher*'s weapons more attention than they needed. Porson whistled thinly through his teeth while he hunted the dark with his instruments. Repeatedly Cray lifted her shoulders and dropped them as if she'd developed a twitch.

They'd all been under too much pressure for too long. Only Emmett sat at his station as if he had nothing to worry about.

Dolph aimed a frown in Min's direction. '*Now* what do you suppose is going on?'

She shrugged. 'Sounds like a gesture. A warning. He doesn't intend to let us push him around. He's still a cyborg. He can defend himself. Or he wants us to think he can.'

She had no confidence in that explanation. She just didn't know what else to think.

Grimly she resumed pacing the bridge.

By chance she happened to be on the far side of the curved space when the bosun and his honor guard escorted *Trumpet*'s people onto the bridge. From her perspective they appeared to be walking on the ceiling; standing upside down.

She was familiar – more than familiar – with the strange orientations caused by the g of internal spin. Nevertheless she strode rapidly along the curve so that she would be able to meet the new arrivals face to face; study every glare and falter in their eyes.

The bridge crew watched in silence as Morn Hyland and her companions approached the command station.

'Captain,' the bosun announced formally, 'may I present the captain and crew of UMCP gap scout *Trumpet*?' His voice shook despite the determination on his features.

With an impersonal scowl, Captain Ubikwe studied *Trumpet*'s people. 'Thank you, bosun,' he rasped. 'You can dismiss your guard now. But I'll ask you to stick around. There may be something you can do for our guests.'

The bosun and the honor guard saluted somewhat raggedly. As soon as Dolph returned an acknowledgment, the bosun sent the others off the bridge. Apparently unsure of what to do with himself, he remained a step behind *Trumpet*'s people.

Min reached the group; stopped. Gripping the butt of her handgun, she cocked her other fist on her hip and confronted six pairs of eyes, six strained, tired faces, as if she were daring them to challenge her.

Between one heartbeat and the next she scrutinized them all, first together, then individually.

Two women. Four men – or two men and two boys. She had no difficulty recognizing some of them. The names of the others became obvious by default.

Morn had positioned herself a little ahead of the others; leading them; taking responsibility for them.

One of the boys, an ash-pallid kid with grieving eyes and an unsteady mouth, looked like he might throw up if anyone offered to harm him; like he'd already suffered enough harm to sicken his soul. But the rest of the group –

In their various ways, most of his companions were vivid with tension. Their postures shouted of dangers Min didn't know how to evaluate.

She remembered Morn well, not just as a little girl, but as a cadet at the Academy. Primarily because of who her parents had been, Min had paid unusual attention to her. But the woman who stood here now was dramatically changed.

As a cadet, Morn had been so beautiful that Min had considered her almost featureless: perfect and bland; with only a hint of chagrin and – perhaps – stubbornness in her gaze to give her face character. Now her airbrushed loveliness was gone. She'd lost weight, a lot of it, as if she'd been burning herself for fuel. And her experiences had chiseled at her features, chipping the blandness off her cheeks and forehead; cutting lines like gutters for pain between her brows, at the corners of her eyes, along her nose and mouth. Her eyes were dark with doubts and hesitations which the sharp demarcation of her mouth belied.

A cast covered her right arm: a sling held it to her chest.

Facing the ED director, her free hand seemed to move involuntarily toward a salute; but she aborted the gesture.

Two men guarded her shoulders, Angus Thermopyle and a much younger man who nevertheless resembled him astonishingly.

Angus stood with his arms relaxed and his palms forward, as if to show that he had no intention of challenging anyone. He seemed essentially unchanged since Min had last seen him. Perhaps the yellow malice in his eyes had deepened: perhaps his feral grin held more threats. In other ways he looked like the same strong, grubby, bloated man Hashi had reqqed and welded. A slight hitch in his stride suggested that he'd hurt a hip.

The younger man must have been Davies Hyland: the damaged kid bore no resemblance to Morn. But Min had automatically expected Davies to look like Nick. She hadn't guessed that Angus was his father. Only the hue of his eyes – exactly Morn's color – indicated that he hadn't been cloned from Angus.

Yet that one detail was significant; crucial. Because of it, his expression reflected Morn's rather than Angus'. The mind behind his father's features hadn't been cramped and clotted with his father's hate.

The other woman – Mikka Vasaczk – glowered harshly past Morn and Angus without meeting Min's scrutiny. A bandage partially obscured her right eye: she'd injured her temple somehow. For that and other reasons, she reminded Min oddly of Warden Dios. She carried herself with an air of competence, and her compact frame and assertive hips gave the impression that she was stronger than she looked.

Nevertheless she seemed almost eager to remain behind Morn and Angus, as if she didn't want to call attention to herself. Or perhaps it was her brother, Ciro, she wished to conceal. She kept one hand on his shoulder as if he couldn't move unless she pushed him; guided him.

Knowing nothing about her, Min guessed that she habitually used anger to control her fear.

Of the six, only Vector Shaheed looked relaxed. His blue eyes held a calm simplicity that contrasted markedly with the tension of his companions. His movements were obviously stiff, presumably painful: Min guessed that his joints hurt him in some way. Yet the pain didn't appear to bother him. His work at Intertech had at last borne fruit. Now he may have been at peace with himself.

'Ensign Hyland,' Dolph put in suddenly, 'you ought to be ashamed of yourself.' His tone throbbed with deliberate anger. 'Apparently you're proud of your parents. Didn't they teach you how to treat a superior officer? That's Enforcement Division *Director* Min Donner you haven't bothered to salute.'

Min didn't glance away from Morn. Morn kept her eyes on Min. The air between them grew more concentrated moment by moment, thickened by exigencies which hadn't been named yet.

More than ever Min believed that Warden's game – the future he played to win – was at issue here. She felt in her burning palms and her clenched handgun that the outcome might be determined by what happened between her and Morn.

At last Morn spoke.

'Director Donner.' Her voice was low; gravid with complex intentions. 'I'm Ensign Hyland. You know Captain Thermopyle. This is my son, Davies Hyland.' She indicated the young man at her shoulder.

As if he couldn't stop himself, Davies breathed quickly, 'Director Donner.' His tone hinted at involuntary respect.

But Morn wasn't done. The hesitation in her eyes didn't seem to affect her. 'It's my duty to inform you,' she went

170

on, 'that the others are under arrest. Vector Shaheed, Mikka Vasaczk and Ciro Vasaczk are my prisoners.'

Captain Ubikwe snorted like a mine-hammer. 'That's fascinating, Ensign. They sure don't *look* like they're under arrest. The last I heard, we use armcuffs when we're outnumbered by our prisoners.'

Min shook her head. 'What do you mean, Ensign Hyland? What's your point?'

Don't keep me in suspense. Tell me what the hell's going on.

Morn held her head high. Only the darkness of her gaze shifted: nothing else wavered. 'My point is that I'm responsible for them,' she answered firmly, 'and I won't tolerate any interference with them while they're in my charge.'

Slowly a fighting snarl pulled at Min's lips. Without transition she no longer cared whose game she was playing, or why. She was the Enforcement Division by God *director*, and *she* was responsible here. No matter how much Morn Hyland – or Warden Dios – meant to her, she had no intention of letting anyone come between her and her oath of office.

'It doesn't work that way.' She made the words crackle like alarms. 'You're only an ensign. You have neither the authority nor the competence to present yourself to me like this.'

Abruptly Angus bared his teeth. They looked as carious as his eyes. 'I warned you,' he remarked to Morn as if they were alone.

She turned to look at him. While a fire-storm gathered in Min, Morn nodded slowly. 'You were right,' she murmured softly. 'We'll do it your way.'

Min had an instant of warning as the clenched tension of Morn's group exploded into action. Just an instant: a fraction of a second; hardly long enough for the synapses of her brain to register the change.

Nevertheless she was fast. Years of experience and training had honed her reflexes to lightning. Before the instant was over, her fist leaped up; aimed her impact pistol at Morn's head.

But Morn had already moved. The doubt in her gaze –

and the cast on her arm – did nothing to slow her; hinder her. As soon as she spoke to Angus, she flung herself headlong at Min.

During the thin slice of time while Min's gun rose into line, Morn's boots lifted from the deck, carried by the force of her spring. She couldn't have stopped even if her reflexes had been as sharp as Min's; even if she'd had time to see Min's gun and recognize that Min was about to kill her.

Other people moved as well – Angus, Davies, Mikka Vasaczk, Vector Shaheed; even Ciro. Their actions were too sudden for anyone else on the bridge to counter. But Min had no time for them. Scarcely a millisecond remained before she tightened her finger; blasted Morn in midleap.

She changed her mind as swiftly as she raised her hand. Snatching the gun down, she stepped aside from Morn's attack.

The adjustment took too long, despite her speed. The interval of Morn's leap simply wasn't large enough to accommodate so many reactions. Before Min finished her sidestep, Morn crashed into her; hammered an acrylic-clad forearm onto her shoulder; grappled for her arm.

Min could have handled that. The force of Morn's blow struck her shoulder numb; but she didn't need it. Plant her rear leg: cock her hip: twist her torso in the direction of Morn's momentum: throw Morn past her. It would have been easy.

Unfortunately Morn's charge had already served its purpose. It was a feint, nothing more: a distraction. Angus reached Min before she recognized the true danger.

If she'd focused on him from the beginning, she could have beaten him. Despite his augmented resources, she would have had time to draw her gun and fire before he closed the gap.

But now –

Now she didn't stand a chance. His fist caught the side of her head with the force of a steel piston; and she went down like a sack of severed limbs.

*   *   *

She didn't lose consciousness. No. She positively declined. She was Min Donner, by God, *Min Donner*, and she was *responsible* for everything that happened here. She *would* not surrender to a mere punch in the head. Through pain that clanged and shivered inside her skull as if the bones were a gong, she clung to the deck and the bridge; refused to let the kind dark carry her away.

For a while she couldn't see anything: Angus had hit her hard enough to shock her optic nerves, her occipital lobes. But she felt the gun snatched out of her limp hand. With her cheek she sensed boots pounding the deck. From the fringes of unconsciousness she heard shouts and curses – Dolph's roar of anger; Bydell's involuntary wail; Glessen's harsh cursing.

Then a woman yelled.

'If you touch that intercom,' the voice cried harshly, 'I'll blow your head off!'

Not Morn. And not Bydell or Cray.

That left Mikka Vasaczk.

Min twisted her head to the side. The movement spiked more pain through her skull; but when it eased she could see again.

Blinking frantically, she looked up from the deck.

'All of you!' Mikka shouted again. 'If anyone lifts a finger, I'll kill him! First I kill him. Then Angus kills Director Donner!'

Min couldn't locate Morn or Angus: they must have been behind her. But the rest of *Trumpet*'s people had spread out around the bridge. Davies had positioned himself to guard the aperture to the bridge. He didn't have as much bulk or muscle as Angus; but he looked quick enough, driven enough, to hurt anyone who tried to get past him. Vector stood in front of Cray, holding his hands over her board so that she couldn't reach the keys to summon help without fighting him for them. Ciro Vasaczk crouched on his hands and knees, crawling toward the nearest bulkhead.

Mikka confronted the command station: a gun in her fist covered Dolph. She must have grabbed it from the bosun. He lay dazed on the deck; eyes dull; holster empty. Min knew at a glance that Mikka was both able and willing to use her weapon.

Captain Ubikwe must have seen the same thing. Nevertheless her threat – and the attack on Min – left him almost apoplectic with fury.

'I don't have to touch the intercom, God damn you!' he raged like a bullhorn. 'This is a UMCP *cruiser*! A ship of *war*! You can kill all of us. *You can kill everyone who comes onto the bridge in the next ten minutes*. But after that you're *finished*!

'By then the rest of my crew will have guns, too. And they aren't stupid, no matter what you think of the cops. They'll override everything from the auxiliary bridge. They'll seal you in here, they'll cut off your goddamn air. And you won't be able to stop them because you don't have the goddamn *codes*!'

Only *Punisher*'s senior officers had the codes he meant – the cruiser's essential priority-codes. Even Morn wouldn't be able to prevent it if, say, Hargin Stoval invoked those commands in order to take over the ship from the auxiliary bridge.

'Either shoot me or get that popgun out of my face,' Dolph demanded hotly. 'I don't deserve to be insulted.'

'You fat asshole,' Angus drawled with a grin, 'what makes you think we care?'

Min was angry, too; as angry as Dolph. But her fury was cold and hard, like forged ceramic. Somehow she dredged her head up from the deck. With a brutal effort, she levered her good forearm under her.

'You should care,' she croaked hoarsely.

You'd better kill me now. Otherwise I'm going to crucify every one of you.

Abrupt hands grabbed the back of her shipsuit. They were strong; impossibly strong: they jerked her upright as if she had no mass, no substance. They planted her on her unsteady feet, then released her with a negligent flick that nearly sent her sprawling.

She flexed her knees against the weight of her pain and turned to face Angus and Morn. Her right arm dangled useless from her numbed shoulder.

174

Angus held Min's pistol aimed at the center of her chest. His free hand clenched and unclenched slowly, as if he were pumping it full of violence.

'Why?' he jeered at her. 'You're the one who reqqed me from Com-Mine Security so Hashi fucking Lebwohl could play his little games with me. After that you pretended you didn't like it, but you let him have me anyway. The way I see it, I owe you nothing but damage. Why should I care?'

Min took a deep breath, reached inward to find a center of balance beyond the clamoring pain. Distinctly she answered, 'Because I won't let you do this.'

Angus widened his eyes mockingly, then narrowed them into a scowl. 'Oh, *I* get it,' he rasped. 'You're planning to stop me, aren't you.' He sank his teeth into the words; seemed to tear them loose one at a time like shreds of meat. 'You're going to use my priority-codes, turn me back into a toy. Aren't you.

'Well, go ahead,' he challenged her. 'Go ahead and fucking try it.'

His manner warned her: everything *Trumpet*'s people had done since *Punisher* spotted the gap scout on scan warned her. Nevertheless she didn't hesitate; didn't second-guess herself.

'Isaac, this is Gabriel priority.' Her voice recovered its force as she spoke, filling the air with compulsion. 'Give me that gun.'

Angus Thermopyle was a welded cyborg, ruled by zone implants and exigent programming; absolutely controlled. Hashi had assured everyone in UMCPHQ that he would never draw another free breath as long as he lived.

But he didn't surrender her weapon.

Instead he laughed like the hunting growl of a predator.

'Well, what do you know? I didn't do it. Isn't that amazing?' His eyes concentrated on her like coherent light.

'And you know what's even more amazing?' he went on. 'I don't have to hold back from hurting UMC-fucking-P personnel. Not now. Not ever again.'

He turned his free hand as if he were aiming a punch in the direction of the command station. Without warning a

175

ruby shaft as thin as a needle lanced between his fingers toward Captain Ubikwe's feet. First the laser scored the deck, deliquescing metal with a plume of smoke, a stink of heat. Then it touched the side of Dolph's boot.

The captain sat like a stone in his g-seat. Not a muscle moved. If he felt so much as a lick of pain, he didn't show it. But the glare he fixed on Angus promised murder.

Through his teeth Angus told Min, 'I already hit you hard enough to get your attention.' Slowly he shifted his laser away from Dolph's boot. 'I can amputate his damn legs if I feel like it.' At last he turned the beam off.

A faint sigh crossed the bridge as Bydell, Porson, Cray and even Glessen let themselves breathe again.

'We changed my datacore,' Angus stated scornfully. 'I don't have to take your orders anymore, or let you turn me off, or make me break my promises. You don't have any restrictions left on me. *Do you hear me?*' he raged suddenly. 'I'm *done* with you! The next time you give me an order, I will *push it back down your throat with my bare hands*!'

'Morn,' Davies put in, half demanding, half imploring, 'tell him to stop. He's made his point. We don't need more threats.'

Mikka's grip on her gun held steady: her aim hadn't wavered a centimeter. 'Whatever it takes,' she muttered. 'Whatever it fucking takes.'

'But he *is* telling the truth, Director Donner,' Vector offered as if he wanted to placate her. 'He doesn't accept orders from us either.'

Min stared back at Angus without moving. For a moment she thought her heart might stop. Her grasp on reality seemed to unravel in the face of his ability to disobey his priority-codes.

Changed his datacore? How? That should have been impossible. Everything was impossible.

Hashi, you miserable, goddamn sonofabitch, this is –

But then another explanation struck her with the force of an electric shock.

– your doing?

176

No. It wasn't Hashi's doing. It wasn't his game at all. It was Warden's.

Warden had used *Punisher* to convey a message to *Trumpet*. The text of the transmission had given Angus' codes to Nick Succorso. But the plain words had been embedded in *some kind of specialized programming language.* And now Angus was free. *Something similar to the one we use to program datacores.*

Warden's doing.

Beyond question the future he was fighting for depended on what happened here.

Morn didn't reply to her son's demand, didn't say anything to Angus; didn't glance away from the ED director. Maybe Min was wrong: maybe it wasn't doubt that darkened her gaze. Maybe it was grief.

'We're not going to kill anybody.' Her tone was full of resolve – and hints of sorrow. 'Not unless you don't leave us any other choice. We don't want bloodshed. And we don't mean to hurt you. We don't even want to insult you.

'All we want,' she said firmly, 'is command of this ship.'

Porson gave a low gasp of surprise. Glessen swore viciously under his breath. Even stolid Emmett flinched.

Dolph was too angry to keep quiet. 'And you expect me to *allow* that?' he barked at Morn. 'What are you, crazy as well as stupid? If you think I'm going to give up my ship just because you're waving a couple of little guns around, you should go check yourself into sickbay. You've gone too far over the edge to function without medical help.'

Min held up her left hand, mutely commanding him to silence. This was between her and Morn – and Warden Dios, whose nameless needs hung over them like a shroud.

'What for?' she asked sternly. 'What do you propose to do if we let you take command?'

'"Let"?' Angus sneered. '"Let" has nothing to do with it. We don't need your goddamn permission.'

Snarling deeply, Dolph bit back a retort.

Still Morn kept her attention on Min as if no one else had spoken; no one else mattered.

'For a start' – her voice was low, but steady – 'we'll go home. Back to Earth.' She shrugged. 'After that it depends on who tries to stop us.'

Back to Earth. Exactly where Min would have taken them.

All at once she seemed to feel a nagging burden of uncertainty and confusion drop from her shoulders.

Between them Morn and her companions carried the most explosive body of information in human space. Morn could testify that Angus had been framed: that UMCPDA had conspired with Milos Taverner to steal supplies from Com-Mine so that the Preempt Act would pass. Vector Shaheed had analyzed the formula for an antimutagen which the UMCP had kept secret, despite its obvious importance to humankind. Mikka and Ciro Vasaczk surely knew about Nick's dealings with the Amnion on DA's behalf. They could describe the Amnion near-C acceleration experiments Angus had mentioned – experiments which might give forbidden space an insuperable advantage if the present uneasy peace turned to war. In some way Davies Hyland represented the knowledge the Amnion needed to create artificial human beings who would be indistinguishable from real ones. And Angus had changed his datacore: therefore everything Hashi Lebwohl had done with welded cyborgs – and, by extension, all humankind's reliance on SOD-CMOS chips – was untrustworthy; founded on a false premise.

If Morn and her companions returned to Earth and revealed what they knew, every dishonorable action the UMCP had taken in recent years would be exposed.

The result would be chaos. At the very least the GCES might dismantle the UMCP. Or pass a Bill of Severance. But the damage would almost certainly go further.

It might go far enough to bring down Holt Fasner.

On the other hand, if Min fought Morn and won – if she outplayed or outwaited *Trumpet*'s people, and took them all prisoner – the harm might be contained. Certainly the Dragon would do everything in his vast power to contain it. The stories Morn and her companions had to tell would be suppressed; lost.

Yet eventually Warden's hand in these events would become known. Angus' datacore would play back every bit of input it had been given. Then Fasner would have no choice but to destroy Warden. It would be all too obvious that Warden had tried to destroy him.

That fact would be significantly less obvious if Morn Hyland was in command when *Punisher* reached Earth.

Min was unaccustomed to surrender. The concept violated her combative spirit: the word itself seemed to violate her mind. But she had larger responsibilities to consider.

'I guess' – for a moment her voice stuck bitterly in her throat – 'I guess you didn't believe me when I said,' swore to you, 'I'm not going to suppress Shaheed's broadcast.'

Morn's head twitched back as if she were reacting to a flick of pain. 'Oh, I believe you, Director Donner. My whole family trusted you.' Then the corners of her mouth knotted with self-coercion. 'I just don't believe you'll have the final say.'

She was right: Min knew that. The Dragon was too strong for her.

'In that case,' the ED director announced like acid, 'you win. The ship is yours.'

Bydell gaped at her in astonishment. Glessen covered his face with his hands.

From the aperture of the bridge, Davies crowed, 'Yes!'

'Min!' Dolph cried out. 'You can't –!'

'I can!' Min wheeled to face the command station; overrode his protest with a shout like a flail. 'I *am*!

'*Listen* to me, Captain Ubikwe. Listen hard so you don't make any mistakes. As long as Ensign Hyland wants to head home, we'll take her there. And we'll take her orders along the way. We are not going to resist her or sabotage her. We aren't going to cause her any trouble at all.'

'Min, please –' His eyes beseeched her.

'No!' She refused to be swayed. Returning sensation sent needles of fire down her forearm into her stunned hand. '*I won't have any more bloodshed.* We've just taken aboard the only six people in human space who've been through more hell than we have. I want all of us to survive the experience, *all of us*. If that means letting a mere ensign issue instructions for a while, we will *do* it.'

If we destroy Warden and bring down the whole UMCP, that's on *my* head, not yours.

'These people are not the enemy, Dolph.' She lowered her voice to a cutting edge. 'Maybe they're out of line. And maybe they're too dangerous to mess with. We'll sort all that out when we get home. Better yet, we'll let Director Dios sort it out. But for the time being' – she delivered each word as distinctly as an incision – 'you will not risk any more of your people.

'Is that understood, Captain Ubikwe? Have I made myself clear?'

'Shit, Min.' He slumped as if he were collapsing in on himself. 'Of course you've made yourself clear. You know that.' With the back of his hand he wiped sweat from his dark forehead. 'But I have to say' – his tone reeked of bile – 'you sure as hell know how to rub salt in our wounds.'

He slammed to his feet, brushed Mikka aside as if she didn't hold a gun. Gesturing at his g-seat, he growled, 'The bridge is yours, Ensign Hyland. I'll be in my cabin. Throwing up.'

Without waiting to be dismissed, he headed for the aperture.

'Sounds like fun,' Angus snorted past his grin. 'I'll go with you. Just in case you decide you don't want to be a good boy. Or Director Donner changes her mind.'

He handed Min's gun to Davies as he followed Dolph Ubikwe off the bridge.

Min understood, although no one said the words. Dolph had just become a hostage.

He seemed to take all the cruiser's courage with him as he left. His people sagged at their stations. Their faces fell: they hung their heads. Even Glessen lost his truculence. Bydell made a small sound that might have been a moan of abandonment.

Abruptly Min's anger returned like the flash of a signal flare. She found herself flexing the fingers of her right hand against the burn; flexing them like Angus. She wanted her gun.

'Don't make this any harder than it has to be, Ensign Hyland,' she warned. 'Our people have already been pushed right to the edge. It'll take just about nothing to make them explode. If your cyborg so much as *scratches* Captain Ubikwe, you'll have a full-scale battle on your hands.'

And I will personally execute the lot of you.

'We know that,' Mikka muttered. 'We know what's at stake.'

Holding Min's gun in his fist, Davies left the aperture to approach Morn and the command station. Bitterly he told Min, 'Angus hasn't hurt anyone since you gave Nick his priority-codes. At the moment he's easier to trust than you are.'

Min wrapped her fingers around the fire in her palms so that she wouldn't retort.

Once again Morn didn't hesitate. She'd committed herself to this course of action. If she had doubts about it, she kept her uncertainty private.

Deliberately spurning her years in the Academy, as well as her whole family history – the respect for rank and authority which she'd surely been taught – she stepped to the command station and assumed Captain Ubikwe's g-seat. Despite the darkness in her gaze, she seemed sure of what she did. The cast on her arm gave her an odd combination of vulnerability and dignity.

Min watched in confusion, baffled by outrage – and by a strange, keen pride that one of her people could rise to a challenge like this.

'Mikka,' Morn said quietly, 'I want you to supervise helm.'

'Right.' At once Mikka stalked over to Emmett's station; positioned herself at the arm of his g-seat so that she had a clear view of his console.

'Davies,' Morn went on, 'you'd better keep an eye on Director Donner. Just to be safe. I want everyone to know she's being held under duress. Like Captain Ubikwe.'

She meant that neither Min Donner nor Dolph Ubikwe was responsible for what *Trumpet*'s people did. In an oblique way she was protecting Min, Dolph and *Punisher*. Perhaps she was even protecting Warden Dios. To that extent, at least, she understood the implications of her decisions.

Quickly Davies shifted so that he had an open shot on Min without risking either Morn or Mikka. Grimacing like his father's grin, he covered Min with her own weapon. But he kept his distance: apparently he'd seen how quickly she could move.

When Davies was in position, Morn turned her station. Following her gaze, Min saw Mikka's brother still huddled on the deck. He'd retreated to the bulkhead; pressed his shoulder against it as if he wanted to hide and had forgotten how.

Gently Morn asked, 'Ciro, are you all right?'

He didn't reply. After a long moment, however, he jerked a nod.

Sighing, Morn returned her attention to the rest of the bridge.

'Communications, I'm sure you have a copy of Dr Shaheed's transmission. Please ready it for general broadcast. As soon as we reach Earth, we'll start transmitting it again.

'Vector, you might want to be sure she gets it right.'

Cray snorted at the suggestion that she might make a mistake. But Vector's response was a grin of relief. 'I think I can handle that.' At once he stopped blocking the communications board and moved around behind Cray's station to support himself on the back of her g-seat.

Morn continued assuming command.

'Helm, please set course for Earth. The best course you can manage with no more than one g of thrust. I don't want to put any more pressure than necessary on this ship.'

'Yes, sir,' Emmett responded automatically. Placing his hands on his board, he started to tap keys.

'Engage thrust when you're ready, helm,' Morn finished.

Punisher was going home.

Gritting her teeth, Min tried to tell herself that she'd done what Warden wanted.

And that what Warden wanted was right.

KOINA

Koina Hannish had isolated herself in her office. The room wasn't Godsen Frik's once-opulent center of operations, which she'd always disliked, and which had in any case been effectively destroyed by the kaze who'd killed the former PR director. It was her own far more austere space. For the time being, at least, she'd delegated to her subordinates the massive job of sifting Data Storage for the truth behind Godsen's fulsome obfuscations. And she'd instructed her receptionist to accept no calls, demands or inquiries unless they came directly from Warden Dios. She'd locked her door, blanked her terminals and readouts, silenced her intercom; dimmed the lights.

Now she sat at her desk and tried to review her life.

This was how she made hard decisions. Whenever she was faced with a difficult choice, she approached it by asking herself who she was, what she wanted, what she believed in.

She'd started doing this a number of years ago when she'd first considered what she wanted to do with her life. What were her convictions? What could she do about them? Her answers had led her into 'public relations', which she defined as the interface between the people who took action and the people who were affected by those actions. To her way of thinking, this was the most potentially fruitful work she could imagine. The interface determined the nature of the relationship between any public organization and its constituents. It was the means by which the organization and its constituents communicated with each other. Even a casual study of governmental – and corporate – entities showed that their effectiveness hinged on 'public relations'.

Later the same answers had inspired her to accept a position in UMCPPR. Nowhere was the interface more crucial than in the dealings between humanity and its defenders.

But the personal and professional dishonesty of the former PR director had forced her to examine her life again. Could she tolerate his misuse of his position, his distortion of everything which passed through his hands in Holt Fasner's name? And if she couldn't, what did she propose to do instead?

In the end she'd concluded that the work of UMCPPR was too important to abandon. Here was where she belonged. Since she couldn't make Godsen honest, she would dedicate herself to cleaning up after him. Among other things, this inspired her to undermine him covertly by, in effect, spying on him for Hashi Lebwohl.

Then, scant days ago, she'd needed another bout of self-examination when Warden Dios had offered her Godsen's job.

Surely this was exactly what she'd been hoping for? A chance to replace Godsen's unctuous lies with the truth? Perhaps not. Warden had permitted Godsen's falsehoods and machinations. He was profoundly responsible for all his former PR director's misdeeds. If he expected her to carry out Godsen's duties in Godsen's fashion, she would have no recourse but to resign.

That was her decision, although the prospect filled her with pain. Humankind deserved better from UMCPPR – and from the UMCP itself – than Godsen had ever given it.

However, Warden had reassured her more than she would have dared hope. In an abrupt, and unexplained, policy reversal, he'd ordered her to do the PR director's job as she believed it should be done: openly, honestly; constructively.

At one stroke he'd changed everything. She couldn't imagine what his motives might be, but she approved completely. He inspired trust, despite his responsibility for Godsen. After years of bad compromises and frustration, her life came into focus. She found that she was eager to be the interface which the UMCP so urgently needed.

But now the task of reexamination had to be done again. The UMCP director had presented her with another arduous choice.

This one was especially cruel.

When she'd left her meeting with Hashi, Security Chief Mandich and Warden, she'd felt sick with grief. Her relief at hearing that she hadn't precipitated the kaze's attack soon faded: her sorrow at other things was with her still. Her efforts to make up her mind were colored by ruin.

She shouldn't feel this way, she told herself sternly. Warden had made the mandate of her duties real at last; given them teeth. Now she would be able to do her job as it should have been done from the beginning.

But the things she'd learned –!

The Amnion had committed an act of war. That would have been enough – more than enough – but it was only the beginning.

On direct orders from Holt Fasner, UMCPDA had framed Angus Thermopyle in order to achieve the passage of the Preempt Act. And Morn Hyland knew the truth. She was alive aboard *Trumpet* – despite the fact that Captain Thermopyle was now a welded UMCP cyborg with explicit instructions not to rescue her from her enslavement to Nick Succorso. Captain Thermopyle's 'escape' from UMCPHQ accompanied by Milos Taverner had been a ruse designed to protect a covert mission against Billingate.

In addition Hashi had produced convincing – if inferential – evidence that the kazes who had attacked Captain Vertigus, killed Godsen and threatened the GCES had been sent by the Dragon himself. Presumably their purpose had been to disrupt Special Counsel Igensard's investigation of the UMCP, as well as to counteract the effects of Warden's – and Hashi's – recent video conference with the Council. In effect, however, the kazes had defeated Sixten Vertigus' Bill of Severance.

Now she, Koina Hannish, had been charged with revealing

all this before the Governing Council for Earth and Space.

Under the circumstances she should have been avid; almost ecstatic with vindication. As Protocol Director for the UMCP, she stood at the fulcrum of events which would affect all humankind. The veil of falsehood and unaccountability which Holt Fasner had woven between the UMCP and the GCES was starting to fray. When she addressed the Council – when she carried out Warden's clear instructions – the fabric would tear.

She should have been thrilled – but she wasn't. Instead mourning ate like acid at her heart. Her sense of clarity and conviction corroded by the moment. Isolated and immobilized, she sat here in the dusk of her office trying to make the most important decision of her life.

Warden Dios had chosen her to destroy him.

When she spoke to the Council – if she spoke – she would put an axe to the roots of Holt Fasner's power over human space. The threat of war would naturally leave the Members chary of interfering with the UMCP. But that threat came in direct response to Angus Thermopyle's mission against Billingate – and to his escape with Morn Hyland. It could be argued, therefore, that Warden was culpable for this act of war. And Maxim Igensard would certainly do so, especially if he had reason to think that Warden could have guessed Milos Taverner would turn traitor. The Special Counsel might well claim that the UMCP was as much a threat to humankind's safety as the Amnion were.

The information that the UMCP had betrayed Com-Mine Security in order to extend its own hegemony would confirm Igensard's argument. So would the apparent breakdown of Hashi's control over his welded cyborg.

The shock of these revelations would increase dramatically if Koina accused Holt Fasner of sending kazes against his opponents.

At the very least the Members would probably reconsider – and perhaps pass – Captain Vertigus' Bill. And they might go much further. They were unlikely to cripple the UMCP at such a time. But if Koina was eloquent enough they might press charges against Holt Fasner. They might decharter the UMC itself.

Whatever else happened, however, the Council would certainly crush Warden Dios. He would be suspended in disgrace: he would be charged with treason. And Holt Fasner wouldn't stand by him. The Dragon would have no choice but to extract from Warden any sacrifice the GCES required, if only to reduce his own losses.

Koina wanted no part of it.

On the surface Warden's behavior appeared unconscionable. Nevertheless she trusted him. Something in the clench of his strong fists, or the probing of his one eye, or the underlying passion of his voice, convinced her that he was honest. Like her, he must have made bad compromises: after all, he worked for Holt. Still she believed that he'd done what he did for reasons which she would have considered honorable.

She didn't want to be the one who brought him down.

So now she had to choose between her duty – as he himself had defined it for her – and her personal loyalty to him. Which could she bear to give up?

Snared by loss, she feared that the challenge would defeat her. No matter what she did, she would have to surrender pieces of herself.

Perhaps this was the kind of pressure which had driven Warden to make unconscionable choices. Perhaps he, too, had been forced to surrender pieces of himself.

She was still gnawing on the problem like an animal chewing its own leg to escape a trap when her intercom suddenly flashed.

She caught her breath: for a moment her heart seemed to stop. That was Warden's priority channel. It made no sound: she'd stilled the chime. Nevertheless it signaled insistently, as urgent as an emergency beacon.

She wasn't ready –

She had to answer it anyway. She would never be able to justify refusing a call from the director of the UMCP.

Instinctively she straightened her back; cleared her throat;

adjusted her clothes. Then she reached out almost firmly and keyed open the channel.

'Koina Hannish,' she announced. 'Director Dios?'

'Koina.' Warden's voice sounded distant, muffled by tension. 'Let's keep this short. I'm in a hurry.

'Len has called an emergency session,' he said without preamble. 'It starts in six hours. Your shuttle leaves in two. You have that long to brace yourself for Igensard.'

Something had happened.

She scrambled to catch up. 'I take it this means you've told the President there's been an act of war.'

'Yes,' he replied. He'd bypassed Protocol entirely – which of course was exactly what he would be expected to do in this kind of crisis. 'As I said, I've been waiting to make a formal announcement until I had a better idea which way events were headed. But now I can't put it off any longer.'

Something *had* happened. Koina held herself still, hoping that her silence would encourage him to go on.

'Another drone just came in,' he explained promptly. He wanted her to know this. 'It's from *Punisher*. She's still in the Massif-5 system – or she was when she launched the drone. But she's on her way out. Chasing *Trumpet*.

'Why *Trumpet* is running from her I can't tell you,' he rasped. 'That's one problem. Nick Succorso has the codes to control Angus. He should have stopped trying to get away from Min by now. But the rest of the news is worse.

'That Amnion defensive was definitely hunting *Trumpet*. Apparently *Trumpet* tried to hide in an asteroid swarm. Massif-5 is littered with them. Even though the defensive was under hard fire from *Punisher*, she parked herself outside the swarm and waited for *Trumpet* to show up.

'Which is another problem,' he muttered. 'How the hell did an Amnioni know *Trumpet* was in there?'

And what was *Trumpet* doing there in the first place? What bizarre breakdown of reason or self-interest had inspired Nick Succorso to head for Massif-5, instead of turning himself over to the protection of Director Donner and *Punisher*?

But Warden didn't raise that question. Sourly he went on, 'When *Trumpet* finally showed herself, the defensive tried to hit her. Not just with matter cannon. She used a super-light proton gun. It's a miracle *Trumpet* is still alive.

'The miracle was that another ship appeared. She must have followed either *Trumpet* or the defensive all the way from forbidden space. And, no, I can't explain that, either,' he growled, although Koina hadn't asked him to. 'But she attacked just in time to help *Punisher* overload the Amnioni's sinks.'

He paused as if he were swallowing indignation or shame, then said, 'Now it gets even worse. When the defensive had to choose between killing *Trumpet* – which was presumably her whole reason for being there – and saving herself, she saved herself. She used her proton gun to destroy the other ship instead of *Trumpet*. Which gave *Trumpet* time to get away.'

At last Koina did interject a question. 'Why is that bad?' She was foundering in new information; implications she couldn't assimilate. 'Aren't we glad *Trumpet* is alive?'

'Of course we're glad,' he retorted heavily. 'What's bad is that the defensive made that decision. It raises the rather frightening possibility that she – or the Amnion – have other responses available, responses we don't know about.'

Like what? Koina wanted to ask; demand. She couldn't imagine what they might be. Despite everything she'd learned recently, she still had no idea what the real stakes were.

What did this have to do with the meaning of her life?

'Anyway,' Warden resumed, '*Punisher* has been too badly hurt to finish the defensive on her own. She broke off the engagement to go after *Trumpet*. The Amnioni got away.'

On that point, at least, Koina understood him. 'I guess you're right,' she muttered. Sorrow made her sound bitter. 'That is even worse.'

Min Donner's decision may have been justified, correct, but it would taint the UMCP's already-tarnished image.

'The risks are too great,' he concluded. 'I couldn't wait any longer. I had to tell Len what was happening.'

189

More and more, Koina's grief came out as sarcasm. 'Did you also tell Holt Fasner?'

'Actually, no.' Warden's tone was stiff, but he didn't pause. 'For some reason I've been too busy to contact Holt.'

Which must have made the Dragon positively apoplectic. Warden was already a dead man: the CEO simply hadn't had time to carry out his execution yet.

'That makes sense,' she said trenchantly. 'I guess.' Of course Warden didn't want to give the Dragon a chance to countermand his suicide. 'Well, for what it's worth, I concur. You did the right thing. It was time to inform the Council.'

For a moment her intercom emitted a troubled silence. Then Warden asked uncomfortably, 'Koina, what's bothering you?'

She wanted to retort, Nothing, I'm fine, what makes you think something bothers me? But she swallowed the impulse. She was tired of lies. The thought of lying to protect Warden sickened her as much as ruining him with the truth.

'Do you still want Director Lebwohl to attend the emergency session?' she asked. Indecision weakened her: she could hardly keep the bereavement from her voice. 'Can he take my place?'

Hashi might enjoy appalling Maxim Igensard with revelations.

'No,' Warden returned. 'I changed my mind. I need him here. And Fane might arrange an "accident" for him down there. I don't want to risk that. Not until he finishes his investigation.'

Cleatus Fane, Holt Fasner's First Executive Assistant, was still on Suka Bator. He would certainly be present for the emergency session.

'I think you're safe,' Warden added in a hard tone. 'But even if you aren't, I want you there.'

Koina bit her lip. If she meant to tell the truth, she would have to go further.

'Director Dios –' she began awkwardly. 'Warden –' For a moment she couldn't put her pain into words. But then she forced herself to say, 'Don't ask me to do this. Send someone else. Anyone –'

'Why?' he demanded at once. 'I thought you were glad for a chance to finally do your job right.'

Come on, Koina, she told herself grimly. Say it. Get it off your chest. Then maybe you'll be able to make up your mind.

When she spoke, her voice was as clear as keening.

'Because this is going to finish you. It'll probably kill you. No matter what else happens, you'll be ruined. When he hears what I have to say, Igensard will cut you to pieces. And the Council won't help you – they'll just sharpen the knives. You won't have any allies left.'

Even brave old Sixten Vertigus, who trusted the UMCP and believed in Warden –

'I don't want to be the one who makes that happen. There must be some other way to accomplish' – emotion thickened in her throat, and she faltered – 'whatever it is you're trying for.'

Still Warden didn't hesitate. He must have come to the end of his personal uncertainties. All his choices were plain.

'Listen to me, Koina,' he ordered sharply. 'Listen hard, because I'm only going to say this once.

'I've earned the right to pay for my crimes.' His voice seemed to echo with absolute commitments. 'All I want you to do is help me pay for them effectively. Help me bring something good out of all these lies and betrayals.

'There's a question you haven't asked me,' he went on before she could demand, cry out, What *good*? 'You haven't asked if I know why the Amnion are so intent on killing *Trumpet*. They must be terrified of something. They wouldn't risk an act of war if they didn't think the alternatives were worse.'

He was right. She'd been so taken aback by the things he'd explained earlier that she hadn't pursued this obvious point.

'Angus has given us several answers,' he grated. 'I'll tell you one.

'Nick Succorso had a mutagen immunity drug. Hashi gave it to him. But the Amnion don't know that's where he got it. I think they want to destroy it before he makes it public. And I think – or Min thinks – *Trumpet* went to Massif-5 to find a bootleg lab so Vector Shaheed could analyze the drug.'

'Wait a minute,' Koina protested in shock and chagrin. *Wait* a minute. 'A *mutagen immunity* drug?' Hashi *gave* it to him? 'Are you saying we have the formula for a mutagen immunity drug' – the idea was too horrific for words – 'and we've been *suppressing* it?'

Hints of ferocity glinted in Warden's tone. 'On direct orders from Holt Fasner, yes. In fact, he would have destroyed the research completely if I hadn't agreed to keep it secret. For the covert use of DA.

'But ever since *Trumpet* left that asteroid swarm she's been broadcasting the formula. That's something else I've kept from Holt. If he finds out before you talk to the Council, he'll get rid of me so fast you won't see it happen.'

Oh, Warden, Koina moaned. Her heart trembled in her chest: it seemed as fragile as a goblet which was about to shatter on the floor. Fasner ordered you to do that, betray your entire species – and you went along with it?

But he wasn't done yet. 'Don't you think that should be made public?' he challenged as if he wanted her to pass sentence. 'Don't you think Igensard needs to know about it?' He might have been asking, Don't you think that's more important than what happens to me? 'What else is PR *for*, Koina?'

She couldn't answer. What *was* PR for, if not for this? Her duty was obvious: to tell the truth about the organization she served – and to hold that organization accountable for its actions. Why else had she come to work here in the first place?

After a moment she pulled herself together long enough to say, 'I'll be on that shuttle, Director Dios. I'll do my job.'

Just make damn sure you do yours.

Then she silenced her intercom so that she wouldn't have to hear him thank her for agreeing to ruin him. But she didn't move to get ready. Instead she put her head down on her arms and let herself grieve.

MAXIM

Special Counsel Maxim Igensard was an ambitious man. Behind his carefully nurtured appearance of nondescript diffidence, he burned with an incandescent hunger. Everything he did, he did for one reason, and one reason only: to satisfy that blaze.

Scruples and doubts rarely troubled him.

His goals seemed so right and necessary to him that he never questioned them. In fact, he seldom thought about them: they were too essential to require consideration. Nevertheless he labored to achieve them with a relentless and single-minded determination which endured no obstacles. Waking or sleeping – although by the standards of his underlings and colleagues he slept little – he worked for what he wanted.

To put what he wanted into words oversimplified it to the point of falsehood. Mere language gave short shrift to the intensity of his desires, as well as to the prospective glory of achieving them. However, if he could have been lured or persuaded to name his goals, he would have said that he meant to become the director of the United Mining Companies Police.

He belonged in that position: it was his natural place. He'd been born to enforce the future of humankind – the vast majority of whom were nothing more than a clot of stupid sheep. And to supplant Warden Dios seemed the finest accomplishment to which a human mind could aspire.

Unfortunately he was still a long way – a *long* way – from

attaining his ambition. For that reason his energies were focused exclusively on the how rather than the why of his goals.

His appointment as the Special Counsel charged with investigating the Thermopyle case on Com-Mine Station was an important step in the right direction: it gave him leverage. Now he could proceed to larger matters.

What he intended, in its baldest terms, was to tarnish Warden Dios, either directly or through his subordinates, so thoroughly that Holt Fasner would have no choice but to replace the UMCP director. This, however, would inevitably incur Fasner's wrath – which would in turn militate against Maxim's appointment in Dios' place. To diminish Holt Fasner's anger, therefore, as well as to subtly demonstrate his own trustworthiness, Maxim was resolved to attack the UMCP director in ways which cast no taint on the UMC CEO.

Thus he was outraged by that old fool Sixten Vertigus' Bill of Severance. It transformed his investigation of the UMCP into an assault on Holt Fasner: it forced him into the position of appearing to support a threat which could only increase the UMC CEO's hostility.

He considered – and discarded – the possibility that he might reach his goal without Holt Fasner's sponsorship. If the UMCP were severed from the UMC, it was of course conceivable that Maxim might find himself selected to replace Warden Dios: conceivable, but unlikely. Taken together, the GCES Members were as stupid a clot of sheep as Maxim had ever seen. They were perfectly capable of ignoring his superior knowledge of the UMCP – as well as his superior abilities – for the sake of investing some fatuous figurehead with Warden Dios' authority and power.

Because of this, he was personally and viscerally furious at Warden Dios and Hashi Lebwohl. Their recent video conference with the Council had dealt him an insidious blow. His ambitions required that he extract evidence of malfeasance or defalcation from reluctant, stonewalling opponents. The importance, the sheer stature, of his investigation was undermined when his opponents voluntarily justified his accusations. That trivialized him. He wanted to ruin Dios in person:

he gained nothing by simply allowing the UMCP director to effect his own end.

When the announcement that the Amnion had committed an act of war reached him – albeit indirectly – from GCES President Len's office, his first action was to call Cleatus Fane. Although such contact was premature, sudden crises required special risks. He wanted to assure Holt Fasner's First Executive Assistant that he would do everything in his considerable power to keep the UMC CEO's reputation clean in the forthcoming emergency session.

To his acute consternation, however, Fane declined to speak with him. Too busy, one of the FEA's aides explained: under the circumstances the Special Counsel surely understood. In other words, Maxim Igensard lacked the significance to gain Fane's notice at a time like this.

Bitterly Maxim queried GCES Communications to learn the truth. But he was informed that for a fact Cleatus Fane *was* busy: the FEA had reqqed every uplink channel which hadn't been reserved by Security, and – according to Communications – was 'emitting enough microwaves to cause sunspots.'

Maxim didn't need to ask whom Fane addressed so feverishly. The answer was obvious. UMC Home Office. Holt Fasner.

Regardless of 'the circumstances', Special Counsel Maxim Igensard had no intention of diminishing himself by explaining his concerns to a mere aide. Seething like magma beneath an almost featureless surface, he went to see Abrim Len in person.

The GCES President had been cast from a different mold from FEA Fane – if a man so malleable and apprehensive could be said to have been 'cast' at all. 'Can't this wait, Maxim?' he muttered peevishly as he admitted Maxim to his office suite. 'I don't have the time. My intercom is flashing like a strobe. Suddenly every constituent on the planet wants to flare his elected representative – God knows why, the newsdogs haven't picked up on this yet. I just finished talking to Tel Burnish' – the Member for Valdor Industrial – 'who has a lot more at stake than any of the rest of us, but I didn't know what to tell him except what we've heard from Warden

Dios. And I haven't even started getting ready. Do you have any idea how much preparation goes into an emergency session? More than I know how to handle, and that's a fact. We've never had an emergency session. At least not since I became President. Not since Captain Vertigus first made contact with the Amnion.

'This is going to turn out badly, Maxim. Mark my words. We're in serious trouble.' Circuitously he arrived back at his point. 'I really have no time to talk to you.'

Maxim gave President Len's sense of harassment the attention he thought it deserved: in effect, none. On the whole island the only thing larger than Len's palatial suite of offices was his staff of aides, advisers, secretaries, receptionists, PR officers and – Maxim suspected sourly – therapists. Nevertheless he offered commiseration while he diffidently steered the President toward one of the more private regions of the suite, away from the flashing intercoms and the tense scurry of subordinates.

'This is difficult for you, I know, Mr President,' he murmured. 'Your responsibilities must be enormous. That's largely why I came to see you. If you'll give me ten minutes of your time, I may be able to simplify your position slightly.'

From Maxim's perspective, Abrim Len was fatuous to the point of brain-death. He was an intelligent man, however, after his fashion. ' "Simplify"?' he retorted as he and Maxim reached a quieter room. ' "Simplify", Maxim? You must be joking. In my experience, when a Special Counsel uses a word like "simplify", what he means is that he's about to make my life miserable.'

Maxim managed a thin smile, although he was in no mood for Abrim Len's sarcasm. 'It may seem so at first,' he admitted. 'But if you'll hear me out, I'm sure you'll appreciate the point I want to make.'

'Fine.' The President folded himself onto a deep sofa like a man who wasn't sure what to do with his limbs. His teeth seemed to protrude over his weak chin. 'I'll listen. At least this way I won't have to take any more calls for a while.'

Maxim sat also. As a matter of policy he kept his physical profile low: at times he appeared to compress himself into the smallest possible space. He found he often gained an advantage by giving the impression that no one needed to fear him.

He began at once. A mind like his seldom hesitated.

'Mr President, you expressed a concern that "this is going to turn out badly". As you say, we are in "serious trouble". But you may not yet have had time to grasp just how "serious" the trouble is. My overriding motivation is to prevent the situation from growing worse – within the context of my duties as Special Counsel, of course.'

'Your sentiments do you credit,' Len remarked sententiously. Perhaps he knew that such vacuous comments irritated Maxim.

The Special Counsel didn't allow himself to be distracted, however. Instead he became unnecessarily pedantic – an oblique form of retribution.

'I have received the full text of Warden Dios' announcement that the Amnion have committed an act of war,' he began. The President's office had broadcast it exclusively to the Members; but of course they had all shown it at once to their aides and advisers, just as Sen Abdullah had shared it with Maxim, and someone – Sigurd Carsin, perhaps – had forwarded it to Cleatus Fane. 'It's frightening enough as it stands. Yet it omits what I consider to be some salient details. And the implications of those details – and of their omission – are even more frightening.

'Director Dios states that a Behemoth-class Amnion defensive has made an incursion into human space. This did not occur near their own frontier – which might be excused – but rather many light-years beyond the limits of any non-hostile rationale. In fact, the defensive has broached the Massif-5 system, where it was engaged in heavy combat by UMCP cruiser *Punisher*.'

Len fluttered his hands. 'I know all that. I can read.'

Maxim ignored the interruption.

'Warden Dios offers no explanation for this incursion, other than to suggest that the defensive is – or was – hunting UMCP gap scout *Trumpet*, presumably seeking to destroy that vessel.' The Special Counsel digressed momentarily. 'In this he must be correct. There is no conceivable strategic benefit to be gained by an attack on Valdor Industrial. Valdor might well repulse the assault.' The Station was massively armed. 'The defensive might be lost to no purpose.'

Then he resumed. 'Fortuitously *Trumpet* has escaped. And now *Punisher* has broken off the engagement, leaving an Amnion defensive alive in human space, in an effort to protect *Trumpet* further. Again Warden Dios offers no explanation, but he patently considers *Trumpet* – or the people aboard her – more important than his sworn duty to defend human space.'

By degrees a look of nausea seemed to take over Abrim Len's weak face. Maxim smiled inwardly as he continued, although his demeanor gave no hint of satisfaction – or scorn.

'Still without explanation, Warden Dios reveals that UMCPED Director Min Donner is aboard *Punisher*. No doubt he cites this detail to convince us that *Punisher* behaved correctly in breaking off her engagement.'

'We're lucky.' The President made an unsuccessful effort to project confidence. He may have been trying to reassure himself. 'Enforcement is her job. And she's good at it. If she couldn't finish that defensive, no one could.'

Still Maxim plowed ahead, cutting the ground along the lines he desired.

'I mentioned omissions. Certainly the omission of any useful account of all these actions is significant. But there are others.

'Warden Dios neglects to observe that *Trumpet* is the vessel which convicted illegal Angus Thermopyle and Com-Mine Security Deputy Chief Milos Taverner' – Maxim permitted himself a trace of sarcasm – 'are purported to have stolen in their escape from UMCPHQ. And he also fails to report what *Punisher* was doing in the Massif-5 system.'

Len gave a sound like a low groan. 'I suppose you're going to tell me she shouldn't have been there. We have warships around VI all the time. For good reason.'

Maxim nodded to placate the President. 'The vessel currently assigned to the defense of Valdor Industrial is UMCP cruiser *Vehemence*. She was sent to relieve *Punisher* after *Pun-*

isher had endured a long and, I believe, damaging tour of duty.

'But *Punisher* never came to dock at UMCPHQ. As soon as she entered the gap range restricted for use by UMCP ships, she altered course and headed outward again.' Maxim had never been able to penetrate the veils of obfuscation which concealed the heart of UMCPHQ, but his authority sufficed to extract this kind of information. 'Min Donner must have joined ship then. Earlier she was known to be on-station. We have reports from her following Godsen Frik's murder.'

His tone conveyed no particular emphasis as he concluded, 'With the UMCPED director aboard, *Punisher* left UMCPHQ control space on a course for Com-Mine Station.'

Abrim Len's reaction was a rewarding blend of surprise and dismay. 'What, Com-Mine?' he protested. '*Com-Mine*? Not VI?'

Maxim noted with some gratification that Len didn't question the accuracy of this revelation.

'You begin to see the pattern, Mr President.' He was sure that Len saw no such thing. '*Punisher*'s stated mission – to the extent that it has been made known to us – was to guard against reports of unusual hostile activity along the frontier near the Com-Mine belt. Yet suddenly we find her in the Massif-5 system. We find *Trumpet* in the Massif-5 system, although UMCPDA Director Hashi Lebwohl asked us to believe that Captain Thermopyle and Deputy Chief Taverner had fled toward Thanatos Minor in forbidden space. And in addition' – he spoke slowly to give each word its full weight – 'by a coincidence which beggars description, we find a Behemoth-class Amnion defensive there as well.'

The President sighed. 'I'm too tired to see patterns, Maxim.' His look of nausea was growing stronger. 'I want them explained to me.'

'Very well,' Maxim replied as if he were acquiescing.

'Mr President, I believe that Captain Thermopyle and Deputy Chief Taverner did not escape from UMCPHQ. I believe they were sent into forbidden space to commit some act – I can hardly guess what – which the Amnion would be unable to countenance. Then they fled deep into human space. This was necessary so that the response of the Amnion would be unmistakable, and yet would present no direct danger to Earth. Any threat to Earth would have been too extreme to be useful.

'*Punisher* went to the frontier with Min Donner aboard to ensure that *Trumpet* was indeed able to flee. Thereafter she followed *Trumpet* to Massif-5, where she awaited this incursion.

'Finally I am certain that all these events occurred because Warden Dios wished it so.'

Gradually Len slid downward until his head rested on the back of the sofa. He stared at the ceiling with his mouth open.

'My conclusion is this,' Maxim pronounced. 'I am convinced that the director of the United Mining Companies Police has deliberately precipitated an act of war in order to stampede the Governing Council for Earth and Space into withdrawing support for my investigation.'

Here he quickened his pace so that the President would have no opportunity to interrupt.

'Evidence has been coming to light which suggests the most heinous kinds of malfeasance and corruption. Warden Dios' probity,' his insufferable air of moral superiority, 'is under question, his power is endangered. Therefore he seeks to protect his position by persuading us that we must not threaten him now. He wishes us to believe that the risk of challenging him is too great at a time when we face the possibility of war.'

Abrim Len flapped a hand, asking Maxim to stop. Maxim complied at once: he was ready to let the President speak.

Len continued studying the ceiling as if it frightened him. After a moment he muttered, 'And you deduce all this from, what, *Punisher*'s presence near VI? Min Donner's presence aboard *Punisher*?'

Maxim's tone sharpened. 'I deduce it from the explanations

200

which have been omitted.' He made no effort to muffle his underlying vehemence now. 'I deduce it from the sheer scale of the coincidences involved. And I deduce it from the knowledge that Warden Dios' position is so precarious as to be untenable.

'Do you doubt me, Mr President?' he challenged. 'Then tell me how you account for the fact that *Punisher* broke off her engagement with the defensive. Min Donner is renowned for her unswerving rectitude, as well as for her pugnacity. Why would she turn aside from her obvious duty, if she had not been given orders to let the defensive live – to reduce the risk that this incursion will become a full-scale war? Warden Dios desires the threat, not the actuality. His malfeasance may be so pervasive that the UMCP is no longer equipped or positioned to pursue a war.'

'*Punisher* was damaged,' Len put in weakly. 'You said that yourself. Warden claims she couldn't beat the defensive.' He paused, then added, 'That ship has super-light proton cannon.'

Maxim nodded, although he conceded nothing. 'No doubt the director speaks factually. But if you think that weakens my argument, ask yourself why *Punisher* was chosen for this assignment. Perhaps it was because she could plausibly claim that she was unable to destroy the defensive.'

There he stopped. He had made his case clear enough for a half-wit to comprehend it. Now he had to await the President's official reaction.

Len scrutinized the doom which he apparently saw displayed overhead. Despite his slumped posture, his tension was palpable. Still he refused to look at Maxim. With an attempt at asperity, he asked, 'Maxim, what do you want? When do we get to the part where you "simplify" my position?'

The distress he caused Abrim Len gave Maxim a bitter satisfaction. He was too well focused to show his pleasure, however. Instead he concentrated on his purposes.

'I have expressed my concerns, Mr President,' he replied, his tone studiously meek. 'Clearly they must be presented to the Council. So much is unavoidable. Humankind's future rests on our evaluation of Warden Dios' integrity.

'Unfortunately this burden falls to you. I lack the official standing to bear it for you. As Special Counsel charged with investigating the Angus Thermopyle case, I have no authority to address an emergency session called to consider an act of war.

'What I "want", Mr President,' he pronounced with his utmost diffidence, 'is to spare you an unpleasant duty. If you will grant the necessary authorization, I will take on the responsibility for prosecuting my concerns.' Just the sort of confrontation Abrim Len loathed. 'In addition, of course,' he expanded speciously, 'I will accept the risk of embarrassment – or perhaps I should say humiliation – if my concerns are shown to be false.'

Len's limbs twitched. With a jerk, he turned a gap-mouthed stare toward Maxim. His nausea had retreated into the background: assessments filled his gaze. He may have been trying to gauge the scale of Maxim's ambitions. Or he may simply have been wondering whether he could accept Maxim's offer.

Finally he closed his mouth, cleared his throat. When he replied, his voice seemed to come from some other room, muted by distance. 'If you can talk Sen Abdullah into giving you his formal proxy – and if it's received in my office before the emergency session – I'll recognize you in his place. It's irregular, but I can stretch the rules of order that far. You'll have as much "authority to speak" as any other Member.'

At once Maxim rose to his feet. 'Thank you, Mr President.' He already knew that he could obtain Abdullah's proxy. The Eastern Union Senior Member hated Warden Dios. Some of his constituents had lost fortunes when Dios had helped Holt Fasner engineer the bankruptcy and absorption of Sagittarius Exploration.

Maxim didn't wait for Abrim Len to dismiss him. As unobtrusively as possible, he left the President's office suite.

By God, Cleatus Fane was going to regret refusing to speak to him. Special Counsel Maxim Igensard had just demonstrated that he was a force to be reckoned with.

MARC

It was typical of his kind that the loss of *Soar* – and of his fellow Amnion aboard – meant nothing to Marc Vestabule.

The ship itself had been merely a technological artifact: temporarily useful as an ally; ultimately more interesting for the methods of production it represented than for itself. Its human crew was exactly that: human rather than Amnion; significant only because they served the Amnion – and might become available for research. And the Amnion aboard *Soar* were expendable. The protein soup from which more Amnion might be grown was plentiful: any Amnioni could excrete it by the liter at need. Therefore any individual could be replaced by another with the same abilities and characteristics.

Even Milos Taverner was not to be lamented, despite his precious heritage. Physically he was a near-perfect transformation; better than Marc Vestabule. The Mind/Union had achieved important advances. But psychologically he was a failed experiment: he had retained too little of his past identity. An Amnioni who appeared human, but who thought, spoke and acted Amnion, would be too easily detected; therefore useless against humankind.

Like all his fellows, Marc Vestabule wasted neither attention nor emotion on the death of *Soar*.

On the other hand, the fact that *Soar* had turned against *Calm Horizons* required a great deal of attention. Specifically it required Marc Vestabule's attention. He had been invested with decisiveness aboard *Calm Horizons*. And he remembered more of his former humanity than any other Amnioni like him.

Because he remembered, he was not replaceable.

Sorus Chatelaine's betrayal had been quintessentially human: no Amnioni could have imagined – much less carried out – such an action. Even Marc Vestabule only grasped it with considerable effort. To contemplate its implications caused him a form of nausea so fundamental that it might have been ribonucleic.

Nevertheless he did contemplate them. The dilemma of *Trumpet*'s escape made that necessary.

Many of his memories were gone, but he could still recollect the end of his time aboard the human ship he had served, *Viable Dreams*. He remembered its capture by treachery. He remembered the vindictive fury of the man who had taken it into Amnion space in order to sell its crew: Angus Thermopyle. And he remembered his own desperation –

The Amnion did not comprehend terror or frenzy. They understood urgency: they were capable of haste. Their dedication to their own purposes was complete – and completely organic. But they were not genetically encoded for desperation. They could not encompass it.

Marc Vestabule still did.

It was the key to understanding humankind. Sorus Chatelaine had betrayed *Calm Horizons* – despite the dictates of her own self-interest – out of desperation. Similarly, desperation had driven Angus Thermopyle to sell the crew of *Viable Dreams*: it drove him and his companions aboard *Trumpet* now. And the results of *Soar*'s treason had been disastrous. *Trumpet* had fled intact. A UMCP cruiser had received *Trumpet*'s broadcast. Beyond question the outcome of *Trumpet*'s escape would also be disastrous.

Once the desperation was grasped, the nature of the disaster became possible to imagine.

Trumpet would approach some large human station – or perhaps Earth itself. Alternatively the small vessel might join forces with its defender, the UMCP cruiser. Then the formula for the mutagen immunity drug would become broadly known. Until a means was devised to circumvent or mask the drug, humankind would be effectively impervious to absorption or transformation.

That invulnerability might inspire the species to initiate a war: a war of ships and weaponry; a technological war, which the Amnion could not win.

Yet even if humankind did not react so extremely, they would be forewarned of Amnion researches into near-C acceleration. Given their mechanistic ingenuity, and their vast means of production, they might well design weapons or defenses to counter the greater velocity of future Amnion vessels. They might devise the means to acquire such velocities themselves.

And their efforts would be inspired by *Calm Horizons'* own actions, which they would doubtless consider an act of war, as well as by *Trumpet's* broadcast.

Lastly – the heaviest blow – the opportunity which the force-grown template called Davies Hyland represented would be lost. If a human could be made Amnion, and yet retain the ability to speak and act and pass as human, the purposes of the Amnion might be achieved at one stroke. That great accomplishment would make possible a war of infiltration and mutation; a war which humankind could not win.

Only an opportunity to study Davies Hyland might serve to counter the other harms which *Trumpet* could do.

Sorus Chatelaine's – and Angus Thermopyle's – desperation had created a dilemma which none of Marc Vestabule's fellows were equipped to evaluate.

He had been invested with decisiveness aboard *Calm Horizons*. After a period of rigorous contemplation – and acute nausea – he concluded that the complex threats of *Trumpet's* escape could only be answered by an act of even greater desperation.

He decided nothing in isolation. The air of *Calm Horizons* was rich with communication of all kinds: information and analysis; emotion and commentary. Pheromones filled with language the sweet atmosphere which the Amnion craved. Marc Vestabule was an Amnioni, alive to the scents and hues of nucleotidal communion; nourished by it.

Yet he was truly unique among his fellows. Furthermore they all recognized his uniqueness: they recognized its value. Without that recognition he would not have been invested. The conclusions he reached were neither understood nor questioned. By a common consent of the most profound form, his uniqueness was granted scope.

The risks were great. Indeed, they were vast. If *Calm Horizons* failed and died, the costs would be terrible. And Marc Vestabule could do nothing to diminish them. Like symbiotic crystalline resonance transmitters, gap courier drones were difficult to grow; hugely expensive in time, effort and expertise. He was fortunate that he had been supplied with the former. He had no access to the latter. Therefore if he acted on his memories of desperation he would be unable to inform or forewarn his kind of their peril.

Nevertheless when *Calm Horizons* reentered normal space beyond the Massif-5 system, the defensive turned at once and began spanning the dimensional gap on a direct course for Earth.

WARDEN

Warden Dios wasn't alone in the CO Room. Techs sat at their stations nearby, linking him to every facet of his domain; listening to their respective communications traffic with receivers set into their ears so that he wouldn't be distracted by incessant chatter; studying the same displays and readouts he watched. He didn't concentrate on what he saw, however: he left that to his staff. While they worked, he focused his energies on trying to think like an Amnioni.

Some of his people – especially those assigned to UMCPHQ Center – believed that he was prescient. They didn't know how else to account for the fact that he so often seemed to be precisely where he was most needed in emergencies. Why was he there, if he couldn't see the future? His reassuring presence in his personal Command Operations Room minutes or perhaps hours before some crisis developed had no other obvious explanation.

But the UMCP director wasn't blessed – or cursed – with foreknowledge. The searching IR vision of his prosthetic eye told him nothing in advance. To some extent his apparent prescience was simply the outcome of his gift for planning ahead. For the most part, however, his knowledge was not of the future, but of himself. He did what he did out of shame and stubbornness – which was to say, out of fear. He was probably no more fearful than anyone else. Unlike most of the people around him, however, he called his fears by their true names. And he paid attention to them.

That was why he sometimes displayed an almost uncanny ability to be in the right place at the right time.

This time he was in the CO Room because he feared the consequences of his own actions.

Lord knew he had enough of them to worry about. Holt Fasner had ordered him to turn Angus over to Nick Succorso, so that Nick might then be persuaded to kill the other survivors of *Captain's Fancy*, all except Davies Hyland, who would be delivered to the Dragon. Warden had obeyed that order – and undermined it at the same time. Had his subterfuge succeeded? If it hadn't, he was finished. But if it had, young Davies might now have control over Angus. What would he do with that power?

According to Hashi, Davies may have been force-grown with his mother's mind. What would *Morn* do, after experiencing so much brutality from Angus – and so much betrayal from the UMCP?

Vital questions. At another time they might have dominated Warden's thinking. But the specific fear which had brought him here revolved around a different set of consequences.

Punisher had broken off her engagement with the Amnion defensive which had pursued *Trumpet* from forbidden space to Massif-5. That was exactly what Warden would have ordered the cruiser to do. He needed *Trumpet*'s people; needed them desperately. And he wasn't likely to get them if *Punisher* risked her life trying to defeat a far more powerful enemy. He suspected that if Min didn't bring them to him, he would never see Morn and Davies, Angus and Vector.

Unfortunately one consequence was that there was an Amnion defensive loose in human space.

That vessel had failed to kill or capture *Trumpet*. What would she do now? How would Amnion minds approach the dilemma of *Trumpet*'s escape?

Clearly they considered the gap scout worth an act of war, despite their demonstrated reluctance to hazard their genetic imperialism in direct combat. They made everything better than humankind did – ships, weapons, computers – but they didn't make many of anything except more Amnion. They avoided open tests of power because they couldn't match humankind's capacity for mass production. In purely material terms, that defensive was more precious than any five human ships Warden could name.

So what would she *do*, now that her incursion had failed? Would she retreat toward forbidden space – preserve her value to her people? Or would she follow the logic of her intentions against *Trumpet* in some other direction?

Sitting in the CO Room surrounded by techs and screens, consoles and communications traffic, helped Warden think as if he were aboard a warship.

He found it difficult to imagine why the defensive would do anything except run for safety. He'd learned from *Punisher*'s most recent drone that before *Trumpet* left Massif-5 she'd begun broadcasting the formula – good God, *broadcasting the formula!* – for Intertech's antimutagen. Apparently Vector Shaheed had made quick use of Deaner Beckmann's bootleg lab. As a result the mutagen immunity drug was now in effect public knowledge. The formula was recorded in *Punisher*'s datacore. Inevitably it had been – or soon would be – picked up by *some*one around VI. And beyond question the defensive had received it.

Another consequence. Directly or indirectly Warden was responsible for *Trumpet*'s broadcast. Now he considered its implications with a strange mixture of horror and hope.

In truth he hadn't foreseen that *Trumpet*'s people might do something so extravagant. Despite his talent for planning, he hadn't guessed that they would take on the challenge of trying to undo decades of covert malfeasance all by themselves.

He was dismayed by the fact that the Amnion had learned the formula for the immunity drug before it could ever be put to its proper use. At the same time he was excited, almost exalted, by the sheer courage and daring of what *Trumpet* had done. If he was right in his belief that Holt Fasner and the UMC posed a graver threat to humankind's future than any alien enmity, then *Trumpet*'s gambit was a veritable beacon of redemption.

Aboard her a handful of men and women had recognized a worthy cause when they saw it – and had committed themselves to it.

That didn't sound like Nick Succorso. It sounded like something Morn's parents might have done.

Her son must have received Warden's ciphered message.

Not incidentally, *Trumpet*'s broadcast also didn't sound like the work of a genetic kaze. As far as Warden was concerned, Hashi's hypothesis had effectively collapsed. To the extent that Morn was a kaze, she'd been aimed at her target by Warden himself, not by the Amnion.

So of course the defensive would burn for forbidden space with all the force of her drives. Of course. The dissemination of Intertech's antimutagen was only a setback, not a defeat. For the present, humankind had developed a way to counter genetic imperialism. But the Amnion were magicians of biochemistry. Given time, they would certainly devise a way to neutralize the antimutagen. The alien warship would do everything in her power to provide that time.

Wouldn't she?

The logic of the situation was plain. Surely the greatest immediate danger to the Amnion was not the formula itself, but rather the possibility that humankind would use the temporary advantage of their immunity to launch a full-scale war. And surely, therefore, the defensive would abandon her intentions against *Trumpet* in order to forewarn forbidden space.

That argument seemed reasonable enough on its face. Nevertheless it was human reasoning. Warden Dios didn't trust it.

Instead of easing, his fear settled deeper into his chest; just behind his sternum. Apprehension seemed to gnaw at the bottom of his heart like buried skinworms.

What if he was wrong about everything, had misjudged everything? What if the Amnion warship did something which defied human logic?

What if the entire elaborate edifice of his desires came crashing down right *now*, when by his own actions he'd made humankind uniquely vulnerable to disaster?

That thought scared him to the marrow of his bones. He already had all the culpability he could bear. He didn't want to carry any more crimes to his grave.

For that reason – and because it was his job – he'd provided as best he could for the defense of Earth and UMCPHQ. Eight gunboats and pocket cruisers held various orbits around the planet, linked to each other by the vast scan net which covered the whole solar system. The battlewagon *Sledgehammer* was still a long way out; but guns as powerful as hers would be able to make a contribution within eighteen or twenty hours. The cruiser *Adventurous* – old and underpowered, but still spaceworthy – was closer: the scan net marked her approach from the far side of the planet. And the destroyer *Valor* would return home soon.

If the crisis waited a week to materialize, another battlewagon like *Sledgehammer* might be ready to emerge from the shipyards.

Unfortunately there wasn't much else anyone could do. None of Earth's orbital stations had been designed as weapons-platforms. The charters of the commercial stations prohibited heavy armamentation. And UMCPHQ had been built on the implicit assumption that any war which came this close was already lost.

Warden Dios wasn't prescient. He was terrified.

Nevertheless he didn't show it. The techs around him would have needed prosthetic vision like his in order to catch any glimpse of his fear. He sat solidly in his command chair, as if he couldn't be moved unless he wished it. His big fists rested like stones on the arms of his seat. His breathing was calm; deep and even. His one human eye glittered with a penetrating concentration which most of his people had learned to trust.

The atmosphere in the CO Room – and in UMCPHQ Center beyond the walls of the Room – was at once more expectant and more relaxed than it would have been in his absence. Because he was here, his people sensed that something was about to happen. At the same time they believed they would be able to handle it – whatever it might be – as long as he watched over them.

Therefore he kept his fear to himself. It was transcended by his determination to fail no one who relied on him: not his own people; not the GCES; not Morn and her companions; not humankind. He'd played his game of complicity against Holt Fasner long enough; perhaps too long. Now he was done with it.

If he could manage it – and if *Trumpet* didn't let him down – he intended to undo the harm of his life's mistakes.

His only reaction was a lift of one eyebrow when a tech murmured suddenly, 'Director, I have a call for you from UMCHO. It's CEO Fasner.'

Warden nodded an acknowledgment; but he didn't accept the call immediately. Instead he took a moment to consider whether or not he wanted to speak to Holt privately. In private his people wouldn't hear how his master treated him. But they also wouldn't hear how he responded.

It was time for him to begin showing where he stood.

'Put it on the speakers,' he told the tech. 'I'll talk to him here.'

'Yes, sir.' The tech tapped keys, and the CO Room speakers came to life with a soft magnetic pop.

Warden turned his head toward his pickup. 'Holt,' he said at once, 'can we keep this short? I've got my hands full here.'

'"Short"?' Holt snorted angrily. He may have assumed that Warden was alone. Or he may not have cared. 'I'm your goddamn *boss*, Ward. You'll talk to me as long as I want, whenever I want.'

'That doesn't make sense,' Warden retorted. He spoke as if he didn't know that all his techs were watching him. 'If I spend all my time talking to you, I can't do my job.'

'Listen to me.' Beneath the surface of Holt's ire, a deeper passion boiled and spat. 'Talking to me *is* your job. You *work* for me. And right now you're hanging by a thread. You're precipitating more disasters than I can manage all at once.'

Not long ago, Norna Fasner had told Warden that her son *fears death too much. It distorts his thinking. He wants to live forever.* At the time the idea had baffled Warden. But now he understood it better. He thought he could hear a hunger for that impossible achievement in the UMC CEO's voice.

For years now, the whole thrust of Holt's policy toward the Amnion had been to maintain an uneasy peace. Peace was essential because it enabled trade; wealth. But if the peace became too secure, too safe, complacency would set in. The UMCP – and through them the UMC – would lose their moral authority, their necessity. Holt's power over human space would diminish. And that in turn would reduce his leverage with the Amnion; his ability to extract profits. He'd pushed to obtain the passage of the Preempt Act for the same reason that he'd sanctioned the covert – and only the covert – use of Intertech's immunity drug: to disturb both the Amnion and humankind; keep the peace uneasy.

Who benefited from this approach? Only Holt Fasner and the UMC. And yet the question inevitably arose: why did Holt care? He was already richer and more powerful than anyone in the history of the planet. What in God's name drove him to the acquisition of still more wealth and more power?

Warden had come to the conclusion that Holt coveted benefits of another kind altogether. Norna had given him the hint he needed to see Holt's ambitions in a new light.

The UMC CEO had ordered Warden to turn Angus over to Nick Succorso. In exchange for a ship, as well as for his own personal cyborg, Nick was supposed to kill everyone except Davies Hyland. Holt wanted Morn's son.

If the Amnion could force-grow young Davies and imprint him with Morn's mind, what was to prevent them from processing any number of human fetuses and imprinting them all with *Holt's* mind? What was to prevent the Dragon from effectively living forever?

If he acquired enough wealth and power to offer the Amnion something greater than mere raw materials – human and otherwise – or technological methodologies, he might

213

be able to make a deal with them. Like Satan himself, the Father of Lies, the Amnion kept their bargains.

All Holt needed was a demonstration that the Amnion were indeed capable of imprinting one human mind on another – and imprinting it intact. Then he would be able to go ahead.

Warden shuddered at the implications while he listened to the UMC CEO.

Holt hadn't paused. He was saying sarcastically, 'The Amnion have committed an act of war, in case you didn't notice. I'm holding you accountable for that – you and your goddamn covert operations, trusting Billingate to an illegal like Thermopyle and a known traitor like Taverner.

'Now the votes are going to hold an emergency session. They'll go crazy. They'll probably think anybody who twitches a finger is a kaze about to explode.' Holt laughed – a harsh, mirthless sound, like breaking sticks. 'I'm holding you accountable for that, too. Thanks to you and your precious Koina Hannish, they're all a-twitter with responsibility. They'll probably try to do something phenomenally stupid, like declaring war on Amnion space. If Cleat can't soothe them somehow, you've done us more harm than a whole damn flotilla of incursions.

'And what are you doing about it? I ask myself,' Holt sneered. 'How do you "do your job"? As far as I can tell, you seem to think the Amnion are going to attack *here* next. First you recalled every warship in reach, which is sure to make the votes even more panicky, even though a hydro-cephalic *child* could tell you that defensive is long gone by this time. And now you've synchronized your goddamn orbit with Suka Bator.'

This was true. With an enormous expenditure of energy, Center had adjusted UMCPHQ's centrifugal rush so that the station maintained a position above the GCES island.

'It's like you think we're already at war,' Holt finished mordantly. 'And we're losing.'

Warden considered shouting his fear at Holt. He considered silencing his pickup and refusing to speak to the Dragon again. Then he responded simply, 'It's a precaution.

I don't want to be occluded. I don't know what's going to happen.' A heartbeat later he remarked, 'I notice you've done the same thing.'

After a series of power-intensive adjustments, UMC Home Office now sailed the dark little more than a hundred thousand k away in an orbit which echoed UMCPHQ's.

'Damn right,' Holt retorted. 'That's because I don't *trust* you, Ward. If you don't want to be occluded, I sure as hell don't. If you decide it's time for something even more destructive than what you've already done, I intend to react fast.'

Warden jerked up his head. Anger drummed in his heart, despite his self-control.

'"Destructive", Holt? Would you care to be more specific?'

He meant to preserve humankind, not destroy it. And the UMCP had a valid function: he intended to preserve that also. But there were other issues as well –

He'd done everything in his power to make sure Holt didn't know about Vector Shaheed's broadcast. If the CEO didn't get that information directly from UMCPHQ, he wouldn't hear it at all until some UMC flunky on VI picked it up and sent out a drone. Or until he learned it from Cleatus Fane at the emergency session. Still Warden wished for confirmation.

'That video conference,' Holt snapped at once. 'Trusting Taverner. Allowing Hannish to tell the votes you're neutral about a Bill of Severance. Letting kazes roam around at will, for Christ's sake. Panicking the votes now.

'I want to know what you're up to, Ward. What in hell do you think you're doing?'

No mention of antimutagens or formulas. Warden nodded to himself.

'What do you *want* me to do, Holt?' he countered.

Holt's reply was a snarl in the CO Room speakers. 'I want you to answer the question. I'm trying to decide whether to fire your ass.'

The UMCP director sighed to cover his ire. He was done acting like Holt's servant; done being the man who did Holt's dirty work. And he ached to let Holt know the truth. He was sick of lies. At the same time he couldn't risk being fired. Not now: not when so many gambles and so much pain had reached the verge of fruition or ruin. He still had to be careful.

'Mostly I'm waiting for news.' Like you. 'Information I can act on.'

He'd already given Holt his rationale for his video conference with the GCES. Long ago he'd explained why he'd chosen Milos Taverner to accompany Angus to Billingate. Now he pointedly declined to comment on – much less justify – Koina's response to Captain Vertigus' Bill of Severance.

Instead he continued in a flat voice, 'Min has gone after *Trumpet*. When she's in range, she'll deal with whoever she finds aboard. I already have your orders about that. They'll come home as soon as they can. Then maybe we'll know where we stand.'

Holt's silence suggested that he was withholding judgment.

Warden tightened his grip on himself. Now, he thought. Do it now. Get it over with.

'As far as those kazes are concerned,' he added, 'DA Director Lebwohl and ED Chief of Security Mandich know who's responsible.' His tone belied the threat he wanted Holt to hear. 'When they finish preparing their evidence, I'll make a public accusation.' To forestall an interruption, he stated, 'But I'm not going to name names until I have *proof*. The culprit is too highly placed.

'Other than that,' he finished as if he hadn't already said too much, 'I'm waiting to see what our encroaching Amnion defensive does next.

'Is that what you want, Holt? If it isn't, you'd better say so. In a few more hours it's going to be too damn late for any of us to change anything. The Council will hold its emergency session, and we'll have to live with the results.'

For a long moment Holt didn't speak. The communications channel between UMCPHQ and UMCHO brought in ambiguous hints of static; anger; apprehension. The fear gnawing in Warden's guts sharpened at the chance he'd taken. Nevertheless he sat motionless and waited, gambling that

Holt wouldn't make any decisions until he knew how much danger he was in.

Finally the CEO said slowly, 'I'll accept the rest for now.' He seemed to be restraining fury. 'Cleat can handle the votes. But I don't like your approach to those kazes.'

'Too bad,' Warden retorted roughly. 'The UMC is a good source of suspects. So is the GCES – hell, so are we. I'm not going to taint our investigation by discussing it with you, or Abrim Len, or anyone else. When the time comes to press charges, I intend to make sure they stick.'

'Listen, Ward –' Holt snapped.

'*No*, Holt,' Warden shot back. '*You* listen. This conversation is on record. My CO staff can hear both ends. I am *not* going to taint our investigation by discussing it with you.'

Again Holt fell silent. The speakers conveyed a muffled, arrhythmic series of beats, as if Holt were pounding his fists on his desk. Warden was certain that Holt would have lashed out at him in private. Only the potential consequences of being 'on record' restrained the CEO.

Abruptly Holt replied, 'I'm going to assume you know what you're doing.' That wasn't a concession: it was a threat to match Warden's. 'I'll let you get on with it for now.

'But when you finish collecting your evidence,' he pronounced fiercely, 'you will discuss it with me before you make it public. That's a direct order. Do you understand me?'

Warden sighed. 'Of course I do.' He'd kept his job. Unfortunately that relief did nothing to ease his deeper dread. 'I've been taking your orders for years. If I didn't understand them by now, I would deserve to be fired.'

'That,' Holt snorted, 'is what worries me.

'I'm watching you, Ward. I'm watching everything. Don't make the mistake of thinking you don't need me.'

Warden shrugged to himself. 'Is that all, Holt? I still have a job to do here.'

'Just one more thing.' Apparently Holt wasn't done warning him yet. 'I have a message for you.

'I talked to my mother recently. She asked me to tell you that it isn't enough.'

Warden wasn't prescient: absolutely not. But Norna Fasner might as well have been. With nothing except video broadcasts and Holt's contrived hints to go on, she'd grasped what Warden was doing. And she wanted him to succeed –

'Tell her I know that,' he answered brusquely.

Before Holt could reply, Warden silenced his pickup, then ordered his tech to close the communications channel.

Obediently the speakers went dead.

With a shift of his shoulders, he settled against the back of his seat and tried to relax.

Norna was right. Without *Trumpet* he was finished. Even if Hashi and Chief Mandich found the proof he wanted, Holt wouldn't fall. He could too easily sacrifice an 'overzealous' subordinate and claim innocence for himself. Because he was the boss, he could even take credit for the UMCP's investigation. The only effective way to challenge him was by attacking the UMCP itself; by turning Warden's deliberate complicity against the UMC CEO. And the only available arena for that challenge was the upcoming emergency session of the GCES.

So it became Koina's job. Warden had given her everything she needed – except proof. Now his fate was in her hands.

And in Morn Hyland's. If she and Davies had received Angus' priority-codes, they would make *Trumpet*'s decisions.

It isn't enough.

He couldn't relax. His fear ate at him too keenly.

From the bottom of his heart he hoped that Min's loyalty to the UMCP – and to him – wouldn't inspire her to get in Morn's way.

'Director –' The tech's throat was so tight that she nearly choked.

Her tone caught him; caught the whole CO Room in a clutch of tension. Instantly alert, he wheeled his seat toward her.

'What is it?'

The woman swallowed convulsively. 'Ship coming in, sir. Just resumed tard. Too close. *Way* too close. She's braking hard, but she's practically on top of us.'

Warden flashed a look at the scan displays, saw the ship's blip perched on a torch of braking thrust. God, she was less than half a million k out. Numbers scrolled rapidly up the screen as computers calculated her deceleration rate. The figures projected that she would be able to stop outside UMCPHQ's orbit. That was good news – so far. But by the time she matched the station's velocity she would be within fifty thousand k.

What the hell did she think she was *doing*?

'Get me id,' he demanded sharply. 'Is that *Punisher*?'

The vector was wrong for *Sledgehammer*: even if she'd attempted a blink crossing, she would approach on a different trajectory. He didn't expect *Valor* to arrive so soon. And *Adventurous* was still occluded: the scan net showed her on the far side of the planet.

'No, sir,' the tech forced out. 'She isn't broadcasting, no id, nothing,' and she should have, any ship this near stations and traffic was insane if she didn't broadcast id. 'But that isn't *Punisher*'s emission signature.'

Warden started to repeat, Get me id! then bit the words back. His people knew their jobs: they were working feverishly. Outside the CO Room, Center had become an electric rush of activity. Traffic officers shouted into their pickups, urgently hailing the stranger for a response; warning other ships and platforms; signaling *Sledgehammer* and *Adventurous*, as well as Earth's cordon of gunboats and pocket cruisers. Collision alarms sounded in case the incoming ship didn't or couldn't complete her deceleration. Klaxons called Warden's people to defense stations. Techs started charging UMCPHQ's few guns. He didn't need to shout for id, or anything else.

In any case the fear eating at his stomach had already answered the question.

'Director!' the tech announced abruptly. 'She isn't one of ours. No signature on record.' Therefore she wasn't a registered human ship. Every ship built legally in human space filed a complete energy profile with UMCPHQ. If she didn't, she wouldn't be given permission to dock anywhere. The woman swallowed again, then finished, 'The computer says she's a Behemoth-class Amnion defensive.'

An Amnion warship. For a moment Warden's heart stumbled to a halt. Here.

She must have been the same one Min had engaged to protect *Trumpet*. Scan made that clear: the vessel's approach vector was wrong for forbidden space, but right for Massif-5.

This was an act of war with a vengeance. Failing to kill *Trumpet* had made the Amnioni desperate.

Unfortunately Warden was virtually helpless. UMCPHQ's cannon were still seconds or minutes away from being charged. Even if they'd been ready to fire, however, they stood little chance against a Behemoth-class defensive's shields and sinks. And the defensive was already near enough to strike.

If the Amnioni attacked, he had no real way to fight back.

ANGUS

Angus was in turmoil. Machine stresses seethed and yowled inside him like ghouls: his welding haunted him. Events and his own choices – the decisions he'd made because Morn wanted them – had pushed him far out along a limb of logic for which his programming seemed to contain no clear instruction-set.

He wasn't allowed to return to UMCPHQ and Earth: his datacore was clear on that. Until someone coded his release from this specific restriction, he was supposed to stay away. But he'd blocked his codes. Nothing Isaac was ordered to do reached him. Therefore the restriction remained in force.

He tried to subvert it by leaving Morn in command and Mikka on helm. Hell, he tried to subvert it by leaving the bridge. *He* wasn't making the decisions, or putting them into effect. Surely if he didn't try to break the rules himself, his computer wouldn't turn against him for letting someone else do so?

To some extent the gambit succeeded. Apparently his commands hadn't been written to prevent others from taking him to Earth. By luck or stubbornness he'd found his way into an area of ambiguity between imposed limitations; a combination of actions and circumstances which Hashi Lebwohl and Warden Dios hadn't foreseen. He could still move and talk and plan without being countermanded by his zone implants.

Yet he *was* going to Earth. And the restriction kept its force. The conflicting impulses of his computer as it ran its inadequate decision-routines filled him with pressure and a strangely impersonal mental anguish, as shrill and weird as banshees wailing over lost souls. Whenever he tried to think, he felt that his skull was about to burst through his scalp.

Other restrictions remained active as well. His threats against Min Donner and Dolph Ubikwe had been pure bluff, empty starshine: he couldn't hurt UMCP personnel. He'd been allowed to hit the ED director only because Morn was in danger. For reasons of his own, Hashi Lebwohl – or Warden Dios, more likely – intended Angus to defend her. Unfortunately that was the absolute limit of what he could do. Even when he struck, his strength was restrained so that he didn't strike too hard. If anyone had risked facing him down, they would have learned that his welded impotence still held.

He hated that. It terrified him. He was a convicted illegal on a ship full of cops, on his way to UMCPHQ; and he couldn't so much as punch anybody unless Morn was threatened.

In addition he had other problems – problems that had nothing to do with his instruction-sets.

Morn wanted to tell her story in public – hers, and Vector's, and his. If she could, she wanted to tell it to the entire fucking Council. And he was helping her despite a visceral abhorrence so profound that it made him shudder.

But it was all shit: too much crap for one mere cruiser to process. God, the stuff was probably hip-deep on the bridge. He hated philanthropists of every description. The stink of their benevolence sickened him. He knew from experience that the people who did the most harm were the ones who said they were trying to do somebody else good. How did they get their goddamn resources to begin with? By raping and robbing the same people they said they wanted to help. As a baby he'd lain helpless in his crib while his mother exercised her madness on him because people who said they wished to do good kept her alive.

Morn didn't fit the pattern, however. She'd freed him from

his priority-codes: she kept saving his life. He did what she asked for reasons as binding as any prewritten commandment. He believed her when she told him what she wanted. And what she wanted – even though it made no sense of any kind – was to hold the cops accountable for their crimes.

If he let himself think about that, he liked it. It was about time somebody held those superior bastards accountable. And her story would make a nice little jolt of revenge for what Hashi Lebwohl and Warden Dios had done to him.

But he couldn't afford to think about it. He knew it was doomed. He didn't believe for a second that Min Donner and Dolph Ubikwe and *Punisher*'s crew and the UMCP and Warden Dios were going to just stand there quietly while Morn shoveled disgrace onto their heads. And if they did, he wasn't sure he would survive to see it. The tumult in his head might kill him long before then.

Despite his feral grin and confident manner, he felt packed with ruin, like a sun about to go nova. None of his turmoil showed as he followed Captain Dolph Ubikwe off *Punisher*'s bridge. Nevertheless it ruled him.

Captain Ubikwe had said that he was going to his cabin. To throw up. Angus had accompanied him, intending to keep him hostage. By the time they'd walked five meters past the aperture into the main body of the ship, however, Angus knew he couldn't do it. His datacore might have allowed it: his fear refused absolutely. If he didn't find some way out of his imposed distress soon, he would begin to gibber and drool like an idiot.

But he was still Angus Thermopyle: welded and constricted; so crowded with other men's malice that there was hardly room for his own; but still himself at the core. He'd butchered and raided his way around Com-Mine for years until his fatal flight from the abyss had brought him into contact with *Starmaster* and Morn. He was at his best when he was terrified.

He followed *Punisher*'s dark, angry captain twenty meters down the corridor in the cruiser's centrifugal g. He followed him into a lift upward. But when they left the lift, he stopped.

'All right, fat man,' he announced. 'That's far enough. I've changed my mind.'

Dolph Ubikwe turned slowly, his eyes wary. In a deep voice he grumbled, 'You've got a hell of a nerve calling *me* fat.'

Angus grinned; slapped his belly with a lunatic show of good humor. 'This isn't fat. It's brains. I think with my guts. That's why I'm still alive.'

The captain snorted. 'Are you sure you've changed your mind? Maybe it's just indigestion.'

Angus shook his head. 'I don't trust you, fat man. Sitting with you in your cabin to keep you out of trouble sounds good in theory. In practice it has a couple of problems.'

Dolph cocked an eyebrow; waited for Angus to go on.

Dishonestly cheerful, Angus explained, 'As far as I'm concerned, you're the most dangerous man aboard. I'm not worried about the high-and-mighty Min Donner. She has her own reasons for letting Morn take over. Hell, she's wearing them like a shipsuit, she can't hide anything.' He dismissed the ED director with a shrug. 'Besides, Morn can handle her.'

'But you don't think you can handle me?' Captain Ubikwe drawled.

Angus grinned again. 'I *know* you, fat man. This is *your ship*. Giving up command isn't easy. Not for you. I think you don't give a good shit what Director Donner orders you to do. I think you're already plotting to get your ship back.'

Dolph made a show of incredulity. 'Like how?'

'*I* don't know,' Angus sneered. 'Maybe you've got an intercom pickup hidden in your san. Maybe you can fart in code, tell your people to mutiny without saying a word.' He laughed humorlessly. His zone implants projected a manic amusement which bordered on gaiety. 'It might be fun to watch you, see how you do it. But there's another problem.'

'Somehow,' Dolph growled, 'I know you're going to tell me what that is.'

'Damn right I am.' Anger and fear he couldn't express frayed the edges of Angus' tone. 'We're in command at the moment,' Morn and Davies and Mikka and Vector held the bridge, 'but that doesn't change the fact this whole exercise is a death-trap. You fucking cops want us dead. Even if you think you don't, you will. And there're just too goddamn many of you.

'We need a back door,' he pronounced, 'a way out.'

Dolph didn't react. He simply stared at Angus as if he thought the illegal had lost his mind.

'Morn doesn't worry about things like that.' Angus gathered sarcasm in place of fear as he went along. 'Which is why she's tough enough to handle your Min Donner. When she goes, she goes all the way.

'But I don't like it. It makes my stomach hurt.'

'Get to the point,' Captain Ubikwe said darkly. 'I don't like standing here.'

Angus bared his teeth. 'You don't really want to go sit in your cabin.' His tone was poisonously sweet. 'If you can't start a mutiny, you'll just feel sorry for yourself. So instead I'll let you come with me. Help me invent a way out.'

'What if I say no?' Dolph countered. 'What if I like feeling sorry for myself?'

'You don't want to do that,' Angus promised. 'For one thing, I'll have to tie you up, drag you along – and that's so undignified. And for another' – he spread his hands – 'you won't find out what my back door is.'

Dolph studied Angus speculatively. 'Do you really think you can tie me up and drag me?' he asked.

'I'm a goddamn *cyborg*, fat man,' Angus rasped. 'You've already seen my lasers. And I've got plenty of other enhancements.' His reinforced muscles and microprocessor reflexes made him more than a match for the captain. 'Of *course* I can do it.

'But I would rather have help.' Abruptly he scowled as if he were making a concession. 'Who knows? You and your queen of muscle might end up needing a way out as much as I do.'

Captain Ubikwe considered for a moment. Fury he couldn't afford to express compressed his lips, tightened his fleshy cheeks. 'Since you put it that way,' he rumbled finally,

'I'll go along. For a while, anyway. It'll be interesting to see how you plan to betray your friends.'

Betray –? Angus felt a sudden desire to bury his fist in the captain's thick abdomen; but his zone implants stifled the impulse instantly. You sonofabitch! You goddamn cops took my *ship* away from me, and you fucking *dismantled* her! You don't have the *right* to accuse me of anything.

Morn was all he had left.

Still none of his turmoil showed. His pain and urgency were as impotent as babies. 'Good,' he jeered. 'You're learning to think with your guts instead of your gonads. Someday you'll thank me for teaching you how to do that.'

Brusquely he turned back toward the lift.

The keypad beside the doors included an intercom. Watching Dolph sidelong so that the captain couldn't take him by surprise, he thumbed the pickup toggle. As soon as the indicators came to life, he drawled amiably, 'Bridge, this is Angus.'

A moment passed before Morn's voice answered. 'What is it, Angus?' She sounded thin with distance and strain; emaciated by the small speaker.

Angus didn't hesitate: he was too scared. 'Captain Ubikwe and I are going to visit *Trumpet*. Clear it for me. I don't want to have to argue with anybody on the way.'

Morn's tone sharpened. 'What're you doing, Angus?' Apparently the effort of outfacing Min Donner, as well as managing Captain Ubikwe's command, took a toll.

'Don't ask,' Angus retorted. 'You don't need to know.' Trust me, Morn. Haven't I done everything you want? I'm just not in the mood to see any of us end up dead. Before she could reply, he added, 'Send Ciro to join us. He isn't doing you any good. He can help me and Captain Ubikwe.'

Ciro could save time and trouble by showing Angus where and how he'd damaged the drives. And there might be other possibilities, if Ciro felt bad enough to listen to them –

The intercom hinted at protests. Mikka or Davies – or even Min Donner – may have been arguing with Morn. But Morn didn't make Angus wait. 'All right,' she answered as if she'd

226

heard his unspoken appeal. 'Consider it done. Ciro is on his way.'

At once the intercom speaker clicked silent.

Dolph had planted his fists on his hips as if he was about to turn stubborn. 'What do you want that boy for?' he demanded. 'He's already scared out of his head. He doesn't need to help *you*. He needs treatment.'

Angus didn't respond directly. Instead he took Dolph's arm, drew him back toward the lift. 'Come on.' Relief and his zone implants made him positively companionable. 'Let's find out how much the fucking Academy taught you about drive repair.'

Captain Ubikwe opened his mouth in surprise; but he didn't hold back.

Angus released his grip. With Dolph beside him, he headed for the airlock which linked *Punisher* to his crippled ship.

WARDEN

U rgent activity concentrated the atmosphere of
Center. Nearly a hundred men and women sat at
their consoles, studying data, typing furiously, bark-
ing or croaking into their pickups. Communications alone
required at least fifty techs. One of them hailed the approaching defensive insistently, demanding some kind of response:
the others had different duties. Some coordinated
UMCPHQ's efforts to protect itself. Others organized the
cordon of ships; flared tight-beamed warnings and instructions to the planet's diverse clutter of orbital platforms;
rerouted in-system traffic; fielded panic from every direction.
A team of specialists managed the massive job of downloading
information – from Data Storage as well as DA's dedicated
computers – to secure planet-side megaCPUs. And members
of Koina's PR staff began the impossible job of preparing
Earth's vast population for disaster.

In addition, data techs worked to glean and interpret every
available fact about the alien vessel. Operations sent platoons
to ready the evac boats. Gunners tested targ, charged cannon.
Engineers rotated the station to present its best guns and
strongest shields toward the defensive.

The result was a constricted tumult which surged and
throbbed like imminent hysteria.

'Unidentified Amnion vessel, this is UMCPHQ Center.'
The tech's voice was already raw with repetition. 'You must
reply.'

Despite the tension on all sides, however, Warden Dios presided over the turmoil as if he feared nothing. Swiftly scrolling readouts and frenetic blips lit his command board, tracing every action around him. From his CO Room he supervised Center as well as UMCPHQ. But he didn't let their urgency infect him. Impassive as stone, he faced the ruin of humankind and his own dreams as if he knew exactly what was about to happen – and what to do about it. His people needed him now: needed his strength, his clarity. For their sake – and because this was his job – he appeared confident and calm; impregnable.

His true fear and shame he kept entirely to himself.

He was responsible for this threat. Directly or indirectly, he'd caused the alien defensive to come here. Now he had damn well better do something about it.

For a start, he meant to take a risk which might not have occurred to five other people on the whole station. Humankind's visceral terror of the Amnion was too acute to allow much room for thought.

'Unidentified Amnion vessel, this is UMCPHQ Center.'

'Hit her *now*,' Chief Mandich urged. He'd reached Center less than a minute after the klaxons first sounded. After a quick look at the situation, he'd joined Warden in the CO Room. 'Don't let her come in on us.'

Warden turned a one-eyed frown on the ED Chief of Security.

'What do you think *that* will accomplish?' His deliberate certainty didn't preclude sarcasm. In any case he had no energy to spare for gentleness. 'Have you noticed the *size* of that thing? She's a *Behemoth*-class defensive. She'll shrug off anything we can throw at her.

'She isn't firing. She could' – the scan displays indicated that the defensive's guns were charged, her targ focused – 'but she isn't. According to her emission profile, she has super-light proton cannon.' Scan confirmed the information Min had sent by gap courier drone. 'She could pulverize this whole station in fifteen minutes. And she still isn't firing.

229

'If you want me to start the bloodshed, tell me why she hasn't already attacked.'

He didn't trouble to add that the danger wasn't limited to UMCPHQ. His station was in synchronous orbit over Suka Bator. With her proton gun, the alien could take out the entire governmental apparatus of the planet. By their very nature, matter cannon were useless through atmosphere. The air itself would dissipate the beam long before it reached the surface. But super-light proton cannon didn't suffer from such limitations. There was no theoretical reason why the Amnion warship couldn't hammer the planet until its crust cracked open.

A Behemoth-class defensive was probably capable of generating enough power to flatten Suka Bator with her proton gun while she used her other arms to cut UMCPHQ apart.

That would be catastrophic: the worst of Warden's fears come to roost on his culpable head.

But she hadn't fired yet.

She would if he struck first. That was inevitable.

'Unidentified Amnion vessel, this is UMCPHQ Center. You must reply. You have encroached on human space.'

'Perhaps she holds back,' Hashi suggested, 'because she desires something from us.' Despite his air of unconcern and his disheveled way of walking, he'd reached the CO Room almost as promptly as Chief Mandich.

'Like *what*?' the Chief of Security retorted. 'If she doesn't plan to hit us and run, she's on a suicide mission. She'll never get out of here. Once she decelerates, she's dead. She'll have eight ships on her back in less than an hour. Nine, if you count *Adventurous*. Ten when *Valor* gets here.' He made no mention of *Punisher*. 'And *Sledgehammer*'s on her way.

'That Amnioni uses slow-brisance thrust.' He pointed at a scan readout for confirmation. 'She may be powerful as hell, but she isn't exactly quick. She can't reacquire enough velocity to risk tach before *Sledgehammer* gets here.'

Vehemently Chief Mandich concluded, 'Whatever she wants, it won't do her any good. She'll be dead.'

Hashi shrugged. His blue eyes gleamed with whetted

230

humor. 'Then perhaps,' he offered, 'she means to surrender.'

' "Surrender"?' Mandich snorted. 'An Amnioni?' His tone said as clearly as words, You're out of your mind.

Since Captain Vertigus and *Deep Star* had first made contact with them, the Amnion had never shown the slightest inclination to surrender. They may not have understood the concept.

'In any case,' Warden observed firmly, 'we can't afford to shoot first.' He had too much to lose – and nothing to gain. 'Right now she has the initiative. I'm going to let her keep it until I find out what she wants.'

Outside the CO Room a hoarse voice went on hailing the defensive. 'Unidentified Amnion vessel, this is UMCPHQ Center. You must reply. You have encroached on human space. We consider this an act of war. If you do not reply, we must assume that your intentions are hostile.

'Our ships stand ready to repulse you. Consult your scan. You will see that you cannot attack us and live. If you do not wish to be destroyed, you must reply.'

Chief Mandich couldn't contain himself. 'If they aren't going to attack,' he demanded, 'why won't they talk?'

'They will,' Warden answered evenly. 'They just aren't in position yet.'

' "Position"?' Mandich protested. 'They could kill us now. You said that yourself. What does position have to do with it?'

Warden shrugged; didn't bother to respond.

'Perhaps,' Hashi mused to no one in particular, 'that will become apparent when we see the position she chooses to take.'

Obliquely he hinted that he knew what was at stake.

Mandich glared at the DA director. Possibly he believed that in a situation like this all positions were the same. If so, he was wrong. He was a competent Security officer; but he wasn't equipped to carry the weight of Min's job in her absence.

'If you do not reply, we must assume that your intentions are hostile.'

The strain of waiting seemed to squeeze sweat from Warden's heart. Nevertheless he sat still and let nothing show.

'Director,' one of the CO techs whispered suddenly, 'she's orienting her guns.'

At once Warden turned to face the man. His hands lay like clamps on the arms of his seat.

'Look, sir.' The tech pointed at a screen, where a 3-D scan projection of the defensive turned: she was firing small jets to adjust her attitude. 'There.' He hit keys, and a luminous pointer marked a spot on the ship's bulbous flank. 'That's her proton cannon emitter. If she has more than one, we haven't been able to identify it.

'That amount of braking thrust distorts some of our readings. But at this range' – the man faltered, then forged ahead – 'we can be pretty sure what her targets are.'

To his cost, Warden himself was past faltering. 'And?' he inquired sharply.

The tech took a deep breath. 'There are five matter cannon aimed at us.' He couldn't keep a tremor from his voice. 'At least three of their torpedo ports have a good window. But her proton gun is aligned on Suka Bator.'

Just as Warden feared. For reasons of her own the defensive still hadn't fired. Nevertheless she obviously understood the tactical possibilities of her situation.

'You have encroached on human space. We consider this an act of war.'

'It's still suicide,' Chief Mandich muttered. 'Suppose she's able to kill the Council, destroy us. Hell, suppose she takes out HO as well. She's still dead.

'And we'll retaliate. We've got nine stations out there, all of them ready to fight. We've got shipyards and manufacturing they can't match. We'll strike so hard and deep into forbidden space they'll think the damage they did here was a slap on the wrist.

'If they want a goddamn war, we'll make them pay for it.'

Warden didn't bother to reply. Of course the Amnioni hadn't fired yet. And she wouldn't – not unless he forced her to it. She'd come here because she'd failed to kill *Trumpet*.

232

The mission which had taken her to Massif-5 hadn't changed.

That gave him no comfort whatsoever.

Hashi peered at the scan projection over his smeared glasses for a moment, then turned to Warden. In an ambiguous tone, he asked, 'I trust that Director Hannish is on her way?'

His question touched the heart of Warden's dread. 'Her shuttle left an hour ago,' he answered dryly. 'Unless someone starts shooting, she'll reach Suka Bator before that defensive finishes deceleration.

'Under the circumstances, the Council will go into session as soon as she gets there. They're receiving all this.' He gestured at the screens. GCES Security had access to the scan net. In addition the Council would be given data by direct downlink from UMCPHQ. 'Some of the Members probably wish they could go into hiding. But they're stuck where they are.' They had no time to escape. 'So they'll have an emergency session instead.'

They couldn't do anything about the defensive, however. The protection of their planet was Warden's job: they were helpless. For that reason – and because they were politicians – they would use the emergency session to assign blame.

'If we can avoid a fight long enough,' Warden finished, 'maybe Koina will have time to do her job.'

From Center a worn voice continued hailing the Amnioni. 'Our ships stand ready to repulse you. If you do not wish to be destroyed, you must reply.'

Abruptly Warden decided that it was time to take a hand in events; remind his people that he wasn't paralyzed. 'Send a message to HO for me,' he instructed one of his techs. 'Address it to CEO Fasner personally.

'I don't have time to talk to him, so I'm not interested in a reply. Just tell him for me that this is *my* problem.' He indicated the defensive's blip. 'I'll deal with it. Advise him to hunker down and concentrate on survival until I've resolved the situation, one way or another.'

'Right away, sir.' At once the tech started coding a transmission.

Hunker down and concentrate – If Warden Dios had been a man who wagered for stakes as minor as money, he would have risked a considerable sum that Holt would do no such thing. The Dragon would probably use this opportunity to try to secure his hold on the GCES. In addition, he might attempt to address the Amnioni directly; bluster the alien into negotiating with him. He might have enough leverage for that: he was the UMC CEO; the man who supplied the Amnion with all their legal trade.

If Holt signaled the defensive, Warden would be able to respond. But the Council was in Koina's hands. He couldn't help her now. Only Chief Mandich and Hashi could do that.

Or Morn and Vector Shaheed.

Tangentially he wondered whether Min Donner knew that humankind's future depended on her. And on *Trumpet*.

He didn't dwell on that kind of speculation, however. Instead he followed his message to HO with action of another kind.

Tapping keys on his board, he opened a station-wide inter-com channel. At the same time he routed his channel to Center so that what he said would reach every human ship and station around the planet. One way or another, his people needed to hear from him.

'This is Warden Dios,' he announced in a voice as crisp and sure as he could make it. 'I'm in UMCPHQ Command Operations.

'You all know by now that there's an Amnion warship coming in on us hard. She's a Behemoth-class defensive. That means she's dangerous. Dangerous as hell. She's armed with super-light proton cannon. And she has enough other guns' – he forced a brief touch of humor into his tone – 'to make us all wish we were somewhere else. But I don't think she wants a fight. She's here to negotiate.'

Chief Mandich stared as if he were amazed or appalled; but Warden didn't pause.

'I can only guess what she hopes to negotiate,' he went on. 'She isn't talking yet. Until she decides to communicate, we'll have to wait. But it looks like we're in no immediate danger. If we have something the Amnion want, we may come through this with a whole skin.

'That could change, of course. Especially if someone on our side gets trigger-happy. So now would be an especially good time to be sure we don't make any mistakes.

'I'm in no hurry to die myself,' he remarked firmly, 'and I don't want to lose any of you, either. I'll do everything I can to keep us all alive. What I need you to do is follow orders, be careful, and don't panic.'

Don't let an Amnioni this deep in human space scare you into thinking you would be better off dead.

'I'm counting on you,' he concluded. 'Dios out.'

With a decisive snap, he silenced his intercom.

He found it both ironic and shameful that he asked his people to trust him at a time when he was responsible for their danger. Nevertheless this was what he wanted: to face the consequences of his own actions; to stand or fall confronting a crisis which he himself had brought about.

But he needed *Trumpet*. Without her he was sure to fail. Koina had everything she required to confront Cleatus Fane and the GCES – except proof.

'We consider this an act of war.'

Chief Mandich had kept still with difficulty while Warden addressed UMCPHQ, but now he abandoned restraint. Bristling, he planted himself in front of Warden's station.

'Did I miss something, Director?' he demanded bitterly. 'When did we start "to negotiate" with aliens that commit acts of war?'

'Chief Mandich –' Warden sighed; rubbed his human eye with the heel of one hand. His prosthesis read the Security Chief's underlying distress and incomprehension clearly; but he couldn't spare the energy to deal with them. 'You're neglecting your duties.'

The man opened his mouth as if he'd been slapped. 'I –'

'You are the Enforcement Division Chief of Security,' Warden said slowly; harshly. 'You're responsible for the protection of the GCES, and for the safety of our personnel here. Among other things, that means you're supposed to pursue your investigation of these kazes' – acid sharpened his voice – 'not stand here telling me how to do my job.' For Koina's sake, he'd specifically instructed the Chief to track down everything he could learn about Clay Imposs and Nathan Alt. 'I don't need a goddamn running critique, Chief Mandich. I need *evidence*.'

'Yes, sir,' Mandich replied as if he were choking. His indignation couldn't withstand a challenge. Warden knew the man well: he was deeply conscientious – and deeply ashamed of his failure to ward kazes away from the Council and UMCPHQ. 'We're working on it. I'll inform you the minute we find anything.'

'Do that,' Warden returned. 'Inform Director Hannish as well. Inform Director Lebwohl. Then back them up. Is that clear? I don't know what they might need from you – but if and when they need it, it'll be urgent.'

'Yes, sir,' the Chief of Security answered again.

His consternation was plain; too vivid for Warden to ignore. Mandich hadn't done anything to be ashamed of: he'd failed for the simple, sufficient reason that people with more power hadn't allowed him to succeed. Rather than let him leave like this, Warden beckoned him closer.

'Sir?' Uncertainly Chief Mandich approached Warden's seat.

Warden put a strong hand on the Chief's shoulder and drew Mandich's head down to his. Whispering so that he wouldn't be overheard, he promised, 'I know what I'm doing.'

Chief Mandich couldn't find a reply; couldn't meet Warden's gaze. His shame was too strong. Without a word, he saluted stiffly, then turned and left the CO Room, walking like a man with fire in his bones and no way to put it out.

'It is with some chagrin' – Hashi tilted his head toward the ceiling as if to convey the impression that he spoke to no one but himself; that he meant no criticism of Chief Mandich – 'that I find myself wishing for Director Donner's return.' He and Min had never concealed the fact that they loathed and distrusted each other.

'So do I,' Warden murmured. 'So do I.'

But there was nothing he could do about it. In spite of all the things he knew and feared, he had to wait like everyone else.

Helpless as a bystander, he watched the screens with his heart caught in a fist of alarm and sweat oozing like corrosion down his chest and sides inside his worksuit.

The defensive continued her approach, remorselessly hauling down on UMCPHQ as she decelerated. If she felt anything like the trepidation which squeezed Center and the CO Room, it didn't show in the throaty howl of her drives, the scan report of her targ, or the unmistakable orientation of her guns. By now it was clear that she would brake in time to shadow UMCPHQ's orbit at a distance of little more than fifty thousand k: point-blank range for her matter cannon.

Hashi had been in and out of the CO Room several times, humming thinly to himself while he went about his duties; but he didn't speak of them. All the rest of Warden's people – like Warden himself – remained at their stations, glued there by sweat and suspense: by the unquenchable genetic terror of being so near the Amnion, who could dispense a ruin far worse than mere cannon-fire and death. One of Center's techs had hailed the big defensive until his voice gave out: then he put his transmission on automatic and let his equipment handle it. Other men and women fielded demands, appeals and hysteria from all across the planet. Still others sat with their hands poised near the keys for UMCPHQ's few guns.

Holt Fasner hadn't demanded Warden's attention; but he wasn't silent. Several downlink channels connected him to Suka Bator. And UMCPHQ scan reported that some of HO's dishes were aimed at the Amnioni. Those dishes were active. Apparently the Dragon was trying as hard as Center to get a response from the defensive. Unfortunately UMCPHQ couldn't intercept any message tight-beamed between HO and the alien. Fortunately none of the approaching vessel's transmitters emitted energy in reply.

Finally Warden decided that he'd waited long enough.

Slapping his thighs to snap his techs out of their transfixed study of the screens, he asked without preamble, 'Would you say that by now she's past the point of no return?'

Despite the tension roiling inside him, he kept his tone calm and clear.

A woman scrambled to catch up with his question. 'Sure looks like it, sir. Unless she has secrets we don't know about, she's already lost too much velocity to attempt a gap crossing. If she comes all the way in, we'll have nine ships' – three pocket cruisers, five gunboats, and *Adventurous* – 'in position to hit her before she can accelerate again. *Valor* should be here soon. And *Sledgehammer* is burning now.' The tech ran a quick series of course and thrust algorithms. 'If that defensive sticks around for eight hours or so, *Sledgehammer* will come into range before she can escape into tach.'

Warden was ready. 'Good enough,' he announced. This was his job: if he couldn't do it now, he deserved the disasters crowded about him. 'She's committed. Now let's find out what she's committed to.

'Tell Center to stop hailing. Then get me a channel for that ship. I'll talk to her myself.'

'If I may, Director Dios –' Hashi put in thoughtfully while Warden's staff hurried to obey. 'It might be advisable to leave the initiative with her. The longer she elects to delay, the stronger our position becomes.' He shrugged, then commented with an air of indifference, 'If we remain passive, it is conceivable that *Punisher* will arrive in time to play a role.'

'That,' Warden answered at once, 'is why I'm not going to wait any longer. Since our visitor is here anyway, I want to make sure she deals with me, not *Punisher*.'

Hashi let out a sigh of comprehension. 'I take your point.' He adjusted his dirty glasses to obscure his vision. 'My suggestion was unsolicited.' A smile twisted his thin mouth. 'Perhaps you will consider it unspoken as well.'

Almost involuntarily Warden grinned at the DA director. 'What suggestion?' For reasons he couldn't explain, there were times when Hashi's sense of humor touched him like a rush of affection. Perhaps it enabled him to feel a little less alone.

That helped.

'Director,' a tech said, 'I have a channel ready.'

'Thank you.' At once Warden turned to his pickup.

'Unidentified Amnion warship, this is Warden Dios, Director, United Mining Companies Police.' His voice seemed to convey a subliminal resonance, as if without shouting he could generate the force for an echo. 'You have committed an act of war. We are in a state of war' – he repeated that word deliberately, reminding the Amnioni that the future of their respective species was at stake – 'and in a state of war *I* am the highest authority in human space. *I* will make the decisions which determine the outcome of your incursion.

'You can no longer escape. Your scan will confirm that we now have enough firepower to stop you. And more of our ships will come into range by the hour.

'I'm tired of waiting. You will talk to me now. If you don't, we will open fire' – he raised a finger to mark the moment – 'in thirty seconds.'

With the back of his fist he silenced the pickup.

The CO Room and Center reacted as if he'd run an electric current through the floor. Men and women seemed to jump at their boards, despite the intensity of their concentration a moment earlier. Battle-alerts sounded like wails. Techs shouted into their intercoms, warning UMCPHQ to brace for combat; relaying Warden's threat to Earth's ships. 'No mistakes!' an officer barked at the gunners. 'Wait for the order! I'll take the skin off anyone who fires without the director's order!'

Ignoring the sudden clamor, Warden made a mental note to commend the officer's caution. He was confident that the defensive would reply.

The response arrived in seventeen seconds. With a crackle of thrust static, the CO Room speakers came to life as if they'd opened directly on vast distances and hard vacuum.

Across the distortion a man's voice announced, 'Warden Dios, this vessel is the Amnion defensive *Calm Horizons*.' He

239

sounded at once strangely human and entirely alien. 'I am Marc Vestabule. I have been invested with decisiveness. You would say that I am the captain.

'Do not open fire. If you do, we will destroy you. Your scan will confirm that we possess the power to do so.

'It appears probable that you are correct. We also may be destroyed. During the interval which remains to us, however, we will crush your station utterly. We will unleash super-light proton fire upon the planetary island which is your site of government. And while we can we will wreak all possible devastation upon your ships and stations.

'Do not fire upon us unless you wish to die.'

The transmission ended in a burst of static. Hot particle noise seemed to fill the CO Room.

'"Marc Vestabule",' Hashi said in surprise. 'That is a human name.'

Warden could hardly help noticing the same thing. 'You mean the Amnion are using human names for some reason? Since when?'

'No.' By some trick of concentration or misdirection, Hashi appeared to reach a board without moving toward it. Rapidly he tapped keys, scanned readouts. A moment later he reported, 'Voice analysis concurs. There are characteristic sound-production stresses when an Amnioni employs human speech. They are absent. It appears that the speaker is physiologically human. He has a human throat, vocal cords, mouth and tongue.

'Unless the Amnion are now able to produce complete human beings from their own RNA,' Hashi concluded, 'Marc Vestabule was once one of us.'

Warden nodded. An interesting detail. Maybe a useful one. 'What does Data Storage say?'

'I've entered an inquiry,' Hashi replied. 'On short notice the results will be less than exhaustive. However –' He looked down at the readout, repositioned his glasses. 'Ah,' he breathed in satisfaction. 'The name "Marc Vestabule" exists in our files.

'A number of years ago,' Hashi summarized from the

screen, 'he was among the registered crew of a vessel named *Viable Dreams*, an in-system hauler which served Com-Mine Station by transshipping ores from the belt. Sadly *Viable Dreams* was lost without trace, taking her "Marc Vestabule" with her. Her fate is – or has been – unknown. Now I speculate that she fell prey to the Amnion in some fashion.'

The DA director paused, then added, 'There are other vocal stresses which would reveal his underlying genetic identity. They cannot be determined without a referent, however. A recording of his voice prior to his mutation would provide a definitive comparison. Again sadly, our files do not extend so far in his case.'

That detail might also prove useful; but Warden let it wait. Still using the back of his fist, he activated his pickup.

'*Calm Horizons*, this is Warden Dios.' His air of poised calm cost him less effort now. For good or ill, the delay was over. He was free to take action. 'With a name like Marc Vestabule, you must have been human once. Maybe you remember that our kind likes devastation. Some of us even like death. You've come a long way to stick your guns in our faces. Unless you like death yourself, I suggest you persuade us to hold back by telling us what you want here.'

Several of the Center techs stopped what they were doing to listen. Two or three of them raised their fists in the air.

Empty static filled the speakers for a moment. Vestabule didn't pause for long, however. Perhaps the decisions he faced were simple for an Amnioni. Or perhaps they'd already been made.

'As you say, Warden Dios, my genetic material once resembled yours. I am now Amnion.' He stated this as if it were beyond question. His way of speaking, stilted and strange, gave the words an intensity his tone lacked. 'Nevertheless the process by which I became Amnion enables me to retain certain resources of memory, language and comprehension. For this reason I have been invested with decisiveness. In dealings with your kind, my former humanity may assist me to function effectively. I will exercise my human

241

resources to satisfy the requirements which have brought *Calm Horizons* here.'

Warden said nothing. He'd presented his demand: now he waited to see how Marc Vestabule would answer it.

'Warden Dios,' the nearly human voice went on, 'there is a matter which I must broach with you. It is an issue of some complexity, in part because it involves a response to concerns which have no meaning to us. I alone aboard this vessel recognize their importance to you. Nevertheless all future relations between our species will be determined by the resolution of this matter. A desirable outcome may only be obtained by' – he said the word as if it were unfamiliar to him – 'discussion.'

Hashi nodded without surprise: like Warden, he'd clearly expected something like this. But some of the CO staff gazed at the director as if he'd confirmed his reputation for prescience.

'I'm listening, *Calm Horizons*.' Pointedly Warden spoke to the ship instead of the man. He wished Vestabule to understand that he was certain of the Amnioni's allegiances. 'What do you want to discuss?'

'As I say, the matter is complex.' Thrust static emphasized Vestabule's awkwardness. 'In addition I find that my former humanity is' – he paused, apparently searching for a description – 'difficult to access. I cannot – discuss – effectively in this fashion.'

Trying to think like the Amnion, Warden guessed that Vestabule was hampered, not by the word itself, but by the concept behind it.

Calm Horizons' 'captain' sounded as alien as the physics of the gap as he concluded, 'I must speak to you in person.'

Muted gasps broke from a few of the CO techs. Out in Center half a dozen men and women rose to their feet involuntarily and turned to stare into the CO Room. In a rare breach of discipline, Center's officers didn't call them back to their duties. The officers themselves studied Warden urgently.

Without transition he felt the fear gnawing at his heart turn cold and fatal, like super-cooled mineral acid. He didn't need foreknowledge to sense what was coming.

'"In person",' he echoed darkly. Despite his determination to appear calm, his tone sharpened. 'How do you propose to arrange that, *Calm Horizons*?'

Vestabule had his reply ready. 'If we are reduced to combat, Warden Dios, the Amnion will lose one defensive. Your losses will be incalculable – in lives, in ships, in stations, in manufacturing capacity. This you know.

'To prevent a conflict which must be catastrophic for you, will you consent to come aboard *Calm Horizons*?'

In an instant all of Center was on its feet. The CO Room burst into a babble of protest, quickly stilled. Hashi Lebwohl gazed at Warden with bemused speculation in his eyes. Even now he seemed to wish for a show of surprise from his director.

Warden ignored them. Between one heartbeat and the next, he found that he had come face to face with his true doom.

Go aboard *Calm Horizons*? Confront the Amnion alone; risk mutation?

For *what*?

For time, he answered himself grimly. For lives. And for freedom from the UMC. For Morn and Koina, Angus Thermopyle and Sixten Vertigus. Humankind's future was at stake in a sense entirely different from the one Marc Vestabule intended.

The UMCP director had been prepared for his own death ever since he'd turned against Holt Fasner. Still he temporized. He had to: if he agreed too readily, he would be misunderstood – by UMCPHQ as well as by the Amnion.

'Are you out of your mind?' he croaked into his pickup as if he had trouble recovering his voice. 'You come here.'

Vestabule had anticipated this counter. Again he was ready.

'That is not acceptable. If I am apart from *Calm Horizons*, I am powerless. You may choose to kill me, knowing that no other Amnioni aboard this vessel is able to replace me. If you are apart from your station, you retain all the strength of your ships and platforms. Your position remains intact in your absence. If we are to discuss' – still the word discomfited him – 'we must meet on equal terms.

'This system is yours, Warden Dios. You must come to me.'

'No,' a tech breathed. Another said the same more loudly: 'No.' In a moment half a dozen men and women from Center added their protests: 'No. No.'

Warden toggled his pickup with a blow of his fist, then slashed a harsh gesture to silence his people before their rejection could take over UMCPHQ's operational heart. Half rising from his seat so that he could look out across Center, he shouted deliberately, 'This isn't a democracy, people! *I* make these decisions! You do *your* jobs – I'll do *mine*!'

Quiet fell like a shutter on the room. In a rush the techs resumed their stations, bent over their tasks.

The nearest officer came to the open CO Room door. 'Sorry, sir,' he offered uncomfortably. 'They just – it's just that they – '

'I understand,' Warden growled back. 'Don't worry about it.'

'Yes, sir.' The officer left the door and began to make a show of supervising the people under his command.

Warden took a deep breath to steady himself, then hit his pickup toggle. 'You say you want me to go there, *Calm Horizons*. Under what conditions?'

'Warden Dios,' the former human being answered promptly, 'you will come to us alone and unarmed. We will hold our discussion under any physical conditions which you consider necessary or comfortable. When we have attained mutual understanding and agreement, you will return to your station.'

'Will you let me remain in contact with UMCPHQ Center?'

'No. You will not speak to your station until our discussion is concluded.'

At the edge of his vision, Warden saw Hashi mouth, This is a trap. But he already knew that. He concentrated on his pickup; on the crackling transmission which linked him to his doom.

'*Calm Horizons*, you are Amnion. I'm human.' The most irreconcilable of differences. 'How can I trust you?'

'Because we *are* Amnion, Warden Dios,' Vestabule replied flatly. 'Unlike humankind, we bargain openly. Also we fulfill our bargains.

'There is this in addition, however. We gain nothing by harming you. If we kill you, another will take your place, and hostilities will continue as before. And if we enforce your mutation, so that you become one of us, the transformation will be detected by your station. Mutation will cause elisions of memory which will betray you. At the same time there will be unavoidable alterations in both your method and your manner of speaking, alterations which your station's instruments will recognize. You would become one of us, but your station would no longer obey you, and so we would gain nothing.'

Vestabule paused, then added, 'You will ask what I offer in exchange. I offer time, Warden Dios. The benefit of delay is yours. As your ships draw closer, our peril grows. Every passing hour diminishes the harm we will be able to commit before we are slain.

'I accept this in the name of discussion. You must accept a similar hazard.'

The Amnioni may no longer have been vulnerable to apprehension, suspense or eagerness. Without discernible inflection, he concluded, 'What is your answer, Warden Dios?'

Roughly Warden closed his pickup. Instead of replying, he took a moment to consider the nature of his dread.

Vestabule's arguments were about what he might have expected. They were also realistic. The Amnioni had a clear grasp on his tactical situation: that was obvious. In a strangely human sense, he knew what he was doing.

No amount of delay would spare Suka Bator. Or UMCPHQ.

Risk mutation –?

That, however, wasn't the true name of Warden's fear. His dread ran deeper.

His complex, insidious attack on Holt Fasner may have brought about the ruin of his own desires. He'd created a disaster which might cost far more lives, resources and hope than humankind could afford. A battle now, here, would effectively undo his long preparations: it would neutralize Koina and Morn, confirm the Dragon's power. In a full-scale war, with UMCPHQ and the GCES gone, the planet would have no one left to trust except Holt. And Warden was sure that Holt would do everything in his power to seize the situation –

This is no ordinary fear of death, Norna had warned. *He wants to live forever. Haven't I seen it? Why do you think he keeps me damned here? I've spent fifty years paying for what I see.*

Warden Dios had no choice. He desperately needed the time Vestabule offered him. Weighed against humankind's future, the cost to himself was too slight to be measured.

The CO Room techs – and half of Center – watched him as if they held their collective breath while he punched the toggle to activate his pickup.

'*Calm Horizons*, this is Warden Dios.' He required all his force of will to keep his voice steady. 'I'll do what you want. I'll come to you.' A mutter of dismay and protest spread outward from the CO Room, but he ignored it. Instead he added sharply, 'Under one condition.'

'Warden Dios, this is Marc Vestabule,' the Amnioni returned almost at once. 'What is your condition?'

Swallowing panic and old shame, Warden took the next step along his chosen path.

'*Calm Horizons*, there are other stations hailing you. So far our scan says you haven't responded to them. My condition is that you talk to *me*. No one else.' If I'm responsible for all this, I will by God *be* responsible. I won't have the ground cut out from under me. 'If you reply to any transmission that doesn't come from this station, our discussion is over, and we will kill you as fast as we can.'

His demand appeared to surprise Vestabule. Without warning, *Calm Horizons*' transmission vanished from the intervening void: the speakers reported silence and cold static. Apparently the Amnioni had stopped to deliberate. Try as he did, Warden simply couldn't think like an alien. He must have struck a nerve he didn't understand; called himself into question somehow.

Biting down curses, he waited for Vestabule's response.

When the former human being replied at last, his tone was as oddly inflected as before; difficult to interpret. Nevertheless it conveyed an unexpected note of caution.

'Warden Dios, permit me to quote you. "In a state of war *I* am the highest authority in human space. *I* will make the decisions which determine the outcome of your incursion." Do you say now that you did not speak factually? Is there another authority which might countermand you? If there is, then I must speak with that authority, not with you.'

Oh, shit! Whatever prescience Warden had must have deserted him: he hadn't foreseen *this*. Possible failures churned in his guts; numberless deaths; treason beyond redemption –

'Let *me* quote *you*,' he retorted, acid with fear. 'You said that you "retain certain resources of memory, language and comprehension." Maybe you can remember that there are always factions in human politics. By law the authority is mine. That doesn't mean other people won't try to make you think you should talk to them instead.

'But no matter who they are, or what they offer you, they can't control this station. They can't control our ships. Our defenses take their orders from *me*. If you make a deal with someone else, it won't mean anything. *I* am the director of the United Mining Companies Police, and *I* will decide whether you live or die.'

Believe that, he demanded mutely; uselessly. I can't think like you. Prove you can think like me.

Apparently Vestabule wasn't convinced. 'Warden Dios,' he stated carefully, 'we are being hailed by the United Mining Companies, in the name of Chief Executive Officer Holt Fasner. Is the United Mining Companies Police not a subsidiary unit of the United Mining Companies? Does Holt Fasner's authority not transcend yours?'

Warden swore under his breath, then snapped into his

pickup, '*Listen* to me, *Calm Horizons*. I'm not going to spend the next several hours teaching a course in human politics.' He let anger mount in his voice until it became as heavy as a club. 'You'll just have to take my word for it.

'You've been "invested with decisiveness". So have I. Warfare is the UMCP's job, *my* job. Holt Fasner can't prevent our ships from opening fire. I can.

'You say you have something you want to discuss. You say we have to discuss it in person. That's your problem, not mine. You can talk to me about it right now. You can put it on general broadcast and "discuss" it with the whole solar system. Or you can accept my condition and get what you say you want.'

Grimly he finished, 'Just make up your mind.'

Raising his fist, he poised it to strike his pickup silent.

Some of the CO Room techs looked like they were praying. Others shook their heads dumbly. A persistent shuffling of feet from Center gave the impression that most of the staff had left their stations.

Warden wanted to look up, see what was happening; but Marc Vestabule's silence held him. His fist hung, paralyzed, over his pickup toggle. In another moment his hand would start to shake.

Without warning the Amnioni answered.

'Very well, Warden Dios.' Vestabule's way of speaking was too stilted to suggest concession. 'This vessel will respond to transmissions from no station except your own. In return, you will come to us alone and unarmed so that we may hold our discussion in person.'

Warden's heart lurched as if he'd been given a reprieve; as if he were eager for a chance to risk his fate aboard *Calm Horizons*. 'I agree,' he replied brusquely. 'Dios out.'

Instead of punching his pickup, he toggled it with a gentle tap.

When he raised his head, he saw the entire staff of Center crowded at the CO Room door.

What –? Despite all his years of discipline and concealment and will, he was too surprised to speak.

For reasons known only to himself, Hashi put on an air of

lugubrious indignation. He may have feigned vexation to conceal amusement. Facing the nearest officer, an earnest man with a deceptively youthful face and a sergeant's insignia, the DA director demanded, 'What is the meaning of this, young man?'

The sergeant didn't so much as glance at Hashi: his gaze clung to Warden like an appeal.

There was too much at stake: Warden needed a minute to pull himself together. Roughly he scrubbed at his face with both hands, trying to force his fear and urgency back from the surface so that they wouldn't show; trying to rub away the sensation that he'd been touched by death. With an effort, he reminded himself that these were his people; that it was their job to serve him, just as it was his job to serve them; that they hung by his fate.

Slowly he lifted his chin and met the eyes staring at him.

They were somber and distressed, hurt by a shared need which he couldn't identify, perhaps because he was so full of his own. The strength of their combined emotional aura seemed to cry out against him. Some of the women and at least a few of the men had to blink back tears.

'Sergeant –' He cleared his throat. Ordinarily he knew all his people; but now for the life of him he couldn't recollect the young man's name. So much focused dismay confused his defenses. 'Maybe you'd better tell me what this is about.'

Stiff with awkwardness, the sergeant could barely speak. 'Please don't think we're shirking, sir.' His larynx bobbed convulsively. 'We'll work twice as hard in just a minute. But I need – we want –'

With a visible effort, he mastered his chagrin. 'It's like this, sir. You can't go. It's wrong. They're Amnion. They destroy people – like they destroyed that Marc Vestabule. We need you here. If you go, they'll turn you into one of them, and then we're lost. We won't have anything to hope for.

'We would rather die fighting for you.'

A throaty murmur of agreement from the techs made it clear that he spoke for everyone in the CO Room as well as in Center.

A bitter retort swelled in Warden's chest, driven by the

pressure of his essential terror. He wanted to shout or wail, What do you mean, *you won't have anything to hope for* if I'm lost? What kind of miracles do you *expect* from me?

Before his grief and shame became strong enough to cripple his self-command, however, another emotion surpassed them: a strange pride, unfamiliar and unbidden, that his people cared for him so much; depended on him so completely.

In another life – a life without the fatal mistake of trusting Holt Fasner – one moment like this would have been enough to make everything worthwhile. He might have been able to believe he'd earned it.

In *this* life, unfortunately, he couldn't afford to feel pride or be comforted. The harm of his complicity in Holt's betrayals wasn't so easily dismissed.

Moving slowly, deliberately, he rose to his feet. As best he could, he meant to look every one of his people in the eyes; face them as equals.

'Thank you, Sergeant, all of you.' He wanted to whisper; but he forced himself to speak so that his voice carried across the gathering. 'I appreciate your concern' – he spread his hands helplessly – 'more than I can describe in words.

'But put yourselves in my place. If you respect me enough to believe I'm worth dying for, then you also respect me enough to know I feel the same way about you. That Amnioni wants to talk to me in person. And every hour we don't fight improves our chances for survival. If I can protect Earth and keep all of you alive even a little longer by risking my life, do you really think I could bear to refuse?'

One after another, he met every gaze around him. Then he straightened his shoulders, squared his chin.

'We are the UMCP. It is our duty – and our honor – to serve and defend humankind.' For years he'd been telling lies he hated; lies that sickened him: first Holt's, then his own. Now he told as much of the truth as he could. 'My life is a pretty small thing to risk for a chance to do my job.'

And it was a small thing to risk for any chance to make sure *Calm Horizons* didn't simply blast *Punisher* as soon as the cruiser arrived. But that truth he didn't tell. Even now he couldn't afford to admit how much he depended on Morn – and Min.

He didn't need his prosthetic vision to see that he'd swayed everyone except Hashi. Their eyes were bright with conviction or blurred with tears: the same loyalty and commitment which inspired their protest left them vulnerable to his response.

To make it easier for them to give him what he needed, he shrugged ruefully and added, 'Of course, doing my job won't mean shit if you don't all go back to your stations and do yours.'

'Yes, sir,' the young sergeant answered in a thick voice. 'Right away.' Almost fiercely, he called the techs, officers and aides to attention. Like an affirmation, they saluted the UMCP director as if they were on parade.

As a rule, Warden never returned salutes: he didn't like them. But he made an exception in this case. How could he refuse?

Nevertheless he took no time to savor the moment, or regret it. He was in a hurry. As soon as the crowd dispersed, he told one of his aides to order his shuttle for immediate departure.

The thought of delivering himself into the hands of the Amnion appalled him. He couldn't afford to put it off.

He wanted to be alone. He'd been moving to meet his doom for a long time, but now that the crisis was upon him he felt a need to gather his resources; harden his heart. Unfortunately he didn't get the chance. Hashi Lebwohl insisted on walking with him to the dock.

Hashi had taken it upon himself to req some supplies for Warden. Before they left the CO Room, a DA tech had arrived in a breathless rush to deliver two things which Hashi then handed mutely to Warden: a breathing mask and an evil-looking black capsule the size of a throat lozenge. Warden had accepted both, thrust them into his pockets without comment. Instead of thanking the DA director, he'd allowed Hashi to accompany him away from Center.

Driven by fears and furies, he set a brisk pace which made

251

no concession to Hashi's slack-heeled gait. Hashi contrived to keep up with him, however.

Hashi held his tongue only until they gained the relative privacy of UMCPHQ's open corridors. Then, in an unusually earnest tone, he spoke.

'Permit me to say, Director, that in my view this is a mistake. The Amnion have nothing to discuss with you. That is pure chicanery.' He sounded certain. 'They desire you as a hostage.'

'A hostage?' Warden knew what Hashi meant, but he wanted to hear Hashi say it.

'To be used against *Punisher*,' Hashi explained. 'How else can they hope to extract what they want?'

'*Punisher* isn't here,' Warden remarked shortly.

'She will arrive soon,' Hashi countered. 'Doubtless Min Donner will invoke Gabriel priority to obtain Isaac's cooperation. Then both *Punisher* and *Trumpet* will return at their best speed.'

Warden had told no one that Holt had ordered him to betray Angus to Nick Succorso.

'There are benefits, of course,' Hashi continued. 'Director Donner will surely silence *Trumpet*'s unfortunate broadcast. That threat to the Amnion will be decreased. Therefore *Calm Horizons* may be less inclined to open fire on both *Trumpet* and *Punisher* immediately upon their arrival.

'Nevertheless they will aggravate the more general threat. When they resume tard, they will recognize the nature of our emergency. They will become part of the cordon closing around *Calm Horizons* – their arrival will strengthen us. It will weaken the defensive's position.

'This Marc Vestabule seeks to purchase the success of his incursion with the only coin he can be certain *Punisher* will respect. The coin of your life.'

Warden had just glimpsed how fatal the loyalty of his people might become. 'That,' he replied heavily, 'is one of the reasons Min Donner is aboard.'

Min may have been the only UMCP officer capable of sacrificing the man she served. Certainly she could be trusted to refuse a direct order – under the right circumstances.

Under *these* circumstances, that made her as dangerous as Marc Vestabule.

'Ah.' Hashi's sigh held a note of awe bordering on reverence. 'You foresaw this also.'

Warden scowled his vexation. 'Not this exactly.' He was in no mood to be probed – and he was *by God* in no mood for awe. 'But something like it.'

Hashi didn't stop. 'Forgive me, Warden,' he pursued. 'I still fail to grasp –'

'Let it go,' Warden snapped. 'It's my problem, not yours.'

At once, however, he felt ashamed of himself. Hashi had always served the UMCP with integrity, imagination and diligence – at least by his own lights. As DA director, his love for covert schemes and baroque interpretations was a positive virtue. It wasn't his fault that he sometimes misjudged the passion which impelled Warden's actions.

To soften the impact of his anger, Warden added more gently, 'I'm going to leave you plenty of other things to worry about.'

'I will do what I can.' Hashi sounded uncharacteristically subdued; diminished in some way. 'In particular I will endeavor to complete our investigation of Clay Imposs and Nathan Alt.'

Just for a moment Warden didn't care about that: he had no attention to spare for kazes or the GCES. Without warning he was overtaken by a desire to be understood.

He'd told so many lies and kept so many secrets for so long that he could hardly bear it. The thought of boarding *Calm Horizons* alone made his self-imposed isolation from everyone who valued or respected him seem insupportable. He stood by his reasons for what he'd done. Still he knew that none of the people he trusted – Hashi, Min and Koina, Angus and Morn – deserved the way he'd manipulated and maneuvered them. Now he felt a profound, poignant desire to bare his soul.

He had no time for a real confession – no time, and not enough courage. But he could give Hashi a hint. For the DA director, a hint would suffice.

'Listen,' he said abruptly. 'I have something to tell you, and I can't wait for another opportunity.'

Although the corridors were empty, cleared by the call to defense stations, he kept his voice low. But he resisted an impulse to bend his head down to Hashi's. Instead he continued to stride ahead, forcing Hashi to keep pace with him.

'I had more than one reason for sending Min aboard *Punisher*. I wanted to protect her from what's about to happen on Suka Bator. From being tainted by Koina's revelations. And I wanted her to help keep Morn alive. In fact, I ordered her to do that. Because I'm hoping –'

He spoke without glancing aside at the DA director.

'Morn and Angus have already gone beyond my expectations. Broadcasting that formula, for God's sake! I never imagined they would have the resources to survive this long and still cause so much trouble. But I'm hoping for something more.'

Hashi made a small, hissing sound through his teeth, but didn't respond in any other way.

'When Morn gets here,' Warden went on, 'I hope' – pray – 'she'll be willing to testify that Angus was framed.' If she did the blow would rock Holt's power to its foundations. 'And if she *is* willing, Min is the only one of us with enough moral authority left to make it happen.' The Council already distrusted Hashi. And Koina would effectively ruin Warden himself. 'She might persuade Morn to talk. She can certainly make the Council listen.'

Is that clear enough? he asked Hashi mutely. Do I have to spell it out?

He wanted Hashi to understand that he'd done everything in his power to bring all his separate attacks on Holt together at the same time.

Still Hashi said nothing. After a moment or two the silence compelled Warden to turn his head.

Hashi cleared his throat without returning Warden's gaze. 'Are you bidding me farewell, Warden?' Unexpected emotions congested his voice. 'Do you assume – as I do – that

254

once you've become Marc Vestabule's hostage he will never release you?'

'Not necessarily.' Warden shrugged grimly. 'Who knows what miracles Morn and Angus can accomplish? But I do assume that whether I live or die I'm going to be charged with treason.'

He only hoped that Holt would fall with him when he finally cut all the ground out from under his own feet.

At last Hashi raised his head to look at Warden.

'It occurs to me that I have not thanked you for revealing the substitution of Captain Thermopyle's datacore.' His eyes emanated a moist heat that Warden had never seen in them before. In some way Warden's openness had touched the DA director's cunning, unscrupulous heart. 'That knowledge shamed me greatly. I had not grasped the true depth of your intentions. Nevertheless I am grateful. I admire your resourcefulness. You have allowed me an insight which I value. Likewise I value your purpose. And I understand the necessity of keeping it hidden.

'I will serve you with every resource at my command.'

To his surprise, Warden found that his fear had suddenly shed some of its sharpness. After all, he was a man who loved the truth far more than his life so far had shown – the truth; and the people who served him.

Smiling crookedly to himself, he faced forward and kept on walking.

For a couple of minutes Hashi seemed lost in thought. Then he broke the silence. 'Speaking of miracles –

'Warden, have you studied the entire contents of Captain Thermopyle's datacore?' He'd composed himself: his voice had regained its habitual wheeze of ambiguity and misdirection.

Warden shook his head. 'I couldn't duplicate your work.' He found it easier to talk now. 'I didn't have time. In any case, I'm not that good. I concentrated on writing new instruction-sets in regard to Morn. Everything else I left alone. I didn't even look at most of your code,' he admitted.

'Then I should tell you,' Hashi said as if he were starting

a lecture, 'that his design includes several failsafes. Most I discussed with you. A few I kept secret' – he chuckled mirthlessly – 'for reasons not unlike your own. The prospect that our lamented Godsen might learn of them disturbed me.

'They take the form of commands which may be invoked without reference to Isaac's priority-codes. Indeed, they supersede all other programming. I believe they will be effective.'

Warden didn't know whether to be pleased or horrified. 'Go on,' he muttered noncommittally.

Hashi clearly had no intention of stopping. 'One such command,' he stated, 'enables full, voluntary access to all his databases. As you know, his primary instruction-sets supply data at need rather than on demand. But if he hears the word "apotheosis" his databases will be released. In effect, he will know all that we know on a variety of subjects' – the DA director gave the words a subtle emphasis, as if he meant Warden to hear something larger behind them – 'among them our ships, UMCPHQ, and many of Earth's orbital platforms.'

Warden paused in mid-stride to stare at the DA director. '"Apotheosis"?'

Hashi grinned smugly. 'You will understand that I required a word which he would be unlikely to hear from anyone but us.'

That was true. But still – *apotheosis*?

With an effort Warden pushed himself into motion again.

Hashi's respiration began to show the strain of matching Warden's pace.

'Another, similar command will free him from all restriction in his response to UMCP – or UMC – personnel. Hearing the word "vasectomy" will enable him to harm or kill anyone who interferes with him. Anyone at all.'

'"Vasectomy"?' Warden shook his head in bemusement. 'Well, damn it, Hashi. Sometimes I'm forced to admire your sense of humor. I just can't help myself.'

He had no idea whether or not Hashi's failsafes would do him any good; but he approved of them anyway. He could imagine – or pray for – circumstances –

256

'Is there more?' he inquired.

'Just one,' Hashi replied shortly. He appeared to lack the breath for complex sentences. 'The word "sepulcher" will invoke self-destruct. His zone implants will fry his brain to jelly.'

Warden winced. He'd already done Angus too much hurt: he didn't like to think that he might be forced to go further.

Unfortunately he could imagine worse fates.

Boarding *Calm Horizons* alone might be one of them. Despite Marc Vestabule's promises, the Amnion had nothing to gain by releasing him.

How much of Vestabule's human capacity for treachery did the Amnioni remember?

That question gave the fears feeding in his chest new teeth. He checked his pockets to be sure he still had his breathing mask and capsule. Then he focused on the simple, arduous task of walking steadily until he reached the docks and his shuttle hanger.

His shuttle was ready: he headed straight toward it as if all the doubt and hesitation had been eaten out of him. At the airlock of the craft, however, he stopped; turned. For a moment he faced Hashi squarely.

With his crew, the dock personnel and UMCPED Security as witnesses, he announced, 'Director Lebwohl, you're in command while I'm away. Your orders are –' He shrugged, tried to smile. 'Well, just don't do anything I wouldn't do.' Then he added more sternly, 'And don't talk to Holt Fasner. He's my boss, not yours. If he wants to throw his weight around, he'll have to do it with me in person.'

Hashi didn't reply. He also didn't salute. Instead he answered with an old, oddly formal bow – the elaborate sweep-and-flourish of a courtier, or a comrade-in-arms.

That was all the comfort Warden took with him as he entered his shuttle and gave the order to leave dock.

KOINA

The PR director's shuttle was halfway to Earth when UMCPHQ reported that a Behemoth-class Amnion defensive had encroached on the orbital platform's control space.

The crew of the shuttle, Koina's PR communications techs and her ED Security guards received the broadcast simultaneously on separate channels. At once the crew routed their reception to the passenger cabin so that everyone could hear it. After the first shock, however, Deputy Chief Forrest Ing – again assigned to ensure the PR director's safety – ordered the cabin speakers silenced. 'If you pipe that back here,' he told the crew sharply, 'we won't be able to hear ourselves think.' Instead he and the PR techs passed around PCRs so that the passengers could listen to UMCPHQ's transmissions and still talk to each other.

For a time, however, no one said anything. They listened in an eerie quiet, as if they were transfixed or hypnotized. The crisis was too great to be discussed – or questioned. Over and over again Koina opened her mouth, but no words came out. There seemed to be no words she could afford to utter.

A Behemoth-class Amnion defensive had arrived with too much velocity too close to UMCPHQ. Earlier the station had shifted to a geosynchronous orbit over Suka Bator. Now the huge defensive decelerated straight for it as if she were aimed like a shaft of coherent ruin at Warden Dios' heart.

Koina couldn't think of anything to say except, What am I going to do now? Dear God, what am I going to do?

Suddenly the mission on which Warden had sent her to Earth looked like the biggest mistake of his life. Right now was the worst conceivable moment for her to begin exposing the UMCP's derelictions and malfeasances. It didn't matter that Holt Fasner was the true target of her attack: Warden would suffer for it long before its implications reached the Dragon. And the hostile warship was armed with super-light proton cannon. Therefore anything which undermined Warden Dios also threatened the UMCP and Suka Bator and all of humankind. If Earth's defenses were prevented from responding effectively, the Amnioni's cannon could dismantle most of the planet.

Now where did Koina's duty lie?

She had no idea.

She ought to say something. She was the highest-ranking person aboard. Her own people, if not Forrest Ing's and the crew, would take their reactions from her. She was PR, wasn't she? Surely it was her job to provide information or explanation; put events in perspective; indicate direction? What else was a 'public relations' interface for?

But she couldn't imagine how to go about it. She didn't know what she was going to do.

In which case, she asked herself bitterly, what in hell was *she* for?

Fortunately Deputy Chief Ing's reaction was of a different kind altogether. He listened hard to his PCR for several minutes. Then he breathed in amazement and pride, 'I swear to God, Director Dios must have seen this coming.'

He spoke quietly; but his voice was audible throughout the cabin. Half a dozen techs and guards jerked around to look at him as if he'd offered them some kind of hope.

His tone was so unlike Koina's stunned fear that it surprised her out of her paralysis. Although the doubt in her mouth threatened to choke her, she swallowed it.

'What do you mean?' she asked softly.

Forrest scowled with concentration. Apparently he was

determined to miss no moment of UMCPHQ's broadcast. He didn't keep her waiting for a reply, however.

'When Valdor's drone first came in, Director Dios deployed a cordon of gunboats and pocket cruisers all around the planet. He called *Sledgehammer*, sent flares for *Valor* and *Adventurous*.'

This was common knowledge, but Koina didn't interrupt to say so. She hardly noticed that Ing had sloughed off his usual meticulous courtesy. Under the circumstances, he had no deference to spare for civilians.

'None of us understood,' he said, 'we thought he was just being cautious. We never imagined something like this. But *he* must have. We're as ready as we could possibly be without knowing which side an attack might come from.'

The Deputy Chief closed his eyes like a man visualizing trajectories and vectors. 'Center is pulling the cordon into position,' he went on. '*Sledgehammer* has been ordered to burn. So has *Adventurous*. *Valor* will be here soon. If that defensive doesn't attack and run, she'll find herself in a crossfire she can't escape. We'll get hurt – but she'll be dead.'

'*Hurt?*' Koina protested without thinking. 'She has a proton cannon, for God's sake. She can destroy UMCPHQ. She can destroy *Suka Bator*. Do you call that "hurt"?'

'All right,' Ing growled vehemently. 'We'll get hurt *bad*. But she'll still be dead.'

He took a deep breath to calm himself. 'Anyway,' he added with less force, 'she hasn't fired. God knows why. And the longer she waits, the less damage she'll do before we get her.'

Intuitively Koina knew why. The defensive had entered human space in order to kill *Trumpet*. But the warship had failed. So she must have made the logical assumption that *Trumpet* – and *Punisher* – would return to Earth from Massif-5. The Amnioni had come to intercept them. She wouldn't attack, wouldn't risk her own death, until she'd made another attempt on the gap scout.

That odd piece of certainty did nothing to ease Koina's indecision.

Now that she'd spoken, however, she was no longer stuck. Gathering her resources, she turned to one of the PR techs. 'Get me a channel to Center, would you? I think I should check in.'

'Right away, Director.' At once the woman began tapping keys on the small box which linked the PR director to UMCPHQ.

The demands on the station's dishes must have been staggering. The tech had to reenter her commands – and invoke Koina's full authority – several times before she was able to report, 'Channel's open, Director.' Quickly she handed Koina a throat pickup.

Koina pressed the pickup to the side of her larynx and announced with as much firmness as she could muster, 'This is Protocol Director Koina Hannish.'

'Center, Director Hannish,' an impersonal voice replied in her ear. 'Forgive the delay. We have our hands full.'

'I know you do, Center.' Koina spoke distinctly to cut through Center's background hubbub. 'I don't want to make your life even more complicated. I assume that Director Dios doesn't have time to talk to me. But I need to ask whether he has any instructions for me. Any message at all?'

Forrest Ing frowned in her direction as if she confused him – as if he thought everything had been made clear – but he didn't question her.

'Just a moment, Director.' Koina heard the distant flurry of a keypad. Then Center's voice came back to her PCR. 'Yes, Director Hannish.' The man sounded so far away that he might have been buried in a crypt. 'There is a message.' If the defensive opened fire, UMCPHQ was doomed. Most of the people Koina knew or loved would die in a conflagration of unnatural physics. 'Director Dios didn't ask us to send it out,' the man explained. He may have been apologizing. 'It's coded to be given to you when you call in.'

'I understand, Center,' she returned, although she didn't understand at all. 'Go on.'

'Here it is, Director.' No doubt the man was peering at a readout. 'It says, "Nothing has changed. Go ahead."'

The voice paused, then added, 'I'm sorry, Director. That's all.'

'It's enough,' Koina pronounced. She didn't want anyone in Center – or anyone around her – to know that her heart was failing. 'Thank you.'

She looked at her tech and nodded. When the woman had closed the channel, however, Koina didn't return the pickup. Instead she rested her head on the back of her g-seat and tried to pull her torn emotions back together.

Nothing has changed. Go ahead.

It's enough.

No, it wasn't. Not at all. It told her only that Warden hadn't changed his mind. It did nothing to resolve her dilemma.

Despite the fact that an alien warship had taken him by the throat, he still wanted her to destroy him. Even though humankind's ability to wage war might collapse in the process.

Surely it was wrong to do this *now*?

The GCES would be terrified: she knew that. Certain Members would retain the ability to think and plan and serve. The rest would turn frantic. The threat of mutation had that effect, even on men and women who were normally stable. More than anything else the Members would want protection. And if the effectiveness of the UMCP was compromised, they would inevitably look to Holt Fasner for their defense; to the broader, but less tangible strength of the UMC.

In the name of God! It was possible that Fasner would emerge from this crisis as the Dictator for Life of all human space.

Yet how could she, Koina Hannish, justify disobeying the direct orders of her director? Especially when what Warden had told her to do was: tell the truth?

Any choice she made might have appalling consequences. She didn't know how to think them through.

She needed help.

It would be dangerous – if not irresponsible – to explain her problem to anyone. Nevertheless she decided to take the risk. She was floundering on her own; getting nowhere. If she didn't do *something*, she might slip back into paralysis.

With an effort, she lifted her head.

'One more call,' she told her tech. 'I need to talk to the UWB Senior Member. Captain Sixten Vertigus.'

The woman was distracted by UMCPHQ's voice in her ear; wild-eyed and vague at the same time. Automatically she said, 'Right away, Director.' But when she turned to her keypad, she seemed to have forgotten how to use it. Her hands fumbled as she began to route a transmission.

Koina didn't try to hurry the tech. She knew how the woman felt. While she waited, she thought about what she could hazard saying to Sixten Vertigus.

The captain was old; almost ancient: half the time he was barely awake. But he was the only person Koina could think of who might understand her dilemma. He valued the UMCP. He hated the UMC and Holt Fasner. And he believed in the Council's responsibility for humankind's future.

Abruptly Forrest Ing leaned toward her from his g-seat. 'I don't think you should do that, Director.'

At least he'd remembered to call her by her title.

As she looked over at him – at his hard face and his soldier's eyes – she realized something that she'd never grasped before. He was capable of killing his enemies. Of spending lives in order to do his job. All of Min Donner's people seemed to have bloodshed somewhere in their minds.

'Why not?' she asked noncommittally.

He took the PCR from his ear as if to show that he was serious. 'We can't guarantee you a secure channel,' he explained. 'Not under these conditions. UMCPHQ can't spare the downlink capacity to relay it for us, and we aren't equipped to do it ourselves.' He seemed to have a prescient knowledge of what she wanted to talk to Captain Vertigus about. Chief Mandich must have briefed him thoroughly. 'Somebody might tap in, overhear you.'

His concern took her by surprise. 'Who would bother?' she objected. 'My God, Forrest, there's a Behemoth-class Amnion defensive armed with super-light proton cannon coming down on UMCPHQ. Right now the whole planet is at stake – and Warden Dios is the only one who can do anything about that. Who's going to care who *I* talk to, or what I talk about?'

This was what she needed: someone to argue with; someone to get mad at. That energy would help her think.

The Deputy Chief shrugged; but he didn't back down. 'Cleatus Fane?'

He was right, of course. No doubt Holt Fasner would tackle the crisis of the Amnion warship personally. His First Executive Assistant's mandate would be to deal with the Council – and with Koina. She couldn't afford to be dissuaded, however.

'Then distract him,' she retorted with an edge to her voice. 'While *I'm* talking to Captain Vertigus, you call *him*. Tell him you're calling for me. Tell him – oh, I don't know' – she fluttered her hands – 'tell him I want to be sure he'll attend the emergency session. Make it sound ominous, like I'm trying to scare him. If you get his attention, I'll probably be safe.'

'All right.' Once again Forrest had abandoned deference. 'I'll do it. But I have to tell you –' He shifted still closer to her; pitched his voice so low that he might have been whispering. 'ED Security is working its ass off to get the evidence Director Dios wants for you. If you compromise that, we won't take it lying down.'

He touched an unexpected spring of anger in her. 'Don't insult me, Deputy Chief,' she snapped quietly. 'Protocol is *my* job, not yours. Director Dios has given me my orders. How I carry them out is between him and me.'

He didn't argue the point; but he kept his hard gaze on her as he jacked his PCR back into his ear and told his own communications tech to put him in touch with Cleatus Fane.

'Director,' Koina's tech offered tentatively, 'I have a channel. Captain Vertigus is waiting.'

'Thank you.'

With her heart throbbing anxiously, Koina set the small pickup to her throat and pushed herself as far as she could into the illusory privacy of her g-seat.

The pickup's sensitivity was her only real protection against the ears around her. It could read the vibrations of her larynx even when she subvocalized every word.

As loudly as she dared, she murmured, 'Captain Vertigus, it's Koina Hannish.'

No one else could hear her PCR. Nevertheless his response seemed dangerously loud. He might have been shouting.

'My dear Koina, you astonish me.' Despite the tremors of age, his tone was strangely cheerful. Perhaps he liked emergencies. They may have helped him stay awake. 'My own aides hardly notice me with all this going on. How does it happen that you can afford the time to call?'

Apparently he didn't expect an answer. 'Are you all right?' he went on. 'You sound strained.' Then he chuckled dryly. 'As if anyone doesn't these days.'

She huddled into herself; but that isolation was as illusory as the protection of her g-seat. She felt small and vulnerable as she breathed, 'I need to talk to you, Captain. I need advice.'

'That's absurd,' he replied at once. 'I've never met a woman who needed advice less than you do. Certainly not mine.'

'I'm serious, Sixten.' Koina found it difficult to insist in a whisper. Speaking softly seemed to emphasize her weakness. She had a command decision to make – and no experience to guide her. 'I don't know what to do.'

He sighed. Volume alone made him sound vexed; disdainful. 'Then I suppose you'd better tell me what's troubling you.'

As soon as he offered to listen, she began temporizing. 'This line isn't secure.' Even now she feared to name her concerns. 'Do you know if anyone can hear us on your end?'

'My dear Koina,' he drawled with bitter humor, 'I'm Captain Vertigus – *the* Captain Vertigus. I'm notorious for being old and irrelevant. In any case, I'm usually napping. Nobody *here* wastes time listening to me.'

His sarcasm cut through some of her anxiety. She didn't want to act like a maudlin waif. She needed to be stronger.

'Well, *that's* not true, anyway,' she replied more firmly. 'After the last session,' when the UWB Senior Member had introduced his Bill of Severance, 'Cleatus Fane would probably kill to know what you'll do next.'

He didn't rise to her riposte. Instead he prompted, 'So what's on your mind?'

Go on, she ordered herself. Do it. If she couldn't trust Captain Sixten Vertigus, she couldn't trust anyone. Certainly not herself.

'This is hard to say,' she began slowly. 'There's too much at stake.

'Of course you know what's going on. You're receiving the downlink from UMCPHQ,' not to mention data from Earth's scan net. 'Obviously the situation is bad enough as it is. But it could get a lot worse.' She faltered, then pushed ahead. 'The timing of this incursion gives me a problem.

'I have some rather explosive information. Information that damns the UMCP.' She barely had enough strength – or enough conviction – to say the words. 'And just about does the same to Holt Fasner.'

'Is it about kazes, Koina?' Sixten interrupted.

'Some of it is,' she admitted warily. Without substantial confirmation from ED Security and DA, Hashi Lebwohl's accusation against the UMC CEO was purely inferential. 'The rest is worse. For us, anyway.'

'And –' he urged.

'I was going to tell the Council about it. Dump it all in your collective laps. When this emergency session was first called, all we had to consider was an act of war around Massif-5. But now the Amnion aren't *out there* somewhere. They're right on top of us.

'I'm afraid' – she made an effort to speak clearly – 'it'll be a disaster if I start unpacking our dirty laundry under these conditions. I'm afraid I'll *cause* a disaster.'

'How?' Captain Vertigus sounded distant, as if he were already thinking of something else.

She started to explain. 'I'm afraid –'

Abruptly he cut her off. 'Never mind. Forget I asked. I don't want to know.' Without transition he was no longer willing to hear her. 'You'll have to forgive me, Director Hannish. I've got work to do.'

His dismissal stung her; his manner stung. 'Wait a minute,'

she demanded. 'What *work*?' As soon as she heard the scorn in her voice, however, she tried to recall it. 'I don't mean to belittle the importance of what you do. But hasn't this "work" come up rather suddenly?'

Don't push me away – not now. Not without telling me why.

Sixten sighed again. As if he were answering her question, he said, 'Maybe you didn't think of this.' Her PCR seemed to multiply his asperity. 'Warden Dios is untouchable right now. He can't be countermanded or overruled. The only legal way to stop him is to fire him – if anybody would be crazy enough to do that at a time like this. The war powers provisions of the UMCP charter give him all the authority he needs. He can do any damn thing he wants.'

'Not quite,' Koina retorted. Sixten's unexpected withdrawal left her acid and angry. 'I'm familiar with the law, Captain Vertigus. The GCES can't restrain or countermand the UMCP director. But the UMCP charter can still be revoked. The Council could do it *today*.' Crazy or not, Holt Fasner could fire Warden, if the Council couldn't. 'And if I expose our secrets right now the situation could get *that* bad.'

Who do you think will take Warden's place? Who *can*?

But the old Member refused to be pulled back to what she needed. 'I'm sure you'll make the right decision,' he said unhelpfully. 'You're a big girl, Koina. You can do your job.'

Damn it, Sixten! she wanted to shout. You aren't like this. What's going on?

Who's listening?

But she couldn't ask him that. It might be dangerous –

While she wrestled with her distress, he spoke again.

'There's just one thing I'm worried about,' he offered impersonally, as if he were discussing the weather with a stranger. 'We have a rumor going around. Even I heard it, so it's probably true. Apparently Special Counsel Maxim Igensard has been sharpening his ax. And he's enlisted a whole platoon of Members to help him swing it. He even has Sen Abdullah's proxy.

'I'm not afraid of your information – whatever it is. But

that ax of Maxim's scares me. If anyone can turn this session into a disaster, he can.'

Sixten's tone sharpened. 'Don't play his game, Koina. Make him play yours.'

Then the Senior Member withdrew again. 'If my aides hadn't all gone stupid with fear and distraction,' he remarked sardonically, 'I wouldn't be required to do any work. But they have. And in any case I don't trust them. So it's up to me.

'I need to get ready to reintroduce that Bill of Severance.'

His manner confused her: for a moment she didn't grasp the import of what he said.

'See you soon,' he finished.

He was gone. Her PCR went dead before she could think of a reply.

Reintroduce –? She had the impression that she hadn't heard him right. Reintroduce that Bill –?

Too late, she caught up with him.

Automatically she took the PCR from her ear, handed the earplug and throat pickup to her tech. There was no point in listening to UMCPHQ's broadcast: Center's reports had stopped making sense to her. Reintroduce –? She couldn't tear her mind away from the sheer audacity of Sixten's intentions.

'Did you get what you wanted, Director?' Forrest Ing asked. His tone suggested discipline rather than politeness.

She shook her head, not in denial, but in amazement. 'He was too far ahead of me,' she said unevenly. 'If he was younger – and knew what we know – he could probably handle this mess without us. We wouldn't even need to be there.'

But Sixten Vertigus did need her: she knew that. He didn't have a prayer of succeeding; not against Cleatus Fane's corruption and Maxim Igensard's ambitions. Not unless she carried out Warden's orders. And even then it might go for nothing, unless Chief Mandich and Hashi Lebwohl did their jobs in time.

Indirectly the UWB Senior Member *had* helped her. Somehow he'd changed the nature of the stakes she was playing for in Warden Dios' name.

MORN

With Morn Hyland in command, Davies on guard and Mikka Vasaczk supervising helm, *Punisher* made her damaged way across the void in the direction of the Earth.

Despite her injuries, the cruiser could have covered the distance more swiftly than she did. But Morn refused to allow Emmett on helm to use more than one g thrust for course adjustments or acceleration. You've been through hell, she told Min Donner. So have we. We all need the rest.

That slowed their progress. Simply bringing the vessel around to a heading for Earth required several hours. And without more velocity *Punisher*'s gap crossings were truncated: she had to translate herself across deep space more often, in smaller increments.

Finally she was hampered by the navigational instability caused by her core displacement. Here again Morn gave orders which reduced the cruiser's accuracy and cost time: she maintained internal spin when *Punisher* went into tach. This was dangerous under any circumstances. Internal spin increased the ship's inertia, which diminished her responsiveness. She became more vulnerable to surprises when she resumed tard. But now the hazards were multiplied by the fact that her core no longer spun true. Her orientation in her own gap field was subtly altered: her crossings often produced navigational errors of 200,000 – or even 400,000 – kilomet-

269

ers. Helm had to compensate for each discrepancy before the ship could risk her gap drive again.

This decision Morn explained as she had the other: There's no hurry. We're tired, we need normal g. And that was true. Human bodies were bred for g. The lack of it exhausted them.

In addition this region of space had been charted many times. And *Punisher* was off the main lanes, unlikely to encounter another ship. The chances of a surprise were small.

The rest of her reasons Morn kept to herself.

So time and the cold deep ticked ponderously by, full of leaden waiting. For reasons of his own, Angus was busy aboard *Trumpet*, assisted by the improbable combination of Captain Ubikwe and Ciro. The rest of Morn's companions – Davies, Mikka, Vector – occupied themselves as best they could.

From a discreet distance, Davies kept an uneasy watch on Min Donner. He'd resolved the denials which had alienated him from Morn earlier: he was committed to her now. Doggedly he did what he could to protect her.

Nevertheless his position aboard *Punisher* created a conflict of another kind for him. Morn knew that, even though he hadn't said anything about it. Most of his mind was still filled with her memories, conditioned by her experiences. And that part of him hadn't been complicated by the particular changes which she'd experienced since his force-grown birth. For him, treating Min Donner as an enemy must have hurt like an act of self-violence.

Morn knew how he felt. She knew it too well.

But he had a separate problem as well, one which she only understood because she'd spent so much time under the control of her zone implant. His heightened metabolism made him restless. His body was too highly charged to sit still. He needed constant movement, duties, exertion. When he was inactive his own energies ate him alive.

At intervals he had to take his eyes off the ED director long enough to get some exercise. Thrusting his gun mutely into Morn's hands, he would burst into a run, sprinting feverishly around and around the bridge until sweat splashed from his skin, unabsorbed by the fabric of his alien shipsuit. Then he would return to the command station, retrieve his handgun and resume guarding Min Donner.

Nevertheless the hours passed heavily for him, and he grew gradually frantic under the strain. He was almost literally dying for something to do; something extreme or desperate enough to make him whole.

As for Mikka, Nick's former second stood like clenched iron at Emmett's shoulder, watching everything he did as if she were prepared to watch helm forever. When – at Min's insistence – the bridge officers were relieved, and Emmett's place was taken by *Punisher*'s helm third, Mikka maintained her supervision. Angus' demand for Ciro's company had disturbed her concentration briefly; but she hadn't objected to it. Her only concession to her mortality was that she'd removed the bandage from the nearly-healed wound on her forehead so she could see better. After that she'd kept her vigil like a woman who had no defense against despair except the duties Morn had given her.

Characteristically phlegmatic, Vector appeared to take a less arduous view of the situation. Once he'd confirmed that *Punisher*'s copy of his broadcast was accurate and ready for transmission, he became – in a sense – superfluous. He was useless with a gun; inexperienced at astrogation. For a while he talked to no one in particular about his time at Intertech: about his antimutagen research; about the experience of having his work stripped from him on the whim of a UMCPDA computer. In his oblique way, he was stating his loyalties so that everyone – especially Min Donner – would know where he stood.

After that, however, he announced to Morn that he needed sickbay. Internal spin may have benefited everyone else, but it aggravated the inflammation in his joints. He'd suffered too much g recently; for too long.

She feared to let him go. He would have made a useful hostage if *Punisher*'s crew had chosen to oppose her. But Min intervened. She used the command intercom to warn the ship that Vector Shaheed was on his way to sickbay, and that anyone who interfered with or troubled him would be liable to court-martial. With no discernible concern, he left the bridge.

When he returned he belted himself into a vacant g-seat and went effortlessly to sleep.

Min herself took an occasional nap. Like Davies and Mikka, Morn stayed awake.

That may have been easier for her than it was for her companions. She'd had far more sleep. But she couldn't have rested in any case. Inside its cast her arm itched acutely, nagging her with memories of gap-sickness and pain. And as she skipped the light-years toward Earth, the confidence she projected to protect herself frayed; slowly went to tatters in the stellar winds of the void. Alarm and chagrin took over her fretted heart. An insidious sense of wrongness corroded her intentions – and she had no difficulty identifying its sources.

One was the dismaying fact that *Punisher* had let *Calm Horizons* live.

The Amnioni's survival was bad enough; dangerous enough. Samples of Morn's tainted blood remained safe aboard her. She'd heard Vector's broadcast, receiving his formula. But the threats didn't end there.

Earlier *Calm Horizons* had allowed *Trumpet* to escape: the warship had chosen to defend herself rather than kill her target, even though the apparent logic of the situation indicated that *Trumpet*'s death was essential. The Amnioni's decision might be explained by the argument that she couldn't be certain of destroying her target, and therefore couldn't risk being destroyed herself. However, Morn could think of other explanations –

At first she'd believed that the Amnion had decided to live so that they could return to forbidden space with their knowledge of Vector's immunity drug. But by now she'd had time to imagine other terrors. Was it possible that the Amnion could attack or neutralize *Trumpet* in other ways? Did they have other ships like *Soar* – human ships in human space, waiting to ambush the gap scout? Had they made covert agreements with Holt Fasner to undermine humankind's future for the sake of his profits?

Entirely apart from the reasons she'd given Min, Morn maintained internal spin precisely because it slowed *Punisher*'s progress. She wanted to reach Earth later than her enemies might expect. That way she could hope to catch them already deployed and visible, rather than lurking out of sight behind her. Spring the ambush before she stepped into it.

Unfortunately other stresses wore at her as well.

She hadn't told Min Donner anything like the whole truth about what she was doing, or why. She hadn't discussed her fear of Holt Fasner's – and therefore the UMCP's – reaction to her intentions. And she'd made no mention of what could happen to her if *Punisher* risked hard g, either now or later. Nevertheless as time dragged on she believed more and more that Min had already penetrated her secrets.

Despite the obvious inadequacy of Morn's explanations, the ED director didn't press her. As closed as stone, Min accepted Morn's command of the bridge in silence, speaking only when Morn asked something of her, or when she thought the cruiser's people needed attention. To that extent, at least, she appeared to consider herself nothing more than a surrogate for Captain Ubikwe. Yet something in the nature of her unresponsiveness conveyed the impression that she knew about Morn's gap-sickness.

Initially that confused Morn. Then, however, she remembered the weeks Angus had spent in UMCPDA's hands, being welded. Min probably knew everything that Angus had ever known about Morn, or done to her, or desired from her, up to the time when Nick Succorso had snatched her away from Com-Mine.

Min knew about Morn's zone implant –

Morn had grown accustomed to Angus' knowledge; to Mikka's, Davies', Vector's. Familiarity inured her to it. But the thought that the ED director also knew filled her with shame; as aggrieved and unanswerable as the burning in her damaged arm. Min Donner was the moral authority on which

273

the entire Hyland family had built its beliefs and commitments.

And Morn had killed most of that family with her own hands. In some sense she'd killed herself: the Morn Hyland who'd served UMCPED no longer existed. Only Davies remained to uphold the allegiance of the Hylands.

As the journey dragged its length across the stars, Morn found it increasingly difficult to face Min without breaking down into explanations or appeals which might cost her more than she could afford.

Min Donner might be as honest as steel: the UMCP was not. Behind her stood men like Hashi Lebwohl and Warden Dios; men with ambiguous intentions, harsh desires. And behind them loomed the Dragon in his malice. Regardless of her personal integrity, Min bore a kind of borrowed corruption. Borrowed or imposed –

Morn kept as much of her own truth to herself as she could.

From time to time – again at Min's insistence – *Punisher*'s bosun brought food to the bridge. This was not for the duty officers, who could visit the galley when they were relieved, but for Morn, the others and herself. Morn ate what she could. Vector roused himself to eat, but seemed more interested in coffee. Mikka gulped sandwiches where she stood. When Min had taken as much as she wanted, Davies devoured the rest.

Nothing else passed the hours except the studied litany of reports from helm and scan: descriptions of navigational errors and open space; announcements of course corrections or tach. No other vessels left blips or particle trails across the cruiser's course. Communications heard nothing. Whatever *Calm Horizons* intended, she'd apparently lost her strange ability to track *Trumpet*'s movements.

By slow increments the distance to Earth diminished.

Angus brought Captain Ubikwe and Ciro back to the bridge shortly after helm announced that *Punisher* would soon be ready for the last gap crossing to Earth.

By then the rotation of watches had returned most of the

officers Morn had first seen to the bridge: a woman named Cray on communications; Porson at scan; a shy, awkward young woman to the data station; a truculent, square-fisted man on targ. Only the helm officer was different: instead of Emmett a man called Patrice guided the ship.

Captain Ubikwe saluted his people gruffly as he arrived. Ignoring Morn, he faced Min. 'Is my ship all right, Director Donner?' he asked in a tired rumble.

Min's gaze had a sardonic cast as she referred the question to Morn.

The sound of voices roused Vector from a final nap. He looked up, straightened himself in his g-seat; smiled a question at Ciro, but didn't speak.

Davies' face showed relief. He may have been reassured by Angus' return. Or he may have been glad to see that Angus hadn't hurt Captain Ubikwe.

Morn was troubled by the sensation that her features had gone numb. She rubbed her cheeks with her good hand, trying to bring them back to life. She would reach Earth soon, after all this time; after so much death and pain. As the weariness of her long vigil accumulated, it seemed to feed her shame. Soon she would be so tired that only her inadequacies remained.

'We haven't done anything to risk her, Captain,' she answered. 'You know that.' He could interpret the gentle interaction of *Punisher*'s spin and thrust as well as anyone. 'Your people have been cooperative, for which I'm grateful. Director Donner insisted, so we've rotated the watches pretty regularly. There hasn't been any trouble.' Distantly she added, 'No sign of any other ships.'

That was about to change, of course. Morn hoped to resume tard as close to UMCPHQ as possible, in the UMCP's dedicated gap range if helm could manage it. As soon as the cruiser entered Earth's solar system, the traffic squall of navigational buoys would reach her, and scan would fill up with blips.

Punisher would have to be much more careful.

Captain Ubikwe grunted an acknowledgment. Something

in his tone – or his manner – tugged at Morn's attention.

He seemed tired to the bone: Angus must have kept him busy almost continuously. But behind his fatigue lay an adjustment of some kind; an amelioration. He looked like he'd been reconciled to the plight of his ship.

Angus must have told him something –

Morn turned to Angus; but he didn't meet her gaze. Instead he studied the display screens, absorbing everything he could about the ship's position and status. He, too, had changed – but it was a change she recognized. He emanated ferocity as if his zone implants emission had risen to an entirely new level.

He was getting ready to fight for his life.

'Are *you* all right, Dolph?' Min asked quietly.

The captain shrugged his heavy shoulders; glanced at Angus like a man who didn't know how much he was allowed to say. Angus didn't react, however. After a moment Captain Ubikwe sighed.

'Just tired. I haven't done that much crawling around in small spaces since the Academy. But I guess we're finished.'

'Finished with what, Captain?' Morn asked. Angus hadn't told her why he wanted both Dolph Ubikwe and Ciro aboard *Trumpet*.

Dolph shrugged again. 'We fixed the drives. Both of them. Sort of. They test green. Readouts sure as hell look stable. But I wouldn't want to pin my life on that gap drive.'

'You won't have to,' Angus muttered.

Captain Ubikwe plowed on, unheeding. 'We couldn't calibrate the hysteresis transducer. Not without activating the drive. So Captain Thermopyle did it by guesswork. I don't care if he carries the specs for the entire created universe around in his head. You can't calibrate the transducer without activating the drive. That gap field could disassemble the whole ship and leave it drifting in tach like so much dust.'

'Captain Thermopyle,' Min drawled, 'I don't suppose you'll consider telling us why you think you need *Trumpet*'s drives?'

Morn also wanted an answer; but Davies distracted her by

gesturing for her attention. When she turned to see what he wanted her to notice, she found herself peering hard at Ciro.

More than either Angus or Captain Ubikwe, he'd become different. He wore a look of hooded concentration; of focus he meant to conceal. Somehow the guilt and horror tormenting him had eased. Or they'd taken root – grown to a kind of clenched, inarguable hysteria. He met no one's eyes; hardly raised his head. But from under his lowered brows, his gaze glinted with intention.

Mikka hadn't seen him yet. She stood rigid at her post beside Patrice, her back to her brother.

Mikka, Morn wanted to say. Mikka, *look*. What's happened to him? What did Angus do to him? But Angus stopped her by replying to Director Donner.

'Sure.' Abruptly he turned from the screens. A grin bared his yellow teeth. 'I'll tell you. Your precious Hashi Lebwohl programmed me to think about things like survival. Keeping people alive. Morn doesn't do that, so it's up to me. *Trumpet* gives us a way off this ship. If we need it.'

Morn studied him in wonder and alarm. Was that really what he was doing? Compensating for her weaknesses, her blind spots; her instinct for self-destruct –?

When I'm in trouble, she'd once said to Davies, *the only thing I can think of is to hurt myself. I need a better answer.*

Was Angus trying to help her find one?

But at once Dolph put in heavily, 'That's not the whole story. Maybe it's true as far as it goes. But he has a pretty extreme notion of "survival" and "keeping people alive". We had a real shouting match about it. He showed this poor kid –'

Angus whirled on Captain Ubikwe. '*Stop* right there, fat man!' he barked. 'I *warned* you. This doesn't have anything to do with you.' He raised his fists. 'It's not too late for a little BR surgery.'

Rolling his eyes provocatively, Dolph closed his mouth.

But Ciro spoke before Angus could prevent him. 'He showed me how to use the singularity grenades.' He might have been staking a claim; announcing who he had become.

'Arm them. Launch them. Detonate them. Suck everything into a black hole.' He smiled – a grin as thin as a cut. 'Like *Free Lunch*. And Nick.'

Showed me –

That shocked the bridge – which may have been Captain Ubikwe's purpose. Involuntarily the duty officers stopped what they were doing and stared. The woman at the data station had gone pale. The man on targ chewed curses under his breath.

– how to use –

'*Ciro!*'

Crying her brother's name, Mikka flung herself around to face him. Vector flinched in consternation.

– the singularity grenades.

For an instant Morn feared her heart would fail. Acid mortality burned inside her cast. With one stroke, Angus had taken away her control of the situation; transformed it into a confrontation charged with blood and coercion. He'd turned Ciro into a pawn in a struggle she hadn't foreseen and couldn't imagine.

Suck everything into a black hole.

And she'd let him do it. Despite all the pain and abasement he'd inflicted on her, she'd trusted him. Trusted his impulse to stand by his commitments to her; trusted his gratitude at being freed from his priority-codes.

Trusted his core programming – and the men who'd designed it.

Like *Free Lunch*. And Nick.

'Christ, Angus!' Davies shouted hotly. Heedless of his assignments, he dropped his watch on Min to face his father. 'What the hell do you think you're *doing*? Don't you suppose he has enough problems already?'

Min didn't need to be guarded. She'd made it plain hours ago that she accepted Morn's command. In some way the actions of *Trumpet*'s people suited the ED director. Nevertheless she didn't take Ciro's revelation calmly.

'Ensign Hyland!' she snapped like the crack of a whip. 'You told me these people were under arrest. That makes you responsible for them. But a man in your custody has just given highly classified and *dangerous* information to a known illegal who *also* happens to be a kid hardly old enough to know his own mind.

'This is on the record, Ensign. If you thought you could protect these people by posing as the arresting officer, you're wrong now. Their conduct incriminates you as well as them.'

Abruptly Patrice remembered his duties. He looked down at his readouts. 'Captain,' he announced to Dolph, 'in five minutes we'll reach our tach window on UMCPHQ's gap range. If we miss it, we'll have to decelerate to compensate.'

Five minutes? Only five?

Angus had shown –

'Ensign Hyland,' Min demanded severely, 'is there anything you would like to say?'

Yes! Morn thought; almost wailed aloud. This isn't what I wanted! The stakes were already too high. I didn't know he was going to do *this*!

She'd killed most of her family. Now she was about to become the cause of even more death.

But when she looked at Angus, the naked appeal on his face closed her throat. Without transition she felt that she'd been translated back to Mallorys Bar & Sleep. He was saying, *I accept. The deal you offered.* Her black box in exchange for his life. *I'll cover you.* He might have been thrusting the control to her zone implant into her hand again: the need which racked his gaze was the same. *I could have killed you. I could have killed you anytime.*

Fiercely she forced down her dismay; her weakness. She didn't want another zone implant control – or anything like it. But this wasn't Mallorys, or Com-Mine: it was *Punisher*. Angus had shown Ciro *how to use the singularity grenades*. The grenades were aboard *Trumpet*, however, and Ciro was here. Whatever Angus had in mind wasn't immediate. She could take the time to think about her choices; try to understand them.

'Helm, I want fifteen minutes.' The steadiness of her voice amazed her. She sounded like a woman who still knew what to do. 'Nudge braking thrust enough to cover the difference.'

Patrice referred the question to Dolph. 'Captain?'

'Do it, Sergei,' the captain rumbled. 'Ensign Hyland is in command. This is her mess. Personally, I'm curious to see how she gets out of it.'

Morn nodded. 'Thank you, Captain.' As soon as Patrice began tapping keys, she felt the viscid drag of *Punisher*'s deceleration tug her against her belts.

Not enough pressure to threaten her –

She didn't wait for the stress to end. Facing Angus again, she demanded grimly, 'I need an explanation.'

'*I* need an explanation!' Davies moved through the inertia of braking toward Angus, clutching his handgun as if he meant to use it. His eyes bulged like his father's. 'God *damn* it, Angus, he's hardly older than I am! Isn't there *anybody* you aren't willing to sacrifice?'

Angus flung a snarl over his shoulder at Davies. 'You mean "sacrifice" the way you "sacrificed" Sib Mackern? You think sending him out to die just so you could get rid of Nick is *better*?'

That stopped Davies: he couldn't answer. He lowered his gun until it dangled at his side, useless to him.

Mikka might not have heard Angus and Davies; or Min Donner. She'd begun to shiver as if she were straining at a leash, held back by ropes from breaking out into blows and fury.

'*Ciro*,' she groaned deep in her throat, 'what in God's name has he done to you?'

Abruptly Ciro retorted, '*Stop* it, Mikka. *You* aren't the one she gave a mutagen to. *I* am. You don't have any idea what it's like, knowing you have to kill everybody you care about.' He turned his head to look at Angus. 'But *he* does.'

'Sib volunteered,' Vector offered quietly. He studied his former second as if he could see the boy dying. 'It sounds like Ciro did too.' Then he shrugged sadly. 'He has as much right as Sib to make his own decisions.'

Angus rasped at Davies, 'You listening to this, boy?' He jerked a thumb in Vector's direction. 'Sib did what he wanted.

So is Ciro. The only difference is, you *liked* what Sib did.'

'I love this,' Captain Ubikwe snorted. 'You're all as charming as snakes. Exactly what *did* you do to poor old Sib? And what's this about a "mutagen"?'

Trumpet's people ignored him. Min kept her attention focused on Morn and Angus.

Angus still faced Davies. 'Well, I don't give a shit what you think. Ciro is working for me now. Instead of kicking him into a corner like a goddamn puppy, I'm giving him something to *do*.'

'Angus' – Morn raised her voice to make him hear her – 'that's not good enough!' Did he call this a better answer? 'I'm not interested in how you justify yourself. *I want an explanation*.'

Angus tore his gaze away from Davies to meet Morn's demand. His whole body was vivid with fury: he looked like he might spring for her throat. But then he seemed to take hold of himself, fight down his vehemence. He may have had some measure of control over his zone implants; may have used them to calm himself. Slowly his passion shifted from anger to supplication.

He didn't speak as if he were begging. Nevertheless Morn saw that he was in the grip of an old terror: the same mortal dread which had ruled his life. Driven by that darkness, he'd offered her her black box in exchange for his own survival.

Stiff with reined brutality, he answered, 'I don't believe Min fucking Donner here is as pure as you think, and I don't believe you can protect any of us. Least of all yourself. One way or another, the cops are going to feed us our guts before this is over. That's their job.'

The corners of Min's jaw knotted, but she betrayed no other reaction.

'You can probably face that,' Angus told Morn. 'Hell, you can probably face anything. But I can't. I am not going to let Hashi Lebwohl and his surgical apes get their hands on me again.'

He moved toward her until he could close his fists on the edge of the command board. Strain whitened his knuckles.

He ignored Min and Dolph and the duty officers; Ciro and Mikka; Vector and Davies: Morn may have been the only person aboard who truly mattered to him.

'I'll back you all the way,' he promised. 'As far as I can. Until you fail. What you want to do can't work. The cops have all the muscle – and muscle always wins. But I don't care about that. I owe you. I'll try anything to help you.

'But I've already been welded once. I won't go through it again. When I run out of choices, I'm going to take *Trumpet* and leave. And I'll take Ciro with me. He's my insurance. If I'm too busy to do it myself, he can launch enough trouble to let us get away.'

He bowed his head momentarily, took a deep breath, then looked at her again.

'Morn, trust me.' Traces of pleading left his tone raw. 'If you can't do that, trust *him*.' A twitch of his head indicated Ciro. 'He's right. None of you understand what Sorus Chatelaine did to him. I can use that.'

'*Use* it?' Mikka wheeled on him, her eyes burning like black suns. 'You sonofabitch, *use* it?'

'Yes!' he retorted. His gaze clung to Morn; but he projected his voice to the entire bridge. 'As of now, this whole damn ship has been taken hostage. You are going to follow Morn's orders, and you are going to fucking like it. Otherwise –'

'Otherwise,' Ciro finished for him, 'I'll go back to *Trumpet* and set off a grenade.' He made the idea sound simple enough to be sane. 'I know how. I know all about it.'

And he might be able to do it. If Angus escorted him.

Captain Ubikwe nodded as if he understood; as if Morn and Angus and Ciro had finally reached the point which had changed his attitude toward being deposed from his command. Before anyone else could react, he cleared his throat loudly enough to catch even Mikka's attention.

'He's protecting us, Min.' He faced the ED director formally, with his shoulders square and his chin up, as if he were expecting a reprimand. Embarrassment twisted his mouth: he didn't like defending Angus. Still he went ahead. 'Sounds

282

silly, I know. But he did a lot of talking while we were sequestered in *Trumpet*. Pretty oblique, most of it – but I got the
impression he's willing to cover our asses as well as his own.'

'You spent too much time listening to him, Dolph,' Min
muttered softly; warning him. 'You aren't talking sense
anymore.'

Dolph cleared his throat again. 'It's like this. The threat
of a singularity grenade makes us innocent. We haven't been
"derelict in our duty". We haven't "given aid and comfort
to the enemy". Nobody can challenge us for letting Ensign
Hyland take over – or for letting her do anything else she
wants.' His voice took on a subtle ring; a hint of excitement
or hope. 'The Dragon himself can't challenge us. And he can't
fault Director Dios, either. Not when *Trumpet* is carrying
singularity grenades, and a kid who's already lost his mind
knows how to use them.'

When he stopped, his words seemed to echo off the bulkheads for a moment, as if their potential refused to die away.

Mikka stared dismay at him. For her he might have been
speaking in an alien language. Perhaps nothing he said could
have penetrated her transfixed distress. But Vector had begun
to grin – a harsh smile, whetted by recognition or remorse.
Davies shook his head slowly, muttering to himself. Captain
Ubikwe's explanation didn't match Ciro's coherent lunacy.

Nevertheless Angus bared his teeth as if he defied argument. He hadn't wanted the bridge to know how he'd
involved Ciro – but apparently he liked Dolph's conclusions.

'It won't work.' Min's tone cut through the hints of resonance. 'Captain Thermopyle is a welded UMCP cyborg. Holt
Fasner knows that, even if the Council doesn't. He'll assume
Angus is acting on my orders. Or Warden's. He probably
won't believe Angus doesn't answer his priority-codes
anymore.'

Morn winced inwardly; took a deep breath and held it to
steady her racing heart. Holt Fasner knew? The possibilities
Captain Ubikwe had raised seemed to vanish as quickly as
they'd appeared.

His shoulders slumped. He ducked his head to cover a

scowl of disappointment. 'In that case,' he answered in a growl, 'I guess it's up to you. Ensign Hyland has the command station. You've let her sit there all this time.' He might have been saying, You let her have my ship. 'But you just reminded her she's responsible for the people in her custody. You used the word "incriminates". Are you going to try to stop her now?'

'No,' Angus snapped defensively, 'she isn't. And you aren't either. I don't give a shit what Holt Fasner thinks. My priority-codes don't work anymore, and I'll kill the first asshole who interferes with Morn.

'You want to try me, be my guest. We don't need you anymore. We'll go back to *Trumpet*. Put a grenade in one of your thruster tubes and *leave*. You'll have some real excitement the next time you try to maneuver.'

His threat seemed to dominate the bridge; but Min wasn't swayed by it. 'Don't lie to yourself, Captain Thermopyle,' she responded. 'You need us. Morn needs us. And she knows it. She wants to go to Earth. We're her safe-conduct. Without us she might as well stay away.'

She faced Morn as if she expected Morn to agree with her.

Clenching with tension, Davies waited for her reaction.

Angus had misjudged his leverage. Morn herself had thought it looked stronger than it was.

She felt crowded in by secret desires and conflicting exigencies. Anything she did, any step she took, would satisfy or frustrate purposes she didn't understand. For days she'd had the nascent impression that she and her friends were groping to find their necessary roles in some huge, blind contest between Warden Dios and Holt Fasner; a contest with stakes so high they appalled her. She couldn't begin to guess what form the struggle took – or what it had to do with her. Still her sense of being enmeshed in a bitter and covert battle grew sharper all the time.

Inadvertently, perhaps, Min had given her confirmation. The ED director might have ceded *Punisher* to her for any number of reasons; but fear or uncertainty weren't among them.

284

One way or another, the UMCP had delivered Morn to Nick. Nick had been allowed to take her off Com-Mine. Yet Angus' programming had compelled him to rescue her.

And later the same transmission which had supplied Nick with Angus' priority-codes had also enabled her and Davies to end Nick's control. Now Angus had blocked those codes altogether.

Could Holt Fasner know that as well? Min believed not.

Could Warden Dios? Angus had said he did.

But when UMCPDA welded Angus, Warden had informed Holt Fasner. Not the GCES.

The time had come for better answers.

Morn couldn't resolve her dilemma by simply taking what the UMCP director did on faith. She had to make her decision by staking everything on the people she knew best. Angus and Davies. Mikka and Vector. Herself.

From Captain Ubikwe's g-seat she replied to Min and the rest of the bridge.

'That's true,' she admitted slowly. 'But this whole discussion is beside the point.' *I'll back you all the way.* 'I'm in command. And I don't care what you think about it.' *But I've already been welded once. I won't go through it again.* 'I've made my decision.

'I'm satisfied with Angus' explanation.'

Harsh relief flared in Angus' eyes, and Davies winced; but she didn't pause.

'I command this ship,' she insisted, 'and I'm going to command her until we do what we're going home for. Ciro will stay here, on the bridge.' Away from the grenades. 'We'll all stay here. But I won't consider myself under your authority again until we've done the job we set out to do.'

Without flinching she met Min Donner's gaze – and her own shame.

For a long moment no one spoke. No one appeared to move. Then Captain Ubikwe shifted his weight. Still scowling, he muttered in a heavy voice, 'I don't know about you, Min, but I'm practically dying to find out what that "job" is.'

Slowly Min turned toward him. Her hard eyes and strict mouth revealed nothing: whatever she felt was contained by a smoldering self-discipline. She let him see that she was sure – of herself; of what she wanted. Then she shifted her gaze back to Morn.

'It still matters what I think,' she pronounced. 'Don't tell yourself it doesn't. You don't command the UMCP – or UMCPHQ. If you want me to let this go, you'll have to convince me.' Before Morn could ask, How? she went on, 'Tell me what happened to Ciro. Tell me about Nick Succorso and Sib Mackern.'

She might have been saying, Tell me what kind of people you've become.

The question surprised Morn. And yet it made perfect sense to her. Like her, the ED director had to take a position based on less than complete information. Morn hadn't revealed what she meant to do. How else could Min make her own decisions?

Morn desperately did not want to lose the tenuous acceptance Min had granted her so far. Min was right: Morn needed her.

'Captain,' Patrice murmured cautiously to Dolph, 'we're three minutes from our new tach window.'

Captain Ubikwe didn't acknowledge him. Neither did Min. For them, as for everyone else on the bridge, Morn's answer took precedence.

She kept it as brief as she could. Three minutes wasn't much time – and she didn't want to dwell on the pain of losing Sib; or of Ciro's crisis.

In a few quick sentences, she explained who Sorus Chatelaine and *Soar* were; why they worked for the Amnion; why Nick hated them. Then she described Sorus' attempt to stop *Trumpet* by using Ciro; Nick's reaction when he lost control of Angus; the destruction of Deaner Beckmann's installation; *Soar*'s pursuit through the swarm; Ciro's cure. She told why Nick had been allowed to set an EVA ambush for *Soar* – and why Sib had gone with him. She admitted that Ciro had sabotaged *Trumpet*'s drives.

Yet even that short summary made her chest swell with distress. Anger mounted in her voice because she hurt. When she finished, she demanded harshly, 'Are you satisfied, Director Donner? Do you think I *like* where we are, or what we have to do?'

She expected a harsh retort. Angus seemed to brace himself to support her. Mikka glowered as if she meant to explode if anyone criticized her brother.

But Min's reply was mild: she sounded almost sad. '"Satisfied"?' she asked. 'Not really. But I don't blame you for that. I'll accept the consequences of whatever you want to do.'

At once she faced Dolph again. 'The answer is no, Captain. I'm not going to oppose Ensign Hyland's command. We've come this far with her. We'll go a little farther.'

A thin sigh passed around the bridge. Relief or regret: Morn couldn't tell which.

Min's assent was provisional at best; but Morn found that she was content with it.

Captain Ubikwe shrugged. 'In that case, Ensign Hyland,' he remarked in a bass rumble, 'I think you better tell the ship we're about to go into tach.'

Davies shook his head. 'Damn it,' he protested under his breath. He seemed unsure of himself in some way. And everything Morn and Angus and Min did appeared to increase his doubt. He peered at the handgun in his fist, grimaced and abruptly shoved it into one of his pockets. 'Why didn't you just say so? Why did we have to go through all this?'

Morn didn't respond. She was in command now; more than she'd ever been before. She had her duties to think about.

'Prepare for tach, helm,' she ordered, knowing she would be obeyed. 'Data, warn the rest of the ship that we're going to drop internal spin.' Around Earth space was usually too busy to tolerate navigational errors and poor maneuverability.

A moment later she added, 'Communications, prepare Vector Shaheed's message for immediate transmission. I want to start broadcasting as soon as we resume tard.'

Min cocked an eyebrow. 'I wouldn't do that if I were you,' she put in quickly.

Angus snorted. 'I'm sure you wouldn't.'

'Why not?' Morn asked.

The ED director gave her a bleak smile. 'I think it's called "look before you leap". You can't know what you're getting into. Hell, *I* don't. How could you? It won't hurt you to take a few readings, listen to the transmission traffic, before you make up your mind.'

'Hell, yes,' Angus sneered. 'That way you can still hope something'll happen to stop us.'

But Morn didn't hesitate. 'All right.' She believed that in some oblique, unspoken way Min was on her side. 'Communications, hold that broadcast for the time being.'

Once the data officer – her name was Bydell – had alerted the ship, Morn tapped keys to disengage internal spin. Hydraulic systems eased g out of the cruiser as her rotation slid to a stop within her hulls. Except for the muffled sighing of the pumps and servos, the process should have been silent. But this time it wasn't. A faint grinding like a visceral shudder carried briefly through the bulkheads. Spin ended with a tangible jolt.

Punisher's core displacement was getting worse.

Min Donner and Captain Ubikwe took g-seats along the walls, belted themselves in. Davies followed their example. Mikka glared miserably at Ciro for a moment, then kicked off in his direction, grabbed his arm and hauled him to a g-seat. He nodded as she swore at him, closed his belts, then coasted to a seat herself.

Only Angus remained standing. Anchored on the edge of the command board with a cyborg's strength, he waited where he was, watching the display screens and the quick scroll of the readouts. His stance was charged and expectant, as if he were guarding Morn – or guarding against her.

'Fifteen seconds to tach,' Patrice announced.

'Fifteen seconds to Earth,' Davies muttered to himself. 'If that's really where we end up.'

Ten.

288

Instinctively Morn held her breath. In the measureless instant when the gap field dislocated her across the light-years, she wouldn't feel anything: no one ever did. The discontinuity which had exposed the flaw of gap-sickness in her brain took place in a realm of physics which human senses couldn't register. And yet most people were like her: they held their breath, or tensed in some other way. Nerves and ganglia reacted with an almost cellular fear – a dread like humankind's genetic abhorrence of the Amnion – to the prospect of being torn without transition from one place to another billions of k apart.

Five.

Scan, data and helm maintained a stream of status reports, their voices low.

Nothing changed until Porson shouted frantically from scan that *Punisher* had dropped short of her intended co-ordinates in UMCPHQ's dedicated gap range by 40,000 k. And *Calm Horizons* was there ahead of her.

WARDEN

Warden rode in the control cabin of his shuttle as the small craft carried him out toward the impending bulk of the Amnion defensive. There was nothing for him to do in the space he was supposed to occupy – the so-called director's cabin – and he couldn't bear to sit idle. He didn't want to spend the time watching some remorseless chronometer tick his life away.

Unfortunately he had no duties here, either. His crew was more than competent for the simple task of ferrying him out to *Calm Horizons*. Nevertheless he could occupy himself by studying the scan displays and command readouts; following the slow concentration of his ships around the defensive; analyzing the Amnioni's heavy profile for signs of damage or weakness.

As a matter of course the shuttle's instruments were linked to Earth's scan net. He could watch for *Punisher* and *Trumpet*.

The longer they took to arrive, the weaker *Calm Horizons'* position would become. Eventually *Sledgehammer* would be in place to unleash the force of her guns. Then Marc Vestabule's leverage would erode to practically nothing. No human power could prevent the defensive from firing on Suka Bator. But after that she would die quickly. Even UMCPHQ might survive the battle.

If *Trumpet* stayed away long enough, *Calm Horizons* would have nothing left to bargain with except the Council's survival – and Warden's life.

Angus' programming had been written to restrict the conditions under which he could return to Earth. He couldn't make that decision for himself: it had to be imposed on him by some authority his datacore recognized. If Nick Succorso didn't order it – and if *Trumpet* managed to evade *Punisher*, so that Min Donner had no chance to intervene – Angus might stay away indefinitely.

In another life – a saner, cleaner existence – Warden would have been praying with all his heart to see no sign of *Trumpet* on the scan net.

In this life, however, his prayers were of another kind.

He needed Morn. Here. Now.

Why else had he undermined Holt's direct orders by giving Morn and Davies the means to oppose Nick – the means to return to Earth? At tremendous cost he'd created a window of vulnerability for Holt Fasner: a small, elusive gap in the Dragon's normally impregnable defenses. But Koina wouldn't be able to hold that window open long. Without Morn – and without concrete evidence from either Hashi or Chief Mandich – she would eventually fail.

And if the Council died, the outcome of this crisis might be the exact opposite of the one Warden had pursued with so much pain. Holt himself might well become the government. At present there was no other power which could make decisions for humankind in a time of war. If Marc Vestabule lost what he hoped to gain by negotiating with Warden, the consequences for humanity would be catastrophic.

Despite his sworn duty to oppose the Amnion, Warden Dios hoped desperately that *Trumpet* would arrive soon. And that the gap scout's people would feel compelled to comply with Vestabule's demands.

Therefore he needed Min. He might convince himself that he had the right and the power to command Morn Hyland; but he had no authority over her son – or Vector Shaheed. And he could no longer trust Angus' priority-codes. If Davies or Morn had freed themselves from Nick, they would be able to countermand any order Warden gave Angus.

Warden needed Min to make *Trumpet*'s people obey him.

Still the scan net gave no hint of *Punisher* or the gap scout. Gunboats and pocket cruisers tightened their paltry cordon around the Amnioni. *Adventurous* lumbered toward the defense from the far side of the planet. Barring some disaster, *Valor* would be in range soon. The net showed *Sledgehammer* on her Earth-bound burn. But *Punisher* and *Trumpet* were beyond the reach of Earth's instruments anywhere in the solar system.

The shuttle had a crew of three: command, scan, communications. At other times the UMCP director traveled with aides and guards; his own communications techs; various UMCP officers. But for this trip he'd left everyone except the crew behind. Jeopardizing the smallest possible number of lives –

Abruptly command cleared his throat. 'Twenty minutes, Director. They've assigned us a docking port. I can put it on a screen if you want to see it.'

Warden shook his head. He didn't care what the port looked like. After a moment he asked communications, 'Is CEO Fasner still yelling at us?'

'Home Office is, Director,' communications answered. 'Not the CEO in person. He's given up.'

'Have they bothered to mention what he wants?'

'You're ordered to reply, Director. That's all.'

'Too bad,' Warden muttered sardonically. 'It might have been interesting to hear him tell me I'm fired. If I had that on record, he would have trouble explaining it to the Council.'

Legally Holt could fire the UMCP director. But the timing would look bad; very bad. The Members might think that Holt Fasner didn't want Warden to keep them alive.

Warden wasn't willing to take the risk, however. Holt might give him orders which would make sense to the Council, but which Warden couldn't or wouldn't obey. Then Holt would have an excuse he could hide behind for replacing Warden.

'Contact HO once I board *Calm Horizons*,' Warden instructed communications. 'Tell the CEO that under the War Powers provisions of the UMCP charter I'm not authorized – much less required – to discuss my actions with civilians.'

He sighed. 'That's a pretty loose interpretation of the law,' he admitted to his crew. 'But maybe it'll make Holt leave you alone.'

The chronometer gave him eighteen minutes.

Punisher and *Trumpet* weren't anywhere on the net.

Command squirmed as if he sat on an uncomfortable secret. 'I think you should take a look at the docking port, Director.'

Warden frowned over a twist of apprehension. 'Why is that?' The man's awkwardness worried him. Had he missed something?

Command glanced quickly at scan. Scan jerked a nod of agreement.

'Just let me show you, Director,' command asked.

Warden folded his arms over his chest to contain his anxiety. 'So show me.'

Quickly command tapped keys. In a moment net schematics scrolled off the main display, and were replaced by a tight video image of *Calm Horizons'* flank. Under other circumstances there would have been nothing to see. The darkness of space was almost absolute. But the defensive had already lit her docking lamps. A wash of incandescence etched her knurled, inhuman skin.

Warden studied the display because that was what command and scan – and communications? – wanted him to do.

'It's a docking port,' he observed impersonally, as if what he saw had nothing to do with him. 'Their airlock doesn't fit ours. Neither do their grapples and clamps. But that looks like an adjustable seal. And we can flex our own. I won't need an EVA suit.' He cocked an eyebrow at command. 'What else do you want me to notice?'

'There, sir.' With a twitch of his hand, command indicated an imprecise bulge at the edge of the screen; the edge of the light. 'That's her proton gun. The emitter.'

Sixteen minutes.

'So?' Warden prodded.

Command turned to scan for help.

'They have us on targ, Director,' scan put in stiffly. 'Guns like theirs, they could fry us in seconds. But if we wait until we're close – another ten minutes – we'll be under their fire horizon. We could veer off, burn –'

'We could crash into that emitter, sir,' command finished. 'Wreck it.'

Wreck –

Oh, shit. New fears cut at Warden's heart. For several seconds he couldn't respond. A clean death – A chance to leave Holt Fasner and the corruption of the UMCP and humankind's future to someone else; someone who didn't have so much shame feeding like a corrosive on his lacerated conscience. Veer off, burn, crash. Die like a hero. Let Morn and Angus, Hashi and Min and Koina pick up the pieces if they could.

But if he did that – he, Warden Dios, who had clawed these wounds into his own soul – there would be nothing clean about it. It would be a coward's death: an abandonment of all the people who had the most right to rely on him.

For him no death would ever be clean unless he took Holt Fasner down with him.

At last he regained his voice. 'And what happens to us?' he asked gruffly.

'Well, Director' – command swallowed a lump of discomfort – 'we're dead, I guess. This craft wasn't built for collision.

'But I'm not sure you're ever coming back, sir,' he went on. 'I'm not even sure we are. Once you're aboard, they can finish us pretty easily.' He hesitated, then faced Warden squarely. 'It might be more useful to take out their proton gun.'

Warden paused as if to consider the idea. 'If we do that, we'll save the Council,' he mused. 'So far, so good. But we'll kill UMCPHQ. Any other station in range will take damage. Some of our ships will die.' For the sake of his crew, he made an effort to sound clear; sure. 'If we burn that defensive's bridges for her, she won't have any choice. She'll have to hurt us as much as she can before she dies.'

He wanted to stop there. The strain of projecting the confidence his people needed hurt him. But the shrouded fear in scan's eyes, and the stubborn set of command's jaw, told him that he had to continue.

'I have a pretty good idea what she wants,' he stated. 'And I think I know how to deal with it. If I'm right, I can keep almost all of us alive. Whether or not I come back' – he shrugged – 'isn't germane.'

Intending reassurance, he added, 'You're safe enough. *Calm Horizons* doesn't want to provoke a fight. She won't attack you.'

But command reacted with flustered indignation, as if Warden had accused him of cowardice. 'That isn't what I –'

Warden winced inwardly. 'I know,' he interrupted. 'If we're going to die anyway, we all want to make it count. Don't you think I feel the same? But suicide is easy.' He forced an edge into his voice. 'The job we swore to do is a little harder.

'I want to make this clear. You're going to deliver me safely to that docking port. And then you're going back to UMCPHQ. *Without* ramming that proton emitter. Or anything else. You do your job. I'll do mine. And maybe' – just maybe – 'something good will come out of all this.'

Scan shrugged. After a moment command lowered his eyes and looked away. 'Aye, sir,' he said softly. 'You can rely on us.'

He may have meant, We're relying on you.

Thirteen minutes.

Warden hugged his chest tighter. 'I know.'

Too many people with too many needs relied on him. And as soon as he passed the threshold of *Calm Horizons'* airlock, he would be almost helpless to do anything about it.

The time seemed to pass swiftly, consumed by *Punisher's* absence, and *Trumpet's*. Communications exchanged stilted approach protocols and confirmations with the Amnioni. By careful degrees the shuttle nudged herself against the docking port.

When the small craft's external seals showed green, Warden

Dios left his g-seat to face the doom he'd brought down on his own planet; his own people.

His preparations were simple. From his pocket he took the black capsule and breathing mask Hashi had given him. The capsule he tucked into his mouth between his cheek and gum. Then he inspected the mask and set its straps over his head so that it rode on his forehead, ready to be pulled down over his nose and mouth when he needed it.

Before he left the control cabin, he recorded commendations for his three officers in the shuttle's log. Contrary to his normal practice, he returned their stiff salutes. Then he turned his back on their clenched faces and headed for the airlock.

He didn't speak to his crew again, or to *Calm Horizons*. Words would have been wasted. Communications negotiated the cycling of the airlocks for him; established the sequence. Scan verified the integrity of the seals. For one terrible moment as the threshold ahead of him opened, he feared that his courage would fail. He'd never seen an Amnioni in person. Apart from old Captain Vertigus, no one he knew had ever been aboard an Amnion vessel. And Morn and Angus deserved better than this from him. Humankind deserved better –

But *Trumpet*'s people were weapons which he'd forged with his own hands. He'd set them in motion – and then he'd set them free. Now he had to trust them, for good or ill.

Settling his mask over his mouth to protect his lungs from the acrid atmosphere the Amnion preferred, he crossed the airlock of his shuttle into *Calm Horizons*.

Sulfurous light appeared to cloy and cling on the odd textures of the walls, so that the grown metal surfaces seemed lambent with energy and intention. The sight made his prosthesis ache in its socket. He had the impression that he'd stepped into one of the antechambers of hell.

The voice of communications reached him from the shuttle's airlock speaker, informing him that the locks were about to close. This was his last chance to flee and die; to spare himself the outcome of his own choices. But he knew better. The shame of his self-inflicted wounds went with him everywhere: there was no escape from it. Instead of retreating, he watched the defensive's airlock iris shut. Then he turned to confront what lay ahead.

Like the outer door, the inner opened like an iris, admitting him to the alien body of the ship. As he crossed the threshold, he caught the first handgrip he could find so that he wouldn't float away; out of control.

Casually adrift in the absence of g, three figures waited for him. Just for a moment, however, he refused to look at them. While he struggled to gather his courage, he glanced around at the hold to which the docking port gave access.

The strong hue of sulfur in the light seemed to thicken the air, throb on the bulkheads. The huge chamber may have been meant for cargo: he saw irregular structures which resembled gantries, festooned with cables like rough vines; stubby transport sleds on magnetic tracks. But the way the Amnion used space made no sense to him. Even for a vessel that couldn't generate internal g, the arrangement of machines and equipment looked incoherent to his human eyes. Was it actually possible to load cargo this way?

Determinedly he distracted himself from panic with simple curiosity until one of the three figures spoke.

'Warden Dios.' Despite the absence of thrust distortion, Warden recognized the voice. 'I am Marc Vestabule.'

Holding his breath in autonomic trepidation, Warden turned.

Two of them might have been clones of each other. They wore no clothes: crusted skin the color of oxidation apparently took the place of apparel. The general shape of their bodies was hominoid. Heads marked with eyes and mouths sat atop torsos with arms and legs. Still there was nothing even remotely human about them. As far as Warden could tell, they had four eyes apiece, spaced around their heads so that they could see in all directions. Teeth as keen as daggers crowded their lipless mouths. Each had three arms and legs positioned on their torsos for near-ideal utility – and agility – in zero g.

They carried no weapons because they needed none. They were at home here; obviously capable of outmaneuvering him. And the crusted mass of their heavy bodies conveyed an impression of tremendous strength. They projected lurid IR auras which told him nothing. He couldn't read their emanations.

They must have been guards for Marc Vestabule, who scarcely resembled them. He was human enough to make Warden's skin crawl.

He was dressed like a man in a black shipsuit made from a material Warden had never seen before; a fabric which seemed to shed light like water. The shape of his limbs and chest and features appeared normal. Above his boots, pale, ordinary flesh reached as high as his knees. However, the legs of his shipsuit had been cut away at the knees to accommodate thick knobs of crusted Amnion tissue. A human hand and wrist extended from one of his sleeves; but his other arm was bare, covered only with scabs or rust from shoulder to forearm. Half his face showed no mark of mutation or injury. On the other side, a viscid Amnion eye stared without blinking over a partially lipless mouth and pointed, rending teeth.

Like the guards', his aura was a nauseating swirl Warden couldn't interpret.

A receiver in his ear and a pickup at his throat indicated that he could talk to the bridge – or whatever the Amnion called their control center – whenever he wished.

Warden swallowed hard to moisten his throat; make himself breathe. Marc Vestabule had once been human: that was beyond question. But the Amnion had transformed him until only parts of his former shape remained.

With an effort, Warden fought down terror – a blind, atavistic dismay which seemed to spring straight from his genes. Somehow, he thought, prayed, it must be possible to deal with such creatures. It must be possible to stifle panic enough to understand them. Or oppose them.

But he could barely force air into his lungs. To speak or move was beyond him. The ghouls of his darkest nightmares had appeared; images of a damnation he'd risked for his entire species. Yet these creatures weren't true damnation. By its very nature, damnation was human. Anguish and terror and excruciation were humankind's essential legacy: every child born inherited them. The Amnion were worse. Ultimately even eternal agony and dread were more humane than the doom they offered.

Understanding – and opposition – were out of the question.

Almost involuntarily, hardly knowing what he did, Warden shifted the capsule in his mouth until it rested between his teeth.

But then, by some trick of fear or will, he heard the answer Hashi might have given him. *Oh, surely it is not necessary to* understand *them*, Hashi replied in Warden's mind. *Their imperialism is genetic. They desire the conquest of all life as we desire air. So much is simple.*

They are only to be feared when they *are able to understand* us.

What had Vestabule said? *The process by which I became Amnion enables me to retain certain resources of memory, language and comprehension. For this reason I have been invested with decisiveness. In dealings with your kind, my former humanity may assist me to function effectively.*

If that was true – and Hashi was right – the time had come for real fear.

Suddenly Warden passed beyond primitive terrors and visceral abhorrence. With a clarity that astonished him, he recognized that he needed his fear too much to let it paralyze him. Fear was strength: it made him human. And if Vestabule could in some sense think and act as if he were human, then only another human might hope to resist him.

Carefully Warden pushed the capsule back into his cheek. The air he pulled into his breathing mask tasted of treachery. Human malice: human deceit. Hope. He grinned as if he'd already won a contest more profound than any challenge Marc Vestabule could present.

'I'm Dios,' he announced through the mask. 'I don't know what you want to "discuss", but I would rather talk about

it someplace smaller.' Less exposed. More private. 'All this'
– he gestured around the hold – 'gives me hives.'

'There will be no difficulty, Warden Dios.' Without the
distortion of thrust static, Vestabule's voice sounded like his
alien skin: caked with rust; as if his humanity had been corroded by disuse. 'Your requirements will be satisfied.

'A chamber has been prepared. There we will negotiate.'
Despite his *resources of memory, language and comprehension*,
he couldn't use words like "negotiate" and "discuss" without
discomfort. 'When we have gained mutual satisfaction, you
will convey your commands to your ships and station.'

He turned. With an awkward gesture, he asked Warden to
follow him.

A chamber – Apparently Vestabule had no intention of
letting the UMCP director see *Calm Horizons'* 'bridge' – or
any other vital part of the ship. Warden nodded to himself.
It was comforting to think that the Amnioni still considered
him dangerous.

From his grip on the wall he pushed off so that he coasted
between the guards after Vestabule.

Neither of them reached out to take hold of him. Instead
they followed at his back – too close for comfort; not close
enough to grab him quickly. Another small comfort:
Vestabule meant to try persuasion before coercion.

From the hold Vestabule entered a corridor like a gullet,
crooked and misshapen. As the space around Warden became
constricted, it seemed to concentrate the light. The surfaces
seethed like brimstone. More and more the passage ahead
resembled a descent into fire.

But he didn't have far to go. After twenty or thirty meters,
Vestabule halted at an irregular depression in the wall. When
Warden reached it, it proved to be a door. Vestabule's palm
on a sensitive plate beside it caused it to slide open.

Vestabule led him into a chamber the size of an interrogation room. Light from sources he couldn't identify filled every
corner. A console had been set or grown into one wall. He
didn't know enough about Amnion technology to be sure of
its function, but he assumed it was a communications ter-

minal. Other than that, the room contained nothing except two chairs rooted to the floor, facing each other. Both offered zero-g belts – presumably for comfort.

Why did the Amnion want him here? To negotiate, Vestabule had said. But he'd also said that Warden would be allowed to return to UMCPHQ when the 'discussion' was done, and that was patently a lie. How many other lies had the Amnioni told?

When Warden had asked, *How can I trust you?* Vestabule had replied, *Because we are Amnion. Unlike humankind, we bargain openly. Also we fulfill our bargains.* Then he'd added, *There is this in addition, however. We gain nothing by harming you.*

The lie was there, but Warden couldn't name it. He would have to wait until it was revealed.

He didn't think he would have to wait long.

Decisively, as if he already had all the answers he needed, he drifted to one of the chairs, pulled himself into it, and closed the belt across his lap.

Vestabule did the same. When he was secure in his chair, he made a series of guttural sounds – speaking into his pickup or addressing the guards, Warden couldn't tell which. However, the guards reacted as if they'd received orders. They retreated from the door. One of them palmed it shut.

Warden Dios was alone with his ghoul.

Defenseless, except for his fear –

He began at once.

'You have something you want to discuss – something you think is worth risking a war over.' He spoke with force, but the strange walls seemed to absorb his voice, depriving it of resonance. 'You said, "all future relations between our species will be determined by the resolution of this matter." And you suggested we might reach a resolution in person because your' – he permitted himself a grimace – ' "background" helps you understand my concerns. Well, I don't know what *your* concerns are, but *mine* are simple.

'I want you out of here. Out of Earth's solar system. Out of human space. And I want you to go without firing a shot.

'Let me be clear about this. No casualties. No damage. No fighting. None. You give me that, and I'll give you a safe conduct as far as your frontier. Then I'll let the diplomats figure out what you can do to make reparation.'

Vestabule replied with a nod which somehow failed to convey assent. The fixed stare of his Amnion eye and the blinking of his human one gave a mixed impression of malice and anxiety. 'That is indeed simple,' he pronounced. 'However, it is not acceptable. If our requirements were comparably simple, we would not have hazarded bringing our species to war.

'We are here.' His shoulders twitched. He may have meant to shrug, but his muscles had forgotten how. 'Our presence must be faced as it is, not as you wish to consider it. You have stated your desires. I will state ours. If our requirements are not satisfied by negotiation, we will conclude that we must fire upon you as hard and often as we can until we are destroyed. We will crush your location of government. We will crush your own station. Then we will –'

'I know, I know,' Warden interrupted harshly. 'You said all that before. But you still haven't told me what your "requirements" are. So far we don't have anything to discuss.'

'I await –' Vestabule's voice trailed off into the distance. For a moment he turned his head: he may have been listening to his receiver. Then he faced Warden again. His alien eye glared like a pool of acid. 'Now I am ready.'

His metallic hostility tightened a knot in Warden's viscera.

'Warden Dios,' the Amnioni scraped out, 'a cyborg in your service was sent into Amnion space to destroy an installation. That in itself was an act of war, meriting reprisal. In addition, however, this cyborg – this Captain Angus Thermopyle – also stole two items of property which had come into the possession of the Amnion through open bargaining and the mutual satisfaction of requirements with another of your agents, Captain Nick Succorso. I refer to the human female, Morn Hyland, and her male offspring, Davies Hyland, force-grown on Enablement Station.'

302

'*You* call them "property",' Warden snapped. '*I* call them "people". Succorso didn't have the right to bargain for them.'

Vestabule stared and blinked like a schizophrenic. 'Your response lacks relevance, Warden Dios. I speak of Amnion requirements. We require the restoration of our property. And in reparation for the wrong we have suffered – so that we will not be compelled to consider ourselves at war with humankind – we require Captain Thermopyle himself, as well as others who accompany him. In particular we require the man named Vector Shaheed.'

He stopped as if he'd said everything that needed saying; as if he knew Warden had no choice except acquiescence.

But Warden was prepared for this. He'd known all along what *Calm Horizons* had come for. And he'd guessed how much Milos Taverner had told the Amnion. He was only surprised that Vestabule didn't demand Nick as well. Did the Amnion know what had happened to Nick?

Because Warden wasn't surprised, he was able to contain his panic. He snorted scornfully. 'And you're human enough to realize demands like that would make anyone who heard them furious for your blood. UMCPHQ would by God mutiny if my people thought I would accept those terms. So you insisted on presenting your "requirements" to me in person. In secret. You think you can extort an agreement from me without risking UMCPHQ's reaction. Not to mention Earth's. You think I can tight-beam orders to *Trumpet*, orders no one else hears – hand you Morn and Davies and everyone else, then tell my forces to let you go unmolested. You get what you want, I get what I want. And nothing bad happens until I have to tell the people I swore to serve what I did.

'It's a nice, tidy picture,' he observed in a snarl. 'Unfortunately it has several flaws.'

Vestabule sat without speaking as if the idea of 'flaws' had no meaning in the language of his kind.

For one, Warden wanted to shout, roar, *I won't do it*. Hell, he wanted to spit in Vestabule's half-human face. But he wasn't ready to go that far yet.

Instead he said trenchantly, 'For one, *Trumpet* isn't here.

And for another, what makes you believe she would obey orders like that if I gave them?'

Apparently the Amnioni didn't consider these significant obstacles. 'She will obey,' he replied, 'for the same reason that you will order her. The cost of refusal will be measured in millions of lives. Also your power over your cyborg will enable you to compel him.

'Our instruments,' he continued, 'and your own system-wide scan network indicate that *Trumpet* is indeed here. The vessel arrived a short time ago. For reasons which you will know better than we, it is transported from the gap by a UMCP cruiser which your network identifies as *Punisher*.'

Involuntarily Warden recoiled. He couldn't help it: he needed a chance to collect his courage – or his wits. *Trumpet* was here? Transported by *Punisher*? He didn't doubt Vestabule for an instant. Nevertheless he couldn't begin to guess what the information meant.

But *Trumpet*'s arrival made the crisis immediate. Vestabule would push for a decision – and action – as quickly as possible. Any delay weakened his position.

Stalling for time, Warden asked, 'What's *Punisher* doing?'

Again Vestabule spoke incomprehensibly into his pickup, listened to his receiver. Then he answered, 'Her targ is fixed on us, as ours is on her. However, she has withheld fire. The orientation of her communications dishes suggests that she is in contact with your station.'

Good. Hashi would brief *Punisher*. He would tell Min what was at stake, here as well as in the GCES emergency session.

Warden had already made the decision to stake his hopes on Hashi's good faith.

He resisted an impulse to fold his arms across his chest. He did that too often; closed his heart. Instead he braced his palms on his thighs for support.

'Why don't you hit her now? Kill her while you can?'

Vestabule's shoulders attempted another unconvincing shrug. 'Your vessels have not arrived in a manner which we deem threatening. And we believe that our requirements will be better satisfied by your intervention.' He paused, then added, 'Doubtless *Punisher* will enforce your orders if *Trumpet* opposes them.'

That may have been true. If Min's loyalty had limits, Warden had never reached them. And her example inspired loyalty in her people. Even Dolph Ubikwe would obey her in an emergency, despite his insubordinate nature.

But Warden believed that she was also capable of refusing –

He needed to take control of his circumstances before they became untenable. For *Trumpet*'s sake, and *Punisher*'s, as well as his own, he countered, 'I don't know what "manner" you're talking about. I guess that's beside the point. Here's the point.

'I won't do it.'

Vestabule's Amnion stare revealed nothing. His human eye seemed to flutter in distress. His heritage of humanity may have been *difficult to access*, but it remained a part of him: the part which made bargains with lies; sealed them with coercion.

'I know why you want Morn and Davies,' Warden went on bitterly. 'They've sent messages explaining the situation. You haven't risked a war over mere "property". You want them because you think they represent the knowledge you need to win. Wipe out humankind completely.' Anger thrummed in his voice. 'And you want Vector Shaheed to help you develop defenses against us.

'It's too much.' At last he let himself shout. 'I will not threaten my entire species by asking or ordering them to turn themselves over to you!'

Despite his outrage and dismay, however, his assertion was dishonest; a lie to match Vestabule's. Humankind's survival was more important than a few million lives. But Warden had reason to fear that losing those lives would lead to Holt Fasner's elevation in the Council's place. Holt might become the government; the only power. And if that happened it also would endanger the survival of humanity.

To keep those few million people alive – and give Koina her chance at the Dragon – might be worth the peril of letting

Calm Horizons have Morn and Davies, Angus and Vector.

In addition there were other possibilities – too nebulous to define, too precious to ignore. Warden hadn't yet decided how he would finally answer Vestabule. He refused in order to force Vestabule's hand; push the Amnioni into exposing his own falsehoods.

Vestabule faced him without moving. For a long moment the Amnioni didn't speak. His aura swirled and seethed like the radiance of a demon. When he replied at last, his tone remained inflexible and unmoved; beyond appeal. Words came from his distorted mouth like flakes of rust and ruin.

'It is a handicap for us that we do not understand deceit. Lies are not' – he seemed to search his memory – 'conceivable?' – he nodded at the choice – 'not conceivable among us. Our communication rests on smell as well as on sound, and to some extent on vision. Pheromones do not lie. Hue and shade do not lie. For that reason we are alone in this chamber. Other Amnion would be distressed by our discussion.'

Distressed to be in the presence of treachery –

'I also am distressed,' Vestabule continued. 'Nevertheless I remember portions of my human nature, and of my experience. In particular I remember mutation. I remember my dismay that my humanity was threatened.'

Warden scowled to conceal his reaction; his prescient dread.

'Because I remember,' the Amnioni continued, 'I know how I must respond to your refusal.'

From a pocket of his shipsuit he drew out a hypo filled with a clear liquid and a vial of small pills.

At the sight fear clenched Warden's guts so hard that he nearly gasped. There it was at last: the lie; the coercion.

'Attend this well, Warden Dios.' Vestabule spoke like old iron. 'I stated accurately that we gain nothing by your enforced mutation. The transformation would be detected. Therefore your people would cease to obey you.

'However, this mutagen suits a special purpose. It is slow

to act. Once injected, it will remain passive for perhaps ten minutes before it begins to alter your genetic identity.

'These capsules' – he raised the vial – 'will cause the mutagen to continue in its passive state. Each supplies an hour of prolonged humanity. The mutagen will live among the false strings of your DNA. But you will be preserved as you are while the counteragent is active.

'I will inject you with the mutagen,' he announced. 'Then I will offer you the counteragent in exchange for your compliance with our requirements.'

Without haste or urgency – inexorable as nightmare – he released his belt. He seemed certain he could do what he said; certain Warden would surrender, paralyzed by panic.

Or perhaps he simply trusted his own strength.

But Warden was ready for this as well, despite the primitive horror writhing in his guts.

He'd never heard of a mutagen or counteragent like this. The prospect of being injected with such an evil appalled him. Nevertheless the threat itself was simple: clear and easy compared with the question of sacrificing Morn and Angus, or of letting several million people die. Beyond doubt Marc Vestabule remembered much of what it meant to be human. For that reason he was dangerous; and vulnerable.

Like the Dragon –

Warden raised his hand as if he had the power to stop Vestabule; the power to command him. 'I hear you. Now *you'd* better listen to *me*. Before you do something rash.'

Secretly he was pleased that his voice held firm. That small show of strength diminished the sting of his shame.

Vestabule paused in the act of rising from his chair.

With a sweep of his tongue, Warden moved Hashi's capsule to the front of his mouth; held it between his teeth so that the Amnioni could see it. Then he pushed it back into his cheek.

'It's called a suicide pill,' he said as if he'd forgotten what fear felt like. 'It's poison. Quick and sure. It doesn't dissolve. I'm safe right now. But if I bite down I'm dead.'

To that extent he trusted Hashi absolutely.

'I'm sure you're strong enough to force that mutagen into me.' He spoke in a slow, fatal drawl. 'I might flounder around the room for a while. Eventually you'll get me.

'But there's no way you can prevent me from biting down.

'You know I'm serious,' he added in case Vestabule missed the truth. 'Maybe you remember how you felt before you were mutated. Maybe you remember that you would have done *anything* to save yourself. But even if you don't, you know you would do the same in my place. To save your people.'

Try me, he dared the Amnioni. Just try me. Don't you know I would sell my soul – if I still had one – for a clean death?

By degrees Vestabule settled back into his seat. His expression was blank: whatever he felt didn't reach his face – or his features couldn't convey it. But after a moment his human eye closed. It stayed shut. He fixed his alien gaze on Warden as if he wanted to see Warden in purely Amnion terms.

Still slowly, ponderously, he directed the hypo at his own forearm; pressed it there until the hypo was empty. He raised his hand to show Warden that the mutagen – and the threat – was gone. Then he opened his fingers and let the hypo's inertia carry it away. The vial of pills he returned to his pocket.

His human eye remained closed as he began speaking into his pickup.

The words sounded so harsh and uncomfortable to Warden that his throat hurt in sympathy. Yet they came naturally to Vestabule. The stilted searching which characterized his human speech was absent.

When he was done, he looked at Warden again with both eyes. Despite its inflexibility, his voice carried an impression of pressure – a new threat, at once more insidious and more lethal than any mutagen.

'Warden Dios, you have caused an impasse. My alternatives

308

have been restricted. Therefore I have ordered *Calm Horizons* to commence combat. In two minutes our super-light proton cannon will destroy your location of government. Then it will be turned on your station. At the same time our matter cannon will attack your approaching ships.

'*Punisher* we will not harm. That vessel is nearer than any other, but has been damaged. We can withstand its fire.'

Warden lifted his eyebrows at this. 'Don't forget Holt Fasner's station,' he suggested hopefully. 'It's in range, too.'

'Still you do not understand,' Vestabule retorted. 'Holt Fasner has made it plain that he desires to bargain with us. He will be allowed to live, his station intact. Perhaps when your government is gone he will be able to satisfy our requirements.

'If he fails us –' Once more the Amnioni attempted a shrug. 'Then we will turn our fire on *Punisher*.'

Apparently he'd remembered enough of his former humanity to call Warden's bluff. Warden was trapped. The choice he had to make couldn't be avoided any longer.

Once *Calm Horizons* opened fire, no human ship would obey an order to stop fighting, no matter what Holt threatened or promised. The defensive would die sooner or later. But Warden knew beyond question that Marc Vestabule and every Amnioni aboard was willing to die; at least as willing as he was himself.

It was time to decide.

Sacrifice Morn and Davies, Vector and Angus. Save millions of lives. And give the Amnion a chance to discover how to mutate men and women so that they retained enough humanity to be undetectable.

Or condemn millions of men and women to death. Prevent the Amnion from acquiring terrible knowledge. And let Holt Fasner have his way with humankind's future.

At last the UMCP director found that he knew his answer.

Why had he put Morn and Angus through so much anguish – why had he bothered – if he didn't mean to trust them?

He cleared his throat. His voice was raw with anger.

MORN

Pandemonium erupted on the bridge of the cruiser. Cray shouted warnings she received from UMCPHQ's traffic buoys: *Punisher* was too close to the station, moving too fast. His voice cracking under the strain, Porson echoed confirmation. His hands raced to sort data from his sensors and Earth's scan net. The man on targ cursed savagely. Patrice programmed helm like scattershot. The data officer, Bydell, made a thin noise like keening in her throat as she scrambled to identify the scan blips.

Davies swore, too – a high, clenched sound, tight with surprise and terror. Ciro didn't react; but Mikka groaned as if something in her chest had snapped. Pale and aghast, Vector stared mutely at the displays. In an instant Angus shifted positions; moved to the side of Morn's console so that he could see the screens and still keep an eye on her. Min strained at her belts, her gaze as keen as a hawk's; eager to strike.

Through the tumult Captain Ubikwe's deep tones cut clearly. 'Deceleration, Sergei. *Burn* it on my order. Prepare for evasive action.' He seemed unnaturally calm; impervious to surprise and danger. 'Charge your cannon, Glessen,' he told targ. 'Ready torpedoes. Stand by to open fire.

'Sound battle stations, Bydell. Deceleration alerts, proximity warnings – hell, sound them all.'

'Aye, Captain.'

At once the lorn wail of klaxons echoed across the clamor.

'Status on that bastard, Porson?' Dolph continued.

'I'm still reading, Captain!' Porson called back. 'Scan isn't clear yet. Too much gap static.' Then he croaked urgently, 'She has us on targ!'

'Do it now, Sergei,' Captain Ubikwe instructed helm. 'Put everything we can spare into it.'

Without transition the muffled thunder of thrust mounted to a roar as if *Punisher* had fallen into a smelter. The ship began to shudder. If she were still under internal spin, she would have torn herself apart.

Hard g; gravitic violence: the essence of reality.

Calm Horizons had reached Earth ahead of them. Because Morn had insisted on making the journey gently –

Fearing what might happen, she'd made exactly the wrong decision. She and her friends might have been safe if they'd beaten the Amnion vessel to Earth.

She was supposed to be in command: of herself as well as the cruiser. Yet she was paralyzed. *Punisher*'s gap drive had translated her from normal space into the domain of nightmare. *Calm Horizons* was here! Of course. What was the worst thing the defensive could possibly have done after failing to kill *Trumpet*? What else but this? – a gambit so extreme and lethal that Morn had never considered it.

She'd failed before she ever had a chance to begin.

And braking thrust shoved her into her g-seat with brutal force. Involuntarily her lips pulled away from her teeth. Her eyes seemed to bulge in their sockets. She could hardly breathe: shuddering thunder filled her chest, clogged her throat. Her arm had shed too much of its pain to protect her.

Cruel and compelling, g drove her out of herself into the place where all things became clear.

Clear as vision. Clear as the voice of the universe, of existence itself. Articulate and irrefutable beyond any possible resistance. She heard the voice, understood the vision; received its necessity like a sacrament.

Self-destruct.

Oh, yes.

She had the means. The universe had provided them for

312

her: clarity provided them. The command board lay in front of her, willing and transsubstantial; as compulsory as a sacrifice. Luminescent certainty marked the keys she should touch, the sequence of obedience. Every question had come to an end. When she reached out her hands, she would be whole; her life made clean at last.

The universe told her what to do – and gave her the strength to do it. She stretched her arms for the keys.

Before she could touch them, Angus hit her so hard that she thought he'd broken her skull –

'*Report*, Porson,' Captain Ubikwe demanded through the roar. His battle-calm overrode the pressure of hard g. 'I can't see the damn screens like this.'

Valiantly Porson squeezed an answer past the mass in his throat. '*Calm Horizons* is orbital. Right on top of UMCPHQ. God, she must be within 50,000 k. Coasting. They're both geosynchronous over Suka Bator.' He faltered, then somehow found a way to raise his voice. 'Captain, *Calm Horizons* has a clear line of fire on Suka Bator! Her proton cannon is already aligned.'

– but she didn't lose consciousness. Not quite. Instead the blow lifted her across the personal gap between clarity and pain. Shards of agony like bone splinters nailed her mind to the hard matter of her skull. She forgot the siren call of the universe. She'd been crucified: clarity and coercion couldn't reach her.

Around her shouts and orders swirled like panic. Davies may have cried her name; may have sworn at Angus: she couldn't be sure. If Angus retorted, she didn't hear it. The pain in her head had become exquisite grief. She was certain of nothing except that she'd lost her last chance to be whole.

There were no better answers: self-destruct was all she understood. And Angus had bereft her of it.

'Ready, Glessen?' Dolph asked.

'Damn right, Captain!' Glessen retorted.

Inaccuracy in the gap had brought *Punisher* too close to UMCPHQ: close enough to aim all her strength at the Amnioni.

'Ease deceleration, Sergei,' Captain Ubikwe commanded. 'I need to *see*. Evasive action on my order. Make her dance. We're in no condition to let ourselves get tagged.'

At once some of the cruel g lifted. Morn could breathe again, thin sips of air like constricted gasping.

'Wait a minute, Dolph!' Min barked promptly. 'Look around! Who's firing? How much support have we got?'

He may not have heard her. 'All right, Glessen,' he growled. 'Let's see if we can do some damage –'

'Captain!' Cray yelled from communications. Fear and g pitched her cry to a shriek. 'Hold fire!'

Hold –?

'Wait a minute, Glessen,' Dolph snapped quickly.

'Orders from Center!' Cray went on. 'They're shouting at us. Absolute priority. Don't fire!'

'Have they lost their minds?' the captain demanded. 'There's a Behemoth-class defensive parked right on top of them, and they want us to *hold fire*?'

'Absolute priority,' Cray repeated.

'No one's shooting, Captain,' Porson announced frantically. 'Not UMCPHQ. Not *Calm Horizons*. We have ships in range. More on the way. They haven't fired.'

With an effort, he fought down frenzy. 'I see *Adventurous*,' he continued, 'but she isn't close enough yet. And *Valor* is here. Looks like she resumed tard ten minutes ahead of us. But she's a lot further out.' Out where *Punisher* should have been. 'Too far to attack yet.'

Morn's pain bled slowly into the lighter g. Angus must not have hit her as hard as she thought. She couldn't speak; could hardly think. But she could listen.

Vestigial clarity flickered at the edges of her mind like heat lightning. The situation made sense in distant bursts. *Calm Horizons* had committed an egregious act of war – and no one fired at her. Of course not. The big warship hadn't come on a suicide mission against UMCPHQ and the GCES. She'd come to stop *Trumpet*. Capture the gap scout if possible; kill her otherwise.

UMCPHQ and the GCES were hostages –

Grimly Morn began to fight the aftereffects of gap-sickness. Once Captain Ubikwe and Min understood the stakes, they might sacrifice Morn and her friends. To save UMCPHQ and the Council. If Warden Dios ordered it –

'Orders from Center,' Dolph snorted. '*Whose* orders? My God, are we *surrendering*? *Who* wants us to hold fire?'

'The order is from Hashi Lebwohl,' Cray answered. She couldn't muffle her shock. 'Acting Director, UMCP.'

In response Min snarled like a predator. '*Hashi*'s in command? How in hell did that happen? What happened to Warden?

'Communications,' she demanded, 'get me a direct channel to *Acting* Director Lebwohl. Absolute priority. I can play that game as well as he can. *I want to talk to him.*'

'Do it, Cray,' Dolph said. But his confirmation wasn't necessary: Cray was already at work.

The Amnioni's targ continued to sizzle on *Punisher*'s sensors. Nevertheless *Calm Horizons'* guns stayed silent.

Captain Ubikwe squinted at the screens. 'Ease deceleration,' he instructed helm again. 'We don't have a lot of room. But we can turn.

'Give me a new course. I want to intercept that warship's line of fire on Suka Bator. Coordinate braking so we match orbits and stay there. If we can't do anything else, we'll at least be an obstacle.'

G dwindled once more as Patrice obeyed. Stress vectors shifted. Morn's pain settled into a basal throbbing she could almost bear. Her limbs and head remained heavier than they should have been, but they felt comparatively light. And the hull-roar of thrust continued to decline: she lost weight as if she were evaporating. Soon she might be able to raise her head.

Her arm had begun to itch and ache again.

'Morn,' Davies called across the bridge, 'are you all right?' He sounded desperate with worry and fear. He must have known why Angus had struck her.

Angus bent over her. 'Say something, Morn,' he muttered as if he was afraid of her. 'Don't make me hit you again.'

She put her hand on his arm, drew him closer. 'You promised to back me up,' she whispered like a sigh. Davies deserved a response; but she didn't have the energy to spare for anyone else. 'I'm trusting you.'

Holding his arm for support, she pulled herself forward so that she could reach the command board.

She feared Hashi Lebwohl more than Warden Dios. Far more.

At last g shrank enough to permit cautious movement. Captain Ubikwe began to unclip his belts. 'While we're waiting, Cray,' he rumbled, 'get me Center.' His tension seemed to increase as the threat of immediate combat receded. 'It's about time somebody told us what the hell's going on.'

'Right away, Captain,' Cray answered.

Heaving against too much weight, Dolph stood up from his g-seat. Clearly he meant to assume the command station.

'Stop him,' Morn murmured to Angus.

For a moment she feared that she'd spoken too softly, weakly, to be heard. But then, without haste, he stepped away from her and aimed his armed fist at the captain's head.

'That's far enough, fat man.' He grinned a warning. His eyes were yellow and carious, like unclean fangs. 'In case you've forgotten, you aren't in command. You don't speak for this ship.'

Davies gaped in consternation. Abruptly, belatedly, he hauled his handgun out of his pocket and raised it; but he didn't know whether to aim at Dolph or Angus. Mikka started to open her belts, then changed her mind and subsided in dejection.

Captain Ubikwe froze between one stride and the next.

'Back off, Captain Thermopyle,' Min rasped fiercely. Her tone threatened him; but she made no move to leave her g-seat. 'Morn's in no condition to command anything. You know that. My God, you had to hit her just to get her through hard g.

'Stay out of the way. This is our job. Let us do it.'

'And what happens then?' Angus countered between his teeth. 'Don't tell me, I already know. Hashi fucking Lebwohl tells you that damn Amnioni is ready to wipe out the cops and the whole government. He's so sorry. You'll have to turn us over to *Calm Horizons*. Unfortunate but necessary. And you'll do it. You're the UMCP director of muscle – you *like* following orders when you don't have to count the bodies afterward.

'Get it through your head,' he finished. '*Morn* is in command. She speaks for this ship.'

Captain Ubikwe scrubbed his face with his hands, then dropped them to his sides. His grin matched Angus'.

'There's just one thing you aren't taking into account,' he drawled cheerfully. 'A small detail, really – but it makes a difference. This is *my* ship.'

Ponderous with augmented mass, he pitched a fist like a bludgeon at Angus' head.

Davies shouted an alarm; slapped to release his belts so he could move. But Angus didn't need his help.

Dolph was too slow for Angus; far too slow. Despite the extra g, Angus' response was so effortless that it seemed almost gentle. Smoothly he caught Dolph's elbow and turned him; locked his arm behind his back; shoved him toward his g-seat.

'That's enough, Angus,' Morn put in quickly. She didn't want to see Captain Ubikwe hurt. Her pain sufficed for everyone. 'He's not the enemy. Neither is Director Donner. They just don't understand.'

Angus didn't reply. He stood with his fist pointed at Dolph until the captain sat down again; closed his belts. Then he resumed his position beside the command station.

Swearing in relief, Davies settled back into his g-seat. He held up his handgun indecisively for a moment, then kept it in his fist.

Min's jaws clenched and loosened as if she were chewing iron; but she said nothing.

'Center is standing by,' Cray announced. Angry disapproval stiffened her tone. 'Tight-beam transmission. The defensive can't pick it up.'

Glessen leaned away from the targ board; folded his arms

317

as if to say that he, for one, wouldn't take Morn's orders. Bydell looked back and forth between Captain Ubikwe and Min, her eyes wide with supplication. But Porson and Patrice kept working: *Punisher*'s survival depended on them no matter who commanded her.

'Thank you, communications,' Morn replied unsteadily. 'Let's hear what they have to say.'

Distorted by thrust static, the bridge speakers spat to life.

'*Punisher*, this is Center,' a man's voice began at once. 'Captain Ubikwe, take no action. That's a direct order. Decelerate to copy our orbit and hold there. Keep your cannon charged. But don't show the Amnioni even a flicker of fire. If you do, we'll court-martial what's left of your corpse after we're all dead.'

'Damn it, Morn,' Min hissed, 'we don't have time for this.'

Morn sighed. 'I'm sorry, Director. I don't have time for anything else.'

With one finger she toggled the command station pickup.

'Center, this is Ensign Morn Hyland.' Now more than ever she needed firmness, calm; needed to sound sure. But she couldn't stifle the tremor of ruin in her voice. 'I command *Punisher*. I don't need orders, I need situation. We have a hostile alien charged to fire on Suka Bator.' Or any other target the defensive chose. 'Why aren't we trying to destroy her?'

'Morn Hyland?' Center's surprise was plain despite the intervening static. 'Who the hell are you?

'Wait a minute.' He must have been running feverish commands on his board. 'You aren't on *Punisher*'s crew manifest. You're –' For an instant he paused in shock. 'Shit, you're *that* Morn Hyland. Off *Starmaster*.

'What happened to Captain Ubikwe?' the man demanded hotly. 'What happened to Min Donner? *What're you doing in command?*

Morn took a deep breath. Min was right: they absolutely did not have time for this. But she saw only one way out of her plight. Open fire: start a battle. Yet that decision appalled her. She didn't have enough information to make it.

'Let me repeat myself, Center. I don't need orders. And I don't need questions. I need to know why we're all just sitting here while an Amnion warship sticks her guns in our faces.' She faltered momentarily, then added, 'If I don't get an answer, I'll be forced to take action on my own.'

If *Punisher* opened fire, UMCPHQ and the rest of Earth's defenses would have no choice but to join her. The cruiser would certainly die. UMCPHQ and Suka Bator might be destroyed. But *Calm Horizons* would die as well. The Amnioni's knowledge of Vector's antimutagen, and her samples of Morn's blood, would die.

That might be a trade worth making.

'Don't!' Center shot back. 'Don't do *anything*!' Distortion complicated the fear in the man's voice. 'Just wait.

'I can't talk to you. I'm not authorized –' The bridge speakers hinted at muffled shouts in the background. Then Morn heard, '*Punisher* – Ensign Hyland – hold on while I connect you to Acting Director Lebwohl.'

He didn't wait for a response. As he silenced his pickup, the spattering hiss of transmission noise filled the speakers.

'You hear that?' Angus sneered at Min. 'Acting by damn Director Lebwohl hasn't got time for *you*, but he'll talk to *Morn*.'

'Leave the Director alone,' Davies put in tautly; pulled tight by vexation and alarm. His loyalty to Min appeared to torment him. 'For all we know, he won't talk to Morn either.'

Min gave him a cold glare which made him wince. Still she kept her retorts to herself.

Morn ignored them. She had other problems. Turning her station, she faced Glessen on targ.

'Listen to me, targ,' she said grimly. 'I'm only going to say this once. If I tell you to fire, I expect you to do it.'

Glessen didn't look at her. His arms gripped his chest truculently. 'Not unless Captain Ubikwe gives the same order.'

'What do you expect, Ensign?' Dolph demanded at Morn's back. 'We have direct orders not to shoot. Do you think we're going to commit treason just because you happen to be feeling suicidal?'

Angus flashed his grin. 'Maybe it's time Ciro went back to *Trumpet*.'

'I know how to do it,' Ciro assented. He sounded eager. 'Angus showed me.'

Without transition Morn's mouth had become cotton. She swallowed roughly, trying to moisten her throat. 'Don't be in such a hurry. We aren't that desperate yet.'

Urgently she swung toward Mikka. 'Mikka, I want you to take targ. This officer has been relieved.'

Glessen started cursing, then bit his lip to stop himself.

Mikka replied with a shattered look, as if something inside her had broken during g, or in tach. Her reserves of intransigence or anger appeared to have cracked and spilled under the pressure of her brother's madness – and Angus' use of it. Even the blow which had cracked her skull short days ago hadn't hurt her so much.

Nevertheless she was as loyal as Davies or Angus; as loyal as anyone. Her commitments held her. Slowly she fumbled free of her belts; left her g-seat by the bulkhead and plodded leadenly toward the targ station.

Glessen didn't move. After one quick glance at Mikka, another at Captain Ubikwe, he sat still, staring straight ahead; immobile with rage.

'Acting Director Lebwohl is standing by,' Cray pronounced acidly. Her disapproval had become bitterness.

A new clutch of tension ran along Morn's nerves. Pointing at Glessen, she murmured, 'Angus, please.' Then she left the problem to him so that she could concentrate on Hashi Lebwohl.

Davies aimed his gun at the targ officer, leaning forward as if he wanted to deal with the problem himself. He must have needed movement; decisions; anything which might help him believe in himself. Being forced to sit still was a kind of torment for him. But again his father didn't require his help.

Angus reached the targ station without apparent effort. Swift as a snake, he reached past the board to unclip Glessen's belts. With his fists knotted in Glessen's shipsuit, he heaved the man bodily out of the targ station.

Glessen had time to hit him once – a blow Angus hardly seemed to feel. Then the targ officer landed heavily; slapped to the deck; skidded.

Mikka trudged mutely past him to take his place at targ.

In a low snarl Captain Ubikwe said, 'You've gone too far, Ensign.' His voice shook. 'If you open fire, we won't wait for *Calm Horizons* to kill you. My people will do it themselves.'

Without lifting his head from his readouts, Patrice muttered, 'Damn straight.'

A moment later the frightened young data officer, Bydell, said clearly, 'Aye, Captain.'

Angus faced each of them in turn with his teeth and his glare and his clenched lasers. Davies brandished his handgun threateningly. But Morn ignored them all.

The man who'd reqqed and welded Angus had somehow become 'acting director' of the UMCP. To her way of thinking, that development was as dangerous as *Calm Horizons'* presence.

Abruptly she toggled the command pickup.

'This is *Punisher*. I'm Ensign Morn Hyland.' The words seemed to stick in her throat: she had to force them out. 'I'm in command here.'

'Ensign Hyland,' a man's voice wheezed waspishly from the speakers. 'I must confess that you continue to astonish me. Indeed, you are an ongoing source of amazement. If more of our brave officers possessed your affinity for the unexpected, civilization as we know it might totter and fall.'

'Is this Acting Director Lebwohl?' Morn demanded. She recognized his voice easily enough, but she wanted to prevent him from taking control of the situation.

Hashi ignored her question. 'This time, however,' he continued as if she hadn't spoken, 'I fear that you have exceeded yourself. My dear young woman, you really must return command to Captain Ubikwe. Then I will speak to Director Donner.

'Unless you have had the temerity to dispose of them?' he inquired severely. 'I do hope not, Ensign. That would be quite unforgivable.'

Morn winced. 'Captain Ubikwe is fine. So is Director Donner.' Hashi's manner grated on her sore nerves. She couldn't afford the time – or the energy – to trade barbs with him. 'But they trust you. I don't. I'm afraid that means you'll have to talk to me. If you won't tell me why you're holding fire while an Amnion warship aims her proton cannon at Suka Bator, then stop wasting my time. We have work to do.'

'Do you?' Hashi's voice countered. 'How curious. I would have supposed that your work was identical to ours, considering that you are – or claim to be – an Enforcement Division ensign. Perhaps you will enlighten me concerning your intentions.' His wheeze sharpened. 'Even you will not expect my connivance in the charade of your command if you decline to tell me what "work" you mean to do.'

'Yes, I'll tell you,' Morn retorted. Hashi's attitude angered her more by the moment. Her arm throbbed in sympathetic irritation. Wasn't he the man who'd programmed Angus not to rescue her? 'We have your formula – the formula for the mutagen immunity drug you gave Nick Succorso. Vector Shaheed analyzed it for us. If I don't get some cooperation – and get it *soon* – we'll tight-beam the results to every ship and station we can reach. We'll downlink it to Earth – to the Council, the major cities, every regional government.

'Then we're going to open fire on *Calm Horizons*.'

With the back of her fist, she toggled the command pickup so that Hashi Lebwohl wouldn't hear her panting to control her ire.

For reasons of his own, Hashi did the same. The bridge speakers fell silent.

In the sudden quiet Vector remarked phlegmatically, 'So I guess it's a good thing we didn't arrive broadcasting. We wouldn't have any leverage now. And we might already be dead.'

Captain Ubikwe gave a snort of contempt. 'I warned you once, Ensign,' he growled. 'I won't do it again. If you –'

'That's enough!' Davies raised his gun at the captain. 'If you don't shut up, I'll stop you myself, and I'll make it *permanent*. Do you think we *like* doing it this way? Do you

322

think it's *easy*? If Ciro hadn't sabotaged the drives, God damn it, we would still be running circles around you, and your only choice would be to *keep your opinions to yourself*!'

Apparently he'd reached the end of his endurance. Inactivity and the strain of defying people he respected seemed to pain him more than he could bear.

Nevertheless his threat didn't touch Dolph. The captain's eyes widened in mockery. 'You're kidding,' he croaked. 'You expect me to believe you'll kill me in cold blood? Shit, boy. You aren't that tough.'

Before Davies could fire a retort, Min Donner spoke.

'Calm down, Dolph.' She sounded unexpectedly mild; composed and sure. Nevertheless the note of authority in her tone was unmistakable. 'What do you want them to do? What would you do in Morn's place – if you were a good cop who's already been sold out once' – Min may have been referring to the UMCP's decision to let Nick take Morn off Com-Mine – 'and doesn't have any reason to think we won't do it again?

'Don't you think that formula should be made public? I know I do. Concealing an effective antimutagen is a crime against the people we're supposed to serve. This mess should have been cleaned up long ago. But if it were up to us, we wouldn't do it. We couldn't release that formula without permission. If she wants to solve the problem for us, I don't intend to get in her way.' The ED director smiled without a trace of humor. 'Since I'm not in command here, I don't have to.

'You said the same thing yourself twenty minutes ago,' she finished flatly.

'Shit,' Angus muttered in Min's direction, 'now I know we're in trouble. I felt safer when you were acting righteous.'

Dolph stared at her. For a moment his mouth hung open. Then he closed it. 'That was before –' he began. But he couldn't go on.

Abruptly the speakers crackled. Without transition Director Lebwohl's voice returned.

'Ensign Hyland, this is Acting Director Lebwohl.' His condescension was gone, replaced by concern and a note of frailty.

'Please listen to me. I must urge you not to take such extreme action. Since you do not acknowledge Captain Ubikwe's authority, or Director Donner's, I presume you will ignore mine as well. For that reason, I do not order you to hold back. But I ask – no, Ensign Hyland, I implore you to reconsider.

'To discuss either our tactical or our strategic situations is entirely outside my mandate. Neither you nor your companions can be allowed to affect the decisions which must be made here.

'If you do not restrain yourself, I must order our forces to support *Calm Horizons*' defense against you.'

'Christ!' Davies protested. 'If *we* don't have the right "to affect the decisions", who does?'

Morn raised her hand to silence him. Hashi wasn't done.

'I will mention one detail, however,' the DA director went on, 'in the hope that you will recognize its significance.

'Warden Dios is aboard *Calm Horizons*.'

Morn flinched involuntarily. Davies yelped like a stung kid. Min stiffened as if an abyss had suddenly opened at her feet. Bydell and Porson blanched. With the heel of one hand, Captain Ubikwe struck himself on the forehead once; twice. Each blow made a moist, smacking sound, like a clap of despair.

'It's got to stop,' Angus remarked through his teeth. 'He said that to me once. Looks like he was serious.'

Hashi's voice didn't pause.

'His shuttle delivered him to the Amnion hardly ten minutes ago. In my view, he is effectively a hostage. Nevertheless the stated purpose of his presence is to negotiate the survival of both the UMCP and the GCES.'

There the DA director stopped. The speakers hissed and clicked with thrust static while he waited for Morn to find some reply which didn't fill her with horror.

MORN

Warden Dios is aboard –
Morn could hardly think.
He is effectively a hostage.

Of course. What else? Like the proton cannon trained on Suka Bator, this threat was really aimed at *Punisher*. At *Trumpet*'s people aboard the cruiser.

Now Morn faced an abyss of her own: a completely different gulf from the one in front of Min; or the same chasm from the other side. She was the wrong person to be where she was, doing what she did. The wrong person altogether. Her loyalty to the UMCP director ran too deep: it had been in her family until it became almost genetic. Could she sacrifice him in order to tell her story; make Vector's formula public? She didn't think so.

Someone else should be in command – someone who could reach decisions without counting what they cost.

Angus couldn't do it. His essential programming prevented him from harming UMCP personnel. And Davies couldn't. His commitment to Warden Dios was clearer than Morn's; less conflicted. Exhaustion and damage precluded Mikka. Like Vector, she couldn't command Angus' support.

Morn needed a better answer.

And she had no one else to turn to.

'Director Donner –' Her voice cracked helplessly. A surge of hysteria took her: the vertigo of the abyss. She had to fight it down before she could speak. 'I'm in command here. But

I'm not really qualified to take Captain Ubikwe's place. I certainly can't take yours.' Was that pleading she heard in her voice? She didn't care. The stakes were too high for her. 'If you're willing, you should talk to Director Lebwohl. Officially. As the director of Enforcement Division.'

Angus faced her like the cut of a lash, his teeth clenched on curses. But Davies radiated a relief so palpable she could taste it. Vector watched her as if she'd become miraculous in ways he couldn't understand.

For no apparent reason, Ciro said distinctly, 'Suck everything into a black hole.'

Min didn't hesitate: she shifted from passivity to action in an instant. Swift and sure, as keen as a hawk, she slapped open her belts, left her g-seat. Despite the added g of *Punisher*'s deceleration, she approached the command station as if she were pouncing. One precise touch keyed the pickup.

'Hashi, this is Min.' A low thrill of release echoed in her tone. 'Ensign Hyland wants me to talk to you.

'I'm sure she's serious about opening fire if she doesn't get some cooperation. But I'm also sure she doesn't want to trigger wholesale slaughter, if we can avoid it. This is official, Hashi. On the record.'

'Director Donner,' Hashi sighed. 'I must say that hearing your voice comforts me. Please offer Ensign Hyland my congratulations for an intelligent decision.'

He paused, then said, 'We have much to discuss. However, you will understand that I am constrained to inquire first how you come to be in such an unlikely predicament.'

Morn understood. He wanted to know what kind of gun was being held to Min's head.

But Min deflected the question. 'It's a long story, Hashi. You don't have time for it. For now I'll just say that we have *Trumpet* in tow. And *Trumpet* carries singularity grenades.' In an acid tone, she finished, 'You might mention that to Holt Fasner the next time you report.'

Her whole body seemed to concentrate on the command station pickup as if it were a weapon. Apparently she wasn't sure she could trust the DA director. His appointment as acting director must have occurred after she'd left UMCPHQ.

'I do not report to CEO Fasner.' Hashi's asperity buzzed from the speakers. He might have been declaring an allegiance. 'He desires that I do so, naturally. Indeed, he is altogether insistent. By good fortune, Director Dios ordered me to refuse. And the Dragon has no authority to coerce me.'

His response dismissed the usefulness of Angus' gamble with Ciro. He may have missed the implications of Min's hint. Or he may have considered them unimportant.

He seemed to mark time for a beat or two. Then he announced, 'However, I will contrive to make it known that I have resigned as acting director. The position is yours, Director Donner, with all the powers and responsibilities' – he sounded almost whimsical – 'appertaining thereunto.'

Morn ignored Captain Ubikwe's surprise. She had no attention to spare for Angus' reaction, or anyone else's. She focused exclusively on Min's voice, and Hashi's, trying to make sense of the undercurrents between them; glean what she needed for her own decisions.

'What?' Min retorted. 'Are you out of your mind, Hashi? You can't do that. Warden gave *you* the job.' She caught herself. 'I mean, I assume he did.'

Hashi's silence conveyed a shrug.

The muscles at the corner of Min's jaw bunched like a fist. 'So I also assume he had a reason. You probably know what that is. I don't. Besides, I'm stuck out here on a ship that doesn't take orders from me. I can't –'

'Nevertheless,' Hashi cut in, 'you will accept the appointment, Min. Warden Dios did indeed elevate me to my exalted state. But he did so for the simple and sufficient reason that you were not here. No other explanation is necessary.'

Without pausing he continued, 'You will ask why I desire to be – as one might say – decommissioned. I must reply that my motives are various.

'Surely you understand that you outrank me. Enforcement

Division precedes Data Acquisition. It is right and proper that you should replace me.

'In addition –' He sighed again. 'I must say this, Min, although doubtless Ensign Hyland and her cohorts can hear me. As Acting Director I am not favorably placed to withstand the Dragon. I am *here*, precariously accessible to the great worm and his minions, as well as to' – his tone became a sneer – 'our esteemed Council. Worse, I am also in communication with *Calm Horizons*. Hence I am vulnerable to any instructions or compromises which the Amnion may extract from Warden.

'Finally I do not desire this responsibility. Command interests me – very little. And I have other duties which I believe require my attention. If my public profile is diminished,' he explained ambiguously, 'the Dragon will find it more difficult to thwart me.

'You are now Acting Director of the UMCP, Min.' Hashi's earlier frailty had returned. 'The transfer of authority has already been logged and recorded by both Center and Administration. If you decline the position, you must name a surrogate.'

Roughly Min toggled the pickup. For a moment she scanned the bridge. Then she fixed her hard gaze on Morn. Her eyes hinted at vast dimensions, terrible depths: she could confront gulfs which made Morn quail. She wasn't afraid to determine the fate of humankind.

'If you're going to stop me,' she said harshly, 'do it now. Once I'm Acting Director, I won't put up with any interference.

'I'll leave *Punisher* to you. I'll cooperate with you as much as I can.' The winds of a chasm blew in her voice, cold and pitiless. 'But if you don't like the decisions I make for UMCPHQ – or for our other ships – you'll have to kill me. *And* Captain Ubikwe.' Dolph nodded. '*And* the duty officers.' So did his people. 'And then you'll have to start on the rest of the crew. If I accept this job, I mean to do it.'

'Morn,' Angus protested quickly, warning her. He stood

near enough to protect her. 'How many times have you told us we can't trust the cops?'

He was right, of course. No matter how she felt about Min Donner, Morn believed that the UMCP was corrupt. They'd stifled Intertech's mutagen immunity research. They were owned by Holt Fasner and the UMC. The threat of *Calm Horizons'* guns wouldn't make them honest.

Yet she lacked the resources to meet that threat. She could open fire: she was capable of that. Butcher millions of people. Get killed herself. Self-destruct – But if there was another way out of her dilemma, she couldn't find it. She'd never been able to find it.

She needed help.

'Davies.' She turned away from Min to look around her. 'Mikka. Vector. Can any of you think of a reason why we should trust Director Donner?'

'Sure,' Davies said before anyone else replied. As if he were Morn's father, the man he'd been named for, he answered, 'She's Min Donner.'

Morn understood. In some ways he remembered Min more acutely than she did. And she had nothing else to go on.

Angus swore. 'What the fuck is *that* supposed to mean?'

Morn faced him briefly. 'It means she's the right person for the job. And I'm not.' Then she returned her gaze to Min.

'Go ahead.'

Min didn't hesitate. A combative flare lit her eyes as she thumbed the pickup toggle. Without preamble she demanded, 'What duties, Hashi? You know I'm not going to refuse. Not with so many lives at stake. Not when Warden is in this much trouble. But if you want to drop this load on my shoulders, you better tell me what I'm carrying.'

The DA director had been waiting for her answer; but his response avoided her question. 'As Acting Director,' he stated formally, distantly, as if his thoughts were already elsewhere, 'your duties are at once simple and ambiguous. The chartered purpose of the UMCP is to preserve and defend humankind. You see the threat. A Behemoth-class Amnion warship armed with super-light proton cannon has violated our space. Her matter cannon and other weapons are more than adequate to destroy UMCPHQ. Her proton gun impends over Suka Bator. Given time, she can ruin much that is vital to us, both planet-side and in orbit.

'The scan net has doubtless made our defensive preparations visible to you. Center will brief you further whenever you wish.

'Clearly you must deal with *Calm Horizons.*'

While Hashi spoke, Davies left his g-seat and came to stand beside Angus at the command station. Captain Ubikwe did the same as if he thought Min might need his support. During the rest of the DA director's speech, they seemed to keep watch.

'The Amnioni's approach has been curious as well as unexpected,' Hashi observed. 'It appears that she has a former human being aboard – one Marc Vestabule.'

Morn gasped involuntarily. Davies drew a hissing breath through his teeth. Even Mikka flinched, despite her emotional exhaustion. They had encountered Vestabule first on Enablement Station, then at Billingate. More than once, he'd boarded *Captain's Fancy* to present the Amnion demand for Davies' life. And Nick had delivered Morn to him. In a cell in the Amnion sector of Billingate, he'd injected a mutagen into her veins.

If she'd thought about it, she might have guessed that he was with *Calm Horizons.* She'd seen a shuttle leave the Amnion sector before *Captain's Fancy* went down; before Billingate was destroyed. He must have been on it.

His presence made *Calm Horizons'* purpose painfully obvious.

Min noticed Morn's reaction, and Davies', but she didn't interrupt Hashi.

The DA director was saying, 'This individual has been "invested with decisiveness". Quaint phrase. Although he came upon us of his own volition, he acknowledges the impossibility of his position. He may harm us on any imaginable scale, but in the end *Calm Horizons* will surely die. And the longer combat is postponed, the less harm we will suffer before the end. In any case, much of our capacity for retaliation and vengeance will remain intact. The potential cost of warfare may be greater than the Amnion can bear.

'Because this Marc Vestabule was once human, he claims the ability to reason in human terms. And he has insisted that there is an issue – an unspecified point of contention – upon which humankind's future against the Amnion depends, and which can only be resolved by personal negotiation. On pain of Suka Bator's destruction, and our own, he has demanded Warden's presence aboard his vessel in order to "discuss" this matter.'

For a moment Hashi seemed more present. His tone sharpened. 'Marc Vestabule has not named his concerns, but you know them as well as I do. Certainly Warden does.' Then his abstraction distanced him again. 'For that reason – among others – he has complied with Vestabule's demand. He is duty-bound to stave off bloodshed and damage if he can. And he hopes to prevent the defensive from attacking you immediately. He has not spoken to us since he went aboard. His shuttle is in transit from *Calm Horizons*.

'When you receive Warden's orders, you must decide how – or indeed whether – to carry them out.'

The suggestion of frailty in Hashi's voice increased. 'Even if the Amnioni's concerns are resolved to his satisfaction, I believe Warden will not be released. *Calm Horizons* will retain him in an attempt to ensure our compliance. Hence I consider him a hostage. I mention this so that you will comprehend all the consequences of refusing his instructions.'

'I understand, Hashi,' Min pronounced acidly. 'Just because I'm ED doesn't mean I'm stupid.'

Hashi ignored her retort. Still wanly, he continued, 'In addition, you must decide how best to answer Holt Fasner's demands. In some sense, his importunity is justified. He owns the UMCP. Were it not for the War Powers provisions of our charter, he would be entitled to req every scrap of data we possess, and to treat with *Calm Horizons* himself. And even under conditions of war, he retains the power to fire

331

Warden. Doubtless he would cite "malfeasance" to account for his action.'

Morn and Davies both winced at the idea. Was Holt Fasner capable of firing Warden while the UMCP director was being held hostage? Despite the fact that Warden was risking his life to save millions of others? Apparently Hashi thought so.

However, Min heard Hashi's statement in other terms. She cocked her head. 'But he can't fire us, Hashi. Can he?'

'No.' Hashi's reply suggested a grim satisfaction. 'Only the UMCP director can do that. The great worm must dispense with Warden and replace him. Until then we are secure.'

Min permitted herself a thin sigh of relief.

'I might also say,' Hashi went on, 'that in my view it is open to question whether UMCPHQ would accept a replacement under these conditions. Our Warden has never inspired more loyalty here than he does at this moment.'

Morn nodded in recognition. She might have felt that way herself.

'All right.' Min straightened her shoulders. 'I have the situation. I'll talk to Center in a minute.' She paused to collect her thoughts, then pursued, 'But you still haven't told me what *your* duties are.'

'Ah, Min.' Hashi's voice seemed to drift away from the speakers. He sounded almost unreachable as he asked, 'Are you entirely certain that you wish me to answer you in the presence of Ensign Hyland and her cohorts?'

'Of course not,' Min retorted. 'I have no idea what you might tell me.' Immediately, however, she corrected herself. 'Yes, I'm sure. They have a right to know what's at stake. And I'm not exactly in command here. Ensign Hyland can shut me down if she doesn't like the way we treat her. I need her support.'

Without transition Hashi's distant frailty disappeared. 'Then I will explain.' His voice became a precise wheeze in the speakers, brisk and clear. Min must have given him the response he wanted: a kind of permission.

Morn had the frightening sense that her position was about

to become even more difficult; that in his oblique way Hashi would put as much pressure on her as he could.

He began by saying, '*Calm Horizons* has come upon us at a complex time. As you might suppose, our estimable Governing Council is in emergency session as we speak. I believe President Len opened the proceedings – oh, perhaps ten minutes ago. Thus events conspire to produce marvels of synchronicity.

'As you might further suppose, our newly anointed colleague, PR Director Koina Hannish, attends the session. She has been charged to speak for Warden while he is otherwise occupied.'

Morn started to ask what had happened to Godsen Frik; then bit the question down. She wasn't sure she wanted an answer. It was common knowledge that he'd worked for Holt Fasner.

'I venture to say, however,' Hashi expounded, 'that no supposition will prepare you for the nature of the mandate which Warden has given her.'

Min listened in a state of coiled poise; but she didn't interrupt.

'Director Hannish,' Hashi pronounced, 'has been instructed to reveal that our Captain Thermopyle is not an escaped illegal – as I personally assured the Council scant days ago, on Warden's direct orders – but is rather a welded cyborg sent to effect Billingate's destruction. By implication, of course, she must admit that Captain Thermopyle's success has motivated the acts of war committed by *Calm Horizons*.'

Angus jerked up his head. 'I'm damned,' he murmured in astonishment. 'He was serious. That fucker was *serious*.'

Morn had no idea what he meant – or why Warden might have ordered Hashi to lie to the Council – but she didn't ask. Hashi wasn't done.

'Further,' he continued, 'she has been told to describe the manipulations by which passage of the Preempt Act was obtained.'

Davies frowned confusion at Morn. He hadn't heard Angus explain the Preempt Act. Min's clenched attention, and

Dolph's closed stare, revealed nothing. Angus glanced at them, then whispered to Davies, 'I'll tell you later.'

'Lastly,' Hashi stated, 'if corroborative evidence can be obtained, she has been authorized to accuse CEO Fasner of sending kazes against both the GCES and the UMCP.'

Min's head jerked aside as if to avoid a blow – an instinctive reaction of which she seemed unaware. One hand clutched at her hip, groping for the gun she usually carried. Captain Ubikwe made a choking sound deep in his throat. In the distance Glessen muttered, 'Fasner? That bastard?'

Kazes –? Mutely Morn turned to Angus.

He shrugged. Apparently this was a subject he knew nothing about.

Only Patrice attended his board – Patrice and Mikka. The rest of the bridge crew stared at Min in shock or incredulity.

Tensely Min asked her pickup, 'Is it true?'

'I believe so.'

Past a veil of thrust static Hashi continued, 'You will be unaware that there has been another attack. In addition to the kaze who threatened Captain Vertigus, and the one who slew poor Godsen, a third attempted detonation during a session of the Council, specifically during a session in which Captain Vertigus attempted – and failed – to obtain passage for a Bill of Severance which would have relieved us of the Dragon's authority.'

Min bit down questions while Hashi said, 'Fortunately our casualties were slight – and included none of the Members. Unfortunately the good Captain's Bill was defeated. However – again fortunately – the kaze's earthly remains hint at his origins.

'Hence our belief that these assaults derive from the great worm in his lair.'

Grimly the DA director finished, 'In essence, both Chief of Security Mandich and I have been assigned the same duties. Each in our own province, we must do what we can to substantiate Director Hannish's accusation. Considering that the emergency session has already begun, the need for evidence is urgent. That is my work, Min, and I mean to do it.'

334

'Good God, Hashi,' Min breathed when he was done. 'He's going after Fasner. He's trying to bring the Dragon down.'

'I drew the same conclusion,' Hashi answered laconically.

Min might not have heard him. A moment later she added, 'This will kill Warden. Even if he succeeds, it'll kill him.'

Again Hashi's voice receded. Clearly he wanted to stop talking and get to work. 'Perhaps that explains his willingness to hazard himself aboard *Calm Horizons*.'

Going after Fasner, Morn thought dumbly. She felt that she'd been stricken stupid. Trying to bring the Dragon down. So much had happened – there was so much she didn't know. Authorized to accuse – Kazes had attacked the GCES and the UMCP? Sent by Fasner? Hashi said it was true, but it didn't make sense.

Why in the name of God –?

Vector stood by the command station. Morn hadn't seen him move: she only realized he was there when he cleared his throat. His eyes shone a clear blue above his soft smile.

Quietly he remarked, 'This might be an especially good time for the Council to hear what we have to say.'

He knew no more than she did; had no more to go on. Yet he seemed to grasp the situation better than she did.

Was he right? Was Min? Was Warden Dios at last trying to clean up the UMCP?

She couldn't think of another explanation. It'll kill him. He was willing to die in order to challenge the Dragon. Willing to be held hostage – willing to risk mutation –

He'd sent this Koina Hannish to Earth to level charges against CEO Fasner. Then he'd put himself out of reach so that Fasner couldn't give him any more orders; force him to commit any more crimes.

Or fire him.

Morn reeled inwardly. Gulfs gaped at her on all sides. The sheer scale of the desperation which must have driven Warden to such extremes stunned her. He understood self-destruct as well as she did –

But what if he was wrong? What if Holt Fasner hadn't sent

kazes – or if Hashi Lebwohl and Chief Mandich failed to find evidence? What then?

Then the UMC CEO might survive the challenge. And the only man in human space who could have opposed him would be gone.

Unless somebody intervened –

Unless somehow Morn did what Vector suggested.

Min had recovered faster than Morn could imagine. She was already in command of herself; prepared to make choices and take action. She may have been training for this crisis all her life.

'All right, Hashi,' she told the pickup decisively. 'Two more quick points, and I'll let you go.

'Can that defensive read our scan net?'

The DA director sighed in the distance. 'Surely. This is Earth, not the frontier. The volume of traffic demands data which is both plainly and promptly accessible. Until now we have had no reason to encrypt the net.'

'Then shut it down,' Min ordered. 'Our ships can get by with their own sensors.'

'*Calm Horizons* also has sensors,' Hashi observed.

'Just do it. The less help we give her the better.'

'As you say,' Hashi assented. 'And the second point?'

'Tell Center to relay communications from *Calm Horizons* to me. Also anything from Fasner. And the emergency session. But keep it all tight-beamed. I don't want eavesdroppers.

'I'll talk to Center as soon as I sort out some of the confusion here.'

Hashi was in a hurry to leave. 'Farewell, Director Donner,' he said at once. 'Your orders will be obeyed.' Despite his eagerness, however, he paused long enough to add, 'I do not envy you your responsibilities.'

Then an audible click silenced his pickup. The speakers were left with nothing but static and open space.

'Good-bye, Hashi,' Min murmured into the void. 'I'll talk to you again. If we both live long enough.'

She set an example which Morn felt compelled to match. Davies' wordless urgency required it: Vector's understanding and Mikka's prostration and Ciro's madness begged for it. Captain Ubikwe and his people deserved it. Even Angus Thermopyle, welded and damned, had a right to it.

A better answer.

She couldn't imagine that Marc Vestabule would allow her time or space to address the Council.

Cray closed the speakers, and a new quiet filled the bridge. Everyone around the command station might have been waiting for Morn to speak.

She didn't look at any of them. Her eyes were fixed on the scan blip which represented *Calm Horizons*, where Warden Dios had gone to meet his doom.

'I think,' she said softly, 'we should try to rescue him.'

There was no one else who could make the attempt.

KOINA

With a war of one kind impending hundreds of k over her head, and a war of another directly in front of her, Koina Hannish entered the crowded chamber which Abrim Len had decided to use until the Council's formal meeting hall could be cleaned and refurbished.

This room was normally set aside for conferences with the planet's newsdogs; but the communications gear and data terminals of the video networks had been commandeered, rerouted and coded for the use of the Members and their aides. The twenty-one voting Members and a restricted number of their aides and advisers clustered at the terminals they'd been assigned, studying UMCPHQ's downlink, while President Len scurried around the room like a frightened hare, fussily arranging people to suit some standard of precedence or common interest known only to himself. Perhaps, Koina thought, he kept himself busy in this way in order to avoid demands or special pleading; attempts to take over the agenda of the emergency session.

In any case no one seemed to pay much attention to him. Most of the room was in the grip of a nascent hysteria which seethed from wall to wall independent of the President. The whole space reeked of visceral terrors like rank sweat.

At first it appeared that there was no place left for her. Despite Len's restrictions, the chamber already held more people than it had been designed to accommodate. Then she spotted three vacant seats in a corner near the dais usually used by Members to address newsdogs. They didn't offer access to a terminal; but she didn't need one. She had two of her PR communications techs with her: one to concentrate on her private downlink, one to keep UMCPHQ informed of what happened here. Deputy Chief Ing and his guards could stand against the walls.

Unfortunately the empty seats were right beside those occupied by UMC First Executive Assistant Cleatus Fane and his staff. Apparently someone – Abrim Len, or Fane himself – thought it was time for the UMC and the UMCP to stand together. The Dragon's FEA also had no terminal, and didn't need one: like Koina's, his people were all communications techs laden with gear – dedicated relays, encryption boxes, transceivers. Cleatus himself had a PCR jacked into one ear and a throat pickup patched beside his larynx. He may have been listening to the downlink, or to instructions from HO: Koina had no way of knowing.

She still reeled inwardly at the most recent news from Center – the news of Warden's departure for *Calm Horizons*. And the idea of sitting near Fane made her skin crawl. He was her most dangerous opponent; more her enemy than Maxim Igensard. To postpone the moment when she would have to endure his proximity, she paused inside the doors to take stock of the chamber.

Because she wanted to see a friendly face, she looked first for Captain Vertigus, the United Western Bloc Senior Member. He didn't appear to be present, however. His Junior Member, Sigurd Carsin, sat shuffling a sheaf of hardcopy between Vest Martingale, the Com-Mine Station Member, and Sen Abdullah, Senior Member for the Eastern Union. In their lesser ways, they were also Koina's opponents. Sigurd Carsin seemed to attack the UMCP for the same reasons that Sixten Vertigus distrusted Holt Fasner. Vest Martingale was responsible for Maxim Igensard's appointment as Special Counsel to investigate the Angus Thermopyle case: her constituency's reputation depended on her efforts to tarnish the UMCP's integrity. And Sen Abdullah – lean, hawk-faced and fanatical, with a perpetual sneer between his dark cheeks and his sharp, silver beard – appeared to be on a personal crusade against Warden Dios out of religious fervor or prejudice. However, rumor suggested that his hatred had more to do with money than religion: his constituency had lost staggering sums when Warden had helped 'arrange' Holt Fasner's takeover of Sagittarius Exploration years ago.

Then Koina spotted Sixten. She'd missed him because he was obscured by the Special Counsel. Although Maxim sat in front of Captain Vertigus, his public posture was typically so condensed and deferential that no one would have been hidden by it. However, Sixten had slumped down in his seat until he was almost invisible. His eyes were closed, and his mouth hung open: he was clearly asleep.

Koina shrugged ruefully and continued scanning the room.

She'd only been the UMCP's PR director for a short time, but she recognized all the Members by name and reputation. Punjat Silat, the Senior Member for the Combined Asian Islands and Peninsulas, was one of the few she believed would make decisions rationally, despite the incipient panic around him. Blaine Manse, the Member for Betelgeuse Primary, was another. Her reputation suggested that she was more interested in sex than politics. But according to Hashi's reports – inherently more accurate than Godsen's – Blaine's countless peccadilloes camouflaged a keen mind with a clear sense of purpose.

Tel Burnish, the Member from Valdor Industrial, usually held himself apart from debates about the UMC and the UMCP. However, now that his Station had been threatened by *Calm Horizons* he might begin to take sides.

Most of the other Members kept lower profiles, especially those with any history of resistance to the UMC. The fear which poured steadily into the chamber from the UMCPHQ downlink caused them to rally around the only obvious, tangible locus of power: Cleatus Fane. This was patently more comfortable for the 'votes' Holt Fasner 'owned' outright: New Outreach, Terminus, Sagittarius Unlimited, SpaceLab Annexe, and both Members for the Pacific Rim Conglomerate. Men and women who'd occasionally voted against the

Dragon, or who'd made efforts to disguise their loyalties, had a more awkward time approaching the only reassurance any of them could imagine.

The UMCP belonged to Holt Fasner. He possessed virtually all the effective muscle in human space. If he couldn't save the Members – who were, after all, trapped on Suka Bator because Warden Dios had sealed the island after the most recent kaze attack – no one could.

Koina Hannish had been sent here to cause even more panic. And the mood of the Council was already against her. Many of the Members were arrayed in opposition. That tightened her own fear to a pitch she wasn't sure she could stand.

Did she really believe that she would be able to carry out Warden's orders? What if undermining him now proved to be the worst mistake she could possibly make? What then?

Then she might find herself praying for *Punisher* to fire down ruin on the island. Death would be easier to face than her culpability for a disaster of such magnitude.

But Warden didn't consider it a mistake.

He'd had any number of opportunities to rescind his orders – yet he'd left them in force. *Nothing has changed. Go ahead.* He'd taken himself to the Amnioni, knowing what Koina would do on Earth: what she might do, if she had the courage; and might succeed at, if Hashi Lebwohl or Chief of Security Mandich supplied her with evidence in time. Then the question became, not, Would she be able to obey him? but, Could she bear to let him down?

Across the room, Abrim Len caught her eye and gestured frantically toward the seats he'd reserved for her. At the same time Forrest Ing stepped to her side and touched her arm.

'You'd better take your place, Director,' he said in her ear. 'From the look of things, Len'll have a coronary if he doesn't get this session started soon.'

She nodded. 'Security has this room covered, I hope,' she whispered. 'A kaze here now –'

A blast in this constricted space wouldn't leave any damage for the Amnion to do.

'We're using all our own people,' Forrest answered softly.

'We've screened them down to their genes. And the Members have vouched personally for everyone with them. I think you're safe.' He paused to frown at the FEA, then added, 'Unless Fane or one of his techs is full of explosives and wants to die.'

Koina nodded again. No doubt Cleatus *was* full of explosives – metaphorically speaking. But she was sure he had no intention of committing suicide. The Dragon didn't attract that kind of loyalty. If Hashi was right, the recent attacks hadn't been designed to destroy the GCES. Instead they were meant to strengthen Fasner's hold on the UMCP.

With the Deputy Chief at her side, she shifted through the crowd toward her assigned seat. When her techs were settled, and Forrest had taken a place at the wall behind her, she sat down.

Cleatus gave her an iron smile as she took her place. Ordinarily he projected the benevolence of a Father Christmas: he had a talent for it. But he'd set aside his air of expansive generosity. His eyes held a lupine glitter, and his beard bristled like wire.

'Director Hannish.' He inclined his head in a small bow. 'I'm here, as you requested.' As Forrest Ing had urged on her behalf. 'I must say, I'm eager to learn why you considered such a message necessary. Or appropriate. Perhaps we'll be able to discuss it later.

'You played your part well in the last session.' His tone repaid the threat Forrest had implied for her. 'But this time we aren't "playing". I hope you realize that. Your Warden Dios has refused to speak to the CEO since this crisis started. Whether you know it or not, he's left you out on a limb. If I have to, I'll cut it off.

'If I have to,' he promised quietly, 'I'll reduce the whole damn tree to kindling.'

Koina replied with a smile of her own – a smooth, bland, professional expression, immaculate and meaningless. 'You're kind to warn me.' She kept her voice low. 'May I ask you a question?'

Fane let her see his teeth. 'Of course.'

'I'm curious. How old are you?'

He closed his mouth. His eyes widened slightly, as if she'd suggested an insult. 'What does that have to do with anything?'

Her smile brightened. 'Nothing at all. As I say, it's mere curiosity. I was wondering whether CEO Fasner has shared any of his medical longevity with you.'

She meant, *How long do you think he'll keep you alive? What do you really think you're worth to him?*

The FEA appeared to understand her. He met her gaze without blinking. 'As it happens, Director Hannish, I'm in exceptionally good health.'

'I'm so glad.' Behind her professional mask, she was secretly pleased – and relieved – that she could still hold her own despite her fear. 'There's already too much death in the air.'

She didn't think he would heed her own warning. But his scowl showed that he'd heard it.

While she'd been speaking to Cleatus, President Len had at last made his way to the dais and picked up his ceremonial mace – what Hashi called his 'cudgel'. Now he began to bang it on the podium.

'Order, please.' He hefted the mace as if he might need it to ward off blows. 'This is an emergency session of the Governing Council for Earth and Space. Come to order, please.'

The tense exchanges of the Members and their aides were stilled almost immediately. Worry throbbed across the silence.

'You all know why we're here.' Len sounded weary to the point of exhaustion; reluctant; beaten. His stance behind the podium seemed oddly vulnerable. Neither his personality nor his experience fitted him to lead the Council in a time of war. 'You've been listening to the downlink. But if you're as scared as I am' – he sighed – 'you may find the whole crisis a little confusing. Just to get us started, I'll ask UMCPPR Director Koina Hannish to explain it. She may know something we don't.'

He turned to Koina, gestured her toward the podium. 'Director Hannish?'

She stood so that she could see faces better; but she didn't

343

leave her place; didn't waste time trying to dissociate herself from Cleatus Fane. She hadn't expected Abrim to call on her. Nevertheless she was ready – at least for this.

'Thank you, Mr President. For the moment I have nothing to tell you that you haven't already heard. In the interest of clarity, however, I'll summarize the situation.

'Because of the incursion of an Amnion warship into our space, Warden Dios has invoked the War Powers provisions of the UMCP charter. The alien vessel is a Behemoth-class defensive named *Calm Horizons*. As you've heard, she out-powers and outguns any of our ships. Only the recently commissioned battlewagon *Sledgehammer* comes close. More to the point, however, is the fact that she's armed with super-light proton cannon.

'That cannon is aimed at us.

'Director Dios has ordered a cordon of our ships to close around *Calm Horizons*. Already it's strong enough to ensure that the Amnioni dies if she fires on us. Soon it'll be strong enough to contain the damage we may suffer.'

'What does that *mean*, Director Hannish?' Sen Abdullah interrupted rudely. He strove to convey command; but his voice had an unpleasant whine which made him sound petulant.

'In twelve hours,' Koina answered firmly, '*Sledgehammer* will come into range. Then our cordon will have enough firepower to protect everything except Suka Bator and UMCPHQ.

'Unfortunately' – she permitted herself a small shrug – 'unlike matter cannon, a super-light proton beam isn't hindered or weakened by atmosphere.' And atmosphere was the island's only defense. '*Calm Horizons* can hit Suka Bator directly and often. She simply cannot be killed quickly enough to save us.

'For that reason,' she finished as if she were offering her audience hope, 'and because we have no way of knowing whether the Amnioni will hold fire for twelve more hours, Director Dios has gone aboard *Calm Horizons* alone in an attempt to negotiate for our survival.'

344

At once questions burst at her from the clenched gathering.

'What does he think that will accomplish?'

'What does he have to negotiate with?'

'Why hasn't that ship opened fire yet?'

The Members were too alarmed to wait for Abrim to recognize them. And he seemed to lack the will to insist on order.

'Why aren't you already shooting at her?'

The last demand came from Sigurd Carsin. Koina answered it first because it led naturally to the others.

'Director Dios held fire because *Calm Horizons* did.'

This was her job: she'd taken an oath to field questions like this. And it was easier than other things she'd sworn to do; duties she hadn't tackled yet.

'It has been obvious from the first,' she explained, 'that the Amnioni threatens Suka Bator. As soon as anyone starts shooting, all of us here are dead. But *Calm Horizons* hasn't fired. Clearly there's something she wants – and she wants it more than she wants to damage us.

'For all we know, she's here to defect. Or to prevent a defection.' Koina suggested those unlikely possibilities in the hope that they might distract some of the dread around her. 'We have many reasons to think the Amnion fear a war.

'Director Dios has gone to *Calm Horizons* to find out what the Amnion *do* want. And, if he can, to discuss ways of satisfying them without compromising our safety in human space, or bringing down unimaginable destruction on our planet – and ourselves.'

Again Sen Abdullah disdained the courtesy of waiting for Len to call on him. 'Does your Director Dios think he has the *right* to make those kinds of decisions?'

Koina fixed her PR smile tightly in place. 'Senior Member Abdullah, you have a terminal. If you wish, you can consult the exact wording of the War Powers provisions. Or you can trust me when I say that Director Dios is doing his sworn duty. Under conditions of war, the UMCP – and the UMCP alone – is responsible for the safety of human space and the survival of humankind.'

At last the President made an attempt to regain control of

the proceedings. 'Calm down, Sen, please,' he said pleadingly. 'We're all familiar with your opposition to Director Dios. I promise – you'll get your chance to speak.' For reasons Koina didn't understand, Abrim turned a quick glance in Maxim's direction. 'In fact, I'll recognize you first. When I'm done.

'Until then, please don't waste our time finding fault with the UMCP director's mission aboard *Calm Horizons*. As Director Hannish says, he's gone there to keep us alive. No matter what you think of him, you can't believe he means to harm us with this. No one has ever accused Warden Dios of treason.'

'Until now,' Abdullah muttered darkly. Instead of continuing, however, he resumed his seat and closed his mouth.

Len sighed his relief, then nodded to Koina. 'Thank you, Director Hannish. I'm sure we'll have more questions later. For now you've summarized the situation admirably.'

Dismissed, she sat down. Now that she was done, she noticed that her knees were trembling. Nervous sweat ran like skinworms across her ribs and down her spine. Involuntarily she looked over at Cleatus to gauge his reaction.

He met her gaze and smiled approval.

At that moment, under the bale of his approbation, Koina Hannish reached a final decision about the meaning of her life. When she realized that her account of events had pleased the Dragon's chief servant, she became sure of herself: who she was; what she meant to do.

As she returned his smile, some of her fear slipped from her, and her knees stopped trembling.

President Len still held his mace, but didn't swing it. 'Members,' he said to the gathering, 'let's begin.' A small tremor weakened his voice at first; but it faded as he went along. 'Director Hannish has outlined the immediate crisis. It's time for us to do the work we were elected for.'

Koina had the impression that he was delivering a speech he'd memorized. Perhaps he feared he wouldn't be able to hold his thoughts together otherwise.

'To begin, we must distinguish between the immediate crisis and the general emergency. The immediate crisis is legally, effectively, in Director Dios' hands. He will deal with *Calm Horizons* to the best of his abilities. In similar fashion, his station, UMCPHQ, has been covering the planet with preparations for disaster. Earlier we were restricted from leaving this island. You know why. Now there's nowhere we could go in time to save ourselves.

'Apart from keeping us alive, however, there's much that can be done, and is being done, for the people we represent. Population centers are being evacuated. Underground installations of all kinds – geothermal tapping stations, storage facilities and repositories, shielded police and military centers, deep-rock research establishments – have become bunkers. Food and water are being gathered against the aftermath of an attack. Secure communication and distribution networks are being activated. Much of the planet's weaponry has been directed into space.

'All this is necessary and admirable. I take it as evidence of Director Dios' good faith – and foresight.'

Again the President turned an unexplained look toward Special Counsel Igensard. As he did so, an abrupt movement brought Sixten Vertigus into view behind Maxim. At last the old Senior Member was awake and listening.

'Nevertheless,' Len continued, 'it's also desperately inadequate. For too long, we've believed that if we fought a war it would be' – he gestured toward the ceiling with his mace – 'elsewhere. Somewhere out among the stars. Not here. We've planned and built and provisioned for a war somewhere else.

'In that sense, we aren't ready for the immediate crisis. And there's nothing UMCPHQ can do to compensate for it.'

Abrim paused. When he resumed, his voice held a note of coercion, as if he were forcing himself to make assertions which discomfited him; assertions which would produce contention rather than consensus.

'However, our unreadiness is part of what I call the general emergency. The general emergency concerns the policies, the institutions and, yes, the personnel which have brought about the immediate crisis. If the immediate crisis is in Director

Dios' hands – as it must be – then the general emergency is in ours. If we aren't ready for a local war, the responsibility is ours. And if any person, decision or organization has called down *Calm Horizons* on our heads, we are again responsible.

'Those are the issues this session must consider,' Len finished tightly. 'I propose to keep you all here until we do consider them.'

As she listened Koina was momentarily bemused. She hadn't expected so much lucidity from Abrim. Behind his congenital fear of conflict, he apparently had a good mind. He may even have had a sense of honor. His statement was the opposite of Sen Abdullah's accusative demands. If a simple majority of the Council could be brought to see the situation as clearly as Abrim did, there was hope: hope of avoiding panic, if nothing else; perhaps hope for one or two intelligent decisions as well.

Unfortunately Len had promised to let Abdullah speak first.

Before the President could go on, however, Cleatus interjected, 'Mr President, if I may – ?'

Abrim turned to face Fane and Koina. His eyes were moist with strain and worry. If he'd allowed it, his weak chin might have trembled. Preparing and delivering a lucid opening statement must have been costly for him.

'Of course, Mr Fane. We welcome comments from the UMC.' He nodded at Koina. 'Or the UMCP.'

The FEA rose smoothly to his feet. At once everyone in the room shifted to stare at him, some avid for any reprieve the Dragon might devise, others in mistrust or disapproval. Koina herself stared, trying to gauge the depth of his game.

As he spoke, complex intentions disguised each other in his tone. She thought she heard concern, scorn, humor, reassurance, threats; but she wasn't sure of any of them. His stiff beard surrounded his mouth with an impenetrable tangle.

'Mr President, your summation of the responsibilities of the Council is especially apt. Some of you may be aware that apart from UMCPHQ the UMC Home Office is the only armed station orbiting Earth. And let me say, by the way, that if they're needed those arms will surely be used in our defense. The point I wish to make, however, is that HO is armed because Holt Fasner – no one else – sets policy for the UMC. I mean no disrespect when I say that he has always taken the dangers of dealing with the Amnion more seriously than the Council.'

Koina allowed herself to cock an eyebrow. Under other circumstances she might have asked, *Our* defense? Who do you mean? Those of us here against *Calm Horizons*? All humankind? Or do you mean just the UMC?

'I'm sure what you say is true, Mr Fane,' Sixten remarked unexpectedly. He didn't stand; ignored dozens of heads craning to peer at him. His voice was high and thin with age, but he managed to make himself heard clearly. 'Are *you* quite sure that arming HO is consistent with the terms of the UMC charter?'

At once President Len intervened to deflect the challenge; the insult. 'Captain Vertigus, please. I must have order. I recognized Mr Fane out of courtesy to an interested guest. If you wish to be recognized, I can only assure you that your turn will come. Any Member who wishes to speak will be heard. But this is an emergency session of the Governing Council for Earth and Space, and it will be conducted in good order.'

'Order.' Sixten flapped his hands dismissively. 'Rules. I'm too old for all this, Abrim. By the time you get around to me, I may be dead. *You* ask him. Ask Mr Fane if the UMC charter provides for an armed station.'

Exasperation hunched Abrim's shoulders. 'Captain Vertigus –'

'I'll answer, Mr President,' Cleatus offered without hesitation. 'Maybe then we can go on.' He brandished his whiskers to suggest perplexity. 'Although why anyone would object to HO's guns at a time like this is beyond me.'

Koina could think of a reason. She had no difficulty grasping Sixten's point. An armed station could defy the law; defy the Council. But she didn't say anything. The time hadn't come for her to speak.

349

The President sighed. 'Perhaps you're right, Mr Fane. If you're willing, please go ahead.'

Fane bowed from the waist. 'Thank you, Mr President.' Then he pointed his smile at Sixten.

'Captain Vertigus, the UMC charter neither provides for nor disallows an armed Home Office. You can look it up if you want to. I'll happily refer you to the relevant subsections.'

'Don't bother,' Sixten muttered.

The FEA shrugged. 'In the absence of an explicit restriction,' he concluded, 'we have cannon – and shields – because CEO Fasner decided we should.'

'Are you satisfied, Captain?' Len made no attempt to conceal his vexation.

'Satisfied?' Sixten's voice cracked; perhaps deliberately. 'Of course not. But I'll shut up anyway. Maybe you'll be kind enough to wake me when it's my turn.'

With another bow, Cleatus seated himself.

On impulse Koina leaned toward him and whispered, 'I take it you think the government should be turned over to CEO Fasner?' She kept her voice too low to be overheard.

Fane's eyes flashed. 'We're staring down the guns of an Amnion defensive because your director screwed up,' he replied softly. 'But he won't face the problem – or the consequences. He refuses to talk to his boss. Instead he's aboard *Calm Horizons* making decisions for the whole human race. Who knows what he's giving away to keep us alive – or cover up his mistakes? And there's nothing the Council can do about it. He can hide behind those War Powers provisions until we all dry up and wither away.

'Don't you think it's time someone with a few brains and a sense of responsibility took charge?'

Koina met his gaze and smiled like sugar. 'Personally, Mr Fane, I would vote for you.'

As soon as she saw his disconcerted frown, she turned her attention back to the dais and President Len. There were times, she thought, when being a woman – and being what others called beautiful – gave her a significant advantage. Which was fine, as far as it went; but she needed more.

350

She needed leverage. Without it the things she'd been ordered to say might give Holt Fasner just the excuse he was waiting for; an excuse to take direct control of the UMCP.

Then he would be the only effective power in human space.

Nothing has changed. Go ahead.

Fervently she prayed that Warden had taken steps to prevent such a disaster.

President Len had made his opening statement. Apparently he had no more to say. 'If we're quite done with interruptions,' he announced now, 'it's time to address the issues of this session. I'm not going to limit the discussion in any way, except to preserve order. I hope, however, that you'll restrict yourselves to the subjects I've outlined. If you don't, I'll accept motions from the floor to cut you off.

'To begin, I recognize the Senior Member of the Eastern Union, Sen Abdullah.'

Carefully Abrim set his mace down on the podium as if he were disavowing responsibility. Then he retreated to a seat at the back of the dais.

At once Abdullah surged to his feet. 'Mr President,' he half-shouted. 'Members!' He may have been trying to camouflage his habitual whine with volume. 'I was not the first to use the word "treason" in this room, but I can promise you I won't be the last. It must be said now, and it must be said often. Treason! Warden Dios has committed *treason* against the GCES, *treason* against the planet Earth, *treason* against all humankind.

'By the rules of order, I yield the floor to Special Counsel Maxim Igensard.'

Len steepled one hand over his eyes. Slowly he nodded.

Oh, shit, Koina thought. So that's how it comes. Not from Cleatus. From Maxim. Of course. Cleatus didn't want to look complicit. Or maybe he wasn't complicit. Maybe he just knew that Maxim would do his work for him.

A moment ago she'd dreaded facing Sen Abdullah's fanatic petulance. But now she realized that the EU Senior Member would have been a far easier opponent than Maxim Igensard. Even the FEA would have been easier – Abdullah would have

351

undermined himself: his hate was too obvious, too partisan and too irrational to sway the Council for long. And Cleatus made too much money in Holt Fasner's service. Maxim had far more credibility, if for no other reason than because he had no constituency; no vested interest. As long as he did his job, he was safe no matter what his investigation uncovered.

With his ego and his intelligence, he was the perfect tool –

Rising from his seat, he moved through the crowd cautiously, like a man trying to minimize his profile. Two steps took him up onto the dais. There he approached the podium, positioned himself behind it, and gripped it by the edges with both hands as if he were anxious and needed support. Although he wasn't as small as he made himself seem, only his head and shoulders showed above the rim of the podium.

'Mr President.' He turned a courteous bow toward Abrim. 'Members of the Governing Council for Earth and Space. First Executive Assistant Fane. Protocol Director Hannish. Thank you for your attention. I won't waste it.

'You may think I exceed my mandate by speaking to you now. I've been charged to investigate the so-called "Angus Thermopyle case" – his arrest, conviction and subsequent escape – not to comment on matters of war policy. For that reason, I wish to make two points immediately clear. First, I am here as the assigned proxy of Eastern Union Senior Member Sen Abdullah.' Maxim nodded respectfully at Abdullah. 'I have both his right to speak and his vote. Confirmation is available from your terminals.'

A rustle of movement followed as Members told their aides to check. Koina didn't bother, however. She was sure that Igensard hadn't made any procedural mistakes.

'Second,' the Special Counsel said, 'I am here because I believe that the "Angus Thermopyle case" has a special bearing on *Calm Horizons'* presence in our space. If I'm right, then what I have to say is directly, explicitly relevant to the issues of this session. And, whether we like it or not, we'll all be forced to use the term "treason".'

Koina couldn't contain herself. 'Forgive me, Mr Igensard,'

she said so that everyone would hear her. '"Treason" is a highly emotional word. You haven't earned the right to use it yet.'

At once Maxim retorted, 'But I will, Director Hannish. Toward that end, I mean to examine you shortly. Perhaps you'll take my charges seriously enough to answer them truthfully. With or without your cooperation, however, I will earn the right.'

Then he returned his attention to the Council.

'As you recall, President Len called this session before *Calm Horizons* appeared here. He called it because he'd received a formal announcement from UMCP Director Warden Dios, informing him that a Behemoth-class Amnion defensive – apparently this same *Calm Horizons* – had encroached on the Massif-5 system. The information had reached Director Dios by gap courier drones from Valdor Industrial and UMCP cruiser *Punisher*. The first, from VI, reported *Calm Horizons*' incursion and *Punisher*'s engagement. The second, from UMCP Enforcement Division Director Min Donner aboard *Punisher*, reported that the cruiser had broken off the engagement, in part because she was too heavily damaged to prosecute her attack successfully, and in part to supply protection for another UMCP vessel, the gap scout *Trumpet*, believed to be the target of *Calm Horizons*' incursion.'

The Special Counsel didn't use notes. Apparently he didn't need them. He gave the impression that he never forgot anything. His voice sharpened as he spoke, and his physical presence seemed to expand, as if what he said made him larger.

'Because we've all been quite naturally appalled and alarmed by Director Dios' information,' he stated, 'we have perhaps failed to notice that much of it makes no sense. In fact, however, the director's announcement is far more significant for what it conceals than for what it reveals.'

'"Conceals"?' Captain Vertigus interrupted scornfully. 'He was in a hurry, for God's sake. What do you want him to do, write you a goddamn white paper on human-Amnion relations?'

'What I *want* is simple, Captain Vertigus,' Maxim shot back. 'The truth. Nothing more. Nothing less.'

Koina applauded Sixten in silence; but she didn't support his objection. Instead she made use of the distraction. She thought she could see where Igensard was headed. I mean to examine you shortly – Turning away, she leaned toward her communications techs. 'Flare Chief Mandich for me,' she whispered carefully, hardly moving her lips. 'Flare Director Lebwohl. Tell them I'm running out of time here.'

The tech responsible for keeping UMCPHQ informed of events nodded. 'Right away, Director,' she breathed.

As the tech obeyed, Koina straightened herself to listen again. Cleatus treated her to a cold smile, which she ignored.

'Time and again,' Maxim was saying, 'we've been given reason to believe the Amnion don't desire war. Their imperialism – rampant though it may be – is of another kind. In the simplest terms, their production methods aren't adequate to supply the ships and *matériel* a war would demand.

'This raises a number of questions.

'Why now have the Amnion elected to violate a peace on which they're dependent? And why did they do so by encroaching on Massif-5, a system far better defended than Earth – indeed, quite capable of repulsing and even destroying the defensive? How can a mere UMCP gap scout justify such action? What is at stake, that having failed to kill *Trumpet* would cause the Amnion to compound their act of war by coming here?

'Director Dios' announcement gives no answer. Perhaps a "white paper" on the subject would have been useful.'

Igensard glared briefly at Captain Vertigus, then continued like a cutting laser.

'Neither does the UMCP director explain why *Punisher* was there to meet *Calm Horizons*' incursion. The cruiser had just finished an arduous tour of duty around VI, and had returned to Earth for much-needed leave and repair. Her replacement, the UMCP cruiser *Vehemence*, had already reached Massif-5. Yet *Punisher* never docked at UMCPHQ.

As soon as Director Donner joined ship, *Punisher* departed on another mission.

'My investigation has revealed – another detail omitted by Director Dios – that the cruiser was sent, not back to Massif-5, but out to the Com-Mine belt.'

Some of the Members reacted with surprise. Koina herself was surprised that Maxim had been able to obtain such information. But he didn't pause.

'Her stated mission,' he sneered, 'was "to guard against reports of unusual hostile activity along the frontier near the Com-Mine belt." Why Min Donner's presence was required for such a mission is not explained.

'How then does it happen that *Punisher* entered the Massif-5 system in time to engage *Calm Horizons*? And how does it happen that a UMCP officer with Min Donner's reputation for probity, valor and determination decided to break off the engagement? Why did she conclude that *Trumpet* was more important than her sworn duty to defend human space?

'Above all, why was *Trumpet* there?' Maxim didn't raise his voice. Nevertheless it seemed to swell until it filled the room like a shout. 'What accounts for the gap scout's presence in the Massif-5 system?'

Koina saw Sixten squirm under the pressure of Igensard's challenge; but the old Senior Member didn't interject a comment. He may have realized that it was already too late for him – or anyone – to defend Warden.

Quietly Cleatus murmured, 'An interesting question, don't you think, Director Hannish?' He seemed to be taunting her. 'I'm afraid your Warden is in more trouble than he can handle.'

Koina kept her attention fixed on the Special Counsel; hid her tension and dread behind a mask of professional detachment.

'One other significant fact is absent from Director Dios' announcement,' Maxim proclaimed as if he wished to draw blood. 'As if he thinks we might not have noticed, he doesn't mention that *Trumpet* is the same vessel in which Captain Angus Thermopyle and former Deputy Chief of Com-Mine

355

Station Security Milos Taverner are purported to have made their escape from UMCPHQ.

'Mr President, Members' – he paused to scan the room – 'I consider the omission of these points to be as significant as their implications.'

No one interrupted him now. The Members and their aides stared at him, rapt, as if they'd fallen under a spell. They'd all received Warden's announcement. Most of them probably remembered where they'd heard of *Trumpet* before. Some of them must have been struck by the strangeness of *Trumpet*'s role in events. But they'd been distracted by *Calm Horizons*' presence; by the threat to Earth – and themselves.

Koina was sure that for most of Maxim's audience the picture he outlined had begun to seem profoundly disturbing.

'A few days ago UMCPDA Director Hashi Lebwohl informed us by video conference that Captain Thermopyle and Deputy Chief Taverner had stolen *Trumpet* and fled toward Thanatos Minor in forbidden space. So much is plausible. Captain Thermopyle is a convicted illegal. By implication, Deputy Chief Taverner is also an illegal. The bootleg shipyard on Thanatos Minor is an illegal installation – a natural destination for such men.

'But how does it occur that two illegals in a stolen ship at a bootleg installation countenanced by the Amnion have damaged or threatened the Amnion to such an extent that *Calm Horizons* was sent to commit an act of war in response?

'I'll propose an explanation. Call it a hypothesis if you wish. I don't pretend to have concrete evidence. Until quite recently' – he glanced at Koina – 'UMCPHQ has not been open with records and information. But I have the evidence of common sense. The evidence of intelligence.

'When I'm done, I'll ask Director Hannish if she chooses to contradict me. If she does, I'll ask her' – now he did shout – '*no, I'll dare her*' – at once he softened his tone again – 'to supply facts that support her position.'

Although she'd seen this coming, Koina felt a new sting of apprehension in the palms of her hands, the pit of her stomach. Still no word from Hashi, or Chief Mandich – In a few more minutes she would have to face Maxim Igensard and the Council with nothing to go on except Warden's orders and her own untried ability to make Hashi's reasoning sound credible.

'Be fair, Maxim,' President Len put in unexpectedly. He sounded deeply tired; but apparently he still felt compelled to smooth out conflicts. 'Do you really expect her to be prepared for a challenge like that? Without any warning?'

Maxim didn't hesitate. 'Mr President, she's the UMCP Director of Protocol. It's her *job* to be prepared.'

'Well, don't keep us in suspense,' Captain Vertigus said with an acerbic quaver. 'If you're so eager to accuse Warden Dios of treason, get it over with. Just what *is* this "hypothesis" of yours?'

The Special Counsel faced his audience again. He looked taller, elevated by eagerness. Something inside him had reached critical mass and begun to expand toward an explosion.

'Members of the Council, the stories we've been told are incredible, and I think they aren't true. I believe Captain Thermopyle and Deputy Chief Taverner did *not* escape from UMCPHQ. I believe they're agents of the UMCP, agents of Director Dios. I believe they were sent into forbidden space to commit some affront or do some harm which the Amnion would be unable to countenance. And when they'd succeeded, I believe they fled deep into human space on Director Dios' orders.

'Because it was already known how the Amnion would respond, *Trumpet* ran to Massif-5, a place so far inside our frontier that no act of war could be excused, and yet so far from Earth that we – and UMCPHQ – would be in no direct danger.

'For her part, *Punisher* went to the Com-Mine belt with Min Donner aboard to ensure that *Trumpet* was indeed able to flee. Thereafter she followed the gap scout to the Massif-5 system, where she awaited *Calm Horizons'* incursion.

'The crucial point is this.' For the first time he let go of the podium. With the heel of one fist he tapped each word onto the surface in front of him. 'I'm certain that all these events occurred because Warden Dios wished it so.

'No, let me be plainer. I believe that the director of the UMCP has deliberately precipitated an act of war.'

Apart from Koina, Abrim Len appeared to be the only person in the room who'd guessed – or known? – what was coming. He didn't react; sat without moving. Once again his hand steepled over his eyes as if he'd seen all he could bear. It was possible that he had known. Some argument must have been used to persuade him to sanction assigning Sen Abdullah's proxy to Igensard. Perhaps this was it: perhaps Maxim had convinced Len that he needed a Member's stature in order to present his accusation.

But everyone else –

The director of the UMCP has deliberately precipitated an act of war.

In one corner, two or three people jumped to their feet around someone Koina couldn't see; someone who'd apparently fainted. From wall to wall men and women turned pale as if the blood were being drained from the room. The distinguished scholar Punjat Silat clutched at his chest; groped toward an aide until the aide pressed a small vial into his hand. Silat jerked back his head to swallow the contents of the vial, then slumped in his seat, his face as gray as ash. Sigurd Carsin and Vest Martingale stared at Maxim with their mouths open. Sixten grimaced convulsively, then began to beat his forehead with the heels of his palms, trying to drive back his dismay; his sense of betrayal. Cleatus waggled his beard by pursing his mouth like a man tasting a bitter pill to see whether he could stomach it.

Deliberately precipitated –

The Council had trusted Warden too long: humankind was too dependent on him. The bare idea that he might have committed the crime Maxim suggested seemed to open a gulf deep enough to swallow the planet.

Could it be true? Even Koina considered the possibility with pain. Oh, God, Warden. What have you done?

In distress she turned a mute appeal to her techs. Her

mouth shaped the word, Anything? But they shook their heads. One of them whispered, 'Chief Mandich asks you to forgive him. Director Lebwohl says he doesn't want to be disturbed.'

She bit her lip to stifle a groan. She had to have *evidence*; needed it desperately. Otherwise everything Warden was trying to do would recoil against him.

Beside her Cleatus subvocalized into his throat pickup: a thin, ragged sound, too low for her to distinguish words. Talking to the Dragon –

A moment later she was startled to hear Blaine Manse raise her voice. 'In God's name, *why*, Maxim?' the Member for Betelgeuse Primary protested. 'What kind of man would do that? I didn't think *anybody* was crazy enough to want a war.'

'I'm sure you're right,' Igensard retorted incisively. 'Director Dios does *not* want a war. The Amnion aren't the real target of his actions. *We* are.'

'How so?' Blaine pursued.

'To put it crudely' – Maxim paused, apparently to focus his audience's attention – 'his purpose was to frighten the Council into withdrawing support for my investigation.'

From the back of the room, Tel Burnish gave a snort of contempt. 'Does the word "megalomania" mean anything to you, Special Counsel? What makes you think you're important enough for Warden Dios to risk starting a war?'

'What makes you think you're important enough to force him to turn his back on a lifetime of dedicated service?'

Maxim faced the VI Member's challenge without flinching. He was primed for a detonation. Gathering pressure seemed to throb under his skin; glint dangerously from his eyes; echo like the clang of a hammer in his voice.

'In the pursuit of my duties,' he pronounced, 'I've been accumulating evidence of the most malign kinds of malfeasance and corruption. Warden Dios' probity is under question, his power is endangered. You were here – you heard him during the video conference. His back is against the wall. *I* pushed him there.

'Now he's trying to protect his position by convincing us

we can't afford to threaten him. He wants us to think the risk of probing and questioning him is too great at a time when we face the possibility of war.

'And he would have succeeded, except for one fatal miscalculation. The actions of Captain Thermopyle and Deputy Chief Taverner were too extreme. They were so extreme that *Calm Horizons* didn't stop when *Trumpet* escaped from Massif-5. Prevented from following by *Punisher*, the Amnioni didn't withdraw, as Director Dios no doubt intended – preserving her own survival, as well as the possibility that peace could eventually be restored. Instead *Calm Horizons* came here.

'Do you think I'm wrong?' the Special Counsel demanded in the hard tones of a prophet. 'Then tell me how you account for the fact that *Punisher* broke off her engagement with the defensive. Min Donner is famous for her unswerving sense of duty. She's also notoriously belligerent. Why would she break her oath as the Enforcement Division director of the UMCP, if she hadn't been given orders to let the defensive live?

'Warden Dios wants the threat of a full-scale war, not the actuality. *Calm Horizons'* destruction might have been more provocation than the Amnion could endure.'

'*Punisher* was damaged,' Sixten objected weakly. '*Calm Horizons* has super-light proton cannon.'

'I'm sure that's true,' Maxim assented. 'It only confirms my point, however. Why was a damaged ship chosen for this mission? Why not this new battlewagon, *Sledgehammer*? Why not *Vehemence*, a cruiser already assigned to Massif-5?

'I think it was because *Punisher* could plausibly claim that she couldn't destroy the defensive.

'Ask yourself why Director Dios has gone alone aboard *Calm Horizons*. Don't you think it's likely he hopes to convince the Amnion that he didn't mean for events to go so far? Don't you think he's offering them restitution for whatever *Trumpet* did?

'It's possible that because of his dereliction the UMCP is no longer able or willing to prosecute a war.'

Koina stifled a protest. She would have loved to shout at the Special Counsel, *Dereliction* has nothing to do with it! We don't have enough *ships*! Or enough people. We don't have the *budget* for a war. Fasner hasn't given us that much money.

But that wasn't what Warden had ordered her to say. He hadn't offered her any excuses. His intentions were more subtle. He didn't want to be let off the hook: he wanted to use that hook against the Dragon.

And he wanted Koina to do it for him; to him.

Without evidence –

Tel Burnish had surged to his feet: he may have been trying to counteract Igensard's grip on the Council. 'No, Special Counsel,' he insisted. 'You're going too fast. You're getting ahead of yourself. Your argument only makes sense if you assume Warden Dios knew there would be an incursion. Otherwise all this talk about "treason" and "dereliction" is just so much paranoia.'

The VI Member had reason to defend Warden. More than any other station except Com-Mine, Valdor had seen the UMCP's ships – and integrity – in action.

But Maxim wasn't daunted. 'Exactly,' he countered. Triumph rang like iron in his voice. Heavy with power and accusation, he turned toward Koina.

'Director Hannish.'

She met his glinting gaze squarely. 'Special Counsel?'

'I have some questions I want to ask you.'

She opened her mouth to say, Of course. That's what I'm here for. I have orders – But her throat closed on the words. It was too late: Hashi and Chief Mandich had taken too long. Without substantiation the things she had to reveal would make Igensard sound sane.

Abruptly Cleatus put his hand on her arm; tugged at her attention. He made no effort to keep his voice down.

'You don't have to submit to this,' he told her. 'I'll answer his questions. Save us all the strain of dragging this out. The UMC is responsible for the UMCP in any case. I'll just have to cover the same ground when you're done.'

He sounded sure of himself: patronizing and impregnable. His face belied his tone, however. Instead of looking at her, he flicked his eyes around the room like a man searching out enemies. His cheeks had lost color, as if his blood had run gray. He held his head cocked slightly toward the PCR in his ear. Concentration clenched the corners of his mouth.

Before Koina could reply, one of her techs murmured, 'Director,' and thrust a small communications board into her hands. Apparently the tech didn't want to chance being overheard. Instead she pointed at a message on the board's readout.

Instinctively Koina held it so that Cleatus couldn't see it. Blinking hard to focus her eyes, she read the transmission.

It was from UMCPHQ Center.

It reported that *Punisher* had arrived.

Resumed tard not far from UMCPHQ and *Calm Horizons*. With Ensign Morn Hyland in command.

In command – ?

The readout also stated that Hashi Lebwohl had stepped down as Acting Director in Warden Dios' absence. Still aboard *Punisher*, Min Donner had taken his place.

Acting Director Donner had ordered the shutdown of Earth's vast scan net.

In *command* – ?

None of it made any sense. Min Donner was Acting Director? Even though she was stuck aboard a ship she didn't command? And she wanted the scan net shut down?

Somehow Morn had – ?

Koina couldn't begin to guess what it all meant.

Nevertheless it explained why Cleatus didn't want her to answer Maxim's questions. The fact that Morn Hyland was here – and in command of *Punisher* – must have appalled Holt Fasner. She was dangerous to him; far more dangerous than Koina herself. In Warden's absence, Morn was more dangerous than anyone.

Fasner knew he'd lost control of the UMCP. Cleatus knew. They knew they couldn't trust Koina.

And without the scan net, HO – like UMCPHQ – had to

rely on its own instruments. To that extent, the Dragon had been blinded. He could no longer see everything that happened.

'Director Hannish,' Maxim rasped sternly. 'We're waiting.'

At once Koina rose to her feet. As if she were as sure as the FEA, she answered, 'I'm ready, Special Counsel.'

That was a lie. She wasn't ready. Without evidence, she would never be ready. Yet she accepted Igensard's demand as if he'd challenged her to personal combat: a test of honor.

Warden had given her his orders. And Cleatus Fane wanted her to remain seated; silent. Now that the crisis was upon her, she had no difficulty choosing between them.

HASHI

Freed from his responsibilities as Acting Director, Hashi left Center and headed for Lane Harbinger's lab.

Despite his shambling gait and his air of distraction, he moved quickly: by his own standards, he was running. In the past hour crises had multiplied around him at an alarming rate. Quantum uncertainties expanded in chain reaction. At the same time – and by the same logic – the window during which he could hope to help shape events shrank. Endorphins and necessity burned in his synapses: his blood felt rich with urgency. He had work to do.

UMCHO had charged its guns. However, they were pointedly not aimed at *Calm Horizons*. The great worm in his lair wished Marc Vestabule to know that he was prepared to defend himself, but that he would not treat the huge defensive as an enemy unless he was forced to do so.

Time had become exquisitely short.

In subtle ways this pleased the DA director. Lesser men and women, lesser minds, had already been left behind by the burgeoning emergency. Now only genius might suffice to fend off ruin.

Hashi Lebwohl was eager to prove himself equal to Warden Dios' vast and dangerous intentions.

Lane's lab was several levels and several hundred meters away from Center. Lifts and service shafts shortened the distance, however, and Hashi knew them all. He reached her workroom scant minutes after confirming Min Donner as Acting Director.

But when he entered the lab – a large space by the constricted measure of an orbital platform – he stopped in surprise.

Lane was alone. Apart from the complex clutter of tables and terminals, instruments of all kinds, sterile chambers and autoclaves, retorts and flasks, probes and sensors and keypads, packets of stim and hype, pots of coffee, bowls overflowing with ash and butts, the room was empty. The numerous aides and techs he'd assigned to her were gone – sent away, he assumed, since he declined to believe that any of his people would have abandoned a project so vital.

And Lane herself was sitting down. In itself that was profoundly uncharacteristic: Hashi wasn't sure he'd ever seen her in a chair of her own volition. As a rule she consumed enough stimulants of all kinds to make a block of wood hyperactive. Yet her condition was worse than uncharacteristic. She sat with her legs sprawled gracelessly in front of her as if she had no further use for them. Her head hung down, unclean hair dangling before her face: he couldn't tell whether she'd glanced at him; whether she'd noticed his arrival at all. Only her mouth moved as she sucked, arrhythmic as a limping heart, on one of her foul nics. Smoke curled up into her face and filtered away through her hair as if she were exhaling her life.

For a moment Hashi was stunned. He lacked Warden's talent for responding to the emotions of his people. Indeed, he seldom cared to let them distract him. By nature he was unprepared and ill equipped to deal with any woman in a state which resembled catatonia.

He had no time for Lane's despair; no time at all. Yet he knew instantly, intuitively, that he would be unable to reach her unless he attended to it. Without warning he discovered that he would be lost unless he could prove himself Warden's equal in completely unexpected ways.

'My dear Lane,' he asked softly, 'what on Earth has gone wrong?'

She didn't react. Smoke seeped out of her hair as if the mind under it had been burned to the ground.

Before he could decide how to approach her, the lab intercom chimed. 'Director Lebwohl?' a voice asked nervously. 'Director Lebwohl, are you there? This is Center. Director?'

Hashi swallowed an arcane curse. Briefly he forgot where Lane's intercom was. The voice from Center seemed to arise from a source he couldn't locate. Then he remembered that the console where she usually worked held her pickup and speaker.

Four vexed strides took him around a worktable to her terminal. With a jerk of his thumb, he toggled the pickup.

'Director Lebwohl,' he announced like a wasp. 'Did I mention that I'm busy?'

'Sorry, Director,' the nervous voice replied quickly. 'I have a flare for you. From Director Hannish. At the emergency session.'

Hashi wanted to retort, I *know* where she is. I *stepped down* as Acting Director. I wasn't fired for incompetence. But he restrained himself. He didn't have time to indulge his ire. Instead he drawled, 'Then perhaps you should tell me what it says.'

'Yes, Director.' Hashi heard the sound of keys. 'To DA Director Hashi Lebwohl,' Center reported. 'From PR Director Koina Hannish. "I'm running out of time here." That's all.

'Any response, Director?'

Hashi flapped his arms. The urgency in his blood needed an outlet. At the same time he couldn't justify covering a mere communications tech – or Koina herself – with his exasperation.

'Inform Director Hannish,' he said brusquely, 'that I do not wish to be disturbed.'

At once he silenced the pickup and turned back to Lane.

Past her hair he caught the glint of one eye. Her nic had been smoked out. She dropped it to the floor beside her, produced another from somewhere, lit it with a small magnesium torch hot enough to start a fire which would gut the station.

He concealed a thin sigh. Not comatose, he thought. Not unreactive. So much was encouraging.

On impulse he reached up, removed the glasses he wore for obfuscation, folded them carefully and dropped them into a pocket of his labcoat. A feigned absence of pretense was the easiest stratagem he could devise on short notice.

'Lane, I can't afford this.' He filled his voice with a vibration of sincerity. 'I need you. Director Hannish needs you. You heard her message. It would be impossible to overstate how sorely you're needed.

'I have no time to play therapist for an autistic child.'

At first he feared she wouldn't answer. And what if she didn't? What then? He could log on to her terminal, access her notes and records, attempt to reconstruct her results. But such a task might require hours. Even if he accomplished miracles of celerity, it would take too long –

Fortunately she'd heard him. She may have been overwhelmed by despair – or perhaps just utterly exhausted – but she was possessed by a mind which had always responded to the demands he'd placed on it. Her voice seemed to ache with reluctance as she murmured past the screen of her hair, 'I failed.'

'What, *failed*? *You?*' Deliberately he stifled the avuncular tone he normally used in times of stress. Nor did he reveal his relief. Despair was in some sense unanswerable – a neurochemical wound which no words could heal. Mere failure was an altogether simpler issue. Perhaps she experienced something akin to the shame he'd felt when he'd realized that Warden's game was far deeper than he'd imagined: the wound to his self-esteem. 'Forgive my doubt. You could only fail by trying to answer the wrong questions. If you appear to have failed, it must be because I have misnamed your assignment in some way.'

After a moment she shook her head – the only movement she'd made except for those required by smoking. 'I can't find any proof,' she murmured listlessly. 'Isn't that what you wanted? Isn't that what you need?'

If she'd been any other woman – even Min Donner – he might have believed that she was on the verge of tears.

Her vulnerability sparked a reaction in him which he hardly recognized. It may have been that his heart went out to her. Slumping on the heels of his old-fashioned shoes, he moved toward her until he was near enough to touch her. With both hands he eased her head back, then parted her hair away from her face so that the smoke of her nic was no longer trapped in her eyes.

'Do I need proof?' he answered. 'Assuredly. But it's an ambiguous notion at the best of times – which these are not. Don't trouble yourself with what I may or may not need, Lane. Tell me what you've learned.'

She didn't meet his gaze. Her attention was fixed on a landscape of pain he couldn't see.

'I found the hollow tooth. Where they stored that apoenzyme.' Nathan Alt's chemical detonator. 'He bit into it and blew up. But I can't prove that. I can't prove some other trigger wasn't destroyed in the blast. I can't tell you who did it to him.'

'We expected that,' he murmured to encourage her. 'Go on.'

A small tightening that might have begun as a shrug seemed to pull her in on herself. 'I tried to locate the original research.' Smoke and grief made her voice husky. 'Somebody must have developed that apoenzyme. Made it. It didn't just happen in his body. But whoever came up with it has done a better job than usual of keeping it secret. Or my clearance isn't high enough. Or it came from the Amnion. I can't find it.'

Hashi let his mouth twist with regret. He would have been delighted to learn that the research had been done by some subsidiary of the UMC.

'The code engine is current and correct,' Lane continued dully. 'I told you that. It doesn't prove anything.'

'No,' he assented. 'But it *is* fascinating. And it serves to eliminate' – he fluttered a hand – 'oh, any number of misleading possibilities.'

Apparently his reassurance meant nothing to her. She pulled herself tighter.

'I did a complete readout of the chip.' Her tone hinted at weeping. 'Took a long time. My last hope.' She discarded one nic, lit another. 'But it didn't tell me anything we didn't already know. Alt's retinal signature wasn't superimposed on Imposs' credentials. Nothing was superimposed. That's not Imposs' id tag. It's a new one. An authentic forgery. Designed to be exactly the same as his. Except it says Alt is him.'

Between one beat and the next, Hashi's pulse accelerated. A new one. Excitement began to throb like hope in his bloodstream. An authentic forgery. She'd told him that earlier; but at the time he hadn't entirely grasped its significance. Now it rejuvenated him.

'That doesn't prove anything, either,' she went on. 'Whoever did this has resources the native Earthers would kill for. So we can ignore them. But you knew that already, too.

'I don't have anything for you,' she finished as if she'd reached the end of her strength. 'We need to trace that chip.'

Perhaps he should have sustained his mask of sincerity for a few more moments. To some extent, however, he'd already forgotten her distress. Excitement carried him elsewhere. Unselfconsciously he snatched his glasses from his pocket, slapped them back onto his face.

'Then we will,' he announced like an affectionate uncle.

His sudden rush of confidence must have struck her as smug, condescending. She flinched as if he'd struck her; recoiled so hard that she nearly lost her seat. Then her despair ignited to fury with such brisance that it staggered him.

She flung herself at him; bunched her fists in the lapels of his labcoat; drove him backward.

'*Don't you think I've tried?*' she yelled into his amazed face. 'My *God*, what do you think I've been *doing* here while you flit around smiling at everybody and pretending to know everything?' When she'd pushed him as far as the wall, she held him there. 'What do you think I've been tearing my *heart* out about?'

Hashi blinked at her in confusion. 'Do you mean you've been unable to identify the id code for that chip?'

'It's too damn *small*!' Lane shouted; tried to howl. '*Haven't I told you that*? If I dropped it in your mouth, you couldn't find it with your tongue. It doesn't have a source or a drain, and it doesn't have a goddamn *id code*! I can't produce evidence that isn't there!'

Abruptly he understood her.

He made no physical effort to pull away. That wasn't necessary. Instead he said gently, kindly, 'Forgive me, Lane. You're speaking of the SOD-CMOS fragment you recovered from Godsen's office. Naturally you were unable to identify its id code. I didn't intend to imply otherwise.

'I was referring to Captain Alt's id tag.'

Her mouth fell open. With a visible effort she closed it. Her breath came in ragged gasps. As if she'd just become aware of what she was doing, she let him go and stepped back.

'Well, shit, Hashi,' she panted. 'Of *course* I traced it. I'm still not stupid. But it doesn't prove anything, either.' Gradually her respiration slowed. 'It was part of a routine shipment delivered to UMC Home Security three weeks ago.

'I suppose you could say that's incriminating. I mean, how did an HS SOD-CMOS chip end up in a GCES Security id tag? But it isn't *evidence*. It just indicates UMCHO isn't exactly secure, that's all. Which is something else we already knew.'

'Lane, Lane.' He waved his arms generously, distributing reassurance in all directions. 'As I say, proof is ambiguous. If you could have asked yourself the right questions, you would have seen that you've already found a strand of evidence.'

And enough strands made a rope.

At the same time, however, he berated himself in silence for not having foreseen this. A routine shipment to Home Security. He could have saved time if he'd guessed that the trail would be so direct; could have taken advantage of his brief tenure as Acting Director –

Perhaps after all he was no match for Warden Dios.

Yet the pressure of the situation left no space for self-recrimination. Without pausing, he remarked, 'Three weeks ago, forsooth. And yet the illustrious Cleatus Fane asserts that Nathan Alt was fired twice that long ago.'

'Fired?' Lane asked quickly.

'From his position as UMC Security Liaison for Anodyne Systems,' Hashi explained.

While she absorbed this information, he went on, 'The fault for your misapprehension is mine. You were inadequately briefed. I have been distracted with other duties.' Other people's emotions. 'Despite my failings, however, you have commenced the work we must do.' The work which had to be done before Koina ran out of time. 'You have begun to trace that chip. Now we will go further. Perhaps we will find strands enough to weave a noose.'

As he spoke, Lane appeared to regain her mental poise, her focus, by measurable increments. 'How're we going to do that?' she asked sharply. Only the trembling of her hands as she extracted and lit another nic betrayed the strain she felt.

In response Hashi allowed himself to resume his accustomed avuncular manner.

'My dear Lane, it has perhaps not come to your attention that I have placed "screaming red" security locks of the very loudest sort on all Anodyne Systems' logs and records. In addition I have covered much of UMCHO with similar seals.

'Here.' Hurrying now, he moved to her terminal, opened a DA authorization query screen and tapped a flurry of keys. Then he pointed a thin finger at the readout. 'I have entered the codes which will grant you access to Home Security records.'

'That won't help,' she objected. Her hard eyes studied him as if she wasn't sure she could trust him. 'They've had plenty of time to edit anything. Or cover it up.'

He shook his head. 'Doubtless that's true. Nevertheless I suspect they have not done so. From their perspective, it was inevitable that Captain Alt's false id would be destroyed in the blast. Therefore no one would ever inquire into its provenance.' He shrugged. 'More recently, of course, both the great worm and his prime spawn have been too heavily occupied to undertake the challenge of tampering with Red Priority locks.

'I believe you will be able to determine the use Home Security recorded for that chip.'

For a moment Lane scrutinized him warily. Something in her apparently wanted to hold back. She was too tired: too much had been asked of her. Or she'd seen through his pretense of concern – and didn't like what she saw. Yet her gaze seemed to slide of its own accord away from him to the terminal. The lure of the investigation tugged at her. Almost against her will, she moved toward the keypad.

He stepped aside to make room. Sucking hard at her nic, she stared at the screen. Tentatively she reached out through a swirl of smoke and began entering commands.

Impelled by a pang which might have been relief or fear, Hashi turned to his part of the task. Trusting Lane to concentrate in spite of him, he thumbed the intercom toggle.

'Center,' he announced peremptorily, 'this is Director Lebwohl. On my personal authority, with the utmost priority, I must speak with Chief of Security Mandich at once. Instantly would not be too soon. Then I require a tight-beam transmission channel to Acting Director Min Donner aboard *Punisher*.

'I will speak with Acting Director Donner as soon as I'm done with Chief Mandich.'

The voice from Center hesitated for a second, then answered, 'Right away, Director.'

Right away, Hashi snorted to himself. Right away would hardly be soon enough. By degrees Lane's hands gained speed on the keypad. As she typed, the tremors of her distress receded. Still the job he'd given her was complex. How much time did Koina have left? How long would Special Counsel Igensard indulge the Council in diatribes and perorations? What scale of obfuscation would the Dragon's First Executive

Assistant put forward? *I'm running out of time here.* What did that *mean*?

While urgency coiled around his heart, he asked himself whether he should have been more explicit with Min; perhaps even with Morn Hyland. He'd given out enough hints to stupefy a half-wit. On the other hand, he had no mandate to direct events. Warden had told him, *Just don't do anything I wouldn't do* – hardly a definitive assignment. This was Warden's game, not his. He believed he understood it. Nevertheless he might cause it to fail if he neglected to concentrate on fulfilling his own role.

And he'd already made too many mistakes –

He was forced to wait another fifteen seconds before Chief Mandich responded.

'Leave me alone, Director Lebwohl,' the harried man rasped without preamble. 'This job is already impossible. I can't do it with all these interruptions.'

Hashi swore to himself. A pox on such emotional people! Was there no one individual anywhere around him who could summon bare intelligence without being coerced? However, he rejected the luxury of sneering at Mandich.

'Chief Mandich, your point is precisely the one I was about to make.' He leaned over the pickup as if he were abasing himself. 'Your duties are impossible. You simply do not have the time to search out and acquire the sort of evidence you have been asked to procure. That's why I'm interrupting you. I require your help here.'

He told the Chief of Security where he was.

Unfortunately Mandich seemed oblivious to Hashi's restraint. 'Don't insult me, Lebwohl,' he snapped. His shame shook in his voice. 'This is bad enough as it is. You *know* I can't help you. You know *I* know it. I'm out of my fucking *depth* with this.

'If I can't do my job, at least let me fail in peace.'

Lane flashed a speculative look at Hashi, but didn't pause in her search.

Hashi resisted an impulse to knot his fists in his hair. 'Chief Mandich,' he pronounced with all the force he could command, 'I would not waste the effort of insulting you in such an emergency. I require your *assistance*. I *demand* it.

'In another minute I will speak to Acting Director Donner. If you refuse me, she will order you to comply. But that will take *time*. Director Hannish has very little left.

'Give me that time,' he ordered. 'Postpone feeling sorry for yourself.' Just this once. 'Come here.'

He didn't allow the man time to answer. Fuming, he hit the intercom toggle; then hit it again.

'Center, I'm ready to speak to Acting Director Donner.'

The speaker emitted muffled sounds which suggested consternation. Indecipherable shouts came from the distance.

Almost too swiftly to be read, Lane's screen scrolled as she hunted for data.

'I'm trying, Director,' Center's voice replied abruptly. 'But we're going crazy here. We don't have any spare tight-beam capacity. And *Punisher* has even less.'

'Whelp!' Hashi wanted to roar, but he produced only a beehive snarl of frustration. 'Did I neglect to mention that the entire future of humankind depends on this? *I must speak to Acting Director Donner.*'

'I'm sorry, Director,' Center said in chagrin. 'I *am* trying.'

The intercom reported more shouts. Hashi was sure he heard someone yell, 'Just do it!'

At last arrhythmic staccato clicks filled the speaker like static as Center rerouted the lab's intercom channel.

'Hashi.' Min's voice seemed to appear as if it had resumed tard in the room. 'Make it quick. This is getting more complicated by the minute.'

Despite his concentration, his heart lurched like a wounded thing. Obliquely he wondered whether his health was good enough to sustain the stress. Nevertheless he did his best to be brief.

'As acting director, Min, you're in command of UMCPHQ. You have authority for Administration. I require the Administration codes which enable terminals here to access the dedicated design computers at Anodyne Systems.'

'Good God, Hashi!' she shot back. 'Why in hell do you want to do *that*?'

Under other circumstances he might have enjoyed her surprise. Or he might have tried to justify himself. But Lane's distress had taken a toll on him: Chief Mandich's frank outrage had left him raw. The sudden poignancy of his desire to be trusted took him aback.

'You don't have time to hear an explanation, Min,' he answered softly. 'I don't have time to offer one.' He sighed at her doubt. 'I'm attempting to carry out Warden's orders.'

At least she hadn't asked, Why didn't you take care of it while you were Acting Director? She'd spared him the indignity of having to say, Because I didn't think of it.

'All right,' she returned decisively. 'Give me a minute. I'll have to route my authorization through Center to Administration so you can open that file. The system isn't set up for this, but I can invoke disaster priorities.'

The speaker went dead as *Punisher* stopped transmitting.

Hashi bowed his head. That may have been as close as Min Donner could come to giving him what he truly wanted. For a brief moment he allowed himself to be grateful.

When he looked up, he found Chief Mandich standing across the room from him, just inside the door.

Mandich's fists were cocked on his hips; his jaw jutted like the head of a cudgel. 'This better be good, Lebwohl,' he snarled. 'The last time a man treated me the way you do, they had to put a plate on his skull afterward to keep his brains in.'

Hashi couldn't hold back. He loathed being held responsible for other people's faults and furies. 'Sadly,' he retorted, 'they neglected a plate for *you*. Without being noticed, your brain must have fallen out on Suka Bator.'

Lane hid a grin behind a fringe of unclean hair.

Hashi ignored her. Before Mandich could muster a reply, he demanded in a tone of utter exasperation, 'Are you not able to grasp the fact that you are essential? Lane and I cannot discover the evidence we seek without your help.

'A terminal, Chief Mandich,' he ordered. '*There.*' His arm rigid and trembling, he pointed at the console he wanted Mandich to use. 'I will work here.' Two quick strides planted him in front of a terminal near Lane's.

The Chief didn't move. Apparently Hashi had caught his attention: the belligerence in his eyes had turned to uncertainty. Nevertheless he stood where he was.

'Tell me what we're doing,' he insisted harshly.

What we're doing. He'd said 'we'. That was all the opening Hashi needed.

With a few quick keystrokes he logged on to his terminal and began hunting for the file which Min had promised to open for him. As he typed, read the screen, typed again, he asked in a calmer voice, 'Lane, what have you learned?'

'One' – she fired instructions at her keypad – 'more' – bit her lip, tried another approach – 'minute.' Then she shouted in triumph, 'Ha! *Got* it.'

Abruptly she looked up from her terminal. The vindication in her voice was so intense that it sounded savage.

'Chief Mandich, nobody tampered with Clay Imposs' id tag. They didn't superimpose Alt on it. They made a new one, one for Alt himself, one that gave him all of Imposs' clearances.'

The Chief frowned, plainly baffled.

'I traced the SOD-CMOS chip,' she went on. 'From his id tag. I just finished.

'It was delivered to UMC Home Office three weeks ago in a routine shipment for Home Security. Ten days later' – she indicated her screen accusatively – 'that chip was assigned to the office of the UMC Security Liaison for Anodyne Systems. To be used for testing code designs.'

Hashi wanted to applaud; cheer aloud; shout at the ceiling. Hidden by the lab table which held his terminal, his feet danced a brief jig. If Mandich hadn't been there, he might have invoked a blessing on Lane's weary, brilliant head.

The Chief of Security stared his incomprehension across the tables.

' "Ten days later",' Hashi echoed eagerly. 'Eleven days ago. Yet great Cleatus Fane in full spate informs us that Nathan Alt was fired as Security Liaison several weeks previously.

'How do you imagine he came to possess a chip which can be traced eleven days ago? If he indeed conspired with the native Earthers, as our good FEA claims, how did he do so with source code which is both current and correct?'

'But –' Chief Mandich protested inchoately. He tried to close his mouth; couldn't.

'But it is not proof,' Hashi said for him. 'There you are correct. For that reason, Lane and I must depend on your help.'

The Chief still didn't understand: that was clear. Nevertheless his truculence had vanished. He lifted his hands uncertainly, then took a step or two toward the terminal Hashi had indicated.

'What do you want me to do?'

As if on cue the file Hashi sought opened on his screen. Min Donner may have been self-righteous and unyielding: she may even have been obtuse. At that moment, however, he loved her. She'd kept her word.

He addressed Chief Mandich more kindly now. Min had restored his benevolence.

'You described the precautions which defend the security of our code designs for the chips produced by Anodyne Systems. First Administration codes authorize a link between our terminals and Anodyne Systems' computers. After that DA codes are required to negotiate the necessary datalink protocols. Then ED Security codes must be supplied to grant the terminal operator access.

'We are three.' He waved his arms expansively. 'I will take the part of Administration. Lane represents DA. You are ED Security in person.'

As if he were entirely sure – and had all the time he could need – he concluded, 'Together we will break into the Anodyne Systems computers and extract the information we need.'

Lane brandished both fists in a mute cheer.

Chief Mandich didn't respond. Clenched in silence, he reached his terminal.

When he was ready he met Hashi's gaze over the top of his screen. His eyes were as feral as the fire in Hashi's blood.

MORN

She'd said, 'I think we should try to rescue him.'

Now she sat isolated at the command station. Captain Ubikwe and Min Donner, Davies, Angus and Vector surrounded her; but she might as well have been alone. Mikka and Ciro were nearby, as well as *Punisher*'s duty officers: they were of no help. With those few words she'd translated herself across a dimensional gap of comprehension, leaving everyone she needed light-years behind.

Davies' instant flare of eagerness separated him from her as much as Vector's bafflement, or Dolph Ubikwe's heavy consternation. The surgical probe of Min's scrutiny, like Angus' livid outrage, isolated her. None of them recognized the utter desperation of her need for a better answer.

For herself. For Warden Dios. For humankind.

Davies agreed with her at once, but for the wrong reasons. She knew him too well; saw the truth flaming in his eyes. Her past had trapped him: he thought and felt and ached like a cop. His metabolism drove him to extremes. And the prospect of falling into the hands of the Amnion appalled him. He burned to attempt a rescue so that he wouldn't have to confront the other issues raised by Warden Dios' presence aboard *Calm Horizons*.

Vector had been taken aback. He'd believed he knew why she was here, what she would do. Now he wasn't sure.

The sources of Captain Ubikwe's distress were less clear. Morn hardly knew him; could only guess at what he felt. He

379

may have been torn between a desire to snatch Warden away from the Amnion and a fear that she was about to doom his ship.

But she couldn't even guess at Director Donner's reaction. Min's calculating penetration mystified her. From the first Morn hadn't understood why Min had allowed her to take command of the ship. Min knew about her gap-sickness; her weakness; her core of shame. Now she was confused by the impersonality of Min's stare. The ED director seemed to see possibilities in her which she herself hardly noticed.

Her role had become too large for her. Like Hashi Lebwohl, with his reluctant revelations and oblique hints, Min apparently thought that Morn had come here to carry out some nameless and essential act of redemption.

So much emotion pouring at her from all sides scared her: she might not have been able to handle it in any case. But there was more. Angus' passion dominated the others. She needed him more than she needed anyone else. Even Min as Acting Director of the UMCP was secondary. Davies himself was secondary –

Angus struck the command board so hard that the metal rang. '*I won't do it!*' His shout was a stentorian clap of fury.

Davies recoiled in surprise; then sprang back with his own anger. 'Angus –!'

Min placed her hand on his arm, shook her head slightly. At once he stopped. The unexpected gentleness of her touch seemed to shock him silent.

Apparently she wanted to hear how Morn would reply.

I won't do it!

Morn's place on the bridge had turned into a cruel joke. She could no more command these people, or this ship, than she could carry out her own suggestion. And yet she understood the necessity of it; grasped it with the clarity of anguish, even though it was out of her hands. Try to rescue him. The man who had caused all this: the only man in human space who stood any chance against the Dragon. Try to –

'You mean it's possible?' she asked Angus softly. 'You know how?'

He lashed the air with his fists in frustration. 'Of course it's *possible*!' A paroxysm of rage or terror distorted his face. 'Everything is fucking *possible*! I won't *do* it!'

He leaned over the console, forced his dismay at her. 'Christ, Morn! Have you forgotten why we're here? Why you *said* we're here?' His yellow eyes and sweat-slick skin loomed like accusations. 'We're talking about *Warden Dios*, the god-damn UMCP *director*! He *did this* to you.' Angus slapped a gesture at her as if her condition were obvious to everyone. 'He did it to *me*. If he wants to pay for some of it now, I'm going to let him!'

Again Davies started to protest: again Min restrained him. Mikka made a low sound like a moan of weariness or exasperation. Despite his perplexity, Vector shifted closer to Morn as if he wanted to protect her somehow.

She faced Angus squarely. 'No, I haven't forgotten why we're here,' she said between her teeth. 'I didn't ask you to do it. I asked if you knew how.'

'Stop that!' He wheeled away from her to make room for the extremity of his outrage. His fists pumped blows in all directions. 'Don't lie to me!

'Do you expect me to believe you're going to ask anybody else? *Who?* Your goddamn *son* doesn't have the resources, any more than you do. Vector can hardly walk. Mikka might as well be comatose, and Ciro's out of his skull.' His anger had become a kind of frantic supplication. 'And the fat man here takes his orders from Min Almighty Donner. They don't give a shit what you want. They're just trying to figure out how to use you.

'Have you forgotten about the Preempt Act? Don't you understand why they framed me? Or why they let Nick have you?'

Abruptly Dolph rumbled, 'I can²t stand any more insults, Min.' He didn't appear to be shouting, but his voice filled the bridge like a rockfall. 'I know he can kill me with both fists rammed up his ass. I don't care. If he doesn't watch his mouth, I'm going to remove it for him. At the neck.'

Without any sign of haste, as if *Calm Horizons* were a

problem she could postpone indefinitely, Min intervened.

'Ensign Hyland, we're getting ahead of ourselves,' she put in quietly. 'We aren't ready to discuss rescuing anybody. We don't know what we're up against. And we have more than one crisis to tackle. Let's do this a step at a time, if we can.

'Captain Thermopyle' – a subtle hardening inflected her tone – 'I'm asking you nicely. Take it down a couple of notches.'

Angus' arms folded a refusal across his chest. He didn't so much as glance at Min: his attention was fixed like a cutting laser on Morn.

Morn's command may have been a joke, but she didn't shirk it. She'd come too far to let her own frailties stop her. She wasn't Min; couldn't match Min's authority. Like Dolph, however, she hated Angus' insults. In one form or another she'd loathed him ever since he'd retrieved her from *Starmaster*'s wreckage. And yet she'd helped him escape the bondage of his priority-codes. She was dependent on him for everything –

'Listen to me, Angus,' she demanded harshly. 'You keep telling me to trust you. Now it's my turn.

'I did not ask you to rescue Director Dios. If you don't want to do it, I can't force you – and I won't try.' She made that promise even though she suspected that she hadn't pushed her strange hold over him anywhere near its breaking point. 'But if you know how, I need to hear it.'

He ducked his head as if he were flinching; then jerked his chin up again. The muscles along his jaw bunched like iron. A smear of rage or grief blurred his yellow gaze.

In a small, almost childlike voice, he whispered, 'Fuck you, Morn.' Then he turned away as if he were abandoning her; stamped across *Punisher*'s deceleration g until he reached a vacant g-seat beside Ciro, and flung himself into it.

With both hands he covered his face as if he couldn't bear to meet Morn's mute stare.

Fuck you, she echoed to herself. That was nothing new. How often had he already done it? How often had she allowed – no, seduced, encouraged – Nick Succorso to use her?

Bitterly she swung the command station toward Min.

'This is your chance, Director Donner,' she pronounced like acid. 'If Angus doesn't back me up, I can't hold the bridge.'

Captain Ubikwe might have acted on the idea without hesitation; but Min dismissed it with a shrug. 'I made a deal with you. I'll stand by it.'

Even though she knew who'd killed *Starmaster* – Without question Min's compromised position aboard the cruiser gave her something she craved; an advantage she couldn't get in any other way.

'But there's something I want to know,' she added promptly. 'Before I start dealing with Center.

'What does this "Marc Vestabule" have to do with you?'

Morn opened her mouth to reply, then found she didn't know where to begin. Min's attitude confused her: her own relief got in her way. And she had too many other things to think about.

I think we should try to rescue him.

Don't you understand why they framed me?

Davies could have answered Min's question; but he was as distracted as Morn. He had too much at stake. *Calm Horizons* wanted him so badly that she'd taken the fatal risk of coming here –

With an unspoken appeal in her eyes, Morn referred the subject to Vector.

He took the hint quickly. 'Nothing, Director Donner.' Despite his bafflement he seemed to see Morn's needs more clearly than she did herself. 'I mean nothing personal. We've met him a couple of times, that's all.

'He was on Enablement. We went there so Morn could have her baby. He handled the "negotiations" after the Amnion decided they wanted to keep Davies. In exchange he gave us components to repair our gap drive.

'Then he showed up on Billingate. He must have arrived on – what was that other ship?' – the name came to him almost at once – '*Tranquil Hegemony*. He still had the job of demanding Davies.

'An Amnion shuttle got off Thanatos Minor before the installation blew up. He must have been aboard. Then I guess *Calm Horizons* picked him up.' Vector shrugged. 'Or *Soar* did.'

The mention of *Soar* seemed to catch Davies' attention. As Morn watched, he made a visible effort to put his anger at Angus aside; concentrate on what was being said.

'*Soar*?' Captain Ubikwe pursued heavily. 'You mean the ship that died fighting for you outside the asteroid swarm?'

Vector nodded. 'She destroyed Deaner Beckmann's lab. She tried to kill us in the swarm. But after that –' Shadows darkened his eyes like memories of what was done to Ciro. 'I guess Captain Chatelaine changed her mind,' he finished.

Abruptly Min aimed a sharp stare at Morn. '*Soar* used to be called *Gutbuster*. Did you know that?'

Morn hadn't mentioned *Gutbuster*'s name when she'd talked about *Soar* earlier. Now she winced as if Min had touched an old wound. The ED director continued to surprise her. How had Min known about *Gutbuster*? And why did she want to discuss *Soar*'s past here?

'Nick told us,' Morn admitted thinly. 'She's the same ship that killed my mother.'

As if she were pronouncing judgment – or asking forgiveness – Min stated, 'She did a lot of harm. But she made restitution.'

Like Min herself? Like Warden Dios?

Davies shook his head. 'She did more than that,' he countered in a low, tense voice. 'She could have helped *Calm Horizons* kill us. She probably should have. She needed an antidote to stay human. But she didn't.'

At one time he'd been so determined to destroy *Soar* that he hadn't been able to think about anything else; understand what he was doing. But events had forced him to reconsider his reaction.

'Instead I think she saved her soul.'

Morn gave her son a look of gratitude. Perhaps she'd misjudged him: perhaps his reasons for wanting to rescue Warden were closer to hers than she'd imagined. He'd reminded her that Sorus had found a better answer. And that there were many worse fates than death –

At Morn's side Vector nodded sadly. Min assented with her stern gaze. In his g-seat against the bulkhead, Ciro leaned over and whispered something to Angus.

Under his breath Dolph muttered, 'It still scares me. Until you told us, I didn't know they had mutagens like that.'

'Fucking right they have them,' Angus growled. 'They're probably giving one to your Director Dios right now.'

A sudden pall covered the bridge. 'Jesus!' Captain Ubikwe croaked. One of his duty officers groaned aloud; Morn didn't see who. Davies flinched as if he'd been burned: his face closed like a fist. Min's brows pulled into a hard frown.

Softly Vector urged, 'I don't think we have much time, Morn.'

Time? There was no time. They're probably giving one – Warden Dios might face the same plight which had broken Ciro. I think we should try –

Have you forgotten about the Preempt Act?

With an effort of will she straightened her back; put on authority as if she'd earned it. 'Vector's right, Director Donner.' Self-coercion rasped in her voice. 'We're running out of time.

'Tell me about the Preempt Act.'

She wanted to hear Min confirm the betrayal Angus had explained to her aboard *Trumpet*. And she wanted Davies to know what had been done to his father.

Davies moved closer to her. 'Director Lebwohl mentioned a "Preempt Act". I didn't know what he was talking about.'

Tension at the corners of Min's eyes hinted at pain; but she didn't turn away. Holding Morn's gaze, she asked over her shoulder, 'Communications, how many dishes do we have available?'

'Depends on who we're sending to, Director,' Cray answered.

'UMCPHQ,' Min replied. 'UMCHO. Suka Bator.'

Cray consulted her readouts. 'Sorry, Director. Two tight-beam transmissions are all we can manage from this attitude.

If you want to reach more than that, we'll have to use general broadcast. Or relay it through Center.' She paused, then added, 'Unless you're willing to turn our blind side on that Amnioni.'

'All right.' Min still faced Morn. 'Keep one on UMCPHQ. I need to talk to Center. Aim the other at Suka Bator. When I get a chance, I want to find out what's happening down there.

'If Fasner has to reach me, he can do it through Center.'

Without transition she said to Morn, 'I'll tell you about the Preempt Act. Since we're on the subject of restitution.' A flick of her eyes referred to Captain Ubikwe. 'You haven't heard about this, Dolph. You aren't going to like it.'

He grimaced. 'I haven't liked anything so far. Why should this be different?'

Hard knots swelled at the corners of Davies' jaw.

Min aimed her frown like a challenge at Morn. Her empty hands clenched and opened at her sides as if she were groping for weapons. Her tone was hard, incisive – a chisel she used to cut down images of herself.

'The GCES passed the Preempt Act a few months ago. It gives the UMCP jurisdiction over local Security anywhere in human space. Holt Fasner has been trying to get legislation like that enacted for years. Finally he succeeded.

'He succeeded because we made the Members think local Security – specifically Com-Mine Security – couldn't be trusted. We used Angus for that. Between the two of them, Nick and Milos Taverner framed him for stealing supplies. It was obvious he must have had inside help. That crime couldn't have happened any other way. So there had to be a traitor in Security.

'Well, there was a traitor,' Min stated brutally. 'But he wasn't working with Angus. He was working for us. Nick and Milos got their orders from Hashi. Warden issued those orders, but they came directly from Holt Fasner.'

The ED director ignored Morn's flinch of pain, Dolph's gathering outrage, Davies' desperate look of betrayal. She paid no attention to the tight consternation of the duty officers, or to Angus' fierce, wounded grin. 'We let Nick have you,' she told Morn like an act of violence, 'because that was part of the deal. Part of what we paid him to do jobs for us. He wanted the satisfaction of stealing Angus' woman.'

Then she allowed herself a stiff shrug. 'Now Fasner needs you dead,' she finished, 'because you can testify Angus didn't commit that particular crime. I assume that's why we sent Nick those priority-codes. We could make another deal with him. He probably would have been delighted to kill you all.'

A stunned silence filled the bridge. The ship muttered and sighed to herself as servos hummed, blips and sensors chirped, scrubbers exhaled. *Punisher*'s deceleration roared in the background. But no one made a sound.

Pressure rose in Morn's chest like the approach of a gale. Deep inside her, voices which might have belonged to her parents wailed out their abandonment like the damned.

Angus had told her the truth.

That was part of the deal.

There was a traitor. But he wasn't working with Angus.

Now Fasner –

Everyone in her family had sworn their lives and honor to people who did such things.

Captain Ubikwe was the first to recover speech. 'Let me get this straight.' He scrubbed his palms over his eyes like a man trying to clear away a film of despair. As he found words, his dark rumble became a snarl of protest. 'You gave her to a man like this Succorso so he would help you betray Com-Mine Security?

'My *God*, Min! That's unconscionable! It's *treason*. I should haul you up on charges – I should arrest you right now!'

Min didn't glance at him. 'You should,' she agreed. Her strict gaze was fixed on Morn as if no one else mattered. 'But you won't.'

'Why won't I?' he demanded hotly; dangerously.

'Because you know it's not that simple,' she told him; told Morn. 'And because you know dealing with *Calm Horizons* takes precedence. If we survive, you'll have plenty of time to ruin my reputation, destroy my career.' A mirthless smile twisted her mouth. 'Who knows? Maybe you can even get me executed.'

Davies had fumed with tension while Dolph spoke. Now he brandished his fists like an echo of Angus' furious rejection.

'I don't care what he knows.' His voice was a constricted cry. 'I don't care whether you think it's simple or not. *Did you have any idea what you were doing to her?*'

At last Min let Morn go; turned to face her son.

'We didn't hear about it until later.' Commandments lined her face. She was determined to shirk nothing. 'Until Hashi interrogated Angus. But we knew his reputation. And we knew Nick. We could guess what it cost her.'

Davies was close to tears. 'And you went along with it?'

'Yes, I went along with it,' Min rasped. 'I was given orders, and I carried them out. I got them from a man I trust.'

'*That's not good enough!*' he yelled at her.

Her self-discipline didn't slip. 'Yes, it is,' she answered firmly. After a moment she added, 'I still trust him. More than ever. He's earned it.'

'I'll tell you what he's earned,' Angus growled across the bridge. 'He's earned exactly what's happening to him right now.'

Aboard *Calm Horizons*. A mutagen like the one Sorus had forced on Ciro –

'Director,' Cray put in raggedly, 'Center is starting to sound frantic. They really need to talk to you.'

'Wait.' Morn held up her hand before Min could move. She had the authority she needed now: the ED director's admission gave her that. But when Min paused like an obedient subordinate, Morn didn't attack or castigate her. Morn had other questions to ask – questions which were more urgent than outrage.

'You said we were on the subject of restitution. *What* restitution?'

Slowly Min's shoulders lifted as if Morn had taken a burden off her back. 'Think about it,' she said quietly. 'You'll figure it out.'

Without hesitation she moved toward the communications console. As soon as she reached it she accepted a PCR from Cray and screwed it into her ear; adjusted a throat pickup beside her larynx; announced herself to UMCPHQ Center. When Center replied, she assumed her duties as Acting Director of the UMCP.

Abruptly Dolph slapped the back of the command g-seat like a man whose need to hit something had become more than he could bear. 'I never thought I would say this, Ensign Hyland,' he drawled, 'but I'm glad you're in command. If I had to think this through, I would give myself an aneurysm.'

At once he pushed his heavy frame toward targ. Peering down at Mikka, he observed almost gently, 'You look exhausted. And I need something to do. Why don't you let me take a turn?'

Mikka raised her head. A smear of prostration she couldn't blink away half blinded her. Hoarse with fatigue and concentration, she countered, 'Why don't you go fuck yourself?'

Captain Ubikwe scowled lugubriously. 'You people amaze me,' he remarked to no one in particular. 'You've all been taking courtesy lessons from Angus.'

Shoving his hands into the pockets of his shipsuit, he wandered back to his g-seat against the bulkhead and sat down.

As soon as Dolph left, Davies crowded closer to Morn's console. Distress congested his features: he'd been hit by too many shocks at once. 'Vector's right,' he breathed tensely. 'We're running out of time. We can't let them get away with this. Framing Angus. Selling you. What're we going to do?'

She might have replied, What we came for. Talk to the Council. Rescue Warden Dios. Stop *Calm Horizons*. But she wasn't ready to say those things aloud. She didn't know how to accomplish any of them. And the idea of restitution had taken hold of her: she needed a chance to gauge its implications.

'At the moment,' she announced slowly, 'I'm waiting for Director Dios to tell us what he thinks we should do. As far

389

as I can see, he created this mess. Maybe he knows how to get us all out of it.'

Min didn't pause in her rapid exchange with Center; but she flashed a quick gaze at Morn – a brief, hard glance like a look of pride.

DAVIES

He paced the cruiser's bridge. He couldn't help himself: his exaggerated metabolism drove him. An acute dread of *Calm Horizons* and Marc Vestabule ate at his nerves. And his heart hurt with a sense of chagrin so profound that it was almost metaphysical. Frustration swarmed through him as if his skin held a hive of angry wasps. His throat ached from yelling at Min.

Did you have any idea what you were doing to her?

As recently as two or three days ago, he would have told himself that Morn was making him crazy with her delays and hesitations, her conflicted priorities; her scruples. But now he knew better. His distress was entirely his own: painful, intimate and unanswerable.

That's not good enough!

In every effective sense he was a UMCP ensign – born and bred to the job. All his instincts cried out for the work the UMCP should do. Defend Earth. Destroy *Calm Horizons*. Protect human space.

But Min Donner had made him ashamed to be a cop. He didn't know how to excuse the crime of framing Angus in order to make Holt Fasner stronger.

She still trusted Warden Dios. Davies no longer trusted anyone except his mother.

I think we should try to rescue him.

That made sense to him. He wanted to fight. God, he *needed* to fight. *Calm Horizons* had come for him: no one else. The warship had come here for no other purpose than to reclaim possession of him. The Amnion intended to use him against his entire species. If he had to he would kill himself to stop them.

But he also wanted to hold Warden Dios accountable –

He was sure Morn felt the same way. She must have: he'd been imprinted with her mind. She could see the need for some kind of action as clearly as he did. But he understood her uncertainty now; her determination to wait for more information. Like him, she'd been made ashamed. Like him, she wasn't sure who to trust. And she desperately wanted to know whose cause her choices would serve when she made up her mind.

For him the question was more personal.

By now Vestabule must have known that he couldn't quash Vector's antimutagen. It had already been broadcast too far to be called back. None of the secrets *Trumpet* had carried from forbidden space could be suppressed now.

No, *Calm Horizons* had come for Davies. The Amnion wanted to study him; learn how to make Amnion like him. If their research succeeded, he would supply the key which would enable them to eradicate all Earth-born life from the galaxy.

But his real problem was worse than that; far more complex.

He believed that Warden Dios would try to give the Amnion what they demanded. How else could the UMCP director prevent *Calm Horizons'* guns from wreaking colossal devastation on the planet? He might not understand what was at stake. Or – if Angus was right – he might be under pressure from the same mutagen which had broken Ciro; ruled Sorus Chatelaine until the end. In either case the result would be the same.

It would be safer to rescue Warden than to take his orders. Unfortunately Angus had already refused. And Davies had no idea how to do it himself. If he made the attempt he might be captured.

On the other hand, the prospect of a direct attack on *Calm Horizons* appalled him. Too many innocent people would die.

So it might be less costly to ignore Warden's plight altogether and concentrate on the Council. Tarnish his reputation and credibility until no one on Earth would expect *Punisher* or *Trumpet* to follow his orders. But if the UMCP director fell, who would take his place? Where would his power go? To Min Donner? Not likely. Not while Holt Fasner owned the cops. Tainting Warden's honor would accomplish nothing but ruin unless the Dragon could somehow be held accountable for Warden's trespasses.

It was no wonder that Morn hesitated; waited – Davies would have done the same – if he could have borne it. But instead he stalked the bridge as if he were hunting for a way through his dilemma. A way out.

He couldn't find one. He was too scared.

He'd said to Morn, *We're running out of time. We can't let them get away with this. What're we going to do?* as if he wanted her to make his decisions for him. But he didn't. His appeal was of a completely different kind.

Since the day he was born, he'd done little or nothing to determine his own fate. Nick had given him to the Amnion. Morn had sent him to the Bill. Angus had rescued him. He'd cut the datacore out of Angus' back because Morn had told him to do it. Whenever he was desperate, Mikka or Morn or Vector or Angus or even poor Sib had picked up the slack of his inadequacy.

He didn't want to be given any more answers. He was looking for some hint that might tell him how to go about saving his own soul. If he'd known what Morn meant to do, he might have been able to think about his plight more clearly.

But no one talked to him. No one shed any light. Morn simply bided her time. Angus had slammed some kind of door; barricaded himself behind his fear and refusal. Mikka was too bone-weary and heart-sick to think about anything except the targ board. Vector's view of the situation was too simple to lift Davies' confusion, and Ciro was crazy.

As for Min Donner, who at least valued the truth enough to tell it –

393

She made cryptic remarks about 'restitution': she confronted this crisis like a woman who saw dimensions and implications Davies couldn't grasp. And her few explanations cast murk instead of illumination. Nick and Milos Taverner had framed Angus in order to secure the Dragon's hold on human space. And Warden Dios had condoned it – initiated it? Min herself had gone along with it? She revealed facts; but she said nothing about what lay behind them.

Think about it. You'll figure it out.

Maybe Morn already had. Maybe that was why she could bear waiting. But she wasn't the one *Calm Horizons* had come to damn.

Now Min was immersed in her dealings with UMCPHQ Center. Except for the helm officer, Sergei Patrice, and Cray on communications, she was the only one who had anything to do. Scan and data processed the same information again and again; Mikka confirmed everything she already knew about *Punisher*'s weapons status; Angus and Ciro muttered to each other like bitter conspirators; Morn and Dolph Ubikwe and Vector remained passive, as if they'd forgotten how to move.

In contrast, Min stood beside the communications board, holding her body like a gun. One hand cupped her PCR to keep what she heard to herself. When she spoke into her throat pickup, her voice was a crisp, low murmur that didn't carry: most of the time Davies couldn't make out what she said.

The weight of her impact gun in his pocket wore against his thigh.

At some point he thought he heard her address Hashi Lebwohl. Most of what she said to the DA director was a covered blur, however, and Davies ignored it. His dilemma didn't hinge on what she and Hashi did together.

Later she recited the names of ships: *Valor*, *Adventurous*, others. By studying Porson's scan display, Davies gleaned the information that she was making adjustments in the cordon around *Calm Horizons*. Deliberately she placed her vessels so that they all had clear fields of fire on both *Calm Horizons* and *Punisher*, as well as on UMCPHQ and Holt Fasner's HO.

Punisher's deceleration edged her closer to the same goal. The Acting Director was keeping her options open –

So was Morn, for that matter. But Davies seemed to have none.

Finally, he crossed the cruiser's g to stand in front of Angus and Ciro. He didn't know where else to turn. He held himself rigid until Angus raised an acid stare to his face. Then he leaned forward and demanded softly, 'Tell me how to do it. How to rescue Warden Dios.'

Please. I need something to think about that doesn't feel so much like destroying everything I want to save.

Angus twisted his mouth in a grin like an act of malice. 'Ask Ciro.' He indicated Mikka's brother with a jerk of his head. 'He knows all about it.'

'I know all about it,' Ciro confirmed. He, too, grinned – a complex, secretive smile that hinted at relief and dismay.

'That won't help you,' Davies told the boy bitterly. 'Not while he refuses to do it' – he slapped a gesture at Angus – 'and won't let anybody else try.'

At once, however, he regretted inflicting his anger on Ciro. The damaged kid lowered his head, shrinking into himself; but before his eyes fell Davies saw them fill up with darkness.

Swallowing a groan, Davies turned back to Angus.

'Vector still has some of Nick's antimutagen.' Misery he couldn't stifle thickened his tone. 'Even if Vestabule gives Director Dios that mutagen, we could help him.'

Angus wasn't swayed. 'You haven't been listening,' he rasped. 'I've said all this before.'

'Your Director Dios knew what he was doing when he sold Morn to Nick. He framed me. Cost me my ship. My life. Her –' He flicked at glance at Morn. 'And he knew what he was doing when he welded me. He called it a crime against my soul. But that didn't stop him. None of it stopped him.

'Now it looks as if he's found a way to stop himself. I want to make damn sure he doesn't change his mind.'

Davies shuddered. As far as he could see, Angus' indictment

of Warden was valid. And Min's obscure talk of 'restitution' did nothing to soften it.

No one helped him answer his own questions.

'Morn,' Vector said unexpectedly, 'I think we should go ahead. Take our chances.' He spoke gently, but his gaze was clouded with concern. 'We can't keep second-guessing ourselves. We've been told too many lies. There's too much we don't know. If we spend all our time worrying about whether we're making a mistake, we'll never do what we came here for.'

Morn didn't reply. She may not have heard him. She sat in the command g-seat with her head back and her eyes closed as if she were asleep. Only the tension in her shoulders and arms, and the way the corners of her mouth reacted to every voice around her, betrayed that she was conscious; paying attention.

Abruptly Porson announced from scan, 'Director, *Calm Horizons* is turning a dish on us. Looks like she wants to talk.'

Davies wheeled toward the communication station; froze. Morn jerked open her eyes and faced Min. Mikka made a small, thin sound that might have been a curse or a prayer.

I'm waiting for Director Dios to tell us what he thinks we should do. As far as I can see, he created this mess. Maybe he knows how to get us all out of it.

Min didn't hesitate. 'General broadcast, Cray,' she instructed. '"UMCP cruiser *Punisher* to Amnion defensive *Calm Horizons*."' She made no effort to muffle her pickup. '"We can't hear you. We've been damaged. We don't have a dish available. If you need to reach us, you can route your transmission through UMCPHQ Center." Repeat that until she does something about it.

'From now on,' she told the bridge, 'nobody has any secrets. If Marc Vestabule wants to say anything – or Warden does – it'll be on the record.'

Logged and stored by Center.

Davies found that he was holding his breath. On the record. With one quick stroke Min had shaken his distrust.

Nobody has any secrets.

Restitution. Honesty.

What the hell was she doing? What did she want?

'I guess she heard us,' Porson reported. 'She's shifting that dish away again.'

Captain Ubikwe straightened himself in his g-seat. 'Can we tell who she *is* talking to, Porson?' Apparently he wasn't as uninvolved as he might have wished.

'We can't tap into tight-beam transmissions, Captain,' the scan officer stated unnecessarily. 'And some of her dishes are occulted. But before the scan net was shut down, we got a pretty good picture of her. Good enough to know she has one dish fixed on UMCPHQ. And another on UMCHO.'

'What about HO?' Dolph rumbled. 'Who are the Dragon's dishes pointed at?'

Porson consulted his instruments; calculated vectors. 'UMCPHQ, Captain. *Calm Horizons*. Suka Bator.' He looked toward Dolph. 'There's one aimed at us, too, but HO isn't using it.'

Abruptly Davies caught the point of Captain Ubikwe's questions. A new pang twisted his heart. He turned to Morn. 'What will we do if Vestabule makes a deal with Holt Fasner?'

'I've got a better question,' Angus put in sourly. 'How are you going to know it if they *have* made a deal?'

Min interrupted her exchange with Center by lifting the pickup from her neck. 'They won't,' she asserted. 'Fasner can't give Vestabule what he wants.' She glanced at Morn, then added ominously, 'But they will, if Warden doesn't satisfy them.'

Angus swore. 'Just what we need. Another threat.' His voice was harsh, guttural with strain, as if he had to fight his zone implants in order to speak for himself. 'When Warden fucking Dios full of mutagens tells us to surrender, you want us to do it so Vestabule won't try to bargain with Fasner. You think maybe an idea like that ought to scare us into submission.

'Well, the good news is, *I don't care*. If Fasner wants to sell off the whole damn planet, I say let him. Makes no difference to me.'

'You don't care,' Davies rasped over his shoulder. 'So you keep telling us. You won't do it.' His desperation demanded an outlet. He feared that if he didn't start shouting – if he didn't do *some*thing soon – his heart would crack. 'But some of us don't feel that way, so why don't you just *shut up* and let us think?'

'You really don't get it, do you?' Angus countered roughly. 'It still hasn't penetrated your thick excuse for a brain that I'm trying to keep us all alive.'

Davies didn't respond. He didn't know how to tell his father that other things were more important than staying alive.

Morn had closed her eyes again as if she wanted to shut out distractions: Davies' face, or Angus'; the scan displays; anything which might confuse her. 'Cray,' she asked tensely, 'does the Council know we're here?'

Min answered before Cray could respond. Without turning her head or silencing her pickup, she said, 'Center has a secure downlink open for Director Hannish on Suka Bator. She knows.

'But the general broadcast for the rest of the planet isn't exactly complete. Center has its hands full trying to manage the crisis on Earth. And shutting down the scan net hasn't inspired much confidence. Most of UMCPHQ's microwave capacity is taken up with disaster procedures.

'If Koina hasn't told the Members, they don't know.' Min paused, then added, 'Unless they heard it from Fane. I'm sure he's in contact with HO all the time.'

Suddenly Cray went rigid. 'Director,' she croaked. 'Center is relaying a transmission from Director Dios.'

Oh, shit! Davies thought in misery. Here it comes.

He wasn't ready.

Morn sat forward with a jerk; opened her eyes. Alarm flared whitely in her gaze. The crisis seemed to set her alight: Davies had the impression that the muscles in her shoulders and neck and arms were on fire.

Vector moved closer to the command station. Davies did the same, drawn by Morn's urgency. Instinctively he closed his fingers on Min's handgun.

398

'I have her on targ,' Mikka muttered in a worn growl. 'I can hit her whenever you want.'

Ciro was her brother. She may have understood better than anyone what the mutagen Sorus Chatelaine had suffered and used could do.

But Min ignored the apprehension around her. She might have forgotten that fear existed. 'Put it on the speakers,' she told Cray quietly. 'And keep me off that channel. I'm busy with Center. Ensign Hyland will speak for the ship.'

Good God, Davies thought. She was serious. She was going to keep her word.

'Aye, Director,' Cray answered. Her hands shook feverishly as she tapped keys; brought the speakers to life in a muted crackle of thrust static.

Morn took a deep breath; braced herself –

A man's voice carried firmly through the distortion. '*Punisher*, this is Warden Dios.' He spoke as if nothing could prevent him from being clear. 'I'm aboard *Calm Horizons*. You already know that.

'Min? Dolph?'

Davies had never heard the UMCP director's voice before. Nevertheless the sound stirred Morn's memories in him. He felt an odd thrill, as if he'd been touched by the call of a trumpet. Warden's power to inspire loyalty, dedication and faith – or Morn's ingrained response to it – reached him across the gap between his experience and hers.

In spite of everything, the director's convictions and commitments defined the UMCP for Davies; gave substance to the honorable work of being a cop. Something in his heart turned at the call of Warden's voice.

I think we should try to rescue him. Yes.

I still trust him.

Apart from Morn, he may have been the only one on the bridge who reacted in that way. Captain Ubikwe sank deeper into his g-seat; bowed his head as if he wanted to hide the shame of losing his command. Patrice attended to his duties, as focused and constricted as Mikka. Porson made a show of studying his sensors and readouts; but Bydell sat at the data station as if she were paralyzed by worry. Glessen clenched his fists and remained rigid, swearing to himself.

At the communications station Min had resumed her exchange with Center as if she no longer cared what Warden might say. Davies envied her composure; her concentration. He couldn't match them. His nerves rang as if he were stuck in a carillon.

With a stiff flinch of her shoulders, Morn toggled the command station pickup. 'Director Dios –' Her voice caught. She grimaced in dismay at her weakness; swallowed to moisten her throat. 'This is Morn Hyland. Aboard *Punisher*. I'm in command.'

For a moment Warden didn't react. Static filled his silence with ambiguity: he might have been hiding behind it. Then he pronounced carefully, 'Did I hear you right? You're Ensign Morn Hyland? Off *Starmaster*?' His tone sharpened. 'And you're *in command*?'

Apparently he hadn't discussed *Punisher* with Center. Or Hashi Lebwohl.

'Yes, sir.' Morn lifted her head; squared her jaw. 'My father was Captain Davies Hyland. But I don't think of myself as an "ensign" now. I resigned my commission when I joined *Captain's Fancy*.

'I took command outside the Massif-5 system. Director Donner and Captain Ubikwe are here. No one's been hurt.' Grimly she finished, 'But I make the decisions for this ship.'

Her tone said, Don't try to give me orders. I don't take them anymore.

Again Warden answered with silence. He may have been shocked. When he replied, however, distortion and distance conveyed the impression that all his emotions had been locked away.

'Forgive me, Morn. I've had too many surprises recently. It's difficult to absorb them all.

'I've just been informed that you did this once before. Took over a ship you had no business commanding.' He didn't explain; but Vestabule must have told him how she'd forced Enablement to return Davies, after Nick had traded

400

her son away for gap drive components. 'Obviously you're good at it.'

Vestabule must have explained how she'd extorted Davies' return.

'I won't ask what you think you're doing,' the UMCP director went on. 'We don't have time to go into it. But under the circumstances I can't take your word for it that Min and Dolph are safe.'

'They haven't suffered anything worse than a few insults.' To Davies Morn sounded as impersonal, as concealed, as Warden did. 'You can confirm that if you want to. But you can't talk to Director Donner. She's busy. I've given her permission to serve as Acting UMCP Director in your absence. In exchange, she's ordered Captain Ubikwe not to interfere with me.'

This time Warden didn't pause. 'Can they hear me?'

'I'm using the bridge speakers, Director,' Morn returned acerbically. 'We can all hear you.'

From now on, nobody has any secrets.

'Dolph?' Warden's distorted voice asked promptly. 'Are you all right?'

Captain Ubikwe opened his mouth to reply, then closed it. Deliberately he looked at Morn for permission.

She glanced toward him over her shoulder and nodded.

'No, Director, I'm not all right.' Dolph's deep tones thrummed with bitterness. 'Nothing is all right. But I don't know what to do about that. I don't even know how we got into this mess. All I can tell you is that for the past few days we've been making decisions that seemed reasonable at the time.'

'I'm sure they were,' Warden responded as if he were promising a pardon. 'I'm not worried about that. I'm just glad for a chance to hear your voice.

'Morn,' he continued, 'is Angus with you? Can he hear me?'

Angus cocked his head in surprise. The muscles at the corners of his jaw bunched.

Davies winced inwardly. For reasons he couldn't name,

he feared hearing Warden invoke Angus' priority-codes. The resonance of loyalty and idealism in Warden's voice held him. He was sick of coercion: he didn't want to hear Warden try it.

But if Morn felt the same way, she didn't show it. 'Yes, Director.' Her tone hinted at acid and blood. 'Everyone from *Trumpet* who's still alive is here.'

Warden didn't ask her who'd died. Apparently he wasn't interested. 'Angus?' he asked. 'It's good you made it this far. You've done well.' He waited, obviously hoping for a reply. When Angus didn't give him one, he pursued, 'Are *you* all right?'

Morn faced Angus gravely; gave him the same nod she'd given Dolph. Pain and need darkened her gaze.

Angus unclenched his jaw. 'That depends,' he growled, 'on what you order me to do.'

Davies clenched his fist on Min's gun because he couldn't reach his sore heart and made a conscious effort not to hold his breath.

A sigh came from the speakers. Now Warden's voice hinted at weariness; the accustomed fatigue of loss. 'I'm not going to do that. I'm sure Min already tried it. If Morn is in command there, I assume you've found a way around your priority-codes.

'We talked about that once,' he added obscurely.

He must also have assumed that Nick was no longer a factor. An easy deduction: if Nick had retained control over Angus, the situation aboard *Punisher* would have been completely different.

Slowly Angus raised his hands to his face, rubbed at his sweat-grimed cheeks. 'In that case,' he retorted, 'no, *I'm* not all right either. The fat man isn't as stupid as he looks. None of us are all right. The difference is, I'm the only one who knows what we're really doing here.'

What we're −? Davies gaped at Angus. − really doing? What was he talking about?

'Which is?' Warden asked warily.

Angus didn't hesitate. As if he were passing sentence, he

402

pronounced heavily, 'We're waiting for you to keep at least one of your promises. I'm sure every one of us has a candidate in mind. Personally, I want to see you keep the one where you stop the crime you've done to me.'

Morn's eyes widened involuntarily, and Davies caught his breath. Like her, he hadn't considered the possibility that Warden might have made promises to Angus as well.

Angus was right: in spite of his truculence and his refusals, he'd named the truth.

'I'm considering it,' Warden drawled across the gap between the ships. 'I haven't made a decision yet. I don't know enough about the situation.'

'Well, while you're "considering it",' Angus retorted, 'let me tell you what *we're* considering.

'We want to know what kind of mutagen Vestabule gave you.'

Warden sighed again. 'Don't worry about it,' he returned. 'I have a suicide pill in my mouth. I'll bite it open if I have to.' Firmly he added, 'I'm not particularly eager to turn into an Amnioni.'

Davies believed him. He was starting to feel capable of suicide himself. And the UMCP director's voice carried conviction, despite the intervening distortion. Morn had spent most of her life believing implicitly in Warden Dios. Now Davies felt that he simply could not doubt anything Warden said.

That made his own position harder to bear. It was easier when he was full of outrage.

Morn pulled her hands through her hair, resisting the persuasion of her memories; tugging at her scalp to remind herself that the cops were corrupt.

'Why are you telling us this, Director Dios?' she asked unsteadily. 'What's your point? I've already said I don't consider myself a cop anymore. I'm not under your authority. Whatever we decide to do isn't going to depend on whether or not you have a suicide pill.'

'I recognize that,' Warden replied at once. The pressure of his position aboard *Calm Horizons* seemed to urge him ahead.

'But I want *you* to recognize who you're talking to. I'm not some Amnion pawn you can afford to ignore. I'm Warden Dios, and I'm trying to do my job.'

By an exertion of self-discipline so severe that it appeared to make her shiver, Min kept her attention fixed on her PCR and pickup; on Center.

Do my job, Davies nodded helplessly. Save Suka Bator. UMCPHQ. A few million lives. How could he argue with that? How could he hold back from offering to sacrifice himself? Didn't he think those lives were worth what he would have to pay for them?

But Morn wasn't swayed. 'I'm sorry, Director Dios. I'm afraid I just don't understand.' She may have meant, Which promise are you trying to keep? 'Why are you aboard that ship? How can you do your job if you're a hostage?'

'What makes you think negotiating with the Amnion won't cost us more than we can possibly afford?'

Her words may have stung Warden. 'You don't need to understand it, Morn,' he responded with unexpected vehemence. 'What you need to understand is that the Amnion are going to destroy Suka Bator, UMCPHQ, your ship and anything else they can aim their guns at if we don't give them what they want.

'And after that what's left of us will be at war with forbidden space. All-out war. Wholesale slaughter. My God, Morn,' he finished brutally, 'we're talking about enough blood to drown a planet. Try understanding *that*.'

She covered the misery on her face with her hands. 'Don't drag it out, Director,' she breathed. 'Tell us what it means. So we'll know what we're up against.'

'All right,' Warden consented grimly. 'I'll put it in plain language for you.

'The Amnion consider Davies Hyland their rightful property. They want him returned to *Calm Horizons*. In addition, as compensation for an act of war committed against Thanatos Minor, they want Angus Thermopyle, Vector Shaheed and you. If the four of you don't come here and surrender yourselves, the defensive is going to open fire.'

His words restored the full force of Davies' dilemma.

Calm Horizons wanted *him*.

In subtle ways the terms of his decision had shifted. The visceral throb of loyalty he felt whenever Warden spoke seemed to alter the valence of the emergency. Involuntarily he forgot Warden's crimes. Yet his fear remained, appalling and paralyzing him. The demands of the Amnion pressed him toward a gap he didn't know how to cross.

Without realizing that he'd moved, he found himself standing in front of Min Donner as if she held the clue he needed; the hint which would unlock him from his impasse. The truth – She hardly glanced at him, however. Although she seemed to hear everything that was said around her, she concentrated like a hawk on the pickup at her throat and the PCR in her ear.

Angus started to say something; but Morn silenced him with a cutting gesture. She faced a dilemma of her own: distinct from her son's, but no less arduous.

'What about *you*, Director Dios?' she asked thickly. 'What do *you* want?'

The speakers crackled. 'You've said more than once that you don't consider yourself bound to take my orders.' Warden spoke slowly, precisely, as if he were suppressing a vast need. 'If you did, I would order you to comply. Since you don't, I'm trying to persuade you.' Harsh with coercion, he added, 'If you refuse, I'll instruct Director Donner to take command away from you and force you to comply.'

Then he went on more gently, 'I don't mind paying for my own mistakes, Morn. God knows I deserve to bear the brunt of this. And *you* know that's true. You've learned everything you need about Intertech's mutagen immunity drug. By now you've probably heard that Angus was framed so we could pass the Preempt Act. If you have, you can figure out that we sold you to Nick so you couldn't tell anyone Angus was innocent. And the final responsibility for *Calm Horizons* is mine. I chose Milos Taverner to go with Angus to Billingate.'

On the record Warden Dios admitted his crimes.

'I'm dead no matter what happens, Morn. If being a hostage, or asking you to give yourselves up, is part of the price

I have to pay, I'll do it. But I simply cannot let millions of innocent people be killed just because I've failed in my duty.'

Min paused; turned to see how Morn would respond. From under his dark brows, Captain Ubikwe studied Morn piercingly. Most of the duty officers neglected their boards while they waited for her answer. Even Mikka raised her head from the targ keys and readouts; looked at Morn with her face full of exhaustion and mute, baffled longing.

Angus muttered curses under his breath. Ciro gave no sign that he understood anything except his own peculiar secrets. He sat with his head back and his eyes half closed, murmuring softly to himself. But Vector listened with pain in his eyes and lines of loss around his mouth.

The Amnion consider Davies Hyland their rightful property.
I'm dead no matter what happens –

Davies' life hung on a decision he couldn't make.

Morn seemed unaware that everyone waited for her. She was caught in the grip of Warden's appeal. Moisture blurred her eyes. A frown twisted her forehead. She gripped the arms of her g-seat as if she needed them for balance.

She was silent for a long moment as if she were listening to echoes of her parents' voices. Then she leaned over the pickup.

Husky with constricted emotion, she said, 'We'll have to talk about it, Director. I can't make these kinds of decisions for other people.

'Stay on this channel. We'll come up with an answer as soon as we can.'

With the tip of one finger, she silenced her pickup gently, as if she were bidding the UMCP director farewell.

Davies hardly heard her. His attention was fixed on Min. He needed to ask her a question which he didn't know how to formulate. The crisis he dreaded most had caught up with him at last. Somehow he had to decide what he was going to do.

Min Donner seemed to be the only person on the bridge who might be able to tell him why he shouldn't put her gun to his temple and blow his brains out.

WARDEN

M orn said, 'We'll have to talk about it. I can't make these kinds of decisions for other people.' Then her voice clicked silent, leaving Warden Dios alone with Marc Vestabule.

His heart trembled as he drifted at the communications terminal grown into one wall of the small chamber where Vestabule guarded him. Sweat beaded on his temples; prickled along his spine. His human eye throbbed at the strain of the Amnion illumination: his prosthesis told him nothing he could use.

Morn Hyland was in command of *Punisher*. The scale of that accomplishment – or the depth of the disaster – stunned him. Somehow she'd persuaded or forced Min and Dolph to stand aside. Now she insisted that she no longer served the UMCP. Dolph plainly considered himself helpless. Min had reached some accommodation which allowed her to serve as Acting Director without opposing Morn's command. And Angus was openly hostile –

Something had happened. Something wonderful – or terrible. With Vestabule looming at his shoulder, Warden was no longer sure he could tell the difference.

Questions seemed to throng at him from the inhuman walls. What would Morn decide? Would Min obey him if he ordered her to surrender Morn and Davies? How had she become Acting Director? What had happened to Hashi?

Effectively a prisoner aboard *Calm Horizons*, Warden Dios

had no choice except to trust the people he'd most misused: Min and Hashi; Morn and Angus.

Slowly Vestabule reached past him to deactivate the board pickup. For a moment the Amnioni used his own pickup to address someone – presumably *Calm Horizons'* command center. Warden couldn't decipher the guttural Amnion sounds; but he guessed that Vestabule was making sure the defensive's channel to *Punisher* remained open.

Then Vestabule turned his attention to Warden.

'Your people do not obey you,' he pronounced stiffly. Like Warden, he had only one human eye. His Amnion side stared at Warden inflexibly; but the human one was moist with distress. 'You are not invested with decisiveness. You cannot satisfy our requirements.'

Oh, shit.

Alarm labored like the acrid air in Warden's chest as Vestabule continued, 'I must open communications with Holt Fasner. Your failure allows no alternative. He states that he is able to command compliance from all effective power in human space.'

Anchoring himself on the communications board, Warden turned quickly to contradict Vestabule.

'If that's what he says, he's lying through his teeth.' He mustered anger to muffle his panic; raised his voice to force it past the obstruction of his breathing mask. 'Ask Center to send you a copy of the UMCP charter War Powers provisions. You'll see I'm telling the truth. Fasner's authority over the UMCP was suspended the minute you began this incursion. Right now *I* am the only effective power in human space.'

Damn you, I'm selling my soul for this! Don't throw it away.

Vestabule's strange features revealed nothing. The blinking of his human eye was too ambiguous to interpret. The aura he cast to Warden's IR sight seethed and pulsed with hues the UMCP director didn't recognize.

'I know it doesn't look that way,' Warden went on harshly. 'Morn Hyland resigned her commission. She doesn't recognize my authority under martial law. And it's obvious Captain

Thermopyle broke out of his programming somehow.

'But I'm not done yet.'

Without inflection, the Amnioni countered, 'Do you not find it difficult to assert that you are "the only effective power in human space" when it is plain that you have no effect? Even among your kind such clear contradictions must cause distress.'

Warden swore to himself.

'I'm not *done* yet,' he insisted. 'You're surrounded by our ships. Right now *Punisher* won't take my orders. But *none* of them will take Holt Fasner's. Any deal you made with him would be useless because he can't make those ships hold fire.

'I still have more to say to Morn. And even if I can't give her orders, the situation itself is pretty persuasive.

'You talk about how much you remember, but I'm not sure you remember what it's like for a human being to believe in an idea that's bigger than you are. Morn isn't just a cop. She believes in what cops are for. Her whole family did, and she's no different. She's been hurt and disillusioned, but she isn't capable of forgetting it's her sworn duty to protect innocent lives.'

Behind the concealment of his anger, he prayed fervently that he was right.

'But even if she ignores me,' he grated, 'I'll still give you what you want. For one thing, Morn can't hold that ship if Director Donner and Captain Ubikwe decide to take it back. The crew will obey them. And both Min and Dolph will obey *me*.

'On top of that, there are codes I can use that will affect Angus. I haven't done it yet' – as if involuntarily, he burst into a shout – 'because I'm *trying to keep as many of my people alive as I can*!' The trembling in his heart spread to his lungs; his voice. His mask seemed to constrict his breathing until he had to pant for air. 'As soon as I turn this into a test of what you call "decisiveness", there's going to be bloodshed.'

In case Vestabule missed the point, Warden explained bitterly, 'No matter how careful Min and Dolph are, Davies might contrive to get himself killed.'

The Amnioni stared back uncomfortably. The strange contrast between his human and alien eyes gave the impression that he was torn by the irreconciled contradictions of his nature.

'The same thing might happen if Holt Fasner gave orders *Punisher* was willing to obey,' Warden growled. 'I'm not in a hurry to take that chance. I don't think you are either.

'We made a deal.' His voice shook as if he were furious. 'I get you what you want. You don't try to bargain with anybody but me. And the Amnion are *famous* for abiding by their agreements.' He made a point of shifting the capsule in his mouth. 'Leave Holt Fasner out of it.'

A slight turn of Vestabule's head suggested that he was listening to the receiver in his ear. He grunted a complex response that seemed to crunch and cut like shards of broken sound; a response full of laceration and death –

In his panic Warden wondered whether he was strong enough to force his capsule into Vestabule's mouth before the Amnioni could bring down ruin on his frantic hopes.

Then Marc Vestabule answered him in a tone like old iron, 'Understand this, Warden Dios. I must have satisfaction soon. What I chiefly remember of being human is desperation. If our requirements are not met, I will have no other recourse.'

Warden ached to ask what Vestabule meant. But he could guess.

'You remember desperation,' he muttered darkly. 'That's a start. Then maybe you can understand that you don't gain anything by threatening me. I'm already committed to satisfying your requirements.

'If you really want me to succeed, give me something I can use. Tell me what happened to Nick Succorso.'

Vestabule blinked erratically. 'Of what relevance is this?'

'I just told you,' Warden snorted through his mask. 'We're talking about desperation. Morn's. Davies'.' Mine. 'The more I know about why they're desperate, the more effective I can be. How much pressure do you think I can put on them if I don't understand what they've been through?

'Not so long ago Nick held Angus' priority-codes. He commanded *Trumpet*. With Angus to back him up, he *ruled* that ship. But now there's no sign of him. And Angus is free of his codes.

'Isn't it obvious how crucial that is?'

For a moment Vestabule considered the question. His unreadable study of the UMCP director didn't waver. The process by which he reached decisions – whatever it was – didn't involve any discernible emotion, any alteration in his aura; any consultation with his fellow Amnion.

When he was done, he acquiesced. Without preamble he stated, 'Captain Nick Succorso was slain by Captain Sorus Chatelaine. I find this incomprehensible. By some means he contrived to board *Soar*, where he threatened her with death. She killed him instead.' His head moved meaninglessly from side to side, as if he'd forgotten how humans expressed bafflement. 'Then she betrayed *Calm Horizons*.

'I remember desperation, but I can remember nothing which would account for her actions.'

Apparently it was Sorus Chatelaine he didn't understand, not Nick – a woman who'd served the Amnion for years before turning against them.

Under other circumstances Warden might have been fascinated by this hint of how an Amnion mind worked. Now, however, he hardly noticed it. He barely absorbed the information that Nick was dead. The manner of Nick's death distracted him.

Abruptly he recalled Hashi's discovery that *Soar* had once been known as *Gutbuster*. In her previous identity *Soar* had killed Morn's mother, Bryony Hyland. And she'd also destroyed the original *Captain's Fancy*, leaving only her cabin boy, Nick Succorso, alive.

A fatal coincidence, for Sorus as well as Nick. And yet the outcome was that Morn and *Trumpet* remained alive. Something in the tangle of hunting *Trumpet*, being hunted by Nick and serving the Amnion had turned Captain Chatelaine against her masters.

Hashi had theorized that Nick and Sorus were working together; but he was wrong. Nick had hated Captain

411

Chatelaine too much for that; hated her so much that even after he'd lost everything else he'd 'contrived to board' her ship so that he could try to kill her: an act of such raw need and loathing that it took Warden's breath away –

In some sense, Hashi Lebwohl – like the Amnion – didn't truly understand desperation.

But Vestabule wasn't done. 'Remembering desperation,' he continued, 'I will tell you another thing for the sake of your effectiveness with *Trumpet*'s people. I am acquainted with Captain Angus Thermopyle.'

As soon as he heard the Amnioni say Angus' name, Warden's attention snapped back into focus.

'In my former life,' Vestabule explained, 'I served as crew aboard a human ship named *Viable Dreams*. Perhaps your records have revealed this to you.'

Warden nodded slowly while a strange new alarm bloomed in his heart like an evil flower.

'Our ship was captured,' Vestabule said. 'It was taken to Thanatos Minor, where its surviving humans were sold to the Amnion. I was one among twenty-eight men and women delivered for experiment and mutation.' His tone didn't waver. 'This was done by Captain Thermopyle.'

Then Warden Dios needed every gram of discipline and abnegation he could muster to conceal his reaction. In brutal self-denial he kept his expression flat and his gaze hooded while a singularity grenade of dismay went off in his chest.

Angus had sold twenty-eight men and women to the Amnion.

Vestabule didn't say what Angus had purchased with so much human blood and horror, but Warden could guess.

Twenty-eight –

Somehow Angus had concealed that fact during his interrogation by Hashi and DA. Despite the intrusion of zone implants into his head, the mental rape, he hadn't let slip any hints: he'd only answered the questions which his tormentors had known to ask. Even when he was helpless, he'd found the strength to preserve one secret. And Warden, who'd guessed the existence if not the nature of that secret – Warden

412

had said nothing to put Hashi on the track of this appalling revelation.

Angus had sold –

And now he had the sheer effrontery to say, *We're waiting for you to keep at least one of your promises*, the malign and colossal gall to suggest, *Personally, I want to see you keep the one where you stop the crime you've done to me.*

So he could do what? Help deliver *Trumpet*'s people – Morn as well as Davies and Vector – to *Calm Horizons* so that he could escape himself? Thumb his nose at everything Warden had hoped for from him – or from Morn?

Twenty-eight men and women!

He wanted to be set *free*?

While a black hole of nausea and chagrin ate at his heart, Warden asked himself whether he had any choice. Millions of lives hung in the balance. He and no one else had chosen Angus; arranged his capture; designed his welding; maneuvered him into his plight. There was no one else Warden could blame. Or hold responsible. Or ask to make this decision for him.

Blinking unsteadily, Vestabule inquired, 'Is this information of use to you?'

Apparently he remembered more about being human than Warden would have thought possible.

But the UMCP director was determined to conceal all his personal desperation. He had no intention of letting the Amnioni watch him shrink and die inside himself. And he'd promised years ago that he would bear the full cost of his mistakes, regardless of how high it ran.

'It helps,' he told Vestabule through the baffle of his mask. 'Now I have a better idea what I'm up against.'

Hashi had given him a code to kill Angus: to induce a cyborg's version of self-destruct. For the first time he began to believe that he would have to use it.

DAVIES

Finally Morn raised her head. In a thick voice, as if she felt like weeping, she breathed, 'Somebody say something.'

Davies tried. He wanted to. Director Donner, tell me – But he couldn't find the words. He still didn't know how to name what he needed from her.

Neither Min nor Captain Ubikwe spoke. Min watched Morn impersonally, as if she'd taken an oath to do or say nothing that would influence Morn's thinking. And Dolph's shrouded gaze hid his thoughts.

Davies was obliquely surprised that Angus kept quiet. Angus looked like he was charged with sarcasm; primed to sneer or jeer. Yet he kept it to himself.

Bydell and Porson pretended that they were busy with nonexistent duties. Cray concentrated like death on managing the complex flow of transmission back and forth between *Punisher* and UMCPHQ Center. Glessen glared truculently at Mikka as if he wanted to club her unconscious.

At last Vector took a step or two forward. 'I'll go.'

A spasm of dread clenched Davies' heart. A wail filled his chest: a cry so primitive and profound that it seemed like the voice of his DNA. *Go? Go there? Submit to that?*

Morn and Dolph wheeled their g-seats toward the former engineer. Angus raised his head; bared his teeth at Vector.

Vector made an attempt to smile, but he'd lost his familiar calm. 'They probably want me because they think they can use what I know about our antimutagen,' he explained unnecessarily. 'But if Vestabule is an example of how much humanity they can retain, they won't get much out of me.'

'Vector –' Morn began; then seemed to choke on her own protest. Clenched around herself, she fell silent.

'Don't argue with him, Ensign,' Dolph muttered darkly. 'If he has the guts for it, you shouldn't stand in his way.

'Personally I want to give him a medal. Although he probably won't appreciate it once the Amnion finish with him. We might have to pin it to his chest with matter cannon fire.'

'Shut up, Dolph,' Min ordered softly. 'I'm not in the mood for your sense of humor.'

Glowering, the captain subsided in his g-seat.

Vector ignored him and the ED director: he ignored everyone except Morn. She was the pivot on which his life had turned. Her arrival aboard *Captain's Fancy* had changed him, just as it had deflected Mikka and transformed Sib – and destroyed Nick. The only response he cared about was hers.

'I don't want to be mutated,' he admitted. 'The idea makes me feel like puking. But to be honest I haven't exactly enjoyed the way we've spent our time recently. A chance to help save a few million lives seems' – he shrugged painfully – 'better than the alternatives.

'Who knows? Maybe I'll finally get rid of this arthritis.'

Go? Davies panted to himself. Go *there*? He was stuck: his distress repeated itself as if fear were the only message his genetic code contained. Submit to *that*?

'This isn't what I had in mind,' Morn groaned. 'When I said I wanted to come here.' Emotion cramped her throat; tightened her chest. 'I didn't intend to sacrifice you.'

Again Vector tried to smile. 'That's all right. I've always wanted to be the savior of humankind.' But his effort to soften the situation failed into a grimace. 'Narcissism, I suppose. Or megalomania. But it looks like this is as close as I'm likely to get.'

Slowly Morn nodded. 'I understand.'

Davies understood as well. But he couldn't match Vector's

courage – or resignation. The Amnion wanted Vector to help them counter Intertech's antimutagen. They wanted him, Davies, to help them destroy humankind.

Morn scanned the bridge; looked into Angus' eyes, and Min's; studied Mikka and Ciro. Apart from Cray's murmured responses to Center, and Min's occasional statements, no one said anything. By degrees Morn's moist gaze cleared. Determination like anger whetted her gaze; pulled her forehead into a knot between her brows.

'I can't go,' she announced grimly. 'I won't. I came here to tell my story. I want to talk to the Council. I want to give Director Hannish my evidence. I want to put a stop to things like suppressing antimutagen research, or framing and selling people to get legislation passed.' She tapped the arms of her g-seat with her fists. 'I can't do that unless I'm *here*.'

She hadn't stated her purpose in Min's hearing before, or Dolph's, but they didn't react to it.

'We aren't to blame for what *Calm Horizons* does,' she asserted.

She was talking to Davies: he knew that. He could hear the way she pitched her voice to reach him. She sounded like Captain Davies Hyland as he remembered her father, explaining his wife's death to his young daughter; trying to convey across the gap of recollection and death that Morn wasn't at fault.

But the Davies who stood on the bridge of *Punisher* facing Min Donner and ruin also heard Bryony Hyland in Morn's voice: the targ officer who'd stayed at her post and died to save the ship she served.

Morn was saying, 'We aren't the ones who decided to play manipulation games with the Amnion. None of us knew what might happen when Nick took us to Enablement so you could be born. It isn't our responsibility. It belongs to Warden Dios. We don't have to help him carry it around.'

Davies wasn't persuaded. He simply couldn't find enough conviction inside himself to answer his fear.

'But telling our story is a different question,' Morn went on. 'That's *my* responsibility. Whether millions of people live or die today, the cops will still be corrupt. And saving those lives now won't help them in the long run. The only thing we can offer humankind that might make a difference is the truth.'

From now on, nobody has any secrets.

She'd told Davies that she needed a better answer. An alternative to self-destruct. Was this it? Was risking wholesale slaughter preferable to sacrificing herself? Was 'the truth' that powerful? Or was her answer something else – something Davies hadn't grasped?

Director Donner, tell me –

Go? Go there? Submit to that?

Tell me what's so bad about self-destruct.

He had Min's gun. He could choose the future for his entire species. Kill himself: force *Calm Horizons* to open fire and die: abandon humankind to Holt Fasner. Or surrender –

When no one else responded, Vector replied as firmly as he could, 'I agree. You should stay here. There are worse things you can do to people than killing them. Like making them believe lies. Or letting them believe lies when you know the truth.'

Morn nodded again, but she didn't reply. Instead she watched Davies as if she feared that he would break her heart. Vestabule wanted four of them: Angus and Vector, Morn and her son. Vector had consented. Angus had said, *We're waiting for you to keep at least one of your promises.* Morn herself had made up her mind to refuse. Only Davies remained in doubt.

'Davies,' Morn breathed softly. She might have been begging. 'You have to decide. I can't do it for you.'

Then she waited. Even Angus appeared to wait. All the tension on the bridge seemed to revolve around Davies as if his uncertainty were a form of gap-sickness.

The Amnion might accept Angus' refusal. They might conceivably accept Morn's. But if Davies rejected their requirements, they would begin to kill –

At last Min looked him in the face. 'Say it,' she ordered dispassionately, as if she didn't care whether he obeyed or

417

not. 'Whatever it is. Nobody can help you if you don't say it.'

Tell me –

If I gave back your gun, would you kill me? Spare me? Or would you point it at my head and make me do what Warden wants?

Abruptly Cray interrupted, 'Director, Center is relaying a transmission from UMCHO. From CEO Fasner.'

Min cocked her head like a woman going into battle. Without hesitation she told Cray, 'Put it on the speakers. Let's hear what he has to say.' Then she turned toward the command station. 'With your permission, Morn, I think I should talk to him.'

Morn swallowed at an obstruction in her throat. 'Go ahead.'

Frustration and alarm pulled tighter around Davies' heart. What the hell did *Fasner* want? What did he want *now*?

'I can't wait,' Dolph grumbled sourly. 'This is going to be such fun.'

As soon as Cray tapped her keys, an angry voice crackled and spat in the bridge speakers. 'Min Donner? God damn it, answer me. This is Fasner. *Holt* Fasner. United Mining Companies *Chief Executive Officer* Holt Fasner. I'm tired of being shuffled around like a poor relation. I want an answer.'

His voice was as sharp as poison; as corrosive as ruin. It sank like pain into the open wound of Davies' heart.

Min smiled harshly to herself. 'CEO Fasner,' she replied, 'this is UMCP Acting Director Min Donner. I'm sorry Center gave you the impression you're being shuffled around. They're trying to manage a catastrophe.'

'You think I don't *know* that?' The force of Holt's retort distorted the speakers like static. 'You think I don't know who *caused* it? I'm tired of bullshit, Donner. I want *action*.'

Min showed her teeth. Anger glittered in her eyes. Nevertheless her tone remained calm; impersonal.

'What "action" did you have in mind, sir?'

'For a start,' he announced at once, 'I want you to aim a

dish over here. It is *intolerable* that everything I say has to be routed through those officious prigs in Center.'

'And what else?' Min asked as if her compliance were a foregone conclusion.

Holt shot back, 'That madman you work for still hasn't bothered to tell me what *Calm Horizons* wants, but I think I can guess. Under *no* circumstances, Donner, *absolutely none*, are you to deliver anything or anyone from *Trumpet* to that warship. Am I being clear? *Calm Horizons* gets nothing from you.

'Put everything and everybody you found aboard *Trumpet* on a shuttle. If you don't have a shuttle, detach your damn command module. Send all of it to me.'

Send –

Angus' face tightened: he rose like a warning from his g-seat. Vector shook his head with dismay in his eyes. Both Morn and Dolph sat rigid, staring their apprehension at Min.

'I wasn't thrilled when you shut down the scan net,' Holt went on, 'but maybe you were right. You can arrange an occluded launch. *Calm Horizons* won't see anything. Your shuttle or the module can go around the far side of the planet. It'll get here soon enough.' Traveling opposite HO's orbit would shorten the journey considerably. 'Just do it *soon*.'

Send all of it –

That's crazy, Davies thought. Did the Dragon want *Trumpet*'s people that badly?

What did he want them *for*?

Quickly Min consulted the scan displays. 'It'll still take time, sir,' she returned carefully. 'I don't think *Calm Horizons* will wait much longer. Have you considered what might happen? Are you prepared to sacrifice the Council?'

Holt swore viciously. 'Get one of your goddamn dishes *aimed* at me, Donner. *I'll* tell you what I'm prepared to do. When we have a secure transmission.'

Min muffled her pickup with one hand. Contained fury seemed to pour off her in waves, but it didn't show in her voice. Ignoring everyone else, she grinned at Captain Ubikwe.

'Pay attention, Dolph,' she advised. 'This may turn out to be more fun than you thought.'

Then she uncovered her pickup.

'With respect, sir,' she replied disingenuously, 'that's going to be impossible. I'm only the acting director. I don't consider it within my mandate to hear or say or do anything that isn't on the record.' She permitted herself a note of stiff piety like a hint of scorn. 'I want to be able to face anybody who questions what I do with a clear conscience.

'Center has recorded and logged your orders. But as it happens,' she remarked as if she trusted the Dragon to agree with her, 'you can't actually give me any orders. Under conditions of war, only Director Dios has the authority to command the defense of human space. The next time I talk to him, I'll ask him if he wants me to do what you tell me.

'At present I have no instructions to surrender anyone or anything from *Trumpet* to you.'

Again she justified Davies' desire to believe in her.

Angus watched her with a twisted frown, as if he didn't know how to interpret what she said. But Morn knew. Deliberately she raised one fist in the air; taunting Holt – or cheering Min.

Dolph sat at attention. His eyes shone. 'By damn, Min,' he murmured, 'you're right. This *is* fun.' Softly he suggested, 'Do it again.'

'Did I hear you right?' the CEO snapped. 'You refuse a direct order from the man who *owns* the UMCP?'

'That's correct, sir.' Still piously, Min added, 'It really doesn't matter who "owns" the UMCP. I take my orders from Director Dios. If you want me to obey, I'll need instructions to that effect from him.'

'*Thank* you, Donner.' Fasner spoke so fiercely that acoustic shatter fretted the edges of his voice. 'Now I have grounds. That's insubordination. It would be a court-martial offense even if we were at peace. Under conditions of war, it's a capital crime.

'Min Donner, you are relieved as acting director of the UMCP. You are relieved as Enforcement Division director.

That's on the record, too. As soon as I'm done with you, I'll name one of my people to take your place. Until this crisis is over, you will consider yourself under arrest.'

Abruptly he broke into a shout. '*Have I made myself clear?*'

Davies stared at the speakers in amazement and alarm. The sudden savagery of Holt's shout seemed to create a clear space in his mind. For the first time in what felt like hours, he began to think.

Did the Dragon want *Trumpet*'s people *that* badly?

What for? What in God's name *for?*

If Holt Fasner held what the Amnion required, he could bargain in Warden's place. That was one possibility. He could make a deal on terms that weren't restricted by what was left of Warden's honor.

But as soon as Davies got that far, he went further —

Min hadn't paused. 'Clear enough, sir,' she told the CEO. For a moment she glanced around the bridge. Then she added with more force, 'Unfortunately you can't relieve me. You don't have the right. I was appointed by the director of the UMCP, and only the director of the UMCP can relieve me. If you want to get rid of me, you'll have to replace Warden first.

'But before you try that,' she warned in a cutting tone, 'I should tell you that while we're under conditions of war I'll consider any attempt to replace or interfere with Director Dios to be an act of madness. On my personal authority,' she drawled as if her voice were a flensing knife, peeling skin from bone, 'and on my oath as UMCPED director, I will order UMCPHQ to ignore any announcement that Warden Dios has been fired. No member of the UMCP will acknowledge or obey a replacement until we receive direct confirmation from Warden Dios himself.'

Decisively Min faced Cray. 'End this transmission, communications. Inform Center that I no longer have anything to say to CEO Fasner. Then verify that his orders and my response have been formally logged as well as recorded.'

At once she turned her back on Cray's station. Slowly she gave the bridge a bloody-minded grin.

'I don't know whether that accomplished anything.' Harsh pleasure rang in her voice. 'Saying no to the Dragon is usually like sticking your head in an incinerator. But I have to admit it felt good.'

For a moment her audacity seemed to stun *Punisher*'s people. Then Glessen began to pound his hands together in applause.

Captain Ubikwe was the first to join him, but an instant later all the duty officers started clapping – Porson and Patrice enthusiastically, Bydell with deep fervor. Davies wanted to applaud as well. The UMCP may have been corrupt; but these men and women were eager to do their jobs without regard for Holt Fasner's needs or desires.

Vector studied Min uncertainly: his distrust of the cops ran deep. Mikka was too tired to care what the ED director did. However, Morn's approval showed in the strict lines of her face and the keenness of her gaze.

Like her son, she seemed to trust Min more and more.

After a moment Dolph said cheerfully to Min, 'I notice you didn't mention singularity grenades – after I went to all the trouble of convincing you we have an excuse for whatever we do.'

Min nodded like a shout. 'I didn't want an excuse. I'm tired of lies.'

But now Davies hardly heard them. Instead he thought furiously, tracing a chain of inferences which started at the hint Holt had given him –

Tell me –

He could feel his doom close like a noose around his neck. In another minute Morn would demand an answer from him. If he failed to reach a decision he could stand behind, he would be lost – as doomed as if the Amnion did what they wanted to him.

She needed an answer that didn't involve self-destruct.

Even though Sorus Chatelaine's body was full of mutagens, she'd opened fire on *Calm Horizons* to save her soul.

Tell me, Director Donner –

Davies wanted to know what he was being asked to sacrifice

himself for. Whose vision of the cops – and the future – was he expected to serve?

What was Warden Dios doing aboard *Calm Horizons*?

Why was Fasner so eager to obtain *Trumpet*'s people?

Urgently Davies put the scattered pieces of his comprehension together.

It was inconceivable that Warden would have betrayed Com-Mine Security, or sold Morn to Nick, or suppressed Vector's research, without Fasner's consent. No, more than that: it was inconceivable without his explicit orders. None of those things would have happened if they hadn't suited the Dragon's designs.

When *Trumpet* had first reached human space from Billingate, Angus had flared a report to UMCPHQ. Warden must have shared it with his boss: he could hardly have avoided doing so. Therefore Holt had known days ago who was aboard the gap scout. He must have known who Davies was, and why the Amnion wanted him.

Days ago. More than time enough to formulate his own dark ambitions for *Trumpet*'s people.

Now both Min Donner and Hashi Lebwohl believed that Warden was trying to bring the Dragon down. He'd sent his PR director, Koina Hannish, to deliver appalling accusations to the GCES. And he'd accepted Vestabule's demand to negotiate aboard *Calm Horizons*. Where Holt couldn't reach him.

Couldn't give him any more explicit, abominable orders.

'Davies,' Morn insisted quietly when the applause had died away. 'It's time. We can't wait any longer.' She hesitated; then finished in pain, 'Don't force me to choose for you.'

Obliquely he wondered what choice she would make. But that was secondary: he could live without knowing.

He trusted Min's evaluation of Warden's actions. So what he really wanted to know was this: How long ago had Warden begun to plan his attack on the Dragon? How far back did his subversion reach? When had his intentions first diverged from Holt's?

Before *Calm Horizons* came to Earth? Earlier?

Before *Trumpet* left for Thanatos Minor?

Before Angus was framed?

Unfortunately Davies couldn't simply pose his question in so many words. Min would tell him the truth as she saw it – he believed that – but her unsubstantiated opinion wasn't enough. He needed facts: information concrete enough to support the weight of his decision.

'Director Donner –' He was sweating, and the alien fabric of his shipsuit chafed his joints. Vast implications hovered just out of reach, waiting for him to translate them into existence; make them real. 'After we left forbidden space – before we hit Massif-5 – you sent us a message.' His voice sounded thin in his ears; stricken by the scale of the crisis. 'In effect, you ordered Angus to give Nick his priority-codes.

'Why did you do that?'

Nobody has any secrets.

Min faced him like a poised predator. Her eyes were the eyes of a hawk stooping for its prey. As if she'd been expecting his question – and knew exactly why he asked it – she replied, 'The order came from Director Dios, but he didn't send it to me. He sent it to *Punisher*. Highest possible priority. Backed by his personal authority. He ordered *Punisher* to relay that message.'

Davies' mouth dropped open. 'The order wasn't sent to you? You mean Director Dios wasn't sure you would carry it out?'

Min didn't flinch from answering. 'That's how I took it. He knows me. He knows how I feel about letting anybody hurt my people.' She indicated Morn with a glance. 'Especially a man like Succorso. And he knows how I feel about him. He knows I trust him enough to assume he wouldn't send a message like that unless Holt Fasner demanded it. He may have thought I would try to protect Morn – and him – by keeping his message to myself.'

That made sense. The Min Donner Davies remembered might well have risked insubordination in order to protect one of her own from Nick.

He tightened his grip on himself. Strain beaded on his

forehead. 'The message we heard,' he pursued, 'was it the same? Exactly the same? You didn't edit it? Add anything? Leave anything out?'

Min shook her head. 'You got what we were told to send.'

Holding her gaze, Davies asked over his shoulder, 'Captain Ubikwe, will you vouch for that?'

'Davies –' Morn objected. 'She's Min Donner. She just told us she's tired of lies.'

Unable to contain his urgency, he wheeled to face her. 'God damn it, Morn! This is important! *I'm the one Vestabule wants!* He can do without you. Angus probably isn't crucial. Even Vector is secondary. But if *I* don't go there and let him –'

Terror closed his throat before he could finish.

'Of course I'll vouch for it,' Dolph put in quickly. 'Hell, if you're worried, Cray can pull up the communications log, run a bit-by-bit comparison. We sent it exactly the way it came in.'

Davies refused the offer with a wrench of his head. As soon as he stopped shouting, he began to tremble. He believed Min. He believed Dolph. In another life he would have been eager to serve under commanders like them. But now there was too much at stake: everything he did mattered too much. He held his fear so hard that his arms shook.

He turned back to the ED director.

'The words were clear enough,' he told her, 'but they were embedded in a bunch of code we couldn't read. What was that? What did it say?'

Who gave Angus permission to show Warden's message to Davies and Morn? Whose game were they playing?

Min shrugged, but her eyes were keen with certainty. 'We can't read it either,' she said as if she were acknowledging a defeat; admitting that she couldn't help him. 'We've been trying to crack it. So far we haven't succeeded.' Then she added, 'But we've figured out what kind of code it is.

'According to our computer study, it's a machine language. The type of language we use to program datacores.'

The type of language Hashi Lebwohl had used to program Angus. UMCP machine code.

Warden's work, not Holt Fasner's.

That meant Warden had begun to oppose Holt before he'd learned that the Amnion were willing to risk a war over Davies. Holt had ordered him to betray Morn and Davies and even Angus by giving Angus to Nick; but Warden had found a way to protect them behind the Dragon's back.

He'd kept at least that one of his promises.

And now he was aboard *Calm Horizons*. The man who defined the ideals which the Hyland family had served for generations was as much at risk as any human being alive. For no apparent reason except to put himself beyond Fasner's reach, he'd taken the chance that the Amnion would destroy him.

Abruptly Davies' tension flushed away. A weakness like sorrow took its place. In an instant the sweat on his forehead turned cold. Nevertheless he no longer trembled. His loss was as sure as the light in Min's eyes.

'All right,' he told Morn without looking at her. 'I've made up my mind.' He didn't have the strength to turn and meet her gaze. 'I'll go. You can tell Director Dios I'll go.'

For an instant a rush of eagerness overwhelmed Min's self-discipline. It flared up in her face like a cheer. She bared her teeth as if she wanted to fasten them in Fasner's throat.

Dolph allowed himself a sigh of relief and dismay. Bydell hid her face in her hands. Glessen nodded angry approval.

But Morn made a tight sound like a groan. 'Oh, Davies.' Her voice labored out of her chest. 'I told you you don't have to do that. I don't want – You didn't bring *Calm Horizons* here. You don't have to let Director Dios off the hook.'

'Morn –' Fighting weakness, Davies shifted his feet until he could look at her.

In her damaged eyes he saw all the hurt she'd suffered for him; all the death she'd held in her hands to keep him alive.

On one occasion she'd had sex with Nick in front of *Captain's Fancy*'s bridge crew, placating him for Davies' sake. Later she'd forced the Amnion to return her son by threatening to blow up *Captain's Fancy* and half of Enablement Station. Still later, despite Nick's murderous rage, she'd broken out of the cabin where he'd imprisoned her so that she could divert Davies' ejection pod away from *Tranquil Hegemony* to Billingate.

Davies did his best to explain.

'You heard the Dragon,' he sighed thinly. 'He wants us. He's probably wanted us ever since he found out we were aboard *Trumpet*. I think Director Donner is right. Fasner ordered Warden to let Nick have Angus' codes. He could bargain with Nick. And Warden had to obey. But he didn't want to betray us, so he wrapped that code around Fasner's orders. He gave us a way out.'

'Those strings didn't make any sense to me,' Angus put in unexpectedly. '*Trumpet*'s computers didn't recognize them. But when I recited them to my computer datalink – like an instruction-set of some kind –' A light the color of sulfuric acid glared in his eyes. 'At first nothing changed. But as soon as Nick left the ship, my datacore made me show Davies the message.'

Not Morn: Davies. The UMCP director had no way of guessing how badly Morn might have been hurt by Angus and Nick. He couldn't gauge what she might do if she controlled Angus. So he'd chosen her son. Without knowing him, Warden Dios had given Davies the same power Nick had.

At the time the decision to free Angus had been too much for Davies. Morn had been forced to reach it alone. But he could make choices now.

– kept at least that one of his promises.

'I can't turn my back on him,' he said to his mother. He felt weak enough to faint. 'Not after he saved us. Not while he's aboard *Calm Horizons*.'

So that he wouldn't collapse, he folded to the deck; sat with his elbows braced on his knees and his hands covering his face. If they could, the Amnion would use him to destroy humankind. In his pocket, Min's handgun seemed to dig at his thigh, but he no longer cared.

ANGUS

A ngus sneered at everyone around him because he didn't
know what else to do.

Ever since he'd announced his refusal to rescue
Warden Dios, he'd been effectively paralyzed. Oh, he could
still move and speak: in some superficial sense he could make
decisions. But on a deeper level he was trapped between
Morn's commitments and his own rejection; between his need
to escape the crib and his utter dependence on the mad,
fractured woman who abused him.

Morn had released him from his priority-codes; from compulsions and torments which Warden Dios had forced onto
him. Yet what she needed from him now was his help extricat-
ing Dios from the hands of the Amnion. He had nothing
else to offer her.

And he couldn't do it. The prospect terrified him. *Warden
Dios* terrified him. Without the support of his zone implants,
he might not have been able to form words when Dios had
spoken to him; asked him, *Are* you *all right?* Only his artificial
resources had given him the strength to say, *We're waiting
for you to keep at least one of your promises.*

Despite his pose of sarcasm and belligerence, he'd nearly
fallen to his knees in drooling, idiot panic when Dios had
told him, *I'm considering it.* He knew what Dios 'considered',
and it wasn't his promises to Angus; or to Morn.

Angus had spent a lifetime fearing and fighting cops: he'd
learned how Dios' mind worked. He was intimately familiar

with Hashi Lebwohl's designs. And he understood failsafes.

He didn't believe for a second that his priority-codes were the only hold Dios and Lebwohl had on him. When Dios had spoken to him, he'd feared he was about to find out what other forms of coercion the UMCP director could invoke.

But he hadn't been coerced. Dios was still *considering it*. He wanted to see how *Trumpet*'s people would answer Marc Vestabule before he took the final step in Angus' welded dehumanization.

So Vector Shaheed, the Savior of Humankind, was willing to let the Amnion have him: that was fine. So Davies had finally talked himself into surrender: that was fine, too. Angus didn't really care. Even Morn's decision not to go meant nothing to him – except that it spared him the maddening humiliation of being forced by his computer to keep her aboard *Punisher* against her will; of having his own volition overridden by Warden Dios' chiseled commandment to preserve her life.

None of those things altered his essential plight.

Morn had set him free from his priority-codes. And now she needed his help; needed him to resubmit himself to compulsion and the crib by rescuing Warden Dios. She didn't know it, but that might be the only way to keep her son human.

Her open distress at Davies' decision touched Angus oddly, in places he didn't recognize. *That* he cared about. He hated seeing her in pain. But he couldn't afford to let her move him.

He refused. God damn fucking *right* he refused. Unfortunately it accomplished nothing. Dios was still *considering*. As soon as he made up his mind, Angus would be driven to obey.

He mocked the people around him because he had no other outlet for his bitterness.

When Davies sank to the deck in emotional exhaustion, Angus told Morn, 'Don't try to talk him out of it.' Fervently he hoped that Davies' surrender would be enough; that Dios would let him, Angus, off the hook. 'Call *Calm Horizons* and tell your precious director he can have most of what he wants. Do it before your kid suffers another moral spasm and changes his mind.'

Davies was his son. Nevertheless Angus did his utter best to believe that he didn't give a shit what happened to the boy. And in fact it may have been true that he didn't care at all whether the Amnion used Davies to help them doom humankind. But it was also true that he saw himself in his son. Davies had been tied into yet another version of the crib; shackled to the slats by 'millions of lives' and Dios' dark authority. Like Angus, he was dependent on those who tortured him.

More than once Angus had killed people who reminded him of his own helplessness. At least once he'd nearly killed Morn for the same reason.

The look she turned on him might have withered his heart, if he hadn't already been so full of desolation. Her eyes were mute wails of loss. Lines as strict as the exigencies of his programming marked her face. Despite everything the cops had done to her – and everything she'd suffered for Davies – she still thought it was her duty to save lives. No matter what that cost her.

Another crib.

'Do you think it's enough?' she countered as if she meant something else entirely. The stress in her voice implied outrage, loathing; desperation. 'You've already refused. I'm going to refuse. Will the Amnion accept a deal like that?'

'Well, hell, they should,' he replied out of the wilderness. 'He's all they really want. The rest of us are just smoke.' He snorted. ' "Compensation for an act of war" is a load of crap. They're trying to hide the truth. Even Vector doesn't count. Davies is the whole point of this exercise.'

'It can't hurt to try, Morn,' Min put in quietly. 'If we don't give them what they want – or at least keep the negotiation open – they might not leave us enough time for anything else.'

Angus was sure he knew what the ED director meant: enough time for Morn to do what she'd come here for in the first place. He hated all cops – but in some strange way he was starting to trust Min Donner. He believed that if Morn satisfied *Calm Horizons* Min would do her best to satisfy Morn.

The idea made him want to kill her. She was a *cop*; Enforcement Division in person: she had no right to be honest.

Slowly Morn turned away from him as if she couldn't bear the sight any longer. Her gaze seemed to rake welts across his soul as it shifted toward Min. For a long moment the two women faced each other as if they were trying to bridge a gulf. Then Morn said in a constricted tone, 'Communications, give me a channel to Director Dios.'

Cray didn't hesitate. Murmuring, 'Right away,' she typed commands to reestablish *Punisher*'s connection through UMCPHQ Center to *Calm Horizons*.

While Cray worked, Min glanced at Captain Ubikwe. 'If I remember right, Dolph,' she remarked, 'we don't have a shuttle.'

'That's true,' he confirmed. 'We'll have to use the command module.' A conflicted nausea darkened his eyes. He looked sick at the idea of surrendering Davies and Vector – and at the consequences of not surrendering them. 'Unless Captain Thermopyle volunteers to run *Trumpet* over there.' But he didn't wait for Angus to reject the suggestion. 'Bydell,' he ordered, 'tell the ship to secure for detachment. Inform the auxiliary bridge I want them ready to take over in fifteen minutes. I'll assign crew for the module as soon as we have a deal with *Calm Horizons*.'

'Aye, Captain.' Quickly Bydell activated her pickup and began sending *Punisher*'s people to their tasks.

Cray raised her head. 'Ensign Hyland,' she announced in a bleak voice, 'I have a channel to Director Dios.'

A new clench of anxiety gripped the bridge. Patrice and Porson straightened themselves at their stations. Like a woman who had no part to play in what followed, Min adjusted her throat pickup and resumed exchanging orders and information with Center. She may have sold her soul to Warden Dios, but she kept her word to Morn.

Morn acknowledged communications with a stiff nod. She thumbed her command pickup; and Cray put *Calm Horizons'* transmission on the bridge speakers.

'Morn,' Dios said at once. Static like the sound of crumpling hardcopy covered his voice. Nevertheless his increasing urgency was palpable. 'Have you reached a decision yet? I can't wait much longer. This ship is running out of patience.'

Davies raised his head, instinctively responsive to the UMCP director. Morn's features had tightened to stone. Vector sighed quietly to himself.

None of them understood what was about to happen.

'Director Dios,' Morn answered. Her own voice held steady, despite the cost of losing her son. 'I realize you're in a difficult position. We're doing the best we can.'

At once Dios retorted, 'I don't want excuses, Morn. I want action.' Somehow he'd turned up a rheostat; dialed the intensity of his tone to a new level. 'I want to get this defensive out of here with as much of the planet intact as possible.'

Angus trembled at the force Warden conveyed. The UMCP director had a gift for command; for making people want to obey him – trust him. Angus himself had almost believed it when Dios told him, *It's got to stop.*

Shaking with tension – inside his shipsuit, where no one could see it – he began to pace the bridge as Davies had done earlier; push his mortality across the cruiser's deceleration g. He needed movement. Hell, he needed to *run*. Get out of here and never look back. Ignite *Trumpet's* drives cold. Hide behind *Punisher* while he put as much distance as possible between himself and *Calm Horizons*. Then burn for the gap –

As soon as Morn answered, Warden would have all the information he needed to make his own decisions. He would know the situation; would be done *considering it*.

And Angus would be lost.

Yet he didn't try to escape. Regardless of the terror which had ruled his life, he remained on *Punisher's* bridge, pacing.

Morn gave no sign that she knew he was taking a stand. She didn't realize what was about to happen. She cared too much about Davies and Dios, about millions of lives and police corruption, to recognize the danger.

'Then I won't drag this out,' she told Dios and *Calm Horizons.* Her tone was cold and distant; desperately compelled. 'Davies and Vector have agreed to give themselves up. *Punisher* will detach her command module to transport them.

'But Angus has refused.' She swallowed fiercely to clear her throat. 'And so do I.'

In response a hollow quiet filled the speakers. Warden must have covered his pickup with his hand – presumably so he could talk to Vestabule. Thrust emission inflected the silence while everyone on *Punisher*'s bridge waited.

Sounds that might have been prayers filled Angus' head; but he hardly knew what he was praying for.

Then Warden said, 'That's not good enough, Morn.' Pressure congested his voice. 'The Amnion don't consider it acceptable.'

Morn closed her fists in front of her; tightened them until her forearms quivered.

'Too bad,' she replied sharply. '*I* am in command here. And *while* I'm in command, nobody will be forced to do something like this. Angus says no. That's his decision. And I say no. That's mine.

'The Amnion have already had their turn with me,' she explained without relenting. 'And I still have work to do.'

She may have meant to remind him of what was at stake on Suka Bator.

'Tell that warship to kill us now or take what we offer.' She sounded as uncompromising as a knife. 'They don't have any other alternatives.'

The speakers reported another covered silence: more discussion or conflict *Punisher* couldn't hear. Angus paced the deck as if each heavy tread were an act of protest. Davies made a tired effort to get to his feet; then changed his mind and subsided. Vector's mouth moved, although he didn't make a sound: he may have been counting the seconds under his breath.

After two or three heartbeats, Captain Ubikwe rumbled

softly, 'Ensign Hyland, I wish you would let Glessen back on targ. If that Amnioni fires, I want someone fighting for us who isn't just about comatose with exhaustion.'

Morn ignored him. Mikka didn't so much as turn her head.

'Stand by,' Min told Center. Her tone was almost gentle. 'I think it's now or never. If *Calm Horizons* doesn't start to shoot in the next ten minutes, we may actually survive.'

'Morn,' Warden said abruptly from the speakers, 'the Amnion accept your refusal. As you say, they've already had their turn with you. They acknowledge that.'

Fucking right, Angus growled to himself. The sight of Morn's suffering when he'd rescued her from the Amnion sector of Billingate still haunted him.

'But they insist on Angus,' Warden continued, as harsh as welding. 'He did more damage than they can tolerate. If he doesn't give himself up, we don't have a deal.'

Angus faltered in his pacing; turned a gaze full of involuntary dismay toward the command station. Min swore viciously, then resumed talking to Center. Davies looked back and forth between Angus and Morn as if he no longer understood them.

Morn kept her attention fixed on her pickup. Davies had agreed to go over to *Calm Horizons*. Nothing else could reach her. For the second time she said, 'Too bad.' Without turning her head, she raised her voice to reach everyone on the bridge. 'Mikka, prepare to fire. On my order.'

Angus stopped moving altogether. Across the bridge he stared at Morn. She was risking war, wholesale butchery – She'd transcended him again; raised her resolve and her self to heights he couldn't match. The things he and Nick and Warden Dios had done to her had made her greater than all of them.

Croaking a curse, Dolph slapped at his belts, surged out of his g-seat. In a rush he moved to the targ station. 'For God's sake, woman,' he hissed at Mikka, 'let *somebody* who isn't half asleep do this job!'

Mikka faced him with a glare like a fist. Her hands on the matter cannon keys had become as steady as servos.

434

At the same time Warden warned quickly, 'Morn, don't do anything stupid. There has to be a way around this.'

Morn's jaws clenched. 'Make it good,' she told the pickup. 'I don't sell human beings.'

What had she said earlier – when she'd decided to help Angus edit his datacore? *We're cops. We don't use people.* Now she showed again that she meant what she said.

Shouts rose against the restraint of Angus' zone implants. He wanted to roar at the speakers, You *hear* that, Dios? There's at least one member of the goddamn UMCP who *means what she says*!

For a moment Warden paused. Morn had shamed him; or he needed to listen to Vestabule. When he spoke again, his voice seemed to freeze the blood in Angus' veins.

'Speaking of selling, is Angus still there? Will you let me talk to him?'

Angus meant to yell, No! before Morn could reply. Don't let him do this to me! But the cry stuck in his throat. She blocked it by looking at him. As far as she knew, there was nothing to fear. Her gaze said as clearly as words, I'm willing to start a war to protect your freedom. What're *you* willing to do?

And he wanted to match her. That may have been the only thing he'd ever truly wanted.

'Oh, hell,' he muttered. His zone implants enabled him to maintain the pretense of steadiness. 'If it'll make him feel better, I'll let him argue with me.'

At once she turned away. 'Go ahead, Director Dios,' she said in a tight voice. 'Angus can hear you.'

Now Warden didn't delay. 'Angus,' he said through the static, 'I'm with an Amnioni called Marc Vestabule. In effect, he's the captain here. He's been "invested with decisiveness". But he used to be human.

'He says he knows you.'

That surprised Angus. He locked his arms across his chest; clamped his teeth together until the corners of his jaw ached. 'He's probably lying,' he snarled back, although he feared

Vestabule might be telling the truth. 'Even if he isn't, what makes him think I care?'

'He used to crew on a ship called *Viable Dreams*.' Heavy with accusation, Warden's reply carried through the static. 'He says you captured his ship, took him and twenty-seven other members of the crew captive. Then you hauled them off to Billingate and sold them all to the Amnion.

'He hasn't told me what you were paid for that, but I think I can guess.'

Oh, shit.

At once a stricken silence fell across the bridge. Min jerked up her head: an instant of fury flamed in her eyes; stretched her lips back from her teeth. Mikka lowered her head to the targ board, covered her skull and the back of her neck with her arms. Curses gathered savagely in Glessen's face; Patrice's; Porson's.

If his zone implants hadn't held him, Angus would have staggered. Dios caught him with a charge he couldn't answer; turned the bridge against him. Morn and Davies knew about *Viable Dreams*: he'd told them to explain how he'd learned to edit datacores. In spite of that, Morn had made the decision to help free him from his priority-codes. But everyone else –

Only Ciro didn't react. Morn hid her face behind her hair. Davies lifted a look of dull speculation toward his father. Min's hands strained for the gun she no longer carried.

In dismay Vector croaked, 'You did *what*?'

Then Glessen and Cray started to shout.

Mikka's shoulders shook as if she were weeping. 'Oh, God. I never knew –' A sound like a sob closed her throat. 'Your own kind, Angus? Your own *kind*?'

Abruptly she wrenched up her head; cried as if her heart were torn, 'What have you done to my brother? *What in God's name have you been telling him?*'

At the same time Captain Ubikwe wheeled to face the command station. 'Christ on a crutch, Ensign Hyland!' he roared. 'And you *listen* to this bastard when he asks you to trust him? Are you *insane*?'

'You amaze me, Angus,' Vector went on. Disgust or grief

crumpled his round face. 'I didn't think I could still be horrified. I thought Nick cauterized that part of me years ago.'

Morn didn't touch her pickup; let Warden Dios hear it all.

Dread rose like fire in Angus' heart. If the revulsion around him mounted high enough, these people might call his bluff; might push him until they discovered that his programming still prevented him from hurting them. As long as they didn't threaten Morn, he might not be able to defend himself at all.

One way or another, they could force him aboard the command module. Even if his datacore allowed him to put up a fight, *Punisher*'s crew could overwhelm him with sheer numbers.

He couldn't bear it.

'*Stop that!*' he yelled like the report of a gun.

His shout seemed to crack against the bulkheads; fracture into echoes and old hurt. Darkness mottled his face: blood and dirt marked his skin like livid stigmata. His heavy arms beat anguish against his sides.

'*Stop* it! You haven't earned the *right* to be so fucking self-righteous with me!'

Instinctively he aimed his rage like despair at Morn. There was no one else he could ask for help. '*Tell them!*' he demanded. '*Tell* them this is the only reason you're still alive!'

She shook her head. She was capable of opening fire on *Calm Horizons*; capable of refusing him. 'You tell them.'

For an instant he gaped at her. Then he whirled; grabbed Davies by the front of his shipsuit; ripped the boy to his feet.

'Tell them!'

Davies resembled his father, but he had Morn's eyes. He met Angus' desperation without flinching; without hesitating.

'She's right. You tell them.'

He might have said, Don't try to make us responsible for your crimes.

With a strangled howl, Angus pushed Davies away.

An emotional convulsion came over him. Alone in the center of the bridge, with loathing all around him, and nowhere to turn, he raised his fists to his head, set his knuckles against his skull. At that moment he was utterly and absolutely

437

determined to cut his brain open with laser fire; squeeze coherent ruin into the core of his pain –

His programming declined to permit it. His zone implants sent out their emissions. Without transition he passed from despair to a sickening, fatal calm. His horror remained. The rage of his personal furies went on. Their wings seemed to labor in the background of his mind, covering him with their shadows; clattering for his heart. But the wildness disappeared from his body. Helpless to do otherwise, he lowered his arms.

Briefly he scanned the bridge. He might have been *considering it* the same way Warden Dios did. Then he picked Min Donner. *You tell them.* Since Morn had abandoned him, Min was the highest authority here. Despite the combative fury in her eyes, the judgment which lined her mouth, he moved toward her.

She met him with her fists poised to strike, as if he were an enemy she intended to defeat with her bare hands.

Dolph started forward to give her his support; but Morn halted him with a sharp gesture.

'Yes, I did that,' Angus told Min's knotted outrage. Stifled vehemence seemed to strangle him; but only a hint of it showed in his voice. 'Sold all fucking twenty-eight of them. And the Amnion paid me by teaching me how to edit datacores.' He grinned at the sudden shock in her gaze; the instant recoil. 'It's supposed to be impossible, but I can do it.'

As if she were unaware of them, Min lowered her arms.

Stiffly he went on, 'That's why Com-Mine Security couldn't find enough evidence to execute me. I deleted it. And it's why I don't have to listen to my priority-codes. I blocked them.'

Everyone on the bridge stared at him. Min studied him as if he were about to reach critical mass. Mikka watched with her face full of tears. Under his breath Vector muttered something that might have been, 'Well, damn.'

From his g-seat Ciro smiled at Angus like a soulmate.

'If I hadn't done that,' Angus said quietly while acid frothed and spat inside him, 'they would all be *dead* by now. Why do you suppose that asshole Fasner wanted Nick to have my priority-codes? So Nick would kill them. But first he would have hurt them so much they would have begged to die.

'I *saved* them,' he insisted. 'Because I *could*. Because I sold Vestabule's goddamn ship.'

And because Morn had released him.

Abruptly he flung out his arm. Trembling with desperation and strain he couldn't show, he pointed an accusation at the speakers.

'*He* knew about it.' The director of the UMCP. 'He *knew*. Before he ever put me aboard *Trumpet*, and sent me to Billingate, and let Milos torture me, he *knew*. He told me so.' At last he found the strength to raise his voice: his data-core allowed it. 'He's been *counting on it*!

'And he's *still* counting on it. I don't know what the fuck he thinks he's doing, but I am shit-positive he's still counting on what I can do! He's *using* all of us, *right now*, the same way he's always used us!'

Now Min's face showed nothing, gave nothing. She concentrated on absorbing what she heard.

Finally Morn intervened. 'That's enough, Angus.' She didn't shout. Nevertheless a vibration of force in her tone stopped him. 'It doesn't make any difference. Not now. Not here. We can all yell about this later.'

She may not have wanted Vestabule to hear him explain what he meant.

Roughly he swung away from Min to confront Morn across the gap between their stations. If he could have acted of his own free will, he would have howled, wailed, Do you think I fucking *care* what fucking *Vestabule* hears? *You don't have the right to despise me!* But now it wasn't his zone implants that restrained him: it was Morn herself. The impacted hurt in her gaze told him how she would respond.

While I'm in command, nobody will be forced to do something like this.

I don't sell human beings.

I need a better answer.

Mikka, prepare to fire.

She may have been the only one here who could imagine

439

how much harm his welding had done him. If he couldn't match her, he could at least try not to get in her way.

He took a step or two toward her, then stopped like a man who didn't believe in himself enough to go on. Instead of resisting her, he groaned in the direction of her pickup, 'Are you listening, Dios? Do you like what you hear?'

Then he lapsed into silence as if his zone implants had shut him down.

His voice conflicted by static, Warden replied at once, 'Oh, I hear you, all right. I hear you fine.' Then he added, 'So does Vestabule. You've betrayed one of their secrets. Now he has even more reason to prefer a war if you don't give yourself up.

'There's just one thing I want to know, Morn,' he went on before anyone could speak. 'Did he tell you about *Viable Dreams*?'

Even more reason –

More reason for everyone aboard the cruiser to make Angus comply with Vestabule's demands.

But Morn didn't hesitate. 'Yes, Director.' Her tone was as cold as the gap. 'He told me. Both Davies and I knew.'

'He couldn't work on his datacore without help,' Warden pursued. 'I assume you helped him. When did he tell you? Before or after?'

'Before,' she answered simply. 'I knew before I decided to help him.'

'I see.'

Warden paused. During the silence Angus felt the last seconds of his life ticking away.

When Dios spoke again, his manner had changed. Almost gently, he said, 'You know him better than I do, Morn. I'll trust your judgment.'

Then his voice changed focus. 'Angus, are *you* listening?'

Angus flinched inwardly. 'I try not to,' he growled. If he could have wept, he would. 'But I can't get you out of my head.'

'You're damn right I've been using you, Angus.' Warden pierced the distortion as if he intended to give Angus orders

440

after all. 'I've been using you and Morn ever since you reached Com-Mine. After *Starmaster* died. I was using you when I switched your datacore. And I'm going to keep right on using you.

'I've heard how you justify yourself, Angus,' he pronounced harshly. 'Now I want you to hear *me*.

'We're facing a total crisis here. An outright apotheosis.'

Between one heartbeat and the next, Angus collapsed on the deck as if he'd been cut off at the knees. In the prison of his skull, a tidal wave of images and sensations broke over him. An inarticulate gargle of shock or surprise bubbled up from his chest. Spasms he couldn't control gripped his shoulders.

Davies gasped in dismay. Morn came half out of the command station, then froze.

Something Warden had said –

He was still talking. He might have been unaware of a reaction he couldn't see. 'Are you *listening*, Angus?' he demanded. 'Vestabule has his guns aimed at Suka Bator. If we don't do what he wants, he's going to give us a super-light proton vasectomy.'

A thick cry tore its way past Angus' teeth. Before his zone implants could intervene, his synapses fired as if he were being transfigured. His knees jerked up to his chest. He tucked his head against them; cowered on the deck while everything he knew and understood came to an end.

Warden may not have heard him. Or maybe he knew exactly what was happening. His voice rang as he proclaimed, 'I will use anybody I can to do my job.'

MORN

For a moment Morn remained frozen; caught between Angus' fall and the instant knowledge that Warden Dios had caused it. In response to Angus' defiance he'd invoked commands no one else knew about, and now the only man who might have helped him lay stricken on the deck, huddling into himself like an infant. The shock held her while she struggled to catch up with it.

Warden did this.

Because Vestabule had told him about *Viable Dreams*, and he no longer trusted his welded cyborg? Because he had no other way to enforce Angus' compliance; fend off the threat of war and untold bloodshed?

I will use anybody I can to do my job.

She couldn't catch up; not like this; not with Angus groveling on the deck, and everyone she depended on stunned to silence.

Abruptly she dropped back into her g-seat; turned to her pickup. 'Director, Angus just collapsed.' She made no effort to hide her urgency. 'I don't know what's happened to him. I'll call you back.'

Warden shouted her name, trying to hold on to her, make her keep her channel open; but she hit her pickup toggle and cut him off in midsyllable.

Around her, everyone stared at Angus as if he were becoming an Amnioni in front of them. The only man who might have helped Warden –

They insist on Angus.

He wrapped his arms more tightly across his knees. His shoulders hunched: he might have been strangling something inside himself.

Christ, Warden! What have you *done*?

'Good God,' Dolph protested softly. 'Somebody help him.'

None of the duty officers obeyed. In their separate ways, they all seemed too shaken to react; too confused. And Mikka had nothing left to give: she used the last of her will, her heart, to hold herself steady on targ.

But Davies lurched stiffly to his feet. Morn may have made the decision to help Angus block his priority-codes; but Davies had done most of the work. He'd cut open his father's back; dipped his hands in his father's blood. When the imponderable stresses of *Trumpet's* singularity grenade had driven Angus into stasis, Davies had spilled more blood to bring him back. Dismay and bafflement filled his face as he moved to Angus' side.

Awkwardly he knelt to the deck; put his hands on Angus' shoulders to roll him over.

As soon as he saw his father's face, he recoiled in surprise. '*Shit*, Angus! What the fuck're you doing?'

A manic grin stretched Angus' stained face. Tears squeezed from his eyes: crazy humor flushed his cheeks. He looked like a man who'd locked himself into a ball so that he wouldn't break out laughing.

'It's got to stop,' he croaked at Davies as if that were the funniest thing he'd ever heard. 'It's got to stop.'

Abruptly Morn felt a new gulf yawn open at her feet. Hidden intentions and vast risks pulled at her like the strange forces of the gap. They would kill her, kill everyone, if she didn't start understanding them *now*.

'Angus –' Her voice caught. She swallowed fiercely, tried again. 'Angus, what's happening to you?' What did Warden *do*? 'What the hell is going on?'

I will use anybody –

With a conspiratorial roll of his eyes, Angus raised a heavy finger to his lips. Whispering intensely, he warned, 'Don't let Dios hear you. Don't let Vestabule know.'

Davies jerked up his head; shot a frightened glance at Morn.

Quickly she turned to communications. 'Cray?'

Cray took a deep breath; forced herself to consult her board. 'We aren't transmitting,' she confirmed. 'We still have a channel to *Calm Horizons* through Center. They're standing by. But they can't hear us.'

An abyss of incomprehension –

Morn choked down a surge of bile. 'All right, Angus. They can't hear us.' Repeating Cray's words seemed to be the best she could do. She took hold of herself; required something better. 'Get up. Talk to me.'

As suddenly as he'd fallen, Angus uncoiled his limbs and sprang to his feet. Without transition his collapse ended – or changed. Wiping his eyes with the backs of his hands, he moved toward her. His burst of amusement was over, but he went on grinning as if he'd been let in on one of life's essential secrets.

When he reached her, he leaned over her console and growled cheerfully, 'Jesus, Morn! If he can do *that*, I bet he can do other things, too. I bet he could have made me kill myself.'

'Why do you suppose he didn't? Get it over with? Put me out of my misery?'

If the idea frightened him at all, he didn't show it. He faced her with his hands braced like defiance on her board and his chin up, still grinning.

Morn ground her teeth in frustration. 'I can't answer that. You still haven't told me what happened.'

Glowering, Dolph raised his voice. 'Captain Thermopyle, I want to know what's going on.'

Min nodded harshly. 'This isn't optional, Angus,' she put in. 'We *need* to know. If we have to fight now, for God's sake *say so*. I can coordinate a first strike, hit that defensive with everything we have. We can't save Suka Bator – or UMCPHQ – but every bit of hurt we put on her will reduce the slaughter.

'Stop smirking' – her voice sharpened to a shout – 'and tell us what Warden did to you!'

Apparently Warden hadn't explained his game to her. She and Morn had that much in common: they were both guessing. Min may have had nothing to go on except her faith in him – and her confidence in her own people.

But her demand didn't touch Angus. He glanced at Dolph; turned a baleful glare on Min. Then he ignored them.

'He did that pretty well,' he told Morn. Moment by moment an eerie eagerness grew in him. Yellow excitement shone from his eyes. 'Gave us the opening we need.' He slapped one palm on the command board. 'Now we can get started.'

His attitude seemed to take her by the throat. She didn't know how to answer him; had no idea what he was talking about. Started? Her arm in its cast seemed to throb with prescient dread. He knew how to rescue Warden –

Nevertheless she held his gaze. 'Damn you,' she whispered thinly, 'tell me what happened.'

Davies came forward a step or two, then stopped as if he couldn't get any closer. Mikka had dropped her hands from the targ board in order to concentrate on Angus and Morn. Mutely her damaged face asked again, *What have you done to my brother?*

Vector had braced himself on the back of the command-g-seat to take some of the strain off his joints. Frowning, he inquired, 'Started on what, Angus?' Mikka's question in different words. 'I thought you refused to get involved in this.'

Angus paid no attention to Vector; focused exclusively on Morn. Perhaps no one else mattered to him. 'Vector's willing,' he reminded her. 'Davies is willing. That's all we need.

'Here's what you're going to do,' he announced while his certainty strangled her. 'First you're going to call Dios again. Offer him the same deal as before. He can have Davies and Vector, but not you or me. Tell him' – Angus grinned maliciously – 'I'm having convulsions, I must have burned out a circuit or something, fried a few synapses, you can't send me over there because you can't control me, I look like I'm already dying. Tell him whatever you want. He'll accept it. This is a goddamn negotiation, isn't it? *Make* him accept it.'

Morn opened her mouth to protest; catch her breath. But Angus overrode her.

'If he still objects, offer him *Trumpet*. Even if Vestabule is still human enough to want me for revenge, he can't ignore bait like that. The datacore of a UMCP gap scout ought to be worth a fucking fortune. Not to mention all those singularity grenades, and that dispersion field generator.'

She stared at him as if he'd threatened to rape her. The pressure he exerted made her want to puke.

'After that,' he went on triumphantly, 'you can concentrate on talking to the Council. Donner'll help you. She'll make them listen.' He sounded certain. Anticipation danced like flames of madness in his eyes. 'Leave the rest to me.'

It made no sense. What had changed? What had Warden *done* to him?

God, she needed to *understand*!

Fighting for breath, she countered, 'The rest of *what*?'

He didn't explain; might have been too eager to see how completely he confused her. Instead he went on, 'Give me Mikka and Ciro. Give me the fat man here.' He nodded at Captain Ubikwe. 'Give me *Trumpet* and the command module. Then you can forget about Warden Dios. Forget Fasner. Forget that fucking Amnioni if you feel like it.

'I'll deal with them,' he promised.

As soon as Angus mentioned the command module, Dolph started fuming. 'That's enough, Thermopyle,' he barked. 'You're going too far too fast. This is *my ship*, God damn it. If you think I trust you enough –'

'It isn't up to us, Dolph,' Min interrupted quietly. Her tone seemed to ache with the force of her restraint. 'This is Morn's decision.' Whether or not she grasped what was happening had apparently become irrelevant. 'That's why she's in command. To make choices like this. Instead of you or me. She's paid for the right. Hell, so has Angus. And we've already been disqualified. Compromised –'

'*Compromised?*' Captain Ubikwe yelled at her. '*How?*'

She shrugged. 'We take Warden's orders. We're cops – that's what we do. We obey. And some of those orders come from Holt Fasner.'

Although the words seemed to hurt her, she said again, 'This is Morn's decision.'

Dolph may have wanted to argue with her, but his own pain stopped him. His dark face closed around the thought that he, too, had been compromised.

Morn held Angus' gaze. 'Why am I going to do all that?' she asked him bitterly. 'Captain Ubikwe has a good point. Why am I going to trust you that much?'

Even though she'd set him free from his priority-codes, repeatedly staked her life on him, she still didn't know what to believe about him.

Angus let out a burst of grotesque laughter.

'Because I was programmed to keep you alive.' Acid mirth left his voice raw. 'I wasn't supposed to be. Hashi Lebwohl told everybody my instruction-sets were written to prevent that. You were supposed to die. But at the last minute Dios gave me a new datacore. Right before I left UMCPHQ. He sent me to Billingate to get you away from Succorso. That may have been the only reason. Blowing up the installation was just an excuse.

'He let Succorso have you in the first place to protect you from Fasner. So Fasner couldn't *suppress* you. As far as Warden Almighty Dios is concerned, you're more important than *God*.'

Her mouth sagged open. Standing behind Angus, Davies gaped like her twin. He must not have guessed – it had never occurred to her – that Warden might have had a good reason for selling her to Nick.

But Angus wasn't done. Without a pause he raised his face to the ceiling, stretched out his arms. Standing rigid, as if he were remembering a crucifixion, he shouted, 'And you're going to trust me *because I'm free*!'

The sheer intensity of his cry shocked the bridge like a static charge. In an instant it seemed to transport Morn into the heart of the gulf; drop her down the long wall of a chasm. She knew at once that he meant a freedom far greater than any mere relief from the compulsion of his priority-codes.

Free to rape and kill; demean; betray.

While she fell, he whirled toward Min Donner.

'You made a deal.' His voice sank to a malign whisper. 'Morn is in command. And you keep telling us how you believe in Warden Dios. You talk about "restitution". Show me you mean it.

'Hold up your hand.'

Min faced him like the muzzle of a gun. Mounting violence beat in her temples; in the veins of her neck. She must have recognized the threat of Angus' demand. Nevertheless her commitments required her to accept it. Slowly she lifted her right hand, the palm open and outward, as if she meant to take an oath.

'Min,' Dolph cautioned her tensely, 'I don't like this.'

Morn tried to say Angus' name, urge him to stop. But an obstruction in her chest blocked her voice. She continued falling; plunging into the depths of an immeasurable realization.

Because I'm free!

Warden had –

Before anyone could react, Angus aimed one fist at the ED director. A thin streak of crimson fire shot out from between his knuckles. Instantly his laser burned a hole through the center of Min's hand.

Morn gaped at the wound as if she'd struck the bottom of the abyss. Betray –

Angus had turned against them.

Warden had turned him against them?

No, this wasn't the bottom: she had farther to fall.

Across the bridge, shouts of dismay and anger rang off the bulkheads. Too late, Davies hauled Min's pistol out of his pocket; charged at Angus. Frantically he jammed the handgun at the side of Angus' head. 'You sonofabitch!' he yelped. 'What do you think you're doing?'

Roaring, Captain Ubikwe hurled his bulk at Angus. Glessen

and Sergei Patrice were already halfway to the command station.

Min froze them with a raw shout: '*Stay where you are!*'

Dolph stumbled to a halt a stride away from Angus. His boots skidding, Patrice stopped. Glessen waved his fists, driven by fury; but Min's authority held him back.

Terrible self-coercion intensified her features. Her cheeks and forehead seemed to burn, set afire by the heat of their underlying bones. Murder and restraint wailed against each other in her eyes.

'Don't you understand?' she rasped at Dolph; at Glessen and Patrice. Her pain echoed as if she were screaming. 'We don't have time for this.'

Angus lowered his fist. 'Oh, put that thing away,' he sneered at Davies. Cruel humor twisted his face. 'You're too scared to think. Deciding to let the Amnion have you has turned you stupid. She'll heal. Hell, laser burns are self-cauterizing. She didn't even *bleed*. And I made a point of not hitting bone.'

Involuntarily Davies lowered the gun. He didn't know how to meet Angus' scorn.

Not hitting bone?

Angus was a cyborg: maybe he could be that accurate.

If this wasn't a betrayal, what was it?

Trembling, Min stalked over to the command station; displayed her burned hand in front of Morn. She'd been called Warden Dios' 'executioner'. Her arm shook with the force of blows she chose not to strike.

Transfixed, Morn stared at the wound. From Min's palm she caught a faint whiff of roasted meat.

Even this hurt, this indignity, the ED director tried to endure in the name of her beliefs.

'Just so you'll know,' she snarled like the cut of a drill, 'I also have orders to keep you alive. They're practically the only orders Warden gave me. He sent me aboard this ship to make sure you survive.

'If you decided to surrender yourself to *Calm Horizons*, I would have to stop you.'

449

For a moment she fixed a killing glare on Angus. She didn't speak: at first she kept her fury to herself. But then her damaged fist flashed out like lightning; struck him high on the cheek. Despite her burned flesh, she hit him so hard his head rocked sideways.

He responded instantly. His return blow reached halfway to her head before she could react – before Morn even saw him move –

– carried that far and stopped. A forearm's length from Min's face, his fist paused, then withdrew. He lowered his arms. A red welt swelled on his cheek.

Grinning like a beast, he remarked, 'I guess that's fair.'

Deliberately he pushed his hands into the pockets of his shipsuit.

Poised on the balls of her feet, Min studied him as if he confused her. Dark speculation thronged in her gaze. Then she seemed to see something she recognized in him. She nodded once, harshly, and turned away.

'Warden must want you alive for a reason,' she told Morn. A stifled clamor frayed her voice. 'I sure as hell hope it's a good one.'

She might have been shouting, Make up your *mind*!

Stiffly she went back to the communications station.

Morn opened her mouth and found herself gasping. Her heart jolted as if she'd been struck, not Angus; as if the blow Min delivered and the one he repressed had both been aimed at her.

For a reason –

With a flash of laser fire and an instant of restraint, Angus had made the terms of her dilemma clear. He'd demonstrated his freedom – and his self-control.

In some way Warden had let him go. She was so precious to Warden that he'd released Angus altogether.

And now Min challenged her to make the choices she'd been given. Trust Warden. Trust what he'd done to Angus. Set aside her fears and her shame; her visceral revulsion.

Or reject –

There: that was the bottom; the final question. Earlier Min

450

had talked about 'restitution'. She believed Warden wanted to end Holt Fasner's power over human space – and human-kind's future. She'd said, *He's going after Fasner. He's trying to bring the Dragon down.* That was restitution of a kind. And submitting himself to *Calm Horizons* was another. By that means he'd preserved his authority over – and his responsibility for – the UMCP: he'd created the conditions under which Min could lawfully refuse Fasner's commands.

And now –

Because I'm free!

Was that yet another form of restitution?

Warden had freed Angus because she'd already done so. Before he caused Angus' collapse, he'd said, *You know him better than I do, Morn. I'll trust your judgment.*

Her judgment? Hers?

Here was the floor of the chasm. Humankind's future, as well as millions of lives, depended on her *judgment*. And self-destruct was the only answer she'd ever truly understood.

It's got to stop.

'Glessen,' Dolph ordered distantly, 'get a first-aid kit for Director Donner.' Impotent passion seemed to drive him deep into himself, where he couldn't be reached. 'Help her take care of that hand. I doubt she'll agree to go to sickbay.'

'Aye, Captain,' the targ officer answered through his teeth. Cursing under his breath, he moved to obey.

'You can sit down, Sergei,' Dolph went on. 'Director Donner will let us know when she wants us to do something for her.'

Without a word Patrice did as he was told.

Morn inhaled with a shudder. A passion of her own gath-ered in her. *I need a better answer.* She felt it mount behind her eyes; flush like fever across her cheeks; burn in her wounded arm. For a terrible moment she seemed to under-stand everything – and she hated it all. Too many people had asked too much of her; cost her too much.

Her time had come.

'Angus, listen to me.' Her voice ripped at him. 'Listen good, because I've had all of you I can stand.'

451

In time with the labor of her heart she struck the edge of the command board with her cast, sending small shards of hurt like splintered glass along her arm.

'That's *Min Donner* you shot. She's been honest with us ever since we came aboard. She's told us the truth. She's kept her word. She's left me in command, even though she knows why that's wrong as well as you do. *You* are a butcher and a rapist, and you *sell people to the Amnion*! I will not *tolerate* any more damage from you!

'*Is that clear?*'

With all her strength she hit the board hard enough to shatter her cast.

An instant of pain stopped her. At first she couldn't tell whether the partly healed bones of her arm held. She didn't care. Peeling away broken pieces of acrylic with her good hand, she flung them one at a time at Angus' face: accusations with ragged edges; raw demands; threats. But when her arm came free from the remains of the cast, she found that she could flex her fingers and elbow without too much discomfort.

Angus didn't flinch as the light fragments struck him; made no effort to avoid them. If he blinked to protect his eyes, she didn't see it. Instead of reacting, he faced her like a man who no longer knew anything about fear. Or maybe his fears had become so profound that they made him sure. He waited until she was done before he let himself rub a hand across his stung cheeks and forehead.

'I didn't hit her,' he murmured thickly. 'Don't you get it? I could have broken her skull.'

He might have been echoing an earlier appeal. *I could have stopped you. But I didn't. Because I made a deal with you.*

'Yes, I get it!' she flamed at him, fierce as impact fire. 'I *get* it, God damn you. Warden removed the restrictions. Now you can hurt UMCP personnel. You can hurt anybody you want. But you haven't answered any of my questions.

'I'm *sick* of it. You're going to start *now*. Or I'll tell Davies to shoot you where you stand!'

Davies may not have understood her; but he didn't hesitate. He moved quickly away from Angus – out of Angus' range – and raised his gun at his father. Like her, his eyes were shouts of panic and determination.

Still Angus faced her without faltering. The muscles at the corners of his jaw bunched and loosened.

'We're going to rescue Dios,' he told her. 'I said I know how. Isn't that what you want?'

He shocked her out of her fury. Despite the glimpses of clarity he'd given her, she hadn't grasped the full truth about him; hadn't gone far enough to guess the changes implied by his new power to harm – and to withhold.

'Did you think Dios was *playing* when he talked to me?' he asked her stricken face. 'Knocking me down just to show he could do it? You know better than that. You know *him* better – He has codes he never told me about. Commands I can't block. And he untied me.'

A note of exultation began to beat in Angus' rough voice.

'When he said "apotheosis", every damn database in my computer came on-line. Most of that stuff is there for emergencies. I couldn't access it unless my programming decided I need it. But now I have it all.

'I know everything there is to know about this ship.' He indicated *Punisher* with a jerk of his head. 'I know everything DA ever heard about Amnion equipment, weaponry, capabilities. Shit, I even know why I was designed this way.'

By degrees Davies' grip on the pistol loosened. His hand sank, pushed down by the weight of Angus' words. Like Morn, he stared as if he'd been rendered helpless.

Min waited, silent and motionless, while Glessen slathered tissue plasm onto her hand, covered her wound with a bandage. Bloodshed filled her eyes; but she did nothing to interfere.

Everyone else on the bridge listened like cold death.

Angus leaned his eagerness closer to Morn.

'But that wasn't all. By itself it wouldn't do me any good. When he said "vasectomy", he shifted my core programming. Erased the command that protects UMCP personnel. I shot

Min Donner in the hand. You saw me. I could shoot her in the *head*, if I felt like it. If she quit being honest.'

Without warning he wheeled away from Morn and yelled savagely, 'I could go around this bridge and cut every one of you bastards in half!'

But I didn't.

An instant later an unnatural calm settled over him. He must have triggered his zone implants. Whether it happened voluntarily or involuntarily didn't make any difference.

He faced Morn again.

'That's why you're going to trust me,' he informed her. 'Because Dios could have forced me to do what he wants. I'm sure there's a self-destruct code he could use. Or he could have given it to you. But he didn't. Instead of putting a gun to my head, he let me go.

'Before he sent me to Billingate, he told me it's got to stop. Crimes like welding me.' Reflexive anger darkened his gaze. 'Making me into a machine. Or suppressing that anti-mutagen. He said they've got to stop.

'Well, he stopped one of them. He kept *that* promise.

'Once I get him off that fucking warship, I'm going to ask him why he picked us to stop the rest of his crimes for him.' At last Angus allowed himself a trace of sarcasm. 'If I don't like the answer, I'll probably kill him.'

Still no one spoke. Davies and everyone else waited like Min for Morn's response.

Kept that *promise.*

Smiling across the bridge, Ciro announced, 'I know what to do. He told me all about it.'

The look in Mikka's eyes as she watched Morn was bleak and beyond hope; desolate as a derelict.

Because she'd lived so long with self-destruct, Morn recognized that in his own mind Ciro was already dead. There was nothing she – or Mikka – could do to save him.

Angus seemed to press himself against the edge of the command board. 'I'll tell you anything you want to know.' Despite his eagerness for freedom, he did his best to persuade her. 'But you don't need that. You just need to accept it.

Stop suffering over what Dios wants, or Fasner, or Vestabule. You know what you came here to do. So get started. Leave the rest to me.'

Morn flexed her sore fingers; rubbed at her aching forearm. She felt strangely naked without her cast, as if she, too, had been released.

Her judgment.

Warden Dios thought she was *more important than* God. He'd saved her from the consequences of his own dishonesty by selling her to Nick. Then he'd welded Angus to rescue her. When the crisis of *Calm Horizons*' encroachment became too great for him to control, he freed Angus to carry out his designs for him.

Humankind's future depended on her.

Ciro knew what to do.

The decision was one she could make.

Nevertheless she postponed it for another minute. Studying Angus closely, she asked, 'How much of all this is in your databases?'

She meant, How much do you know about what Warden wants?

If the UMCP director kept one promise, he might keep others.

Angus scowled at her delay. 'Some of it.' He contained his frustration, however. 'Resources, mostly. Possibilities. Applications. I don't think even Dios saw this exact disaster coming. He's just good at planning for emergencies.

'But I know how to use it,' he avowed. He might have been taking an oath – the same oath Min took when she'd raised her hand as a target. Then he laughed like a burst of thrust distortion. 'Maybe *that's* why he picked me. There's nobody better.'

When she felt sure he'd told the truth, she was ready.

Days ago, in another lifetime, he'd pleaded with her to let him edit his datacore. *I made a deal with you,* he'd reminded her. *I gave you the zone implant control. You let me live.* Then he'd said, *I kept my end. Whether you kept yours or not.*

As far as she could tell, that was the truth as well.

When I hurt you, I hurt myself.

She knew how to trust him.

'All right.' To herself she sounded unnaturally calm; as calm as he was. Somehow she reached past her fears to the answer she needed. If lost Deaner Beckmann's hypothesis was accurate, the sheer gravity of her plight had pulled her to a new kind of clarity. Davies had already agreed to take the risk. 'We'll do it your way. As soon as you tell us exactly what you've got in mind. You're playing by new rules. So am I. Maybe we can change the rules of the whole game.'

Then she leaned back in her g-seat and let an unfamiliar quiet settle over her heart.

WARDEN

Warden had plenty of time to think while he waited for Morn to reestablish contact; all the time he needed. More than enough to realize how much he'd staked on her.

God, he'd gambled *everything* –

Unless or until Hashi found the evidence he hunted, she was the only witness who could support Koina's accusations against Holt Fasner. Without her, anything Koina said depended solely for its credibility on Warden's personal statements – which might be dismissed as self-serving fabrications.

In addition Morn was in command of *Punisher*. She'd reached some kind of accommodation with Min Donner; enlisted Min's fierce integrity to back her up. Now she held the physical force to plunge the whole solar system into battle and ruin if Warden couldn't convince Marc Vestabule to agree to her terms.

She and Davies had helped Angus edit his datacore. She'd admitted as much. And she'd known about *Viable Dreams* before she made that decision. For some reason he'd told her the most damning thing he could about himself. Yet she'd trusted him.

Warden Dios was directly, personally responsible for much of the abuse and degradation she'd experienced since *Starmaster*'s death. But now he had no choice except to leave the fate of everything he needed and desired in her hands.

He could have killed Angus. Hashi had told him how to

do it. Instead, however, he'd elected to risk humankind's future on Morn's judgment.

Angus' death would gain nothing.

On the other hand, setting him free might be worse –

The UMCP director had time enough, and more, to consider all these things while he waited to hear from Morn again. Five minutes at least – probably closer to ten. If the small chamber where Vestabule kept him held a chronometer, he couldn't read it. But there wasn't enough time in all creation for him to convince himself that he'd made the right choice.

The best he could say on his own behalf was that he'd committed his loyalty – and surrendered his life – to the two people in human space who had the greatest right to demand such things from him.

Finally an indicator on the alien console caught Vestabule's attention. With his human hand, he activated incomprehensible controls; and at once Morn's voice entered the room.

'Director Dios, this is Morn Hyland.'

The sound was almost frighteningly clean, immediate. *Calm Horizons'* equipment filtered out *Punisher's* thrust distortion with preternatural ease. Morn might have been speaking to him from the far side of the room.

Warden took hold of the edge of the console, pulled himself closer to the pickup.

'This is Warden, Morn.' Despite the potential cost of anything he said, he responded firmly. 'We need to resolve this now. I can't keep *Calm Horizons* waiting any longer.'

'I understand that, Director.' Morn's calm was deeper than his: it hinted at depths he couldn't measure. 'But our position hasn't changed. Vector and Davies have agreed to surrender themselves. I refuse. And Angus –'

Vestabule hardly moved. Nevertheless his posture conveyed an increased tension; a poised threat.

'Director,' Morn went on as if she feared nothing the Amnioni could do, 'Angus can't make this kind of choice. When you spoke to him, he collapsed. Whatever you said hit him hard. And since then he's been like a crazy man. If I begged him to do what you want, he wouldn't listen to me. If I held a gun to his head, he would probably laugh at me.

'As I've already told you' – her severity could have drawn blood – 'I will not impose the decision you want on anyone. I would rather die fighting. If Angus can't choose to go of his own free will, then he isn't going.'

Warden flicked a look at Vestabule's closed face. 'Morn –' he began urgently.

She overrode him. 'I heard you the last time. The Amnion don't consider that acceptable.'

The accusations she might have leveled against him were present in the room; as clear as her voice.

'Director Dios, I'm willing to fight about this' – for a heartbeat or two she paused – 'but I would prefer to reach some other agreement. Tell Vestabule he can have *Trumpet* instead of Angus. She's intact. Her drives failed – we had some sabotage – but everything else is undamaged. Datacore, weapons systems, everything.'

He can have *Trumpet*?

Caught by fear and wonder, Warden stared at the console speaker. The place where her words reached him was all he could see of her.

Have *Trumpet*? Are you serious?

That's brilliant!

Or insane.

She was saying, '*Punisher* doesn't have a shuttle. Vector and Davies will be using the command module. But that's not a problem. The module can piggyback *Trumpet* at the same time.'

Crisply she finished, 'Tell Vestabule that's our best offer.'

Before Warden could reply, Vestabule silenced the pickup. He faced the UMCP director squarely. His human eyelid fluttered with discomfort in the acrid air. Colors which might have indicated distress seethed through his aura.

'It does not suffice,' he pronounced.

At once Warden cried, '*It must!*' He no longer cared how much desperation he betrayed. The time had come to show it.

You inhuman bastard, are you bluffing?

Vestabule shook his head. 'You cannot control your cyborg,' he stated inflexibly.

Perhaps he meant to accuse Warden of lying. Earlier Warden had said, *There are codes I can use that will affect Angus.* He'd deliberately misled the Amnioni. Now he had to accept the outcome.

Nevertheless he protested falsely, urgently, 'Something happened when he edited his datacore.' Protecting Angus as well as he could. 'He made changes I don't know about. They must have corrupted parts of his programming. Are you going to throw away Davies and Vector and millions of lives over *that*?'

Through his teeth, he countered, 'I'm not the one who taught him how to edit a SOD-CMOS chip. *You* are.'

Again Vestabule shook his head. That motion of denial may have been the last remaining vestige of his former identity.

'There is human treachery here.'

If he knew that, he wasn't bluffing.

Still Warden tried to argue. As if he were breaking under the strain, he croaked, 'What do you want from me? You can have Davies. You can have Vector. You can have *Trumpet*, for God's sake. You've even got me. What more do you think I can do?'

Vestabule didn't use his throat pickup; didn't speak to any other Amnioni. Apparently he felt no need to consult with his kind. He'd been invested with decisiveness.

Slowly he extended his human hand, palm upward, toward Warden. 'Give me your suicide capsule.'

Your humanity –

Quietly, as if he no longer needed it, Warden's heart seemed to stop. He stared at Vestabule for a long moment, trying to guess how much treachery the Amnioni understood.

But Vestabule's features made it clear that he'd come to the end of his capacity for negotiation. He gazed blank, brutal ruin into Warden's face.

When he saw that there was no other way he could save his kind from Holt Fasner and war, Warden jerked up his breathing mask, took Hashi's black capsule out of his mouth, and placed it in the Amnioni's palm.

Vestabule accepted it stolidly. His conflicted features gave no hint of triumph.

For the last time he activated the console pickup. 'Tell Morn Hyland that her offer has been accepted. We require that *Punisher*'s command module will be detached to convey Davies Hyland, Vector Shaheed and *Trumpet* here within ten minutes.

'If you are wise, you will remind her that the consequences of any false dealing will be extreme.'

Warden nodded dully.

He'd seen Vestabule dispose of the 'slow' mutagen with which he'd been threatened earlier. Maybe that particular mutagen was in short supply aboard *Calm Horizons*. Maybe there was none left.

The man responsible for humankind's future had nothing else to hope for.

DOLPH

Six minutes later Captain Dolph Ubikwe sat where he belonged: at the command station on the bridge of the UMCP cruiser *Punisher*.

His restoration pleased him.

Everyone else was out of place, however. Only Davies Hyland and Vector Shaheed kept him company. All his duty officers had left the bridge, taking the rest of *Trumpet*'s people with them. They'd passed through the aperture to the main body of the ship as the cruiser's command functions were transferred to the auxiliary bridge. Even Min Donner and the woman who'd usurped him, Morn Hyland, were gone.

Now servos whined as they closed bulkhead doors to seal the aperture, isolating the module. At the same time the module's separate maintenance systems and power came to life. Between the hulls relays unclipped instrument and computer leads, shut down atmosphere connectors, disengaged communications channels. When the module's thrust drive had warmed enough to take over from the energy cells, and diagnostics had confirmed her integrity, her spaceworthiness, the massive clamps which gripped her to the rest of the cruiser would release, and she would drift free.

Then she would begin the short voyage which would deliver her lonely human cargo to the doom of the Amnion.

In a sense, nothing was as it should have been. *Calm Horizons*' guns held Suka Bator, UMCPHQ and much of the planet hostage. And Director Dios was effectively a hostage as well. Grimly he bartered human beings to satisfy the Amnion. Meanwhile the new PR director, Koina Hannish, had been sent to Earth to level appalling accusations against the organization Captain Ubikwe served – charges which were apparently true. Morn Hyland intended to contact the GCES so that she could add her testimony to the specifications of malfeasance and corruption.

On top of all that, Dolph had nothing except the command module. Ensign Hyland still held the rest of his ship. And the UMCPED director, Min Donner herself, had given her loyalty to *Trumpet*'s people, despite the personal harm they'd done her.

Beyond question the whole situation was an atrocity. Captain Dolph Ubikwe, a good cop, and *Punisher*'s rightful commander, should have writhed in chagrin and outrage; seethed with counter-plots to recover his place in the moral order to which he'd committed his life.

Well, he must have lost his mind. All this stress – chasing *Trumpet* and fighting *Calm Horizons*, dodging betrayal, absorbing terrible revelations, losing his ship – must have stripped the gears of his cerebral mechanism. He wasn't upset. Hell, he wasn't even angry. While he ran his board, prepared the module for detachment, a song seemed to tug at the edges of his heart. From time to time he caught himself whistling through his teeth.

Separation from *Punisher* freed him from an essential conflict. He no longer needed to oppose events, or suffer indignities in silence, or watch passively while other people played for humankind's future. He was back where he belonged. His insubordinate spirit surveyed a solar system crowded with terrors and treachery, and approved.

From the simpler, cleaner perspective of the command module, Dolph saw that Min was doing the right thing. By her own standards, so was Morn. The decision which both Vector and Davies had made to surrender themselves showed a kind of courage which left Dolph in awe. And that damn cyborg, Angus Thermopyle –

Angus was doing the right thing absolutely.

463

While they'd repaired *Trumpet*'s drives together, Angus had revealed quite a bit about how his mind worked. Apparently he had a talent for desperation, an instinct for extreme solutions, which Dolph couldn't help admiring. When Angus explained how he proposed to rescue Warden, *Punisher*'s captain had been the first to approve.

Despite the danger, Dolph Ubikwe was positively delighted to offer that malign, welded rapist and butcher all the support he could.

Now he ran helm, scan, data and communications – the only functions the module still possessed – from his board alone. He didn't need help. All the other stations had been shut down. The module was no more than a shuttle; almost a cripple. But her commander had no complaint. Small as she was, this vessel was his. Angus had given him that, and he was satisfied.

Perhaps Angus had recognized the piratical nature of Dolph's approach to law enforcement. In a situation like this, the cyborg could trust Dolph completely.

When the last of his diagnostics showed green, Captain Ubikwe looked up at his companions and growled happily, 'Christ on a crutch. If my dear, departed mother had known I was going to end up in a mess like this, she would have drowned me at birth. It's a good thing she couldn't see the future. One look at the entrails of a chicken would have sent her off her head. Then they probably would have had to tie her down to keep her from killing my father too.'

Neither Davies nor Vector laughed. They were in too much peril for jokes: if anything went wrong, they would be the first to pay for it. Nevertheless the geneticist mustered up a wry smile. 'If I may say so, Captain,' he murmured, 'your mother must have been a remarkable woman.'

'Say what you like,' Dolph allowed expansively. 'There aren't any rules here. This is about as down-and-dirty as it gets. If you worry too much about being polite, you'll just wear yourself out.'

After a moment he asked more seriously, 'Do you have everything you need?'

464

Vector had settled himself into the helm station g-seat. Davies sat at the blank targ board. Both of them had already put on their EVA suits, leaving only the helmets and gloves aside. Vector's expression was calm, but wan; worn by fatigue and the old pain of severe arthritis. He rested as much as possible, husbanding his strength.

For a while earlier Davies had conveyed the impression that he'd been exhausted by the moral strain of making his decision to surrender. But now his features had recovered some of their intensity. His gaze showed better focus: the lines of his face were sharper: he paid more attention. Paradoxically, the change seemed to increase his resemblance to both his parents. He'd inherited Angus' calculation as well as Morn's conviction: he, too, understood extreme solutions.

He didn't answer Dolph's question with words. Instead he picked up his left glove, reached into it, and pulled out one of the weapons Angus had given him. It was a meter of monofilament line weighted at both ends and crusted with fused polysilicate granules as sharp as diamond chips – a tool normally used to saw steel in small spaces. Then he opened his belt pouch to reveal a shard of rigid plastic whetted like a dirk. According to Angus, they would escape detection, but anything more useful – especially a gun – would be caught.

Davies returned the coil to his glove, sealed his pouch, and referred Dolph's question to Vector.

Shaheed also carried a dirk; but he didn't appear to consider it important. Instead he held up a vial. 'This is the antimutagen Hashi Lebwohl gave Nick,' he said slowly. 'What's left of it, anyway. We've used more than I thought we would.' He shrugged. 'We're down to two capsules. They're good for roughly four hours each.

'Davies will get one when we reach *Calm Horizons*. I'll take the other.' He cleared his throat. 'Just in case Marc Vestabule turns out to be more treacherous than we are.' Then he looked squarely at Dolph. 'Unfortunately, that doesn't leave any protection for Director Dios. We'll have to hope he can defend himself with his suicide pill.'

Dolph frowned. Warden's vulnerability worried him. Ever

since he'd heard about the mutagen which had ruled *Soar*'s captain and damaged Ciro, he'd felt a visceral alarm on Warden's behalf. The bare idea of such a mutagen made his skin crawl. The possibility that Warden might be injected with it –

But Warden's fate was out of Dolph's hands, at least to that extent. He was doing everything he could for the UMCP director by transporting Davies, Vector and *Trumpet* to *Calm Horizons*.

'All right,' he told Vector. Deliberately he turned back to his board. After scanning his alerts and readouts, he announced, 'Secure for detachment.'

A couple of keys opened a communications channel. '*Trumpet*,' he said to his pickup, 'this is Captain Ubikwe. You about ready? I got the impression Vestabule is in no mood for delays.'

'We've *been* ready, fat man,' Angus broadcast at once. His voice rasped in the speakers: a concentrated threat. 'Sealed and drifting. You can pick us up as soon as you're clear.

'But for God's sake,' he warned, 'watch your attitude. And leak as much emission as you can. Once we're piggybacked, I want to be occluded all the way. Make *Calm Horizons* think that's normal. The scan net is down, so they won't be able to see us until we get close. I want to hide the fact that our systems are live as long as possible.'

Occluded all the way. That was going to be a tricky piece of navigation. Dolph had his work cut out for him.

He didn't hesitate. Keying another channel, he announced, '*Punisher*, the command module is secure for detachment. Give me the word, and I'll hit the clamps.'

After no more than a heartbeat, Morn answered distantly, 'We're ready here, Captain. *Trumpet* is clear. You can go anytime.' She paused, then added, 'Just be careful.' Her tone hinted at fervor and loss.

Before Dolph could reply, Davies surged out of his g-seat and approached the command pickup. Without asking Dolph's permission, he answered, 'Don't worry about us, Morn. You do your part. We'll be okay.' His voice echoed

Angus' harshness. 'Vestabule isn't as human as he thinks. No matter what happens, we'll give him a few surprises.'

He glanced at Dolph, then stated distinctly, 'I didn't say it before, but I think this is the right answer.'

'I hope so, Davies.' For what may have been the first time since she'd boarded *Punisher*, Morn sounded like she was smiling. 'I sure don't have a better one.'

As far as Dolph was concerned, she didn't need one. He liked this answer just fine.

Davies returned to his station. He and Vector closed their belts. Dolph confirmed that his companions were secure, then began typing the commands to initiate detachment.

The metallic clangor of the locking clamps as they released sounded like the opening salvo in the battle for humankind's survival.

MIKKA

Crowded with sorrow, Mikka Vasaczk sat at *Trumpet*'s command station while Captain Ubikwe maneuvered to grapple onto the gap scout's hull, and Angus transmitted his last instructions to both the module and *Punisher*.

Her brother meant to die. If Angus understood that, he didn't admit it. Instead he made bizarre, implausible provisions for everyone's survival. But Morn knew. Mikka had recognized the knowledge in Morn's eyes when Morn had asked her if she would aid Angus. And she suspected that Vector knew as well. Sadly, awkwardly, he'd hugged Ciro before they parted; and Ciro had smiled his demented smile, but he hadn't returned Vector's clasp.

Yet they all – and Ciro more than any of them – wanted Mikka to help him end his life.

'We've *been* ready, fat man,' Angus had told Captain Ubikwe aboard the module.

When the module reached them, the grapples would take hold of *Trumpet* and position her so that one of her airlocks met an emergency access port in the module's hull. There magnetic clamps would grip her while Captain Ubikwe conveyed her across the fatal gap between *Punisher* and *Calm Horizons*. But there was nothing Mikka could do to secure the gap scout; nothing for her to do along the way. Her duties wouldn't begin until they reached the warship, and Angus and Ciro left the ship.

Ciro meant to die. Somehow Angus had offered him a way

out of the distress Sorus Chatelaine had inflicted on him, and he intended to take it.

He wanted Mikka to help him. When Morn and Angus had asked her to run *Trumpet*'s command board, they were asking her to assist as well as condone her brother's suicide.

'If this works,' Angus transmitted to Morn while the gap scout drifted, 'I'll get my ship back.' Presumably he meant *Trumpet*, not *Bright Beauty*. His old tincan vessel was dismantled months ago. 'That makes it worth the risk.'

Did he think the cops would let him go? Turn a welded cyborg loose, with all those enhancements, all that capacity for destruction? If he did, Min Donner didn't contradict him. Maybe she trusted Warden Dios to control him.

'I hope so,' Morn replied distantly. 'This whole gamble is your idea. If you don't see it through –' She paused as if she couldn't find an adequate threat, then finished like a shrug, 'I'll kill myself.'

Angus snorted a guttural laugh. 'No, you won't. Not anymore.' At once he added, 'But you better jump like hell when the excitement starts. Even if everything goes right, there's going to be a gap where *Calm Horizons* can take a crack at you. You can bet your ass she'll do it.'

His life depended on that gap. So did everyone else's. Even his useless provisions for Ciro's survival depended on it.

'I understand,' Morn answered. 'I think Patrice can handle it.'

That was all the farewell they said to each other.

It was more than Mikka and Ciro had done.

Earlier – long hours of exhaustion ago – Angus had taken Ciro and Captain Ubikwe aboard *Trumpet*, ostensibly to repair the gap scout's drives. By the time they'd returned to *Punisher*'s bridge, Ciro's fractured mind had found a focus. He'd learned how to name the death he desired.

Before Angus could stop him, he'd announced, *He showed me how to use the singularity grenades.* And when Mikka protested, he'd answered, *You don't have any idea what it's like, feeling like you have to kill everybody you care about.* Although

469

Morn must have known. Then he'd referred to Angus. *But he does.*

In turn Angus had defended him. *Ciro is working for me now. None of you understand what Sorus Chatelaine did to him.* As if he considered it an act of compassion, Angus had told the bridge, *Instead of kicking him into a corner like a goddamn puppy, I'm giving him something to do.*

At the time Mikka had been too stricken to argue. Or fight. Trapped by dismay, she'd made no effort to tear Angus' head off. And perhaps she truly had not understood. But later, while she'd watched over *Punisher*'s targ, brutalizing herself to perform that small service because everything else was beyond her, she'd learned to understand.

Angus was right. Ciro's plight was worse than Morn's.

In the end it wasn't the fact that *Soar*'s captain had forced a mutagen into him which had broken Ciro. It was his own compulsory terror. After he'd revealed what she'd done to him – and after Vector had flushed the mutagen out of his cells – he'd taken his first opportunity to obey her; sabotage *Trumpet*'s drives. At the time he must have believed that was necessary. He was no geneticist: any evidence Vector had shown him to convince him he was safe probably seemed too abstract to outweigh his fear. Involuntarily, instinctively, he must have *believed* Sorus' threat more than Vector's reprieve.

But then the hours had passed; and the antidote Sorus gave him had run out; and he'd remained human. And then his sanity had cracked. The knowledge of his own weakness had been more than he could bear.

The death he named for himself was a form of restitution.

Mikka understood. She would have been more than willing to die herself if anyone had offered her a chance to repair the harm she'd done Ciro by taking him aboard *Captain's Fancy*, introducing him to Nick.

For that reason, when Morn and Angus had asked her to run *Trumpet*'s command board, she'd agreed. Who could take her place? Angus, Morn and Davies all had other parts to play. And no one else knew the gap scout as well as she did.

For the same reason, she'd gone to sickbay as soon as she reached *Trumpet* and keyed the systems to dispense every stimulant available: stim and hype; caffeine tablets; complex pseudoendorphin supplements. Her weakness was as great as Ciro's. She'd run out of strength and courage: her mortality was too heavy to lift without drugs. Everything Angus had in mind for himself and Ciro, for Davies and Vector, for the command module and *Trumpet*, would be wasted if she failed to stay alert.

Because she understood so well, she was going to help her brother kill himself.

Like Angus, he'd already put on his EVA suit, although they were in no hurry; the trip to *Calm Horizons* would give them plenty of time. Only his head remained exposed: he'd left his helmet beside Angus' on the second's g-seat while he wandered around the bridge, whistling softly to himself. Mikka recognized the tune – a lullaby familiar from her childhood, when her mother was still alive to sing to her.

The sound made her want to wail.

For as long as she could, she ran diagnostic and parameter checks on the gap scout, making sure that Angus' repairs were stable; that thrust was ready for cold ignition; that passive scan was adequate to give her the information she would need; that the energy cells still held enough power to handle the load of the dispersion field generator. Unfortunately no amount of hype and stim could relieve her loss. After a while her concentration frayed into anguish.

Ciro's whistling was going to drive her mad.

The next time he passed between her and the display screens, she snapped, 'Do you have to do that?'

Inwardly she cringed at her unnecessary harshness. But his reaction hurt her more.

He stopped in front of her, faced her with sudden terror in his eyes and a bland, dissociated smile on his mouth. 'No, I don't.' His voice sounded as bleak as hard vacuum. The idea of singularity grenades had already sucked him away. And yet he offered softly, earnestly, 'I won't do it if you tell me not to.'

In dismay she saw that he was offering her the greatest and most terrible gift he could imagine: the gift of his life; of refusing his part in Angus' plans.

I won't do it –

At once Angus wheeled like a burst of flame on the boy. He may have wanted to shout in rage. You *what*? he might have protested. You little shit, *we're counting on you*! But he must have seen the death in Mikka's gaze. He caught himself in time; clamped his teeth shut.

– if you tell me not to.

She couldn't bear it.

They had alternatives. They could trade places. She could teach him how to initiate cold ignition. How to use the dispersion field. What to look for on scan. She could try to do his job for him. But the cost would be too high for both of them.

'Never mind,' she told him. She felt her heart tearing like a sheet of hardcopy; but he needed this gift from her more than she needed his. 'You know what you have to do. That's good enough for me.'

Roughly Angus turned away as if he wanted to hide his relief.

By degrees the terror faded from Ciro's eyes. After a moment he began to whistle again; resumed wandering the bridge.

He intended to die. The prospect didn't scare him at all.

KOINA

From her seat near Cleatus Fane, she moved through the crowded tension of the GCES Members and their aides toward the dais where Maxim Igensard presided on the strength of his position as Sen Abdullah's proxy.

The Special Counsel had demanded, *I have some questions I want to ask you.* Questions about Warden Dios and *Calm Horizons.* About *Trumpet* and treason. But Holt Fasner's FEA had intervened at once. *You don't have to submit to this,* he'd assured her. *I'll answer his questions. The UMC is responsible for the UMCP in any case.*

Both Maxim and Cleatus must have been accustomed to men like the late Godsen Frik – men for whom Protocol meant ambition and manipulation, not honesty. Now, in their separate ways, for their separate reasons, they may have begun to suspect that Warden's actions had brought them to the brink of disaster. But neither of them knew Koina. They had no idea what they were dealing with.

She'd ignored Fane's efforts to stop her. Hiding her trepidation behind a mask of bland professional confidence, she'd risen to her feet and told Maxim, *I'm ready, Special Counsel.*

To some extent, she accepted the perilous burden of carrying out Warden's orders precisely because Cleatus Fane had warned her against doing so. He was afraid of her: the strain on his face made that obvious. Through his PCR link to UMCHO – and Holt Fasner's informants in UMCPHQ – he probably knew as much as she did about

473

what was happening in space. Like Holt, he must at last have seen that events were moving in directions the Dragon hadn't anticipated and couldn't control. Perhaps he was starting to guess just how much damage she'd been sent here to do.

The nature of his loyalties helped her be sure of her own. His desire to silence her confirmed her determination to speak.

The UMC is responsible for the UMCP.

If it was possible, she intended to rub his nose – and Fasner's as well – in that responsibility.

'Director *Hannish*,' he hissed after her; but she didn't turn her head.

Clearly the Special Counsel didn't want her to join him on the dais. No doubt he preferred to thunder his accusations at her from above; overwhelm her with the sheer stature of his righteous indignation. *I've been accumulating evidence of the most malign kinds of malfeasance and corruption.* As soon as she left her seat, he raised his hands in a frustrated attempt to halt her.

'That isn't necessary, Director,' he snapped irritably. 'We can all hear you from there.'

For the moment she ignored him as she'd ignored Cleatus. She had much to say: questions to answer; risks to take; fears to face. But her first priority was to weaken Maxim's grip on the chamber, if she could. Despite the objections and incredulity of Members like Tel Burnish, Blaine Manse and Sixten Vertigus, Maxim had already half convinced the Council that Warden was guilty of treason. And in a sense he was right: *Calm Horizons* was here, with her super-light proton gun fixed on Suka Bator, as a direct result of Warden's decisions and actions. Before Koina did anything else, she needed to defuse the emotional force of the Special Counsel's accusations.

She made her way up to the dais in order to claim as much stature as he had.

Physically that was easy: she was a good fifteen centimeters taller. But the ominous intensity he radiated, the sense of critical mass he conveyed, made him seem larger. He gave the impression that there was no limit to how far he might expand.

On the surface, she had nothing to oppose him with except her beauty, her feigned calm – and her determination to tell the truth. But she also possessed a certain low cunning which she'd learned from Godsen Frik. His restless machinations had taught her a great deal.

As she joined him at the podium, Maxim turned to Abrim Len as if her presence were a point of order. 'President Len?'

Len had seated himself at the back of the dais while Maxim had the floor. He didn't rise to Maxim's demand; but he lifted his head with a cornered glitter in his eyes. 'You asked her to speak, Special Counsel.' His tone carried more resolution than Koina had expected from him. 'If you want her to answer your questions, she might as well stand up here where we can all see her.'

Before Igensard could reply, Captain Vertigus put in sharply, 'Give her the floor, Maxim.' The old Senior Member had his own reasons for outrage. As one of the UMCP's staunchest supporters, he must have been profoundly shaken by Maxim's allegations. 'We already know what your questions are. Her answers are what matter now.'

From the other side of the room, Punjat Silat offered, 'For what my poor opinion may be worth, I concur.' It was the first time Koina had heard the Senior Member for the Combined Asian Islands and Peninsulas speak. Apparently the drug he'd taken a short time ago had calmed his unsteady heart, at least for the present. Like his illness, his diffidence seemed to give him dignity. 'As spokeswoman for the UMCP – and, by extension, for Warden Dios himself – her response to these troubling charges is of paramount importance.'

Maxim acceded gracelessly. Scowling, he began, 'In that case, Director Hannish –'

Koina faced him with a cool smile. 'A moment, please, Special Counsel. It's my job as UMCP Director of Protocol to answer your questions, and I'll do it. But first –'

She shifted her attention to the Members and aides around the dais. At once her knees started trembling again. Every eye in the room clung to her urgently. Several men and women were sweating profusely, as if the air-processing had broken down. Others looked dangerously pale.

As smoothly as she could, Koina rested a hand on the podium for support.

'Because I *am* the UMCP Director of Protocol,' she stated as if she were in no danger, 'my dedicated channel to UMCPHQ Center carries more information than the general downlink.' She nodded toward her communications techs. 'Just now I received some news which isn't publicly available yet.

'I think you should know that *Punisher* has come home.'

Someone – Tel Burnish? – breathed fervently, 'Good.'

No one else spoke.

'Apparently,' Koina went on, 'her mission to "retrieve" *Trumpet*'s people – if that's the right word for it – was successful.' Ensign Morn Hyland was in command of the cruiser. 'She's joined our cordon of ships around *Calm Horizons*.'

Deliberately she made no mention of Morn. She wasn't ready to go that far. She had no idea what Morn's improbable authority aboard *Punisher* might signify. And she wanted to mislead Cleatus Fane. If he'd already received the same information from HO, he might think that she suppressed Morn's name in order to protect the Dragon; that he and his master could trust her after all.

While Maxim fumed at the delay, Koina continued, 'You all know that when Director Dios left UMCPHQ for *Calm Horizons* he named DA Director Hashi Lebwohl as acting director in his absence. No doubt Special Counsel Igensard will view Director Lebwohl's appointment in the worst possible light' – subtly she tried to weaken the ground under Maxim's feet – 'but the simple fact is that at the time he was the highest ranking UMCP officer on station. He became acting director by the plain logic of the chain of command.

'However, ED Director Min Donner has now returned aboard *Punisher*. Therefore Director Lebwohl has stepped down as acting director, and Director Donner has assumed those duties.'

476

Although her manner was grave, Koina put a smile into her voice. 'Frankly, I consider this good news. I respect Director Lebwohl more than the Special Counsel does, but after Warden Dios I can think of no one I would rather have command our defense than Min Donner.'

A rustle of approval crossed the chamber. Her ploy was working. Warden and Hashi may have been suspect, but Min's reputation held firm. Even Maxim had admitted as much.

Unfortunately Koina's knees refused to stop trembling. Her real work was still ahead of her.

'If this session had allowed you time to study the downlink,' she informed the Members, 'you would already be aware of at least one step Director Donner has taken for our protection. She's ordered the shutdown of our system-wide scan net. This deprives *Calm Horizons* of a valuable source of data.'

Sen Abdullah interrupted her in a spasm of indignation. '*Blinded* us?' he protested. 'What is *that* supposed to accomplish?'

Koina had no military experience: she was out of her depth on such subjects. Nevertheless she retorted sternly, '*Calm Horizons* has been blinded, Senior Member – at least in part. *We* haven't. Our ships can still share all the data they need with each other.

'Of course, the defensive's scan is more than adequate to maintain her proton cannon fix on us. That goes without saying. But she can no longer see everything in our solar system. This gives our own ships greater flexibility. It may improve their effectiveness.'

'I wouldn't have thought of it,' Sixten muttered, 'but it's probably worth a try. Hell, *any*thing's worth trying.'

Thank you, Koina told him silently. When she'd spoken to him from her shuttle earlier, she'd asked him for help with her decisions. At first he'd appeared to refuse her appeal. *You're a big girl, Koina*. But then he'd given her more assistance than she'd ever expected.

With the Council and Cleatus Fane watching her, however, she couldn't afford to admit aloud how much she was in the old captain's debt. Instead she turned to look at Maxim.

'I'm ready now, Special Counsel.' As ready as she would ever be without evidence. To some extent she'd succeeded at disrupting Igensard's sway. There was nothing left for her to do except answer his questions, defy the FEA, and pray that some kind of corroboration arrived in time to save Warden's hopes. 'Where do you want to start?'

With her smile and her collegial manner, she made it as difficult as she could for him to treat her like an opponent.

But his particular hostility was impervious to her charm. Apparently her interference with the role he'd arranged for himself confirmed her status as his enemy. The concentration in his gaze sharpened and swelled. He no longer fumed. Unlike a number of the people around him, he seemed proof against sweat. In a flash of insight, Koina guessed that any personal irritation he may have felt was subsumed by a larger ambition: to best her in front of the assembled Council; to wrest what he wanted from her despite her resistance.

To prove himself against her –

She had no idea what he wished to prove. Or to whom he wished to prove it. But she recognized the peril.

Maxim Igensard would stop at nothing.

'Unfortunately, Director Hannish, I have so many questions that I hardly know which one to ask first.' He spoke to her, but he didn't look at her: he faced the Members – and Cleatus Fane. His stare seemed to quarter the room as if he were searching for weakness. 'As I've already suggested, my investigation into the Angus Thermopyle case, and my concerns about what President Len calls "the immediate crisis", have given me an impression of almost global corruption and wrongdoing. All of it must be accounted for, in one way or another.'

'I agree completely,' Koina put in earnestly. Maxim's voice wasn't particularly high or shrill, but it had a quality which reminded her of a sonic cutter. The longer he spoke, the more his tone abraded her nerves. Was the man incapable of making a point without all this self-righteousness?

'That's admirable, Director,' he rasped in vexation. He didn't like being interrupted. 'I hope you mean it.

'Since we must start somewhere,' he resumed, 'let me

478

remind you of a statement you made moments ago. You said that *Punisher*'s "mission to 'retrieve' *Trumpet*'s people was successful". As you confessed yourself, "retrieve" is an interesting choice of words. You didn't say "capture", which is a duty we might reasonably expect of a UMCP cruiser. After all, *Trumpet* is a UMCP gap scout supposedly stolen by a convicted illegal and his accomplice. And you didn't say "rescue", which might well be *Punisher*'s appropriate response when a human ship is hunted by the Amnion.

'Director Hannish, what's so special about Angus Thermopyle and Milos Taverner that they have to be "retrieved" instead of "arrested" or "saved"? Maybe if you can tell us that we'll begin to understand what both *Punisher* and *Trumpet* were doing in the Massif-5 system.'

Koina met his opening with her best professional detachment. 'A fair question, Special Counsel.' Her tone betrayed none of the quivering in her legs. 'I'll try to give you a fair answer.'

But if he didn't consider it necessary to look at her when he spoke, she saw no reason to reply as if her answer were directed at him. Leaning only slightly on the podium, she gazed out at the strained faces around her.

'However, I feel I should first explain that I was extensively briefed for this session. In one form or another Director Dios and I have discussed most of the issues which now confront the Council. He gave me explicit orders to answer the Special Counsel's questions as accurately as I can.'

It was vital for the Members to understand that Warden had authorized everything she would reveal; that he'd instructed her to damn him.

'Bear with me, please. This gets complicated.'

She paused as if to collect her thoughts; but in fact she was mustering her courage for a plunge which might carry humankind to disaster. Then she announced more formally, 'When Director Dios and Director Lebwohl addressed the Council by video conference a few days ago, they did not tell you the truth about Angus Thermopyle, Milos Taverner and *Trumpet*.'

At her side she felt Maxim expand with vindication.

'Personally, I deplore this,' she said. 'Professionally, I grant that it may have been necessary.' Necessary to advance Warden's struggle against Holt Fasner; to expose Fasner's responsibility for the UMCP's crimes. 'Putting the matter crudely, Captain Thermopyle was being sent on a dangerous mission, and he needed "cover". Director Dios and Director Lebwohl lied to you in order to protect that mission. Any hint of the truth would have been fatal.'

Vivid consternation roiled the chamber. Someone rasped, 'Fatal how?' Sigurd Carsin pronounced, 'That's bullshit.' Other Members swore, muttered; consulted with their aides. But Blaine Manse's voice carried over the protests and indignation.

Rising from her seat, she demanded, 'Was *anything* we heard during that conference true? What about Director Lebwohl's statement that you gave one of your ensigns – wasn't her name Morn Hyland? – to a DA agent so he could use her in some kind of covert operation against Thanatos Minor?'

Usually the Member for Betelgeuse Primary affected a bantering detachment from every subject except sex; but now an almost sensual anger throbbed in her tone.

'Director Lebwohl said something about faking an antimutagen for his agent to sell. And letting the agent have poor Morn Hyland so he could save himself by selling her if he got caught in his own trap.'

Confronting Koina, Blaine wore her sexuality like an accusation. She may have guessed that Morn had been sold *to* Nick rather than given to him to sell elsewhere.

Hashi had said more. He'd told the Council, *Ensign Hyland was irretrievably compromised. We believe Captain Thermopyle's vileness toward her beggars description. In our opinion no hospital or therapy can restore her.*

Therefore we elected to make use of her in another way.

That was the truth; but it disguised more lies. More harm.

'Member Manse –' Koina cleared her throat. 'I'll answer you. I'll tell you all I know about it. But, as I say, the things

480

I need to explain are complicated. It'll be easier to keep them straight if I take them in a different order.'

For a moment the Member for Betelgeuse Primary held Koina's gaze. Then, apparently – woman to woman – she decided to trust Koina. Pouting her frustration, she resumed her seat.

Under her breath, Koina murmured a soft thank-you. At once, however, she widened her attention to the rest of the Council. She didn't want to give Maxim room to assert himself again.

Clearly she announced, 'The truth about Captain Thermopyle's "escape" from UMCPHQ is this. After his conviction for crimes against Com-Mine Station, he was reqqed by Data Acquisition and made into a cyborg.' A stirring of surprise crossed the room; but she didn't pause. 'The process is called "welding". By the use of zone implants, he was bonded to a computer. The result was a near-ideal DA operative – notoriously illegal, therefore free to go anywhere illegals go, and yet completely controlled by DA's programming.

'He did not "escape" from UMCPHQ. He was given *Trumpet* and dispatched on a mission to destroy the bootleg shipyard called Billingate on Thanatos Minor. Because the Amnion allowed this installation to exist inside the borders of forbidden space in clear contravention of their treaties with us, we considered it a valid target for a covert operation.'

'So Warden Dios sent Angus Thermopyle to commit an act of war,' Sen Abdullah sneered harshly.

'No.' Koina couldn't restrain her desire to defend Warden. 'Captain Thermopyle was sent to carry out an act of sabotage against an installation which the Amnion should not have allowed to exist. His mission can be easily justified under the terms of the UMCP charter.'

Sen snorted in derision, but didn't argue the point.

Firmly she resumed, 'Once Captain Thermopyle had carried out his mission, he fled forbidden space. *Punisher* had been sent to the Com-Mine belt to provide support in case he needed it. When his flight took him to Massif-5, she followed.'

So far she doubted that Fane had any quarrel with her responses. Her edited version of events must have reassured him. But that was about to change –

'Do you call this complicated?' Tel Burnish put in dryly. 'It seems simple enough.'

Ah, but she hadn't yet told him the real story.

'Why Massif-5, Director Hannish?' Member Silat asked in an unassuming tone. 'Are you able to account for this?'

'Yes, I can –' Koina began.

'*No*, Director Hannish,' Maxim intervened like the crack of a whip. 'I won't allow you to skip so blithely over the most crucial questions.' He had no idea how crucial what she would have answered was. 'Why did *Calm Horizons* pursue *Trumpet*? *That's* what we need to know.

'You claim Captain Thermopyle's mission can be "justified under the terms of the UMCP charter". But "an act of sabotage against an installation which the Amnion should not have allowed to exist" wasn't likely to inspire this incursion. In terms of treaties, they can't pretend they weren't in the wrong. So why is *Calm Horizons* here now?

'What did Captain Thermopyle *really* do in forbidden space? What was his true mission?'

Koina fixed a trenchant stare on Igensard. 'Special Counsel,' she stated acidly, 'Captain Thermopyle's "true mission" was exactly as I've described it. His actions aren't responsible for this incursion. As far as our present crisis is concerned, his only fault is that he rescued some of our people before he fled forbidden space. If you call that "fault".'

Obliquely she wondered, Was that part of his 'true mission'? Had Warden sent him to Billingate to bring Morn home? Hashi had said no: Angus' programming had been written *to preclude the possibility that he might save Ensign Hyland's life*. And Warden hadn't contradicted him. Yet Koina found that she believed otherwise. Morn was too vital to be left in Nick's hands – or the Amnion's.

Turning away from Maxim, Koina asserted, 'The blame for *Calm Horizons*' presence belongs to two other men.'

She nodded to the CAIP Senior Member. 'Bear with me,

please, Senior Member Silat. I can answer your question better if I tackle the Special Counsel's first.

'The two men I mentioned are Com-Mine Deputy Chief of Security Milos Taverner and Captain Nick Succorso.'

'What, *Taverner*?' Vest Martingale objected. As the Member for Com-Mine Station, she took accusations against Com-Mine Security personally. 'Are you still blaming *him*?'

'Member Martingale –' Koina's frustration and anger at being badgered showed in her tone. She made no effort to suppress it. 'Milos Taverner was sent with Captain Thermopyle – among other reasons – to serve as a kind of "control". To supervise his actions. To adjust his programming as circumstances might dictate. The plain fact is that no set of instructions, however sophisticated, can cover every situation or decision a welded cyborg might conceivably encounter. Deputy Chief Taverner's job was to make any corrections which might become necessary to keep Captain Thermopyle "on course".

'Unfortunately Taverner betrayed Captain Thermopyle and *Trumpet* to the Amnion. Sold them out.'

'I don't believe that,' Maxim snapped. Each time Koina shifted her attention away from him, he moved slightly toward the front of the dais, as if he wanted to force her to look at him; upstage her before the Council. 'Thermopyle's mission must have succeeded. Otherwise the Amnion wouldn't have any reason to pursue him. But how could he succeed if he was betrayed?'

Koina took a deep breath, held it briefly, so that she wouldn't shout at him. Everything she said took her closer to the most painful parts of her explanation. But anger gave her strength; steadied her resolve. Unnoticed, her knees had stopped trembling. Despite the interruptions, she didn't lose the thread of her explanation.

'Captain Thermopyle,' she articulated distinctly, 'succeeded because the deputy chief's treachery was foreseen. Director Dios and Director Lebwohl were aware of the danger, and took precautions against it.

'But Milos Taverner had other secrets to reveal.' Koina had

inferred this after her last conversation with Warden, when he'd told her why *Trumpet* had gone to Massif-5. Since then she'd gleaned indirect confirmation from Angus' only transmission to the UMCP director. 'He had reason to know –'

'Wait a minute.' The Special Counsel simply couldn't leave her alone. 'What do you mean, "aware of the danger"? How did they know?'

'I'll get to that,' she snapped back. 'If you keep interrupting me, I won't be able to answer *any* of your questions.'

Before Maxim could retort, President Len spoke unexpectedly from the back of the dais.

'Special Counsel, I'm warning you. So far I've let all of you harry Director Hannish as much as you want. But if you keep this up, I'm going to impose strict rules of order.' Apparently his exasperation – or perhaps his sympathy for Koina – had become greater than his instinct for conciliation, at least for the moment. 'After that, anybody who says *any*-thing without being recognized will be removed from the room.'

Koina looked toward him gratefully. 'Thank you, Mr President.' A bit of her anger melted, and she gave him what she hoped was a ravishing smile. 'That helps.'

Gracelessly Maxim muttered, 'I apologize, Director Hann-ish. I'll repeat the question later.'

Koina ignored him.

Despite his interference – and the Council's – she'd reached the line which separated Warden's intentions from Fasner's desires; the brink of disaster. Now she had to take her first step into a land of ruin –

With no word from either Hashi or Chief Mandich.

If she hadn't chosen to believe that Warden had sent Angus to rescue Morn, she might have faltered. But her unsupported conviction sustained her.

'Here's part of what you wanted to know, Member Manse,' she said more quietly; holding her anger in reserve. 'Deputy Chief Taverner knew that the drug in Captain Succorso's possession – the "fake" antimutagen Director Lebwohl mentioned – was in fact a true, effective mutagen immunity drug.'

484

At that moment the shock in the room was so great that no one made a sound. For an instant even Fane's subvocalized running commentary to UMCHO fell silent. *A true, effective mutagen immunity drug.* Her words had the effect of a kaze's blast. Igensard almost staggered; seemed to shrink in surprise. Punjat Silat made a series of small, stunned, clutching gestures, as if he were reaching out for a support which no longer existed. Sen Abdullah gaped like a man who couldn't breathe well enough to grasp the opportunity Koina had given him; bereft of air and wit by the enormity of the treason she confessed.

Stiff with strain, Sixten Vertigus lurched to his feet. He may have wanted to cry out against this revelation; denounce it – Betrayal filled his old eyes. For decades he'd backed Warden Dios against Holt Fasner. But dismay seemed to seal his throat. Koina's heart went out to him as he groped for words he couldn't find. When he collapsed slowly back into his seat, she feared he would never stand again.

Because he needed the only help she could give him – and because she couldn't retreat now – she told the appalled stillness, 'Building on research done by Intertech, primarily the work of Dr Vector Shaheed, DA developed the formula some time ago. But the information was never released. On direct orders from Holt Fasner, the use – and even the knowledge – of the drug has been restricted to DA covert operations.'

Do you hear me, Sixten? she thought toward the old Senior Member. Maybe you were wrong to back Warden. I don't think so – but maybe you were. But you were right to oppose Fasner.

Captain Vertigus may not have understood her. The stricken pallor of his face and the distress in his eyes gave her the impression that he was beyond reach.

Abruptly Fane found his voice. 'That's a *lie*,' he almost shouted. A flush of fury showed through his tangled beard. 'Holt Fasner did no such thing. He knows nothing about this.'

At the same time Maxim rallied to demand, 'Are you saying

the UMCP have had an effective antimutagen for years, and have been *suppressing* it?'

Koina gripped the edges of the podium and continued to address the Council as if neither man had spoken.

'Captain Succorso had the drug with him. Director Lebwohl gave it to him so that he could carry out operations for DA in forbidden space.'

'Did you hear me, Director Hannish?' the FEA blared like a trumpet; loud as a horn of doom. 'I said *that's a lie*!'

Still Koina ignored him. While she could, she explained, 'That's one reason the Amnion have risked an incursion. They want that drug. They can't be sure Captain Succorso got it from us. They're hoping to destroy it before the formula reaches the rest of humankind. And if they can't destroy it, they want to study it, learn how to counter it.'

'*Lies!*' Fane roared. 'The drug doesn't *exist*! And even if it does – even if Dios has been lying to us all this time – Holt Fasner *knew nothing about it*. If you're going to make these accusations, by God, you'd better *prove* them!'

Without a glance at him, she answered, 'I have Director Dios' word for it.'

And Vector Shaheed's, she might have added. Nick Succorso's. Morn's. Davies'. But she wasn't ready to go that far yet. She was hoping for something else –

'Do you have any record of the order?' the FEA countered fiercely. 'Is it logged anywhere?'

'Not that I know of,' she admitted. Now she used her anger to keep her calm. 'As a rule CEO Fasner delivers his orders to Director Dios in person.' Deliberately she put aside any pretense that her attack wasn't aimed at the Dragon. 'In the privacy of UMCHO. If any record exists, he has it.'

'Then it's Dios' word against mine,' Fane snarled. 'And you've already admitted that he's been lying to the Council.'

Koina didn't argue. Instead she left his challenge hanging in the air while she took a deep breath to calm herself. Her attack on Fasner's authority had hardly begun: she had a great deal more to say. But all her accusations lacked the corroboration which would make them unimpeachable. If Hashi and Chief Mandich didn't find evidence for her soon, she was going to fail. Everything she said would recoil against her. Warden would look like a man who wanted to cover his own crimes by blaming someone else. And she would look like his puppet.

Rather than contradicting Cleatus directly, she told the Members, 'When *Trumpet* first left forbidden space, Captain Thermopyle flared a message to UMCPHQ through a UMC listening post. It said, in part, "The Amnion know about the mutagen immunity drug in Nick Succorso's possession." Whatever the First Executive Assistant disputes, I think we can take *that* as fact.

'I believe Milos Taverner also knew. He and Captain Succorso did business together for years. When he betrayed Captain Thermopyle, he also betrayed a familiar partner.'

As well as the rest of humankind.

Maxim was charged with too much intensity to keep quiet. 'So when Director Lebwohl told us this Taverner betrayed Com-Mine with Angus Thermopyle,' he sneered, 'that was another lie?'

Koina nodded firmly. 'It was.' But she kept her attention fixed on the faces below the dais. 'The Special Counsel asked what I meant when I said that Director Dios and Director Lebwohl were "aware of the danger" Milos Taverner represented. The truth is that we – I mean Director Dios and Director Lebwohl – had what you might call a special relationship with Taverner. The deputy chief was a man of' – she considered a choice of descriptions – 'flexible loyalties. Putting it crudely, he was for sale. He sold what he knew and what he could do to anyone who paid him.

'We know that because *we* paid him.'

Vest Martingale snatched a sharp gasp through her teeth; but no one else reacted. Even Cleatus was silent; too busy with his throat pickup and PCR to say anything. And the rest of her audience, Koina suspected, had already received too many shocks. They were too shaken to protest against every new revelation.

Too bad. She was just getting warmed up. Her voice hardened as she went on.

'Angus Thermopyle was accused and convicted of stealing supplies from Com-Mine. But he didn't do it. He was framed. *We* framed him. Or, more precisely, we paid Milos Taverner and Nick Succorso to frame him.

'Taverner was paid in cash.' She made each word as clear as a cut. 'Succorso was paid with Morn Hyland.'

That was too much for Blaine Manse. 'Good God!' she objected; almost wailed. 'You admit it? One of your own people?

'*Why?*'

Koina knew that Blaine meant, Why did you sell Morn? Hashi had said, *Ensign Hyland was irretrievably compromised.* In one sense that may have been true. But in another it was entirely false; a piece of misdirection to confuse Warden's foes. However, the PR director replied as if Blaine's question referred to Angus.

'We wanted to be sure he was convicted of a crime that didn't carry the death penalty so we could req him. And –' Even now she found these things difficult to say. But the anger in the marrow of her bones carried her. 'And we wanted to undermine Com-Mine Security's credibility.

'I'm sure you all remember how the Preempt Act finally passed into law. We introduced it several times, but you always voted it down. You didn't favor it until we found a way to convince you local Station Security wasn't trustworthy.

'We used Angus for that.'

She kept her voice quiet, her tone level. Nevertheless the weight of what she said seemed to fill the chamber like a shout. 'Let me be completely clear. We can't afford any confusion about this. We framed Angus Thermopyle with the explicit intention of persuading you to pass the Preempt Act.

'Once again,' she finished, 'Director Dios and Director Lebwohl did this on the direct orders of CEO Fasner.'

She expected some new outburst from Maxim; watched him peripherally so that she could brace herself. But instead of swelling to an explosion, he seemed to shrink. Some kind of personal dismay leeched the blood from his cheeks, damped the core of his energy. His shoulders sagged, and his eyes flinched away from her; away from the Members.

'No,' he moaned so softly that Koina barely heard him. 'No. This is all wrong. It won't work like this. Not if Fasner –'

By now he must have realized that Koina – and Warden Dios – were playing for higher stakes than he was prepared to face.

While Igensard sank, Captain Vertigus pulled himself up in his seat. His hands trembled as if they were full of infirmity; but a keen fire shone in his old eyes. He may have grasped one of Koina's unspoken points. To suppress a true mutagen immunity drug was a crime of one kind: to deliberately mislead the Council into passing the Preempt Act was malfeasance of another kind altogether. If an accusation like *that* could be nailed to the Dragon's door –

Despite his earlier chagrin, he now looked like a man who did, indeed, have *work to do*.

Koina sighed to herself. It was really too bad that she still had no evidence.

Indignation left the Member for Com-Mine Station almost apoplectic. Punjat Silat sighed as if his worst fears had been confirmed. But no one spoke. The whole Council seemed to feel out of its depth. Most of the Members were waiting for Cleatus Fane's response.

He didn't keep them in suspense. Chuckling harshly, he waved his hand to signal for attention. A slight tilt of his head suggested that he could hear his master's voice in his ear while he rose to his feet. That didn't interfere with his ability to address the Council, however.

'My dear Director Hannish, this is preposterous,' he said with feigned amusement. A smile like an act of violence crinkled his eyes, then fell away as if it cost him too much effort. 'At last I think I understand what's going on here.

'Please believe me when I say that I'm sure you're behaving in good faith. I don't doubt that you're giving us information exactly as it was given to you. If more PR directors did the same, the world would be a better place.

'But – correct me if I'm wrong, Director Hannish – you have no record of *this* order, either. Holt Fasner is *alleged* to have ordered the suppression of an effective antimutagen. He is *alleged* to have ordered the framing of Angus Thermopyle so the Preempt Act would pass. But you have no evidence.'

'That's not quite true,' Koina interrupted quickly. 'I've been authorized to open DA's financial records to Special Counsel Igensard's investigation. Given time, his accountants will be able to trace payments made to Deputy Chief Taverner.'

Cleatus dismissed the point with a swipe of his palms. 'That's admirable, I'm sure.' Without transition his air of amusement shifted to sarcasm. 'Very forthcoming. But the mere existence of payments proves nothing. It won't confirm what they were *for*. And on that crucial subject you're just telling us what Warden Dios told you.'

Then he turned from her to face the Council.

'It's all clear, isn't it, Members, Mr President? Koina Hannish delivers Warden Dios' accusations against Holt Fasner. Naturally we believe her. We have every reason to presume she's honest. And we're all properly horrified.'

Abruptly he raised his fist. 'But *consider the source*. Look at what Director Hannish has just told us. Warden Dios selected Milos Taverner to "control" Captain Thermopyle. Warden Dios knew that Taverner had "flexible loyalties" – that he was "for sale". Of *course* he knew. He bought Taverner himself. And yet he chose that same man to supervise a welded UMCP cyborg on a dangerous and highly sensitive mission inside forbidden space.'

Despite the precariousness of her position, Koina took grim comfort from the fact that Cleatus didn't challenge her explanation of the reasons Angus had been framed. He had to accept part of her story in order to attack the rest. He couldn't defend the Dragon without letting her damage Fasner's credibility as the man who was ultimately responsible for the UMCP.

'On the surface, Members, Mr President,' the FEA said, 'that was a strange decision. A *bizarre* decision. But really it

490

makes perfect sense. For one thing, it got Taverner out of the way, so we can't ask him to tell us his side of the story. And for another –' He tightened his fingers until his knuckles showed white. 'Warden Dios knew Taverner would betray Captain Thermopyle! He was *counting* on it. Because he wanted the Amnion to commit an act of war. Exactly as Special Counsel Igensard has already suggested.

'When Warden Dios chose Taverner to "control" Thermopyle, he brought *Calm Horizons* here as surely as if he'd flared the Amnion an invitation.'

Fane's voice tightened like his fist. 'Now this same Warden Dios is using his own PR director to confuse the issue with accusations against Holt Fasner so that the Council won't recognize the enormity of his treason.'

'He's right.' Maxim scrambled to support the FEA. In fact, he seemed to address Cleatus instead of the Council. 'Mr Fane is right.' Under pressure his pose of diffidence became a kind of hunger, urgent and abject. Apparently his ambitions required him to undermine the UMCP without tainting the UMC. 'It's the only answer that fits. Dios is just trying to confuse us.'

With a severe effort, Koina kept her professional mask in place. 'That may be true.' She shrugged against the vulnerability and loss straining at her nerves; the anger throbbing in her heart. 'I can't prove what I've said, one way or the other. I can't prove that Director Dios didn't lie to me.

'I *would* like to point out, however, that the Preempt Act doesn't benefit the UMCP. We're stretched too thin as it is. We don't have either the personnel or the ships to police all of human space. We need Station Security.' We need a budget that lets us do our job. 'Extending our jurisdiction that far benefits only the UMC.'

Before Cleatus could protest, she went on, 'But all this is really beside the point I was trying to make.'

Again Abrim Len surprised her by speaking. Earlier he'd sounded exasperated; worn down; unhappily resigned to conflict. Now his tone had a decisive quality she'd never heard him use before. In a clear voice he prompted her, 'You were giving us Warden Dios' explanation for the fact that an Amnion defensive has her super-light proton cannon aimed at this island.'

He had no history of opposition to the UMC. Nevertheless, like Sixten, he seemed to draw strength from the plain thrust of Koina's revelations. Perhaps he was finally starting to believe that it might be possible for the GCES to meet what he'd called 'the general emergency' with a substantive response; that he and his fellow Members might at last begin to do their jobs.

'Thank you, Mr President.' Koina nodded. 'That's correct.'

Fighting an impulse to hurry, she resumed revealing Warden's secrets.

'I mentioned two reasons. One is that Milos Taverner told the Amnion Nick Succorso has an effective antimutagen. Captain Succorso himself is directly responsible for the other.

'I've already explained that we hired Succorso to help Taverner frame Captain Thermopyle. And we paid him with Morn Hyland. Since then we've learned that Morn was pregnant. Either she was pregnant when Captain Succorso took her, or she became pregnant shortly afterward. Under the circumstances – considering the character of the two men who could have victimized her – I wouldn't venture to guess which is the father.'

Koina suppressed a shudder at the thought of what Morn must have suffered. Here before the Council in Warden's name, the PR director already faced as much violation as she could stand. Yet Morn had endured much worse –

Warden himself might endure worse aboard *Calm Horizons*.

Sternly Koina pushed herself ahead.

'I can't account for what happened after that. I'm not inside Captain Succorso's mind. I can only tell you what he did.

'Whatever his reasons may have been, he took Morn into forbidden space, to Enablement Station. There he somehow persuaded or tricked the Amnion into using a process called "force-growing" on her fetus. The result was that she ended up with a mature son in a matter of hours instead of years. She named him Davies, perhaps because that was her father's name.'

The poor man had died with *Starmaster*, killed by Morn's gap-sickness.

'Apparently the outcome of this "force-growing" wasn't what the Amnion had expected, however. There's something special about Davies, something I don't understand and can't describe. But in his flare to UMCPHQ Captain Thermopyle said, "Davies Hyland is Morn Hyland's son, force-grown on Enablement Station. The Amnion want him. They believe he represents the knowledge necessary to mutate Amnion indistinguishable from humans."'

She paused to let the Members absorb the horror of this news; then concluded, '*That* is why the Amnion have risked an act of war. More than anything else, they want to be able to make themselves look and act just like us so they can infiltrate our space and destroy us without firing a shot.' Anger was all that kept her from trembling at her own words. 'From their point of view, the stakes are more than high enough to justify the risk.'

For a moment Members and their aides gaped dismay at each other; at Koina; at Cleatus Fane. Then President Len put in as if he wished to forestall a panic, 'Forgive me, Director Hannish, but you still haven't answered the question.' Like everyone else in the room, he probably had nightmares about the possibility she'd just described. 'Why is *Calm Horizons* chasing *Trumpet*?'

He was asking her to say it all. Make everything plain.

She accepted the burden. She'd promised herself – and Warden Dios – that she would do her job.

'Because, Mr President, they're all aboard. Nick Succorso. Morn Hyland. Davies Hyland. Even Dr Shaheed, who did most of the research on Intertech's mutagen immunity drug, before DA took his work away from him. Captain Thermopyle rescued them all from Billingate before he destroyed the installation.'

'So if *Punisher* retrieved *Trumpet*'s people,' Blaine Manse murmured in amazement, 'Morn Hyland is here.'

Cleatus Fane swore under his breath. He must have known the truth; but for obvious reasons he didn't want it spoken.

In the privacy of her heart, Koina prayed that Warden had never meant to abandon Morn; that Angus had brought Morn back on Warden's orders.

'Member Manse is right,' she stated. '*Calm Horizons* has her proton gun aimed at us because she's holding us hostage. The people who were aboard *Trumpet* are her real target.'

Now she began to speak more quickly. Because she feared a panic as much as Len did, she tried to prevent another interjection. The Members needed time to master their emotions. And she wanted to reach the end of the things she could say without support from Chief Mandich or Hashi Lebwohl. Her ability to restrain her anger was fraying; worn out by ruin.

'Incidentally' – she referred back to Punjat Silat's earlier question – 'I think we can assume that Captain Succorso's antimutagen explains why *Trumpet* headed for Massif-5. When *Punisher* engaged *Calm Horizons*, the Amnioni had stationed herself outside an asteroid swarm where *Trumpet* happened to be concealed. I'm sure it's no coincidence that one of the largest bootleg labs in human space is located in that swarm.'

'I know the one you mean,' Tel Burnish confirmed. 'Deaner Beckmann's facility.'

Koina inclined her head toward the VI Member. 'And when *Trumpet* emerged from the swarm, she came out broadcasting the formula for the drug. Shouting it in all directions as loudly as she could. Clearly *Trumpet* went to that swarm and that lab so Dr Shaheed could analyze the drug he did so much to help create.'

There she stopped. She was finished – stuck – without outside help. At least she'd carried out Warden's orders: she'd done her job, for whatever that was worth. Nevertheless a clenched sense of outrage was all that kept her from despair. Without evidence she might as well have stayed on

UMCPHQ; let Igensard and Fane do what they wanted with the emergency session.

When she glanced over her shoulder at Forrest Ing, she saw a look of dumb misery on his face. He may have been surprised, even horrified, by some of the things she'd said; but he knew what she'd tried to do — and knew she'd failed.

Neither of her communications techs met her gaze. They concentrated tensely on their separate links with Center; hardly seemed to be aware of anything else.

White-lipped with strain, Cleatus spoke swiftly, hoarsely, into his pickup. Koina expected outrage from him — an expression of the Dragon's hot fury. But she was surprised to see that he didn't look angry. The stress in his eyes resembled frenzy; terror.

Maxim had a different reaction, however. Here was his chance to step forward — resume control — and he took it like a snapping predator.

'This is too much,' he objected. 'I really can't allow you to go on like this.' He was struggling to recover some of the moral superiority he'd generated earlier. 'You're doing it again, Director Hannish. Skipping over the points that matter most. Trying to baffle us with obfuscation.'

Koina sighed wearily. 'In what way, Special Counsel?'

'Angus Thermopyle was a "welded" cyborg,' he retorted, 'isn't that right? "Completely controlled by DA's commands and restrictions," you said. So when he took Dr Shaheed to that lab he was following orders. Warden Dios' orders.

'What kind of game is your boss playing now?'

Cleatus was still on his feet, using his bulk — and his alarm — in an attempt to dominate the Council's attention. 'For that matter,' he added tensely, 'how does it just happen that Dr Vector Shaheed, of all people, ended up aboard *Trumpet*?'

So she wasn't done. Finished — but not done.

Despite her fear that Warden's hopes had crossed the brink of disaster, Koina did her best to outmatch her opponents.

'It "just happened", Mr Fane, that Dr Shaheed was a member of Captain Succorso's crew. He served as Captain Succorso's engineer. Reports from Billingate indicate that

Captain Succorso's ship, *Captain's Fancy*, was destroyed in the attack. Apparently only a few of his people survived. When he joined *Trumpet*, Dr Shaheed was with him, as well as his command second, Mikka Vasaczk, and her brother, Ciro, Dr Shaheed's second.'

Argue with *that*, you sonofabitch.

Brusquely she turned to Maxim.

'Special Counsel, Captain Thermopyle was *not* following orders when he fled to Massif-5. Director Dios knew that if Milos Taverner turned traitor Captain Thermopyle would be left without a "control" to adjust his programming. And without appropriate adjustments he might become dangerous when faced with situations or exigencies not covered by his instruction-sets.

'For that reason, his instruction-sets were written so that if he was betrayed he would have enough freedom of movement to provide for his own and *Trumpet*'s survival. In addition he was barred from returning to Earth until a new 'control' could be supplied. That was one of Min Donner's duties aboard *Punisher*. She was supposed to replace Milos Taverner. When *Trumpet* escaped Massif-5, however, Director Donner hadn't yet succeeded – perhaps because *Punisher* was too busy fighting *Calm Horizons*.

'Whatever Captain Thermopyle's and Morn Hyland's reasons may have been, they went to Massif-5 on their own.'

Igensard tried a righteous sneer, but he was too harried and tight to carry it off. 'Do you expect us to believe that?'

Koina let her anger answer him. 'I'm the UMCP PR director. I have a great deal more information than you do. If you can't prove I'm wrong, I think you owe it to this Council and the people of Earth to start believing me.'

For a moment silence answered her challenge. Members refused to meet her eyes. Their aides studied her as if she'd become oddly repulsive. Then President Len asked, 'What will Warden Dios do? Why is he aboard *Calm Horizons*? Does he have any hope of keeping us alive?'

She understood his real question; his indirect attempt at conciliation: Will Warden surrender *Trumpet*'s people to save us?

'I don't know, Mr President.' For a moment grief swelled in her chest. 'He didn't tell me that.'

'Can we talk to Morn Hyland?' Blaine put in suddenly. 'Surely we can aim a dish at *Punisher*? Or route a channel through UMCPHQ?'

Koina bowed her head. 'I haven't been authorized to do that, Member Manse.' She was beaten and desperate: she would have jumped at the chance to do as Blaine suggested. 'Director Dios didn't mention it. And I'm not in contact with Acting Director Donner. I don't know whether she would sanction it or not.'

If Warden had to surrender *Trumpet*'s people in order to preserve the Council, Morn might already be out of reach. Sold again –

'*Ask* her,' Blaine urged. 'What have we got to lose?'

Cleatus flapped his hands dismissively. 'I'm sure the acting director has her hands full,' he snorted. 'She won't have time to deal with us. Considering Dios' behavior so far, she's probably our only hope. I for one don't want to distract her.'

I'm sure you don't, Koina thought. But she kept her opinion to herself. She didn't have the heart to provoke him further. It was plain that too many of the Members agreed with him.

Without warning Captain Vertigus tottered to his feet.

'Director Hannish, I have a question.'

Maxim squared his shoulders and opened his mouth, clearly intending to cut Sixten off. To forestall him, Koina replied quickly, 'I'll answer it if I can, Captain.'

Sixten gripped the back of Maxim's empty seat as if he needed it to hold him up. His head wobbled weakly on his old neck. All the energy he could muster was focused in his voice.

'I've been listening to these revelations with more than a little nausea. If I hadn't had so many years to get used to the way Holt Fasner does things, I would probably be puking by

497

now. But the single thing you've told us that sickens me the most can't be blamed on him.

'How in the name of conscience do you justify selling Morn Hyland to Nick Succorso?'

He gave the impression that he held Koina accountable for Warden's actions; but she knew better. She was simply the only person here who might tell him what was in Warden's mind. He had *work to do* – work as hazardous as hers, and as necessary – but he needed something from her before he could do it.

She let him see the distress on her face as she said, 'I understand how you feel. Giving Morn to Nick Succorso when she'd just spent weeks as Angus Thermopyle's victim was' – she opened her hands to show that her heart was open as well – 'abominable. But we didn't know how else to keep her alive.

'She's a witness to the fact that Captain Thermopyle was framed.' That the Council had been tricked into passing the Preempt Act. 'If Com-Mine took her into custody, we were sure she would end up dead. CEO Fasner has a long reach. And he doesn't want anyone to know the Preempt Act rests on a lie.'

Sixten nodded. He seemed to accept her explanation; to believe her. A combative smolder showed in his eyes, and he straightened his back like a man who was about to go into battle.

'In that case –'

But he didn't get to finish. Cleatus had started shouting.

'That's *enough*, Director Hannish!' he raged. 'You've gone too far!' He seemed to draw strength from his PCR. 'You admit – over and *over* again – that you don't have any evidence. And yet you *persist* in these baseless accusations. It's *slander*, and I won't tolerate any more of it!'

'Mr Fane,' Sixten yelled back, 'I have the floor!'

'No, you don't!' Maxim sounded frantic; on the verge of howling. '*I* do. *I* have the authority to question her. You're just *interrupting*!'

'Igensard!' Cleatus roared furiously.

At once Maxim flinched backward a step; shrank into himself. In a thin voice he announced, 'I yield the floor to FEA Cleatus Fane.'

'*Thank* you,' Cleatus snapped.

Heavy as a battlewagon, he strode to the dais, mounted it, and aimed his bulk at Abrim Len as if he meant to browbeat the smaller man.

'Mr President, I object to this whole debacle.' Iron indignation clanged in his voice. 'You've allowed Director Hannish to retail the most malign falsehoods without restraint. This isn't a court of law, but it should be. Warden Dios is on trial. Not Holt Fasner – *the director of the UMCP.* You can't go on letting Dios' mouthpiece taint this Council with irresponsible hearsay and unsubstantiated charges! If she can't supply *evidence*, you should make her *stop.*'

Apparently Abrim's unfamiliar decisiveness had deserted him. It cost him too much: he couldn't outface the Dragon's minion. He seemed to recede into his chair as he asked Koina hesitantly, 'Director Hannish, do you have an answer?'

'Not a good one, Mr President,' she admitted tiredly. If she hadn't sworn an oath as Warden's Director of Protocol, she might have been tempted to concede defeat. 'I've simply been trying to save time by telling the whole story as I know it. To help the Council make informed decisions.'

But she *had* sworn an oath. And Warden had staked his life aboard *Calm Horizons* to *save* these people. In spite of her despair, she couldn't bear to back down while there was still something, anything, she might say.

Before President Len – or the FEA – could continue, she added, 'And, frankly, I had hoped the evidence I need would have arrived by now.'

'*What* evidence?' Cleatus sneered like vitriol. 'From *whom*?'

Koina confronted him squarely, her anger swelling to match his. 'From Hashi Lebwohl. From UMCPED Chief of Security Mandich. They're investigating these recent kazes.'

In response he brandished his beard at her like a club. He'd been practicing innocence for a long time. He was good at it. 'My God, this is *unconscionable*! Are you going to blame *that* on Holt Fasner, too?'

She didn't try to stop. She didn't want to. Risking what was left of her credibility, she snapped, 'Yes, I am. I believe he sent those kazes. I believe he's the one who wants to confuse this Council. And I believe he'll do worse if he isn't stopped.'

Her charge may have sounded like lunacy to everyone else; but Cleatus was ready for it. His PCR gave him information and advice she couldn't hear. The baldness of her accusation didn't make him falter for a second.

Wheeling away from President Len, he proclaimed, 'Members, we've had too much of this farrago. Director Hannish has made a *shambles* of this session.

'But it won't go on like this. That's a fact, not a challenge. I've just been informed' – he indicated the receiver in his ear – 'that CEO Fasner has relieved Acting Director Donner of her duties.

'Because the CEO doesn't believe the Amnion will ever let a man as valuable as Warden Dios go, no matter what kind of deal he makes with them, Director Dios will be replaced. A new director will be named shortly. And I'm sure one of his first actions will be to put a stop to Director Hannish's malfeasance.'

Koina winced in shock. Involuntarily she flung a look at her techs; mouthed the words, Is that true?

One of the women had the blessed presence of mind to rise to her feet. 'Director Hannish' – only a slight quaver marred her voice – 'we've received a report from UMCPHQ Center. On your dedicated downlink.'

'What does it say?' Koina asked quickly.

The tech cleared her throat. 'Acting Director Donner has refused to be relieved.' Her tone grew stronger as she summarized Center's transmission. 'According to the terms of the UMCP charter, her authority derives from the director. She insists that Holt Fasner has no right to relieve her. He must first replace Director Dios. But Director Dios can't be fired without due notification. This is especially true under conditions of war. Since Director Dios hasn't been replaced, Director Donner has refused CEO Fasner's orders.'

At once the woman sat down as if she wanted to get out of the crossfire.

Thank God! Abruptly Koina's knees started trembling again. She leaned an elbow on the podium to support herself.

Cleatus didn't contradict the tech. Obviously he knew her information was accurate: his PCR had already given him the same news. Instead he protested savagely, 'That's not our fault. For the last twenty-four hours he's refused to speak to Mr Fasner. And now the Amnion are holding him incommunicado. We've done everything we can to give him notification.'

'But the point is' – Koina offered a bitter smile – 'that Director Dios has not been fired. Under the circumstances, UMCPHQ has lawfully refused to recognize any authority except Min Donner's.

'Why did you lie to us, Mr Fane? Did you think you could bluff your way out of this?'

But Cleatus was ready for that, too. His downlink from UMCHO seemed to cover everything. Without pausing to collect himself, he blared at the Council, 'If I hadn't been interrupted, I would have told you what you just heard. The *point* isn't that Dios hasn't been fired. It's that he's blocked CEO Fasner's *lawful* authority at every turn.

'Do you need more *proof*? Do you have to be hit by *proton cannon fire* before you recognize the treason here? Warden Dios has betrayed his office. He's betrayed the UMCP. He's betrayed humankind. *How many more crimes have to come to light before you do something about it?*'

'Like what?' Koina demanded so that Sixten would have an opening. 'What do you think the Council should do, exactly?'

The old captain didn't hesitate. His voice quavering with age and urgency, he pronounced, 'Pass my Bill of Severance. Now. While we still can. Take the cops away from the UMC so they won't be influenced by a man like Holt Fasner.'

Fane shook his head brutally. 'That's not good enough.'

He seemed to be prepared for everything. 'It leaves Warden Dios free to do what he wants. I have a better idea.

'This Council should decharter the UMCP. Right here, right now. Revoke their existence. Then recharter them with somebody else as director. My God,' he cried, '*anybody* else! If you actually believe any of this shit about Holt Fasner' – his scorn rang off the walls – 'you can give Captain Vertigus the job.' He flung a gesture like a blow at Sixten. 'It doesn't *matter*. Only staying *alive* matters. And putting an end to these *lies*.'

When she looked around the room, saw the dismay and dread on the faces of the Members, Koina had no doubt which proposal they would accept. They were too troubled, too unsure, too scared to reject the power of the Dragon.

And Warden was lost.

MORN

The quiet she experienced when she made the decision to trust Angus with her son's life, and Warden Dios', comforted her; but it didn't last long. First came a rush of activity as everyone hurried to their places: Captain Ubikwe, Vector and Davies with the command module; Angus, Ciro and Mikka aboard *Trumpet*; Min Donner, *Punisher*'s duty officers and Morn herself on the auxiliary bridge. Then followed the tense work of detaching the module and releasing *Trumpet*. Min stood impatiently at the communications station while Cray routed Center's transmissions to her PCR and throat pickup. Patrice activated the helm console swiftly. Restored to his post at last, Glessen ran targ with grim satisfaction. Porson and Bydell working together brought up the main displays – scan schematics, orbit and course vectors, targ windows – and added blips for the command module and *Trumpet* as Dolph began transporting the gap scout along his cautious route toward *Calm Horizons*.

Among them, Morn settled into the command g-seat. The auxiliary bridge felt like a completely different place from the one she'd just left: oriented differently in *Punisher*'s deceleration g; with different sounds and pressures. And the air was colder for some reason. It seemed closer to the outer dark; the absolute chill of space. More exposed –

Unlike the people around her, she had no duties. The cruiser would have obeyed her orders, but she had none to give. Captain Ubikwe's officers took care of *Punisher*. Min handled everything else. And Morn had no part to play in Angus' plots, or Davies' risks. Finally she'd arrived at the position she'd sought ever since she'd returned to consciousness beyond Massif-5. She was free to do what she'd come here for.

Tell the truth. Accuse the men and women she'd been raised to serve of crimes she abhorred.

That crisis loomed ahead of her like the last gap crossing of her life; the ordeal she dreaded most. She'd talked about it as if she were certain of herself; believed completely in what she meant to do; as if she had no room for doubt. But now she feared it might prove to be a new form of gap-sickness – a more fatal form.

Possibilities of ruin seemed to throng like furies about her, calling for blood. She would have to bare her soul to the Council; open her shame for every Member of the GCES to see and condemn.

Because she needed Min's help, she looked for some way to catch the ED director's attention; encourage Min to leave Center's demands aside for a moment and talk to her. But Min's link to Center – and, through Center, to the planet – required harsh concentration. She was responsible for Earth's defense in every sense: both planet-side and out in space. At times she appeared to answer multiple questions simultaneously; issue orders on several different subjects at once.

A nagging itch troubled Morn's sore arm – a sign of healing, she supposed. Grateful for it, she scratched at it occasionally while she awaited her opportunity.

After a while the command module and *Trumpet* finished their last transmissions. Then Porson confirmed that *Trumpet* was well occluded, her telltale electromagnetic activity masked by the module's emissions. Still Morn didn't speak. Despite her complex fears – and a mounting sense of urgency – she waited until Min made time to glance in her direction.

But then she found that the words she required were hard to say. Once they were spoken, she wouldn't be able to call them back: simply articulating them would make them irrevocable; a promise she had to keep. In chagrin she stalled for courage by asking the first question she could think of.

'How's your hand, Director?'

If Min considered that an odd question, she kept her reaction to herself. She may have understood why Morn asked it. Flexing her fingers, she inspected the bandage Glessen had applied for her.

'Funny thing,' she muttered, frowning. 'That damn cyborg has good aim. Hitting him hurt worse than getting shot.' Her mouth twisted. 'Someday I'll learn to keep my temper. But that probably won't happen anytime soon.'

The auxiliary bridge was definitely colder than it should have been. Morn checked her maintenance readouts; saw that a couple of temperature sensors and air circulation relays weren't working properly. They must have been damaged somehow.

She tried again.

'Director –' Her throat closed. Min –

'You know about my gap-sickness. You know what Angus did to me.' She didn't wait for Min's assent. 'But I never told you that Vector broke my black box. My zone implant control. Angus gave it to me. But Vector broke it to keep me from killing myself. When Nick had Angus' priority-codes.

'Since then,' she explained lamely, 'my gap-sickness has been more of a problem.'

The lines of Min's face became sharper. 'I wondered why Angus hit you when we hit hard g. At the time that seemed' – she frowned at the memory – 'excessive.'

Ignoring her duties, she waited for Morn to go on.

Morn swore at herself. Why was this so hard? Hadn't she grown accustomed to her shames *yet*? Surely by now she might have come to understand that *Starmaster* was gone – that no amount of self-torment would bring her family back?

With an effort she set her reluctance aside.

'I need your help, Director,' she admitted unsteadily. 'I want to talk to the Council. Tell my story.' Give my testimony. Now or never. 'But I can't do it alone. Center doesn't take orders from me. GCES communications certainly doesn't. I need you to open a channel. If you don't, I'm helpless.'

Her request didn't surprise Min. The ED director must have heard enough hints to guess what Morn had in mind. Perhaps she approved: perhaps this was why she'd let Morn take command in the first place. Deliberately she removed her PCR, lifted the pickup off her throat. Her eyes searched Morn like a hawk's.

'You don't have to talk to them.' She sounded distant, noncommittal, like a woman withholding judgment. 'They need to hear your story, but you don't have to tell it in person. You can record it. Then I'll talk to them for you. Give them a playback. Answer their questions.'

'In your spare time?' Morn countered ruefully. She'd already observed how tightly Min's responsibilities stretched her. The strain was palpable every time Min addressed her pickup.

'I can do it,' Min insisted. Then, more gently, she added, 'You've already done enough. More than any of us.'

Morn bowed her head. The unexpected kindness of Min's offer touched her; but she wasn't tempted to accept it. 'It's my job, Director,' she sighed. My story. 'I think they should hear it from me.'

When she looked up again, she saw a gleam that might have been pride or hope in the ED director's gaze.

'In that case –' Min shrugged. 'Give me a few minutes. Suka Bator isn't exactly calm at the moment. And even when they are calm, what they do best is dither. I may have to put the fear of God into a few techs before they'll do what I tell them.'

Without hesitation she returned her attention to her PCR and pickup. Morn heard her issuing crisp instructions in a tone that left no room for argument.

A few minutes.

Morn was glad for the delay. Despite the pressure of events, she felt now that she could use every moment Min gave her. Gripped by her gap-sickness, she'd killed her whole family. In order to protect her shame, she'd bartered Angus' life for

506

her zone implant control. And then she'd driven herself into zone implant addiction so that she could lie to and seduce Nick Succorso. If her pregnancy and Davies' birth hadn't changed the way she made decisions, she might have continued ruining herself until she joined her mother and father.

The Council needed to hear her story.

She needed all the time Min gave her to harden her heart.

CLEATUS

Cleatus Fane knew what might happen.

That's why he was so angry – and so scared. He knew what might happen. He could see it in the way some of the votes struggled against his proposal to decharter the UMCP. He could hear it in Holt's incisive, unscrupulous voice from his PCR. He could visualize it in the fatal progress of *Punisher*'s command module toward *Calm Horizons*. Now more than ever, events and the FEA's master hinted at terrible possibilities.

Cleatus was so scared that his bowels squirmed. The studied bonhomie with which he usually faced the votes had deserted him entirely. It was his job to ensure that nothing terrible happened; that Holt saw no need to make anything terrible happen. And he appeared to be succeeding at it. Certainly the Council gave that impression, despite the Hannish woman's infuriating allegations, and the few remaining instances of resistance among the sheep. But he knew he couldn't afford to relax even slightly until Dios was officially and legally out of a job: until someone else took over as director of the rechartered UMCP. Then *Calm Horizons* as well as *Punisher* could be informed that Dios no longer had the authority to make deals, and any accommodation he might have hammered out was void.

Punisher's command module was on its way to the defensive. With *Trumpet* in tow. So Holt had informed his FEA.

Dios had devised some kind of accommodation: that was obvious.

Whatever it was, it had to be stopped. Holt wanted the Hyland kid for himself. He wanted Morn dead. He wanted that damn antimutagen crushed out of existence – and Vector Shaheed with it. And he wanted the Amnion to *finish* Dios for him. But if Dios' deal held, very little of that would take place.

Dios himself was definitely out of the picture. Cleatus didn't believe for a second that the Amnion would ever release him. But if the module wasn't stopped, Davies would be lost to Holt. Morn might protract her improbable survival long enough to cause more trouble. And blind, self-righteous Min Donner might take it on herself to release Shaheed's formula. She was arrogant enough. The only way to keep her in line was to give her a boss with enough authority to overrule her. The kind of boss Dios should have been.

The module was still almost two hours away from *Calm Horizons*. Cleatus had that long – only that long – to make reality match his master's wishes.

Unfortunately there was nothing he could do about it at the moment. He'd countered Hannish's revelations as vigorously as circumstances allowed. For the second time he'd disrupted the efforts of that old fool Sixten Vertigus to pass that insipid Bill of Severance. And he'd presented Holt's counter-proposal in terms which made it hard for the sheep to balk. But he didn't run the Council. Instead he had to sit on his hands and watch the Members debate an idea they should have voted into law by acclamation.

Fortunately Holt was at his most lucid in emergencies. His powers of concentration helped make him dangerous. He didn't waste time with useless demands or impossible orders. One of the FEA's techs delivered a verbatim report of the proceedings: Cleatus supplied explanations and commentary. On that basis Holt grasped the situation as accurately as Cleatus did. He didn't expect Cleatus to work miracles; didn't hold Cleatus accountable for the actions of others.

Not in an emergency.

Nevertheless the CEO's precise pragmatism made Cleatus' guts clench in alarm. More than anyone else in this room – or anyone else in human space, for that matter – Cleatus knew how far Holt's grip on practical reality might take him.

From his seat beside Dios' pet PR director, Cleatus Fane projected outward calm and stewed inwardly while the sheep blundered about the business of achieving a vote.

The process took longer than it should have; much longer. Len acted like a man who wanted to be sure each word he said was unimpeachable. The supercilious twit insisted on dotting every legislative i, crossing every procedural t – which used up time. In addition several of the votes did their best to turn the session into a true debate.

That promiscuous slut from Betelgeuse Primary harped endlessly on the emotional observation that Dios risked his humanity aboard *Calm Horizons*. After all, he had no real reason to think the Amnion would ever release him. She'd figured that out. So the accusations against him were pointless, she insisted, since he obviously gained nothing from his so-called crimes except this chance to suffer mutation.

In his most effete tones, the Council's resident intellectual snot, Silat, advanced the more ominous argument that if the UMCP were dechartered, Dios would lose his authority to make deals – surprise, surprise – in which case, any arrangement he conceived would be meaningless. The new director would have to start from scratch, which would take time. And time worked against the Amnion. They might conclude that proton cannon fire would serve them better than protracted renegotiations.

And useless Tel Burnish pointed out that the entire UMCP organization might rebel if both Warden Dios and Min Donner were replaced. Loyalties within UMCPHQ, and aboard UMCPED's ships, might be strong enough to leave Earth – not to mention Suka Bator – defenseless.

Even that defeated idiot Vertigus added his irritating voice and scrawny objections to the obstacles which slowed the sheep's progress toward a vote. Hannish obviously admired his willingness to flog a lost cause: her eyes shone every time he opened his mouth, as if she considered him honorable, or even heroic. But Cleatus felt otherwise. He would have cheerfully had the old captain shot.

In fact, he hated them all – Manse, Silat, Burnish, Vertigus; Hannish and Len. He would have been generously, *magnanimously* delighted to see every one of them dead.

Manse probably isn't worth the trouble, he told his pickup. Neither is Silat. But we ought to kill Burnish.

He already knew what Holt thought of Vertigus.

We'll worry about that later, Holt replied crisply.

The good news was that Hannish couldn't do anything to encourage all this obfuscation. Like Cleatus, she had to sit and watch. And he'd done everything in his power to undermine her credibility. The votes couldn't believe a thing she told them unless they were prepared to side with Dios against Holt.

A few minutes ago she'd accepted a PCR from one of her techs. Presumably she was listening to her dedicated downlink from UMCPHQ. If so, Center must have told her about the command module and *Trumpet*. But she didn't announce the information. She may have realized that she'd reached the end of her string. Or – the thought wrung Cleatus' intestines – she may still have hoped someone would rescue her.

The sheep were *taking* too long. He interjected comments and offered arguments whenever he got the chance, but he lacked the clout to force a conclusion. Meanwhile the chronometer was running. If the Council didn't vote soon, Holt would give up on legal solutions to the problems Dios had caused.

Terrible –

Grimly Cleatus reminded himself that he still had at least ninety minutes. Surely that would suffice? God, it ought to! If no more surprises hit the Members, Holt was going to win. And his First Executive Assistant would live.

He nearly lost control of himself when he saw an aide leave a console near the chamber doors and hurry toward the dais, waving his arm to attract Len's attention.

Damn, this was bad news. Had to be. Otherwise the man

wouldn't have been in *such* a hurry, stumbling against chairs and tripping past legs in his rush to reach the dais.

Len scowled at the man; shook his head to reject the interruption. Good boy. But the aide sprang up to the dais, caught Len's arm, drew him back from the podium, and began whispering tensely in his ear.

One after another, the votes stopped talking. A clutch of suspense froze them. Nameless fears crowded the room: proton cannon; war and mutagens; the fatal dark of space. Cleatus felt them himself. He rose half out of his seat, then thought better of it and stayed where he was, murmuring worry into his pickup.

Holt said nothing.

Vertigus covered his face. That raving fanatic Sen Abdullah gaped as if he were choking on vexation. Poised on the edge of his chair, Igensard sat ready to leap up and fling objections; trying to be helpful –

Damn. Len nodded abruptly to the aide, gestured the man back to his console. More delays. While the aide hurried away, Len returned to the podium. Despite the rank dread around him, he took his time: bowed his head; drew several deep breaths; gripped his ceremonial mace carefully. Then, still slowly, he straightened his spine, lifted his chin, settled his shoulders.

His eyes held a look Cleatus couldn't read. It might have been desperation or resolve.

'Members,' he announced unevenly, 'Director Hannish, First Executive Assistant Fane, this vote will have to wait.'

Cleatus felt a knife bite into his guts. He barked a protest like a yelp of pain. At the same time Igensard shouted something Cleatus didn't hear; something about voting first –

The next moment he watched in amazement and horror as Len raised his mace and hammered it against the podium as if he wanted to shatter one or the other.

'I said *this vote will have to wait*!'

The blow – and Len's unexpected vehemence – jolted the sheep like a shot of stun. Several Members jerked in their seats. Some of the aides lost flurries of hardcopy. Even Len flinched as if he'd shocked himself; as if he hadn't known how much strain he was under, or how deep his revulsion ran. He recovered quickly, however. In a milder tone, he explained, 'One of my aides has just informed me that we're receiving a transmission from Ensign Morn Hyland. Aboard *Punisher*.'

Damn! Damn it all –! Cleatus couldn't think of an oath powerful enough to express his terrified fury. Dios and his lackeys were going to get everyone on this island killed!

Subvocalizing furiously, he reported to Holt.

Stop them, Holt instructed. He didn't tell Cleatus how.

In an instant Hannish reached her feet. Like a woman galvanized by hope, she blurted out, 'Let's hear it.'

Then she seemed to remember her place. 'Forgive me, Mr President,' she added breathlessly. 'I don't mean to intrude. But Morn is *there*. Where the decisions our survival depends on are being made. You must talk to her. It's vital.'

'I agree.' Somewhere Len found the strength to produce asperity. 'That's why I said –'

'But *I* do *not* agree!' Cleatus blared. Stop them? *Stop* them? He bounded upright; shoved past Hannish to put himself between her and Len. 'What's *vital* is dechartering the UMCP! That woman has no business being *alive*, much less presuming to contact us. After what she's been through, she's probably insane. Or she and your Captain Succorso want to run some scam. She's just an *ensign*, for God's sake! Let her wait until we finish saving humanity!'

'Don't you understand?' Hannish shouted at his back. 'She knows what's going on!

'*Punisher* has detached her command module. The module is headed toward *Calm Horizons*. And she's towing *Trumpet*.' Without the Hyland woman, apparently. 'Director Dios has made some kind of deal with the Amnion, and *Ensign Hyland knows what it is*! If she wants to talk to us, we have to hear her. We *must*!'

Cleatus didn't waste time cursing her for that revelation. He had a more urgent fear.

Morn might want to give evidence.

For God's sake, he told his pickup. Open fire on *Punisher*.

What's the point? Holt retorted. If I go that far, I'll have to go further.

'*No*, Mr President!' Igensard also was on his feet. He didn't take frustration well: he looked as if he was on the verge of a paroxysm. 'This is inexcusable! We are the Governing Council for Earth and Space' – he'd conveniently forgotten that his status as Abdullah's proxy was temporary – 'and we're making the most important decision of our lives! You have no right –'

With a sweeping motion, Len raised his mace like an ax over his head and aimed it at the podium.

Oh, shit! Cleatus bit back his outrage. Igensard clamped his mouth shut in midspate. Even Hannish stopped. What had happened to Len's instinct for conciliation – his cowardice? He seemed to be losing his mind.

If he suffered a breakdown right here in front of the votes, they would lose *more* time –

When he was sure of the silence, he lowered his arms; dropped his mace like a rock onto the podium.

'Mr Fane.' His voice cracked with strain, but he didn't waver. 'You're a guest here. You've already had your say. If you don't hold your tongue, I'll have you removed from the room. Forcibly, if necessary.'

What, *removed*? Holt Fasner's *representative*? 'You wouldn't *dare* –' Cleatus fumed.

'*I* would,' a guard barked from his station against the back wall. Forrest Ing, Deputy Chief of UMCPED Security. Another Donner lackey. 'My men and I would consider it an honor to obey President Len.'

Cleatus flung a murderous glare at the man; but he could see Ing was serious. The blunt threat on Ing's face promised that he would enjoy manhandling the FEA. Shaking with anger, Cleatus hid a bitter retort behind his beard.

Hannish looked like she could hardly restrain a cheer.

Accept it, Holt ordered. We'll find some other way. She can't connect us.

Len didn't wait for Cleatus to answer. He wheeled on Igensard.

'As for you, Special Counsel –' Unprecedented anger burned in his eyes. 'Don't talk to me about "right". I've had enough. When you told me why you wanted Sen Abdullah's proxy, I couldn't think of a reason to refuse. Now I can.

'If you had a gram of professional integrity, you would leap at a chance to hear anything Morn Hyland might say. *She pertains to your investigation*. But apparently you care more about crucifying Warden Dios than learning the truth.

'If that's true, get out of here and let the rest of us carry out our responsibilities,' Len commanded harshly. 'I'm sure Senior Member Abdullah is more than qualified to speak for himself. He doesn't need you.'

Jesus! Cleatus groaned. What in God's name had *happened* to Len? Where was the timid, weak and above all manipulable President Cleatus knew?

Was he *taking sides*?

'For reasons I don't understand,' Len told Igensard and the Council fiercely, 'Ensign Hyland has been forced to suffer in ways we can't imagine. She's been abandoned and sold by people she should have been able to trust, and' – his voice rose – '*we are going to hear her!*'

Igensard gaped like a fish at the reproof. Involuntarily he turned an appeal toward Cleatus. Stupid – He may have been an ally of a sort, but Cleatus had no help to give him. Slowly he shrank back to his seat; dwindled like a deflated bladder.

'I'm sorry, Mr President,' he murmured thinly. 'Of course we should talk to Morn Hyland. I'll wait my turn.'

Hannish was obviously delighted.

For a moment amazement or chagrin held the room. Then Vertigus lurched to his feet. Raising his thin arms high, he began to applaud. At once Manse jumped up and joined him enthusiastically. Burnish contributed a hard, rhythmic clap, like impact pistol fire. After a brief hesitation, Vest Martingale – who should have known better – added her approval.

The rest of the votes had better sense. Abdullah snarled whining curses. Sigurd Carsin covered her face. Even Punjat

Silat studied Len with a noncommittal expression on his stubby features. Others consulted their aides in urgent whispers, or buried themselves in their notes, as if they suddenly needed bits of information they couldn't recall.

Suffer in ways we can't imagine, Cleatus thought bitterly. So that was it. Len had always been a sentimental bastard. Now he'd been seduced by the idea of Hyland's pain. He'd lost himself to a woman he hadn't even met.

Through the applause a look of weakness washed over the President. For a moment Cleatus hoped he was about to faint. It was possible he'd never been so forceful in his life: the effort may have exhausted him. Leaning closer to the podium, he propped his elbows under him for support.

Hannish resumed her seat like a good girl. Manse and Vertigus did the same. At first Cleatus remained stubbornly on his feet: he wanted to confront Morn standing. But then he reconsidered. *Accept it,* Holt had told him. *We'll find some other way.* Subvocalizing tensely, he retreated to his chair and sat down.

'Unfortunately we weren't expecting this,' Len said weakly. 'We aren't set up for it. But my aide is routing a channel through the newsdogs' speakers and pickups. We should all be able to hear Ensign Hyland. She may be able to hear all of us.'

He made an effort to sound more assertive. '*Strict* rules of order, Members. This woman has been through hell. No matter what you think of Warden Dios – or Holt Fasner – she's one of the victims. I won't let her be harassed.'

Then he told his aide, 'When you're ready.'

That emasculated twit has turned against us, Cleatus muttered to his pickup. He thinks Hyland is some kind of martyr. If he gets a chance, he'll let Vertigus reintroduce Severance.

Not if you do your job, Holt retorted.

My *job*? Cleatus thought – but didn't say. What do you *think* I'm doing?

'I'm ready now, Mr President,' the aide answered promptly. Bending over his console pickup, he said, 'Ensign Hyland, stand by for President Len and the Governing Council for

Earth and Space.' Then he keyed in a quick series of commands.

The room speakers clicked to life.

They seemed to expand like a window into deep space. The background hum of thrust distortion muffled by noise-reduction circuitry gave an impression of depth, size; cold and uncomprehended distances just out of reach. Cleatus had the strange sense that he was listening to the interstellar mutter of a solar furnace as it broadcast unattainable light and heat across the void.

Len mustered the energy to lift his voice into the deep. 'Ensign Hyland? Can you hear me? I'm Abrim Len. President of the Council.'

'President Len,' a woman's voice answered. 'I'm Morn Hyland. Aboard *Punisher*.'

Cleatus had never heard Hyland speak; but he was instantly sure the voice was hers. The strain in the speakers grated across his nerves like nails on slate. There was no one in human space he wanted to listen to less.

His guts fumed with acid and anguish as he braced himself for disasters.

'I'm sorry you had to make me wait,' she continued sharply. 'This is urgent.'

'I'm sorry, too, Ensign.' Len sounded sincere. 'Representative government is unwieldy sometimes.

'The whole Council is here. I think we can all hear you. And I suspect we all have questions we want to ask. But if your reasons for contacting us are urgent, perhaps it would be best if you simply go ahead. When you're done – if you're willing – we'll ask our questions.'

At once the woman inquired, 'Is Director Hannish there?'

Cleatus saw Hannish cock an eyebrow in surprise. She hadn't expected this. Nevertheless she didn't presume to respond.

'Yes, she is,' Len acknowledged.

'Has she spoken to the Council?'

He, too, was surprised. He frowned uncertainly. 'Does it make a difference?'

517

'Time.' Static whetted the edges of Hyland's tone. 'That's the difference, Mr President. If I know what she's already told you, I can save time.

'*Trumpet* and *Punisher*'s command module will reach *Calm Horizons* in seventy-one minutes. I don't know what'll happen then. But I'm pretty sure whatever we do after that won't change anything. If we want to affect the outcome of this crisis, we have seventy-one minutes.'

Cleatus' PCR confirmed this.

'Tell me what Director Hannish told you,' Hyland demanded.

Len looked past the votes at his aide, slid one finger across his throat. At once the man silenced the pickups and speakers.

'Opinions?' Len asked. His manner warned the Members to be brief.

Silat spread his heads. 'It seems a reasonable request, Mr President.'

Cleatus couldn't let that pass. 'Unless she wants to make sure her story fits what we've already heard.'

Vertigus and a few of the sheep shook their heads. But none of them ventured to contradict Cleatus. His authority to speak in Holt's name still carried that much clout, anyway.

Len winced; rubbed his hands unsteadily up and down his face. Then he signaled his aide to open the channel.

'Forgive me, Ensign Hyland. I don't mean to make your circumstances more difficult than they already are. Please believe me when I say that anything you tell us will be more useful if it hasn't been edited to fit what we expect to hear.'

Chewing his lip in suspense, he waited for a reply.

After no more than a heartbeat of hesitation, Hyland conceded, 'All right. I want to talk to you. That's why I'm here. Nobody told me to do this. I'm not under any pressure. I just think you need to hear what I know.'

Cleatus was sure he could guess what she meant to say. Appalling prospect – But he took some comfort from Hannish's plain tension. When she thought no one was looking, the PR director gripped the arms of her seat; tightened her fingers until the sinews stood out on the backs of her hands.

She wasn't sure Hyland's story would match hers.

Her anxiety wasn't enough to satisfy him, however. He wished he could make her suffer as much as he did. But that was out of the question. She had absolutely no idea how much trouble they were all in.

As if she were delivering a formal report, Hyland began, 'My first deep-space assignment for the UMCP was aboard the destroyer *Starmaster*. We were sent to patrol the Com-Mine belt. There we witnessed the destruction of a mining camp by Captain Angus Thermopyle's ship, *Bright Beauty*. When we hailed him, he fled. We went after him. Unfortunately during the pursuit I developed gap-sickness, which caused me to initiate *Starmaster*'s self-destruct. I was the only survivor.

'Captain Thermopyle captured me from the wreckage and forced me to serve as his crew by giving me a zone implant. This had the advantage of managing my gap-sickness. In other ways, I was effectively his slave.

'Under his control, I used my UMCP credentials to protect him from Com-Mine Security's attempts to investigate *Starmaster*'s disappearance.'

The sheep were shocked. Some of them squirmed in their seats. Others hugged themselves with their arms. They hadn't known any of this. Cleatus himself was vague on some of the details: UMCPHQ's reports to Holt about Thermopyle's welding had been suspiciously imprecise. But the brutality of what Morn revealed – and the strict, strained way she mortified herself by telling it – kept the votes quiet.

'While Captain Thermopyle and I were on Com-Mine,' she went on, 'he was framed for stealing Station supplies. I can testify that he could not have committed that crime. At the time I only knew that he was framed by Captain Nick Succorso. But since then I've been given reason to believe that Captain Succorso was helped by Com-Mine Security Deputy Chief Milos Taverner.

'I'll return to that point in a minute. First I must explain that when Com-Mine Security came to arrest Captain Thermopyle, he tried to get rid of the evidence of his crimes against me. He offered me the control to my zone implant.'

Hyland faltered momentarily, then stated, 'I took it.'

That explains a lot, Cleatus breathed to Holt.

What, exactly? Holt asked.

If she controls her own zone implant, Cleatus replied, she's a goddamn superwoman. No wonder she's still alive.

Holt rejected the idea. That's not enough. Even superwomen don't have force-grown brats in forbidden space and survive. She must have had help.

'I took it,' she was saying, 'even though I understood its importance as evidence.' Even though she was a cop sworn to preserve evidence. 'I knew I was helping him avoid a sentence of death. I took it because I needed it. I'd become dependent on my zone implant. I wanted to control it myself. For that I was willing to let Captain Thermopyle live.

'Then I left Com-Mine with Captain Succorso aboard *Captain's Fancy*. I believed I had no other choice. Captain Succorso wasn't likely to discover my secret. If I surrendered to Com-Mine Security, they certainly would. And Captain Thermopyle would be killed.'

No shit.

'I'm telling you this,' she informed the Council, 'I'm explaining my own crimes so you'll know how I came by my information.'

Hannish had bowed her head, listening hard with her expression hidden by her hair. Cleatus couldn't read her reaction. He assumed she thought Hyland was some kind of hero.

Before Morn could go on, Manse waved her arm feverishly, demanding a chance to speak. Len glanced at her and nodded, but didn't recognize her. Instead he cleared his throat.

'Please forgive an interruption, Ensign Hyland. There's a point I would like you to clarify.

'According to Director Hannish, you were given to Captain Succorso as payment for his part in framing Captain Thermopyle. But you've just suggested that you went with Captain Succorso voluntarily. How do you –? '

'One doesn't preclude the other,' Hyland cut in: a woman

who knew what she was talking about. 'Captain Thermopyle's use of my zone implant left me practically insane. I made a whole series of bad decisions. Like joining *Captain's Fancy*. The UMCP may have asked Com-Mine Security to let me go. They could do that. I was an Enforcement Division ensign. But at the time' – she meant before the Preempt Act – 'they didn't have the authority to issue orders. If I'd surrendered myself, Com-Mine Security would have been forced to accept jurisdiction.

'I went with Captain Succorso. The UMCP persuaded Com-Mine Security to let me go.'

She'd sold herself for the control to her zone implant.

Which may have been the *only* thing she'd done that made sense to Cleatus. If zone implants weren't so damn illegal, he would have had one wired into his head years ago. As long as no one but him could touch the control.

Still Hyland condemned herself with virtually everything she said. That helped.

'Thank you, Ensign,' Len murmured. He sounded strangely wounded, as if he could imagine too many of the things she didn't say. 'Please go on.'

Morn's voice was harsh with static as she resumed.

'Since then I've been told that Captain Succorso and Deputy Chief Taverner were paid by UMCPDA to frame Captain Thermopyle. I'm told that his arrest and conviction served a political purpose for the UMCP. I don't know anything about that. But I am a witness to his innocence of the crime for which he was arrested.

'And I know where to find evidence of Deputy Chief Taverner's involvement with Captain Succorso. A playback of *Bright Beauty*'s datacore will show that Captain Thermopyle had traced a transmission link between *Captain's Fancy* and the Deputy Chief.'

Cleatus' guts clenched as he relayed this to Holt.

'Aboard *Captain's Fancy* I discovered I was pregnant.' God, the woman was remorseless. 'And I met the ship's engineer, Vector Shaheed. Dr Shaheed is a geneticist. At one time he worked for Intertech in the field of mutagen

521

immunity. He was close to success when his results were suppressed and his research stopped by UMCPDA.

'Captain Succorso confirmed this. He told me that DA had completed Dr Shaheed's research, and that he, Succorso, had the results in his possession. They were given to him so that he could carry out covert assignments for DA in forbidden space.'

That's hearsay, the FEA said into his throat pickup. He would need every lever he could find to shift the weight of Hyland's appalling narrative.

'I have no direct knowledge of the source of the drug.' As if deliberately, she admitted the weaknesses of her story before anyone could challenge them. 'But I can vouch for its effectiveness. Because I was pregnant, Captain Succorso took me to Enablement Station in forbidden space, where my unborn child was delivered and force-grown in an Amnion lab. At the time I observed that Captain Succorso relied on the drug for protection. On another occasion I tested it myself. When *Captain's Fancy* reached the bootleg shipyard Billingate, Captain Succorso gave me to the Amnion. They injected me with mutagens. More than once. I remained human because I'd stolen some of the drug, which I used while I was held prisoner.

'I hope this is clear, President Len. I can testify that an effective mutagen immunity drug exists, and that it is currently available to UMCP agents in the name of Data Acquisition.'

Too bad it didn't fail, Cleatus commented bitterly.

Damn, Holt murmured in his ear. I never should have let Ward talk me into giving Lebwohl that research.

Len cleared his throat uncomfortably. 'It's clear enough, Ensign Hyland. I don't expect you to tell us why Director Dios countenanced this kind of malfeasance.' He glanced sidelong at Cleatus. 'But I think you have a right to know that so far your story confirms what we've heard from Director Hannish.'

Hyland's voice seemed to fade out of the speakers briefly. When she spoke again, she sounded more distant; weakened by relief. 'Thank you, Mr President. I'm glad to hear that.'

Almost at once, however, she recovered her harshness.

'While I was held by the Amnion, Captain Thermopyle and *Trumpet* reached Billingate. I saw very little of what happened, but I've been told that Deputy Chief Taverner betrayed both Captain Thermopyle and Captain Succorso. I can't testify to that. I only know that Captain Thermopyle rescued me from the Amnion. He rescued my son, Davies Hyland, from the Billingate authorities. We were joined by Captain Succorso and Vector Shaheed, as well as by three more of *Captain's Fancy*'s crew, Sib Mackern, Mikka Vasaczk and Ciro Vasaczk. Together we escaped forbidden space during the destruction of Billingate.

'Later I learned that Captain Thermopyle had been reqqed by UMCPDA after his arrest and made into a cyborg. I can vouch for this also. I've seen his datacore.'

What? Cleatus wanted to demand. *Seen* his datacore? How?

'He was given zone implants,' she pronounced darkly. 'He was controlled by a computer. In that condition, the UMCP sent him to destroy Billingate and rescue me.'

She's lying, Cleatus panted to Holt. Must be. Dios had orders —

Seen his datacore?

No, Holt retorted. It's true. Just for an instant his concentration cracked. *Ward did this.* Then he recovered. Norna warned me, but I didn't guess what she meant.

Perfect! Cleatus snorted to himself. Dios' treachery went that far back. My God, he'd planned for all this!

Hannish's reactions no longer comforted him. He didn't care that she, too, hadn't expected Hyland to actually see Thermopyle's datacore.

Morn hadn't stopped. Ignoring the effects of her information, she plowed fatally ahead.

'But I guess his programming wasn't adequate to manage him after his mission succeeded. It's probably impossible to write instruction-sets to cover every eventuality indefinitely. For a while he was left free to make some of his own decisions.

'At my urging, and Dr Shaheed's, he took us to Massif-5.

We hoped Deaner Beckmann's bootleg lab would allow Vector to analyze Captain Succorso's antimutagen. Our intention was to discover the formula and make it public.

'Suppressing an effective mutagen immunity drug,' she explained grimly, 'is a crime against all humankind, and we meant to put a stop to it.'

Put a *stop* –? The woman's arrogance left Cleatus gasping.

Earlier Hannish had reported, *When* Trumpet *emerged from the swarm, she came out broadcasting the formula for the drug.* But she hadn't said why. Apparently she hadn't known. As she listened to Hyland now, her eyes shone with admiration.

But Hyland was angry. Her voice sawed across the static, driven by outrage.

'Unfortunately we were overtaken by a transmission from UMCPHQ, relayed to us by UMCP cruiser *Punisher* and ED Director Min Donner. It gave the priority-codes which controlled Captain Thermopyle to Nick Succorso.'

As Holt had ordered. To that extent, at least, Donner had kept her insubordination to herself.

What went wrong?

'This is important, President Len,' Morn insisted fiercely. 'Captain Thermopyle was a UMCP cyborg. In some ways he'd been set free. Nevertheless underlying UMCP restrictions and priorities still ruled him.

'That transmission took away the last of his volition. He became Captain Succorso's puppet.'

She paused; may have been trying to calm herself. Cleatus had time to wonder why she seemed so loyal to Thermopyle. Had she fallen in love with the murdering sonofabitch? More likely she was addicted to his particular brand of abuse.

When she continued, her tone held less violence. Instead she sounded tired to the bone; vulnerable to the cold dark implied by the speakers.

'Captain Succorso now commanded the ship. And he had no intention of releasing the antimutagen. He made that obvious. He wanted the formula, but he wanted it for himself.

'Fortunately there were other intentions at work as well. We learned later that the same transmission which betrayed

Angus to Nick also issued new programming to his datacore.'

Cleatus held his breath.

'When Captain Succorso and Vector Shaheed left the ship to use Deaner Beckmann's lab, that new programming caused Angus to reveal his priority-codes. For reasons we didn't understand, Davies and I were given the means to resist Nick.'

There! Cleatus thought. Black murder filled his head. *That's* how Dios did it. Even when he followed orders, he undermined them. And now terrible possibilities loomed overhead, straining to be born.

The votes may have been too stupid to grasp the implications; but Cleatus didn't miss them.

Dios *wanted* this. He made it happen.

Despite the force of that insight, however, Hyland's next words shocked the FEA.

'We didn't use them,' she reported brusquely. 'Instead Davies and I cut out Captain Thermopyle's datacore and let him reprogram it to block his priority-codes.'

Cleatus was too scared to contain himself. Blaring indignation, he shouted, 'You *what?*'

Len whirled to face him. 'Mr Fane, this is your last warning!' the President barked. 'Deputy Chief Ing, if the FEA speaks out of turn again, don't hesitate. Remove him.'

'Yes, *sir*, Mr President.' Ing sounded eager.

Fuming, Cleatus closed his mouth. But he left his demand hanging in the air. Good God! he protested to Holt. She's even more dangerous than I thought.

In disgust Holt muttered, Ward's been so goddamn busy rubbing the lamp he didn't notice it wasn't a genie coming out. It's a fucking nightmare.

With a final glare at Cleatus, Len turned away.

'Ensign Hyland,' he said apologetically, 'that was Cleatus Fane, First Executive Assistant to Holt Fasner.'

'I know the name.' The sound of knives filled Hyland's voice. 'Mr Fane, I've been the victim of a zone implant. I won't treat another human being that way. No matter who he is. Suppressing an antimutagen is a crime. So is welding illegals. I'll do anything I can to stop it.'

No question about it: the woman was an addict.

Vertigus raised a weak fist in approval. Hannish touched her palms together as if she wanted to clap. But neither of them spoke. Apparently they didn't want to risk exasperating Len further.

'I understand, Ensign,' Len sighed weakly. 'Please go on.'

Hyland paused for several heartbeats – so long that Cleatus wondered whether she'd given up. But then she returned.

'I'm almost done.

'When Dr Shaheed finished analyzing the drug, Davies and I made Captain Succorso prisoner, and we left the lab. But then we found both *Punisher* and *Calm Horizons* waiting for us. *Punisher* covered us while we escaped across the gap. Later both our gap and thrust drives failed, and *Punisher* was able to catch up with us. We joined ship and returned here.

'If you want to ask questions,' she finished, 'do it fast. We have fifty-six minutes left. I need the time.'

Cleatus Fane desperately wanted to know what she needed the time *for*. He understood too well how Holt might use it.

MIN

The acting UMCP director was desperately busy: sweating with strain; concentration stretched to tearing point. From the communications pickup on *Punisher*'s auxiliary bridge, she commanded nearly a dozen ships positioned for Earth's defense. She ruled UMCPHQ; directed preparations for damage-control and evacuation; supervised Center's efforts to ready the planet for war; chose or rejected information and instructions to be included in UMCPHQ's system-wide downlink. And she did what she could to protect the other stations within *Calm Horizons*' range. Those platforms with the capacity to adjust their orbits she sent on new trajectories: the rest she covered with her cordon. Her PCR brought in three, four, sometimes five channels at once. She responded as fast as she could key her pickup.

Valor on one. Confirm targ priorities.

Center on two. Nonessential personnel duty assignments?

Two of the pocket cruisers and at least one gunboat seemed incapable of comprehending the coordinates they'd been assigned.

SpaceLab Station on four. What happened to the scan net? We can't alter orbit blind.

Downlink control on one. Planet's screaming for the net. What explanation shall we give?

At the same time she felt desperately useless.

She'd come all this way: from her meeting with Captain Vertigus, when she'd given him Warden's Bill of Severance, to *Punisher*'s encounters with *Free Lunch* and *Trumpet* near the Com-Mine belt; across space toward Massif-5 and battle with *Calm Horizons*, beyond the VI system to retrieve the gap scout; homeward with Morn and Angus in command. And yet now there was nothing she could do except manage the crisis while *Trumpet*'s people determined the fate of Warden Dios, the UMCP, and humankind.

She needed –

God, she hardly knew what she needed; had no time to think about it.

Center on three. Suggest evacuation of nonessential personnel now.

Min said no. Where the hell were they going to go?

Gunboat *Flash Attack* on two. What's wrong with our position?

You're off line to intercept fire on PolyMed Station, she answered. Compensate. Get targ priorities from Center.

She needed to help Warden make restitution. She'd carried out his orders, even when they appalled her: she was as much to blame for the UMCP's crimes – and for *Calm Horizons'* presence – as he was. She would never forgive herself if she didn't do something to save him.

But there was nothing. In every effective sense, Morn had relinquished the cruiser when Dolph and the command module had carried *Trumpet* away. Yet that gave Min no relief. She'd decided long ago – was it only hours, or days? – to let the children of Warden's secret desires carry out the roles he'd prepared for them as they saw fit. Her frustration no longer centered on *Punisher*.

Everything that mattered was in someone else's hands. Since she couldn't go along with Dolph and Angus, she would have to live without her own forgiveness.

Center on two. *Sledgehammer* confirms targ priorities. Give her eight hours and she might be able to use them.

PR uplink from the emergency session on one. Vertigus wants to reintroduce his Bill of Severance. Fane proposes dechartering instead, rechartering with someone else as director.

Damn Cleatus Fane!

Valor on five. Reconfirm targ priorities? You want us to include UMCHO?

Min keyed an acknowledgment. She feared instinctively that Fasner might interfere with the command module and *Trumpet*.

Warden had put her in this position for a reason. Presumably he wanted her to survive so that she might pick up the pieces of humankind's defense after his efforts to bring down the Dragon had destroyed the UMCP. And presumably he'd picked her instead of someone else because he'd believed or hoped that she would let Morn and Angus make their own choices. She didn't know anyone else who would have done the same.

It wasn't enough for her. She meant to do the job he'd given her; intended to fulfill her oath of service to the absolute limit of her abilities. But it was no consolation –

Earth uplink on four. All major cities report escalating riots. Local police demand support.

We don't have any, Min snapped back. Tell them to concentrate on protecting disaster installations, planetary defenses, lives, in that order. They can worry about property later.

She needed more.

This whole gamble is your idea, Morn had told Angus before *Trumpet* broke radio contact. *If you don't see it through* – She may have shrugged. *I'll kill myself.*

No, you won't, he'd snorted back. *Not anymore.* Then he'd warned, *But you better jump like hell when the excitement starts. There's going to be a gap where* Calm Horizons *can take a crack at you. You can bet your ass she'll do it.*

I understand, Morn had answered. *I think Patrice can handle it.*

Min had seen Patrice in action: she knew what he could do.

She envied him the simple exigencies of helm. Demands labored at her as fast as *Punisher*'s dish could bring them in; but nothing she answered would make any difference if Angus

529

and Morn failed. Patrice could at least try to keep the ship alive.

Center on four.

Adventurous on one.

Downlink control on two.

Morn was doing her part. After a few difficulties, most of them procedural, Min had forced a link through Suka Bator communications. Then Morn had persuaded the GCES to hear her. Fane and Igensard had objected. Of course. But Len silenced them. Apparently the President had discovered a backbone Min didn't know was there.

Past the PCR babble in her ear she listened to Morn's transmission as Morn began to tell her story: the story for which she'd kept herself alive, commandeered *Punisher* and come home; the story for which she risked her son on Angus' good faith. The story of Warden Dios' crimes –

Min told Center to cancel her feed of the PR uplink. *Punisher*'s speakers brought her everything she needed to hear from the emergency session. She would have cringed at the things Morn said if Hashi hadn't warned her that Warden had ordered Koina to betray the same secrets.

Projecting relief and vehemence, Glessen had resumed the targ station when Mikka left. Porson ran scan at a scramble, pulling together input from UMCPHQ and all the other ships. Bydell helped him frantically. Cray worked communications support so that the gabble of channels in Min's ear wouldn't overlap each other.

At the auxiliary command station, Morn slumped over her pickup as if she were about to collapse. Her hair hung in her face. Her elbows propped her on the arm of her g-seat. She'd been through hell – and not least during the last twenty-four hours. All the strength she had left was focused in her voice.

If we want to affect the outcome of this crisis, we have seventy-one minutes.

Her voice held. Min was certain that the Council – and above all Cleatus Fane – had no idea how close to exhaustion Morn was.

Center on two. Message from UMCHO. CEO Fasner states that the GCES is about to strip Director Dios of his authority. A new director will be lawfully appointed. You're warned the consequences will be severe if you refuse to obey orders.

Ignore him, Min instructed harshly.

Adventurous on one. We have power-spikes. Matter cannon unstable. Must be a short in some of the old conduit. We'll trace and reroute as fast as we can. Until then we aren't good for much. Sorry, Director.

Flash Attack on four. We can cover for *Adventurous*.

Hold your position, Min ordered through her teeth.

Director, we're just sitting here!

So *sit*. If you want to commit suicide, do it on your own time.

Min fought to remain focused on her PCR, her duty. But she kept slipping away. The sound of Morn's voice tugged at her.

I went with Captain Succorso. The UMCP persuaded Com-Mine Security to let me go.

It was the truth. Min hated hearing it anyway. If she was useless now, how useless had she been when Morn went through the Academy? Or when she'd brought to Morn's home the stiff official condolences and empty honors for Bryony Hyland's death? How had she so completely failed to convince Morn that no UMCPED ensign was expected to suffer hell alone?

She'd failed because the truth was more convincing. If Morn had turned herself over to Com-Mine Security instead of running off with Nick, some other way would have been found to silence her; get rid of her. Holt Fasner would have seen to it. So that the Preempt Act would pass.

They injected me with mutagens. More than once.

Min winced. She hadn't known that. Often she'd asked herself if this Ensign Hyland was really the woman Warden wanted Morn to be; a woman he could trust. Now she was sure. Morn had been in Angus' hands for weeks – and Nick's for months. She'd been sold to the Amnion. They'd injected

531

her with mutagens. And yet she'd retained enough of her essential identity to come here and tell her story.

The ED director wished that she herself could do half as much to repay Warden's trust.

Downlink control on four. There are too many people for the disaster installations. We're doing what we can. Contingencies are ready for your approval.

Flash Attack on three. Tell *Calm Horizons* your command module has thrust failure. Dispatch us to complete the tow. We'll get in close, then smash that proton emitter before she can use it.

Center on one. Nonessential personnel are panicking. If we don't evacuate them, they'll go spaceshit.

Useless. Procedural details. All the real work belonged to Koina and Morn, Angus and Davies and Dolph.

Because she was useless, she toyed with *Flash Attack*'s suggestion. Then rejected it. Suka Bator would be saved. Maybe. But Warden, Angus and Dolph would die. So would the others.

And Angus' plan might work. If he did what he'd said. If he was telling the truth. If she didn't interfere.

Center on two.

Earth uplink on one.

Out of the confusion she heard Morn say, *I've seen his datacore.*

Min froze in midsentence. Seen –? A sensation of electric distress burned along her nerves. How? She forgot her PCR; forgot Center and her cordon of ships. *Why?*

As if to answer Min, Morn told President Len and the Council, *Davies and I cut out Captain Thermopyle's datacore and let him reprogram it to block his priority-codes.*

For an instant Min couldn't breathe. Shock paralyzed her synapses. Cut out – She hadn't known that, either; hadn't guessed – Angus had revealed that the Amnion taught him how to edit datacores. In exchange for *Viable Dreams.* He'd altered his datacore to block his priority-codes. But no one said Morn had anything to do with it.

And yet he must have had help. That was obvious. Min

should have realized it earlier. He couldn't cut open his own back to remove the chip. He might have programmed *Trumpet*'s sickbay to do it for him – but then hardwired stasis commands would have left him helpless to edit anything.

My God, Morn was a fool. Completely crazy. A man like Angus –

But she was also wonderful. Somehow she'd kept alive the dreams the cops should have served; the ideals they should have lived by. No matter what it cost her.

Suppressing an antimutagen is a crime, she told Fane. *So is welding illegals. I'll do anything I can to stop it.*

Min couldn't see. She had sudden tears in her eyes and a knot of grief in her throat.

Her PCR continued to demand her attention.

Director Lebwohl on five. I should talk to Koina, Min. He sounded breathless with haste. I've reviewed her uplink. She needs help.

Without transition Min found herself blinking at one of the auxiliary bridge displays – a scan plot of her cordon of ships – as if she'd noticed it for the first time. *Punisher* was there. *Valor. Adventurous. Flash Attack* and the others. The command module with *Trumpet.* Clustered around *Calm Horizons.* And UMCPHQ.

But because of the positions she'd assigned them they were also poised around UMCHO. She didn't trust the Dragon. That was the real reason she'd shut down the scan net in the first place.

Help?

Had Hashi succeeded?

Koina had explained Warden's secrets to the Council. With the passion of her personal experience, Morn was covering much of the same ground.

But Hashi –

He could raise the charges against Fasner to an entirely new level. If he hadn't failed. If he knew what he was doing.

And Dolph was on his way toward *Calm Horizons.* He and Angus and Davies, Mikka and Ciro and Vector, as well as

Warden: they might all survive – if Angus could keep his promise.

If he couldn't – if anything got in his way – they were as good as dead.

Abruptly Min understood the problem.

Timing.

The divergent pieces of Warden's hope needed to come together in a certain way. So that they would help each other succeed.

And she knew what she could do to help.

Please go on, President Len prompted Morn.

With a swift slash of her burned hand, Min gestured for Morn to stop talking.

Morn raised her head. A bleak question filled her battered gaze.

Director Lebwohl on three. Director Donner, this is urgent. Authorize a channel. I must speak to Director Hannish.

Min ignored him. 'We have a deadline,' she told Morn softly, intensely. 'When I give you the signal, get off that channel. Finish what you're saying and get off.'

A frown of strain and coercion had settled into Morn's face: it was becoming permanent. 'What deadline?'

'That's my problem. I'll handle it.' Trust me. But Morn needed more; deserved more. Quickly Min explained, 'If you go on too long, Fane will run out of time. We need to make sure he has room to hang himself.'

After a moment Morn nodded. The look she gave Min might have been the same one with which she'd received Min's condolences and honors years ago.

The ED director waited until she heard Morn announce to her pickup, *I'm almost done.* Then Min attacked the communications board with all her heart's thwarted, iron conviction.

Center, Director Lebwohl can have a channel to Suka Bator when I say so. Not before. Tell him to start the instant I give the word.

The delay would infuriate him. Nevertheless she believed

he would do his part. She'd learned a new respect for him when he'd resigned as acting director.

Stand by to relay targ priority changes, she ordered. All ships. All guns.

Rapid as automatic fire, she coded new commands. Dazed with exertion, Cray transmitted them for her.

The response was immediate.

Center on two. Are these priorities right, Director? She heard hints of hysteria. Are you serious?

She showed Center how serious she was. Do it, she snapped grimly. Then get me a channel to *Calm Horizons*.

Almost at once her PCR shot a burst of confusion into her ear.

Valor on four. *Adventurous* on one. *Flash Attack* on five. Reconfirm targ priorities!

Center on three. *Calm Horizons*, Director? Please confirm.

She was still waiting for a transmission link to the Amnioni when the countdown in her head told her that the time had come for Morn to stop.

CLEATUS

Get ready, Holt warned the FEA. Len won't let you tackle her yet. He's being too damn protective. But you'll get your chance when she's done.

After no more than a moment, several of the votes shot their hands into the air. Despite Holt's warning, Cleatus wanted to ask her, Why the hell do you need *time*? But he was too angry to wave his arm for permission to speak like a goddamn schoolkid.

For no apparent reason, Len indicated Silat. 'Senior Member Punjat Silat,' he announced formally to Hyland, 'Combined Asian Islands and Peninsulas.'

Ponderous with superiority and heart trouble, Silat climbed to his feet. 'Ensign Hyland,' he offered sanctimoniously, 'I will not delay you by describing how profoundly I admire your resourcefulness and courage. However, we must be clear on essential matters.

'Why does *Calm Horizons* pursue you? Why are the Amnion willing to risk a war in order to stop you?'

Morn had her answer ready. Unfortunately Cleatus felt sure she would support Hannish's accusations.

'They know we have an antimutagen. They know we're willing to broadcast it. They want to silence us if they can.

'And they want Davies.' The strain in her voice gave the impression that she held her arms locked over her chest. 'They were surprised by the results when he was force-grown.'

In fatigue and ire she explained, 'Simply turning a fetus

into a physiologically mature organism isn't enough. The new child needs a mind. Something to take the place of years of development. With their own kind, they imprint the mind of the host on the offspring. I guess it works for them. But in the past it hasn't worked for human beings. When they tried it, they lost the host. Apparently having your mind copied makes you insane. I think it's a fear reaction.

'But I didn't go insane when my mind was copied. My zone implant protected me. I had the control with me.

'They knew I had an implant. They could tell. But I guess they never thought of using one that way. They don't understand how fear affects humans.' She sighed. 'So now they think maybe they can use zone implants to let them copy human minds onto Amnion. Or Amnion minds onto humans. And they want to study Davies to find out how successful the imprinting was.'

Several of the sheep bleated aloud. Her explanation seemed more plausible than Hannish's bald statement earlier: it made the idea of Amnion that could pass as human look real. But Silat received the information as if it were only of academic interest. 'Thank you, Ensign Hyland,' he said impersonally as he sank into his chair. 'A fascinating insight.'

The smug bastard was probably planning his next monograph.

Damn it, Cleat, Holt insisted harshly, I want that kid! He's *perfect*. I can make a deal –

As soon as I get the chance, Cleatus promised. After I've torn her apart, even these morons will vote to decharter.

His grip on his bowels was so tight it made his chest hurt.

More hands. Len had reduced the Council to a kindergarten class.

His choices made no sense. He recognized Vest Martingale as if he felt sorry for her tarnished constituency; announced her to the room pickups.

Martingale stood up. 'Ensign Hyland, where is Captain Succorso now? Can we talk to him? His side of the story might shed some light.'

Com-Mine was blamed everywhere for the passage of the

Preempt Act. Martingale wanted to know what Succorso might say about Hashi Lebwohl and Milos Taverner.

'Captain Succorso is dead,' Hyland answered flatly.

That was a blow to Martingale's desire for vindication. 'Dead?' she demanded. 'What happened to him?'

'Member Martingale –' The woman sounded tired of trying to account for herself. 'When we left Deaner Beckmann's lab, we were under attack by Amnion surrogates and mercenaries. Captain Thermopyle used a singularity grenade to turn the battle. But Captain Succorso and Sib Mackern had left the ship to attempt an EVA ambush. As far as I know, they both died in the black hole.'

'Wait a minute,' Martingale shot back. 'Captain Succorso left the ship? *After* you made him prisoner?'

Cleatus hoped devoutly that Hyland would admit she'd had Succorso murdered.

No such luck. 'The ambush was his idea,' she retorted. 'He thought he could damage one of the ships we were fighting, an Amnion surrogate. And he had as much to lose as we did. We let him try.' For a moment her voice seemed to ache in the gap between her pickup and the Council's speakers. 'Sib Mackern went along to make sure he didn't turn on us.'

Martingale bit her lip in disappointment. 'Thank you, Ensign Hyland.' She sat down heavily.

Another flurry of hands. The sheep seemed to thrive on being treated like children.

Len surprised Cleatus by nodding to Igensard. 'Special Counsel Maxim Igensard,' he told Hyland, 'in proxy for Eastern Union Senior Member Sen Abdullah.'

Igensard jumped up so fast he almost tripped himself. The misguided idiot probably wanted to redeem his credibility.

'Ensign Hyland,' he began as if he meant to sneer but had forgotten how, 'you've had time to study the situation. You've talked to Director Donner.' They'd had plenty of opportunity to decide on a story. 'You said – I assume you were telling the truth – the transmission you received from *Punisher* included two sets of contradictory instructions. In retrospect, how do you account for that?'

He must have struck a nerve. Morn snapped, 'Special Counsel, I've come too far to waste my time lying to you.' But she didn't refuse to answer his question.

'The orders that gave Captain Thermopyle's codes to Nick Succorso were perfectly clear. Anybody who received that transmission would have understood them.' Including, presumably, Donner herself. And *Punisher*. 'But the programming which caused Captain Thermopyle to reveal his codes to us was encrypted. It was written in a kind of embedded machine language none of us recognized.

'We asked Director Donner if she had anything to do with it. She states that UMCPHQ's transmission was relayed exactly as the cruiser received it. *Punisher*'s communications log confirms this.

'The transmission was coded from Warden Dios. He wrote it.'

Oh, hell, Cleatus groaned in disappointment. She knew. The damn woman had figured out what must have happened.

Why wasn't she *dead*, where she belonged?

As if she had the right to make such statements, she pronounced, 'I believe that when Director Dios issued his plain instructions he was carrying out someone else's orders. Or he wanted to mislead someone he feared. The encrypted instructions represent his true intentions. He meant to foil whoever wished Nick Succorso to have control of Angus.

'As far as I know,' she finished in a spatter of static, 'the only man in human space who can give orders to the director of the UMCP – or threaten him – is Holt Fasner.'

Of course. Another accusation. But Cleatus didn't bother to comment on it. He knew in his guts there was worse to come.

Igensard made a desperate effort to recover his earlier righteousness. 'You're speculating, Ensign Hyland,' he countered. 'You can't prove any of that.'

'True.' She was sure of herself; so sure that she didn't falter for a second. 'But I can tell you *this*, Special Counsel.

'Captain Thermopyle has told me – and Director Donner

has confirmed – that DA wrote his programming explicitly to prevent him from rescuing me. I was considered dangerous because I could testify that he was framed. But I couldn't do any harm as long as I was with Nick Succorso. If he didn't kill me, someone else would. Unless Captain Thermopyle interfered.

'So why am I alive?'

She paused as if she wanted to be sure all the votes were listening. Then she said, 'I'm alive because Captain Thermopyle was given new orders. Just before he was released from UMCPHQ, Warden Dios switched his datacore. His new programming included instruction-sets which required him to save me.'

The bastard! Holt rasped in Cleatus' ear. So *that's* how he did it. I knew she must have had help.

Fiercely Hyland concluded, 'The Warden Dios who wants me alive is not the same man who handed Captain Thermopyle's priority-codes to Nick Succorso. Nick would have cheerfully killed me. As soon as he could think of a way to do it with enough pain and degradation.

'I'm here telling you my story because Warden Dios made that possible.'

Panting, Holt explained, He's been planning this ever since he sent Thermopyle to Billingate – no, ever since he let Succorso take that fucking woman off Com-Mine. By God, he started to betray me months ago!

Cleatus shook his head in dismay, appalled by the realization that Dios was so dangerous; so much more dangerous than he'd ever imagined. Even when the bastard was stuck aboard *Calm Horizons*, he worked through puppets like Hyland to ruin –

Igensard looked helplessly at Cleatus; but Cleatus offered him no assistance. If he couldn't think of a way to attack Hyland's assertions, that was his problem. His ambitions meant nothing to the FEA.

'None of this makes sense, Ensign,' Igensard protested weakly. He was too distraught to notice that he was simply feeding her the questions she wanted; helping her score her points. 'Dios has been the UMCP director for years. Why has he started countermanding his own orders now?'

'Maybe,' the woman retorted at once, 'this is his first real chance to show you that Holt Fasner isn't fit to be responsible for the UMCP.'

Gray failure tinged Igensard's face as he slumped down into his seat.

Fit? Holt snarled. His fury seethed like Fane's guts. *She doesn't think I'm* fit? *If I get my hands on her, I'll teach her a thing or two about* fit.

At the moment Cleatus could think of nothing he wanted in life except to help Holt crucify Hyland. The votes had been right on the *edge* of enacting his, Cleatus', proposal. Now he would have to start the whole process again.

Gritting his teeth to curb his exasperation, he lifted his hand like a good little boy.

Len ignored him. Goading him – The effete twit may have wished to provoke an eruption so he could carry out his threat to have Cleatus removed. Ing was stupidly eager to obey.

Cleatus contained his indignation as Len recognized Sixten Vertigus. At once Vertigus levered his old bones upright.

'It's an honor, Captain.' Interference marred Hyland's transmission, but she sounded sincere. 'I wish we could have met under other circumstances.'

Inanely Vertigus flapped a hand she couldn't see. 'The honor's mine, Ensign.' His voice wobbled. 'You're a valiant woman.' With a visible effort he tightened his grip on himself until he was able to speak more steadily. 'I wish I could tell you everything you've done will be worth what it cost. But none of us are sure how this mess is going to turn out.'

He looked at Hannish as if he were talking to her as well as to Hyland.

'Director Hannish has told us *Punisher*'s command module is towing *Trumpet* to *Calm Horizons*. What's going on, Ensign? Director Dios must have reached some kind of agreement with the Amnion. We need to know what it is.'

For the first time Morn hesitated. When she answered, her tone had lost some of its certainty.

'We're responding to *Calm Horizons'* demands.'

Apparently she wasn't sure how much she could afford to let the votes know.

Her caution brought Cleatus to the edge of his seat. Instinct told him that she was about to give him the opening he needed.

Vertigus frowned. He didn't know how to take Hyland's response. 'I assume you've been in contact with Director Dios.'

'We've talked to him, yes,' Hyland said distantly.

'Is he all right?'

Again she hesitated. 'He sounds all right.'

Static surrounded her words like an aura. What she said – or what she meant – was embedded in it. Nevertheless Cleatus thought he heard hints of distress through the distortion.

Vertigus missed them. Or he believed that what he wanted to know was more important. Instead of probing her hesitation, he rephrased his question.

'What did he tell you to do?'

'He didn't tell us to do anything.' Her discomfort made her impatient; cryptic. 'He relayed *Calm Horizons'* demands. Now we're responding to them.'

Vertigus scrubbed his face with both hands like a man trying to wake himself up. 'Forgive me, Ensign. You aren't being clear. Or I'm being stupid.' Bingo. 'Do you mean to say Director Dios did *not* reach an agreement with the Amnion?'

Hyland sighed. 'That's right.'

'But if *he* didn't,' the old fool protested, 'who *did*? Somebody must have. Isn't your command module on the way to *Calm Horizons*? With *Trumpet*?'

An instant of silence from the transmission conveyed the impression that Hyland tapped depleted reserves; summoned the last of her strength. Then she said harshly, 'I did, Captain.'

Vertigus gaped at the speakers. Most of the sheep did the same. His voice cracked as he demanded, 'On whose authority?'

'On *mine*,' she snapped. '*I'm* in command here.' A woman

542

on the brink of an abyss. '*I* have the bridge. I stopped taking Warden Dios' orders when he abandoned me to Nick Succorso. We're responding to *Calm Horizons* on *my* authority.

'Ask UMCPHQ Center,' she finished. 'They'll confirm it.'

If Cleatus hadn't been forewarned, he would have been as shocked as the votes. Fortunately he was ready. He'd known for some time that Hyland commanded *Punisher*. By intuition he'd grasped the implications.

A mere ensign had arrogated to herself the responsibility for humankind's survival. And for keeping the Council alive.

Exactly the opening he needed.

Before anyone in the room could speak, the speakers emitted the metallic pop of a toggled pickup.

'*I'll* confirm it,' a new voice barked; another woman.

Cleatus recognized her as soon as she said her name.

'This is Min Donner, UMCP Acting Director, aboard *Punisher*. Ensign Morn Hyland is in command of this vessel. She and Captain Thermopyle took the bridge when they came aboard.

'And it's a damn good thing they did.' Intensity clanged like iron in her voice, but Cleatus couldn't interpret it. Fury? Desperation? 'She's negotiated an arrangement that may actually keep you alive. Which is more than I could have done. If it were up to me, we would all have fried by now.'

Vertigus struggled to control his chagrin. 'Acting Director, this is Captain Vertigus. What arrangement?'

I swear, Holt spat, every idiot in human space works for Ward. He's pulling too many strings. If we don't start to cut them soon –

He didn't finish the warning. He didn't need to. Cleatus understood him perfectly.

As if she were stifling curses, Donner replied, '*Calm Horizons* has agreed to leave without shooting at us. Morn has agreed to let them have Davies Hyland, Vector Shaheed and *Trumpet*. Captain Ubikwe is using the command module to keep our part of the bargain.

'Davies is her *son*,' she asserted. She must have thought that was important.

Before Vertigus – or Len – could challenge her, she snapped, 'Donner out,' and silenced her pickup with a violent click.

Cleatus feared that *Punisher*'s transmission had been cut off. But the cavernous hiss and spatter of the speakers told him the channel was still open.

Go! Holt ordered. Now!

Cleatus jumped. For the moment, at least, Vertigus was too shaken to find words. And Len seemed to founder in confusion. None of the other Members knew what to do.

The FEA didn't say a word; didn't give Len any excuse to remove him. Leaping to his feet, he flung his hand like a mute shout at the President.

Hannish opened her mouth to object, then bit it shut again.

Under the circumstances, Len couldn't refuse. His gaze flinched and wavered in alarm. Apparently he needed his grip on the podium to keep him upright.

'Ensign Hyland –' The words stuck in his throat. He swallowed thickly, then tried again. 'Ensign, will you answer a question from UMC First Executive Assistant Cleatus Fane?'

The damn woman may have thought she no longer had anything to fear. 'We're on a countdown here, Mr President.' Already her attention seemed to be elsewhere. 'He's got two minutes.'

Len turned a look like a groan at Cleatus. 'Mr Fane.'

Cleatus fought down his squirming trepidation. Quietly, hiding his hopes, he asked, 'Ensign Hyland, you said Director Dios "sounds all right". I get the impression you aren't sure. Why not? What're you worried about?'

That got her. She hesitated again. The background noise of the speakers suggested groping.

His heart thudded without mercy while he waited.

Abruptly she answered, 'The Amnion have a special mutagen, Mr Fane.' Her voice had changed. It carried an ache Cleatus couldn't name. 'A delayed reaction mutagen. It doesn't start to work until ten minutes or so after it's been injected. And they have an antidote. It's not a cure. It just keeps the mutagen inert. As long as you have the antidote in your system, you don't mutate. As soon as it runs out, you turn into an Amnioni.

'They use this mutagen for blackmail. They inject you with it. Then you do what they say, or they don't give you the antidote. We know about it because it was done to one of us. Ciro Vasaczk.'

She paused, groping again, then admitted softly, 'We're concerned that Director Dios may be under that kind of pressure.

'He says he has a suicide capsule. I don't doubt him. But I'm not sure even that would be enough to protect him.'

There Cleatus identified the change in her voice. It was a note of farewell. She'd already given up hope for Warden Dios.

Good-bye.

And good riddance.

That was all Cleatus needed from her.

He remained on his feet, even though his question had been answered, and votes around him flapped their arms like scarecrows. From the knotted tension in his guts to the throbbing pulse in his temples, he was sure that Hyland hadn't told the truth; not the *whole* truth.

He believed her 'concern' for Dios. He knew that much of what she'd said was dangerously accurate. But she'd stated more than once that she felt pressed for time. She'd just announced, *We're on a countdown here*. Earlier she'd said, *We have fifty-six minutes left. I need the time*. And she hadn't explained why.

If her side of her bargain with *Calm Horizons* could be fulfilled by her kid, Shaheed and *Trumpet*, what else did she have to do? What *countdown* was she talking about?

She was keeping secrets. Plotting something. Lying –

He conveyed this to Holt; but it didn't disturb him. In fact, he was counting on it. Let her try any desperate trick she could think of: on *Calm Horizons*; on UMCPHQ; on Holt. Cleatus didn't care. Not as long as she *shut up* and let him get to work.

There was a moment of confusion while Len scanned the

room, trying to decide which of the sheep he should recognize next. Then Hyland took the choice away from him.

'Mr President,' she announced roughly, 'I can't afford any more time. I hope I can tell my story in more detail when this is over.'

Before Len could reply, she said, '*Punisher* out.'

At once her transmission disappeared from the speakers. Cold space punctuated by particle noise took its place until Len's aide closed the channel. Then the Council's link to the contest of ships far overhead was gone.

Finally!

The sheep turned glazed, vacuous stares toward each other, stunned by their own incomprehension. Vertigus fumbled at a console he apparently didn't know how to use. Hannish watched Len with her legs poised under her, no doubt champing for a chance to point out how neatly Hyland's story supported hers. Burnish and Manse consulted urgently with each other. Martingale hissed fury at her aides like a woman who wanted to tell the entire created universe that Com-Mine had been maligned. Carsin kept her horrified gaze on her Senior Member, Vertigus, as if she thought he might start to show signs of mutation.

Cleatus' downlink told him that *Punisher*'s command module was thirty-eight minutes away from *Calm Horizons*.

'Mr President,' he ventured, 'may I address the Council?'

He'd lost ground; a lot of it. That was obvious. Anything which confirmed Hannish's facts suggested the illogical implication that her conclusions were also accurate. Most of the votes were too stupid to tell the difference between evidence and inference. Martingale had gone over to the enemy. Carsin was wavering. Hell, even Igensard had collapsed.

But Morn Hyland had given Cleatus the opening he needed.

With an air of defeat, Len conceded the floor. He seemed to be the only one in the room besides Cleatus who'd grasped the significance of Hyland's last revelation.

'Thank you, Mr President.' This time the FEA left his place and ascended the dais. Now it was essential for him to dominate the Council. He took any advantage he could get: elevation; physical presence; fear.

With an effort of will that made him sweat, he kept his tone mild. He would lose even more ground if any hint of his underlying desperation showed; if he betrayed by any word or inflection or gesture that he was fighting for his life.

Some of the votes were hostile. But most of them were simply frightened; scared out of their small minds by proton cannon and mutation and treason. Deliberately Cleatus set himself to direct their fear where it would do the most good.

'Members, it's time for action.' The voice of reason, stating the irrefutable, pointing out the inevitable. 'Ensign Hyland's story has made that obvious. It's urgent that you reach a decision now. As she said herself, if you don't act before *Punisher*'s command module and *Trumpet* reach *Calm Horizons*, nothing you do will make a difference.

'You don't need me to tell you that it's the task of this body and this session to make a difference.'

Determined to succeed, he forced himself to relax against the podium.

'You have two choices. Only two, that I can see. The UWB Senior Member's Bill of Severance. Or my proposal to decharter the UMCP so that they can be rechartered with a new director. You must pass one or the other.

'Unfortunately' – Cleatus sighed with false regret – 'I think a Bill of Severance has just ceased to be an option.'

He was the Dragon's First Executive Assistant. Even his enemies didn't presume to treat him the way Hannish had been treated: interrupted and hectored at every turn. Only Len had dared insult him – and the weak little man clearly had no intention of doing so again. The votes who were dependent on the UMC hung on his every word, waiting for him to save them from their dilemma. Those who weren't actively hostile gave him a chance to persuade them. And the rest didn't risk offending him.

With nothing except Holt's voice to distract him, Cleatus was allowed to speak for his master unimpeded.

'The whole point of such a bill,' he explained, 'is that it

547

preserves the present hierarchy, operations and personnel of the UMCP. It shifts accountability from the UMC to the GCES. Everything else is maintained intact.

'In other words,' he stated heavily, 'Warden Dios remains as director.'

He sighed again. 'Well, you heard Ensign Hyland. She's "concerned" that Director Dios is being blackmailed. And I, for one, take her concerns seriously. I think she knows what she's talking about.

'To be injected with a delayed-reaction mutagen would be a terrible thing. But it would be even more terrible to let a man in that condition keep his job.'

Good, Holt murmured. Don't stop.

In case the sheep weren't scared enough, Cleatus asked, 'Do any of you think you could stand up to that kind of blackmail? Do you think Warden Dios can? For myself, I'm not sure.

'If you *aren't* sure,' he asserted, 'it would be inexcusable to let him stay on as director.'

Vertigus fluttered an arm like a drowning man; tried to inject a protest. The idiot refused to give up. Even Hannish had enough sense to hang her head; but Vertigus went on floundering.

Cleatus talked over him.

'Captain Vertigus wants to suggest an alternative. Perhaps an amendment to his Bill, stipulating that Min Donner assumes the position of UMCP director until the immediate crisis is past, and Warden Dios can go to a lab for some bloodwork.' The look on Sixten's face showed that Cleatus had guessed right. 'I'm sorry, that isn't good enough. Min Donner is aboard *Punisher*, a ship she doesn't command. Her own life is in the hands of renegade cops who may or may not be telling us the truth about what they want.

'In fact,' he digressed, 'we have reason to think they are not. I'll get to that in a minute.'

Then he resumed, 'My point is this. If she can't control her own movements, or make her own decisions, she certainly can't take charge of the UMCP.

'And who else is there?' Grimly he restrained his impulse to shout the sheep into flight. 'Director Lebwohl? Do you want him to command our defense? No, I'm afraid a Bill of Severance is no longer a viable alternative.'

Argue with that, you silly bastards. I dare you.

Enough, Holt pronounced. They're convinced. Unless they're too stupid to live. Go on before you lose them.

Cleatus swore mutely at the voice in his ear; but he obeyed.

'On the other side' – visceral outrage gave his voice an edge he couldn't suppress – 'Director Hannish has raised some rather distressing objections to my proposal. She blames virtually every crime the cops have committed on Holt Fasner.

'For her part, Ensign Hyland doesn't go quite so far. She only accuses Holt Fasner of wanting her dead so she can't testify that Captain Thermopyle was framed – of wanting her dead so badly that he ordered Director Dios to give control over DA's welded cyborg to Nick Succorso.

'I'll respond to those charges.'

He paused to let his anger grow. If he couldn't contain it, he might as well use it. Still he chose his words carefully.

'I think we'll have to take Director Hannish's facts as given. Ensign Hyland has confirmed a number of them. And since she's safely sequestered aboard *Punisher*, we can't examine her evidence. Because we have so little time left, we must assume that Director Hannish, at least, has told us the truth.'

As it appears to her, Holt prompted unnecessarily.

'As it appears to her,' Cleatus intoned.

'I've already talked about this. I don't want to belabor the obvious. Everything Director Hannish has revealed was supplied by Director Dios – the man directly responsible for the crimes she reports. And she can't prove any of her charges. They're all based on inference and distrust.

'Do you believe her? As I said earlier, consider the source. Warden Dios betrayed Com-Mine Security, framed Angus Thermopyle, tricked you into passing the Preempt Act. He suppressed an effective antimutagen and maneuvered the Amnion into committing an act of war. And now he's been caught. He's stuck in a mess of his own making. So of course he wants to pin the blame on someone else. That's his only hope.' The FEA's tone hinted at bloodshed. 'He knows he'll be executed if he can't convince you he was just following orders.

'What else do you expect from a man who's capable of the crimes Warden Dios has committed?'

He paused, trying to give his question the force of an indictment. Then he went on, 'It's a fact Director Hannish can't dispute that Warden Dios has refused to speak to Holt Fasner since this crisis began. And for almost twenty-four hours before that he kept himself incommunicado. He's declined to explain himself or his actions to the one man in human space who could have held him accountable.'

Good, Holt murmured in approval. Good.

Since Holt was satisfied, Cleatus took the next step.

'Where Ensign Hyland is concerned, I'm not convinced she's telling the truth.'

Now he did his best to sound rueful: the sorrow of a man who hated impugning Hyland after all she'd suffered, but whose responsibility to the Council left him no choice.

'Again consider the source.

'For one thing, she's patently insane.' He ticked off indications at random. 'She kept her zone implant control. She let the Amnion force-grow her baby. She broadcast Dr Shaheed's formula while *Calm Horizons* could hear it. She freed Thermopyle from his priority-codes. She took command of *Punisher*.

'Which she must have done at gunpoint,' he added. 'Or by threatening them with those singularity grenades. I can't imagine that Min Donner would have let it happen otherwise.'

Then he continued tallying the evidence against Morn Hyland. 'In addition, she took it on herself to negotiate for our survival. And she sold her own son to keep herself alive.' That was enough. 'It's all madness. And this lunatic theory linking Holt Fasner with Nick Succorso proves it. After everything she's done and endured, she's plainly demented.'

Be careful, Holt warned. *The votes feel sorry for her. Don't give them a reason to react the wrong way.*

'But that's not all,' Cleatus said at once. 'If it were, I wouldn't mention it. Who am I to question her decisions after everything she's been through? I have to ask, however' – he made a show of shouldering an unpleasant burden – 'exactly what *is* her relationship with Angus Thermopyle?'

He had the satisfaction of seeing the Hannish bitch wince. The rest of his audience stared at him, rapt or dumbfounded.

'She concealed evidence that would have led to his execution by Com-Mine. She freed him from his priority-codes. And did you notice that her deal with *Calm Horizons* doesn't include him?

'What's going on here? Is this an example of the hostage syndrome, where women fall in love with the men who trap and abuse them? Since she admits the crime of keeping her zone implant control, how can we believe her when she says Thermopyle was framed? Her only evidence conveniently exists in the datacore of a ship which has already been dis-mantled.

'She's a cop. She knew what she was doing. Like Warden Dios, she's ruined if she can't pin the blame on someone else.'

Damn it, Holt snapped, *I told you to be careful!*

Gritting his teeth, Cleatus forged ahead. 'And isn't it really Angus Thermopyle who's in command of *Punisher*? That would make more sense. He has some strange power over Ensign Hyland. He has singularity grenades. And he has a reason – he might call it a good reason – to hold *Punisher* as well as Director Donner under duress. He's a welded cyborg. He may be slime, but he's had every vestige of choice and dignity stripped away from him. He must want revenge. He wouldn't be human if he didn't.

'Everything you just heard from Ensign Hyland – including her implausible "deal" with *Calm Horizons* – could be Angus Thermopyle's revenge. If he wants to destroy the UMCP for what they did to him, he could hardly hope for a better way to go about it.

551

'Why do you think the scan net is down? Do you really believe Min Donner ordered that? Do you believe it actually restricts what *Calm Horizons* can see without limiting the effectiveness of our ships? I don't. I think the net is down because that suits what Captain Thermopyle has in mind.'

Nice recovery, Holt gibed. He sounded more cheerful. *I'm* convinced.

Just wait, Cleatus muttered into his pickup. I'm not done.

'But even that's not all,' he told the votes. 'There are two other points I want you to consider.

'According to Ensign Hyland, the Amnion had her in their hands twice. What if she's lying about the effectiveness of this antimutagen? What if it didn't come from DA, isn't based on Shaheed's research? What if the Amnion have already gotten what they wanted from Davies Hyland? What if the whole story is a fabrication?

'What if Morn Hyland is no longer human? What if this entire disaster is some incomprehensible Amnion plot to discredit the UMCP and Holt Fasner just when we need them most?'

Are you listening, bitch? he asked Hannish mutely. Do you think you have a monopoly on tainting people with unsubstantiated charges?

Shit, Cleat! Holt yelped. I warned you to be careful! You've gone too far. They don't want to hear that!

He was right. Some of the sheep muttered protests. Manse mouthed, No, no, in shock and refusal. Burnish exchanged whispered objections with his aides and Carsin. Len shifted forward as if he meant to intervene. Just loudly enough to be heard, Silat observed, 'This charade seems rather too elaborate and – if I may say so – too human to be attributed to the Amnion.'

Quickly Cleatus retreated a step. 'It's just speculation, of course,' he admitted with apparent candor. 'It would explain a lot – but I really don't have a scrap of evidence. Hell, *I* don't have any way of knowing where Succorso got his antimutagen. Or how good it is. But if I were a Member of this Council,' he added sententiously, 'I would want to take every possibility into account, no matter how farfetched it sounds.'

That mollified the votes somewhat. Manse and Len subsided. Silat inclined his head condescendingly. After a moment Burnish silenced himself like a man biting his tongue.

Behind her expressionless mask, Hannish's face was pallid with misery. She seemed to think he'd already won.

He wasn't sure. Hurrying to recover his momentum, he stated, 'One more point, and I'll sit down. I've saved this for last, but it may be more important than all the others.'

Some of the sheep groaned; but he ignored them.

'I said earlier we have reason to think Hyland may be lying. Actually, I'm sure she is.' Before Hannish or Vertigus could react, he asserted, 'She hasn't told us the truth about her deal with *Calm Horizons*.'

He hoped his audience would hear the words he didn't say: *And if she's willing to lie about that, she could lie about anything.*

'Obviously she's under some kind of pressure,' he explained. 'Otherwise why did she say, "I can't afford any more time." At first we all thought she was referring to the deadline of the command module's dock with *Calm Horizons*. But that's still twenty-two minutes away,' according to his downlink, 'and yet she couldn't "afford any more time" ten minutes ago.

'*Why* is she out of time? It doesn't make sense. If she really made a deal – if the Amnion have agreed to let us live in exchange for Davies Hyland, Dr Shaheed and *Trumpet* – what's left for her to do? What *can* she do?

'There's only one explanation.' Abruptly he stiffened; let veiled outrage into his voice. 'She has something planned. Something she doesn't want us to know about. Something that will have a direct effect on the outcome of this crisis.

'It may be she intends to cheat *Calm Horizons* somehow,' he suggested bitterly. 'Or it's possible she's actually agreed to give away a hell of a lot more than she admits. For all we know, we've been doomed without the decency of any forewarning. Or maybe we'll have to live with an arrangement that's too expensive for humankind to sustain.

'She's crazy, remember. Whether you want to hear that or not, she's crazy.

'Whatever happens,' he sneered, 'it will happen because an abused ensign took it into her head to negotiate our survival on terms she isn't willing to explain.'

All right, Cleat, Holt put in. You've made your point. Now let them vote. We can still pull this off.

Cleatus couldn't stop. 'Am I the only one,' he demanded harshly, 'who can smell Angus Thermopyle's reek in all this?'

Yet he had to stop. Holt was right: the time had come. If the bastards couldn't make up their minds now, they were beyond hope. They deserved any terrible thing that happened to them.

But, God! Cleatus Fane did not want to share their fate.

Suddenly he felt as tired as Len looked. 'Members,' he sighed, 'I've answered your objections as well as I can. It's up to you. The future of our species has to be decided now.'

Heavily he left the dais, returned to his seat. For a moment he had no idea where matters stood. Exhaustion filled him like defeat, and he couldn't begin to estimate the mood of the Council. There must have been more he could have said; some better way to meet Holt's demands; some sentence or argument that would have turned the fear of the sheep to his purposes. He simply couldn't imagine what it might be. He'd done his best. Now he had to leave his personal terror in the hands of a gaggle of twits and cowards.

When he heard Len ask for a motion from the floor, however, and saw how the votes treated his proposal to recharter the UMCP, he knew that he would live.

CIRO

Ciro Vasaczk knew he was insane; but the fact didn't trouble him. He had more important things on his mind.

First among them was *Calm Horizons*.

The huge defensive was still half an hour away when he and Angus climbed out of *Trumpet*'s airlock in their EVA suits; cleated their belts to the gap scout's sun-streaked metal skin; settled themselves to wait.

'They won't spot us,' Angus had assured him earlier. 'I can emit jamming fields. Several kinds. They'll cover me. Both of us while we're together. After that you're on your own. But you'll be under their targ range. Behind the module and *Trumpet*. And they'll be distracted. You should be safe enough.'

'I want to get out there early.'

The sweat in his voice told Ciro he was lying; coercing himself. With the insight of his insanity, Ciro recognized that Angus was terrified of EVA; of being confined and helpless in the vast dark. His breathing wheezed hoarsely from his intercom.

'That bastard's so big – I need time to study her. Figure out the dangers. Plan my moves.'

Ciro hadn't argued. He had moves of his own to plan. From the lift to the airlock and then outside he'd followed Angus.

There he got his first human look at his enemy.

Because the solar furnace would have scalded his eyes in their sockets, he'd dialed the polarization of his visor high. As a result, *Calm Horizons* seemed to loom ahead like a dark beast crouching in the unutterable night of space; a predator poised to spring from the concealment of midnight. Nevertheless he could see her clearly enough. Lights blazed from ports, emplacements, airlocks: she already had spotlights and video fixed on the approaching vessels; already had the dock she intended for the command module etched in illumination.

Despite the shroud of blackness, she revealed enough of herself to show him that she was enormous. Her bulk blotted out half the heavens, and the few stars he could see past the rim of her hull looked paltry and unattainable, like forgotten dreams.

The sight scared him. *Calm Horizons* was his doom; as fatal as mutagens and proton cannon fire. But that didn't shake his commitment. It didn't shake his trust in Angus.

The Amnioni meant to use Davies and Vector against humankind. On top of that, she was the only available source for the particular antimutagen which had kept Sorus Chatelaine human.

She was responsible for what Sorus Chatelaine did to him.

He could make out UMCPHQ as well, a ball of steel half-licked by sunfire. The orbital platform showed lights of all kinds, as if the cops thought they could manage the dark by emblazoning their place in it. Vaguely Ciro recognized that UMCPHQ was an altogether bigger construct than the defensive. But distance shrank the station: light shrank it by limning it so precisely. UMCPHQ merely caught the sun and gleamed: *Calm Horizons* dominated the cold gulf between the planets.

Other sparks too close for stars indicated more ships, according to Angus – part of Min Donner's cordon. Other stations must have been out there, too. If Ciro squinted against the sunlight past *Trumpet*'s stern, he could identify *Punisher*'s obscure shape, nearly lost in the dark. But he paid no attention to the cruiser. On those occasions when he felt afraid, and wanted to look away from *Calm Horizons*, he preferred to turn toward the bright planet hanging like a backdrop beyond UMCPHQ.

Earth.

Sunshine burned blue across the wide oceans, picked islands and continents like brown intaglio out of the azure. By some trick of the light, or his visor's polarization, he couldn't see any clouds. The whole lambent atmosphere of the planet seemed untrammeled, as clean as the seas, warm, welcoming – and utterly defenseless; exposed to violence.

Ciro had never witnessed in person the effects of a super-light proton beam; but he knew enough physics to imagine *Calm Horizons'* cannon striking a shaft of ruin into the heart of one of those brown, populated features and reducing it to char. A wound that profound would be visible from a distance far greater than his.

He wasn't born there. Neither were his parents. But *their* parents were. It was his planet. His genetic code remembered it, even though his mind held no recollection. Belted to *Trumpet's* skin while the command module towed her toward *Calm Horizons*, he was as near as he would ever come to his homeworld.

If he and Angus failed, that ineffable, aching swath of blue would become humanity's graveyard.

For the third time Angus checked Ciro's anchor. It was always possible that the approach protocols *Calm Horizons* assigned would force Captain Ubikwe to use thrust suddenly.

Ciro's belt was secure. He wasn't crazy in a way that made him think he could hold on with just his hands.

'You know what to do?' Angus' voice gasped inside his helmet. 'You're sure?'

Ciro understood that the Amnioni couldn't hear them on this channel. He and Angus were linked to each other, and to *Trumpet* and the command module, by specialized fre-quencies which the enemy wouldn't recognize. Still he wished Angus didn't talk so much. The sound in his ears made him feel exposed, as if words might betray him to the defensive.

He hefted his impact rifle. It was secured to his belt by a flexsteel line. 'The hatch is open,' he breathed softly. Angus had opened it before they left *Punisher*. 'Everything's ready. I won't let you down.'

To some extent that was a lie. He'd already figured out exactly how he would disobey Angus' orders.

Angus knew the truth, of course. He grasped everything else. But for Mikka's sake – or his own – he acted like he expected Ciro to do what he was told.

'Make sure you don't,' he panted back. 'I don't care how crazy you are. We can't afford any screwups.'

Angus himself was only armed with a pair of laser cutters. He carried nothing else except an extra EVA suit strapped to his back and a heavy canister of plexulose hull-sealant clipped to his belt. If Ciro hadn't trusted him, the boy would have wondered how much damage Angus could do with such puny weapons.

'Leave him alone, Angus,' Mikka muttered from *Trumpet*'s bridge: automatic protectiveness, with no force behind it. 'If he does screw up, you won't die any faster than he does.'

'You like the view out there?' Captain Ubikwe asked before Angus could reply. He spoke in a soothing rumble, trying to defuse tension between Angus and Mikka. 'They tell me it's spectacular, but I don't enjoy it much. I guess I've spent too much time behind metal walls. Open space makes me want to puke.'

'Then it's a good thing you don't have my job, fat man,' Angus croaked. He might have been choking.

'Damn straight.' Captain Ubikwe sounded cheerful; almost happy. 'I'm fine where I am.'

If everything else went wrong, he was supposed to cut *Trumpet* loose and try to ram *Calm Horizons'* proton emitter. Apparently he didn't mind imagining that kind of death.

Ciro disapproved. He felt diminished by Captain Ubikwe's good humor. He was sure the captain didn't trust him.

'I wish you would all shut up,' he put in petulantly. He hated his own voice. It was too much like a kid's. 'I already have enough to think about.'

To his surprise, both Mikka and Captain Ubikwe fell silent. Angus didn't. But Ciro had heard it all before: to some extent he could tune it out. Instead of listening, he concentrated on *Calm Horizons* – and on the woman, *Soar*'s captain, who had made him what he was.

In some sense he'd fallen in love with her. She'd injected a mutagen into his veins. She'd ordered him to destroy *Trumpet*. Now she was dead – and he'd failed to carry out her wishes. He was bound to her by attachments as intimate as passion.

He considered himself responsible for her epitaph; the way she would be remembered. Because she owned him, the outcome of her life was his to define, and he meant to do it justice.

He intended to follow her example in directions she would never have dreamed were possible.

LANE

Lane Harbinger felt poleaxed by exhaustion – a disconcerting sensation for a woman who often lived on an exclusive diet of artificial stimulants. She hardly knew what to do with herself. Should she put her head down? Close her eyes? That was tempting. But then she would miss –

Instead she lit another nic, gulped down the remains of a flask of coffee laced with hype, and stumbled away from her console toward the lab foodvend for a refill.

Strange – She could hardly keep her balance. Her knees no longer seemed to hinge normally, and her feet had an imprecise relationship with the floor. Had she ever been this tired? Ever in her life? She couldn't remember.

That, too, was strange. She liked to think of herself as a woman who remembered everything.

She must have been expecting some kind of epiphany. Some small blaze of vindication. Perhaps just a little shaft of triumph. Maybe that was why she felt so disoriented. Nothing of the sort had happened. Her eyes had simply lost their ability to focus, and a minor vertigo had begun to tug delicately at the side of her head.

Reality as she'd always known it had just undergone a radical transformation – and all she could think of to do about it was lie down.

She needed hype. Caffeine. Hell, she needed IV stim. Maybe then she would be able to sort out the situation.

After a couple of swallows of coffee, which the foodvend supplied hot enough to raise blisters on anyone else's tongue, she noticed that Hashi was ranting.

He stormed back and forth in front of Chief Mandich as if he thought Mandich might appreciate why he was so incensed – as if he'd forgotten that Mandich was Enforcement Division, therefore brain-numb almost by definition. For a moment all Lane heard were dissociated accusations like 'irresponsibility' and 'arrogance' and 'monomania'. Monomania, ha! He was a fine one to talk. But then she concentrated harder and recognized several words in a row.

'– refused to authorize a channel!'

Something like nausea squirmed in Lane's stomach. She felt her disorientation getting worse.

'I'm sure Director Donner has a good reason,' the Chief of Security retorted stiffly. He should have been as tired as Lane was, but he didn't look it. Instead he looked like he wanted to hit Hashi.

'Of *course* she has a good reason!' Hashi fumed back. 'She is the acting director of the UMCP' – he sneered the words – 'and she's developed a passion for it. She adores control. Is that not what ED is *for*?' He flailed his scrawny arms. 'Henceforward no one will be allowed to breathe or think or shit his pants without Her Lordship's authorization!'

Lane was vaguely amazed to hear herself ask, 'What's going on, Hashi?' She hadn't realized that she could muster the strength for any more confusion.

He wheeled on her with such vehemence that his glasses slipped off his nose. He caught them expertly in midair, however, and slapped them back onto his face.

'Min Donner in her vast wisdom,' he snarled savagely, 'refuses to let me contact Koina.'

Oh, dear. That was a problem. What was it all for, everything she and Hashi and Mandich had done, if they weren't allowed to tell the Council about it?

But Mandich snapped, 'That's not true, and you know it.' The brainless fidelity of Min Donner's underlings was legendary. 'She didn't say you can't have a channel. She said you can't have a channel until she gives the word. Until she's ready.'

'A distinction without a difference.' Hashi seethed and spat with exasperation like a beaker of fulminating acid. 'Our efforts are wasted. As is the ordeal Koina has been forced to undergo without evidence. And I can scarcely *bear* to contemplate the consequences for Warden, who has labored with such cunning to bring about precisely these circumstances.

'Min Donner,' he asserted bitterly, 'grasps neither the significance nor the urgency of what we have accomplished!'

The Chief's fists strained in front of him. Lane wondered whether he would actually strike Hashi. If he didn't, she worried that he might start to trash the lab.

If he did, what would she do? Call ED Security? Ha! That was a joke.

'Bullshit,' he snorted. 'I'm sure she understands it as well as you do. If she doesn't, it's because you didn't explain it to her. You're so goddamn *cryptic*' – he punched at the word as if it meant *dishonest* – 'you can't answer a straight question, or tell a straight truth.'

Hashi brushed that accusation aside. It might have been as insubstantial as the smoke from Lane's nic.

Suddenly he rounded on Mandich. 'But *you* could req a channel for me. As Chief of ED Security, and acting ED director, you have the authority. Center will obey you.

'You need not tell them why you desire a channel. Your general duties will suffice as explanation.' His voice snarled like a hive of wasps. 'You have it in your hands to redeem the UMCP as well as Warden Dios.'

The Chief stared back in disbelief. Then his face closed. 'Go to hell, Lebwohl. I'll see you dead first.

'Do you think I like being the man who let a kaze get Godsen Frik?' Dark fury gathered in his eyes. 'The man who missed Alt? I've got so much goddamn responsibility for this mess I can hardly carry it around. If I screw up again, I might as well be dead. I'll sure as hell be useless.

'The only thing I know is my duty. I get my orders from

Director Donner. I'm not going to betray my job and my oath by letting you pressure me into insubordination.'

'*But I must talk to the Council!*' Hashi yelled.

To her amazement, Lane thought she heard desperation in his voice.

She sighed. Her gaze slipped out of focus. He and Mandich blurred into the background.

He wanted to talk to the Council. He loved to talk. Sometimes she suspected that he loved talk more than life.

Thinly she murmured, 'Maybe she has a reason.' Where had that idea come from? 'One you haven't thought of.'

But Hashi didn't react with the same indignation he heaped on Mandich. She'd snagged his attention somehow. He stared at her with his mouth open; bit it shut. The smears on his lenses caught the light in streaks.

'A reason I haven't thought of?' With unexpected restraint, he asked, 'Such as?'

He may have recognized that she was nearly comatose.

She levered her shoulders into a shrug. 'Your guess is as good as mine.' After a momentary lapse she added, 'She knows more about what's going on than you do.'

Mandich nodded fiercely.

Hashi peered at her as if he, too, couldn't focus his eyes. Or couldn't believe what he saw. In an ominous wheeze, he inquired, 'Are you suggesting that I must trust Min Donner?'

'*I'm* suggesting that,' Mandich rasped.

Hashi and Lane ignored him.

'You picked her as acting director.' Lane wasn't quite sure why she considered this relevant. 'I didn't.' She seemed to be speaking in her sleep.

'Is her high-handedness my doing?' Hashi protested querulously. But at once he flapped his hands to dismiss the question. 'I take your point, however. Why did I ask her to assume my duties, if I was reluctant to trust her? If I was wrong then, I can hardly correct the error now.

'It follows, as you say, that I'm forced to guess what her reason might be. Otherwise I run the risk of undermining her'

– he flung a glare at Mandich – 'presumably commendable intentions.'

'My God,' the Security Chief muttered to himself, 'an outbreak of reason. I can't believe it.'

Hashi didn't reply. He might not have heard Mandich. Hooking his glasses off his face, he held them with one finger while he rubbed the heels of his palms into his eyes, trying to grind his vision clear.

Obliquely Lane remembered the flask of coffee in her hands. She lifted it to her mouth – it seemed to come up from an astonishing distance – and emptied it. Damn, it was already cold. She needed the burn to help her concentrate. Time for a refill.

She got as far as discarding the butt of her nic and lighting another. Then she forgot what she was about to do.

Hashi had put his glasses back on. 'Very well,' he said as soon as she looked at him. 'If she claims the right to choose when the Council will be addressed, I will determine who speaks for us.' He squared his shoulders. 'Attend your pickup, Lane.' He pointed toward her console. 'When Director Donner allows us a channel, *you* will contact Director Hannish.'

She nearly fell. Her flask did: when her fingers went numb, it slipped away from her and clanged plaintively on the deck. Had she dropped her nic as well? She must have. It wasn't in either of her hands. She couldn't feel its reassurance between her lips.

Without warning tears began to stream down her face.

'No,' she groaned. 'Hashi, please. I can't. I'm too –'

All at once she knew exactly what kind of vindication she wanted. She wanted to sit quietly and listen while someone else used the results of her work to make a difference. If she took that risk herself, it would all fall apart.

'You're out of your mind, Lebwohl,' Mandich objected. 'Look at her. She can barely stand.'

'You *must*,' Hashi insisted through her tears. 'I am forced to guess at Min's intentions. Therefore I speculate that they concern credibility. She hopes to choose a moment when the Council will be receptive to our evidence.

564

'But if that is a valid concern, then it is also valid to consider how our evidence is presented. And I am –'

He faltered. For a moment he couldn't speak. He had to move closer to her, stand right in front of her, before he could go on.

'I'm tainted, Lane.' She had the odd impression that he was humbling himself: a sacrifice he made for the sake of something more important. 'In recent days I've issued too many statements which the Council – and most especially FEA Cleatus Fane – will deem falsehoods. No doubt I'm perceived as Warden's creature, in service to him rather than to the facts. If he has committed treason, then I have also. That argument will be used to erode the impact of my testimony.

'Chief Mandich is similarly disqualified by his famous loyalty to Enforcement Division.'

Mandich scowled at this assertion, but didn't argue with it.

'The truth' – Hashi used that word as if it made him uncomfortable – 'will carry more conviction if it comes from you.'

He may have been right. Or not. She couldn't tell. But his appeal reached her all the same. The thought that the Members might refuse to believe the truth simply because they heard it from him was more than she could bear. The only part of herself she valued, the only part she took pride in, was her ability to sift through the rubble of facts until she found bedrock. And she respected Hashi, not because he was admittedly brilliant, but because he'd never hampered or misused that part of her.

If she had to confront humankind's future in person in order to affirm the results of her work –

'In that case,' she told Hashi weakly, 'you'd better order up a hypo of stim from the infirmary.' She couldn't stop crying. 'Otherwise I won't be able to stay on my feet.'

Instead of returning to her console, she folded to the deck and covered her face with her hands.

KOINA

For the sake of her professional pride, she refused to cringe in shame and regret while President Len called the Council to vote on Cleatus Fane's proposal.

She'd failed in the worst possible way: her efforts to weaken the Dragon's grip on the GCES – and the UMCP – had only made it stronger. Cleatus had outplayed her. In the end, everything Warden had dreamed or desired would die because Holt Fasner's people served him more effectively than she did.

What could she have done? she asked herself over and over again. The question was important to her. She had no evidence. Nevertheless she could hardly face Members like Sixten Vertigus, Blaine Manse and Tel Burnish without weeping. She couldn't rid herself of the conviction that there must have been *some* way she could have made a difference.

Still nothing came to her. No desperate gesture or extravagant appeal would work now. The simple truth was that she'd failed. Cleatus would win. And the consequences for humankind's future would be devastating.

Poor Abrim had wanted her to succeed: his extraordinary assertiveness made that obvious. Morn's plight had touched a source of unexpected strength in him. And even now he did whatever he could to postpone the inevitable debacle. After the FEA's proposal had been moved and seconded, he insisted on hearing its precise language for the record. That took a few moments. Then he launched a slow, tedious roll-call vote, asking the Members one at a time by name where they stood; announcing their positions back to them; logging the tally in the Council's official minutes. Despite the urgency of the situation – and Fane's fuming impatience – he led the Members on a weary trudge through the procedure of Warden's ruin.

Koina admired the attempt, but she knew it was wasted. The tally had already reached eight: six in favor, one opposed, one abstention. As soon as the count on Holt's side reached eleven, a simple majority, he could take the vote as law, even if Abrim required all the remaining Members to commit themselves.

She was vaguely surprised by that one nay. It came from Sigurd Carsin, the UWB Junior Member. Captain Vertigus was her Senior Member; but for years she'd opposed him as if she considered his criticisms of the UMC and Holt Fasner contemptible. Apparently, however, she'd reevaluated her allegiances. After casting her vote, she'd reached over and touched Sixten's shoulder as if she wanted to express commiseration or support.

That small, unexpected victory should have meant something to Koina, but she no longer had the energy to appreciate it. Her waning resources were fixed on the cruel task of sustaining her facade while each vote drove Fane's stake deeper into the heart of the UMCP she wished to serve.

There were now seven in favor and two abstentions. So far no one had joined Sigurd Carsin.

At Koina's side Cleatus seethed in silence. As far as she could tell, he wasn't using his throat pickup. Apparently one of his techs had the job of reporting the vote's progress. If the Dragon spoke to him, he showed no reaction. Instead he watched the Members – and especially President Len – with a corrosive glare which seemed to promise trouble for his opponents.

Sixten looked like he was asleep, overtaken by age and defeat. Tel Burnish and Blaine Manse hadn't voted yet. Neither had Punjat Silat. They might bring the total opposed to five. But that was nowhere near enough. And who else would join them? Who had the courage? Vest Martingale, perhaps: her outrage might carry her. On the other hand, the UMC was the majority shareholder in Com-Mine Station –

Eight in favor. Maxim Igensard delivered Sen Abdullah's proxy in a voice that shook with disappointed fervor.

Koina began to think that she should excuse herself; leave the room before the end. Then she would be able to weep in peace. But her duty called her to witness this slow death: the incremental murder of humankind's hope. She remained where she was while her heart brimmed over with desolation.

She hardly reacted when one of her techs shifted toward her, touched her arm.

'Director,' the woman whispered, 'I'm getting a call from Lane Harbinger.'

Koina stared straight ahead while her brain limped to comprehend. Lane –? She didn't recognize the name. Or did she? It left a tingle she couldn't identify somewhere in her tired synapses. One of Center's officers, probably, calling to ask her some painful question, or to give her more bad news.

'Dr Lane Harbinger,' the tech prompted, covering her urgency. 'She works for DA.'

DA –?

As if by magic, Koina remembered the precise tone of Hashi's voice when he'd asked her, *Are you acquainted with Lane Harbinger?* They'd been aboard her shuttle from UMCPHQ, on their way to hear Sixten's Bill of Severance fail. For his own obscure reasons, Hashi had remarked, *You have much in common.*

'She wants to address the Council,' the tech explained tensely.

Without transition an eerie sense of dislocation took over Koina. She no longer seemed to have any control over her own behavior. In fact, she might have sworn that she took no part in it. As far as she knew, she was asking her tech – or herself – What for? Doesn't she know how important this is? I'm surprised Center gave her a channel.

According to Hashi, Lane had uncovered some tiny but significant bit of information about Godsen Frik's murder.

568

Apparently she'd been able to determine that the SOD-CMOS chip of the kaze's presumably faked id tag contained current GCES Security source-code – a detail which Hashi had considered almost preternaturally fascinating. Koina couldn't remember why.

But all that was beside the point. Traces of evidence left behind by Godsen's killer had no relevance here. No scrap of source-code, however suggestive, could avert Warden's downfall.

So what in God's name did Lane *want*?

Nevertheless Koina asked none of those questions. Her thoughts had no connection to what she did. Her body had reasons of its own. As if it belonged to someone else, it leaped upright instantly; flailed its arms for Abrim's attention.

While her brain struggled with its confusion, her mouth called out, 'President Len!'

To her dismay, she didn't have the slightest idea what she meant to say.

'Director Hannish!' Cleatus blared at her like a decompression klaxon. 'Sit down!'

He was right, of course. She was out of order; had no business speaking; she'd already failed. Stricken with shame, she sank back to her seat –

– while her body remained on its feet. Her limbs balanced themselves like a fighter's, as if she intended to strike anyone who interfered with her. 'President Len!' she called again. 'You have to hear this!'

Cleatus swore viciously at her back. Several of the Members tried to shout her down. Sixten raised his head to give her a bleary, baffled stare. She ignored everyone except Abrim; everything except the expression on his face.

Christ, what was she *doing*? In another minute she would be ejected from the room. Abrim wouldn't have any choice. He'd threatened to have Cleatus removed: for the sake of consistency, if not for some better reason, he would feel compelled to carry out his threat on her.

At first, however, he was too surprised to censure her interruption. 'Hear what?' he asked with a perplexed frown.

569

Koina didn't know that. She didn't know anything.

She must have known. Otherwise how could she have answered?

'Mr President,' she announced, 'Dr Lane Harbinger is on my downlink from UMCPHQ.' Her voice held firm despite her bewilderment. 'She works in Data Acquisition. She wants to address the Council.'

Abrim groaned a protest. 'Director Hannish, you can't *do* this.' Angry, exhausted regret filled his face. 'We're in the middle of a *vote*, for God's sake!' His mouth twisted as if he wanted to spit out something that tasted nasty. 'We've already allowed you to say everything we can stand to hear. Now you have to let us finish. While there's still time.'

Time: that was the problem. Koina needed to understand herself, but she couldn't; she'd run out of time –

Then she did.

Time. Of course. The linchpin of Cleatus' persuasion: the goad he'd used to drive his proposal forward. For his master's reasons, if not his own, he was frantic to beat the deadline of the command module's dock with *Calm Horizons*.

At that moment her dislocation passed.

Aboard her shuttle wasn't the only time she'd heard Hashi talk about Lane. He'd also mentioned the researcher during that last meeting with Warden Dios, when he, Koina and Chief Mandich had met in one of the UMCP director's private offices.

Lane was involved in the investigation of Nathan Alt.

With a rush Koina caught the inference she'd missed earlier; grasped the argument she should have presented.

'I'm sorry, Mr President,' she stated firmly. 'It's *not* an important vote. In fact, it's meaningless.'

The President's jaw dropped. Maxim blustered a contradiction. Several of the Members who'd already voted yelled at her.

While Cleatus summoned a blast of denial, Koina explained, 'The whole thrust of Mr Fane's proposal is that Warden Dios is under suspicion of treason, and we can't afford to let an accused traitor make deals with the Amnion for us – deals that could affect humankind's entire future.' With the intensity of a shout, she proclaimed, '*But Warden Dios isn't making any deals*. Morn Hyland has done that. She told us so herself. And she's going to keep right on doing it, no matter *who* the UMCP director is, or who issues the orders.

'You *heard* her,' Koina insisted. 'She doesn't recognize any authority except her own.

'As Mr Fane pointed out, she obviously hasn't revealed the whole truth about her dealings with *Calm Horizons*. If she won't even tell us what her intentions are, she certainly won't change them simply because we've replaced Warden Dios.

'The First Executive Assistant's proposal doesn't need to be voted into law right now. It's just not that crucial. It won't make any immediate difference.'

At once Cleatus bounded to his feet, bristling in outrage. His PCR seemed to fill his head with pain. Or fear.

'That's *preposterous*!' he yelped. 'Mr President, this is obviously a desperate –'

Koina raised her voice to carry over him. Clarion and sure, she trumpeted, 'UMCPHQ Center would not have assigned Lane Harbinger a channel – and Acting Director Donner certainly wouldn't have authorized it – if what she wants to say weren't vitally important. This Council needs to hear her!

'We've been debating extreme accusations for hours. If you asked me to guess,' she finished, 'I would say that Dr Harbinger wants to give evidence.'

President Len bowed his head as if he couldn't carry the weight of his dismay.

Before Abrim could reply, Cleatus started again. Like a burst of impact fire, he barked, 'This is obviously a desperate and *irresponsible* attempt to interfere with the will of the Council. It's a *ploy*, Mr President. While we've been dragging out this *interminable* vote, Director Hannish has been in contact with UMCPHQ. No doubt she's asked them to arrange some kind of disruption. To save Dios' hide, of course.

'*Lane Harbinger*, for God's sake,' he sneered with scalding indignation. 'One of Director Lebwohl's stooges. Clearly this is the best they could cobble together on short notice.

'*Listen* to her, if you think it's worth the effort.' He flapped his arms as if he were done. 'Go ahead. I'm curious myself.' Then he yelled with such vehemence that he seemed to knock plaster off the walls, '*But finish the goddamn vote first!*'

The struggle on Abrim's features was painful to watch. He'd already exerted more force during this session than in all the years of his tenure put together. By nature – and perhaps by conviction – he favored conciliation, compromise. That was how he held onto his office. A more commanding president would have been voted out long ago, forced to step aside by the Dragon's vast constituency.

But today he'd faced down Cleatus Fane; bent Maxim Igensard to his authority – The effort had left him in a state approaching nervous prostration.

He held the sides of the podium so tightly that Koina could see his elbows quivering. His mace lay in front of him, forgotten. Sweat on his upper lip caught the light like beads of misery.

'Members –' he began; then faltered and fell silent.

She watched in horrified suspense as he strained to recover. If he collapsed, who would take over? As a body the GCES determined precedence by rotation rather than seniority. Whose *turn* was it? She couldn't remember.

Abruptly one of her techs stood. The woman was pale and wide-eyed, frightened by her own temerity. Nevertheless she was determined to speak.

'Mr President,' she reported meekly, 'Dr Harbinger insists that what she has to say is of the utmost importance. She swears that if you don't hear her you'll never forgive yourself.'

Then she sat down; composed herself like a woman who wished she had someplace to hide.

Koina nodded in silent approval. Apparently she wasn't the only one who wanted UMCPPR to do its job right.

President Len tried again. 'Members –' His voice was a hoarse whisper, raw with strain. 'I will allow this interruption. We'll continue voting after we've heard Dr Harbinger.'

'*By God!*' Cleatus roared; then cut himself off; staggered;

clapped a hand to his ear as if his PCR had started screaming at him. For a moment he groped around him, unable to find his balance. Then he seemed to steady himself by sheer force of will. Turning his back, he withdrew to his seat. As he sank into his chair, sweat stood on his forehead, and his eyes seemed to roll in terror.

Koina guessed that Holt Fasner also wanted to hear what Lane would say.

Quickly she told her techs, 'Route Dr Harbinger's channel to the room speakers. President Len's aide will patch you in. Tell her we'll be ready in a minute.'

As Abrim's aide hurried to handle UMCPHQ's transmission, the President slumped against the podium. 'This is your idea, Director Hannish,' he croaked as if he'd damaged his larynx. 'You talk to her.'

Weakly he beckoned Koina to the dais.

She couldn't hesitate now; couldn't afford uncertainty or fear. Striding rapidly, she approached the dais; ascended to stand beside President Len.

While she waited for his aide to complete the connection from her downlink, she forced herself to face the Council again.

She'd found that difficult the last time, but this was much worse. She had no idea what Lane might say; couldn't imagine what kind of evidence Lane might have uncovered. And where was Hashi? Or Chief Mandich?

What if Cleatus was right? What if Lane *had* no evidence? What if Hashi – or Min – had ordered her call in a last-ditch effort to delay Warden's inevitable ruin?

Koina didn't think she could bear to take part in another failure; not like this, with everyone in the room watching her, and Warden's damaged hopes on the line.

But failure and success were out of her hands. In the name of her commitments she could only do her job and accept what happened. Blaine Manse and Sixten sat on the edges of their chairs. Punjat Silat rubbed his chest as if he wondered how much longer his heart would go on beating. Tel Burnish squirmed with tension. None of them had anything else to hope for. When Abrim's aide signaled to her, she buried her fear behind her professional mask; cleared her throat and began at once.

'Dr Harbinger, this is Director Hannish.' Thank God her voice didn't quaver. 'We're using a patchwork communications setup here. Can you hear me all right?'

'Director Hannish,' a woman replied stiffly from the speakers. 'I'm Lane Harbinger.' Her transmission was cleaner than Morn's had been. Apart from a hint of echo and a faint crackle – the gain on her pickup may have been set too high – no distortion touched her voice. 'You're coming through fine. Can the Council hear *me*?'

'Yes, Dr Harbinger,' Koina assured her. 'All the Members are here, as well FEA Cleatus Fane and myself. You're perfectly clear.'

'Good,' Lane muttered. 'I'm too tired to wrestle with technical difficulties.' The rasp in her tone sounded like irritation, but it may have been fatigue. 'I'm living on pure stim as it is. I almost fell asleep waiting for you to make up your minds to hear me.'

Koina winced inwardly. 'The issues before the Council are complex, Dr Harbinger. The Members are moving as fast as they can.'

She meant, *Help* me, Lane. Don't make this harder by alienating them.

Lane sighed. 'I suppose they are. I'll try to keep it simple.' For a moment her voice seemed to fray out of the speakers. Then she went on more sharply, 'Before you reach any conclusions, you should know that the UMC is guilty of treason.'

Softly Cleatus growled, 'Here we go again.'

Several of his supporters nodded. Koina guessed that they were growing restive under the threat of the Dragon's ire.

Lane had said 'the UMC', not 'Holt Fasner'. Was that significant, or was she just being cautious?

'"Treason" is a provocative word, Dr Harbinger,' Koina countered before anyone else could take up Cleatus' objection. 'Perhaps you should start at the beginning.'

Lane didn't hesitate. 'I'm a research tech for UMCPDA,' she stated at once. 'I don't have anything to do with policy or politics. I deal in facts. Tangible reality. What other people do with those facts is their problem, not mine.

'I've been assigned to study the physical evidence from that last kaze. The one that almost got you. Determine the facts.'

Then, however, she faded to silence. The speakers emitted a rough wheeze of respiration, as if she'd dropped off to sleep.

My God, Koina thought in dismay, how long have you been working on this?

Carefully she prompted, 'What physical evidence?'

Lane's voice returned with a thud, as if she'd dropped something heavy beside her pickup. 'Well, the body, of course. But we also have his id tag and GCES Security credentials.'

'How is that possible?' Koina asked. 'The man blew himself up.' She knew the answer: she was simply trying to help Lane.

'Director Lebwohl grabbed them. Before the kaze went off. I've been working with them since then.'

Koina didn't risk so much as a glance at Cleatus. She wasn't sure she could bear it if she saw that Lane's statement didn't surprise him.

'I see. Please go on.'

The researcher sighed again. 'If you've read ED Security's preliminary reports, you know the id tag and credentials identified a GCES Security sergeant named Clay Imposs, but the man using them was really Nathan Alt.'

Now the Council could hear every breath she took. Koina had the disturbing impression that Lane had put her head down with her mouth right on her pickup. Each hoarse intake and exhalation seemed to fill the speakers with a claustrophobic urgency.

'Captain Nathan Alt was UMCPED until Director Donner court-martialed him for dereliction. Since then he's had a number of jobs. Most recently the UMC hired him as Security Liaison for Anodyne Systems.' Unnecessarily she explained, 'Anodyne is a subsidiary of the UMC. They manufacture the SOD-CMOS chips we use in datacores – and id tags.'

Cleatus raised his voice to announce, 'I revealed all this to Warden Dios yesterday.'

Lane took a sharp breath. 'Is that Cleatus Fane?'

'It is, Dr Harbinger,' Koina answered.

'Good. I like it.' Lane's tone seemed to gather strength, as if she'd found a new source of energy – or been given another dose of stim.

'Mr Fane,' she rasped. 'According to our log of that conversation, you told Director Dios Nathan Alt was fired six weeks ago. Because he had dealings with the native Earthers.

'Is that right?'

'It is,' the FEA said firmly.

Koina thought she heard a bitter grin in the researcher's voice as Lane retorted, 'Well, you're lying.'

Half a dozen Members gasped. President Len covered his eyes with one hand to conceal his reaction. Unselfconsciously Sixten clenched his old fists in front of his chest like a kid wishing with all his might for a miracle.

Cleatus started to launch a furious rejoinder, then clamped his mouth shut on it. Apparently his master had called him to heel again. Instead of defending himself, he wrapped his arms across his belly and let Lane say what she wanted.

The rest of the room was paralyzed by the crowded strain of her breathing. Simply listening to it made Koina's chest hurt.

'The body told us a lot,' Lane resumed. 'For one thing, it was full of hypnagogic drugs. For another, the bomb had a chemical trigger. The catalyst was contained in a false tooth. Of course, the man himself can't testify. He's too dead.' The raw edge of her respiration suggested another grin. 'But the circumstantial evidence is clear. Alt entered the Council chamber in a state of deep hypnosis. On a preconditioned signal, he bit down to break his false tooth. The catalyst entered his system. A minute or two later he exploded.

'It's also clear that he must have been given the signal by someone in the room. Someone he could see. Or hear. He was in no condition to make decisions himself. So you had a traitor with you during the last session. Since no one's been allowed to leave the island, he's probably still there.'

'Except Hashi Lebwohl,' Cleatus interrupted. 'He was here then. But he left. He hasn't returned. And he was in a better position than anyone to give a signal. He could easily have triggered the explosion, and then switched credentials to supply the "evidence" that makes you think I'm lying.'

He was floundering. Koina half expected him to accuse her, as well – or Forrest Ing. But he didn't.

'I guess that's true,' Lane murmured. 'Interesting idea.' She paused like a woman swallowing a yawn. 'On the other hand, it's relatively easy to prove Director Lebwohl hasn't had access to any SOD-CMOS chips for several weeks. Especially not this particular chip.'

As she went on, she began to breathe harder. The speakers carried a heavy throb of exertion. She was near her physiological limits.

'Obviously the id tag and credentials are crucial. They're our best clue to where this kaze came from.

'How were they doctored to identify Nathan Alt as Clay Imposs? That's supposed to be impossible. You can't do it unless you have an intimate knowledge of the code engine that drives GCES Security clearances. Which leaves out the native Earthers, I think,' she remarked. Then she said, 'But still the doctoring should show. If you know how to look. You can't edit SOD-CMOS chips. You can only add layers of new programming.

'In this case the chip wasn't doctored. It isn't Clay Imposs's original id tag. It's a new tag specifically written to identify Nathan Alt as Clay Imposs. That's probably easier to do. Harder to detect. But you have to be able to get new chips. Not a simple problem. And the job still requires you to know that code engine. An even tougher problem. In fact, that knowledge may be our most closely guarded secret.

'But Nathan Alt had it. Or he did until he was fired.' She snorted wearily. 'As UMC Security Liaison for Anodyne Systems, he helped design the code engines.'

Koina chafed under the pressure of Lane's difficult respiration. Time was growing short: the command module and *Trumpet* must be within fifteen minutes of *Calm Horizons* by now. She already knew about Alt's work with Anodyne. She needed to hear something she could use.

'Where is this leading, Dr Harbinger?' she put in. 'What conclusions have you reached?'

Lane didn't answer directly. 'The interesting thing about this id tag,' she said between gasps, 'is that it's so recent. The programming isn't the only part that's new. The chip is new, too.

'We logged it in a routine shipment to UMC Home Security three weeks ago. Ten days later, according to HS records, the same chip was reqqed by the office of the Anodyne Security Liaison. For use in testing code designs. So it went to Anodyne, where the design work is done. The traitor must have acquired it after that.' She let out a shuddering gust, then sneered, 'But of course Alt was fired six weeks ago.

'You can see the problem. How is it possible that a man with the knowledge to fake a GCES Security id tag got his hands on a SOD-CMOS chip from his former office nearly four and a half weeks after he was fired?'

Involuntarily Koina held her breath. Her body seemed to think it could counter Lane's stress by refusing air itself.

'We've just completed a legal search of Anodyne's records. In particular we searched the computers Anodyne uses for code engine design. It wasn't easy. As I say, those secrets are closely guarded. You need three different kinds of access, all working together. Without any one of them, the other two are useless. But we learned that on the Security Liaison's authority that chip was used to study methods for faking id tags. And the same chip was reqqed back from Anodyne by the Security Liaison's office four days ago.'

A yawn Lane couldn't suppress came from the speakers.

'In both cases the orders were logged by Nathan Alt. Now five and a half weeks after he was allegedly fired.'

At last! A flare of hope seemed to go off in Koina's heart.

Her relief was so intense that she nearly staggered. Without noticing it, she began to pant for air. At *last*!

If the Members hadn't been trapped in the sound of Lane's breathing, more of them would have reacted. Some of Holt's supporters slumped as if they were collapsing. Others gaped in disbelief and consternation; betrayal. Blaine tried to speak, but couldn't find her voice. However, most of the Council simply stared at the speakers like men and women who were too aghast to understand what they heard. The ground they'd walked on all their lives – the power and position of the UMC – had begun to crack under them.

In the shocked silence Sixten jumped to his feet and thrust his fists triumphantly at the ceiling.

'This is crazy,' Cleatus croaked. The blood had been stricken from his face: he looked as pallid as a cadaver. 'Alt must have planned it all along.' His lips quivered. His gaze raced around the room, as if he were looking frantically for an escape. 'He must have betrayed our entire Security. We fired him. Somehow he got back in. Weeks after we got rid of him.'

The sight of his fear was all the evidence Koina needed. It confirmed that Lane was right.

'No, Mr Fane.' The researcher seemed to fight her fatigue down for the last time. 'You said yourself you changed your security after he was fired. That's on the record. In any case, no one person can break into Anodyne. We've just proven that. Alt must have had clearance from Home Security, as well as the full authority of the Security Liaison's office, in addition to his personal codes. Otherwise he wouldn't have been able to get his hands on that chip.

'There's only one possible conclusion. You've been lying all along. Alt was still working for the UMC when he made his plans to replace Clay Imposs. And the traitor who detonated him is still in that room.'

Lane faded away; then returned with an effort. 'Everything we've done has been logged and recorded. You can access it whenever you want verification.'

Still in that room – The idea took a moment to penetrate.

Then it seemed to sting the Members out of their stunned dismay. In a rush they all started talking at once; to each other or their aides; to anyone they could reach.

Koina pitched her voice to carry over the sudden hubbub.

'One last question, Dr Harbinger. I know you're exhausted. You've done brilliant work, and you deserve rest. But the last I heard this investigation was assigned to Director Lebwohl and Chief of Security Mandich. Where are they now? What have they been doing?'

If she could, she wanted to remove any taint that Hashi's tarnished reputation might cast on Lane's testimony.

Lane whimpered softly. Her breathing shook as if she were feverish. Nevertheless she rallied to answer.

'We've been working together. They're back in the Anodyne computers. Getting more evidence. We may be able to trace the id tags for all three kazes to the same source.'

Somewhere she found the strength to finish, 'Lane out.' But she couldn't toggle her pickup. The speakers produced a thin, snoring rasp until someone closed her channel for her.

Cleatus' eyes rolled, and sweat splashed down his face: he looked like an animal in torment. His hands made clutching motions he couldn't complete, grasping after support he didn't get from his downlink.

'*Why?*' he objected wildly. '*Why* would anybody do this? Why would *Holt Fasner*? My God, you can't believe it. Send kazes against the Council? It's insane! There's been a mistake. Or that' – he sputtered in outrage – 'that Harbinger is making it up. You could have been killed.' His voice broke into a cry. '*I could have been killed!*'

His fear was too extreme to be explained by failure. Nevertheless Koina took no pity on him. Suddenly Warden's dreams had come back to life; raised from the dead by Lane's inspired exhaustion and Hashi's cleverness and Mandich's loyalty. The Members had been shocked to the core: they *believed* her now. She would see Cleatus Fane in his grave before she let this opportunity pass.

'I don't think you were in any danger,' she retorted, loud and clear as the ring of a carillon. '*I* think you're the one who gave Captain Alt his signal to die. You were safe because you could choose when and where he exploded.'

Cleatus shook his head. Denials bubbled like froth on his lips. But she didn't stop.

'As for why, I think that's obvious.' She hammered the words as if she were nailing shut a coffin. 'The Members might have passed Captain Vertigus' Bill of Severance if that kaze hadn't scared them so badly. In any case, Special Counsel Igensard's investigation could have been dangerous to you. God knows it *should* have been. Under the right circumstances, it might have been fatal.

'Holt Fasner began to suspect that Warden Dios intended to make their crimes public – crimes committed by the UMCP on your CEO's orders. Those kazes were sent to pressure the Council into protecting Fasner by getting rid of Warden Dios without weakening the UMC's hold on the UMCP.'

She would have gone on. After all her years of distress and dishonesty under Godsen Frik – and all the pain of helping Warden do himself so much harm – she was more than angry enough to match Cleatus' alarm. She wanted to pour acid by the vatful on his undefended head.

Sixten interrupted her, however. While she gathered her accusations, he called out like a trumpet, 'Mr President, I move we forget this proposal to recharter and enact my Bill instead.'

His old voice carried a grim thrill of vindication.

'Seconded!' Sigurd Carsin, Blaine Manse and Tel Burnish shouted together.

Before Abrim could respond, Cleatus burst to his feet, jutted his beard at the ceiling. '*No!*' he howled. 'Stop!' He might have forgotten that the Council existed. Desperately he tried to raise his voice across hundreds of k to UMCHO. 'What're you –? *Don't!*'

But apparently Holt no longer heeded him. He ripped the PCR from his ear, flung it away. 'You *fools!*' he raged at the Members. 'You're going to get us *killed*! Don't you know that he won't *tolerate* this?'

He seemed to be raving.

With a quick nod, President Len sent Forrest Ing and his guards to take the terrified FEA out of the room.

According to one of Koina's techs, the command module and *Trumpet* were three minutes off *Calm Horizons* when the Council passed Sixten's Bill by acclamation.

HOLT

olt Fasner considered himself a true visionary, one of the last. After listening to the debacle of Cleat's efforts to control the Council, he thought he might be the only one left.

Apparently that gaggle of self-important, gutless twits had no grasp on the *real* issues humankind faced. They probably couldn't even have guessed what those issues were. Instead they were too busy acting like a damn guttergang to put one coherent idea in front of another. They were in a frenzy to tear down whatever they could reach, despite the fact that they'd benefited for decades from what they destroyed.

A visionary, *any* visionary, could have told them that the entire system which gave them their pretense of importance and authority was doomed.

Did they really think their misguided species could ever win against the Amnion? Did they actually imagine that an ideal police force – backed by an ideal budget, of course – could protect them from Amnion imperialism? They were wrong. Oh, in the short term human production methods gave them an advantage. But over the long haul that would prove to be an illusion. Amnion genetic imperatives were steadier and more relentless than almost any amount of human political will. The aliens would study human production, human tissue, human decisions, and grow stronger. The process might take years or decades: it might take centuries. The Amnion didn't care. The moment humankind's determination wavered, the whole life-form would be swept out of existence.

Holt would have explained all this to the votes years ago if he hadn't been so full of scorn for his own kind. But the truth was that he didn't think his species as it stood deserved to survive. The very ease with which he'd acquired his empire and his power, crushed his opponents and manipulated every faction on the planet disqualified his supporters as well as his enemies from continuance. With virtually no exceptions, Earth's offspring were too small-minded and fearful to even comprehend – much less appreciate – the grand scale of Holt's vision.

So he wasn't surprised that men like Ward tried to fight him. He'd used them from the beginning. Knowing that no police force could succeed at its stated mission, he'd created the UMCP to cover him while he worked at his larger aims. And he'd bent and twisted the GCES to give the UMCP exactly the right amount of strength: enough to appear effective; enough to threaten the Amnion; not enough to interfere with his larger designs.

As the votes on Suka Bator had just demonstrated – again – it was pathetically easy for small people with little minds to convince themselves they'd been betrayed.

His species *as it stood* didn't deserve to survive: that was the crucial point. Therefore humankind had to change. They had to learn from the Amnion as much as the Amnion learned from them.

They had to become capable of what the Amnion could do.

Force-growing infants.

Imprinting minds.

Practical immortality.

The Amnion had it already. They passed their peculiar consciousness undisturbed from one generation to the next. Their bodies had become tools, organic artifacts, to be shaped, used and discarded as necessary: when one suffered damage, grew old, or died, they simply imprinted themselves upon another. For that reason their ultimate victory over humankind was inevitable. There was no limit to how much they could learn – or how long they could wait.

But if human beings acquired the same capability – if they developed the skill to pass their minds from one inadequate, mortal body to the next – if Holt could prolong his own life indefinitely – Ah, then the nature of the real contest would be altered. Then humankind's innate talents for treachery and mass production would enable them to overwhelm their genetic enemies. And Holt would lead humanity into a limit-less future.

Death would never be able to touch him.

The mere prospect was enough to seize his heart and make his head reel with urgency.

Unfortunately his visionary efforts were hampered by petty, self-absorbed and above all *numerous* men and women who were congenitally unable to look at their lives from his vast perspective. They valued small truths and empty scruples more than the existence of their species; or they craved baseless prerogatives, minor wealth and incomplete power too much to care about anything else. The votes had just demon-strated that harsh fact to Holt again – as if he needed confir-mation.

His mouth twisted in distaste at the Council's pig-headedness – and Cleat's final breakdown into hysteria. The poor fool should have gone out with more dignity. Better yet, he should have considered the possibility that the fucking cops might get their hands on Alt's id tag. Even those assholes in ED Security couldn't do everything wrong: it was statisti-cally inconceivable. And Hashi Lebwohl wasn't stupid. Blinded by ego and misplaced loyalty, but not unintelligent. The minute Lebwohl walked into the extraordinary session, Cleat should have realized the danger.

Of course, once Lebwohl spotted Alt the bomb had to go off. There was no other way to get rid of the evidence. But Cleat should have made damn sure he *did* get rid of the evidence. Instead he'd panicked. When the DA director accosted Alt, Cleat had lost his nerve; triggered the bomb too late. And as a direct result the whole visionary edifice which Holt had erected to procure humankind's survival was in danger of crumbling.

Well, he would have to adjust. His long life had taught him many things, one of the most useful of which was that every opportunity he lost created new openings to take its place. All he needed was the wit to see them – and the will to act on them. If he couldn't get rid of Ward in order to continue using the UMCP as cover, he would simply go in another direction.

He wouldn't miss Ward. He wouldn't even miss Cleat. Or the UMCP. And certainly not the GCES. No, his only real regret was that he wouldn't be able to get his hands on Davies Hyland. He wanted to see the results of imprinting for himself; to secure some vindication for his vision.

But it couldn't be helped. Sixten Vertigus' Bill of Severance forced Holt to let such luxuries go. His extended years had also taught him that regret was useless. Otherwise he might have wasted time cursing his decision not to have the fucking 'hero' of *Deep Star* butchered decades ago.

As matters stood, Holt had only one significant cause for concern: the Donner bitch and her cordon of ships. While her authority held, he still faced enemies capable of taking action. But he believed he knew how to deal with the insubordinate harridan. If his timing was good – if he waited until the command module docked and Davies Hyland and Vector Shaheed were aboard, and Marc Vestabule discovered Morn Hyland's treachery – he could set *Calm Horizons* off like Cleat activating Alt's chemical trigger. Then Donner's ships would be compelled to engage the Amnioni. And by the time they'd all destroyed each other, he would be in control of the aftermath.

Still some lingering uncertainty nagged at him. An irrational desire to visit Norna before he committed himself plagued him. Despite everything he'd done for it, his body was just too old to carry so much stress without faltering. Independent of his mind, his viscera seemed to think he would be reassured if he talked to his mother.

After all, he asked himself, why *had* he kept her alive for so many years, when she was fit for nothing but death? Behind his rationalizations, and his frank pleasure in tormenting her, what was his real reason for preserving her? Did he still hope that she might ultimately say something he could trust to guide him? Or was he simply afraid her death would carry him one step closer to his own?

Damn that woman. Deliberately he rejected the idea of seeing her. He didn't have time. And he already knew what to do. His plans were so clear that even Cleat had understood them. He didn't need an inert lump of female baggage to tell him whether he was right or wrong.

It was too bad HO didn't have super-light proton cannon. But the votes would have given him trouble for that: they would never have believed he needed such guns. His lasers were as powerful as any in human space, however, and his matter cannon were almost as good. His researchers had learned that if they first punched a hole with lasers they could drive matter cannon fire through atmosphere with virtually no resistance. The effect lasted for mere fractions of a second, but it would suffice.

Toggling his intercom, he called Operations and made sure his station's cannon were ready to open fire on Suka Bator.

WARDEN

Marc Vestabule remembered Angus Thermopyle and treachery too well. That became obvious as soon as Warden was released from the small chamber where he'd been sequestered during his negotiations with Morn.

For what had seemed like a long time, they'd stayed where they were. Vestabule hadn't spoken. To the extent that he'd exposed any humanlike concentration, his attention had been fixed on his PCR and pickup; on the communications channel linking him to *Calm Horizons'* operational nerve-center. He might have forgotten Warden's existence. Unlike Warden, however, he seemed to have no difficulty waiting.

For his part, Warden had locked his fears behind the bars of his arms and kept silent. Without his black capsule, he was utterly defenseless. And useless: there was no longer anything he could do to shape events, or fend off the ruin he'd set in motion. Morn and Angus, Koina and Hashi, Min and Holt Fasner would save or damn humankind without Warden's participation. He'd kept his mouth shut because he hadn't wanted to give Vestabule the satisfaction of hearing him babble in apprehension.

But then the Amnioni reacted to something he heard from his PCR. For a moment he replied in an alien tongue so guttural and threatening that it hurt Warden's ears. Then he addressed Warden at last.

'The command module approaches, transporting *Trumpet*,'

he announced. 'We are in communication with Captain Dolph Ubikwe, who pilots the craft. He assures us that Davies Hyland and Vector Shaheed are aboard, and are prepared to surrender themselves.'

Poor Dolph, Warden thought obliquely. It must have galled his soul to let Morn take command of *Punisher*; but his present assignment was no better. How did he feel about delivering the means for humankind's destruction to the Amnion? Bitter and betrayed, probably. Unless he trusted Morn? Or Angus –?

What could they do? What would they be willing to try? Warden had no idea. He found that he was no longer able to imagine what the people he'd created and abandoned might attempt.

'Preparations are complete,' Vestabule continued. 'We will await them at the port designated for their arrival.' He indicated the door. Apparently he meant that he and Warden would receive Davies and Vector. 'When they are aboard, *Calm Horizons* will announce a departure trajectory to your vessels, and commence acceleration.'

Warden's heart thudded in his empty chest. Inside his breathing mask, his tongue hunted for a protection he didn't have. 'What about me?'

He assumed the Amnion would keep him, no matter what they'd promised before he left UMCPHQ. Despite his failures, he was a valuable prize. And they would want a hostage. His life might improve the chances that *Calm Horizons* would be allowed to leave unmolested.

Vestabule's human eyelid fluttered uncomfortably.

'You will be permitted to join Captain Ubikwe aboard the command module, if that is your wish.'

Just for a second Warden's head reeled as if he'd been granted a stay of execution. Permitted to join – He almost believed – The Amnion kept their bargains, didn't they? They were notorious for it. Maybe they would keep this one?

But he knew better. Vestabule recognized too well the kind of danger *Calm Horizons* faced. He'd already been forced to give up on Morn and Angus: he would never let Warden go. If he said anything else, he was lying.

With an inward groan, Warden tried to brace himself for what might come. He hadn't realized that Vestabule's human heritage extended as far as outright falsehood.

Vestabule raised his arm awkwardly toward the door, gesturing Warden in that direction. For a moment Warden didn't move. He couldn't: a visceral dread paralyzed him. But then he remembered the price which Davies and Vector had agreed to pay for humanity's sake; and he realized that he had to do whatever he could to match them. The fault for their plight was his. If nothing else, he owed it to them to look them in the eyes when they sacrificed themselves.

Grinding his teeth, he nudged himself into motion and drifted toward the door.

It slid open as he neared it.

Two Amnion awaited him in the uneven passage outside the chamber. They may have been the same ones that had guarded him earlier: they each had four eyes so that they could see all around them, mouths full of whetted teeth, three arms and legs, skin as rough as rust. And they were still unarmed. What need did they have for weapons? He was no threat to them.

Too late, he saw that one of them carried a hypo.

Marc Vestabule remembered Angus Thermopyle and treachery with a vengeance.

Frantically Warden slapped at the door frame; tried to alter his trajectory by sheer force of desperation. He flung a wild kick at the hypo, then scissored his legs to turn him. But Vestabule was right behind him. As soon as he started floundering, the half-human Amnioni grabbed him by the back of his shipsuit; caught him in a hold he couldn't break.

Panic and hysteria closed his throat. Gasping with urgency, he fought while the guards closed on him. But he had no physical strength to compare with theirs. They gripped his wrists like iron; blocked his legs; stretched out his arms until he hung crucified in the air between them. Then the Amnioni with the hypo pushed back his sleeve and plunged clear liquid destruction into his forearm.

Mutation. Genetic ruin.

Involuntarily his brain went white with terror. Cellular dismay sent him into convulsions: he thrashed and flinched spasmodically. Contractions he couldn't control wrenched through his muscles hard enough to tear them.

Without apparent transition, Vestabule came around in front of him. One hand held the vial of pills Warden had seen earlier – the drug which rendered this particular mutagen temporarily inert. For a moment Vestabule watched his absolute, autonomic revulsion. Then the Amnioni opened the vial, rolled out a small capsule and held it up in front of his face.

'I remember fear,' Vestabule grated rigidly. 'It is wasted.' His own humanity had been taken from him by violence. 'If you wish to retain your genetic identity, I have the means.'

With a flick of his fingers, he lifted Warden's breathing mask and dropped the pill into his straining mouth.

Appalled and shameless, Warden crushed it between his teeth; choked down the bitter powder as fast as he could.

The corrosive taste brought him back to himself.

Shameless – Ah, God. He belonged to Vestabule now. Belonged to the Amnion. Like the guards, his native fear was too strong for him. After all his years of plotting, endurance and pain, he'd been beaten as easily as a child.

How had he become such a coward? When had he earned the right to protect himself without counting the cost?

Slowly Vestabule nodded as if he recognized the horror in Warden's eyes. A rough word released the hands of the guards. At once pain pulled Warden's arms around him, raised his knees to his chest. He drifted weightless in front of the Amnioni like a man reduced to infancy; barely self-aware enough to push his mask back into place. But his gaze never left Vestabule's face.

For some reason Vestabule told him, 'We have received a transmission from *Punisher*. The woman who speaks names herself Acting UMCP Director Min Donner.'

Min – Oh, Min! Warden suddenly feared that he might

start to weep. She would have been braver than this. If everything else failed, she would have spat out that pill; would have chosen to become completely Amnion rather than be used to betray the people she'd sworn to serve.

Vestabule's human eye fluttered, but the Amnion one held firm. 'She states,' he went on, 'that our presence has produced a –' He paused briefly, hunting for concepts that meant nothing to his kind. 'A political crisis. A conflict among factions. And she claims to fear that this conflict may become combat. Some among your ships or stations may open fire on the others.'

What? A last spasm closed Warden about himself. Then by degrees his muscles began to unclench. Fire licked damage alerts along his nerves as he straightened his arms, unfolded his legs. Combat? At a time like *this*? What the hell is going on?

Was Holt *that* desperate?

Vestabule didn't answer such questions. Instead he said, 'She asserts that if this occurs those who are attacked will respond. But she assures us that these hostilities will not be directed at us. They will not threaten us. No attack will target us. Therefore she begs us to take no hostile action ourselves.'

Christ! Warden thought in amazement. Hashi must have succeeded. He and Koina and Morn must be nailing Holt's coffin shut right now. Otherwise Min wouldn't be worried about what the Dragon might do next. Not so worried that she felt she had to warn *Calm Horizons*.

'There is human treachery here, Warden Dios,' Vestabule pronounced without inflection. 'It may be that this Min Donner means to deal falsely with us. Or it may be that your Morn Hyland intends some ruse to harm us.

'I assure you that we will take extreme action if we are cheated – or hindered.' He made an almost human effort to emphasize what he was saying. 'And I assure you also that you will commit your utmost efforts to ensure that Morn Hyland's promises are kept.'

In that instant all Warden's terror and dismay transformed themselves to savagery.

Everything *hadn't* failed. If Hashi and Koina and Morn had succeeded, he could afford to hope again. He could stop feeling beaten, victimized; go back to acting like the director of the UMCP. Min thought Holt was desperate. She was ready for him. Now all Warden had to do was trust Angus. And prepare himself to help as much as he could.

'If those promises are kept,' Vestabule finished, 'and if we are not threatened in any way' – his human eye seemed to give off a glint of satisfaction – 'you will be granted an opportunity to join Captain Ubikwe.'

Now Warden believed the Amnioni spoke the literal truth.

Using pain for strength, he asked acidly, 'How long did you say this pill will keep me human?'

Vestabule didn't hesitate. 'One hour.'

Perfect, Warden snorted to himself. Long enough to get him aboard the command module and away – if events played out the way Vestabule wanted. Not long enough for Dolph to take him anyplace where he might find salvation.

'How many will you give me if I decide to go?'

'None.'

From somewhere deep inside him Warden Dios dredged up a slow, fierce grin.

'That's what I thought.' With a twist of his hips, he turned; pushed off from the rough wall to float along the passage in the direction of the cargo hold and docking port where he'd first entered *Calm Horizons*. 'Come on. Let's go see what we can do to make Davies and Vector feel welcome.'

Vestabule remembered treachery, but he'd forgotten the rest of being human.

Streaked by solar fire, and half-fixed in the flare of spot-lights, Angus rode *Trumpet*'s metallic skin like a limpet with Ciro beside him while Dolph Ubikwe nudged the command module onto its final approach vector for *Calm Horizons*. He was armed with nothing but a pair of laser cutters, a stubby cylinder of hull-sealant and a spare EVA suit. The fact that he intended to tackle an Amnion defensive with such paltry firepower would have been laughable if it hadn't appalled him so badly.

He felt completely dehydrated. Sweat slicked the inside of his suit; and he'd already been out here for what seemed like hours, watching *Calm Horizons*' fatal bulk block out the heavens. Despite the efforts of his suit's systems to regulate his body temperature, he always oozed like a pig when he went EVA – an autonomic reflex his zone implants could scarcely control.

But his cruel, blind, irreplaceable programming had prompted him to drink at least a liter of fluids before he put on his EVA suit – an essential precaution which his human mind usually forgot. Terror had that effect on him. The sheer scale and cold of space horrified his crib-bound perceptions. The merciless and impersonal death which reached to infinity in all directions was the only thing he'd ever known that matched the universe of pain he'd received from his mother's love.

So of course he'd spent most of his life fleeing in small

metal ships like coffins through the deeps of a horror he could never escape. Tenuously protected by hulls of steel and will and fear, he'd spent every minute on the run. On his good days the engulfing abyss had touched him only through the abstract schematic and binary data supplied by his instruments.

But most of his days were bad –

The occasion beyond Beckmann's installation when he'd left *Trumpet* to fling a singularity grenade at *Free Lunch* had been one of the worst. Then only stark desperation had saved him from his own terror – desperation, and Morn's crazy decision to run helm in hard g – after which the hungry stresses of the black hole had dislocated his hip; sent him into stasis; damn near killed him.

And now EVA had been forced on him again. He'd been out here for a long time, studying the defensive's ominous side while Dolph tugged *Trumpet* slowly closer and closer to an entirely different kind of ruin. The crib had tightened its grip on him once more. And once more he had to beat it or die.

By rights his heart should have thumped hard enough to burst. But his datacore restrained it.

A gnawing desire to talk to Morn tormented him.

The impulse was madness. According to the specs for his suit transmitter, he could still reach *Punisher*. But the power drain of dialing his signal that high would have weakened his jamming fields. And the Amnion were bound to detect a transmission that strong. Angus himself had ordered Morn, Min Donner and Dolph to keep their radio mouths shut.

Nevertheless while *Calm Horizons* blotted out half the galaxy and the moment of docking slid closer, his ache to hear Morn's voice grew so acute that he could hardly stifle it.

Are you all right? he wanted to ask. Is the Council listening? Does telling them what happened to you change anything? But more than that he wanted to ask, Why did you do it?

He knew she hated him. He'd seen it on her face so often that he wanted to kill her for it. Or himself: he could hardly tell the difference. So why had she helped him escape his priority-codes? Why was she letting him make decisions that could easily kill them all?

Only his old passion for survival kept him from calling out to her.

How long before the command module touched against the defensive's docking seals? Nine minutes? Less? His computer could have given him a precise projection, but he didn't want to know. He was already scared enough.

Sweat leaked into his eyes. He couldn't wipe the sting away. He had to squeeze his lids together so tightly that his face hurt in order to clear his sight.

He might have felt less frantic if Ciro had talked to him. That was safe enough. *Calm Horizons* would never hear them on this frequency; at these power-levels. He didn't care how demented the kid might sound, or how deep his fixation on Sorus Chatelaine ran: Angus would have listened to *any*thing as long as Ciro didn't become confused about what he had to do, or when, or how. But the damn boy was silent most of the time. If he wasn't prodded for a specific response – some short, unhelpful sentence like, *The hatch is open*, or, *I won't let you down* – he left Angus alone with his sweat and his fears.

Just once Ciro had broken out of his detachment. *I wish you would all shut up*, he'd snapped at Mikka aboard the gap scout. *I already have enough to think about*. Other than that he kept his madness to himself.

So how the hell was Angus supposed to endure being out here? Minutes or hours ago he'd mapped his route; planned for every contingency he could imagine. For the remaining eight minutes, or seven, he had nothing to do. He'd abandoned the false, necessary safety of *Trumpet* much earlier than necessary. He'd consigned himself to this hell as if he'd believed the experience would be good for him.

Stupid shit.

For as long as he could remember he'd been at his best when he was terrified: faster, stronger, smarter than under any other circumstances. But it wasn't true now. He'd become a man he didn't recognize, and everything he did was alien to him.

That bastard's so big – he'd told Ciro. *I need time to study her.* But he'd been lying. The truth was that he'd hoped the sight of so much terrible emptiness would help him recover himself; turn him back into the man he remembered.

What was he *doing* here? What in God's name had made him think this was a good idea? The Angus Thermopyle he remembered would have cheerfully stayed aboard *Punisher*; let Warden fucking Dios and UMCPHQ and Suka Bator and the whole damn planet rot in their own brutality. Or he would have broken *Trumpet* away from the command module; fired the drives; taken his chances burning for open space. But he hadn't done that. Not him: not the new, smitten, brain-numb Angus. Instead he'd offered to rescue the whole motherless lot of them. Or get himself killed in the attempt.

What had *possessed* him?

A datacore with a crippled instruction-set? Not likely: he hadn't felt the coercion of his zone implants.

Or was it Morn? Maybe. She'd been totally, abjectly in his power after *Starmaster*'s end – and yet she'd saved his life when Nick's trap sprang on him. She'd released him from his priority-codes for the simple, silly, imponderable reason that she believed welding him was wrong. And she'd gone on trusting him, despite the accumulated risks. She'd eaten her way into his heart somehow: he couldn't forget what he owed her.

Nevertheless as far as he could tell the one – or the final – thing which had removed him from his own recognition like a sated mother when he'd suffered as much as she needed was the fact that Warden Dios had kept a promise. He'd told Angus, *It's got to stop.* And he'd made good on his commitment. He'd erased every restriction which might have prevented Angus from killing him.

By the harsh logic of Warden's mercy, Angus found that he now had no choice except to rescue the bastard. One kept promise – and Morn's trust – were enough: they compelled him like a hardwired command.

Despite everything he'd suffered – and everything he'd learned from so much pain – he could still be seduced into idiocy.

'Shit,' he rasped to Ciro because he thought he would snap unless he heard a human voice soon, 'if the fat man doesn't slow down he's going to ram that damn port. Crumple us like tin when we hit. We'll bleed to death in our fucking suits before the Amnion figure out we're here.'

That wasn't true, of course. His computer calculated trajectory and deceleration automatically: he knew Dolph was bringing them in safely. By now *Calm Horizons* was so near that she'd stopped growing. Her size and the polarization of his faceplate conveyed the illusion that he could reach out and touch her whenever he wanted. He cursed and complained for the simple reason that in moments he would have to do things which scared him like all of space concentrated into one complex sequence of hazards.

It was almost time. In another minute or two he would cast his life to the solar winds – and take as many of his enemies with him as he could.

For the tenth – or the hundredth – time, he checked to be sure his cutters were fully charged, then adjusted his polarization to compensate for *Calm Horizons'* chaos of spotlights and shadow.

Ciro surprised him by remarking distantly, 'You did that already.'

Angus secured the cutters at his sides. 'I know,' the man he didn't recognize sighed. 'I'm just scared.' God, when had he started admitting things like that? 'If I don't get to them in time, they'll all be Amnion. Then I'll have to kill them.' Struggling to remember himself, he finished harshly, 'In case you screw up.'

'I won't screw up,' the kid answered without distress. He seemed to have the patience of the damned. 'I remember everything you told me. I can do it.'

Angus snorted. 'Just don't forget you'll be exposed as soon as I leave,' he warned. 'My jamming fields don't have a hell of a lot of range.'

'I can do it,' Ciro repeated. He sounded almost tranquil.

Abruptly Dolph's deep rumble filled Angus' helmet. 'You could get started, Angus,' he suggested. 'We're close enough. Your suit jets are faster than walking.'

Like Angus, *Punisher*'s captain was worried about Davies, Vector and Warden. If Angus took too long crossing the defensive's huge hull – or if Dolph failed to break the command module free from the docking seals in time –

'No.' Angus shook his head bitterly inside his helmet. 'I can hide myself, but I can't cover up jet emission. If those fuckers spot it, they might guess what I'm up to.'

Marc Vestabule might remember enough of his humanity to jump to the right conclusions.

'Then,' Mikka put in, 'you'd better be damn fast.' A raw edge of stim ran through her exhaustion. She might have been close to hysteria. 'Davies is probably desperate enough to take on a whole platoon of Amnion. But Vector doesn't know how to fight – and he isn't exactly tough.' Grimly she added, 'God knows what condition Dios is in.

'The Amnion are too strong, Angus,' she finished raggedly. 'Too many – You won't have much time.'

'We need a diversion,' Dolph muttered. 'Something to slow them down. Unfortunately I can't think of anything to help us. Or anybody.'

Angus swore under his breath. It was true that a diversion might save them. It might distract the Amnion enough to make them miss Ciro. It might give Davies and Vector a few precious extra minutes. But it might also prod *Calm Horizons* into opening fire too soon. Then all their lives would be wasted.

In any case, Dolph was right: there was no help available.

'Are Davies and Vector ready?' Angus asked while his eyes and his computer measured distances, estimated timings.

'They've been in the airlock for the past ten minutes,' Dolph reported. 'But they'll try to delay as much as they can without being obvious about it.'

He didn't need to add that if Davies and Vector made the Amnion suspicious *Calm Horizons* might fire before Angus could carry out any of the tasks he'd assigned himself.

'All right.' Angus' machine projections approached the synchronization he wanted. 'I'm on my way in thirty seconds.'

If they all died, he would have only himself to blame.

Despite the harm Dios had done him, he found that he was grateful for his welding. Between the stark, hot beams of the spotlights, shadows as impenetrable as tombs shrouded *Calm Horizons'* uneven hull. Without the support of his zone implants and his datacore, he would have been sure to fail.

Roughly he turned to Ciro. 'Don't screw up. I mean it. Get set up. Then *wait for my signal*. If you jump the gun, this is going to backfire so fast you won't even see it happen.'

He couldn't see through Ciro's faceplate; but the kid's helmet inclined like a nod. 'I understand.'

'Just do it, Angus,' Mikka interrupted. 'We don't have time to *discuss* it anymore.' Grimly she continued, 'I'll start warming up the drives as soon as you head back this way.'

'They'll still have matter cannon,' Angus returned – a last warning. 'This fucker can pound us to powder as soon as she gets a targ fix.'

Then *Calm Horizons* would smash UMCPHQ. And *Punisher*.

And Morn.

'I know.' Fatigue and strain fretted Mikka's tone. 'I've studied myself blind on this dispersion field generator.'

Angus' plans depended on that generator – and on Mikka's timing. But they also rested absolutely on Ciro's shoulders. And on his own. On his implanted equipment as well as his quickness, determination and cunning.

In addition, they hinged on Dolph, Davies and Vector.

There were too many variables: the whole damn sequence was too vulnerable. If just one small piece fell out of place, it would all collapse.

He braced himself to move; but Mikka wasn't done. 'Angus –' she offered softly. 'I wanted to say –' Her voice had become a low moan like a prayer. 'Ciro and I, Sib, Vector – we didn't have anything to do with framing you. Nick kept it secret. He handled it himself.'

Angus heard her unspoken appeal as clearly as words. Save Ciro. Please. If you can. Her brother wasn't responsible for delivering him to fucking Hashi and UMCPDA.

He could have promised that he would try, but there was no point. The kid had already chosen his own doom.

Instead of insulting Mikka with dishonest reassurance, he retorted acidly, 'I already knew that. Why do you think I've been so damn nice to you?'

Hadn't he been nice to her? On Nick's orders he'd nearly crushed her skull. But he'd measured his force to let her live.

It was time. His zone implants enabled him to move without hesitation, despite the sweat stinging his eyes and the fear laboring in his veins. While the command module and *Trumpet* coasted across the last fifty meters toward the emblazoned docking port in *Calm Horizons'* side, he unclipped his belt from its anchor in one smooth motion.

Trusting the strength and precision of his welded resources, he launched himself away from Ciro into the direct blaze of the spotlights. Weightless and silent, covered by every jamming field he could project, he sailed straight as the stroke of death toward the distant emitter of the warship's super-light proton cannon.

DAVIES

He and Vector stood together in the airlock while Captain Ubikwe eased the command module along its final approach to *Calm Horizons*. They wore their EVA suits, but hadn't put on their helmets yet. The act of sealing themselves in completely seemed too final; too fatal.

And without their helmets they could talk privately. Even Captain Ubikwe wouldn't hear them unless they used the intercom: Mikka, Angus and Ciro wouldn't hear them. Once they locked their helmets in place, their suit transmitters would link them to *Trumpet* as well as the command module, if not to Angus and Ciro. And the Amnion would be able to pick up their signal –

That was deliberate, although Davies hated it. They could have tuned their communications to the same frequency Angus and Ciro used. But if they did so the Amnion might somehow acquire that channel. They might trace it from the suits; detect it from the helmet speakers. For that reason Angus had told Davies and Vector to use a separate frequency, one *Calm Horizons* might monitor. Captain Ubikwe would still hear them; but the other communications on which Angus' plans depended would be protected.

Davies accepted that. Hell, he didn't even complain about it, even though it meant the Amnion might hear him gasping in dread. He had enough other worries: he didn't waste time fretting over whether or not he would sound scared to his enemies when he went to face his doom.

He'd volunteered for this – before Angus had suggested other possibilities. When he'd said, *I'll go,* he'd assumed that he would surrender himself to mutation; a ruin far more complete and cruel than any kind of death. And Vector had stepped forward on the same terms: that was the bond between them. Yet now they had dangerous and demanding roles in a scheme so elaborate – and so utterly reliant on variables none of them could control – that it still took his breath away whenever he thought about it.

He felt that he was being pulled apart by conflicting emotions. The airlock could have held eight or ten people, but it seemed too small to contain his tension. The restrictions of his suit frustrated his elevated metabolism. If he hadn't been able to talk to Vector, his concentration might have snapped.

Part of him ached like an amputation because he wasn't with Morn. She was doing what a cop should do – giving evidence about crimes she'd witnessed and experienced, no matter how much the truth hurt her. To some extent humankind's future rested on what she said. And her son had been imprinted with her mind: he wanted to be with her while she spoke. He burned to support her testimony with his; to stand beside her and for her when she was questioned; to cram her conclusions down the throats of those who doubted her.

Another part of him needed to be where he was, however. The sheer ingenuity of Angus' plans entranced him. And they fed his desire to *fight* – a deep, thwarted yearning which he'd never been able to satisfy. Like Director Donner and Captain Ubikwe, he craved to confront humanity's enemies with guns and violence. An acute hunger for gunfire filled his heart; for blows struck in the good cause of humankind's survival. He'd been bred for extremity in Morn's womb, and he *needed* to act on it.

And yet another part of him, more profound than consciousness – his visceral, genetic being – quailed in horror at the prospect of facing the Amnion again. The danger to which he submitted wasn't simply that he would be transformed to the stuff of nightmares. It was far worse. If the Amnion succeeded with him, he would be used to impose the ultimate nightmare on his entire species. At the base of his brain, mutely, while the rest of his mind struggled to contain its conflicts, he gibbered with fear so sharp that it threatened to unman him.

God, it might have been kinder if Angus had just let them go die. That way he and Vector would at least have known where they stood. They could have tried to make their peace with despair.

This way —

Apparently Vector felt the same. Despite the familiar self-mockery in his tone, his blue eyes were troubled as he said, 'I'm glad I don't have to do this alone. Somehow being the savior of humankind hasn't turned out quite the way I imagined.' He smiled ruefully at his own foolishness. 'This may sound strange, but I think it might be easier if we just gave up.'

Davies looked at his companion sharply. 'Is that what you want to do?' If Vector decided to die, Davies was effectively finished. He couldn't tackle *Calm Horizons* alone.

Vector avoided Davies' gaze. 'I suppose there's something attractive about an heroic surrender,' he mused. 'Martyr ourselves to save Suka Bator, UMCPHQ, and half the planet. We would be legends in our own time. Or in our own minds, anyway,' he added sardonically.

'But thrashing and clawing to stay alive, floundering around in a fight we can't really hope to win while we pray for God or Angus to arrange some improbable stay of execution — which isn't likely to happen even with the best will in the world because the whole scenario is so damn precarious, and it could all go wrong in half a dozen different ways at once —' He gave an exaggerated sigh. 'Well, it's not exactly dignified, is it? We're never going to achieve the status of legends if we can't end with a little dignity.'

Scowling, Davies repeated, 'Is that what you want to do? End with dignity?' The idea that Vector might abandon him — and Director Dios — gnawed at his heart. 'Turn Amnion without a struggle?'

Vector spread his hands. 'Hell, Davies, that's what I've always done. I can't remember the last time I *resisted* something.' He snorted in deprecation. 'I mean, besides gravity.' Then he explained, 'When the cops shut down my research at Intertech, I could have put up a fight. If I'd gone public fast enough, made myself conspicuous enough – or just been clever enough – I might have survived long enough to tell my story. I might even have made a difference.'

Morn's example seemed to weigh on him. More than anyone except Davies, and perhaps Angus, he appreciated the cost of what she chose to do.

He shrugged. 'But even if I'd decided I didn't want to die exposing a secret like that,' he went on, 'I could have put up a little resistance in other ways. I knew what Orn Vorbuld was like. I could have refused to turn illegal with him. And I certainly didn't have to join Nick when he did.'

With an air of effort and chagrin, he met Davies' gaze. 'It does seem that surrender is what I do best.'

Davies shook his head. Anger and fear clanged against each other in his chest. He wanted to protest, So you're just going to let it *happen*? We're all depending on you. Don't you think even *one* of us is worth a little indignity?

Do you think *I* want to turn Amnion?

But the distress in Vector's gaze stopped him. It was too personal. Vector had volunteered first, before Davies found the courage: he'd been prepared to face this doom alone. He deserved a better reply.

Kicking himself mentally, Davies tried to imagine what Morn would say; tried to find her inside himself. After a moment he ventured, 'That doesn't make sense, Vector. Letting someone steal your research isn't the same as surrendering yourself to save millions of lives. You can't compare them.'

'I suppose you're right.' Vector's eyes drifted away again. His mild tone hinted at regret. 'But it does make restitution.'

'In *this* case,' Davies countered more harshly than he intended, 'so does staying alive. And it's better than dying.'

As far as he was concerned, *anything* was better than the oblique death of mutation.

A short time ago he and Vector had taken the last of Nick's mutagen immunity capsules. Even if everything went wrong, they had roughly four hours of humanity left. But now that seemed more like a curse than a blessing. Five extra minutes might give Angus time to reach them: four more hours would supply nothing except absolute horror.

Maybe Vector feared those four hours more than he dreaded an undignified struggle.

'Do you really think we can trust Angus?' he asked carefully, as if he didn't want to give offense. 'He's your father. Maybe you've inherited something that helps you understand him. I certainly don't.

'Why does a man like that change his mind? What does he get out of acting like a hero, when until now the only thing he's ever fought for is a chance to go on breathing?

'What if the only reason he's here – the only reason we're all doing this – is so he can snatch *Trumpet* and try to escape?'

'No.' Davies did his best to sound certain despite his mounting alarm. 'When he makes a commitment to Morn, he keeps it. I don't understand that any better than you do, but I'm sure it's true.'

He trusted his father for another reason as well. He had no choice. If he didn't, he would lose his grip on himself and start to scream. But that wouldn't comfort Vector.

Vector shrugged; said nothing. The trouble in his eyes deepened.

A moment later the airlock intercom chimed. When Davies toggled the speaker, Captain Ubikwe announced, 'Six minutes to dock, boys and girls.' He seemed to like living this close to disaster. He sounded almost indecently relaxed. 'I'll make this as gentle as I can, but you might want to hold onto something.

'Angus and Ciro are still in position,' he reported. 'I suggested Angus could leave now, get a head start. But he pointed out the Amnion might spot his jet emissions. He's probably right. He knows more about those jamming fields than I do.'

Yet the longer Angus waited the longer Davies and Vector would have to resist Marc Vestabule's fate.

'What if he doesn't go at all?' Vector asked the intercom.

'Dr Shaheed,' Captain Ubikwe replied cheerfully, 'you have a suspicious mind. If that happens, I don't think Mikka will like it any more than I will.' A deep chuckle rattled the speaker. Ciro's life was at stake as much as anyone's. 'In fact, we've already talked about it. She doesn't intend to let him back aboard unless he does his job. Instead she's going to charge her guns and try to take out that proton emitter before it fires.

'I guess we aren't exactly brimming with trust ourselves,' he admitted. His tone suggested a fierce grin.

Sweat licked frustration down the small of Davies' back. His suit was full of itches he couldn't scratch.

'Any news from Morn?' he asked. Stupid question: the command module and *Punisher* had broken off contact with each other as soon as the module secured *Trumpet*. Angus hadn't wanted to give the Amnion any cause for alarm. Still Davies couldn't stifle his desire for some kind of news.

Moment by moment he felt that he was losing the battle against terror. He needed an anchor – and Morn was the only one he'd ever had.

Captain Ubikwe appeared to understand. Without hesitation he answered, 'Scan tells me *Punisher* spent a while using the dish aimed at Suka Bator. But they stopped transmitting ten or fifteen minutes ago. So I assume Morn finished giving her testimony, and now the Council has to debate it.'

'Thanks.' Davies silenced the intercom quickly to disguise the fact that Captain Ubikwe's reply wasn't enough. He needed something more solid to hang onto.

He needed to believe in himself. At the moment his only real conviction was that the Amnion would use him to destroy humankind.

Vector faced him again. Regret pulled at the corners of the older man's mouth.

'I'm sorry, Davies. I guess I shouldn't have asked you about Angus. There's nothing we can do about him anyway.' He paused awkwardly, then tightened his jaw and forced himself to say, 'I'll tell you what I'm really worried about.'

A defensive clench lifted his shoulders. 'The truth is, I'm not much good in a fight.' His strained gaze admitted that he meant *no good*. 'I'm afraid I'm going to let you down. You'll hold up your end, but you'll fail because of me. And I'm not sure I can live with that.' He grimaced. 'As long as I'm still human, anyway.'

Claustrophobia and confusion brought up bile into Davies' mouth. His throat worked, but he couldn't swallow the taste. He no longer felt like yelling at Vector. Now he wanted to burst into tears.

'In that case,' he offered thickly, 'maybe you'd better stay behind. I'll tell them I killed you. So they won't get your knowledge. That'll break the deal, but it won't be Morn's fault. They can't blame her. And they don't have time for more negotiations. As long as they have me, they probably won't open fire.' On Thanatos Minor he'd protected himself from the Amnion with lies. 'If I can confuse them enough, they may still give Angus enough time.'

Vector studied him closely for a moment, then sighed, 'Ah, well.' Slowly the former engineer turned away. 'I don't think I could live with that, either.'

While Davies fought to recover some semblance of courage or control, the intercom chimed again. He rapped the toggle with his knuckles; but then he couldn't find his voice to respond.

Captain Ubikwe sounded strangely eager. 'Two minutes to dock.' He must have thought he was having fun. 'Angus is away. Right on target, by God – and moving fast. Ciro won't start until we hit the seals, but we're committed now.

'Let's make this work.'

Angus is away. That was an anchor of sorts – the best Davies could hope for, since he had so little reason to trust himself. Right on target. Angus intended to keep his word. If his son could do the same –

When neither Davies nor Vector said anything, Captain Ubikwe went on, 'I told Angus you'll give him an extra minute or two, if you can. If you're willing to take that kind of chance.'

Vector glanced at Davies, then faced the intercom himself. 'I don't think so, Captain.' The resignation in his voice might as well have been despair. 'We might upset Vestabule. Then a whole lot of people won't live to regret it.'

'I understand,' Captain Ubikwe answered more quietly. 'Secure for dock impact. Then kill a couple of them for me.'

Vector took hold of a handgrip; but Davies ignored the danger of a jolt. Instead he spent the last of his concentration checking his weapons.

He'd coiled his sharp monofilament line into his left palm inside his glove. His plastic dirk rested in his belt pouch. That was all he had to defend himself with. Angus had promised him they would pass *Calm Horizons'* sensors.

Davies feared that the Amnion would knock him unconscious before he could even begin to put up a fight. Then he would be lost: ten minutes or four hours of mutagen immunity wouldn't make any difference. Nevertheless he faced the outer door of the airlock as if he couldn't wait to bring his lifetime of confusion and distress to an end.

CIRO

He may not have been as crazy as he thought. He was still sane enough to understand Angus' plans – and to fear for their success. As the command module carried *Trumpet* across the last twenty meters to the docking port marked by incandescence in *Calm Horizons'* side, he stayed where he was; clung to his rifle; and tried to weigh the dangers against each other.

He should already have started to work himself: that was what Angus had told him. *Don't wait around. Open the hatch. Get that damn thing in position as fast as you can. Otherwise you'll be in trouble.*

At a certain point – after Davies and Vector boarded the defensive – Captain Ubikwe would fire thrust to break free of the docking seals. Unless Ciro had manhandled his doom past the module and away across the defensive's hull by that time, the sudden force might do him real harm. He could easily break a limb, or damage his suit, unless he was anchored and braced. Worse, he might lose control of the grenade. If it bounced off the module's hull, or *Trumpet's*, and out of reach, everything would be ruined. Even using the full power of his suit jets, he might fail to retrieve the grenade in time. It had too much mass to be managed quickly. Then Davies and Vector, Angus and Warden Dios, Captain Ubikwe and Mikka – they would all die for nothing.

There was another factor as well, although Ciro had already

decided to ignore it. For Mikka's sake, Angus had instructed him to position the grenade *as fast as you can* so that he, Ciro, could return to the command module before it moved out of reach. But he foresaw at least two problems. He didn't trust his aim: he would miss unless he fired at close range. And he feared setting the grenade too near the docking port – too near the module and *Trumpet*.

Still he should have moved by now. That was the plan. Nevertheless he lay flat against the gap scout's metal skin while Captain Ubikwe guided the module meter by meter into the maw of the docking port. *Calm Horizons* lowered in front of him like a wall of sky, her darkness slashed with spotlights; and Ciro clung where he was as if her sheer size paralyzed him.

Angus' orders seemed to make sense, but they had one fatal flaw. He'd admitted as much, if not in so many words. *You'll be exposed as soon as I leave.* That was the danger. Ciro was small enough to be missed: even *Trumpet* dwarfed him. And he'd made his profile even smaller by lying down. But spotlights searched every meter of the gap scout and the command module constantly. At least half a dozen video pickups studied the approaching vessels. He was certain that some watching eye would spot him as soon as he rose into motion.

And then –

Ah, then: disaster. The Amnion would realize that they were threatened. They might not guess the nature of the threat, but they would recognize its reality. And they would make the same decision human beings would make in the same crisis: they would open fire.

One super-light proton cannon burst might be enough to raze Suka Bator. Two would certainly do the job. And when UMCPHQ, *Punisher* and the rest of the ships returned *Calm Horizons'* matter cannon barrage, *Trumpet* and the module would be pounded to powder almost instantaneously.

Ciro may have been crazy; but he knew this danger was greater than the one he'd been told to avoid.

Defying Angus' explicit instructions, he lay like a blister on

Trumpet's hull and waited for Angus to carry out the first part of his mission.

He'd positioned himself so that he had a clear view of Angus' progress. The cyborg appeared to sail unnaturally fast: with his artificial strength, he'd launched himself hard at his target. Straight as a laser, he soared toward the distant proton emitter. But *Calm Horizons* was huge, and he still had a long way to go. Spotlights glared off his suit as they hunted for foes. At intervals he seemed to burn against the backdrop of the heavens like a star gone supernova. If any of his jamming fields failed – or if he'd misjudged their effectiveness – he would be noticed at once.

Ciro concentrated exclusively on Angus; didn't know how close the command module had come to its destination. The sudden jolt-and-scrape as the module hit the port guides and slid along them toward the docking seals took him by surprise. Inertia pushed him onto the hull, then rebounded through him, nearly lifting him from the surface before he caught himself.

He didn't take his eyes off Angus.

Without a sound, but palpable through the ships' metal, maneuvering thrust forced the module down the guides to mate against the docking seals. For a moment *Trumpet* shuddered on the module's back. Then the seals took hold. Gradually thrust faded, and both vessels came to rest.

Shit. In another minute or two, Davies and Vector would leave the airlock to meet Marc Vestabule and Warden Dios aboard *Calm Horizons*. No matter what Captain Ubikwe said, they couldn't delay without making the Amnion suspicious. And Angus still hadn't reached his target. And when he was done there, he would have to come all this way back, running on magnetized boots – or coasting in zero g – so that his jets wouldn't betray him.

Now surely it was time for Ciro to start; time to take the risk, accept the consequences. The job ahead of him would test his strength – and his craziness – to their limits. Nevertheless he remained motionless and went on waiting. He was still sane enough to pray –

There. Angus had stopped; snagged himself to a halt on the projecting muzzle of the emitter. Instinctively Ciro held his breath. The distance was too great; and his faceplate's polarization cost his vision depth: he couldn't see what Angus was doing. But he knew the plan. And he may have been the only person living who trusted Angus implicitly.

Angus meant to sabotage the emitter. But he had to do so in a way that concealed the damage. Once the Amnion realized they'd been hurt, they would open up with all their other guns. Angus needed an undetectable means to disable the proton emitter.

That was why he carried a canister of hull sealant.

With no one to witness him except Ciro, he sprayed sealant down the emitter's muzzle; enough sealant to replace ten cubic meters of blown bulkhead. It hardened in seconds. If he was right – if his databases hadn't misled him – the gun was ruined now. Simple as that. When *Calm Horizons* tried to use it she would blast a hole the size of a pocket cruiser in her own side.

If he was right –

Ciro's chest tugged at him, demanding air; but he held his breath as if he thought that act of self-denial might keep Angus alive. *It's easy*, Angus had told Morn. *All I have to do is get there. Ten seconds later your damn Council is safe.* If a theory no one had ever tested turned out to be accurate, Marc Vestabule had just lost his hostages. But Angus still had to get away. If *Calm Horizons* fired her proton cannon while he was anywhere nearby, he would be caught in the explosion. Metal and wreckage would tear him apart like shrapnel.

Now Ciro saw Angus start back toward him. Angus had kicked himself into another fast glide. Apparently he thought that would be quicker than running. In two more heartbeats, or three, he would be out of immediate danger. As long as Marc Vestabule didn't know what had just happened –

Davies and Vector must have emerged from the module's airlock as Vestabule expected. The Amnioni must have believed that he still had the power to destroy Suka Bator. That *Trumpet*'s people intended to keep their bargain with him. No explosion shook the defensive. She didn't do any-thing that would bring Director Donner's cordon of ships into battle with her.

Slowly Ciro began to breathe again.

Beyond question it was time for him to get to work; past time. In Sorus Chatelaine's name he'd accepted a role that demanded strength, timing, accuracy. And he lacked the raw muscle to keep his promises quickly. Any moment now Angus would start to yell at him, cursing him into action.

But when he heard a voice, it wasn't Angus'. It was Captain Ubikwe's.

'Mikka, Ciro hasn't moved.'

Immediately Mikka demanded, 'What's happened to him?'

'I don't know.' Dolph's deep tones thrummed with worry. 'He's paralyzed.'

Mikka didn't hesitate. 'I've got to go out there.'

Ciro could imagine her slapping at her belts, thrusting herself from her g-seat.

'You can't,' Captain Ubikwe countered urgently. 'We still might survive if he doesn't do his part. If you don't do yours, we're dead.'

Mikka's groan seemed to ache inside the confines of Ciro's helmet.

Yet his reasons for staying where he was still gripped him. If he moved now – and the Amnion spotted him – all the rest of Angus' plan would fail.

He hoped the Council was safe. On the other hand, those people meant nothing to him. Davies and Vector, Angus and Mikka – they meant a lot. He didn't want to cause their deaths.

Filled by madness like wisdom, he clung fervently to *Trumpet*'s hull and went on waiting.

Sometimes prayers were answered. With part of his mind, he wondered if Sorus Chatelaine had known that. Just when the pressure to move threatened to become more than he could bear, he saw hot laser fire streak the dark, followed almost simultaneously by the nacreous visible punch of matter cannon.

The strange double blast arose from one of the distant specks he'd assumed was an orbital platform. And it came nowhere near *Calm Horizons*. Instead it left a scorching trail of incandescence on its way through atmosphere toward a planet-side target.

Almost at once black space became a blaze of violence as every ship in the cordon unleashed her guns.

Ciro Vasaczk had no idea what was going on, and he didn't care. He cared only that none of the fire was directed at *Calm Horizons* – and *Calm Horizons* didn't return it.

He'd been given the diversion he needed.

Without hesitation he unclipped his belt from its anchor and flipped himself toward the compartment which held *Trumpet*'s singularity grenades.

MIN

She couldn't control the fire in her palms – the burning desire for weapons and action which had earned her her reputation as Warden Dios' 'executioner'. It spread outward from the place where Angus had shot her. Waiting imposed such complex demands that she doubted her ability to stand the strain. Her PCR brought in four, five, sometimes six overlapping channels. From her place at the communications station on *Punisher*'s auxiliary bridge, she handled as many of them as she could; gave out every answer she had. She was the center around which every aspect of Earth's defense against *Calm Horizons* turned. But it was all just *waiting*. Her chance to take part in determining humankind's future hadn't come yet.

Downlink control on two. Planetary authorities report widespread panic, riots, violence. They blame losing the scan net. Urgently request restoration.

Tell them no, she ordered. She didn't want to let Holt Fasner see her cordon of ships that clearly.

Adventurous on three. Rerouting cleared the power-spikes. We're back in business. Ready on your order.

Center on five. ED Security is afraid of violence at the evac stations. Nonessential personnel are going crazy. If we don't give them something to do, we'll have a whole new kind of trouble on our hands.

By degrees a blaze of urgency spread from Min's wrists up

into her forearms. Any minute now she might burst into flames –

PolyMed on one. Director, you've got to help us. We're sitting ducks. We have priceless data here. And patients. We need downlink facilities and personnel carriers.

PolyMed couldn't adjust its orbit. Nothing protected hundreds of patients and invaluable zero-g medical research except one small gunboat, *Flash Attack*.

But Min had no downlink facilities or personnel carriers to spare – and no attention. PolyMed wasn't an immediate target. Everything except the disposition of her ships was chaff, harassment, distraction. Whatever happened, Angus and Dolph were out of her hands. With most of her concentration and all of her heart, she focused on the reports from Suka Bator.

PR uplink on six. Dr Harbinger states that she's been able to trace the SOD-CMOS chip from Nathan Alt's id tag.

Min flinched involuntarily. Dr *Harbinger* states –? What the hell had happened to Hashi? Why was Lane speaking for him? He was supposed to contact the Council as soon as Min authorized a channel. But when she gave the word, it wasn't Hashi who obeyed: it was Lane Harbinger.

Center, she ordered, maintain that PR uplink. I don't care who has to postpone talking to me. Give me a constant feed.

She didn't wait for an acknowledgment. Grimly she told Cray, 'Put six on the speakers. I want everybody to hear it.'

Especially Morn. To some extent Morn had caused this crisis: she needed to know the outcome of her testimony. Min couldn't think of any other way to help her.

'Aye, Director.' Cray obeyed numbly; exhausted by the stress of directing Min's communications traffic.

Hell, they were all exhausted. Porson and Bydell worked as hard as Cray, collecting and sorting data of every description so that it would be available when Min needed it. And Patrice had run helm hard and often in the past forty-eight hours. Only Glessen on targ looked steady and strong, eager to fight.

One way or another, Min meant to make sure he got the opportunity.

Center on three. Scan reports your command module and Trumpet *on final approach. Estimate dock in seven minutes.*

UMCPHQ had a clear view of *Calm Horizons* on that side: *Punisher* did not. Without UMCPHQ's scan data, the cruiser would have had no way of knowing what the two small vessels did, or what happened to them.

Earth uplink control on one. Provisioning inadequate. Shortfalls expected within hours. Resupply essential.

Min ignored that. The emergency would be over in minutes, not hours. Battles in space were like that: appallingly swift; done before anyone could comprehend the scale of the forces which had been unleashed. She would worry about the aftermath later.

Valor *on three. Damn it, Director, that's a* human *station! We're facing a Behemoth-class Amnion defensive – and you want us to fix targ on a* human *station?*

Flash Attack *on two.* Adventurous *on five. Pocket cruiser* Stiletto *on four. Director, we need an explanation. These targ priorities don't make sense.*

Just *do* it! she fired back at them all. If I'm wrong you can insist on a court-martial later.

Then she told Center, Remind Vestabule I warned him. He's safe as long as he has that proton cannon.

By God, she needed to shoot somebody!

More than that, she needed to be right. She owed it to Morn as much as to Warden – and to her sworn duty as acting director of the UMCP.

Morn had obeyed promptly when Min told her to end her transmission to Suka Bator. Despite everything she'd endured, all the ways she'd been betrayed, she still trusted the ED director that much. Under other circumstances, Min would have felt touched, gratified; perhaps humbled. But now she didn't have time.

Nevertheless she was acutely conscious of Morn. Angus Thermopyle's victim, and Nick Succorso's – and Warden Dios' – had brought herself and her people all this way by sheer grit so that she could make one valiant, costly attempt to change the course of humankind's future. And now she had nothing left to do except remember her own pain.

She'd told her story; explained the crimes she'd experienced and witnessed. In some absolute sense, she was done. She still sat at the command station; but she no longer gave orders, or offered suggestions. Angus and Davies were beyond her help.

She was done – but she wasn't satisfied. Nothing had been resolved.

After she'd silenced her intercom, stopped talking to the Council, she sat almost motionless in her g-seat, with her head resting against the back and a haunted look in her eyes – alone and lost; almost out of reach. Her bruised stare suggested horrors Min could hardly imagine. She knew what it was like to be injected with mutagens.

Davies had gone to surrender himself to the Amnion. And no one could save her son except a man who'd raped and brutalized her for weeks.

Min probably should have sent her to sickbay. Had her dragged there if necessary. But she deserved better than that. She'd earned the right to remain where she could watch and hear what happened, even if there was no longer anything she could do about it.

For her sake as well as Warden's – and for humanity's – Min hoped fervently that the Council would make the right decision.

'According to Dr Harbinger,' the PR uplink echoed from Suka Bator, 'Anodyne Systems records show that Nathan Alt reqqed that chip just a few days ago. He still had UMC access and clearance to Anodyne five and a half weeks after he was allegedly fired.'

Lane's statement didn't make much sense to Min. She knew too little about the situation: Hashi hadn't had time to give her all the details of the third kaze's attack. Nevertheless the importance of Lane's evidence was plain, if only because Koina's communications tech relayed it with so much hushed intensity.

The Dragon had been dealt another blow –

Abruptly Morn moved. Her commitments wouldn't let her rest. With a palpable effort she pulled herself upright at the command station. Her worn gaze caught Min's.

'Director,' she asked softly, 'who is Dr Harbinger?'

Min turned from the communications board. At that moment she would have answered any question Morn asked, no matter whom she kept waiting.

'One of Hashi's techs,' she said past her throat pickup. 'She's brilliant, one of the best. But I don't know why he wants her to talk for him.' As soon as she said that, however, an explanation occurred to her. 'Unless he's worried about his credibility.' In the Members' eyes – and in the context of Morn's testimony – he must have been dangerously tainted. Cleatus Fane could have used that against him. 'He may think the Council is more likely to believe her.'

Morn nodded slowly. 'He's right.' A vibration of anger sharpened her voice. 'He's already done too much harm. I wouldn't believe him if he told me my own name.'

Now I would, Min thought. But she didn't try to explain what had just changed for her.

If her guess was accurate, Hashi had done something unprecedented. He'd refused an opportunity to display his own cleverness.

Even Lane couldn't have penetrated Anodyne's security alone: that wasn't possible. She must have worked with Hashi every step of the way; and, presumably, with Chief Mandich. Why else had the DA director asked Min for those Administration codes?

Yet he declined the spotlight; declined a chance to deliver one of his notorious lectures. Min had always considered him a rampant egomaniac, but apparently there were things he valued more than his own pride. In its way his loyalty to Warden's vision of an independent UMCP must have been as clear as hers.

'The FEA is objecting,' the PR uplink reported – an intent, subvocalized murmur amplified by transmission gain. 'He's objecting hard. He claims Dr Harbinger's evidence must be false because it doesn't make sense.'

'Typical,' Min sneered like the fire in her hands. Her heart had begun to soar. 'Lane's investigation makes the Dragon look bad, so of course she must be lying.' The more Fane protested, the more guilt he betrayed. 'Maybe he doesn't know she's the kind of woman who would probably throw up if she tried to say something that wasn't true.'

Come on, you bastard, she urged Fasner. I *dare* you to let this pass. You haven't got the *guts* to give up.

The husky voice from the speakers held the bridge. 'Director Hannish is answering. She accuses him of triggering that kaze. Now she says CEO Fasner suspected that Director Dios intended to make his crimes public. The CEO sent all three kazes to scare the Council into rejecting the Bill of Severance.'

Morn's chin came up. Glints of vindication complicated the haunting in her eyes. She must have understood what she heard less than Min did. Nevertheless the eagerness of Koina's tech made its implications clear. Through her pain and weariness Morn seemed to catch her first real glimpse of hope.

If the Members took the next step –

Center, Min warned her throat pickup, stand by. All ships, all guns. On my personal authority.

She wanted to add, If you've ever believed in me, trust me now. But she didn't have time.

Too excited to whisper, the PR tech announced, almost shouted, 'The Council has dropped Fane's proposal to decharter the UMCP. The Bill of Severance has been moved and seconded. They're going to pass it! My God, they're passing it by acclamation. *Holt Fasner no longer owns the UMCP.*'

No longer owns – Min found herself on her feet, snatched erect by years of desire realized at last. She felt like flames leaping high. Warden had succeeded. By God, he had *done* it! The strength of his complicity and regret had broken Fasner's legal grip on human space.

Now only illegal methods of control remained.

Only treason and violence.

'Fane is hysterical,' the uplink crowed. 'He's being escorted from the room.'

Of *course* he was hysterical. He knew what was about to happen.

Center on three. Your command module and *Trumpet* are almost there. Dock in ninety seconds.

'Captain Verti –' Koina's tech seemed to choke in surprise. 'I don't believe it. Captain Vertigus is *dancing* on his chair. Most of the Members look too stunned to react, but some of them are applauding him. Blaine Manse, Tel Burnish, Sigurd –'

Suddenly everything in Min's life had become simple. She no longer had to worry about politics and humankind's future, plotting and doubt: she'd been restored to her chosen place as the UMCP's ED director, and her duty was plain.

That's enough, she told Center. Cancel feed on six.

Center obeyed promptly. Without transition the uplink fell silent as if Suka Bator had ceased to exist.

Now, she thought in Holt's direction. Do it *now*.

Morn might have been waiting for this moment. She closed her eyes for a few seconds like a woman marshaling her last resources. Then she opened her belts and stood up from the command station. The look of relief on her wounded face bore an acute resemblance to mourning.

'Director Donner,' she pronounced quietly, 'you have the bridge. I'll get out of your way.

'When this is over, I hope you'll remember that they were all my prisoners – Mikka and Ciro, Vector, Angus. I'm responsible for anything they did that might count against them. If you don't think they've earned a reprieve, take it out on me.'

She'd let her son go. Whether he lived or died, she'd spent him to purchase her chance to address the Council. And now she had no way to help him. She'd done the best she could for him when she'd decided to trust Angus.

It was no wonder that her success seemed to fill her with grief.

Center on four. Docking complete. They've arrived.

The fire had reached Min's eyes, as hot as tears. An unexpected lump closed her throat momentarily. 'Ensign Hyland –' She started again. 'Morn – I consider it an honor to know you. As far as I'm concerned, the Vasaczks and Dr Shaheed are as innocent as the day they were born. And Captain Thermopyle already works for us. On my word as UMCP Acting Director, nobody is going to "take" anything "out on" any of you. You are –'

She would have said more; wanted to find *some* words that might convey what she felt. But she'd run out of time.

In a burst of urgency, Porson and Center together cried at her, 'HO is firing! Lasers and matter cannon! My God, they're trying to hit *Suka Bator*!'

Min Donner had planned for this. With nothing to go on except Morn's courage, Hashi's stubborn genius, and her own faith in Warden Dios, she'd judged the Dragon rightly.

Now at last she could help the man she served make restitution.

Blazing with pure passion, she yelled, '*Fire!* All fire! Fire *now*!'

Almost at once, almost in unison, every cannon in the cordon and every gun UMCPHQ could bring to bear unleashed a barrage of devastation at Holt Fasner's HO.

DAVIES

Even though he was braced for it, the hit-and-scrape as the module struck the port guides and slid along them into the docking seals jolted Davies' heart. He wasn't ready for this; didn't know how to be ready. He had to remind himself constantly that Angus and Ciro – and Director Donner – had no intention of letting the defensive escape with knowledge which could doom humankind. Unless every single aspect of Angus' plan failed, Davies and Vector were far more likely to die than to end as Amnion. Their artificial immunity would last long enough to spare them.

The scraping became a shudder as the guides forcibly adjusted the module's approach. Moments later, however, the seals caught the module and locked it to a halt. There the stress ended. With a faint sigh of hull-strain, the small vessel settled to rest against the Amnioni's side.

For what he feared would be the last time, Davies looked at Vector's face.

They still hadn't put on their helmets. As soon as they did, they wouldn't be able to say or hear anything they didn't want to share with *Calm Horizons*.

Vector held Davies' gaze gravely; but the former engineer didn't speak. They'd come to a place where they had no more words to offer each other.

Almost at once the airlock intercom chimed. This was Captain Ubikwe's last chance to talk to them without being overheard. Apparently he hadn't run out of words.

Or he may have had something vital to convey –

Davies thumbed the intercom awkwardly. The tension in his muscles stiffened his movements; deprived him of grace.

Not for the first time he was amazed by the ease in Captain Ubikwe's deep voice. Vocally, if in no other way, *Punisher*'s dispossessed commander comported himself like a man with nothing to fear; nothing at stake.

'We're in,' he announced unnecessarily. 'Davies, Vector, this is your last chance to change your minds.

'Personally, I want to rescue Director Dios. I think the risk is worth taking. But I'm in no danger of ending up Amnion if absolutely everything goes wrong. I can't make a choice like this for you.

'I won't argue with anything you decide. Say the word, and I'll blow the seals, tear us back out of here. Hell,' he chuckled, 'it won't be the first time I haven't done exactly what I was told. And we might even survive for a while. I'll be surprised if a fucker that big can fix targ on us when we're this close. We'll still go out in a blaze of glory, but it won't be until the real fighting starts.'

He was probably right. As soon as *Calm Horizons* recognized the betrayal, however, she would unleash her attack on Suka Bator. Or on UMCPHQ and *Punisher* if her proton cannon failed. Then the command module and *Trumpet* would be ripped apart in the crossfire.

Drifting near the intercom, Davies asked the only question that mattered to him now. 'Where's Angus?'

'On his way,' Captain Ubikwe answered promptly. 'But he still hasn't reached the emitter. I would rather wait where we are until he heads back this way. Unfortunately Vestabule has already ordered us to open the airlock.' He snorted like a subterranean explosion. 'I don't think he's in the mood for suspense. In any case, I don't know whether Angus' plan is going to work. I have no idea what happens when you fill a super-light proton cannon emitter with hull sealant.' Calmly he finished, 'So it's up to you.'

Vector cleared his throat. 'What about Ciro, Captain?'

'He's out there.' Dolph's tone conveyed a shrug. 'But I'm

not sure we can count on him. We'll probably have to rely on Mikka and *Trumpet* to keep us alive.'

Davies heard a hint of concern behind Captain Ubikwe's composure; but he didn't have time to pursue it. Vestabule *has already ordered* – Mutely he looked at Vector for confirmation.

Vector met Davies' eyes again and nodded. A rueful smile twisted his mouth.

Davies' throat closed on a groan. Swallowing roughly, he said to the intercom, 'Tell Vestabule we're on our way. As soon as we get our helmets on.'

Vehement with dread, he closed the toggle.

Shit. They had to go. Now or never. Whatever happened.

He snatched up his helmet, jammed it over his head, set the seals. Almost at once the status indicators on the readout inside the helmet showed green. He adjusted the polarization of his faceplate to improve his vision as much as possible, then turned for a last look at Vector.

Vector's helmet was already in place. The reflective surface of his faceplate concealed him completely.

'I suppose,' his voice breathed in Davies' internal speaker, 'I ought to say something about death before dishonor. It's traditional.'

'Fuck that,' Davies muttered. 'I want to make a tradition of surviving.'

Morn had done it under worse conditions than these.

Grimly he coded the sequence to open the module's airlock.

But his hands shook on the keys. Everything he did felt brittle. His life had become breakable as glass, and he feared that his own distress would shatter it before anyone else had a chance to threaten it.

Vector was right. Surrender would have been more dignified.

Alerts signaled from the control pad as the doors began to ease aside. Servos worked the mechanism with a palpable hum. Davies' external pickup brought in a low sigh as the airlock's atmosphere equalized with the specific pressure of the docking port. Inside his helmet Captain Ubikwe offered, 'Good luck.' Then the command module stopped transmitting.

The doors unsealed to a wash of acrid light. Both the outer and inner iris-doors of *Calm Horizons'* airlock stood open, letting the kind of radiance the Amnion preferred flow through. It was the same sulfur-hued illumination into which Davies Hyland had been born on Enablement Station. He remembered it vividly: the memory made him want to throw up. That light seemed to catch and breed on the rough textures and uneven surfaces of the ship, as if it were nourished by every Amnion thing it touched.

He didn't wait for Vector. Passing himself rigidly from handgrip to handgrip, he left the command module and entered the defensive.

Vector followed less awkwardly. G afflicted him with constant pain. He moved more easily weightless.

Davies assumed that he and Vector were scanned while they crossed *Calm Horizons'* airlock; but he couldn't identify any of the sensors or instruments. The Amnion grew their technology in ways he couldn't begin to understand.

For no apparent reason, he found himself wondering how *Calm Horizons* had found *Trumpet* in the immense labyrinth of Massif-5. Presumably *Soar* must have guided the defensive in. But how in hell had Sorus Chatelaine and Marc Vestabule contrived to communicate with each other?

The Amnion had almost achieved near-C velocities. They could communicate effectively across imponderable distances. In some ways their technological resources were as fearsome as their mutagens. Perhaps their sinks could shrug off the combined fire of all Min Donner's ships.

Did they know he and Vector were armed? Could they tell? Angus had said not – but he wasn't here. Marc Vestabule and the Amnion were.

Beyond the port airlock, Davies and Vector faced a huge space like a cavern left behind by a receding flood of brimstone and lava. Maybe the light actually did feed on the walls. Every span of the bulkheads and equipment seemed to glow with implied heat. Davies guessed that the high chamber was a cargo hold. Structures which resembled trees formed of poured concrete stood as if rooted to every surface: they were probably gantries, positioned for zero g. Cables like vines spread at random angles from their limbs and trunks. Among them the decks and walls were crisscrossed with magnetic rails for transport sleds.

Despite its alienness, the hold eased one of Davies' worries. He'd feared facing Marc Vestabule and Warden Dios in some featureless, constricted room where nothing was possible.

The actual situation was bad enough –

Ten meters beyond the airlock, four Amnion held the floor. Two of them looked like replicas of each other: each with four eyes so that they could see all around them; each with three arms and legs. The other two had been grown to a different design. One had four arms, the other five; and their legs also might as well have been arms. They carried ambiguous pieces of equipment, which they used with separate limbs. Pouches hung from various shoulders. But all four of them wore the gnarled crust which took the place of clothes for the Amnion. And all four had the lipless mouths, lamprey teeth and merciless eyes of their kind.

'A reception committee,' Vector murmured. 'How nice.'

Davies ignored him.

He didn't see any guns. None of these Amnion held anything comparable to the weapons he'd seen on Enablement.

That, too, eased a worry.

In front of the four creatures floated two men; or rather one man and a mutated human being. Davies recognized Marc Vestabule. He'd encountered the Amnioni once before; wasn't likely to forget Vestabule's approximation of humanity. The human side of Vestabule's face wore a vestigial look of concern, which his alien features contradicted. He had what must have been a PCR jacked into one of his ears and a pickup fixed to his throat. If he commanded the defensive, he needed such things to stay in contact with the bridge.

His companion was Warden Dios.

Davies had never met the UMCP director; never seen the man before. However, Morn's memories filled the gap as effectively as personal knowledge. In some strange sense, he'd known those strong, square fists and that thick chest longer than he'd been alive. He recognized the patch which covered Warden's left eye socket above the breathing mask: he knew it concealed an IR prosthesis which enabled him – so they'd said in the Academy – to detect lies no matter who told them. And the direct force of Warden's human eye was familiar, as if he'd stood under its scrutiny more than once.

He knew Director Dios couldn't see him, not through the polarized mirror of his faceplate. Nevertheless he seemed to feel Warden's gaze searching him as if the UMCP director wanted to understand what kind of son Morn had brought into the world.

Davies' metabolism burned too hotly for comfort inside an EVA suit. Droplets of sweat broke free of his face, left odd bits of refraction and distortion on the inner surface of his faceplate. In spite of the power drain, he dialed internal cooling as high as it would go; increased the oxygen balance supplied by his tanks. Still his skin felt flushed, as if he were feverish – or ashamed to face the UMCP director.

In his memories, Warden Dios was a man who demanded the best from everyone around him – and had the right to demand it because he gave the best himself.

Davies looked around quickly to make sure there were no other Amnion in the hold. At the edge of his faceplate he noticed that the iris of the airlock remained open behind Vector. A kick of adrenaline carried new fear through his veins. Were the Amnion planning to force their way aboard the command module? Was that what all this equipment was for – to pry open or cut through the module's seals?

If the airlock itself stayed open, Captain Ubikwe might cause Warden's death before Angus could try to rescue any of them.

For a moment neither Vestabule nor Warden Dios spoke: they simply stared at the faceless EVA suits. Then the former human turned to Warden. In a voice like flakes of oxidation, he said, 'The way is open, Warden Dios.' He indicated the airlock. 'Will you depart?'

Depart –? Davies bit his lip to contain his alarm. Were the Amnion willing to let Warden go? A hostage as valuable as the UMCP director? What kind of deal had he made with them?

What had they *done* to him?

Warden replied with a snort of derision. Nudging the deck with one foot, he moved a meter closer to Davies and Vector; ahead of the Amnion. As if he understood how they might take Vestabule's offer, he said gruffly, 'Don't worry about it. He knows I can't leave. This is just his confused idea of a joke.'

Behind him, Vestabule intoned, 'The statement was made that you would be permitted to return. I have abided by it.'

The Amnioni added a guttural sound to his throat pickup. At once the hold airlock irised shut.

Warden snorted again. 'One of the pleasures of dealing with the Amnion,' he rasped, 'is the way they keep their promises.'

Before Vestabule could respond, the director asked harshly, 'Which of you is Davies Hyland?'

Davies raised his right hand as if he were taking an oath. A clutch of panic gripped his chest, but he forced himself to say, 'I am.'

Warden stared at him hard, then glanced toward Vector. 'In that case, you must be Dr Shaheed.'

Vector inclined his head. 'As you say, Director Dios.' A small movement of his hands implied a shrug. 'I hope you'll forgive these suits. We aren't particularly eager to start breathing that air.'

Warden dismissed Vector's apology with a frown. 'There's nothing to forgive.'

'Do not delay, Warden Dios,' Vestabule warned. 'We must initiate thrust. You will ensure that there is no resistance.'

Warden's chin jutted as if he were grinding his teeth.

'I'm not going to waste time thanking you for this,' he told Davies and Vector. 'You deserve more gratitude than I can express. But I do want to make my position clear.

'Our host has given me the benefit of a delayed-action mutagen. I imagine you're familiar with it. I'm still human because he also gave me a temporary antidote. But when the antidote wears off –' The corners of his jaw knotted. 'That's why I can't leave.'

'Director Dios belongs to us,' Vestabule stated flatly.

Warden grimaced. Bitter as acid, he drawled, 'So please don't torment yourselves thinking there must be something you can do for me. You'll end up as confused as he is.'

He may have meant, If you've got something planned, leave me out of it. I can't help you. And there's nothing left of me to save.

Davies' heart dropped. A flash of despair filled his throat with ashes: for a moment he could hardly breathe. Angus was right. A delayed-action – Like Ciro. Everything Angus planned, everything Mikka and Ciro and Captain Ubikwe risked had already come undone.

Now there was no reason to do anything except surrender.

But Vector reacted differently. 'I'm sorry to hear that, Director Dios,' he murmured. 'I know the mutagen you're talking about. It shouldn't happen to a dog.' Then he added stiffly, 'It's too bad "our host" hasn't offered you a supply of that temporary antidote. I assume he has one.'

Warden's eye glinted fiercely. 'Oh, he has one, all right. He's just keeping it to himself.'

Vector must have understood how Davies felt. Nevertheless a hint of resistance in his tone caught at Davies' attention. Apparently he hadn't given up. Instead he was fighting for time. Every word, every sentence, gave Angus a few more seconds.

There was no reason to struggle –

No reason except anger and grief and humanity.

Davies took hold of himself; swallowed roughly. Angus' inheritance beat in his veins. No matter what happened, Morn's rapist and Warden's victim wouldn't surrender.

And if Davies could get the antidote from Vestabule –

Tension in the human parts of Vestabule's body suggested

impatience. 'Our departure is imminent,' he announced. 'We await the resolution of the political conflict which your Director Donner warns us may turn to combat. She assures us that we will not be threatened in any way. Nevertheless we will retain our line of fire on the site of your Council until we have witnessed the truth. Then we will commence our return to Amnion space.'

Davies gulped in surprise. Political conflict? Turn to combat? My God, what had Morn told the Council?

But Vestabule hadn't paused. Inflexibly he commanded, 'You will remove your EVA suits.'

The two Amnion carrying equipment and pouches drifted forward.

Grimly Davies put Morn out of his mind.

It was time. Now or never. Time to face his terror.

Ciro would destroy *Calm Horizons*. Or Angus would. Or Min Donner. One way or another, they'd all promised Davies that he had nothing to lose except his life.

Trembling with more adrenaline and dread than he could contain, he snapped harshly, 'I don't think so.'

The Amnion stopped. Vestabule's human eye blinked puzzlement or alarm.

Warden's scowl betrayed no reaction.

Davies snatched a breath of clean air, then reached up, opened the seals of his helmet and lifted it off his head. Deliberately he let the Amnion and Warden Dios see who he was; recognize his father in him. After that he replaced his helmet and sealed it again.

His eyes stung from the touch of *Calm Horizons*' atmosphere. More sweat spattered the inside of his faceplate; too much moisture for his suit to process all at once.

'I'm Davies Hyland,' he told Vestabule. 'You know me. But I know you, too, and I'm offended by everything the Amnion did to you. As long as I prefer the taste of human air, I'm going to stay in this suit.'

Vestabule stared at him. 'Then we will force you from it.'

'No, you won't,' Davies countered. He did his best to sound certain. 'Dr Shaheed and I came here to surrender, and that's what we're going to do. You can't force us if we cooperate.'

Surprise them, Angus had told him. *Confuse them. Keep them off balance.*

'Here.' Cursing the tremors which shook his arms, he snatched off his left glove, shoved it under his belt, and jammed his sleeve back to expose his forearm. 'Shoot me up.' With his fingers clenched and his sharp-edged line hidden in his palm, he pointed his fist at the Amnion. 'Transform me. Then I'll take the suit off myself. It probably won't fit me anyway.'

Warden thrust his hands deep into his pockets like a man who wanted to show everyone that he wasn't doing anything.

Vestabule started to reply; but something distracted him. A slight cock of his head gave the impression that he was listening to his PCR. He rasped a few alien sounds in response.

A subtle tension eased its grip on his human muscles.

'It appears that your Director Donner has spoken honestly,' he reported as if he considered this relevant to Davies' behavior. 'The station identified as UMCHO has opened fire on your center of government.'

Davies clenched his teeth to control his reaction. For a moment he couldn't pull his eyes away from the open flare of concern and hope on Warden's face. UMCHO meant Holt Fasner. The man who owned the UMCP was trying to destroy Suka Bator.

The 'political conflict' had become 'combat' with a vengeance. Somehow Morn's testimony had sent humankind to war against itself.

Warden's expression said as clearly as words that he'd caused this to happen. Directly or indirectly, he was responsible for it. He'd given Morn and Davies a chance to master Angus so that she would be able to come here and tell her story.

'Your ships respond with a concerted attack on that station,' Vestabule continued. 'Our scan reports that the station's shields are inadequate to withstand such an attack.'

Before he could conceal what he felt, Warden's alarm

ignited into a look of pure exultation. His fists formed knots of victory in his pockets as Vestabule added, 'We estimate that UMCHO will be destroyed before significant harm has been inflicted on our target.'

Perhaps because the Amnioni remembered some of his humanity, he kept insisting that he still had hostages. Yet he didn't seem to grasp the significance of Holt Fasner's defeat.

As if Min's forewarning had led him to this conclusion, he told Davies, 'Your Director Donner stated that we would not be threatened. She has dealt with us honestly. We will accept your surrender.'

Without any discernible instructions or signals, he sent the two Amnion with all the extra arms toward Davies and Vector.

In the space between one heartbeat and the next, everything else vanished from Davies' head. The implications of Warden's accomplishment; the danger to Angus and Ciro; *Punisher*, Suka Bator: everything. His entire being sprang into focus on the moment of his worst nightmare.

As they advanced each Amnioni unlimbered a pouch from one of its shoulders. Hands opened the pouches: more hands reached inside and brought out hypos.

Lambent with sulfur and brimstone, the fluid in the hypos looked like liquid ruin.

Some of their equipment had begun to wink and murmur like mass detectors. Davies guessed that the devices performed some kind of tissue scan. Perhaps they measured and evaluated the effects of mutagens.

The Amnion may have intended to give Vector the same mutagen they'd forced on Warden. Then they could use his humanity as a lever to help them extract his knowledge. But Davies was sure that they had something different in mind for him.

Hell, the drug meant for him might not be a mutagen at all. It might be – His heart hammered as he realized the peril. It might be a nerve-block; an alien version of cat; something to paralyze him so that the Amnion could study him at their leisure.

'I don't think I can do this, Davies,' Vector croaked. The

vibration of fear in his voice sawed against his impulse to resist. But it wasn't the hypo that scared him.

'*Do* it,' Davies demanded in panic.

Hesitantly Vector removed one of his gloves and tucked it into his belt. His hand seemed to drift away from him of its own accord, extending itself to the nearest Amnioni.

Davies had promised himself that he would wait until after he'd been given the injection – until after the Amnion relaxed because they felt sure of him. Angus needed the time. But the danger had suddenly become too great. As his designated victimizer approached him, he threw out all his plans.

He opened his bare hand, slipped one handle of his monofilament line between his fingers.

Too soon, *too soon*, he flung himself into motion.

While the Amnioni reached its hypo toward him, he whipped out the line so that its weighted end lashed it around the creature's wrist. Then he leaped at the alien, planted his boots in the center of its chest, and heaved on the line with all his might.

His elevated endocrine system supplied more force than his muscles naturally possessed. And the polysilicate chips crusting the line were as sharp as scalpels. The line tore through tissue and bone; rip-cut the Amnioni's hand off.

From the rent stump a geyser of greenish blood sprayed the air, formed a weightless fountain across the acrid light; so much blood a man could have drowned in it. It splashed heavily onto the front of his EVA suit, half blinded his faceplate.

The Amnioni gave out a hoarse wail like a klaxon of pain. Shrill as anguish, the sound rang in his helmet. Nevertheless the creature grappled for him with other arms; struggled to capture him while its life gushed out of it.

For an instant he ignored the clutch; fought it only enough to turn in the air and slash a kick at the severed hand – at the hypo. His boot shattered the hypo, added drugs or mutagens to the spume of blood.

Vector hadn't moved. He stood as if he were frozen in shock.

635

At once Davies turned again, into the Amnioni's grasp. Two arms caught him, three, wrapped around him, hugged him close. He used the creature's pressure as well as his own to pull his line toward the creature's head; loop it around the creature's neck.

But he had no leverage now. Human muscle couldn't match Amnion. The arms closed on him; began to crush him. The alien should have been growing weaker by the second, yet it remained powerful enough to break his bones.

He heard a distant crumpling noise – a muffled explosion; the kind of sound that should have been followed by decompression alerts. But if *Calm Horizons* cried a warning he couldn't hear it; or didn't understand it.

The alien arms squeezed harder.

Without transition Warden appeared at the Amnioni's back. Strong as stones, his hands gripped the creature's head. His fingers gouged more pain into its eyes.

Its wailing scaled higher. Its embrace loosened.

Davies couldn't break free, but he could shift backward. Jamming his free hand to the keypad on his chest, he activated his suit jets.

A waldo harness around his hips controlled the jets. When he jammed his pelvis to the side, a burst of pressure snatched him out of the Amnioni's arms.

His line cut through the creature's neck until it snagged on bone. The handle and his fist were slick with blood: the power of the jets jerked the weapon from his grip. Then his jets carried him away.

Twisting his hips, he shot toward the forest of gantries. As he soared, he slapped at his faceplate, trying to clear off some of the blood.

Vector still hadn't moved. *Damn* it, he was paralyzed by his fear of fighting. At the last moment he'd decided to let his life end without a struggle –

No, Davies was wrong. Vector *had* moved. He must have.

The Amnioni assigned to him drifted limp in front of him now, its arms slack, its hypo gone. Its instruments winked uselessly. Deep in one eye it wore a long sliver of plastic sharpened like a dirk.

Yes. Two down.

Slowly, methodically, Vector pulled his glove back onto his exposed hand like a man who could afford to take his time because his job was done.

Alien voices shouted incomprehensible commands or warnings.

Davies' jets made him faster than any unassisted Amnioni. He ducked past a cable in his way, caught hold of the first gantry-arm he reached, and swung around it in time to see Vestabule intercept Warden Dios.

Warden must have kicked himself away from the deck after Davies. He may have tried to hook a ride on Davies' jets and missed. Coasting weightless, he couldn't deflect his trajectory when Vestabule came after him.

Vestabule's legs were stronger: his leap lifted him faster than Warden could move. At the last instant Warden scissored a kick at Vestabule's head; but Vestabule slapped Warden's boot aside, clamped a fist onto his thigh. Climbing Warden hand-over-hand, Vestabule struck him a sweeping blow which snapped his head back; may have cracked his spine. He slumped in Vestabule's grasp, his head lolling.

Jets at full power, Davies dove at Vestabule before he realized that the two remaining Amnion, the guards, were closing on him.

By pure chance his maneuver surprised them. He flashed through their arms; drove past them toward Vestabule. Inertia carried them on to the gantry.

With almost human vehemence, Vestabule threw Warden's inert form at the nearest bulkhead. Then he wrenched himself around in midair to face Davies.

Davies' hands had already found his belt-pouch: his fingers snatched out his whetted plastic shard. As Vestabule grabbed for him, he hammered his weapon at Vestabule's face.

His strike had all the force of his jets and his arm behind it. Vestabule stopped it with the only defense available: he put his hand in the way. Davies plunged his dagger into the

Amnioni's palm and then ripped it away again as he roared past.

More blood. Shit, the atmosphere was already *full* of blood –

He slewed his hips to turn; launched himself in a desperate effort to catch Warden before Warden struck the bulkhead.

He saw at once that he was too late. Vestabule had hurled Warden too hard for Davies to overtake him. But Vector had no one to fight: he could react more quickly. Rising unexpectedly from the deck, he drifted along the bulkhead in time to interpose himself between Warden and the rough metal.

Warden's momentum slammed both of them into the wall. But Vector's body cushioned the impact. Cradling Warden in his arms, he rebounded slowly toward a nearby gantry.

A hand closed on Davies' ankle. One of the guards had sprung back from a gantry-limb at an angle that intersected Davies' trajectory. Before the guard could improve its hold, he slashed at the hand with his blade, jerked his ankle free, and wheeled off in an uncontrolled tumble of evasive jet blasts.

A voice he seemed to recognize screamed in his ears. It might have been his.

'Angus, God damn you! Get in here!'

The next instant an explosion like a massive fist of thunder staggered the entire hold. God, it must have staggered the whole ship! Cables lurched drunkenly: gantry-arms bobbed and swayed. One of the structures bowed as if it were about to topple – but of course it had nowhere to go in zero g.

The explosion echoed inside Davies' helmet; clanged pain into his ears. A moment passed before he realized that he could hear the unmistakable sizzling hull-roar of matter cannon fire.

At the same time *Calm Horizons'* drives came to life, yowling for power until the bulkheads seemed to shriek in distress.

The last battle was underway.

That explosion may have been the destruction of the proton

638

cannon. Davies prayed it was as he flipped himself around a gantry to scan the hold.

Vestabule and the two guards had apparently decided to ignore Vector and Warden. They all fought their own inertia and weightlessness in order to converge on Davies – the prize for which *Calm Horizons* and everyone aboard was willing to die.

From an entryway opposite Davies' position, four more Amnion appeared. Summoned to Vestabule's aid – They wore jet-pods on their hips: they carried guns. Clustered for assault, they left the deck and sailed in his direction.

Seven Amnion. Four with guns. And he was effectively alone. No sign of Angus. Warden was unconscious – or dead. Vector had already done more than he would have believed possible.

At the start of Davies' life, Morn had told him, *As far as I'm concerned, you're the second most important thing in the galaxy. You're my son. But the first, the most important thing is to not betray my humanity.* She'd faced worse than this in the name of that conviction. And she'd found an answer that was better than gap-sickness and suicide; better than surrender.

Calm Horizons was already as good as dead.

His elevated metabolism gave him all the strength he needed; all the courage –

Cocking his hips, he blasted into motion. A mad howl overwhelmed his suit's external speaker.

'*Come and get me, you bastards!*'

His own last battle had also begun.

ANGUS

The part he didn't give a shit about was easy. Save the Governing fucking Council for Earth and Space. What fun. Several different jamming fields cloaked him until he reached the super-light proton cannon. And hull sealant hardened almost instantly. A database told him more than he wanted to know about it. In 1.7 seconds it stiffened enough to stand against decompression: in 4.2 it became so hard that it could face limited amounts of impact fire and matter cannon as if it were steel. Proton fire would tear it apart, of course – but he only needed five seconds to fill the emitter with so much sealant that the gun would probably shatter itself at the same time.

Call it twelve seconds altogether, and the Amnion lost most of their hostages. The fucking Members were safe.

The rest of what he had to do would be a hell of a lot harder.

If he had any sense – if he were still the man he remembered being – he would head back to *Trumpet*, take his ship away from Mikka. When the fighting started, he could protect himself with the gap scout's dispersion field until he got a chance to burn for open space and the gap.

But he didn't do that. He hardly considered it. Instead he launched himself with all his reinforced strength toward the docking port where *Punisher*'s command module rested against *Calm Horizons*' side.

He'd become someone he didn't know at all.

He'd offered to sabotage the proton cannon in order to placate Morn; so that she would agree to the rest of his scheme. But his promise to her wasn't the only reason he'd actually done it. He needed the diversion. His plans to rescue Dios, Davies and Vector – and to destroy *Calm Horizons* – were desperately precarious. Any one of a thousand things could go wrong. So he was forced to hope that Vestabule would realize he'd been betrayed and try to destroy Suka Bator. When the proton cannon shattered, it might do enough damage to distract the Amnion.

As he sailed toward the docking port, he blocked his terror of EVA and his fear of death by correlating databases on matter cannon, EVA suits and his own welding. He remembered vividly the terrible blast of pain which had nearly finished him back in Deaner Beckmann's asteroid swarm, when the quantum discontinuities of *Trumpet*'s battle with *Soar* – and the effects of *Trumpet*'s dispersion field – had hit his EM prosthesis like a sledgehammer. Now everything depended on the enhanced vision Lebwohl's medtechs had given him. If any of these damn ships or stations opened fire for any reason, or if *Calm Horizons* tried to use her proton cannon unexpectedly, he might find his head burned open by distortion on bandwidths hot enough to slag the neurons of his brain. Killed by his own augmentation –

He absolutely could not afford to be blinded. Not now: not while he was still so far from the docking port, and Davies and Vector were fighting for their lives, and Ciro wasn't even close to being in position. If he reached the port without the full, effective use of his prosthesis, he might as well unseal his helmet and let the cold dark have him. Everything would be lost.

So he followed trails of numbers across the gathered knowledge Dios had made available to him; adjusted the polarization of his faceplate to compensate. Then he checked the numbers again. Through his datalink he did what he could to ready his zone implants for a catastrophe.

As he'd feared, there was no setting which might ward off the EM side effects of a super-light proton explosion.

God, this fucking warship was *big*! He'd crossed less than half the distance, and he was already close to contact with the hull, drawn off his trajectory by *Calm Horizons'* mass. In another few seconds he would be forced to touch down so that he could kick himself into flight again. Or else he would have to activate the magnetism of his boots and try running.

Either way, he would lose time.

He looked up at *Trumpet* through a smear of sweat; cursed viciously when he saw that Ciro hadn't moved. The damn lunatic lay where Angus had left him, even though he should have been halfway to his position by now. If he didn't carry out his part of the plan on schedule *Trumpet* and the command module were almost certainly doomed, along with everyone aboard – Mikka and the fat man, not to mention Angus himself, Davies and Vector, Warden Dios.

Angus understood that Ciro had no intention of surviving. But he'd believed, *trusted*, that the demented kid didn't want to waste his own death.

He keyed his helmet pickup; filled his lungs to howl at Mikka's paralyzed brother.

Before he could start, distant space erupted with fire.

Wrenching himself around, he turned in time to see lasers and matter cannon strike out from a station orbiting beyond UMCPHQ. In the first instant of the attack, he didn't know which astonished him more: the assault itself, defying Min Donner's explicit orders; or the target of the barrage.

For some insane reason, the station used lasers to punch a hole through Earth's atmosphere so its matter cannon could pound a target on the surface.

It made no sense. Someone on that station had gone stark staring spaceshit crazy.

Nevertheless it was a gift. By God, it was a damn *blessing*. He could see that because his faceplate protected him.

And it got better a few seconds later, when every ship in Donner's cordon – and UMCPHQ as well – opened on that station. Without transition the black void came to life in hot streaks of matter cannon fire punctuated by the broad, blurred-edge roar of impact guns, the coherent ruin of lasers.

Torpedoes followed, freighted with slower death. Destructive fury concentrated on the station from several directions at once. Suddenly the whole platform took incandescence as its shields and sinks shrieked at the force of the bombardment.

Donner must have been ready for this; must have seen it coming –

Angus didn't stop to wonder how.

He wanted a diversion? Shit, he got one. The Amnion weren't likely to spot him – or Ciro – while they had a fireshow like that to worry about.

He was distracted himself. Abruptly he plowed into the hull, slammed along it with the full force of his inertia. For an instant he couldn't breathe, couldn't think: his brain went blind in terror while he waited for the swift, excruciating death of decompression. But his suit didn't rupture: his thin EVA skin held against the impact.

Machine logic came to his rescue immediately. In a rush of emission his zone implants quelled his panic. He bounded up from the hull as fast as he'd hit.

The distant station had begun to throb and flare with coruscation like a sun about to go nova.

Trusting Donner's diversion, Angus sent power to his jets, cocked his hips and dove into flight toward the docking port.

To his relief, he saw Ciro move at last. Like him, the boy used his suit jets. Ciro hadn't been paralyzed: he must have been waiting for something like this to cover him. More quickly than Angus would have thought possible, he lifted off *Trumpet* with a singularity grenade tethered to his belt; hauled its uncompromising mass toward *Calm Horizons*.

Now! Angus yelled at Dolph. Do it now! But he silenced his pickup first. Dolph Ubikwe didn't need any urging to carry out his assignment. Mikka might lose control of herself when she thought about her brother; but the man who'd lost command of his ship to Morn wouldn't fail.

Dolph waited until Ciro was clear. Then the module aimed a kick of thrust at *Calm Horizons'* side. Not enough to send the module and *Trumpet* wheeling away, out of reach: just enough to break the grip of the defensive's docking seals.

Followed by a small gust of escaped air, the module drifted slowly off the port guides – ten meters, fifteen, twenty. There a gentle braking nudge stopped the vessel's movement; held it stationary in relation to the port.

The module and *Trumpet* still clung to each other, attached airlock-to-airlock and gripped by magnetic clamps.

Dolph had opened the way for Angus.

Past the module Angus caught a glimpse of Ciro, arcing along the warship's flank with his fatal burden in tow.

Be *careful*, he warned Ciro mutely. That damn thing weighed more than five hundred kg. Now that he had it moving, it wouldn't stop just because he told it to.

But he'd already said that to Ciro; more than once. He had to trust that the boy would do his part; keep his promise.

Angus also had promises to keep. Adjusting his hips to steer his jets, he flew into the gap between the module and *Calm Horizons*, and plunged like a projectile down the guides toward the sealed outer iris of the defensive's airlock.

At the last moment he flipped to reverse his head and feet; used his jets for braking. His boots struck the iris with stinging force, but his reinforced joints absorbed the impact. His momentum threatened to rebound him toward the module: with a slew of his hip, he redirected himself sideward. Before reflected inertia could drag him away, he grabbed a zero-g grip beside the airlock's exterior control panel.

Alerts flashed at him inside his helmet: he was breathing too hard; sweating too much; dehydrating – He steadied himself with a flick of his zone implants. An Amnioni could open the airlock from here, but the keys and codes were incomprehensible to him. He was prepared for that, however. With one hand he reset the polarization of his faceplate for maximum clarity; switched off all his suit lights and indicators so that they wouldn't hamper his EM vision. Then he unclipped one of his cutting lasers from his belt and raised it in front of the control panel.

He couldn't work the keys; but if he cut exactly the right circuits in exactly the right order, the iris would open for him – and he would still be able to close it from the inside.

If he didn't succeed – if he got inside and failed to shut the door again – he might very well die in the explosive decompression when he unsealed the inner iris. Dios would certainly be killed. Davies and Vector might not survive.

He couldn't have done it without his zone implants: he was too scared to concentrate. This was going to take too long, he didn't have time for it. But emissions directed by his computer imposed calm on the troubled centers of his brain. His vision slowly shrank as other kinds of input ceased to affect his optic nerves. By degrees he began to discern a faint EM tracery, echoing the circuits behind the panel.

They were as legible as words – a language which his computer, his databases and a lifetime of desperate experience knew how to interpret. The delicate lines of electronic command, ineffable as the links between synapses, ran *there*. If they were disrupted *here*, shunted *that way*, they would follow *those* microscopic pathways.

His cutter had already been set so fine that its red beam was scarcely visible: it should have been impossible to control. But his attention was cybernetically fixed to the EM field of the panel. His muscles moved by machine increments: his computer and his zone implants held him firm. A minute line of ruby burned into the surface; burned into the circuits.

The next moment the iris slid wide, releasing one swift expulsion of air into the embattled dark.

At once Angus pushed off from his handgrip; swung into the airlock.

The lock was thick with EM fields, scanning against dangerous intrusions. His equipment jammed them all: he could almost see the sensors' bandwidths lose coherence; break up in confusion. Nevertheless the Amnion might guess that he was here – that some kind of treachery was at work. Their instruments would tell them the outer iris had been opened. Circuit diagnostics would report damage.

There was nothing he could do about that. Now only speed would save him.

But he didn't know how to reseal the airlock. Simply

pounding on the control panel might not work. Cutting the circuits again would take time.

Tentatively he touched one key; another; several in combination. Nothing.

He had no way of knowing whether Davies and Vector were still alive. They'd already been in there too long; anything could have happened. If he was right – if Dios had been injected with a mutagen like the one which had ruled Sorus Chatelaine, made Ciro crazy – the UMCP director may have helped Vestabule capture or kill Angus' bait.

Grimly Angus tapped the keys of his suit's receiver; tuned his radio to the same frequency Davies and Vector used.

At once he heard gasping, strain; violent exertion.

Shit! He was too late. The fight had already started.

He snatched up his cutter, pushed his face close to the internal control panel, *begged* his zone implants for help –

'*Angus, God damn you!*' Davies' shout slammed through his helmet like a blow from a mine-hammer. '*Get in here!*'

I'm *working* on it! Angus retorted in mute savagery. Give me a fucking *minute*!

Contract his vision; narrow his eyes against distraction; focus on the impalpable electron filigree of the circuits.

Do it.

Before he could get started, a concussion like the hit of a cannon crashed through the ship. *Calm Horizons* lurched with impact as if she'd been rammed by a battlewagon. The bulkhead holding the control panel jerked at him; struck him hard in the center of his faceplate.

Instantly his faceplate starred into a fretwork of cracks, delicate and fatal; but he didn't see it happen. He was blinded by a scream of randomized proton fire which wailed past the rim of the iris into his prosthesis. His EM sight shrieked on every wavelength it could perceive. Howling white pain ripped along his nerves, tore open his brain, shredded his mind –

For an aeon which his computer measured in picoseconds, Angus Thermopyle ceased to exist.

Then his zone implants threw up a wall against the pain,

shut down tortured synapses all across his cortex; and he seemed to fall back into his body. Sweating like a pig, shaking feverishly, retching in agony, he became conscious of his EVA suit again; felt echoes of anguish crawl along his skin; saw alerts winking fear at him from his helmet readouts.

For a heartbeat or two, he stared at the web of cracks in his faceplate without understanding what it was.

Or why he wasn't dead.

Well, why *wasn't* he dead? Why hadn't his faceplate failed in the vacuum of the open airlock?

And what had happened to the boson fury of the proton cannon's self-destruction? The EM storm of a detonation like that should have lasted longer than this.

Residual pain left him stupid. Two or three more seconds passed before he noticed that the outer iris had sealed itself. The explosion must have triggered automatic damage-control responses all around the ship; overridden the airlock circuits.

But he should have died anyway. The lock still held vacuum, not air.

Somehow his faceplate had retained a degree of integrity.

How much integrity, he didn't know. He only knew that the plexulose hadn't finished shattering itself, blown outward by the pressure inside his suit.

A distant roar reached him: the scorching blaze of matter cannon, transmitted through the hull until the whole ship seemed to sizzle. The bulkheads shuddered with strain as *Calm Horizons'* thrust came to life in a tremendous howl of power.

He couldn't think. There must have been something he was supposed to do, something important – something besides fight against puking. If he let himself vomit now his own spew would smother him in minutes. But he had no idea what was expected of him. His programming seemed to have fallen into stasis, burned to quiescence by the effects of the proton blast.

His stunned confusion lasted until he heard Davies howl, '*Come and get me, you bastards!*'

Abruptly he forgot his need to vomit. His zone implants

force-fed desperation into his veins; fired his heart with enough adrenaline to boil blood. Shit, *Davies*! Vector and Warden Dios. Mikka and the fat man.

And a crack-starred faceplate.

Shitshit*shit*.

He gave up on being careful.

With both his cutters in his hands, he set them to full power; gave them the force of laser pistols. First he raked a pair of red beams through the panel of the inner iris, reduced the command wiring to slag. Then he burned a short-circuit into the leads of the door servo.

Autonomically responsive, the servo swept the iris open.

With a sound like a blow, unequalized air pressure slapped into the lock; caught him hard enough to fling him against the outer seal. But he ignored the impact, the pain; the danger to his suit. Gathering his strength, he recoiled headlong toward the opening ahead of him.

His jets carried him across a cargo hold awash with bitter light, empty of shadows. Gantries stood at various angles, extending their limbs like crusted skeletons with the ruined sinews of cables draped over them. Plumes and splashes of thick Amnion blood decorated the air, drifting lost in zero g. Two alien corpses hung nearby, one nearly beheaded, the other with a plastic spike in one of its eyes.

At the edges of his vision, his prosthesis registered the EM crackle of impact guns. Wheeling his hips in the suit's waldo harness, he spun to scan the hold.

Cracks distorted the view through his faceplate. Inside his helmet, alerts signaled frantically for his attention. With an effort of will and zone implants, he focused past the obstacles to locate Davies and Vector.

At a swift glance, he counted ten figures scattered around the high space, seven of them Amnion. Three of the ten struggled together in a knot a few meters from one of the bulkheads. The others whipsawed back and forth past each other among the arms and trunks of the gantries, dodging blows and impact fire.

The three were Vestabule, Dios and – apparently – Vector.

Neither Vector nor Dios could match Vestabule's Amnion strength. But Dios had caught Vestabule in a headlock, his powerful arms straining against the back of Vestabule's neck. And Vector held onto Dios, using his suit jets to control both men; keep Vestabule between Dios and the Amnion with guns. Because they were all weightless and floating, Vestabule didn't have the leverage to break Dios' grip.

The remaining six Amnion flung themselves around the gantries in a grim, concerted attempt to trap or kill Davies.

Only four of them held guns; but that should have been more than enough. Davies' jets were all that kept him alive. He could move faster than any of his opponents; change direction in midair; flash between enemies so that they couldn't risk shooting at him.

Shit, with those odds, Angus gave the kid about five more seconds –

Vector and Dios would have to fend for themselves. Angus concentrated on the armed Amnion.

Wrenching himself to a new trajectory, he fired both lasers simultaneously. Guided by computer calculations and zone implants and terror, precise as an infernal machine, he burned one Amnioni through the head; ripped open the chest of another –

– and jammed his hips to the side so that he careened away in a mad tumble, slewing insanely through the sudden roar of the impact guns aimed at him.

'*Angus!*' Davies yelled, so fiercely that he might have torn his vocal cords. 'By *God!*'

Impelled by his jets, Davies dove at a cable, caught hold of it and swung; drove his boots like pistons into the face of the nearest Amnioni firing at Angus.

Angus lashed out with another double burst of coherent force. He should have been out of control; disoriented by his cartwheeling flight; spin-drunk; unable to see. But he was a master of zero g combat: he'd spent decades training for fights that involved hurtling mass, evasive maneuvers, abrupt attack. And his programming didn't suffer the confusion of sensory input. Both his lasers gutted another Amnioni before the creature could adjust its aim.

Over and over again Davies hammered his plastic dirk into the throat of the last armed alien. Thick blood sprayed his faceplate and suit as he pounded his blade at the creature's life. Maybe he couldn't see; didn't know the Amnioni was already dead. Maybe he couldn't see its impact gun drifting past him a meter from his head.

Strangled rage echoed in Angus' helmet.

Angus hauled on his jets, struggled to stabilize his trajectory. Too late he saw the rough trunk of a gantry rush at his head. With a yowl of propulsion and panic, he snatched himself aside.

The trunk struck him a glancing blow as he passed. His head snapped backward. For a fraction of a second, his vision turned gray at the edges; melted toward darkness. Then his computer tightened its grip on the neural network of his cortex, jerked him back from unconsciousness.

His sight sprang clear to a glare of damage alerts from his internal indicators. Atmosphere hissed past his cheeks. He found himself staring at a crack that ran through his faceplate from top to bottom. His mouth and lungs tasted the acrid bite of Amnion air.

His suit had lost vacuum integrity. He was stuck aboard *Calm Horizons*.

Shitshitshit*Christ*!

'Angus!' Vector's voice croaked in his ears. 'Davies is in trouble!'

Cursing savagely, Angus wheeled against his inertia; saw an Amnioni attach itself to Davies from behind and start twisting his head off. Blinded by blood, Davies hadn't seen the creature coming. A rifle floated out of reach in front of him.

Angus had lost track of the last Amnioni – and didn't waste time worrying about it. Risking a precious second, he skidded sideways to improve his angle of fire. Then he slagged Davies' attacker through the center of its misshapen skull.

Davies flopped free of the Amnioni, twitching as if his neck were broken.

Angus' panic struck so swiftly that he couldn't name it. The man he'd become seemed to have no choice: instead of whirling to scan the hold, locate the last creature, make sure Vector and Dios hadn't lost their grip on Vestabule, he flung himself toward his son.

Before he'd covered half the distance, Vector cried out another warning.

Angus ignored him; ignored the danger. In a dumb confusion of alarm and relief, he watched Davies slowly raise one hand, wipe a smear of blood off his faceplate, then reach out for the impact gun drifting near him.

His neck wasn't broken. He couldn't have moved like that with a crushed or severed spinal cord.

Before Angus remembered Vector's warning, an Amnioni with at least twice his mass slammed into him like the rock-shattering punch of a mine-hammer.

The impact drove the air from his lungs: for an instant it overwhelmed his zone implants. More arms than he could count wrapped themselves around him. Hands he couldn't see grappled for his cutters. One of his lasers was forced out of his fist.

He let it go. Desperately he fought to twist in the Amnioni's grasp so that he could bring his other gun to bear before the creature hit him with a blaze of focused flame.

Even his welded strength was no match for the Amnioni's. He didn't have enough arms to struggle adequately. But struts reinforcing his joints gave him leverage: terror and zone implants augmented his natural muscle. Too late, too slowly, he shifted against the creature's embrace. Give him two more seconds, and he would be able to reach his assailant's torso with his laser.

He didn't have two seconds. At the edge of his ruined faceplate, he saw the Amnioni aim its laser at the side of his helmet from point-blank range.

Without realizing what he did, he screamed in fury and horror – a howl from the bottom of his soul.

Deafened by his own cry, he didn't hear the bark of the impact rifle as Davies fired.

The gun's force wailed across his prosthesis – a yell of energy as vivid as his terror, but more effective. The neural convulsion as the Amnioni died gripped him tight, then flung him free. Momentarily stunned, he tumbled away.

His helmet speakers reported Davies' voice.

'Angus? Angus! Are you all right?'

Davies sounded concerned. That amazed Angus as much as the fact that he was still alive.

Because he knew how Davies felt, he coughed into his pickup, 'Can't you tell? I thought I was still screaming.'

He slowed himself with a twitch of one hip; controlled his flight so that he could look around the hold.

'God, Angus,' Davies returned weakly, drained by exertion or relief, 'that was close. I didn't think we – What took you so long? Another minute and we were finished.'

A moment later he groaned, 'Oh, shit. Angus, your faceplate – It's cracked.' Shock stretched his voice to a whisper. 'And we only have one spare suit.'

The suit Angus still carried strapped to his back.

Gasping against the harsh cut of the Amnion air, Angus nudged the jet waldo to change directions. The alerts inside his helmet were going crazy: dehydration and hypothermia; lost atmosphere. With a jerk of one hand, he canceled the status displays, shut down all the suit's systems except air and temperature regulation. The circuits and readouts were useless to him now. If he wanted to survive, he would have to take risks so extreme that they violated every condition the suit's designers had ever imagined.

Or he would have to use the suit he'd brought for Dios; let the bastard die here.

Fervently he wished that he was still capable of abandoning the UMCP director. Short days ago he could have done it easily; without a qualm. He might have enjoyed it. And he'd been released from the programmed restrictions which kept him from harming UMCP personnel: he should have been able to leave Dios behind. Hell, he should have been able to kill the motherfucker himself. But other inhibitions held him, as compulsory as his datacore.

Inspired by dread, he searched one database after another for alternatives.

'Angus,' Vector panted urgently, 'we need to get out of here. This ship is moving.' New g and the distant yowl of thrust made that obvious. 'We still have to deal with Vestabule. And there must be more Amnion on the way.'

Angus didn't doubt that. Vestabule had what must have been a PCR jacked into his ear. He made guttural sounds Angus couldn't translate. Calling for help –

Beyond the bulkheads, matter cannon fried the dark. If Mikka and the fat man screwed up now –

With all his alerts and indicators dead, Angus turned between the gantries; rode his jets back toward Vector, Dios and Vestabule.

Vestabule had stopped struggling. In fact, Dios had let him go. Davies drifted in front of him, gripping an impact rifle with its muzzle aligned on his chest.

The accumulating g of thrust pulled them all slowly toward the deck as they confronted each other. They would have fallen already if *Calm Horizons* hadn't been handicapped by slow brisance drives.

One of Davies' hands was bare. The sulfurous illumination made his skin seem unnaturally vulnerable – closer to death than the Amnion corpses settling as *Calm Horizons* gathered momentum. Other than that, his suit appeared intact. So did Vector's. Angus couldn't tell what condition his companions were in: reflection and polarization hid their faces.

But Dios was completely exposed – defenseless without an EVA suit. He looked pale and strained, bleached of strength, like a man with a concussion. A heavy blow had left a swelling lump over his eyepatch. Pain glazed his human eye, muffling its penetration, its light of command. Nevertheless he watched Vestabule and Angus without flinching.

Angus was dimly surprised to find that he recognized Vestabule. Over the years he'd had too many victims: he couldn't remember them all. *Viable Dreams* alone had carried twenty-seven other men and women. And he hadn't known any of their names. Yet Vestabule's face had stayed in his mind.

Marc Vestabule had fought so hard against being turned over to the Amnion that he'd almost killed Angus.

He was silent now. Any help he'd been able to summon was on its way. Angus searched his face for signs of the atavistic terror which had enabled him to retain vestiges of his humanity. But it was gone. Even the frantic signaling of his human eye revealed nothing.

'Angus Thermopyle,' he pronounced harshly, 'you have done great harm.'

'I hope so,' Angus muttered. Obviously the Amnioni knew whom to blame for his defeat. But no amount of harm to the Amnion would compensate Angus for his ruined faceplate.

As their boots touched the deck, Vector sighed, 'Shit, Angus. You can't go outside like that. You'll be dead before we leave the airlock.'

He hesitated for a moment or two, then offered regretfully, 'I'll stay. I'm surplus personnel anyway. And this tub won't last much longer. I'll die human. You can use my helmet.'

He raised his hands to the seals as if he were determined to sacrifice himself somehow.

'It will not be forgotten,' Vestabule stated.

Angus forestalled Vector. 'Fuck that.' His zone implants helped him master his breathing. He knew all his suit's design parameters, every detail of its construction. 'We've got other things to worry about. And we haven't run out of options yet.'

The more *Calm Horizons* accelerated, the harder it would be for Ubikwe to hold the command module and *Trumpet* in position. But the defensive needed all the force she could generate for her guns, shields and sinks. And her thrust was inherently slow. She couldn't acquire velocity quickly.

'The Amnion will not forget it,' Vestabule continued.

Angus wished the Amnioni would shut up.

He unclosed his own helmet and took it off so that he could face Dios without the obstruction of his faceplate. At

654

once the full acid of *Calm Horizons'* atmosphere bit into his lungs. Spasms of revulsion tightened in his chest; but his zone implants controlled them.

Warden Dios had called him a *machina infernalis*. He'd said, *We've committed a crime against your soul.*

And he'd said, *It's got to stop.*

Now he was at Angus' mercy. He'd released the restrictions that might have compelled Angus to spare him.

He waited without speaking under Angus' scrutiny, as if he knew he was being judged. Angus almost believed that the UMCP director was a man of his word.

'While you live,' Vestabule intoned, 'the Amnion will seek your death. There will be no haven for you in any space, at any time. You will never be safe. Nor will any shred or particle of your DNA be allowed to endure. The offspring which you name your son will not be forgotten. Every inheritor of your flesh will be remembered for death.'

Angus didn't so much as glance at the Amnioni. Threats like that meant nothing to him.

'You kept one promise,' he told Dios roughly. 'Let's see you do it again.'

With a flick of his hand, he tossed his laser cutter to the man who'd framed him and reqqed him so that he could be welded.

Dios caught the laser in his fist, settled it into his palm; glanced at it to confirm that it still held a charge. Then he met Angus' gaze again. He seemed to understand the question he was being asked. But he didn't answer it directly.

Instead he countered, 'Do you think this is why I set you free?'

'That's what I'm trying to find out,' Angus rasped.

Dios sighed. 'I told Davies and Dr Shaheed already,' he said carefully through his breathing mask. 'You were right. He gave me a mutagen.' A twitch of his free hand referred to Vestabule. 'As soon as I run out of immunity, I'm finished.'

A suggestion of hope fluttered in Vestabule's human eye. The Amnion side of his face awaited his fate without expression.

Angus said nothing. Davies and Vector remained silent. They knew as well as he did that they couldn't save Dios. They'd used the last of Nick's antimutagen to protect themselves.

With an effort, Dios blinked some of the blur from his eye. His tone sharpened. Lines of command and mortality etched his face. 'I'm sure *Calm Horizons* hasn't been passive during this little raid. What happened to Suka Bator?'

He might have asked, How many lives have you spent to rescue me?

Angus snorted: he was too frightened to laugh. 'You heard the blast. The big one. Right before I came in. That was their proton emitter. I sprayed it full of hull sealant.

'They still have matter cannon, but we're the only hostages they've got left.'

Make up your *mind*, he demanded mutely. Kill one of us. While there's still time. Show us where you stand.

A fierce grin lifted the edges of Dios' mask. 'I swear to God, Angus,' he drawled trenchantly, 'sometimes I'm so proud of you and Morn I almost forget to be ashamed of myself.'

His fist tightened on the cutter's firing stud. Precise as a cyborg, he drilled red fire straight through the center of Marc Vestabule's face.

Vestabule's human eye seemed to widen in surprise as he toppled backward. His lifeless form measured the extent to which he'd been betrayed on the rough deck.

Davies seemed to slump inside his suit. 'Thank God,' he breathed thinly.

A strange pang of relief and regret touched Angus' heart. At last Warden Dios had committed himself.

Which seemed to imply that he'd decided he would be the one to stay behind.

That made sense. He was beyond saving: Vestabule had accomplished that, if nothing else. He was the logical candidate.

Angus should have been glad. He *was* glad. He needed Dios' helmet. Nevertheless the man he'd become felt the loss of something more precious than an undamaged faceplate.

He was afflicted by the same cutting sense of bereavement which had confused him a long time ago when he beat up Morn: the sense that he diminished himself by exacting his own fear from someone else.

'We're out of time, Angus,' Vector put in tensely. 'That module wasn't made for maneuvers like this. And even if Captain Ubikwe can hold his position, one of our ships might hit him.

'We've come this far. Let's finish it.'

'No,' Davies contradicted at once. 'He won't get hit. Director Donner said she'll hold fire until we're clear.'

Maybe he still hoped they could think of some way to save Dios.

'That's a lot to ask,' Vector murmured dubiously. 'She's ED.'

'But she keeps her promises,' Dios stated without hesitation. 'That's one of at least six things I love about her.'

He sounded oddly cheerful, almost happy, like a man whose attempt at restitution was nearly complete.

He tossed the laser cutter back to Angus; then approached Vestabule's corpse and hunted in the Amnioni's pockets until he found a small vial. A wry grin twisted his mouth as he showed the vial to Angus, Davies, Vector.

It contained at least half a dozen small capsules.

'Things aren't as bad as they look. Each of these lasts an hour. I'll stay human long enough.'

Long enough to reach UMCPHQ, where DA had more of the antimutagen Hashi Lebwohl had given Nick.

Oh, shit, Angus groaned. Shit and damnation. Abruptly his relief and regret flip-flopped; became stark panic and resolve.

Dios wanted to go with them.

Someone else would have to stay behind.

Or Angus would have to take a risk so desperate that the mere idea made his guts slosh like water.

The man he'd become seemed to have no choice. In one swift motion he unslung the extra EVA suit from his back, tossed it to Dios. 'Put this on,' he ordered through his teeth.

'Fast. Vector's right. The fat man won't be able to hold his position for long.'

And Vestabule must have called for help.

'Wait a minute,' Davies objected. 'Does that mean you want Vector to stay behind?'

The tension in his voice suggested that he thought he should volunteer for another sacrifice.

'No,' Angus snapped bitterly. 'It means I want you to shut the fuck up and let me concentrate.'

He knew everything the UMCP knew about his EVA suit; every tolerance and molecule. According to his databases, he should be able to –

His EM prosthesis was useless now. He would have to trust his human sight – and the machine accuracy of his computer. A millimeter too much, and his faceplate would be too weak to hold. A millimeter too little, and the cracks wouldn't be sealed. Either way, the plexulose would blow out at the first touch of vacuum.

Either way, he would be effectively blind when he died.

Gripping his helmet in the crook of his arm, he set the cutter to its lowest power, its widest beam, and began to stroke coherent crimson across the surface of the faceplate, melting and fusing plexulose along the worst of the cracks.

God, this was *stupid*. No way in *hell* it could ever work. His databases insisted this kind of plexulose could be laser-formed. Sculptors used it because they could cut and shape it without stressing the molecular lattice. But no one had ever *tried* to restore a faceplate's integrity by hand.

And whether he succeeded or failed the plate's polarization was ruined. If Mikka had been forced to raise *Trumpet*'s dispersion field, he would be defenseless against the EM agony of the boson storm.

He wanted to believe he'd never done anything this *stupid* in his whole life. The idea conveyed a peculiar reassurance. Nevertheless he knew this was only the culmination of a long series of terrified decisions and cruel mistakes. He wouldn't be where he was if he hadn't done *that* and *that* and *that*; if he hadn't fled from violence to violence across all the years of his life.

Whatever happened now, he would have to face it without the comfort of a convenient lie.

In a minute he was done. Live or die, there was nothing else he could do. He put the laser in a belt pouch so that he could reach it easily.

Dios had already suited himself; sealed his helmet; adjusted his hips in the jets' waldo harness. He, Davies and Vector were ready to go.

Fiercely Angus set his own helmet in place, locked it to the suit's neck-ring, and powered up his systems, filling the thin material with atmosphere and circulation.

Status indicators inside his helmet came to life. Most of them flashed danger at him. But the integrity blip showed green.

For now.

'Angus.' Davies' voice crackled in his speakers. 'Can you see?'

'No,' Angus admitted. His faceplate was almost completely opaque: it blinded him like a cataract. 'There's a strip along the edges I can use,' enough visibility to let him deal with the airlock, 'that's all.' Words stuck in his throat. He had to force himself to say, 'I'll need help.'

Help finding his way across the gap to the command module.

'No problem.' Dios sounded like he couldn't stop grinning. 'What are friends for?'

Angus wanted to explain exactly what he thought of the UMCP director's 'friendship'. But he didn't have time. And he'd forgotten that part of himself.

He'd taken too long, concentrated too hard. He knew the danger, but he'd ignored it. He was helpless as a child when he heard servos open one of the far doors of the hold.

He yelped a warning; tried to wheel away from threats he couldn't see. Bodies blundered against him, blocked his way. Vector yelled, '*Look out!*' His cry rang in Angus' helmet, carried on the leading edge of impact fire.

Insanely precise, Angus' computer sorted through the roar and identified three guns, all blasting at once.

Hands shoved him aside. Simultaneously he heard a raw shout from Warden and the hard punch of return fire from Davies' rifle. Then a wall of force seemed to land on him out of nowhere. It drove him backward until he slammed against the bulkhead. Something – or somebody – seemed to hold him there.

'*Cover*, Davies!' Dios howled. 'God damn it, *get to cover!*'

Davies' gun blazed incessantly, as if he were laying down a barrage.

Angus couldn't see. They were all about to die because he'd taken too long; and he couldn't fucking *see*.

Desperation and his zone implants filled him with a transcendental rage. In an instant he crossed the gap between mortality and violence.

With one blow of his fist, he shattered his opaque faceplate. Shook shards of plexulose out of his face.

Found himself hidden against the bulkhead behind what was left of Vector's body.

Blood sprayed everywhere from Vector's shattered limbs and crumpled chest. Wounds like bomb craters gaped in his torn suit, his mangled flesh. He must have been hit by the combined force of all three enemy rifles.

Must have jumped in front of Angus to protect him because he couldn't see –

With his peripheral vision Angus saw Warden emerge from the airlock, take hold of Davies and heave him by main strength toward the thin cover inside the iris. Impact fire answered furiously, slashing the air, scoring the bulkhead. But Davies' return fire had forced the Amnion to dodge and scatter. He and then Warden reached the airlock intact.

Curses Angus hardly heard bubbled in his chest, frothed in his throat. Vector was already dead; beyond pain. Angus reached up, unsealed Vector's helmet and stripped it aside. Then he strode unarmed away from the bulkhead toward his assailants, holding up Vector's corpse as a shield.

His computer was right: there were three of them. As he

advanced they shifted their attention from the airlock. Blast after blast, their rifles pounded Vector to pulp in his arms.

He'd used a weapon like that to kill Captain Davies Hyland, Morn's father.

He knew what impact rifles were for.

One of the guns lay on the floor no more than ten meters ahead of him, beside the body of the Amnioni which had carried it earlier. He felt the power of every blow that struck Vector; but he stalked forward remorselessly, augmented by rage. When he reached the rifle he stooped to snatch it up.

Then he activated his suit jets, released Vector and jumped.

Davies fired wildly to cover him as he arced into the air. His jets weren't strong enough to overcome the defensive's thrust g; but they lifted him higher than the Amnion expected. Taken by surprise – and distracted by Davies – the Amnion aimed too low. Their beams slashed death beneath Angus' feet.

Quick as a machine, and accurate as targ, he picked them off from above before they could recover. Riding the pressure of his jets, he hit them onetwothree. Killed them all. They were dead by the time he passed the top of his arc and started downward.

The Amnion will not forget it.

The sight of their spewing blood left him as cold as deep space. He checked their bodies to see if they carried PCRs and pickups. They didn't. So they hadn't called for more help. Too bad. He was in the mood to kill any number of them.

You will never be safe.

But Warden shouted across the hold, asking him if he was all right. Davies cried out Vector's name, then swore and sobbed as if something inside him had broken.

Angus didn't have time for more killing.

He used his jets to help him hurry toward the place where he'd discarded Vector's helmet. When he saw that it was undamaged, he pulled it over his head; sealed it to the neck-ring of his suit. At once the status indicators began to flash green as they took power from his suit.

Vector had volunteered to stay behind once too often.

'*Angus*,' Davies cried softly, 'oh, Vector. God, Vector! Angus, he saved –'

Angus took his son by the arm, shook him roughly. 'Tell me later!' he snapped. 'We don't have time for this!'

'He's right, Davies.' Warden's voice found an echo of loss in the helmet speakers. 'We need to go.'

Angus didn't wait for them. Grimly he moved into the airlock.

The inner iris was still open: he'd done so much damage to the wiring earlier that *Calm Horizons* couldn't override it. But that posed another hazard. When he opened the outer seal, explosive decompression would vent the entire cargo hold through this relatively constricted passage. He and Davies and Warden would be hurled outward like rounds from a projectile cannon. If the blast itself didn't kill or stun them, they would be in danger of shooting far past the module and *Trumpet*; or of colliding with those vessels hard enough to crush ordinary human tissue and bone.

Nevertheless Angus didn't hesitate. He was too angry for doubt; too cold. As Davies and Warden joined him, he positioned himself in the center of the airlock and focused his EM vision on the circuitry which controlled the outer iris.

Dios stood beside him and clipped their belts to each other; fixed his fate to Angus'. Davies did the same on the other side.

There was nothing else they could do; no other precautions they could take. In the small space of the airlock the constant fury of *Calm Horizons*' matter cannon barrage mounted like endless lightning.

Angus grabbed the laser from his pouch; sighted his prosthesis; ran calculations and adjustments through his computer. As if he were committing murder, he pressed the firing stud.

As soon as the iris began to cycle open, a hard fist of atmosphere flung him and his companions like debris out into the embattled dark.

MIKKA

Somewhere underneath her exhaustion and loss, her physical pain and tearing sorrow, Mikka Vasaczk found the will to survive.

To some extent she was held together by drugs. She'd taken enough stim and hype to convulse a weaker woman; pushed her body far past her normal limits with chemical enhancements. But that only helped her stay awake. It didn't make her strong.

And her efforts to accept Ciro's intentions didn't give her strength. She recognized that his need to follow the logic of his distress to its conclusion was more compulsory than life. Yet he was her brother: he was all she had. Letting him go did little to help her live.

In part she was sustained by the companionable sound of Captain Ubikwe's voice. By intercom from the command module, he talked to her constantly, feeding her information and commentary in a deep, comfortable rumble which soothed her strained nerves. Apparently the last of his personal concerns had been relieved by Ciro's departure. He gave the impression that he was no longer worried about anything.

He couldn't possibly be as sure as he seemed. She refused to believe it. Nevertheless he projected nothing but confidence and relaxation as he described Angus' progress toward *Calm Horizons'* airlock; or UMCHO's attack on Suka Bator, and the withering fire of Min Donner's response to the station; or Ciro's awkward – but effective – journey with his grenade. He warned Mikka cheerfully when he was ready to break the grip of *Calm Horizons'* docking seals so that Angus could reach the airlock. He told her everything she needed to know in order to power up *Trumpet*'s drives safely; charge her guns; prepare the dispersion field generator.

He couldn't restrain a fierce cheer when the Amnioni's proton cannon abruptly exploded, shattering itself to scrap in a hail of quantum discontinuities and debris, as well as ripping a brutal hole in the big defensive's hulls. And after that he was briefly silent while *Calm Horizons'* matter cannon roared violence at every human target they could reach. Instead of talking he routed scan and status data to her screens so she could watch the assault; so she could see that Min Donner kept her promise not to strike back while Angus tried to rescue Davies, Vector and Warden Dios. At the same time he brought up thrust to hold the module and *Trumpet* close to the Amnioni's airlock – and below her field of fire – as *Calm Horizons'* drives raged for acceleration.

He must have been desperately busy. He had to reestablish contact with UMCPHQ and *Punisher*, and coordinate their tactical input with his own maneuvers. But after only a couple of minutes his voice came back on Mikka's intercom.

'Well, thank God for slow brisance thrust, that's all I can say,' he announced happily. 'At this rate we'll be able to keep up with her, at least for a few minutes.

'Looks like Ciro almost missed his chance,' he went on with no discernible anxiety. 'Guess he didn't expect that big fucker to burn when she did. But his jets saved him. He's on the hull now. And he's got his grenade tethered.

'I wonder what Vestabule would do if someone told him he's taken on a little extra cargo. Might be fun to see an Amnioni go spaceshit crazy.'

Mikka didn't reply. She couldn't think of anything she could bear to say.

Apparently Captain Ubikwe didn't expect a response. He talked on as if he trusted her completely. First he described the efforts of UMCPHQ and Director Donner's cordon to fend off *Calm Horizons'* fire. Then he relayed everything he could glean about the damage to UMCHO.

According to UMCPHQ Center, Holt Fasner's station had lost firepower and thrust; most of its operational capability. But the bulk of the platform remained intact. Distress flares indicated a high percentage of survivors.

Reports from Earth confirmed that the GCES was safe. Suka Bator hadn't suffered any significant destruction: Min's counterattack had prevented UMCHO from sustaining its barrage.

That supplied another small piece of Mikka's will to endure. She cared about the Council only in the abstract. But the fact that Holt Fasner had felt compelled to attack Suka Bator meant to her that Morn had succeeded; that Morn's story had persuaded the GCES to reconsider the fundamental structure of power in human space. And Morn's determination to expose the crimes of the UMCP mattered to Mikka. It affected her in ways she could hardly name. Without Morn she would never have turned against Nick. Instead both she and Ciro would almost certainly have died with *Captain's Fancy* and Billingate.

The course she'd chosen in Morn's name, under Morn's influence, had exacted a terrible price. She'd paid blood for it herself. Ciro was about to pay with his life. Nevertheless it was better than staying with Nick: supporting his crimes, enabling his betrayals, while he scorned her for the simple reason that she couldn't heal the wounds Sorus Chatelaine had cut into him. Despite the cost, she didn't regret anything Morn had persuaded her to do, directly or indirectly.

Morn's success gave a touch of vindication to Mikka's part in making it possible. That helped her cling to life when her brother had already chosen to die.

Ultimately, however, her commitment to survival arose from another, more essential source. Drugs kept her awake. Captain Ubikwe's voice kept her company. Accepting Ciro's sacrifice helped her manage her grief. Morn's vindication confirmed that she'd made the right decisions. Yet in the end it was something else that swayed her. She held the frayed and weary strands of her spirit together because Angus, Vector, Davies, Warden Dios and Dolph Ubikwe would all die if she didn't.

At the core she was a woman who served. Nick and *Captain's Fancy*; her brother; Morn: she was the sum and culmination of her loyalties. They defined her. Without them she could hardly say that she'd ever existed.

Morn had asked her to do this. People she valued – especially Davies and Vector – were depending on her. In the deepest part of her heart, she would rather die than let them down.

So she did everything that had been asked of her, even though her brother was lost to her, and her throat knotted with sobs whenever she thought of him. She powered up *Trumpet*'s drives: slowly at first, leaking energy into them by minor increments so that she wouldn't attract *Calm Horizons*' notice; then as fast as she could while the defensive was distracted by Director Donner's attack on UMCHO. She charged the gap scout's matter cannon, even though she couldn't imagine being able to use them. She ran complex calculations through the helm computer, measuring the module's mass and *Trumpet*'s thrust against the potential hunger of a singularity fed by *Calm Horizons*' great bulk. And she made herself as proficient as circumstances allowed with the dispersion field generator.

The command module had neither the raw power nor the defenses to save any of them. And Captain Ubikwe was far too busy to cover for her. Whether this mission lived or died rested in Mikka Vasaczk's exhausted hands.

Alone on *Trumpet*'s bridge, alone aboard the gap scout, she readied herself to carry out Angus' orders.

How much time did she have left? Not much, apparently. According to Dolph, Angus had made his way through the Amnioni's airlock. He would either find Davies, Vector and Warden Dios or not; rescue them or not; emerge from the huge defensive or not. But no matter what happened, it wouldn't take long.

She surprised herself by hoping that Ciro wouldn't lose

heart – or patience – and react too soon. All their lives depended on him as much as on her.

Abruptly Captain Ubikwe called out from her intercom, 'I just heard from Davies!' Complex excitement crackled in the speakers. 'They've reached the airlock. Vestabule is dead! Angus is going to cut the lock circuits to get out.

'My airlock is open. I'm ready for them. We'll go the second they're aboard.'

He would reorient the module and *Trumpet* to put the gap scout's more powerful thrust between them and *Calm Horizons*. The rest would be up to her.

'I'm set, Captain,' she told him so he wouldn't think she'd fallen asleep. 'If it can be done, I'll do it.'

'Mikka –' he began, then faltered unexpectedly. When he spoke again, strain complicated his eagerness. 'They lost Vector. The Amnion killed him.'

She groaned. Oh, God. *Vector*. Poor arthritic, valiant Vector Shaheed: brilliant as a geneticist, but barely adequate as an engineer: kind, humorous and calm. Ciro's teacher. Morn's friend. Even though he was hopeless in a fight, he'd volunteered for this mission before anyone else.

I've always wanted to be the savior of humankind.

She might have wept if Dolph hadn't continued talking.

'I know Angus told Ciro to wait for his signal. But we're running out of time. You'd better tell him to get back here. We can use your guns to set off the grenade.'

The captain must have believed Ciro meant to return. No one had told him otherwise.

Mikka swallowed a knot of tears. Even if Vector was dead, Davies and Angus still needed her.

'I can't,' she answered. 'I've run projections on the effects of that grenade. If we want to escape that much g, we need more distance.' But distance would bring them within reach of *Calm Horizons'* cannon. 'That means we need the dispersion field. And I can't fire through it.'

Beyond the gap scout, *Calm Horizons'* guns raged. The shields and sinks of Min's ships – and UMCPHQ – lit *Trumpet*'s scan like a pyrotechnics display: blooms and bursts of power, flowers of violence, coruscating up and down the spec-trum, shedding color and emission on every bandwidth the instruments could receive. But Mikka didn't look at the fire show, for the same reason that she didn't use her sensors to keep track of Ciro. She needed her attention for other things.

For an instant Dolph was silent. The intercom seemed to convey shock; outrage. Then he growled through his teeth, 'Mikka, are you telling me Ciro has to *stay* here? He has to set off the grenade *in person*?'

Dully she replied, 'If the rest of us want to live.'

There was no other way. When *Calm Horizons*' matter cannon failed to kill the module and *Trumpet*, the defensive would use impact guns, lasers, torpedoes. Then the task of destroying her would fall to Min Donner's ships. The Amnioni might do incalculable damage before she died.

'He'll be killed!' the captain protested. 'We might as well *murder* him.'

The cruelty of being asked to defend Ciro's decision turned some of Mikka's grief to anger. 'He volunteered,' she snapped. 'It was his idea.'

'Then it's suicide,' the deep voice countered.

Abruptly she started to yell. '*No*, it's *not*!' She hardly knew what had ignited in her, but it exploded like the impact of *Calm Horizons*' guns. She seemed to fling a lifetime of pain and anger into the intercom pickup. 'It's *heroism*, you self-righteous sonofabitch! If he were a *cop*, you would call it *valor above and beyond the call of* fucking *duty*!'

Shaken by her own fury, she stopped.

Dolph didn't respond directly. He may have understood her; guessed the implications of a life spent as an illegal. Or he may have realized that no answer of his would help her.

'Christ!' he muttered. 'This must be what he had in mind from the beginning. He's been talking about it for days.

'How long ago did you realize –? No, don't tell me. I don't want to know.

'God, Mikka,' he finished, 'I just hope *you* aren't feeling that valorous. I'm still not ready to die.'

Mikka Vasaczk sank her teeth into her lower lip until she tasted blood. Damn it, Ciro! she groaned. Do you have any idea what all this *valor* is costing me?

She was not a gentle woman. Under other circumstances she might have asked her brother that question aloud – and demanded a reply. But she didn't have time.

Suddenly Dolph reported, 'Here they come! And they're moving *fast*. Too fast. That's one hell of a decompression blast. If they don't brake, they'll –'

Events had begun to accelerate out of control. A rush of expelled atmosphere carried them headlong toward the brink of success or disaster.

'Yes!' the captain crowed. 'One of them is using his jets. Now they all are. Braking. Adjusting to reach us. Shit, that was close. A few more seconds at that velocity, and they would have hit too hard to live through it.'

Mikka rested her hands on the command board. She'd already planned her vector away from the locus of g, at an angle to the grenade so that centrifugal force would help the small ships win free. And she'd programmed everything to two keys: one for thrust and helm; one for the dispersion field. All she had to do was wait –

Angus and the others must have covered the distance at an insane rate. Sooner than she would have believed possible, she heard his voice from the intercom, gasping with urgency and relief. 'We're in! We made it!'

But he didn't pause to savor his survival. Instead he panted, 'Now or never, Mikka! Get your brother back. Or leave him. Just make up your mind!'

He understood Ciro's condition as well as she did. Nevertheless he passed the decision to her as if it belonged to her; as if she'd ever had any say in the matter.

She swallowed blood to reply; but Dolph answered for her. 'We can't do that, Angus.' Trying to spare her. 'If we stay near enough to use our guns we won't escape the black hole. And we're losing position. *Calm Horizons* is pulling away. Even if we burn, we're going to cross her fire horizon before Ciro can get here.'

Yet Angus insisted, 'Mikka?' Apparently he wanted to hear it from her. 'He's your brother.'

Somehow Mikka mustered the instinct for action with which she'd earned her place as Nick's command second. 'I'll tell him.' That talent may have been the only part of herself she'd ever truly respected.

'Secure for hard g. This is going to be rough.'

'She's right,' Captain Ubikwe rumbled in confirmation. 'I'm initiating reorientation now.' Then he added, 'Welcome aboard, Director.'

She heard an unfamiliar voice in a hurry respond, 'Thank you, Captain. This is turning into a real thrill ride.'

Dolph snorted a laugh; and at once inertia pushed Mikka against her armrest as he fired maneuvering thrust, turning the command module and *Trumpet* to align the gap scout's tubes.

While the two vessels swung to their new attitude, she keyed her pickup to Ciro's frequency. 'Ciro, can you hear me?' Her voice glowered like a threat despite her grief. 'It's time.'

To her surprise, he answered immediately.

'I hear you, Mikka.'

Across the static of *Calm Horizons*' barrage he sounded distant and frail; utterly alone.

'They're back,' she said. 'All except Vector. The Amnion killed him.' Ciro had loved Vector. Quickly she continued, 'But we got Dios. We're on our way.'

Through her teeth she added, 'I told Angus I would give you the signal. I wanted a chance to say good-bye.'

For a moment he didn't say anything. If he felt Vector's loss, he didn't show it. Instead he offered simply, 'Good-bye, Mikka.'

The finality in his voice made her think that he was about to silence his transmitter.

'Listen to me!' she rasped. 'In a few seconds we're going to burn. Watch our thrust torch.' Otherwise *Trumpet* would be hard to spot against the background of the battle. 'And wait! We need distance. Wait until you see *Calm Horizons* open fire on us. Then *kill* that fucker.'

Now he didn't hesitate. 'I'm on it.' Without transition his voice took on a new quality – a sound like the grip of his hands on his impact rifle. 'Thanks, Mikka. I have to finish what Captain Chatelaine started. And pay them back for Vector. I'm glad I can try to save you at the same time.'

His last words carried past the emission-roar of guns; the killing emptiness of the gap between them.

'I love you.'

Mikka said, 'I love you, too, Ciro.' But she couldn't hear herself. She'd already touched her first key; and the fierce thunder of *Trumpet*'s drive drowned her out.

ANGUS

He wanted to reach *Trumpet*. That was the only escape he'd been able to imagine for himself. Board the gap scout before Mikka started burning: close the airlocks connecting the two vessels. Then he might stand a chance. If Ciro's grenade devoured *Calm Horizons* – and *Trumpet*'s thrust was powerful enough to break the grip of the black hole's feral g – and Min Donner's ships relaxed their guard when they saw the Amnioni die: then Angus might be able to take the gap scout and run.

If he did all that, he would have to take Mikka with him. But the idea didn't trouble him. She would be the best second he'd ever had. And he didn't think she'd object. Ciro would be dead; no longer in need of her. On top of that, she might not like the uncertainty of her future in the cops' hands. She might welcome the chance to get away from them.

Angus had endured a lifetime of terror during the crossing between the defensive and the command module. The velocity of his expulsion from *Calm Horizons* had increased his usual fear of EVA by several orders of magnitude. Instinctively he believed that if his zone implants hadn't protected him his own blood pressure would have burst his heart.

Once the module's airlock had cycled shut behind him, however, surrounding him with sweet, safe air so that he could breathe again, rip off his helmet and really *breathe*, he forgot everything except escape. He needed a ship: needed

to *run*. Nothing else could relieve his fury at the Amnion –
or his dread at what Warden Dios and Hashi Lebwohl might
do to him now.

But *Trumpet* was denied to him. Dolph Ubikwe had already
sealed his airlocks – a predictable precaution in case the
grapples failed and *Trumpet*'s power pulled the two small
ships apart.

And there was no time. Mikka hit thrust so hard, generated
so much acceleration g, that even Angus' reinforced strength
might not have been enough to preserve him while he fought
to gain *Trumpet*'s bridge. He was barely able to flip himself
into one of the module's g-seats and close the belts before
the howl of the drive threatened to squeeze him unconscious.

He couldn't escape. He was a welded cyborg: the child of
the crib. He'd spent his whole life fleeing; but he'd never
escaped anything.

Once he'd confirmed that Davies and Dios had also reached
the protection of the g-seats, he let his tired limbs settle into
the cushions as if he were surrendering to his mother; to
Warden Dios and despair.

He didn't see chaos erupt across the module's scan as
Trumpet's dispersion field transformed matter cannon beams
to boson madness. He wasn't looking. But he felt the birth
of the black hole. A terrible gravitic fist slammed against him
when Ciro's grenade bloomed into ravening and incalculable
hunger.

Then he knew absolutely that Dios had won. Ciro's rifle
had supplied enough energy to spark the grenade's nascent
singularity. The forces he'd unleashed had killed him nano-
seconds ago – a quantum eternity within the discontinuities
of the event horizon. Now those same forces fed on *Calm
Horizons* – dragged the immense defensive down to the size
of a pinpoint –

– fed and grew stronger.

Just for an instant Angus wondered whether Mikka had
considered how the black hole's power would increase as it
consumed *Calm Horizons*. But after that he wondered nothing; thought nothing. In spite of his zone implants, the

pressure of g drained the blood from his brain, and he fell from consciousness into his mother's forlorn embrace.

Finally fatal g faded to lightness like crossing the gap into death: a lifting evaporation so poignant that he didn't think he could bear it. After aeons of cruel mass – ages which his computer measured in far smaller increments – the burden of his mortality dropped away, and he felt himself drift through relief and darkness as if in some nameless, essential form he'd been cut loose.

Somehow during the past few days he'd learned how to access his datalink without thinking about it. His computer informed him coldly that he'd been unconscious for thirteen seconds. So apparently he wasn't dead. A dead man might not have been able to extract an answer from the machine window in his head.

Yet everything that had ever weighed him down was gone: mass; flesh; dread. Thirteen seconds had brought him to the far side of an inner abyss – a personal fissure like the cracks in his discarded faceplate.

Deaner Beckmann had speculated that a human bred for g might be able to survive inside a black hole; might pass through it to an entirely different kind of life. When Angus remembered that, he began to wonder what had happened to him.

He blinked his dry, sore eyes until they ran. Slowly the blackness dissipated as if it were being vented like waste from an overstressed scrubber; released to vacuum. With tears on his cheeks, he looked up at the command module's display screens.

Scan was clear. For some reason that surprised him: he'd expected the wild aftereffects of a boson storm – or the distorted spectrum inside the black hole's event horizon, Dopplering backward toward extinction. Yet the screens reported data he could recognize. A helm schematic marked the module's position relative to UMCPHQ, *Punisher*, Donner's ships and the vanished Amnioni. Status indicators reported that the grapples still held *Trumpet*; that the last traces of matter cannon emission had faded; that the pressure of g was gone; that the module retained structural integrity; that UMCPHQ, *Punisher* and several other ships signaled for contact. Instead of burning, *Trumpet* and the module now coasted gently along the rim of a planetary orbit. Mikka must have programmed helm to take over when she lost consciousness; to assume this heading and drop thrust once the danger of the black hole passed.

But of course it made sense that scan was clear. Ciro's singularity had gulped down the boson storm as easily as it had swallowed *Calm Horizons*. And since then the module's instruments and computers had had plenty of time to reestablish their grasp on reality.

Morn had feared the singularity's hunger. A force powerful enough to crush *Calm Horizons* might also snag UMCPHQ from its orbit; suck down *Punisher* and the other ships; even threaten Earth. But Min Donner had assured her that wouldn't happen. The ED director seemed to know by heart every spec and capability of every weapon the UMCP designed. She'd told Morn small black holes burned hotter than large ones – and the hotter they burned, the faster they consumed themselves. A black hole with the mass of a star would remain cool enough to feed and grow. But a black hole with no more mass than a planet might well be less than a centimeter in diameter – a tiny thing, despite its vast g; hot as the core of a sun. And Ciro's singularity had only *Calm Horizons*' mass to sustain it.

One of the module's screens reported that the entire lifespan of this black hole had been 5.9 seconds.

Long enough to transform every exercise of power in human space; every interaction between humankind and the Amnion from now on. And every connection in Angus' head.

He knew he'd lost his only chance to escape. If Dolph had sealed the module's airlocks, Mikka must have done the same to *Trumpet*'s – for the same reason. By the time Angus reopened this lock and coded his way aboard the gap scout, other people would regain consciousness. The fat man or Davies would start talking to *Punisher*. Dios would start talking to UMCPHQ. They would be able to warn Donner when *Trumpet* broke the module's grapples – and her ships would have plenty of time to fix targ before Angus acquired the velocity for a gap crossing.

He couldn't run. Just for the moment, however, he didn't mind. The lightness of his body seemed to fill his head, as if the black hole had eaten away everything that normally drove him, everything he recognized about himself, leaving him as weightless as a new soul.

Entirely by coincidence, he'd belted himself into the module's communications station. But the board lay lifeless in front of him: its functions had been routed to Dolph's console. Demands for contact from UMCPHQ and *Punisher* blinked at Dolph's face, not his. He felt free to ignore them.

While the sensation lasted, he let himself enjoy it.

It lasted longer than he would have believed possible. Parts of it were still with him when Captain Ubikwe abruptly jerked against his belts, blinked his g-stressed eyes and peered urgently at his command readouts.

'Welcome back, fat man,' Angus drawled. 'You've all been out so long I might have thought you were dead. If I hadn't heard you breathing.'

Dolph flinched a look toward the communications station. His heavy mouth hung open, but he couldn't swallow enough moisture to speak.

Piqued by an unfamiliar sense of affection, Angus added, 'You snore, you know that? In fact you're pretty damn good at it. On a scale of ten you rate at least eleven.'

Dolph's throat worked for a moment. At last he choked out, 'How long –? '

'Only about four minutes,' Angus answered. 'You can relax. We aren't in any trouble.' He bared his teeth in a predator's smile. 'But you missed the good part.'

Punisher's captain frowned in confusion. 'The good part?'

Angus gestured at the displays. '*Calm Horizons* doesn't exist anymore. She fell into a black hole. Then I guess the black hole fell into itself.' He spread his arms expansively, stretched the muscles of his back until his spine popped. 'I think this means we won, fat man.'

With an effort Captain Ubikwe consulted his readouts again. Slowly he seemed to gather strength from his board; the screens; *Punisher*'s familiar bridge. Data and circumstances he understood restored him like a transfusion.

He looked at Davies and Dios long enough to reassure himself that they were alive. Then he asked, 'What about Mikka?'

Angus shrugged. 'If she's awake, she hasn't said anything. Since we survived, I assume she did, too.' He was obliquely worried about Mikka himself. In another minute or two the man he'd become would feel compelled to go check on her. 'But we're safe enough,' he continued. 'We don't need *Trumpet*'s thrust. We can coast like this for quite a while before we need to worry about anything.'

Dolph considered the situation. 'Well, by damn,' he muttered. His voice began to emerge from his chest more easily. 'That's amazing. Utterly –'

By degrees his mouth spread into a wide grin. 'Of course,' he told Angus, 'I had complete confidence. You have that effect on people. You can't help it. It just happens. Automatic trust. Sort of like snoring, only less benign.

'I don't know what Min's going to do about you.' His eyes glittered humorously. 'She'll have to do something. You're probably too dangerous to live. But if she decides to terminate you, I'm going to make sure you get a commendation before you die. That's a promise.' He held up his hands as if to ward off thanks. 'Anybody who accomplishes what you just did should have a commendation nailed to him somewhere, even if it has to be on your coffin instead of your chest.'

'How nice,' Angus growled in the same spirit. 'I wish I could tell you how good that makes me feel. But it doesn't. I'm so pleased I could puke.'

Because he knew Dolph was joking, he didn't mention that he was prepared to fight for his right to go on living.

The captain replied with a relaxed chuckle. 'I know what you mean. Sometimes I think they really do nail those

677

commendations into you. Drive them right through your heart. Some people never recover.'

He might have gone on; but the UMCP director groaned suddenly. Warden made a convulsive effort to shift his hips as if he needed to adjust the vector of his suit jets. Then he jerked his eye open.

'Angus,' he croaked hoarsely. 'Dolph. Where are we? What's going on? Where's that Amnioni?'

He could probably guess most of what Angus, Dolph, and Mikka had done. He'd seen it happen. But no one had told him about Ciro –

Dolph couldn't restrain a quick laugh. 'Gone!' he crowed. 'Eaten by a black hole.' And then flung outward in an evanescent hail of subatomic particles when the black hole died. 'Mikka Vasaczk's brother, Ciro, set off one of *Trumpet*'s singularity grenades. The briefings I've read say those things don't have much tactical use, but I'm here to tell you they work like magic if you do it right.'

Scowling, Dios rubbed his organic eye; slapped his face; straightened his back; pulled himself together by force of will. 'Captain Ubikwe,' he ordered sharply, 'start again. I didn't understand a word you just said.'

On command Dolph dropped his levity. 'Sorry, Director.' At once his gaze grew troubled; disturbed by images of Ciro – and Vector. 'Nothing's free,' he sighed. 'We wanted to save you and Suka Bator. We wanted to save everything we possibly could. We're just lucky the price wasn't a hell of a lot higher.

'Ciro Vasaczk was an illegal. He served under Nick Succorso. But he gave his life to kill that Amnioni.'

Angus thought he ought to explain how Ciro had reacted to Sorus Chatelaine's mutagen – the same mutagen Vestabule had inflicted on Dios. But he didn't have the heart for it. An explanation would have made Ciro seem crazy. The boy deserved better.

Apparently Dolph felt the same way. He didn't mention Ciro's history. Instead he said, 'He went EVA with a grenade. Attached it to *Calm Horizons*' hull. After you joined me here, Mikka Vasaczk used *Trumpet*'s thrust to haul us out of range.

She covered us with that dispersion field generator. Then Ciro fired an impact rifle at his grenade from point-blank range.

'We're still here,' he finished simply. 'The defensive isn't.'

Dios happened to be at the targ station. A frown clenched his forehead, and he drummed his fingers on the edge of the inactive console, as if he were thinking furiously. His gaze flicked between Dolph, Angus and the screens: he might have been measuring them against each other; estimating possibilities –

Damn, Angus breathed to himself. Damn it to hell. Warden was still scheming. He'd already won. If Fasner's attack on the Council was any indication, Dios had gained everything he wanted. And yet he wasn't done.

'It's probably churlish to point this out,' Dios told Dolph gruffly, 'but you took a hell of a risk.'

Captain Ubikwe's eyes narrowed. All his muscles seemed to tighten, drawing his bulk into a harder shape. Grimly he answered, 'Acting Director Donner sanctioned it in person.'

Without warning Davies raised his head, swung the data station to face Dolph and Dios. 'Did you tell him this was all Angus' idea, Captain?' he put in harshly. He must have been conscious for the past several minutes, listening with his eyes closed while he gathered his strength. Like Angus and Warden, he'd discarded his helmet in the airlock. The after-effects of strain left his features livid and angry. 'Vector and I were just going to sacrifice ourselves. We didn't want the Council killed. Or a war. But Angus convinced Morn to let him do it this way instead.'

Bitterly Davies finished, 'Did you tell him that's the only reason he's still alive?'

Angus stared at his son. Davies' support surprised him. For a moment a strange emotion that might have been gratitude swelled in his chest. Apparently the man he'd become actually felt glad he had a son.

Lightness and release. Gratitude? Shit, his entire head had been filled with emotions he wasn't used to and didn't know how to handle.

If Dios was surprised, he didn't show it. He faced Davies, searched the kid with his IR vision. Then he nodded to himself. 'Davies Hyland,' he pronounced firmly. 'You probably don't need me to tell you you look like your father. But you think like your mother. That's something to be proud of.'

Already his voice had recovered its natural authority. Angus remembered it vividly. The UMCP director had sounded much the same when he'd replaced Angus' datacore.

We've committed a crime against you. In essence, you're no longer a human being. We've deprived you of choice – and responsibility.

At the time, however, Angus had heard hints of self-loathing behind Warden's ease of command. Now they were gone.

He'd avowed, *It's got to stop.* And he'd kept that promise. If anything, he'd become even more dangerous.

'Don't worry about Angus,' he told Davies. 'I have a pretty good idea how much I owe him. And I can at least guess what it cost him. I won't forget.'

Then Dios turned back to Captain Ubikwe. 'And I don't object to the risk, Dolph. I'm just amazed by it. Grateful and humbled. You've given me a chance to finish what I started. I'll try to make it worthwhile.'

Dolph nodded noncommittally. His heavy jaws chewed words he didn't say; reactions he kept private.

Angus swore to himself. He thought he knew how *Punisher*'s commander felt. *Make it worthwhile*, shit. More plotting – more schemes. He'd had enough of Dios' underhanded intentions. They were too expensive. He didn't want to hear any more.

Before the director could go on, he rasped, 'If you don't call Mikka, fat man, I will. She's been quiet too long.'

'You're right,' Dolph agreed quickly. He seemed glad for the interruption. At once he thumbed his intercom. 'Mikka?' he asked the pickup. 'Can you hear me? Are you all right?'

Angus had watched him enough to understand that Dolph Ubikwe had his own reasons for outrage at Warden's manipulations; a cop's reasons. Maybe he didn't think Warden's actions were justified by Fasner's defeat.

A moment passed before Mikka answered. When she finally spoke, her voice sounded thin and fragile; hoarse with coughing. 'Sort of.' The voice of a woman who'd been beaten up. 'I think –' She gasped weakly. 'I think I'm bleeding somewhere. Inside. I'm going to sickbay –'

She faded out of the speakers as if she'd fainted.

'Damn it!' Angus slapped at his belts. 'She needs help. I've got to –'

Davies cut him off. 'No. *I'll* go.' He gestured at the communications indicators on the status display. 'Looks like *Punisher* and UMCPHQ are flaring us as hard as they can. I think there are some decisions that have to be made.' Suspicion and weariness stretched his voice taut. '*I* don't need to know what they are. *You* do. They shouldn't be made behind your back.'

More quietly he finished, 'I can help Mikka as well as you can.'

Angus started to object, then relaxed back into his g-seat. Davies was right. If the UMCP director intended to *make it worthwhile*, Angus had to be ready to defend himself.

Dios' victory was tarnished in ways Angus hadn't expected.

Without waiting for a response, Davies unclipped his belts; drifted toward the airlock while Dolph cycled it open. But at the inner door he paused.

'Ciro was just a kid,' he said to Dios. 'About my age – if I had an age. He was an illegal because that was the only life Mikka had to offer him. He didn't deserve any of this.'

Warden nodded as if he understood; as if every suggestion of distrust made sense to him.

'Captain Ubikwe,' he commanded firmly, 'log an order to Acting Director Min Donner. My last order. Full pardons for Mikka Vasaczk, Ciro Vasaczk, Vector Shaheed, Morn Hyland.' Morn had committed a capital crime when she'd accepted her zone implant control from Angus: she'd stolen the evidence against him – and used a zone implant on herself. In addition she was guilty of insubordination; perhaps even of mutiny. 'They can have anything they want. Relocation, treatment, money, jobs, new id – *any*thing. All they have to do is name it.

'Angus doesn't need a pardon. He already works for us. And you haven't done anything illegal.'

While Dolph murmured, 'Aye, Director,' Warden held Davies' gaze as if he wanted to ask, Does that help?

Angus could see that it did. Davies' eyes softened, and some of the strain left his muscles. Relief or regret twisted the corners of his mouth.

'Thank you, Director,' he answered thickly.

With a quick jerk on the nearest handgrip, he pulled himself into the airlock and disappeared.

Remembering lightness, Angus waited to learn what Dios would do next. Whatever it was, he didn't think he was going to like it. Nevertheless he was willing to be patient – at least for a little while.

He wanted to know whether Warden would leave him any choice.

'Director –' Dolph rumbled uncertainly. He pointed at the communications blips on his board. 'I have to answer these. They're getting frantic.'

'No!' Dios snapped at once. 'Don't answer them. That's my last order for you.'

His voice had teeth: it could bite and tear when he let it.

'Min can stand the wait,' he went on. 'And she can certainly deal with UMCPHQ. I don't want you to say a word to either of them until Angus and I leave.'

'Leave?' Angus drawled. 'I like the sound of that. Where are we going?'

A dark scowl closed Dolph's face. 'Director –' he began again. 'I'm a UMCP officer. It's my duty to report.'

Warden shook his head. 'Of course. But not yet.

'Listen to me, Dolph. This is important.' He held himself still while intensity poured off him in waves. Yet his physical restraint only increased the force of what he said. 'I want you to take Davies and Mikka to UMCPHQ. And protect them.

Make sure Min understands I want them protected. Just in case the Council suffers a spasm of self-righteousness and decides to punish somebody.

'If I can persuade him to join me, Angus and I will use *Trumpet* to go visit Holt.' He permitted himself a stiff shrug. 'You can talk to Min as soon as I'm gone.'

Angus felt a sting of surprise. Persuade? he wondered. *Persuade* him? To go visit Holt? Did Warden mean that? Or was *persuade* just a polite word for coerce?

Captain Ubikwe stared distress at the man he'd served ever since he became a cop. 'My God, Director,' he protested, 'that doesn't make any sense. You should talk to her yourself. Holt is finished. You can forget about him. You should –'

'No.' Dios spoke softly now, but his tone implied a shout. 'Koina told the Council everything. Every crime I've helped commit – everything that makes you wonder whether you can trust me. I'm tainted, Dolph. I'm complicit in Holt's crimes. As much responsible for them as he is. Even if the Council decided to pardon me, I would still consider myself responsible.

'If Min does *her* duty, her first action will be to place me under arrest for treason. She'll order you to make me your prisoner and take me to UMCPHQ. And that might break her heart. *She* still believes in me.' He sounded certain. 'I don't want to put that kind of pressure on her. If she doesn't arrest me, the Members won't trust her. She'll be tainted, too.'

He didn't mention that Dolph might find it painful to arrest the director of the UMCP. He didn't need to: the truth was plain on Dolph's face. He recognized the accuracy of Warden's prediction – and it horrified him.

Dios didn't give him time to respond. The director's vehemence mounted as he continued, 'And Holt's still alive. *That* I guarantee. Most of HO is intact. You can see it on scan.' He indicated the screens with a twitch of his head. 'You can bet he made sure he was safe before he ordered that attack on Suka Bator. He is still alive.

'Worse than that, he still has most of his power. All his

683

contracts and knowledge, databases, leverage – everything his real muscle is based on. He can probably ruin half the Members if they take direct action against him. He can destroy the entire fiscal structure that supports us against forbidden space. Hell, if he wants to he can even sell the whole lot to the Amnion. You know he has ships and drones that weren't damaged. Right now there's nothing to stop him from packing his entire power-base aboard that yacht of his and hitting the gap with it.'

'Min's cordon will interdict –' Dolph croaked weakly.

For an instant Warden's control slipped. He punched one hard fist in the direction of the displays. Almost shouting, he retorted, 'Those ships aren't in *position*.'

Angus believed him; but he glanced at the helm schematic to confirm it. No question about it: a ship could flee untouched from the far side of Fasner's station.

Which suggested some interesting possibilities –

Dolph's heavy frame slumped. In dismay he murmured, 'Do you really think he would sell all that?'

Dios closed his arms like restraints across his chest. 'The Amnion can force-grow fetuses,' he said through his teeth. 'They can imprint minds. They can make him immortal. And they'll be glad to do it when they see what he has to sell. *Yes*, I think he might go that far.

'That's why I want you to let Angus and me go over there. Let us stop him. Permanently. Before he has time to commit a crime that's worse than anything else he's done.'

More gently he concluded, 'And I want you to do it without disobeying orders from the acting director. You shouldn't have that on your record. Which means you can't talk to her until after we're on our way.'

Dolph propped his forehead on one hand to hide his eyes as if he couldn't bear to look at Warden anymore – or couldn't bear the way Warden looked at him. For a moment he didn't say anything. His shoulders knotted as he squeezed at his temples.

In a muffled voice he sighed, 'You aren't coming back, are you' – a statement, not a question.

Dios gripped himself hard. 'What would be the point?'

A sound like a buried groan leaked past Dolph's fingers. He didn't go on.

'Fine,' Angus snorted. He couldn't wait any longer: he wanted to know where he stood. 'Let's pretend everything you say is reasonable. And sane. Here's my question.

'How do you propose to "persuade" me to go along with you?'

Slowly the director turned his g-seat so that he could look straight at Angus.

'You need me, that's obvious,' Angus stated. 'If Fasner's still alive, then he still has defenses. You won't have an easy time tackling him alone.

'But why should I bother?' The first time Warden had talked to him, at the start of his mission to rescue Morn, Angus had hardly been able to meet the man's piercing, augmented gaze. Now he held it easily. The more honest Warden became, the less Angus feared him. 'Are you planning to threaten me with some kind of self-destruct? Some code that'll fry my brain, or scramble my instruction-sets, or short-circuit my datacore? I'm sure you can do it. Hashi fucking Lebwohl wouldn't miss a chance to hardwire me with something that nasty.'

Dios didn't look away. 'No,' he said flatly, 'I'm not going to threaten you. I'm through extorting the kind of help I need.'

Then his voice showed its teeth. 'You'll go with me because I'm taking *Trumpet*. You'll have to kill me to stop me. You may even have to kill Dolph.' He flicked a glance at Dolph, but didn't wait for the captain to say anything. 'And once I leave, you're stuck. You'll end up in custody on UMCPHQ. Unless you force Min to open fire on you. In which case Davies and Mikka will die with you.

'Either way, I don't think you'll like it much.'

Angus faced him with a feral grin. 'Or,' he countered, 'I could go with you part of the way and then kill you. I want a ship of my own. *Trumpet* suits me pretty well.'

Even then Warden didn't look away. He'd been staring at

the consequences of his own actions for so long that nothing could make him flinch. 'I'll take that chance.'

Angus sighed inwardly, where it didn't show. For no good reason except that the director had finally begun to keep his promises, Angus believed him. Min Donner was right: Dios was trying to make restitution.

Still grinning, Angus shifted his attention to Captain Ubikwe. 'There's something he hasn't told you, fat man. Vestabule gave him a mutagen.'

That hit Dolph hard. He snatched down his hand, jerked up his head. His eyes flared dumb anguish at Warden.

'It's the same kind Sorus Chatelaine used on Ciro,' Angus explained harshly. 'He'll stay human as long as he takes the drug to keep it passive. Which he has in his pocket. A few pills – a few hours.'

Dolph tried to ask a question, but he couldn't make his throat work.

'So it's really worse than it looks,' Angus went on. 'If you take him back to UMCPHQ, you can cure him. Lebwohl's antimutagen will do it. Then you can execute him for treason. Or you can let him go after Fasner. Let him finish himself off.

'The way I see it, he's tainted in more ways than one. He's been a cop too long. He's finally realized the same rules he kills other people for breaking should apply to him, too.'

'I'm starting to like that about you,' he remarked to Dios.

Then he told Dolph, 'I don't think your acting director is going to thank you for bringing him in. She won't want to watch what happens to him.'

For a moment Dolph seemed to stagger on the brink of a personal precipice, fighting for balance. Despite his insubordinate nature, he'd served Warden Dios – and Min Donner – with his life. But now all ordinary definitions of fidelity appeared to fail him. He looked as lost as Angus had ever felt in an EVA suit as he confronted his choices and tried not to fall –

By degrees he slumped forward until only his elbows kept him off the command board. Bowing his head, he muttered,

'Oh, well. I should have known this was all too easy. You're a hard man, Warden. Sometimes I wonder why everybody who works for you doesn't commit seppuku.'

He nodded toward the open airlock and *Trumpet*. 'If worst comes to worst, I can always say you were gone before I woke up. When sickbay's done with her, Davies can bring Mikka over here. I'll release the grapples as soon as we seal the locks.'

Softly he ended, 'Warden Dios, you *owe* me for this.'

Dios nodded. A film of moisture blurred his human eye. He had to swallow a couple of times before he could say, 'I'll pay.'

But he didn't allow himself time for emotion. He may have feared that his self-command could break. At once he asked, 'Angus?'

'Shit,' Angus growled cheerfully, 'I can't miss *this*. I've done all kinds of hunting, but I've never gone after a dragon.'

He no longer recognized himself at all. Between the two of them, Morn and Warden had welded him in ways he didn't understand and couldn't measure. Some essential part of him had been transformed by people who kept their promises.

The situation was full of possibilities.

ANGUS

While Warden Dios prepared his final briefing so that Dolph could relay it to Min Donner, Angus boarded *Trumpet*. Hints of lightness remained with him, buoyed by an ineffable sense of opportunity. He no longer felt heavy enough to be held back. The more honest Dios became, the wider Angus' horizons seemed to grow. Warden had 'persuaded' him to accept exactly the same choices he would have made for himself.

Trumpet was a good ship; but he'd begun to think he might be able to do better.

From the gap scout's airlock, he rode the lift to the corridor which ran the length of her core. But then he had to stifle an impulse to head for the bridge. He wanted to see what condition she was in after having twice fought loose from the grip of a black hole; wanted to examine her fuel cells and inventories, confirm her remaining capabilities. Unfortunately he didn't think he could afford the time.

Holt Fasner wasn't likely to just sit around waiting for the UMCP director to catch up with him.

Angus coasted along the corridor to sickbay, keyed the door and went in.

Mikka lay asleep on the surgical table – unconscious or drugged – with IVs plugged into her forearms and a new bandage that smelled of tissue plasm and metabolins high up on one side of her abdomen. An old scowl gripped her features as if she'd been angry so long that she couldn't let it go. But her mouth hung open, slack-jawed and vulnerable. Her breathing carried suggestions of pain her medicated body couldn't feel.

Davies sat limp in the corner of the compartment, resting there while the sickbay systems worked on Mikka. Once he'd settled her on the table, anchored her with restraints and keyed the computer for diagnosis and treatment, there was nothing else he could do for her.

Of course, he could have returned to the command module; listened to what Warden, Dolph and Angus told each other. But he didn't look like he could bear to hear much more. The emotional ordeal of accepting Vestabule's demands and the physical strain of fighting for his life had left him exhausted, despite his elevated metabolism. Obviously he needed rest. However, his slumped posture conveyed the impression that he'd folded into the corner so he could grieve – for Ciro; or for his own fears.

He raised his head when Angus entered the chamber. At first he didn't seem to recognize his father. Then he sighed thinly. 'That didn't take long.' With the heels of both hands he tried to rub a little life back into the muscles of his face. 'I thought the three of you would have to yell at each other for quite a while.'

Angus gave Davies the same fierce grin he'd shown to Dios and Captain Ubikwe. 'Turns out I didn't have to yell much. Now that the director of the United Manipulating and Conniving cops has decided to tell the truth, things have become simpler. The only hard part was convincing the fat man to put off arresting anyone for a few more minutes.'

He pulled himself to the edge of the table, studied the status readout on Mikka's condition, then went on, 'Looks like she's stable. She needs to go over to the module. Can you handle it, or do you need help?'

'I can handle it.' Davies nudged himself off the deck; straightened out his legs so that he drifted upright in front of Angus. 'But I'm probably going to feel lousy about myself later if I don't at least ask what you decided. I don't expect

689

you to care what I think. But *I* care. Or I will when I've had some sleep.'

Deliberately he studied his father's face. 'How bad is it?'

Angus chuckled. How bad was it? That depended on how he looked at it. For Warden things could hardly get worse. Or better. The man had chosen an expensive way to keep his promises. But for everyone else –

'Not bad,' Angus assured Davies. 'In fact, the only bad part is' – sardonically he parroted phrases he'd heard repeated to the point of nausea during his years in reform schools and juvenile lockups – 'you won't get to spend your formative years nurtured by a nuclear family. Morn'll be there. She'll probably hover until she makes you want to scream. But I'll be gone.

'If I have any say in the matter,' he stated, 'neither of you will ever catch sight of me again.'

Shit, he was making promises himself. Warden's influence had begun to rot his brain.

Davies replied with a sigh of resignation. 'You'd better tell me what that means.'

Angus snorted. 'Gone is gone. Not here. Why isn't that clear? Light-years away across the gap. As far as I can get from cops and Amnion who want to rule the galaxy.'

As far as possible from all the people who'd made him into a man he didn't recognize.

In response Davies blinked at him wearily. 'That's not what I meant. I meant –'

'I know what you meant.' For Davies' sake Angus restrained the way his thoughts – and his heart – wanted to leap and run in all directions. 'From here on everything's simple.

'The fat man'll take you and Mikka to UMCPHQ. Protective custody. Until the Council or the cops decide whether they have the courage to admit you and Morn saved the whole planet's ass.

'In the meantime' – he grinned again – 'the almighty Warden Dios and I are going after Holt Fasner.'

Davies nodded slowly. He may have been too tired to

690

consider all the implications. 'What happens after that?'

Angus swallowed another harsh chuckle. Before he could stop himself, he countered, 'What makes you think there's going to be an "after"?'

'That's not what I meant,' Davies said again. 'You'll be gone. I heard that. And I guess maybe Director Dios will finally be satisfied. If he can arrest Fasner. But what about Morn? What happens to her?'

Urged into motion by eagerness, Angus keyed the sickbay computer to remove its IVs from Mikka's arms, then began opening her restraints so she could float free of the table. He was absolutely sure that Dios had no intention of *arresting* the Dragon.

'If Morn doesn't watch out,' he answered, 'Min Donner'll probably erect a statue in her honor. Make every damn cop alive stop by at least once and kiss its feet. She'll be so safe she won't know what to do with herself.'

After a moment Davies mustered another nod. Apparently he still trusted the ED director.

Angus didn't. Oh, he believed she would protect as well as honor both Morn and Davies with her life. But she might not do the same for him. He could easily imagine her having him shut down like an unstable nuclear pile. If fucking Hashi Lebwohl didn't get to him first; do something worse.

When Mikka came loose from the table, he steered her toward Davies. Davies accepted her with both arms; adjusted her against him so that he had one arm free without putting pressure on her injuries.

'You know, it's funny,' he mused softly. 'I can remember everything you did to her.' He'd been imprinted with Morn's mind; Morn's memories. He lowered his head, shrouded his gaze; keeping his grief to himself. 'But I still think she'll be sorry she didn't get to say good-bye.'

That touched Angus: he seemed to have no defense against it. Hints of pain and brutality spread out from the point of contact. For a moment he lost the lightness that had carried him out of himself. Weight dragged at him like a burden of regret.

'Tell her –' he began gruffly. At first he had no idea what

he wanted to say. But then it became clear, as if his computer had opened a datalink to the parts of himself he didn't recognize. 'Tell her I'm sorry I wasn't better.'

He was sorry she'd chosen Nick to save her. If she hadn't helped Nick frame him, everything after that would have been different. In spite of himself, however, he understood. Nick hadn't given her a zone implant.

At last Davies looked up at him. His son faced him squarely as if he, too, had finally become honest.

'None of us are that good,' Davies murmured. 'I think you've done all right.'

Angus turned away. He'd had all the support he could stand. It touched him too deeply. With his back to Davies, he opened the sickbay door.

'Just tell her.'

'I will,' Davies promised.

'In that case –' Angus pointed at the corridor. 'Get Mikka out of here. Dios and I need to burn.'

Davies didn't say anything more. Pulling on a handgrip, he carried Mikka through the doorway; swung her with him along the corridor in the direction of the lift.

At the same time Angus launched himself toward the bridge.

He didn't recover his sense of lightness until Davies had transferred Mikka to the command module; until Dios came aboard and the airlocks sealed; until Dolph opened the grapples. But as *Trumpet* hummed to life under his hands, and the first nudge of thrust settled him into his g-seat, he started to soar again.

He was done with Morn and Davies and vulnerability. *Done* with cops, orders, legal violence, fear. The time had come to cross the gap which had always blocked him.

The minute Warden reached the second's station and closed his belts, Angus fired thrust hard. *Trumpet* burned like a missile armed with ruin toward UMCHO.

Their approach to Earth's largest orbital platform presented no difficulties. Min Donner's barrage had effectively stripped away HO's ability to defend itself. Thousands of people remained alive on station: the sheer number of distress signals HO transmitted, and the volume of emergency communications, made that obvious. But the platform's guns had been crippled. Most of its power was gone. Short of sending out an EVA team, there was nothing Holt Fasner – or Home Security – could do to prevent Angus Thermopyle and the UMCP director from docking at one of the personnel craft ports located in the hub of HO's revolving torus.

Angus felt sure Fasner was still on station. As soon as he'd left the command module behind, he'd started scrutinizing the huge platform with all *Trumpet*'s sensors and sifters, searching for any hint of the Dragon's escape. And his instruments had the support of Earth's system-wide scan net: minutes after *Calm Horizons*' death, Min Donner had ordered the net reactivated. Angus could pull in data from every ship and station, every navigational buoy and scan relay, around the planet. His screens told him that several dozen ejection pods of various sizes had left HO – most in the direction of UMCPHQ or SpaceLab Station, a few sliding down the gravity well toward Earth's surface – but that no craft of any kind had fled toward open space and freedom.

If Fasner ran, he wouldn't use an ejection pod: no mere pod could carry his treasure of data and secrets. And he wouldn't head for any destination where he would be arrested as soon as he docked or landed. Therefore he was still within reach when Angus eased *Trumpet* into the first available port and locked her seals to hold her in place.

Angus didn't power down the drives: he wanted the gap scout ready for him if he needed her. But he code-blocked the command board so that no one else – not even Warden Dios – would be able to take her.

Riding a new wave of eagerness, he asked Dios, 'Now what?'

The director hadn't spoken since he'd come aboard. Once he'd taken the second's g-seat, he'd covered himself with silence like a security screen, ignoring anything Angus happened to say. For the most part, he'd also ignored the scan data Angus studied. Instead he'd concentrated on running a playback of *Trumpet*'s datacore. At first Angus had wondered why Warden bothered. But then he'd realized that the UMCP director was probably the only important man in Earth's space who hadn't heard Morn's story. Apparently Dios was more interested in what she and Angus had done and endured than in anything else.

So Angus had left him alone. In spite of himself, he was starting to understand the director. One way or another, Dios had staked his entire attack on the Dragon and all his hopes for humankind's future on Morn and Angus. The same convictions which had driven him to take a risk like that left him hungry to know what his success had cost them.

Now he didn't answer Angus' question. As soon as *Trumpet* clamped into her berth, he flipped open his belts and pushed himself out of the second's station toward the bridge companionway.

'Shit,' Angus remarked to the display screens. In another minute Dios' silence was going to make him angry. The man was entirely too eager to end up dead. Like Ciro, he was crazy with mutagens. Or he'd been crazy all along –

Clearing the command board, Angus released his belts and followed the director.

He caught up with Dios at the weapons locker. Warden had shucked off his EVA suit, and was helping himself to everything he could carry: an impact rifle and several charge clips; two laser pistols; a dagger with a serrated edge; half a dozen concussion grenades.

Angus whistled through his teeth. 'I guess we're expecting trouble.'

Dios fixed a gaze of pure concentration on Angus – a look of such focus that it seemed to admit no weakness, allow no emotion. 'You could say that.' The authority in his voice had become as hard as a fist. Like a predator he meant to go for the kill while his opponent was weak.

'Home Security has worked up here for decades,' he explained. Helping Fasner. 'They probably think they won't like what happens if they don't resist. When she gets around to mopping up, Min will have the lot of them arrested. They'll face all sorts of charges, starting with that attack on Suka Bator. As long as they hope there might be a way out of this mess, they'll fight.'

Angus tried to imagine 'a way out' for them. A ship? A bargain? Some kind of executive miracle? But he didn't care what it might be.

At least Warden was talking to him again.

'So what's the plan?' he asked while he peeled off his own EVA suit; got rid of the encumbrance.

Dios clipped the handguns to his belt, stuffed his pockets with grenades. All the hesitation had been burned out of him long ago. 'I want you to go after Holt.'

Angus raised his eyebrows. He hadn't expected Warden to give him his chance this easily.

'How am I supposed to find him?'

'Look for his gap yacht,' Warden answered. '*Motherlode*. She's probably berthed somewhere in the hub. If he isn't there now, he will be eventually. She's *his* way out.'

Shaking his head, Angus moved to take his turn at the weapons locker. 'I don't think so.' He'd already studied that possibility. 'From the hub he won't have a window on open space. Two of Donner's ships are close enough to hit him before he reaches gap velocity. He'll have a berth somewhere out on the rim.'

At the right moment in HO's rotation, Fasner would have a clear escape vector.

But the outer perimeter of the torus stretched for at least twenty k. Angus would need hours to search that much of the station.

Warden paused. 'In that case –' He thought for a moment, then said, 'You should probably talk to his mother. She might not tell me where he is. But I'm sure she'll tell you.'

Angus didn't try to hide his surprise. He wanted to ask, Fasner has a *mother*? Still? Isn't he too old? But he had no time for secondary considerations. Instead he countered, 'Why would she do *that*?'

Grimly Dios assured him, 'You'll figure it out when you see her.'

Before Angus could argue, the director gave him a quick set of directions which made sense to one of his databases.

'All right.' Angus set his uncertainty aside. He didn't intend to let it weigh him down. From the locker he selected two impact rifles and a double handful of charge clips. 'What do you want me to do if I catch up with him?'

Again Dios looked at him: a stare like a flare of urgency – or a promise of murder.

'I trust you. Just do what comes naturally.'

He seemed to think he could have imposed restrictions on Angus, if he'd chosen to do so.

Angus grinned fiercely. 'A free hand. I like it.'

Shoving the charge clips into his pockets, he slung his rifles over his shoulders and headed for the lift.

'All right,' he repeated as the lift sank toward the airlock. 'Assume it all works. His mother' – shit, his *mother*? – 'tells me how to find his yacht. I get there in time. What'll you be doing?'

'I'm going after his data.' Warden tapped on the keypad to open the inner doors of the lock. 'That's his real power. If he's still downloading it to his yacht, I'll cut it off. I want to make sure it can't be used to do any more damage.'

'You know his codes?' Angus asked incredulously.

The director shook his head. 'I don't have to. Hashi put security locks on most of the main HO computers. I know *those* codes. The locks won't prevent Holt from accessing anything he wants to copy. They only block deletions, changes. But they'll let me find the same files.'

Apparently he'd thought of everything.

He reached up to cycle the outer doors; but Angus caught his arm, stopped him. Effortlessly Angus pulled Warden around to face him. A sense of doubt nagged at him. The man he'd become felt concerns he couldn't forget.

Deliberately he raised the same question Davies had put to him. 'What happens after that?'

Dios' single gaze held no compromise; surrendered nothing. 'Then all hell breaks loose,' he pronounced harshly. 'And Holt is finished.'

Another promise. Warden made too many of them. They were starting to scare Angus.

The director had only two or three hours of humanity left. After that his supply of the drug he'd taken from Vestabule would run out. If he didn't find an antidote in Fasner's data, he was finished himself – as truly and completely ruined as the Dragon.

With an effort of will, Angus tried again to reach past Warden's defenses. Although the memory hurt him, he said, 'Davies told me Morn would be sorry she didn't get a chance to say good-bye. She probably feels the same way about you.'

Warden's glare didn't flicker. 'Don't worry about it. I'll send her a flare.'

And another. 'Oh, stop it,' Angus snorted. In disgust he let the director go. 'You and God. You can handle everything. The rest of us don't have to *worry about it*.'

Then he found that he couldn't stop himself. A strange fury took fire in his veins, ignited by Dios' rebuff. An allegiance he didn't want and couldn't stifle filled him with outrage. Abruptly he started shouting.

'But you *don't* handle everything. Morn and I carried you this far on our fucking *backs*! Didn't you actually *read* that playback? Shit, you *know* she has gap-sickness. I told you that *myself*! Hard g triggers it. She goes crazy for self-destruct. But she saved us in the swarm. *I* set off the grenade. That was all I could do. *She* ran helm. *In the fucking g of a fucking black hole!* She figured out that pain blocks her craziness. So she kept herself sane and saved us by letting g shatter her arm.

'Don't tell me not to *worry about it*,' he snarled savagely. 'You didn't come here to finish Fasner, or snatch his data. You came here to get yourself killed. So you won't have to go on trial for your crimes.'

For a long moment Warden stared back at Angus' indignation. He didn't contradict anything Angus said. Instead his organic eye softened slowly, and some of the resolve which closed his face relaxed. He seemed to respond to accusations when nothing else could touch him.

At last he sighed. 'I passed sentence on myself a long time ago. I don't see any reason to commute it now.' Then his voice sharpened. 'But I passed sentence on Holt, too. Whatever happens, I want that one carried out.'

Through his teeth, he demanded, 'Don't just kill him, Angus. Tear his goddamn heart out.'

Without transition Angus' anger seemed to release him; set him free. Dios had finally shown him something he could understand. Tear his heart out – That wasn't a cop talking: it was a man full of pain who wanted revenge.

A man like Angus himself.

He took a deep breath, let it out with the last of his doubts. 'That's better.' He gave Dios a bloodthirsty grin. 'Now we can go to work.'

He didn't make any promises. He'd spent them all on Morn. But he had no intention of disappointing the UMCP director. He unslung one of his guns and growled cheerfully, 'Don't just stand there. Open the door.'

In an instant Warden resumed his determination. Holding his rifle ready, he keyed the outer doors of the airlock.

Together Angus Thermopyle and Warden Dios left the ship to topple Holt Fasner's empire.

At first they were lucky. The hub was full of people, all desperately hunting for some craft to take them off station; but none of them were HS guards. There weren't more than five guns in the whole mob. And everyone recognized UMCP Director Warden Dios. Faced with the almost tangible blaze of his authority – and with a pair of charged impact rifles – the crowd gave way; let Angus and Warden through to the lifts.

That was fortunate. So much trapped panic could have overwhelmed the two men. Any number of civilians would have died; but eventually Angus and the director would have fallen.

They were also fortunate that the station's maintenance and support systems still had power. The lifts worked: light and air-processing held steady: most of the status monitors and intercoms remained active. Apparently Min Donner's barrage had crippled the generators which supplied HO's guns, shields and thrust, but hadn't cut deeply enough to kill the platform.

However, the lift carried Angus and Warden down quickly into the grasp of the station's rotational g. That slowed them: instead of floating, they had to carry their own weight. And when they reached the level where Dios had decided they would separate, they found themselves in a pitched battle as soon as the lift opened. Someone in the hub must have called to warn Home Security.

From the cover of the doors Angus laid down fire with both rifles, strafing a swath across the corridor. When he'd cleared enough space, Warden tossed out a brace of concussion grenades. At least twenty guards lay dead, dying or stunned by the time Holt's enemies left the lift. They had to pick their way through the carnage as if they were on a battlefield.

'Damn,' Warden panted. 'I hope there isn't much more of this. I don't like killing people.'

Angus laughed shortly. 'I do.' He didn't give a shit how many of Fasner's guards he took down.

'Well, don't stop now.' Dios glanced at the corridor markers to confirm his location, then headed away at a run, holding his rifle in front of his thick chest like an ED officer, trained for combat.

Angus let him go. From now on the director was on his own. Angus' nerves burned with fear and eagerness; endorphins and zone implant emissions. His instincts fed on the smell of blood, the urgency of death. HS didn't scare him as much as the Amnion did: he knew he was faster, stronger, more accurate. But the guards could still kill him. Guns equalized the contest.

He took an instant to compare Warden's directions, the corridor markers, and his computer's structural schematic of the station. Then he, too, broke into a run, moving with a cyborg's speed to find — the idea still amazed him — Holt Fasner's *mother*.

Clearly HS hadn't had time to coordinate more than one defensive stand. He encountered isolated guards; small knots of terrified civilians; techs still trying to do their jobs. Efficient as a microprocessor, he shot everyone who carried a weapon; left the rest alone. He probably should have tried to kill them all so that they couldn't muster HS behind him. But he'd lost his taste for cold murder. Another change he didn't recognize.

She might not tell me where he is. But I'm sure she'll tell you.

That didn't make any sense.

A sequence of corridors and lifts led him into one of the more heavily shielded sectors of the platform. Markers matched Dios' directions.

Who the hell *was* this woman? Fasner's real mother? Bullshit. He was supposed to be a hundred and fifty years old.

Fire dogged him in rapid bursts. He ducked and dodged; ran; flung bloodshed past his shoulders with machine precision.

You'll figure it out when you see her.

He ran hard; but despite his speed his zone implants kept his pulse firm, charged his blood with oxygen. Past the acrid reek of impact fire, he began to smell the disinfectants of a sterile med-sector.

Warden's directions fit the markers. *That* door.

Unguarded. Abandoned. The whole sector echoed with emptiness. If Fasner's mother was there, he didn't care enough about her to take her with him.

Unless he'd already evacuated her —

Angus hooked his rifles over his shoulders to free his arms. Trusting the lasers built into his hands, he moved carefully to the door; tested it.

Locked.

The mechanism was more elaborate — more secure — than he expected it to be. Nobody but a cyborg would ever walk in *here* without the right codes and clearances.

His EM vision read the circuits. A touch of laser surgery released the lock.

As the door slid aside, he sprang at an angle through the entrance, then crouched down against the marginal protection of the wall, making himself a smaller target while he scanned the room.

Shit! For a heartbeat or two, an emission shout from the far wall nearly blinded him. Voices babbled against each other, dozens of them punctuated by music and sound effects, men and women all talking as if the others weren't there. He searched wildly; saw –

– video screens. Jesus, *video* screens! Twenty or more, the damn wall was full of them. All on: all projecting muted seriousness and urgency into the darkened room. In fact, they gave the only illumination. Someone had switched the room's lights off.

Most of the screens showed newsdogs in full spate, pretending they understood events which had left them behind hours ago. A few channels still carried ordinary programs, however, as if they were too important to be interrupted by the mere threat of war and mass slaughter. Entertainment carried more weight than the fate of the planet. Angus spotted at least one sweaty romance and two canned sports broadcasts among the newsdogs.

Slowly he rose out of his crouch. *None* of this made any sense. If Fasner's mother lived here, the room had been designed for a madwoman.

A moment passed before he realized he could hear one voice which lacked the transmission quality of the video channels. With an effort, he looked away from the screens to finish scanning the room.

At once he saw her. The screens shone full on her mummified face; reflected from her staring eyes. The phosphor glow emphasized her apparent lifelessness: she looked like an effigy of death carved in old flesh. But she wasn't dead. Her eyelids blinked sporadically. At intervals she tried to swallow some of the saliva leaking from the corners of her mouth.

She lived because machines refused to let her die. IVs

festooned her arms: some tapped directly into her neck. A device that did her breathing for her enclosed her chest; circulated her blood. Below the equipment her legs protruded along her medical crib like rolls of antique hardcopy.

So swiftly that he hardly noticed what he did, Angus moved to leave the room. But at the door he caught himself; stopped on the edge of fleeing for his life. Shit, the crib! An autonomic terror had taken hold of him before he could control it. She was *in the crib*. If his computer hadn't helped him, he wouldn't have been able to control it now.

There was nothing to be afraid of. He told himself that harshly while panic roared in his ears, throbbed in his temples. *She* was in the crib. *He* wasn't. He *wasn't*. Morn and Warden had set him free. He didn't need to be scared. Instead of feeling all this terror, he ought to gloat over her, glad to see someone else in that position for a change.

But she was *in the crib*. His mother had tied his wrists and ankles to the slats. IVs and equipment nailed this woman in place. His mother had twisted his whole life with pain which Holt Fasner's mother understood absolutely.

He couldn't feel glad: that malicious pleasure was beyond him. His fear ran too deep. At one time he'd been perfectly capable of selling twenty-eight men and women to the Amnion. For all he knew, he might still be able to do it. But he believed that even in his worst and most brutal rages he could never have done *that* to another living being.

No, he was wrong: he *had* done it. Even that last perception of himself was false. Didn't he think of his welding as a kind of crib? And hadn't he forced a zone implant into Morn's head? Imposed his own version of welding on her? Reduced her to a machine – a *thing* that lived only to satisfy him?

Now finally he understood that terrible moment aboard *Bright Beauty* when he'd wept over the damage *Starmaster* had done to his ship – or over the damage he'd done to Morn. Even then he hadn't been sure which caused him the most pain. But he knew now.

Murder was a small crime by comparison.

He remained, paralyzed, at the door until he heard the woman mutter insistently, 'Is someone there? I thought I was alone.' Repeating herself for the second or third or tenth time.

Still awake: still conscious inside her terrible prison.

As if the situation had suddenly become simple, he left the doorway and crossed the room to stand in front of Holt Fasner's mother. She was still conscious; still suffered the torment he'd fled all his life. That changed everything. Violent tremors ran through him like spasms of revulsion; but his zone implants concealed them. Nevertheless they couldn't stifle the grief and rage that congested his face as he looked at her.

'You're not alone,' he answered her hoarsely. 'I'm here.'

As far as he could tell, she didn't so much as glance at him. Her eyes flicked past him from side to side, hunting her screens for sanity or death.

'Captain Angus Thermopyle.' Her voice was a husky whisper. 'Killer. Rapist. Illegal. I recognize you.

'You're in my way.'

The sound made his scalp crawl; sent skinworms of distress along his spine.

'I know.' He wanted to step aside; wanted to hide his distress in the gloom beyond the screens. Ruled by his computer, his body stayed where it was.

Her toothless gums chewed over his refusal to move for a moment. 'In that case,' she breathed thinly, 'you must want something. What is it?'

The taste of her helplessness sickened him. He bit down hard so that he wouldn't gag on it.

'Tell me where Fasner is.'

Her eyes went on searching past him, pecking up grains of comprehension from the screens. 'What do I get out of it?'

His throat closed. He fought down bile. 'What do you want?'

A small gust of mirthless laughter pulled through her. Spit drooled down her chin. 'I can't tell you. I've been living this way too long.'

Involuntarily Angus matched her strained whisper. 'That's all right,' he assured her. 'I know what you want.'

She might not have heard him. She was silent for a while. Then she remarked obliquely, 'Warden is doing better. But it's still not good enough.'

Angus had no idea how much she knew; what she understood. She was probably crazy. Yet he believed instinctively that she'd grasped everything.

Pressure mounted in him. Clenching his fists, he retorted, 'Will it be "good enough" if he brings this station down around your ears?'

The woman's eyes showed a hint of moisture. Small bits of light and images from the screens reflected in her gaze.

'Only if he does it in time.'

'Then let me help him,' Angus urged quickly. 'Tell me where Fasner is.'

She laughed again. 'Promise me first.' That may have been as close as she could come to sobbing. 'Give me your word of honor. As a gentleman.'

He knew why she hesitated; why she feared him. She knew too much about him – and too little.

He moved closer to her, pushed his face at hers. 'I'm not a *gentleman*,' he rasped grimly. 'I don't know what honor is. I don't even know your name. But I wouldn't leave a fucking *Amnioni* like this.'

That was true now.

'You hate him,' he told her. 'Because he did this to you. That's what keeps you alive. If you don't help me stop him, he's probably going to live forever.'

For the first time the woman looked straight at him.

'Warden was right,' she breathed. A damp film distorted or purified her vision as she studied him past the confines of her crib. 'He staked everything on you. And that Hyland girl. I thought it was a mistake. But I was wrong.'

In a voice he could barely hear, she told him how to find *Motherlode*'s berth.

Without hesitation he snatched both rifles from his shoulders. No flinch or flicker marred his resolve as he aimed his

704

guns at the machine which breathed for her and smashed it to scrap; blasted her imposed life out of her.

At once her old eyes filled up with rest, then glazed to darkness as her torment finally let her go. But he didn't stop there. Instead he blazed fire like a saturation barrage around the room, ripping apart the rest of her equipment, pulverizing her video screens, tearing chunks of plaster out of the walls and ceiling. He didn't release the firing studs of his rifles until he'd reduced the whole place to gloom and debris.

He kept that promise. In some ways he was becoming more like Warden Dios all the time.

Leaving ruin behind him, he burst from the room at a run to keep another.

WARDEN

He didn't have far to go. A lift or two; a few corridors. One more crime: the most spectacular – but by no means the worst – crime of his compromised life. The place where he and Angus had separated was closer to UMCHO Center than to Norna Fasner's sickchamber. Angus probably had less time than Warden did. On the other hand, the cyborg was much faster. And he killed more easily.

In spite of everything, Warden Dios still wanted to keep his own body count to a minimum.

UMCHO Center wasn't the real nexus of Holt's vast empire. But Red Priority security locks would give Warden access to Holt's data from any board in the HO network. And Center had resources he needed; resources which would be easier to use there than from some remote console. In addition, he was hoping for help. If he couldn't persuade or coerce at least one Center tech to assist him, his last crime would be much more difficult to carry out. A lot more people would die –

He ran steadily, but didn't push himself; tried to balance speed and caution. It would be too pitiful for words if he came all this way only to let some nameless HS guard kill him prematurely. But he didn't encounter any guards. The few people he met were unarmed and scared; consumed by the danger; no threat to him. He reached the corridor outside Center without firing at anyone.

The Center doors were guarded, however. He'd been sure they would be. In general Holt didn't inspire the kind of loyalty that would hold men and women at their posts when he'd obviously abandoned them. The guards were there, not to keep other people out, but to keep the techs in.

Left to themselves, HO's civilians would have welcomed anyone who suggested rescue or escape. Unfortunately a darker commitment drove Home Security. The guards knew that if they were taken they would be held accountable for any number of Holt's actions. Their only hope was to believe that the CEO might still find a way to save them.

Warden knew they were mistaken: Holt had no intention of saving any of them. But he was also sure these guards wouldn't listen to him if he tried to argue the point. Before they spotted him, he flipped a concussion grenade at their feet; ducked around a corner while it went off. Then he hurried to the doors.

As a precaution, he slung the guards' rifles over his shoulder, shoved their sidearms into his belt. Armed like a guerrilla, he thrust open the doors and strode into HO Center.

The hall itself was hardly distinguishable from any center of operations in human space. Function dictated form. Displays ranked the walls: rows of consoles lined the deck: flat, impersonal lighting washed out shadows and ambiguities. Except for its size, this could have been UMCPHQ Center.

It was built to a larger scale, however. The staggering amount of data processed here dwarfed UMCPHQ's operations. Holt could have run a planet from this room – if he hadn't been so busy trying to manipulate all of human space.

But the place was practically empty. As he came through the doors, Warden counted five techs and a guard. That was all, in a room where hundreds of men and women usually worked. If the rest had fled, and a guard was required to keep these five at their consoles –

Warden jumped to the conclusion that the techs weren't working for HO. They weren't directing an evacuation, running support systems, allocating resources, restraining panic; weren't doing any of the jobs a damaged station full of terri-

707

fied people needed. Otherwise more of the techs would have stayed.

So they were processing Holt's download. Whether they knew it or not, they were helping him copy the data which would enable him to bargain with the Amnion.

Warden had his rifle in the guard's face before the man could reach his weapons.

'I'm Warden Dios,' he barked even though anyone who worked for Center or HS would recognize him, 'UMCP Director Dios. I'm taking command. From now on you're all under my authority.' He jabbed his rifle at the guard. 'You, drop your guns. Techs, stay at your consoles.'

Fatigue or despair turned the guard's features gray. Sweat gleamed on his upper lip. Apparently he lacked the courage – or the desperation – for suicide. His IR aura twisted with defeat as he dropped his rifle; tossed his handgun aside.

Warden heard the doors bang shut. He wheeled toward them, swept his rifle into line; but saw nobody.

One of the techs had fled.

Damn! He jerked back to cover the guard again.

The man hadn't moved. The other techs remained at their stations.

Warden took a deep breath, held it to steady his heart. When he let it out, he told the guard, 'You can go. If you think this is a good time for HS to attack me, you're stupider than you look. We're going to begin arranging evacuation procedures, get people off this platform as fast as we can. If you interfere – if HS starts a firefight that cripples this room – you'll all die here, and you won't have anyone to blame but yourselves.

'Do you understand me?'

'I understand, Director,' the guard sighed.

Warden read his aura clearly; saw his resignation. The man wanted to live. He would leave Warden and Center alone.

As soon as the guard left, Warden turned to the techs.

All four of them were on their feet. A show of respect? He doubted it. They radiated too much fright. More likely they wanted to run –

Their boards stood in a row partway across the room: the guard had probably ordered them to work side by side so that he could watch them comfortably. Warden moved toward them, letting the muzzle of his rifle drop to diminish the threat he projected. He hated the sight of their fear. He'd become a cop because he wanted to reduce the perils of being human, not because he liked scaring relatively innocent men and women half to death. But he had no reassurance to give the techs unless they agreed to help him.

One of them took him completely by surprise.

A young man stepped past the others toward Warden. He was a kid, really; couldn't have been more than twenty. He had blond hair so pale it was nearly invisible: patches of sweat on his scalp showed through it like stains. His eyes gaped as if he'd gone blind with alarm.

The id patch on his worksuit identified him as 'Servil.'

From one of his pockets he produced a projectile gun and aimed it at Warden's chest.

'I'm sorry, Director.' His voice shook, but his hand didn't waver. 'I can't let you interrupt us. We have work to finish.'

Warden froze. He'd completely misread the nature of the young man's fright. The other techs may have needed a guard to keep them at their posts: this kid didn't. He was still young enough to believe in Holt – as young as Warden had been when he'd first fallen under the Dragon's spell.

He could have taken Servil easily. As soon as the kid brought out his handgun, the other techs scattered; ducked away among the stations; hurried crouching along the rows toward the doors. That distracted him. He took his aim off Warden, instinctively looking for a way to make the other techs return. Warden could have snatched the gun from him without effort.

But Warden Dios didn't move. Didn't raise his rifle to protect himself. He *needed* this kid. And he understood instantly that coercion wouldn't work. It wouldn't have worked on him when he was that age. If he wanted help, he would have to persuade Servil out from under Holt's influence.

When he saw that he couldn't stop the other techs, Servil pulled his gun back into line on Warden's chest. He clutched it with both hands to hold it steady. Distress flared in his eyes – more distress than his nerves could handle.

Warden let his rifle clatter to the deck, then held up his hands to show the tech they were empty. As soon as his IR prosthesis told him that a bit of the kid's tension had eased, he asked quietly, 'Is Holt's download that important to you?'

Servil flinched. His aura said clearly that he hadn't expected Warden to know what he and the others had been doing.

'Don't you know what it's for?' Warden pursued.

The tech tightened his grip on the gun. 'I don't need to know.' The tremor had settled into his voice: he couldn't get rid of it. 'The CEO ordered us to handle it. That's enough.'

Warden shifted his arms so that the other rifles fell from his shoulders. 'We're not going to fight about this.' With the tips of his fingers he pulled the handguns from his belt and dropped them. 'You can go back to work if you want. I won't raise a hand to stop you.' Deliberately he spoke as if he were in command. The only weapon he allowed himself was his authority; his ability to convey conviction. 'But I'm going to tell you what that download's for. And I'm going to tell you what I want you to do instead.

'If you want to shut me up, you'll have to shoot me.'

Servil frowned his confusion. 'I don't trust you.'

Warden grinned humorlessly. 'You don't have to trust me. I'll sit here.' He took a seat in front of the nearest active console. Its readouts showed the status of the download. 'You can keep your distance.' He indicated a board three stations away. 'You'll be able to pick up your gun and kill me faster than I can get to you.'

Without hesitation he started to type as fast as he could.

Center had already processed an enormous amount of data. The download had only fifteen minutes left to run. Then Holt could leave with his treasure intact.

That was nowhere near enough time. Already Warden was being forced to choose between his desire to see Holt dead and his determination to save as many lives as he could.

Forced to trust Angus absolutely –

He didn't try to disrupt the datastream. If he did that, if he warned Holt in any way, the Dragon might rush launching *Motherlode*. Instead he keyed his board to other functions – which might slow the download slightly – and began sifting through codes and clearances to reach the platform's status-and-resource records.

'What're you doing?' the tech demanded anxiously.

'Just what I said I would do,' Warden retorted. 'Arrange evacuation procedures. Figure out how to save all these people. *Your* job.'

'Save them from what? We're damaged, sure. But the platform is stable.'

The director snorted. 'Don't bet on it.'

HO's megaCPUs could multitask on several different levels, carry out quite a few vast – and exclusive – tasks simultaneously. When he found the records he wanted, he separated his readouts. On one of them he searched the docks and berths and holds for any conceivable means to offload large numbers of people.

Servil leaned forward, gripping his gun. 'What do you mean?'

On another screen Warden organized what was left of station communications. With a little ingenuity he managed to orient a hub dish toward UMCPHQ. From a third readout he called up damage control to identify every viable power cell and generator, every energy source, that remained active.

Finally he recalled a display of Holt's download so that he could keep track of it. So that he would know when Holt was about to leave.

'I mean,' he answered Servil, 'as soon as we get as many people as we can away from this hunk of metal I'm going to blow it apart.'

'Stop!' the young man yelped at once. '*Stop* it.' He jumped out of his seat; aimed his gun at the side of Warden's head. 'Take your hands off that board.'

Warden ignored the order.

'Director, I can't let you do this!'

He ignored that as well.

'Listen to me,' he growled through his concentration. 'Holt didn't tell you what this download is for because he was afraid you might be horrified. If you refused, he would be in trouble. He needed at least one tech he could trust. But I'm willing to risk a little horror.

'You know *what* he's downloading. He must have given you a data req.' Even unquestioning assistance required instructions. 'He's copying everything that gives him power. Secrets and deals. Contracts and blackmail. Personal and personnel records, illicit orders, payment logs, corporate protocols. Evidence of every crime he's ever committed. Everything that lets him dictate policy to the GCES.'

Warden's prosthesis read Servil's dismay. The young tech was dangerously close to pressing the firing stud.

'My God, boy,' Warden said like a groan, 'you didn't think he got this far by force of personality, did you? *Nobody* is as pure as he claims to be. And you have to be suspicious of anyone who gets rich off the Amnion. I know for a fact that Holt Fasner cheated, stole, killed and manipulated his way here.

'I *should* know,' he added bitterly. 'I helped him do a lot of it.'

Uncertainty eased the pressure of Servil's fingers. Apparently he didn't know what to make of Warden's frankness. Like most of Earth's people, he'd probably been raised on the idea that the UMCP was honest – and necessary. Holt had projected that illusion at every opportunity. And Warden had done as much as he could to give the conceit substance.

'Why does he need all this information now?' he asked grimly. 'Have you considered that question? He's finished, isn't he? He tried to destroy the *Council*, for God's sake. What good are his records now?'

In a small voice the tech admitted, 'I don't know.'

'Well, I do,' Warden snapped. 'He can *sell* them.

'The power is still there. He can sell it to illegals. Give them a chance to own their own Council Members – even their own stations. He can buy their help for whatever he wants.'

He paused, then stated flatly, 'Or he can sell it to the Amnion.'

Servil flinched. 'Why would he –?'.

'Because,' Warden explained like a splash of acid, 'they'll pay more for it than anyone else can. He's a hundred and fifty years old. He should have died decades ago. They have the ability to give him a new body whenever he needs one. They can imprint his mind from one body to the next without damaging it. They can keep him alive and in his prime – practically forever.

'Hell, he might end up *owning* human space. He can offer the Amnion a deal so rich they'll give him anything.'

With his enhanced sight he saw the threat of Servil's gun withdraw. Turmoil seethed, crimson and violet, through the tech's aura, but it was the wrong kind of tension for an attack. He retreated to a seat as if his legs weren't strong enough to hold up his consternation.

Apparently he couldn't find a fault in Warden's reasoning. Despite his naive loyalty, he was starting to see the truth.

Warden quashed a sigh of relief; ran commands on his board as quickly as he could. If he could have spared the attention, he would have used another readout to monitor Norna Fasner's sickchamber, hoping to mark Angus' progress. But that was beyond him: he'd already stretched his concentration to its limits.

The download would be done in ten minutes. UMCPHQ signaled constantly, calling for a response. HO's small supply of ejection pods was trivial compared with the computer's estimate of survivors. If he meant to save more than a fraction of them, he needed some other approach.

After a moment Servil asked in a shaking voice, 'If that's all true – if you believe it – why aren't you trying to stop him?'

'I *am* trying to stop him,' Warden muttered. 'I'm just not doing it in person. He's abandoned all these people. *Somebody* has to rescue them.'

He wished like hell that he knew where Angus was.

'They won't need rescuing,' the tech countered unsteadily, 'if you don't blow up the station.'

Warden bit the inside of his cheek to keep himself from shouting. 'And what happens if I don't? *Think* about it. Use your brain. I don't blow the station. His data remains intact. Who do *you* trust with it? It's the most destructive body of information in human space.' He would have been willing to take a chance on Min – but even for her the burden might be too much. 'Who do you trust to have that much power and not use it?

'Not the GCES, that's for damn sure. Some of the Members are honest – and some aren't. And I wouldn't want to make my people live with that much temptation. Even the best of them might not be able to resist.'

He hit keys to refine his search for some means to evacuate the platform. While sub-routines flashed down his readout he told Servil, 'There's only one way to defuse those secrets. Make them public. Every bit of that data. Destroy ten or twenty thousand lives and reputations. Cripple a few corporations, a few stations.' Unleash the damage before anyone could manipulate it. Make all Holt's supporters and victims pay for their mistakes simultaneously. 'But we can't do that. Even if we use every dish we've got,' every dish Min's onslaught hadn't shattered or crippled, 'it would take weeks to downlink that much information.'

Holt could copy it all so much faster because *Motherlode* was plugged directly into the HO network.

Abruptly a damage control alert flashed on his console. He checked it automatically.

A small screen told him that every system in Norna Fasner's med-sector had gone dead. Even the dedicated uplink which still fed her video channels: everything. Some kind of fire or explosion had devastated the medical crypt where Holt had kept his mother entombed for almost ninety years.

Angus had gotten that far; done that part of his job.

Good.

But he didn't have much time left. Once the download

was complete, Holt could sever his links with the platform; set his berth's palt to fling *Motherlode* outward when the rotation of the torus gave him an attractive window on open space. He would be gone in a matter of minutes.

Frustration and urgency accumulated in Warden's chest like a nuclear pile approaching critical mass. He'd placed too many demands on himself; made too many promises. Damn, he needed *help* –

'Unless we delete it,' he croaked suddenly.

Erase Holt's data instead of blowing up the station. That would serve the purpose. Unfortunately it would also leave Warden alive. He would have to convince someone to kill him before his supply of Vestabule's drug ran out: he did *not* want to turn Amnion at the end of his life. But everyone else on station might survive –

He wheeled his seat to face the tech. 'Do you know how to do that? Do you have the codes?'

'No,' Servil admitted as if the idea shocked him.

Warden swore under his breath. 'I don't either.' He thought quickly, then asked, 'Can we stop him from launching his yacht? Will these systems do that? Can we get our hands on him and make him tell us the codes?'

'No,' the tech said again. A penumbra of dumb misery swirled around him. 'The overrides have been set. He has complete control.'

Shit! Warden ground his teeth. As he turned back to his board, he demanded, 'Then what choice do you think I have?'

Servil slumped in front of a console. His aura modulated through a series of emotions. Warden caught suggestions of pain, defeat, weariness, resignation. Softly the young tech asked, 'What do you want me to do?'

A kick of hope caught Warden's heart. In a rush he began, 'Help me –'

To his chagrin, his voice shook like Servil's. He was under more pressure than he'd realized: he'd kept himself too busy to realize it. Relief and desperation he couldn't contain nearly made him groan. He swallowed hard and tried again.

'Help me save some lives.'

Once he'd made his decision, Servil didn't hesitate. He raised his hands to his board, held them ready.

'How?'

Warden's human eye burned, dangerously close to blurring. He blinked it clear; scanned his readout of the station's resources. After a moment he found what he wanted.

'There.' Swiftly he copied one of his displays to Servil's console. 'Cargo 11.' A hold out at the rim of the torus: a bay so big *Punisher* could have docked in it. 'Those ore cans.' The computer reported five of them. 'They're empty. If you do it right, you can use them.'

Before it became UMCHO, the core of this station had been the home of Space Mines, Inc. Holt's vast empire had begun as a small ore smelting operation, orbiting Earth to take advantage of the asteroid belt. Since then HO had grown tremendously; but the platform still performed some of SMI's functions. Smelting was no longer done, but a certain amount of ore transshipment took place.

Ore cans were huge cylinders, too large for most ships to carry; designed to be towed rather than transported. And they were airtight, sealed against vacuum to protect their contents, not during shipment, but at their transshipment points and destinations. Some of the metals, isotopes and rare earths humankind mined could only be processed if they hadn't been exposed to atmosphere.

'You can probably get two hundred and fifty people in each of those things,' Warden explained as Servil went to work. 'With enough air for at least a couple of hours. When they're sealed, you can open the bay, use station rotation to spin them out. If you time it right, you can aim them at UMCPHQ.

'I'll tell UMCPHQ Center what's going on. Their tugs should be able to tow those cans in before the air runs out.

'That should take care of almost everyone,' he finished. 'When they're on their way, you and whoever else is left can use the last ejection pods.'

'What about you?' Servil asked in a small voice.

'Somebody has to stay here,' Warden answered harshly, 'and make sure nothing goes wrong. That's my job.'

With an effort of self-control, he didn't add, Unless you want to watch me turn Amnion.

Servil nodded. 'I suppose you're right.' He rubbed the heels of his hands into his eyes as if he wanted to force the uncertainty out of them. Then he started typing.

His fingers gathered speed and assurance as he ran commands to route power and air for the hold, confirm that the ore cans were empty, prepare the bay doors. He called up a platform rotation schematic; calculated the hold's window on UMCPHQ; then activated an intercom so that he could issue orders to the whole station in Holt Fasner's name.

Despite his relative youth, he obviously knew his job.

Warden allowed himself a moment of profound relief – a brief pause of appreciation for Servil's aid. That was all the time he could afford. Almost at once he threw his hands at his board; tackled the problem of making UMCHO destroy itself.

In order to wrest an explosion from the power cells and generators, he would have to route a feedback loop which would drive them past their tolerances. That should have been impossible. Stations were too vulnerable: therefore they had safeguards. Under normal circumstances, the cells and generators were well protected from any destructive tampering.

But Min's guns had damaged a number of the systems. Some of the safeguards had failed: others weren't stable. And Red Priority security locks gave him access to codes which in turn released controls he wouldn't ordinarily have been able to touch.

In addition he'd recently spent a number of hours studying every available detail of HO's design and construction; preparing himself in case this day ever came. He probably knew a great deal more about how the platform worked than the young tech did.

He could do it; cause a blast to gut the station. The explosion wouldn't be as powerful as he wanted: not powerful enough to catch and crush *Motherlode* with its wavefront once the gap yacht was launched and away. But at least he could do it without endangering any of Min's ships.

If he worked fast enough: if he didn't make any mistakes. If he blew the platform before UMCPHQ or any other station sent out craft to answer HO's distress flares.

His hands flew on the keys as if he'd spent his life studying self-destruct sequences.

Where was Angus? Could he reach the yacht? Get aboard? Or would he be caught on station? Warden had no idea. He wished now that he'd arranged a signal of some kind; a means for Angus to communicate success or failure. But he hadn't thought of it.

How many other crucial details had he neglected? He couldn't afford to worry about that. Couldn't afford to let his visceral desire to see Holt die distract him. He'd reached the end of his life. Circuits and relays sprang to life under his hands, filling HO strand by strand with a web of ruin. Holt's download would end soon. The time had come to trust other people with humankind's future. Min and Angus, Morn and Koina, Hashi: they would have to pick up any pieces he might have dropped.

Servil would need at least half an hour to arrange his evacuation – if HS helped him organize the survivors; if HS believed his orders came from Holt. Otherwise the process might take much longer.

Warden had to communicate with UMCPHQ. He couldn't put it off anymore. And he'd promised Angus – But he couldn't bear the prospect of actually speaking to Center; hearing those familiar voices remind him of the life he'd compromised and abandoned. And his heart might break if any of the people he trusted and loved tried to talk to him. He preferred to face the culmination of his old shame alone.

Instead of risking voice transmission, he wrote out a message, warning Center that HO was about to die. He urged men and women he'd once commanded to keep ships away from the station; out of danger. He asked his former officers and friends to rescue Servil's ore cans as soon as they cleared the wavefront.

Finally he added a series of quick personal messages – one for Min and another for Hashi; one for Morn. He gave each of them the best farewell he could. Then he set HO's dish to broadcast his transmission automatically, repeat it as long as possible.

When his console informed him that *Motherlode* had been launched on an escape vector which kept her safe from attack or pursuit, he cursed her blip as if he believed in the power of words to wreak transcendent harm. But his anger at Holt had become curiously abstract. It no longer drove him. For good or ill, he'd left the Dragon to Angus. Now he found that he was content to have done so. None of the people he'd trusted had failed him so far. Even Servil hadn't failed him. And he'd come to the end of himself. He'd completed his web of circuits and relays, of complicity and subterfuge: there was nothing left for which he could take responsibility – except his own tainted soul. An unfamiliar peace eased through him as he watched the gap yacht recede in the direction of her fate.

As soon as Servil sent the cans on their way, Warden gave him ten minutes to reach an ejection pod. But he actually waited longer than that; until he was sure the tech had escaped.

Then, however, he didn't hesitate. He'd told Angus that he'd passed sentence on himself a long time ago. Now he carried it out.

With a few keystrokes, the discredited director of the United Mining Companies Police closed his final relays and tore the foundation of Holt Fasner's malign empire to shreds.

HOLT

Finally humankind's last and greatest visionary was safe. He'd made mistakes: he acknowledged that freely to himself, although he might not have admitted it to anyone else. One was that he'd trusted Ward too long; let the man go too far. Another was that he'd attacked Suka Bator without first gaining control over the Donner bitch and her cordon. And mistakes were always dangerous. They were often fatal. He should have fired Ward as soon as his mother had named his own fears by warning him that the UMCP director would get him into trouble. Failing that, he should have made sure *Calm Horizons* would extirpate the votes for him, instead of risking the attempt himself.

He still didn't understand why *Calm Horizons* hadn't blasted Suka Bator when the shooting started. Apparently Ward's treachery ran deeper than he'd imagined. Or Donner and Morn Hyland had conceived some ruse to trick the Amnioni –

Nevertheless Holt told himself that he had no regrets. In spite of his mistakes, he was safe. A visionary's advance planning – and a visionary contempt for lesser beings – had saved him. He and all his essential data were safely aboard *Motherlode*. And *Motherlode* had already put a couple hundred thousand k between her and HO, accelerating gently toward the gap and deep space on a trajectory which protected her from Donner's ships.

In addition, of course, *Motherlode* was more than just a

luxury gap yacht, furnished, appointed and supplied to transport him in a monarch's opulent comfort. She had the guns of a cruiser; the drive-power and range of a battlewagon; the shields, sinks, and defenses of a space-fortress. Personally he had no particular taste for luxury. When he'd commissioned *Motherlode*, he'd lavished so much wealth on her accommodations because he meant to daunt and manipulate his occasional guests, not because he himself liked ostentation. On the other hand, he valued his own survival highly. If Donner's ships had attacked him at this range, his shields would have shrugged their fire aside like so much solar wind. And if he chose to run not one of them could have kept pace with him.

There was nothing to stand in his way. He was *safe* – as safe as riches and forethought could make him. Protected from death by every resource of human ingenuity: entirely beyond harm. When *Motherlode* finally began to skim the light-years toward forbidden space, he would be close to immortality.

She didn't go into tach, however. Not yet. For some reason, he was reluctant to give the order. Instead of hurrying his escape toward the visionary triumph of force-grown bodies and imprinted minds, he watched *Motherlode*'s screens and waited for something to happen.

He was on the bridge; at the command station. His entire crew – three men – sat at their boards in front of him, facing the same screens. His yacht could have used a crew of ten, but she only needed that many when she carried passengers – and the passengers happened to be demanding. The ship herself required no more than three. In fact, any one of her officers could have handled her alone. Holt could have run her by himself. But he was intimately familiar with the weaknesses of his old body. He'd brought crew with him for the same reason that he didn't risk hard acceleration: he distrusted the condition of his heart. He'd felt his pulse fluttering ever since Donner opened fire on him. A new tightness in his chest refused to go away, despite the drugs which had kept him alive for so long.

721

Because he feared the strain of running *Motherlode* alone, he needed crew. The three of them could take turns; rest enough to stay alert.

Yet he didn't trust ordinary men any more than he trusted his own mortality. They might have questioned him. Might have made the mistake of thinking their lives were more important than his. These three were special.

They all had zone implants. Their zone implant controls were also implanted. And the controls were voice-activated; keyed specifically to *his* voice. With a word he could fill them with enough pleasure to drive them mad; enough pain to kill them. They would do anything for him.

For that reason, he didn't trouble with code-locks for the bridge consoles. His crew would obey him absolutely – and kill anyone who tried to give him trouble.

He was completely and utterly *safe*.

Nevertheless he withheld the order for tach. Despite the fluttering and pressure in his chest – warning signs that he should try to reach forbidden space quickly – he kept *Motherlode* within reach of Earth's scan net. Instead of fleeing, he used the net to watch what happened to UMCHO.

Something would happen: he was sure of that. He just hoped he would be able to recognize it; grasp what it meant.

As soon as Donner had restored the scan net after *Calm Horizons'* astonishing death, Holt had seen *Trumpet* approach HO. *Punisher's* command module had headed for UMCPHQ, but the gap scout had braved Holt's station. Well before *Motherlode's* launch, *Trumpet* had docked in the hub.

Now *that* was an unexpected development. Beyond question something was about to happen.

Who was aboard the gap scout? What did they want? What did they think they could accomplish?

For a while he'd received no hint of an answer. Certainly nothing had interfered with *Motherlode's* launch, or her gradual acceleration. Nothing had threatened him. But then in surprise he'd watched the platform loft a series of ore cans toward UMCPHQ. And he'd seen UMCPHQ send out tugs to receive the cans.

The answer was there, if he could figure it out.

Casually he asked his crew, 'Any idea what's going on?'

The man at the scan station also handled communications. 'Yes, sir,' he replied without hesitation – or interest. 'They aren't keeping it secret. It's on all the in-system relays. Those cans are full of people. They're evacuating HO.'

Evacuating, hell, Holt snorted to himself. That wasn't just evacuation. It was desperation. Nobody who wasn't desperate would leave a stable station in a goddamn ore can.

What were they afraid of?

Apparently they believed the platform wouldn't remain stable much longer. Either Donner's bombardment had done more damage than Holt had realized, or –

Holt's eyes widened in surprise.

– or this was another of Ward's by God oblique, malicious gambles. The final ploy in his vast, impenetrable charade of service to the UMC and humankind.

Holt found the possibility so amazing that he believed it instantly.

Suppose the command module had taken Ward off *Calm Horizons* before the defensive died. What did he have to live for? Why had he bothered to arrange his own survival?

His attack on his rightful master before the Council had destroyed his reputation, his career. He'd given his charges weight by confessing his complicity. By now the votes must be convulsed with self-righteousness. They would almost certainly have him executed. So why had he done it? What was this whole elaborate exercise *for*?

Ah, but what if it had all been for *this*: to give Ward access to HO? He could probably handle HS. If nothing else, he could say Donner was about to gut the station. He could organize a desperate evacuation – and virtuously offer to remain behind, pretending he cared that everyone else got away safely.

Then he would be free to take Holt's data. *For himself*. And with that lever he could defy them all – the UMCP, the GCES, the other stations; the whole planet. He would have the power, the evidence, to topple corporations, platforms, governments.

If he used it carefully, he could make the votes pardon him.

And after that there would be virtually no limit to what he might acquire –

The mere idea almost stopped Holt's heart. He blinked astonishment at the screens, whistling thinly through his teeth. By God, he'd made *another* mistake. He should have deleted his data as he copied it. His mother had warned him and *warned* him – and yet he'd left all that power intact for his worst enemy.

If he'd listened to her, he wouldn't have lost his empire. Or his station. Instead of being forced to flee alone, he would have been able to take his species with him on his visionary journey toward the only future which would allow it to endure.

For a moment his bitterness and regret were so acute that he could barely contain them. Outrage accumulated in his veins. His heart limped from beat to beat, staggering when it should have throbbed safely. Ward's victory was intolerable. Holt should have strung him up by his *balls* at the first hint –

Fortunately one of the crew broke into his thoughts. 'Sir,' the man at the targ station announced quietly, 'I'm getting a malfunction alert.'

At once Holt snatched himself back from his mounting fury. Grateful for the distraction, he asked, 'What is it?' His frailty had reached frightening proportions. He was in no condition for so much anger: he *had* to take better care of himself.

'Routine diagnostics, sir.' The targ officer wasn't worried. 'We aren't in a hurry, so I took the time to run a few checks. One of the airlock servos doesn't respond. The lock is sealed. There's no danger. But that servo ought to read green, and it doesn't. May be a faulty circuit. It's probably been that way since the last diagnostic.'

Since before *Motherlode* had left HO.

Holt nodded. Caution of all kinds was a standing order

724

aboard the yacht. Whatever else happened, he meant to survive.

'Can you fix it?'

The man inclined his head. 'Whenever you like, sir. But I'll have to go down to the airlock.'

'Do it later,' Holt ordered. 'I want you here.' Just in case Ward had more surprises for him.

Whatever happened would probably happen soon. The ore cans were on their way to safety. There would be plenty of time for minor repairs after *Motherlode*'s first gap crossing.

As his distress receded, however, and his pulse recovered a more familiar rhythm, he found he couldn't stop thinking about Norna. The truth was that he'd been thinking about her all along: he just hadn't wanted to recognize it.

He missed her. He'd kept her alive so long – and had profited so much from her hostile insight – that he felt bound to her in ways he couldn't describe. He liked her, despite her grim hunger for his ruin. Over the decades her malice had helped him stay alert; helped him thrive. Without her –

Without her he made mistakes. And mistakes might kill him.

He couldn't have brought her with him. That was out of the question. But now he began to wonder how he would live without her.

'Sir!' the scan officer called sharply.

Holt jerked his attention to the screens in time to see an explosion tear through HO.

In a rush of brisance the whole steel skeleton of the platform crumpled like hardcopy. All the generators and power-cells must have blown simultaneously. Soundless across the kilometers, HO's death seethed on the screens, as poignant and immedicable as a rupturing heart. Incandescence and fire shone briefly through the shattered ribs of the infrastructure, then were sucked back into darkness. Within seconds empty space had swallowed the debris and corpses, leaving only a few charred steel bones to mark the station's place in the affairs of humanity.

Norna was dead.

But so was Ward. The man's ambitions had failed in the end, sabotaged by the platform's vulnerability. Some resourceful HS guard had set that explosion. Or Ward had triggered it himself by accessing the station's computers clumsily. Holt didn't care which. He cared only that Ward had at last suffered the ruin he'd tried so hard to bring down on Holt's head.

And Norna's wish for her son's destruction had also failed.

Her death was a small price to pay.

In addition, Holt's now-exclusive data had just experienced an exponential increase in value.

He released a long sigh of satisfaction. 'Well, that takes care of the high-and-mighty Warden goddamn Dios,' he drawled to the bridge. 'The sonofabitch finally got what he deserves. I wish I could have seen his face when he realized HO was about to explode. All that plotting to get his hands on my data, and suddenly he finds he's going to die for it. I'll bet he shat *blood* when he –'

Without warning a hand closed in Holt's thin hair, wrenched his head against the back of his g-seat. 'I'll bet he didn't,' a voice he'd never heard before snarled cheerfully. 'I'll bet he did it himself. I'll bet he was just so *sick* of you he couldn't bear to let anything you've ever touched survive.'

The crew swung their stations, gaped in shock past Holt at the intruder.

'He kept his promises,' the man went on. 'All of them. That's supposed to be a good thing, but it's really the shits. It makes a bastard like me feel like he has to do the same.'

The pressure on Holt's scalp threatened to choke him; break his neck. He couldn't speak.

Without orders his men didn't move.

'Vestabule cursed me. Can you believe it?' The stranger spoke in a cruel drawl. 'He threatened to eliminate my DNA from the galaxy. I guess he didn't think I would end up with a ship like this, just *full* of interesting secrets. But a mistake is a mistake. Since I can't make any more deals with forbidden space, there's really no reason why I shouldn't do what Dios wants.'

Terror labored in Holt's old chest. Frantically he twisted against his g-seat to ease the strain on his throat. Nearly strangling, he croaked out the word that sent his men into combat mode.

They reacted instantly, obedient to his compulsion. As one they slapped at their belts, jumped to their feet, reached for their guns – and died. The intruder let go of Holt's head. One thin ruby beam burned a hole into the targ officer's forehead, then slashed across the throat of the man on scan, spilling a scorched spray of blood. A second laser devoured most of the helm officer's face.

'Nice trick,' the harsh voice remarked. 'Most men can't move in unison like that. Did you use voice-command zone implants on them? Oh, dear. I'm afraid that's against the law.'

A heavy hand turned Holt's station.

When he saw Angus Thermopyle's face, recognized it from newsdog broadcasts and Ward's files, he started screaming.

MORN

Two days later, when the Governing Council for Earth and Space met formally to consider recent events, Morn Hyland watched the proceedings on a video screen.

President Len had insisted on convening this session in the Council's kaze-damaged meeting hall. He'd announced that he considered the venue symbolically important: he wished the split doors and cracked floor, the concussion-gouged plaster and paint, to serve as tangible reminders of the cost of what had transpired. In other words – according to Min Donner – he meant to rub the Members' noses in the mistake of trusting Holt Fasner and the UMC. So humankind's GCES representatives sat in their assigned places around the large, half-oval table which occupied much of the floor, with their aides, advisers and secretaries ranked behind them in tiers of seats rising to the walls. Morn recognized the scene, although she'd never been to Suka Bator: it was familiar from any number of news broadcasts and UMCP briefings.

Within the oval chairs had been arranged for the Council's guests. Davies and Mikka sat there, accompanied by UMCP Acting Director Min Donner, PR Director Koina Hannish, Captain Dolph Ubikwe, ED Chief of Security Mandich and Hashi Lebwohl. The former DA director currently had no title: he was officially under suspension pending a review of his role in Warden Dios' – and Holt Fasner's – crimes.

Morn wasn't with them because she'd refused to attend.

She'd already told her story; laid bare her shame and pain in front of these same people. And she felt weighed down by loss. Ciro's death, and Vector's, and Warden's, seemed to lie on her heart like slabs of lead. The memory of Sib Mackern's abandoned end ached like a bruise. For a time even Angus' disappearance had troubled her in ways she couldn't name. She was afraid she might start to weep under the eyes of the Council – and once she began crying she wouldn't be able to stop.

That crisis would come. It had to. But when it did, she meant to confront it in her own way; at her own time.

Somewhere Mikka Vasaczk had found the strength to face the assembled authority of humankind, despite her injuries. And Min Donner could do the same, even though she'd lost the man she served. But neither of them had accepted the control to a zone implant from a killer and rapist – or believed they couldn't survive without it. Morn Hyland was no longer willing to endure the anguish of answering questions, or standing up under scrutiny.

Fortunately Min had accepted her decision; supported it. The acting director had assigned her a suite of rooms in UMCPHQ, given her codes to lock her doors against anyone. The suite was supplied with video screens and data terminals, if she wished to use them. She even had her own foodvend. And the entire station had standing orders to leave her alone; let her come and go as she pleased.

As much as possible, she was allowed to make her own peace with what had happened.

She didn't think that she would ever be at peace again. Nevertheless she was deeply grateful for Min's consideration. Real privacy comforted her even when it failed to relieve her pain. She didn't keep to herself all the time, however. During the two days since *Calm Horizons'* death and UMCHO's destruction, she'd spent hours with Davies and Mikka, talking about what they'd done – and how they bore it. And she'd given Min as much time as Min asked for; done her best to explain and describe everything so that Min would understand the whole story.

But she found no solace in words, no matter how much she cared about the people who said them. Mikka's courage and Davies' desire to help did nothing for her. Messages of congratulations, thanks and praise from the GCES and Koina Hannish, Earth's planetary governments, other stations, even corporations once owned by the UMC: all arrived at her data terminal stillborn. She felt no triumph over what she and *Trumpet*'s people had accomplished; no vindication. The way Warden Dios had used her and the others – the way he'd trusted them – neither incensed nor gratified her. Apparently only solitude could reach her where she grieved. She clung to the loneliness of her quarters, unwilling to venture forth until she was ready.

During those two days, only one small bit of news lifted the edge of her sorrow. UMCPHQ had received a flare from *Motherlode*, tight-beamed moments before the gap yacht had disappeared into tach. Min had shared it with Morn as soon as it came in.

Dios told me to stop Fasner, Angus had sent. *So I did. But I'm going to keep his ship. I like it.*

Tell Morn that Fasner was easy. Dios did the hard part.

And tell her I told him to say good-bye.

For reasons she didn't question, Morn was pleased that Angus hadn't died on HO.

Min allowed her a moment to absorb the message. Then the acting director remarked, 'You know what this means. Angus has Holt's data.'

According to one of HO's surviving techs, a man named Servil, the Dragon had downloaded all his essential files to *Motherlode* before leaving the station.

Quietly Morn asked, 'Does that worry you?'

Min chuckled without much humor. 'Not really. We have codes to fry his brain. He knows that. I don't think he'll want to call attention to himself by using that data.

'And Hashi assures me he still can't come here. He's been freed in other ways, but his datacore won't let him do that. Which limits the amount of damage he can do.'

Then she added, 'On the other hand, those secrets give

730

him a lever. We don't want to risk provoking him. If he thinks he's being hassled, he might decide to strike back. It's a standoff of sorts. We'll all be happier if we leave each other alone.'

Morn was glad that he was alive. She was even glad that he had the means to defend his freedom. And she was profoundly glad that he was gone. At last she could let go of the sore, conflicted part of herself which cared what happened to him.

For the rest of the time before she began to watch this session of the Council, only being alone helped her; protected her. The lock on her door was all that held back the consequences of her ordeal while she tried to gather her courage.

Shortly after *Punisher* had reached UMCPHQ, Min had informed Morn that Warden Dios had sent her a message before he died. He'd sent one to Min as well – and to Hashi Lebwohl. Morn's was available on her terminal whenever she wanted to look at it. But she hadn't read it. For two days she'd told herself that nothing Warden could say to her would make a difference now. In fact, however, she needed to isolate herself from him as much as from the GCES and most of UMCPHQ. She feared his message would break down the fragile barrier which prevented her from collapsing into her grief.

After a certain number of formalities, President Len began the session by describing briefly the aftermath of *Calm Horizons*' incursion. The entire intricate complex of the UMC was in disarray, he explained, with staggering implications for the financial structure of human society; but few lives had been lost. Most of the deaths were the result of Acting Director Donner's necessary strike against UMCHO – and of Warden Dios' more ambiguous destruction of the platform. Financial structures could and would be repaired. Considering all the dangers that had been averted – by actions of almost unimaginable valor and resourcefulness – the planet should deem itself enormously fortunate.

Other issues were more disturbing. Len was sure that *Calm Horizons* must have communicated with forbidden space

731

before approaching Earth. Therefore the Amnion possessed the Shaheed formula. And therefore it was only a matter of time before the formula was rendered ineffective.

For that, at least, Morn had forgiven herself. Long before Vector had begun to broadcast his formula, the Amnion had obtained it from her blood. She'd placed her entire species in danger for the sake of her own survival. But she'd preserved her humanity. Her only alternative had been surrender: a kind of self-destruct. She'd come to believe that the need for *a better answer* was more important than keeping Nick's anti-mutagen secret.

Some of the Members, President Len now proclaimed, would argue that humankind should attack the Amnion immediately, while the Shaheed formula remained viable. A decision would be made in a few days. But he warned that he would strenuously oppose any hostile response. In his view, an assault on forbidden space would be desperately shortsighted: too unsure of success; too expensive to carry out. War was the worst possible solution to interstellar conflict, and he meant to stand in its way as long as he held office.

Apparently he, too, felt the need for a better answer.

When he'd finished stating his position, he asked for preliminary reports from Acting Director Donner and Chief of Security Mandich. Stiffly Min discussed the disposition of Earth's forces and the defense of human space in case the Amnion attempted a preemptive strike of their own. She also described the charges against the Home Security guards who had escaped UMCHO. Mandich talked about how the UMCP meant to handle the rest of HO's survivors. He detailed the failure of security which had allowed Holt Fasner to send out kazes with legitimate id and credentials, and suggested procedural changes to protect against similar problems in the future.

With those issues out of the way, the Council turned its attention to the events which had brought *Calm Horizons* to Earth – and to the people who had saved the planet from both the Amnion and Holt Fasner.

In a tone that brooked no objection, Min explained Morn's absence. Then President Len asked Davies to address the Members.

He was the logical choice to speak for *Trumpet*'s people. He had all of Morn's memories up to the moment of his birth. And after that he'd participated in most of what she and Angus and *Trumpet* had done. But he was also the logical choice in another, more personal sense.

During the past two days, Morn had seen that he was changed. His confrontation with the Amnion and his own fear in order to rescue Warden Dios had transformed him in some way. She had the impression that he'd inherited a part of Angus she didn't understand and couldn't measure. He'd faced an even more global version of the fear she'd felt when Nick had delivered her to the Amnion. He'd committed himself absolutely to the fight for Warden's humanity – and his own. And he'd succeeded. In that way he was directly responsible for Holt Fasner's final defeat; for the destruction of HO, and Angus' presence aboard *Motherlode*.

A fundamental doubt had been burned out of him. Despite Morn's memories, he'd begun to believe in who he was. For that reason he could face the Council with more certainty – and clarity – than she would have been able to muster.

Standing before the assembled Members, he told her story again; but it was also his own story, and *Trumpet*'s. He went into more detail than she had two days ago: he emphasized different aspects; arranged his explanations in a different order. But it was essentially the same story, extended to include her indirect dealings with Marc Vestabule and the rescue of Warden Dios. When he was done, her only regret was that he seemed to confuse shame and courage. He'd made her sound braver than she was.

She may have helped topple the Dragon's empire; but she wasn't yet brave enough to leave her rooms.

The ovation which greeted Davies' tale nearly cost Morn her ·tenuous self-command. Surging to their feet, the Members thundered applause around him until her eyes burned and a thick heat filled her throat. He was her *son*.

The voices which had questioned and challenged her when she'd spoken to the Council were nowhere to be heard. Everyone in the hall clapped and *clapped* as if they had no other language for their gratitude.

Swallowing tears, Morn left the screen; went to the san for a drink of water. She didn't return until the applause had subsided.

Once the Members and their staffs had resumed their seats, President Len asked Mikka if she wanted to add anything.

Mikka shook her head. She didn't rise. 'I'm just a witness,' she answered gruffly. 'I don't have anything to say. I'm only here to make sure you don't believe any lies about Ciro or Vector. Or Sib Mackern. Or Morn Hyland.

'I'll speak up if I hear something that isn't true.'

She may have been an illegal; but she seemed to sit in judgment on the Council itself. Her part in saving the planet – and her bereavement – gave her an unimpeachable authority.

The President cleared his throat uncomfortably. 'Are you satisfied so far?'

Mikka snorted, apparently at the idea that anything here could satisfy her. Instead of answering, she countered, 'What's going to happen to us? Applause is nice. I would rather have something more tangible.'

Min leaned forward, whispered to Mikka. But Mikka didn't stop.

'I'm an illegal. Morn broke the law. Davies would make an interesting research subject. Director Donner helped Warden Dios commit his crimes. And Captain Ubikwe let him go blow up a station, when it was obviously the captain's duty to arrest him.

'There's nothing you can do to Angus. I'm glad of that. But the rest of us have been sitting on our hands for two days, wondering what we'll have to suffer. I would like to know how you propose to treat us.'

Morn smiled wanly at the screen. There were times when she admired Mikka more than she could say. Nick's former command second didn't hesitate to put the Governing Council for Earth and Space to the test.

However, Len's expression and tone made it obvious that he took no offense. 'Mikka Vasaczk,' he responded, 'you've already suffered more than we can imagine. We certainly don't intend to add to your distress by leaving you worried about your fate. But you can appreciate that the issues we face are complex. A number of select committees have been at work virtually around the clock since the crisis ended, studying various aspects of our situation. I won't impose on your patience by asking you to hear what they all have to say. For this session we'll only listen to recommendations from three of them.'

Without delay the President introduced Captain Sixten Vertigus, the United Western Bloc Senior Member.

The old man rose unsteadily to his feet. His hands shook until he braced his arms on the table. But his voice was clear and firm, and his eyes shone as he spoke.

'My committee,' he said directly to Mikka, 'was charged to consider what we've been calling "*Trumpet*'s people" – you and your brother, Davies and Morn Hyland, Dr Shaheed and Sib Mackern. And I have to tell you frankly that we've been given the benefit of Warden Dios' opinion on the subject. His last officially logged order was addressed to Min Donner. It reads: *Full pardons for Mikka Vasaczk, Ciro Vasaczk, Vector Shaheed, Morn Hyland. They can have anything they want. Relocation, treatment, money, jobs, new id* – any-*thing. All they have to do is name it.* Apparently the director didn't mention Davies because there aren't any charges against him.

'But we don't need that kind of guidance. Our gratitude toward you all is greater than any words can suggest. Whatever mistakes you've made, whatever misdeeds you've committed, you've spilled your own blood and risked your own lives for humanity's sake. Cops are expected to do that. Illegals aren't. The less reason you had to do it, the more we prize what you've done. You've humbled us all.

'My committee urges the Council to accept Warden Dios' recommendations.' At once applause erupted again, filling the hall until the video pickup crackled. Captain Vertigus wasn't done, however. Somehow he made himself heard through the ovation. 'But those recommendations aren't enough. You deserve more.'

By the time he sat down, the Members had voted the Emblem of Valor, the planet's highest civilian honor, for Mikka Vasaczk and Davies Hyland; for Ciro Vasaczk, Vector Shaheed and Sib Mackern posthumously; and for Morn Hyland in absentia.

Again Morn blinked at damp fire in her eyes, swallowed against the pressure in her throat. Bit by bit her restraint was being broken down. She feared what would happen when it failed, but there was little she could do to stop the process. Perhaps its time had come. She hardly heard President Len explain that the Emblem of Valor carried a sizable pension – as well as the moral equivalent of diplomatic immunity.

Gently he asked Mikka, 'Does that help?'

With an effort she nodded. 'Yes, it does.' Like Morn, she may have been close to tears.

While Morn struggled to compose herself, Len called on Tel Burnish, the Member for Valdor Industrial. His committee had been assigned to consider the future leadership of the new Space Defense Police, with special attention to questions which had been or might be raised concerning Min Donner's conduct and Hashi Lebwohl's self-confessed dishonesty.

Burnish replied without hesitation. 'We're unanimous, Mr President,' he reported crisply. 'We recommend Min Donner's confirmation as Director of the SDP. We see no reason to challenge either her qualifications or her integrity. Her loyalty to Warden Dios served him well. It will serve us better.'

Min bowed her head. Only the tightening in her shoulders betrayed what she felt.

'Further,' Burnish continued, 'we recommend Captain Dolph Ubikwe's appointment as Enforcement Division Director. His courage and dedication under all sorts of pressure is beyond question. And we respect his decision to let Warden Dios go to UMCHO. We think he should be honored for it.'

Dolph muttered something the pickup missed. A huge grin stretched his dark face.

'Finally,' the VI Member concluded, 'we urge Hashi Lebwohl's reinstatement as Data Acquisition Director. However, we do so primarily at Min Donner's request. She observes that his skills and qualifications are irreplaceable. We've seen evidence of that in his efforts to expose Holt Fasner's kazes. But in addition she's shown us a transmission which she received from Warden Dios immediately before HO's destruction. The director's final message defends Director Lebwohl's complete probity, and takes full personal responsibility for any actions which might cast doubt on DA. Warden Dios – and Min Donner – believe that no man can or will serve SDPDA better than Hashi Lebwohl.'

Some of the Members appeared surprised by this; but no one objected. When President Len asked the Council to respond, all three appointments were accepted by acclamation.

Disguised by his smudged glasses, Hashi's face revealed nothing.

Morn approved dimly. She didn't trust Hashi Lebwohl; but she owed both Min and Dolph a debt she would never be able to repay. Under the pressure of her mounting grief, however, she felt too fragile to let their vindication touch her strongly.

She moved to key off the video screen. The session had become more poignant than she could bear. She wasn't ready to let go of her defenses yet. But she stopped with her fingers on the keypad when she heard President Len announce that Punjat Silat would speak next. He was the Senior Member for the Combined Asian Islands and Peninsulas; and his committee had been formed to pass judgment on Warden Dios.

She didn't want to hear this – yet she was transfixed by it. She'd hardly known Warden Dios the man. But Warden Dios the icon, the symbol and embodiment of the ideals and service of the UMCP, was one of the central figures of her life; perhaps *the* central figure. Her whole family had revolved around his ideas, his beliefs; his power of conviction.

Instead of blanking her screen, she sat down to listen as if she believed that any judgment of Warden Dios would be a judgment of her as well.

The scholarly Senior Member spoke in the slow, dignified tones of a eulogy. Nevertheless his presentation was admirably concise and coherent. For two days, he reported, he and his committee had gathered and studied all the information available on the actions – and intentions – of the former UMCP director. The committee had questioned Min Donner, Hashi Lebwohl and Koina Hannish at length, asking them to place their personal knowledge in the context of both Koina Hannish's and Morn Hyland's testimony before the Council. In addition, the Members had examined the most readily accessible of Warden Dios' private records – a scrutiny which Hashi Lebwohl had made possible by supplying some of the former director's codes.

'Beyond question,' Punjat Silat stated, 'Warden Dios violated his oath of office, as well as his own professed ideals, in profound and fundamental ways. That he did so knowingly, with full awareness of the implications of his actions, is made plain by his personal records. However, his records also indicate that he committed his crimes for the clear, unwavering and single purpose of breaking Holt Fasner's grip on humanity's future.

'This is confirmed – albeit often inferentially – by the most trusted of his subordinates. And it is given circumstantial support by Morn Hyland's remarkable evidence.

'Does that excuse him? Certainly not. His actions tainted the entire structure of humankind's defense against the Amnion. They inspired an act of war. Millions upon millions of lives might have been lost, incalculable damage done. By that measure, his conduct was unconscionable in the extreme.'

For a moment Morn couldn't see the screen through her tears. Now more than ever she missed her zone implant control; wanted to be able to stifle and manage her own reactions.

But Vector had cursed her – or saved her – by breaking it. She had no artificial defense against herself; no induced strength.

Perhaps she didn't need it. Somewhere inside her there had to be a better answer than self-destruct.

'However,' Silat was saying, 'my fellow Members and I found that we could not ignore a question which Warden Dios himself often raised in his private records.

'What else could he have done?

'The path of his duty was sufficiently plain. From the moment when he first recognized Holt Fasner's crimes, he should have worked to expose them. At the least he should have resigned his position. But he should have done more. He should have arrested CEO Fasner and charged him before this Council.'

The Senior Member didn't raise his voice. His dignity and gravity sufficed to fill his words with passion.

'Do any of you believe that he would have succeeded? At that time the GCES – and all humanity – were dependent on the UMC. Holt Fasner owned the UMCP. Both personally and publicly, our lives hung on his decisions. A man willing to send out kazes might have cheerfully murdered Warden Dios and defied the Council to hold him accountable. Or he could have simply threatened enough of us with ruin to block any investigation.

'Warden Dios was unable to endure the prospect of failure.

'Our committee believes that his actions were unconscionable. We also consider them profoundly realistic. Instead of offering a relatively small and premature challenge to the most powerful man in human space, he chose to risk the dangerous path of complicity. By participating in Holt Fasner's crimes, he gained the CEO's vulnerability. And when those crimes at last became large enough, heinous enough, to sway even this dependent Council, he took steps to expose them.

'In this way his own crimes became the weapons with which he put a stop to Holt Fasner's larger wrongs.'

Oh, Warden. Morn groaned aloud without hearing herself.

His name clogged her throat. Became the weapons – In her own, smaller way, she'd used the same argument to justify accepting her black box from Angus.

'Most difficult to forgive,' Punjat Silat admitted, 'is the former director's decision to instigate an act of war. There, however, my fellow Members and I believe that events ran beyond his control. His inclusion of the Amnion in his manipulations is clearly culpable, justified only by a desire to ensure that any challenge to the UMC would not be allowed to weaken the UMCP. However, he could not have known that Morn Hyland would give birth to a son in forbidden space – or that Davies Hyland would be a prize for which the Amnion would hazard an assault on Earth. He could not have known that *Captain's Fancy* would learn Amnion secrets while Morn and Davies Hyland were aboard.

'And he did everything in his power to pay the price of his culpability. He went to *Calm Horizons* alone in a desperate and valiant attempt to negotiate for our survival. Remember this. He absolutely could not have known that he would be rescued, or that *Calm Horizons* would be destroyed, by the very people who had suffered most for his actions.'

Measuring out his words with the heavy tread of a funeral march, Silat concluded, 'Our committee acknowledges the malfeasance of the former UMCP director. We recommend a full and complete pardon. If our mortality permitted us to truly honor the dead, we would drop to our knees at Warden Dios' feet.'

It was too much. No longer sure what she did, Morn stumbled away from the screen. As the session ended, Len spoke of commendations for Koina Hannish and Sixten Vertigus; but she wasn't listening.

A full and complete pardon. For a man who hadn't known her at all – and yet had understood her well enough to abuse her to the core. Understood her so well that he could abandon her to Angus and Nick, and yet believe that she would act on the ideals he'd betrayed. That she would keep those ideals alive for him.

You're a cop, she'd once told Davies. *From now on, I'm*

going to be a cop myself. And she'd kept her promise. *We don't do things like that.*

We don't use people.

In the end Warden had put a stop to it.

Through a blur of tears, she found her way to a seat in front of her terminal. Her hands shook as she tapped keys to access his last message. Hugging herself to contain her distress, she picked his words out of the phosphors on her readout.

Two days ago he'd written:

Warden Dios to Morn Hyland

Morn, I'm sorry I didn't get a chance to talk to you in person. There's so much I want to say, and I have only a few minutes left. This message will suffice because it must.

Most importantly, I want to assure you that it wasn't personal. I didn't pick you for your ordeal because of who you are. I picked you because you were available at the right time – aboard Bright Beauty, *in Angus' power, when I needed you both. I would have used any UMCP officer in your position. Then I simply prayed that you would find it in yourself to meet the challenge I'd placed in front of you.*

And you did. You did everything I could have asked for – if I'd had the right – and far more. First you raised the stakes beyond anything I dared imagine. You went to Enablement, gave Davies birth – and brought Calm Horizons *down on my head. My fault, of course. You're completely blameless. My only point is that my plans went awry there. Events became too great for me to manage them.*

But you managed them for me. As the stakes went up, you grew to meet them. You took a problem that I would have called unequivocally insoluble, and you dealt with it.

Don't sell yourself short about this, Morn. Don't tell yourself that Angus did the real work, or Davies took the real risks, or Min held the real authority. You dealt with it. You kept Davies alive. You freed Angus from his priority-codes when Holt forced me to betray you. You commandeered Punisher and came to Earth in the only way that allowed humankind to survive my mistakes.

I didn't hear it, but I'm sure your testimony before the Council changed everything.

Do you understand what I'm saying? I didn't pick you because of who you are. I'm not wise enough. You picked yourself. Or perhaps I should say that you picked yourself up after I'd hit you hard enough and often enough to pulverize a concrete bunker. You picked yourself up and became more than any man or woman I've ever known.

In the end humanity's future depends more on individuals like you than it does on any organization like the GCES – or the UMCP.

Sobs rose in her chest before she finished reading. Hungry for comfort, she hugged herself the same way her father had held her when he'd told her about her mother's death.

And tell her I told him to say good-bye.

Angus had suggested this?

Straining against her grief, she finished Warden's message.

I don't really know you, Morn. I can't begin to guess how much pain and fear you've borne, or what they cost you. But I knew Davies and Bryony Hyland well. You were raised by two fine UMCP officers. Most of your family served with courage, distinction and honor. And I suspect you've always thought you were unworthy of them.

The tragedy of your gap-sickness must have hurt you terribly. You may have imagined that it demonstrated your unworth. But your parents would have grieved over your illness, not condemned you for it. And I'm sure they would have been desperately proud of you.

As I am.

Morn Hyland, you saved my dreams for what the cops should be.

I hope you'll give yourself a chance to heal. Min will help you as much as she can. So will Koina.

Whatever you do, you have my blessing.

Farewell.

Message ends.

There, her last restraint broke, and a storm of tears swept through her; carried her out of herself into shattering and unanswerable sorrow. Wailing like a child, deserted and bereft, she battered her hands on the board of her data terminal; pounded on her upper arms and thighs. For her this was the reality of being human and mortal, undefended by zone implants: utter pain; the opposite end of the universe from the clarity of gap-sickness. Sobs poured from her so hard that they seemed to tear her throat; seemed to cramp the muscles of her chest like spasms of nausea.

She wept for her parents and family. She wept for what Angus had done to her – and for the cowardice of accepting her zone implant control from him. She wept for the lies she'd used to manipulate Nick Succorso. She wept over the way Davies had been made to suffer by Nick's justified outrage; wept over Angus' welding. She wept for Mikka's grim courage and Min's determination. Finally she wept for the dead: for poor Sib Mackern, frightened and abandoned, whose self-sacrifice had helped protect them in the asteroid swarm; for calm, lonely Vector Shaheed, the 'savior of humankind'; for Ciro Vasaczk, following Sorus Chatelaine's example to its conclusion; and for Warden Dios, the last UMCP director, who had used Morn to preserve humankind's future – and died proud of her.

She cried for a long time.

But when the storm finally receded, she found that she understood something she'd never grasped before.

She could bear it. She sufficed. Because she must.

Almost tottering in the aftermath of so many tears, she went into the san to clean her face. Instead of washing it, however, she immersed her head in vacuum-chilled water and let the cold baptize her until the sting had brought her back

743

into her body; restored her relationship with herself. While she dried her hair, she stared at her reflection in the mirror as if she wanted to memorize her own face; confirm that it was hers.

Eventually she discovered that she could look herself in the eyes.

Once her hair was dry, she put on a fresh shipsuit. Then she unlocked her doors and went out to meet the future.

It is common knowledge that Director Donner argued for my reinstatement. And it is also known that the last message she received from Warden Dios urged her to do so. However, I am confident that the primary motivation behind my public 'forgiveness' was and is concern for the functional – as distinct from the ethical – integrity of the new Space Defense Police. The Members fear a preemptive strike from the Amnion, an attempt to cripple our defenses before we can disseminate our antimutagen and attack *them*. Therefore my experience and knowledge have been allowed to outweigh any inaccuracies which might be laid to my charge.

Put more cynically, the Members fear that Min Donner is too honest and direct to oppose the Amnion effectively. They believe they need a man with my reputedly imprecise scruples.

. . . remarkable also was the Council's vote to pardon Warden Dios. I was gladdened by it, although it does little to palliate my sense of loss. In my view, it would be right and just to honor him as both hero and martyr. Few among us would have enjoyed the fate Holt Fasner prepared for us. I believed, however, that his self-sacrifice would be met by more resentment. His actions reminded the Members in the most overt and humiliating way of their own failure as humanity's representatives. Therefore they would seek to diminish him so that they could think better of themselves . . .

. . . apparently Abrim Len declined to permit it. There is another remarkable aspect of the session: the clarity and unity which President Len forged from the collapse of Holt Fasner's power. I had not guessed that he could conjure so much toughness past the veil of his characteristic conciliation.

Nevertheless from my own perspective one event was more remarkable than all the others – remarkable, at least, in the sense that I am positively unwilling to forgo remarking on it. That was young Davies Hyland's behavior toward me.

For two days between his arrival on-station and his appearance before the GCES, his actions were scrupulously correct. He answered questions as circumstances required – principally regarding Morn Hyland and Captain Thermopyle – but of himself he revealed nothing. Nor did he hint at any personal emotions concerning me while he addressed the Council. Yet when the session had reached its conclusion, young Davies approached me. In full view of all the Members and their retinues, he struck me a blow which broke the left side of my jaw in three places.

'That's for Angus,' he informed me. 'He wanted to do it himself. But he was afraid you would fry his brain.'

Which in fact I could have done – but would not. It is not my custom to destroy my tools when they have served their purpose. Captain Scroyle and *Free Lunch* are an exception which I regret deeply . . . Unlike Warden, I err when I attempt to direct the quantum mechanics of events.

Young Davies has caused me no small measure of inconvenience. Sadly, I could not prefer charges against him, even if I wished to do so. He is proof against me – immunized, as it were, by the privileges conferred by the Emblem of Honor.

. . . I am forced to type this record, rather than dictate it in my accustomed fashion. My mandible has not yet healed enough to let me speak without pain. Indeed, I can hardly swallow liquids without acute discomfort.

Pain, I find, is a wonderful aid to concentration.

. . . 'complete probity', forsooth. I confess that I was surprised – and gratified – by Warden's support when I first read of it in his last transmission to Director Donner. He spoke thus of a man who had understood him ill enough to endanger his deepest desires before they could bear fruit. I am forced to think that Warden was able to forgive me in the end. Or that he considered my subsequent service an acceptable form of restitution.

I prefer the latter. It salves the quality of ego or dedication which functions as my conscience. However, I fear that the former lies nearer the truth – ambiguous though that concept may be. I have read widely in his personal records, journals not unlike my own. His last message to me supplied the codes which have allowed me to unlock his files. And the picture of him that emerges humbles me in ways I do not like and cannot answer . . .

. . . his records paint him as a man who condemns himself so severely that he judges no one else. Literally *no one* – not even the great worm in his lair. He does not fault the Dragon. He faults himself for his failure to comprehend and counter the Dragon's essential nature from the beginning. He faults himself for the naïveté or misunderstanding which left him no means except complicity to correct his mistakes. It was an unrelieved self-judgment which compelled him to make use of Morn Hyland and Captain Thermopyle as he did – and then to stew in anguish over the sufferings he exacted from them. Decision after decision, he exacerbated his own accusations against himself until they became great enough to topple the man truly responsible for them . . .

If shame on such a scale is 'truth', then I will gladly spend my days in the universe of mere fact.

But his last message did more than supply me with his codes. Although he was about to die by his own hand, he troubled himself to reassure me.

I trust you, Hashi, he wrote. *Don't think otherwise. I trust you as much as I do Min or Koina – in some ways more. Together, the three of you have everything I have – and everything I lack. I couldn't have beaten Holt without you.*

Then he added, *Take care of Min for me. Her disdain for ambiguity is a great strength, and a dangerous weakness. The truth is usually messier than she thinks it is. Make her listen to you. Trust your own point of view. And back her up when she doesn't take your advice.*

She did that for me. As you did. And she'll need you as much as I ever did.

Curious proposition. I would grieve over it – and for the man who conceived it – if I found it less intriguing. In what sense can it be avowed that the human species, as well was Min Donner, might *need* a man who is not ordinarily disturbed by questions of 'truth'? If the redoubtable Min can be taken to represent the law officer Warden Dios wished to be, then I may be regarded as an exemplum of the law officer he actually was. How can it be that the one does not preclude the other?

On that point, albeit indirectly, I have questioned Director

Donner in person. I wished to know how she proposes to treat with the Amnion, now that our relations with them are somewhat strained. In her typically hostile fashion – typical, at least, of her attitude toward me – she replied, 'I'm going to tell them the exact truth. Keep every bargain I make with them to the letter. And cost them blood if they don't do the same.'

Uncharacteristically, she then elaborated upon this rather outré philosophy. 'Take Billingate for example. If you and Warden – and good old Godsen – had left it up to me, I wouldn't have launched a covert strike. Since that shipyard violated their treaties with us, it was their problem. I would have told them I wanted *them* to destroy the whole planetoid – and I meant to do it myself if they didn't. I would have given them a time limit. And if they refused to comply, I would do exactly what I warned them I was going to do. Send in an armada, reduce Thanatos Minor to powder. And *dare* them to take offense.'

She appeared to sneer at me, but I believe she may have simply attempted a smile. 'They might get the message. You've said yourself, it violates their genetic identity to "deal falsely". One reason they want to destroy us is that we *do*.'

Frankly, I took offense myself. Every fiber of my being is outraged by such simple-minded foolhardiness. And yet I am forced to concede that the Amnion might indeed "get the message". A bloodthirsty honesty can hardly serve humanity's future less well than did the Dragon's policy of monomaniacal manipulation.

Doubtless I will oppose her at every turn. Occasionally she will heed me. And when she does not, I will reread Warden's records, and be humbled.

Perhaps humankind will survive without its gods.

———

This is the end of
THE GAP INTO RUIN
THIS DAY ALL GODS DIE.